THE SAILOR CRUSOE

BY
PERCY B. St. JOHN

1

THE

SAILOR CRUSOE.

BY

PERCY B. ST. JOHN.

WITH

TWENTY-FOUR ILLUSTRATIONS.

BY R. J. PROWSE.

LONDON:

"LONDON HERALD" OFFICE, 13, CATHERINE-STREET, STRAND,

AND ALL BOOKSELLERS.

CONTENTS.

ILLUSTRATIONS.

THE
SAILOR CRUSOE.
BY
PERCY B. ST. JOHN.

ILLUSTRATED BY R. PROWSE.

LONDON:
"LONDON HERALD" OFFICE, 13, CATHERINE STREET, STRAND,
And all Booksellers.

No. 1

THE
SAILOR CRUSOE.

BY

PERCY B. ST. JOHN.

CHAPTER I.

THE SAILOR.

> . . . . Oh! the cry did knock
> Against my very heart! Poor souls, they perished!
> SHAKSPEARE.

> . . . . In solitude
> What happiness! Who can enjoy alone?
> Or all enjoying, what contentment find?
> MILTON.

My father had been a sailor in his younger days, but having married early in life, had abandoned his original intention of ploughing the seas for a living, and taken to tilling the more fertile earth. Another reason for his retirement was, that he had inherited a small patrimonial estate on the eastern coast, which, being a man of simple tastes and domestic habits, amply sufficed for all his wants.

I was his first-born, and though he had many other children, a secret instinct seemed to tell me that I was his favourite. Not that he allowed any undue preference to be seen, but there are little nameless nothings, which steal upon the heart, and reveal what even a parent might wish to conceal.

I could do what I liked with him. As he let the larger portion of his land, and only kept a few acres for his own use and amusement, he had a great deal of leisure time upon his hands, and his delight used to be to take me out with him, and, walking along hand in hand, to expound to me, from the treasures of a well-stored mind, such knowledge as suited my age and character.

He was fond of botany, and would explain to me, in simple and clear language, the mystery of this part of creation; he would point out to me, from the properties of the meadow grass, which trembles at the touch of the butterfly, and bends before the sweeping wind, to that of the almond tree, with its gradually whitening blossoms, or the flower of the hedge bank—eye bright—"whose gaze is like an infant's."

He would point out to me at what season to expect each coming stranger; to know, that in January, when He "scattereth his hoar frost like ashes," we could scarcely expect any visitant save the daisy that never dies, the holly and the mistletoe; how when, in April, God greeteth the earth by the south wind, the hedges are white with blossoms, and so on throughout the year.

He explained to me the uses of every tree and plant I noticed, a knowledge which served me in after days.

I will give you one instance of my father's personal character.

We had been out since morning. He had brought a book with him, that he might read while I played in the meadows, and culled a bouquet of wild flowers for my sister Ellen, two years my junior. I had strayed away some little distance, a somewhat unusual thing, as I generally kept him in sight. The day was warm, the air balmy, and the fragrance of the flowers delicious. The grass twinkled in the sunshine, the daisies opened their round eyes by thousands, the buttercups gleamed in rich profusion.

Suddenly I heard a fearful roar, and turning, saw, at the distance of about a hundred yards, a furious bull coming full tilt at me. I uttered a piercing shriek, and ran. Never, while memory lasts, shall I forget the bounds with which my father came rushing towards me. He seemed advancing to certain destruction, but I am sure he never thought of himself. The savage beast was about ten yards from me, when my father caught me by the hand, and, turning, faced the advancing brute.

Astonished and confounded, he paused, his eyes glared wildly at my father, his feet pawed the ground, his bellowing woke the distant echoes, and then, once more lashing himself into his former fury, he plunged headlong at us.

This was what my father had expected. But it gave him breath. Catching me wildly up, he threw me on his back. My arms clung round his throat, while my little heart ceased to beat with fear. Away he flew, the bull after him. I am sure no man ever ran so fast before. He headed for a hedge. But there seemed no hope. The infuriated beast was close upon us, when my father, rousing up all his energies, made a fearful leap, and fell, with me still clinging to him, down a slope of some thirty feet, and then into the waters of a small trout stream, which skirted our house.

We were saved. But my father was ill for weeks. He never, however, complained. All his thought appeared to be that I was safe and unhurt.

We lived near the sea, and nearly all the people in our neighbourhood were fishermen.

With the exception of the rector, we had little society, and I, who, boy-like, liked to play with those of my own age, was a great deal with the youths who were, at an early period, to man the smacks and luggers engaged in the fishing trade.

Our residence commanded a view of a lovely kind of cove, which I shall call St. Margaret's Bay. Into this secluded spot fell the river which ran past our house.

As it had long been understood that I was to follow in my father's footsteps, and become a tiller of the soil—unless, indeed, I selected a profession—my father raised no objection to my following out my taste for boats and the water.

I could swim admirably. This useful art my father had taught me; and, at twelve years old, I could reef, steer, and do all kinds of odd jobs on board a small vessel.

Like most boys, I loved the sea, and had I not have know

the inborn dislike my mother, especially, had of everything connected with the water, I should have looked forward to the day when I could make long voyages and see strange lands, such as those I read of in my father's library.

But I knew that I was expected to succeed my parents as the head of the house, and though I often sighed, in secret, for the free life of a jolly sailor, I kept my aspirations to myself, nor ever showed any disinclination for the position to which Providence and my parents had appointed me. Nor did I ever, in the course of a long life, have cause to regret, that, though my faults were great, I was ever a good son.

My fondness for water excursions could not, however, pass wholly unnoticed, and dear Ellen, my younger brothers and sisters, and Polly, my cousin, often, in fun, would call me the sailor. Ah me! there is surely a fate in all things, and perhaps never more so than in my case.

How I came to receive another name, which will, I believe, go down with me to the grave, shall now be told.

CHAPTER II.

THE ISLAND.

IN our part of the world we used to call what other persons call lakes or lochs by the name of broads. It is a local appellation, but soon familiarizes itself even to the ear of a stranger.

Now it was my delight both to sail and swim in these vast expanses of water, in some instances, many miles in extent. My father would often accompany me. I was still a somewhat delicate boy, and though, as I have said, a good swimmer, not very fond of going out of my depth. He would, therefore, swim alongside of me, guide me, and, if need be, assist me. These were, indeed, happy and halcyon days to me.

I only wish that every boy, in after life, had such happy hours to look back to as those I then enjoyed.

Now it happened that my father had occasion to go to London on some very important business.

An elder brother of his had emigrated to Virginia, and a very friendly intercourse took place, by letter, between the families. Every now and then, James Challoner—that was my uncle—would require goods from England, in exchange for merchandize sent from America, and he always liked his brother Alfred—that was my father—to transact his business for him.

He had often wished my father to go out, or, at all events, to send me out, as my uncle, though married, had no children; but a fondness for home and its comforts, and an intense dislike to part with me, made my father ever return evasive answers to all invitations.

He would often talk, however, of going to see his brother, some day; but the increasing cares of a large family for a long time prevented any serious thought on the subject.

Well, as I said, my father had gone up to London. It was during my holidays, and, therefore, I was allowed to do pretty well as I liked. Sometimes I would go out with my sister Ellen and my cousin Polly, both about two years younger than myself, nutting, or merely for the sake of picking flowers. But my favourite pastime was fishing, and this pursuit I followed alone.

Our house—I think I see it now—was situated in a delightful little valley. It was a kind of cottage, half hidden by jessamine and honeysuckle. Three miles up the river that passed before our door, and fell into St. Margaret's Bay, was one of those broads I have already alluded to.

It was about eight miles long by about five in width. I had never failed to obtain a profusion of fish whenever I visited it, and so one morning started early in the hope of obtaining a fine day's sport. A friend of mine, who was, however, absent at this time, always allowed me to use his boat; and in this I put off about eight o'clock.

It was a splendid morning, though the sky was overcast, and the heat sultry. As I glided over the glassy pool, towards an island in the middle of the broad, I paused to examine, with interest, the white water-lily, its rose-like flower sitting on the water beside the yellow water-lily, both with oval leaves, so smooth and shiny that the water runs over them as if their surfaces were oiled. But I halted not long, my mind was too much absorbed in the idea of sport.

I had with me, besides my rod and line, a basket of provisions, and a bottle of wine and water, so that I was well provided for the day. No sooner did I reach within a stone's throw of the island, than I cast anchor and began to fish. My endeavours were crowned with great success, and about twelve I adjourned towards the island, with the double view of taking some refreshment, and of seeking shelter against a coming storm, that already began to agitate the trees, and move the water into wavy ripples.

The island was about an acre in extent, its borders being skirted by willows, whilst its interior was partly composed of grass and partly of a thick copse of trees and brambles. Removing all my provisions, and fastening my boat to a bending willow, I landed.

No sooner had I done so, and before I could reach the shelter of the copse, a storm of wind and rain burst upon me, such as I had never seen before. The wind did not come moaning through the trees, as I had heard it, nor did the rain fall slanting, but it came down perpendicularly from the black and angry heavens.

I rushed beneath the overarching boughs of a beach tree, some of the branches of which swept the ground. Despite the extreme violence of the storm, the shelter was complete.

As I had never witnessed anything so severe before, so also was it of short duration; ere half an hour the sky had cleared, the wind had fallen, the grass sparkled with myriad gems, and the feathered choristers of the woods poured forth their joyous song in varied notes. I now sallied forth, refreshed and happy. I thought nature had never looked so gloriously lovely. It was now about one, and having strolled about a little I began to think of returning home, as I had promised sister Ellen and cousin Polly to take them for a walk.

I shouldered my rod, having collected all my fish in a basket, and made for the landing.

The boat was gone.

I rubbed my eyes in dismay, and was about to examine the whole of the island shores, when I saw the boat about half a mile off, slowly moving towards the river, which passed my father's house, and which ran through the lake.

Like a child, as I was almost, I sank upon the wet grass, in utter despair.

Not a soul knew my destination. I had not, when I started, even made up my mind as to where I was going. The broad was rarely frequented, especially at this season of the year, and to the best of my belief it had no other boat within some miles.

At first I thought of swimming, but a very little reflection caused me at once to abandon this idea. I was two miles from the mainland, and I knew that my strength would not suffice for the journey.

Had my father have been at home I should not have been

so uneasy. Not only should I have counted on his strong affection, but on his knowledge of my favourite haunts. Now my deliverance was a work of chance. I had read of men cast away on desert islands—of those who had voluntarily selected such a life, but I never imagined the possibility of my being a prisoner on an acre of land in the middle of a Norfolk broad.

I thought of a raft, but I had nothing in my possession in the shape of tools. True, I had a clasp knife, but long before I could cut down branches and boughs stout enough, succour must come. If not, I thought, surely I must die; and who knows but next spring, when picnic parties visit the island again my bleaching bones well tell the tale?

I shuddered, and taking my bottle of sherry and water from the basket, took a sip. This renovated me a little, and I began to look around me. It was quite clear that one night was to be passed in that dreary place; I accordingly began to think of a hut. There was a certain quantity of wood cut ready for removal. This I decided to use for walls, and, by great exercise of energy, contrived, in about two hours, to erect something like an Indian cabin, roofed with green boughs in abundance.

At the end of this time I was hungry. But my provisions were exhausted. I had, it is true, abundance of raw fish, but I did not even think of that, as the very idea would in all probability have made me ill. There were a few blackberries, and other wild fruit of the same kind, upon which I made a most unsatisfactory kind of meal. Then, exhausted and weary, I crawled into my hut, and soon was in a sound sleep.

It way broad day when I awoke. The birds were singing on every bough, but though their voice was music indeed, it was as the hooting of an owl, compared with that which fell upon my ear next moment. It was my father calling aloud,—

"Alfred! Alfred! My dear boy! Where are you?"

The boat had been found at daybreak by some labourers, who at once went to my father's house, and said they had seen me using it on the previous morning.

Filled with awful dread—thinking first, that I had been capsized in the storm—he hurried to the broad, pulled frantically to the island which he knew I was in the habit of visiting, and there, unable to restrain his anguish, called upon my name.

His delight may be conceived, nor was that of my mother and sisters any less. When, however, the first excitement wore off, they would laugh at my adventure, call me the Sailor Crusoe, and insist on a visit to my desert island, which for many a long day afterwards was one of our favourite haunts.

CHAPTER III.

MY UNCLE.

The life of a youth in the country, devoted to study and the sports of the field, has few events in it worth recording. I went regularly to the school kept by our rector, I assisted my father in his orchard and garden, and became more of a companion than ever. Having married when very young, he was not forty when I was eighteen, so that we had more sympathies in common even than father and son usually have.

His great desire was that I should follow his example, marry and settle down very early in life, an idea which, when I thought of my orphan cousin, Mary Anne, appeared to me a very sensible one.

But I still cherished the old idea of wandering, and would, I fancy, have bartered a year or two of my existence to have made one voyage round the world.

But now an event occurred which changed the whole current of my existence.

I was, as I have said, eighteen years of age, when my father received another most pressing letter from his brother. He was not well; his plantations were now very valuable, and, being unmarried, he had no one to look after his interests. His overseers and servants were robbing him, and, worse still, utterly neglecting his concerns. He could not understand why my father, who had a large family, could not spare one of his children, and that the eldest, to come over and be unto him as a son. However, as he was quite determined and would take no further denial, he was on his way to England, and should arrive almost as soon as his letter. He begged my father to secure a furnished house for himself and a retinue of servants—the house to be as near to him as possible.

At first my father was all excitement at the idea of seeing a brother who, though always known to him pleasantly by correspondence, was in person quite a stranger. Then I saw a change come over him. If ever man did give up his whole mind to domestic joys—the love of home and his children—it was my father. To take away one from his nest, was to commence that breaking up of home so painful to the attached parent. And yet I knew that from the first he had made up his mind to the sacrifice. He knew he could not refuse his brother, and he fancied that my worldly interests were too deeply interested for him to hesitate.

The house was easily found. My father had many friends, who gladly offered their services. One of these obliging offers was accepted.

At last he came. He was a man of imperious manner, brusque ways, but with a noble heart. The meeting between the brothers was most affectionate and tender. I saw at once that my father would do anything for his elder brother. Uncle James at once fixed upon me, and declared that he would not think of returning to America without me.

Then came a long series of conferences, from which I was excluded.

At last my mother was admitted of the conclave, and the three sat in council, off and on, for about a week.

My father one morning announced, at breakfast time, that, having once seen his brother, he could not think of parting from him; that Uncle James had determined to take Alfred away; and so, as a compromise, he had agreed to sell his paternal estate, emigrate to Virginia, and settle beside his brother, with all his household.

All the family brightened up, especially cousin Polly, for I do believe they all loved me dearly.

The emigration of so large a family was not to be the work of a day, and I found that my uncle James had decided to wait our time. There was the land to dispose of, an outfit to prepare, and many things which could not be done in a day. All, however, began sedulously to prepare for the journey; though my mother, sisters, and my cousin, Mary Anne, disliked the sea, they were prepared for any sacrifice rather than be separated from me.

It was agreed that we were to sail in October, as my uncle particularly wished to be home at Christmas time, which we understood was made much of in Virginia, almost as much, indeed, as in old England.

I was enraptured. My darling aspirations, my dearest hopes, were about to be realized. I should witness the ocean in its might and grandeur; and I should see those far-off places of which I had read so much. Every spare moment I could find I read books of travels, narratives of shipwrecks and disasters at sea, while, though almost a man, I would even sometimes steal to my island on the broad, to read "Robinson Crusoe."

Happy he, who, at eighteen years of age, can find delight in such simple and really enobling pleasures.

CHAPTER IV.

WE SET SAIL.

THE name of the vessel we were to sail in, was the bark, Reformation, John Thomas, master.

It was one Monday morning when, our luggage and cargo having been safely stowed the week before, we went on board.

There was my father and mother, myself, my sister Ellen, my cousin Polly, and six younger children. There was my uncle James and his household, thus oddly composed; Peter, Jack, London, Crœsus, negroes; Cajoe, a child; Hagar, Bella, Sarah, negresses; and Venus, an Indian girl, whom he had saved from the slaughter when her family was massacred.

About midday, the bark, after having been warped to the end of Yarmouth pier, started fairly on its way, and I, while the others gazed with mournful eyes at the receding shore, almost danced with delight, as I felt the vessel bounding over the waves, and as I feasted my eyes with a sight of the great wilderness of waters.

It was a lovely day. Light, fleecy clouds were wafted along the clear blue sky. The waves danced merrily to the warm and genial pressure of the wind, and all nature seemed to smile upon our voyage. But, strange as it may appear —I often thought of it afterwards—my father, my uncle, and my mother, were very sad. 'Tis hard to tear ourselves away from the home of our affections, at all times; but in my uncle's case, this was not so. He was bound *for* home, and yet his habitual smile rested not on his countenance.

We were at war with France, so that we hastened to join, as soon as possible, a convoy, which had been waiting for a favourable wind, for several days. Our bark, however, was very swift, and tolerably well armed, with a good crew, so that our skipper determined to run the gauntlet of the privateers as soon as he got an opportunity.

The frigate which had charge of the convoy was commanded by a strict old martinet, who was very careful to keep his flock close under his wing. Every night he was signalling for half an hour, and occasionally firing a gun, to keep them altogether.

But I am anticipating.

My relatives, as soon as we lost sight of land, under pretence of examining their berths, went below, to conceal their agitation; but I, who was in my element, remained on deck. I was delighted at everything; the very singing of the wind, the straining of the cordage, the swearing of the sailors, the the creaking of the ship, all seemed to increase my excitement. At last, I was on board a real, genuine ship, and bound for the long voyage.

Presently, my father and uncle came on deck. They were calmer now. All the rest were suffering, already, from the abominable malady which attacks all who have never before left the land.

We conversed freely now, and my uncle becoming eloquent, told us some fine stories of his plantations in Virginia, which sounded all the more real when I looked at the grin-

ning negroes, who formed his favourite attendants, and watched Cajoe climbing up in the rigging, like a monkey.

That night and the next day it was quite calm, and the convoy got scattered, to the great indignation of the frigate's captain. Our skipper, however, little heeded his signals, keeping on as long as the tide drove us to the westward, and then anchoring.

About eleven o'clock, it came on to blow. It was one of those sudden squalls, against which no prudence can avail, and, before we could recover ourselves, the ship dragged, the cable snapped, and we lost our anchor.

We were now compelled to run before the wind, which we did for some hours, when seeing two lights, our skipper fancied that we had fallen foul of the French fleet. We accordingly tacked, and stood direct for the English shore, which we made a little after daylight. Then came a kind of tornado off the land, and our master, being on the deck, slipped over a coil of rope and broke his leg, which was a great misfortune both to him and to us. But my father and uncle, after some little difficulty succeeded in setting it.

The guidance of the barque was now, necessarily, placed in the hands of the chief mate, who was neither so good a seaman, nor so skilful a navigator, as Captain Thomas. Still he was a man who tried to do his duty. But everything was against him. We either had squalls, or baffling winds, or calms for days, so that we made no progress. Every day we expected to fall in with the convoy, but we saw no sail save fishing-smacks, which, doubtful of our character, kept at a respectful distance.

On the 25th of October we made Cape St. Vincent. The mate wished, as much as possible, to run up the coast for the trade winds, but, owing to a contrary wind at north-east, he was compelled to steer at a great distance from the land, and this for many days, until he was quite out of his latitude, in a region with which he was totally unacquainted.

Then we shifted, and ran in for the land for twenty-four hours, when we sounded and found fifty-five fathoms, which again deepened to ninety towards evening, the wind remaining very variable and uncertain.

Both my father and my uncle began to be very uneasy. They were well provisioned, but only for a tolerably successful journey, and now, through the accident to the captain, and a subsequent low fever which attacked him, we were uncertain as to our whereabouts. Now I saw the evil of my not having properly learned navigation. A very moderate knowledge of that great science would have been invaluable.

On St. Martin's Eve, the 10th of November, the storm augmented in violence, attended by a prodigious swell. When morning broke, it was worse than the night had been, and a sudden shift of wind coming on about mid-day, threw the ship into the trough of the sea, which struck her aft. The rudder broke loose, five of the hinges gave way at the stern, the gudgeons being torn asunder, and the ship being tossed about, utterly at the mercy of the wind and waves, was driven to the westward. The pumps were now sounded, and the terrible news announced, that there was four feet of water in the hold.

At this moment our brave and gallant skipper came on deck, and, though weak and ill, exerted himself to the utmost of his power to encourage his crew, who, with considerable labour and incredible hardship, slung the two long stern ropes to the quarter of the rudder, but it again breaking loose, was dragged, as the captain calculated, three hundred miles after her for the space of three days, when, by means of the utmost efforts, it was once more recovered and made fast.

Still we knew not where we were, and the water increasing, the pumps were rigged, and the negroes and half of the crew put to them, while the other half strove to discover and moderate the leak. After incredible labour and much heartsickness, we did discover its position, but it could only be partially moderated, the gangs still working hard at the pumps.

Clouds began to thicken round more than ever, and the whistling of the wind was something awful. A fresh dreadful storm now commenced from the north-east, which, swelling and roaring, was for some hours more violent than at others, and at length seemed to exclude all the light of the heavens, and leave us in utter darkness. The blackness of the sky, and the howling of the wind, were such as to inspire the boldest of our men with terror, for the dread of death is always more terrible at sea, as no situation is so entirely destitute of comfort and relief.

Our sails were all close clewed up, as if we only showed a reefed foresail to guide the vessel, four and sometimes six men were not enough to steer her, which may partly indicate the strength of the gale, in a manner swelling the sea above the clouds. It did not rain, but it poured, and the wind seemed to grow more loud and tumultuous always as the sheets of water fell. During the whole of this time the heavens were so overcast, that it was impossible to take an observation, for neither was the sun to be seen by day nor the stars by night.

Being, as it were, in spirit, one of the crew, I had taken my watch regularly, and so had my father, all the rest of the family remaining below. That night, as I and my father stood on the quarter deck, we observed a little round light, like a tremulous star, streaming along, and sparkling with a blaze, sometimes shooting from shroud to shroud, and appearing as if about to settle on some of the fore-shrouds at half the height of the main-mast. For half the night it kept with us, frequently running along the main-yard to the very end, and then returning; but towards the morning watch, we lost sight of it, and knew not which way it was gone.

The superstitious sailors form many presages from this sea fire, which, nevertheless, is common in all storms. Perhaps it is the same which the Genoese, in the Mediterranean, call Castor and Pollux. If only one light appeared without another, they considered it an evil omen of a great tempest. The Italians and others, on the Adriatic, call it a sacred body; the Spaniards, St. Elmo fire, and have an authentic and miraculous legend concerning it. Be it what it will, we had other prospects of safety or destruction than its rising and falling. Could it now have enabled us to take an altitude, we should have been disposed to consider it miraculous. But we ran, like men hood-winked, sometimes north-north east, north and by west, then varying two or three points, and even half the compass. We endeavoured, as much as possible, to steer east and by south, which was not at all easy to do, though the ship was greatly lightened by throwing many articles overboard, and staving many casks of beer, oil, cyder, wine, and vinegar. All our ordnance was hove over to the starboard side.

All this time the leakage filling the hold prevented us getting at beer or fresh water, nor could any fire be lighted in the cook's-room to dress any meat, so that we were fain to put up with rain water and hard biscuits. As we all took our turn at the pumps and buckets, this added to our need of proper refreshment. Grief, apprehension, and fatigue, fairly banished sleep from our eyes.

I calculated that the pumps gave four thousand strokes in a watch—about one hundred tons every hour. From the

Tuesday until the Friday, in all about two thousand tons. Had we ceased one single moment, we must have sunk.*

CHAPTER V.

THE STORM.

Now again, on this terrible Friday, our rudder got loose once more, and as our vessel was driving with her broadside before the wind, two rudders of a triangular form, were, by our carpenter's advice, constructed out of masts and spars, to check her course. However, they were soon carried away, and a rudder which they contrived to hang, proved but an indifferent substitute, and was also swept away by the fury of the waves.

On the 27th of November all on board began to give themselves up for lost. When I went down I always found my mother, and brothers, sisters, and cousin Polly in prayer. My uncle would cry, and reproach himself bitterly as being the cause of all our misfortunes, forgetting that he, like us all, was in the hands of Providence. As for myself, and my father, we had long since abandoned all idea of seeing land again, and only worked because we felt it to be our duty.

Suddenly, however, the unexpected moderation of the weather gave us some relief; but now a new difficulty occurred. Owing to the excessive rain, and the terrible stress of the gale, the sails were so much weakened that at any attempt to hoist them, they successively split asunder. Thus the barque was tossed about, wanting those indispensable portions, sails and a rudder; and now her straining again opened her seams to the admission of such a quantity of water, that, by all our efforts, it could scarcely be kept under.

The lead had continually been cast without finding soundings, now, however, eighty fathoms was got in the morning and one hundred and twenty at night.

On the 4th of December, the vessel sank deeper in the sea, from the effect of four successive waves breaking over her. Once such an immense sea broke over us, that it covered the ship from stem to stern, as if with a sheet of water. For a time it actually filled her brim full within, from the hatches up to the spar deck. The force of the water dashed the men from the helm—we had just hung a makeshift rudder—forcing the tiller out of their hands, and on their attempting to recover it, they were dashed from starboard to larboard, in such a manner that it was wonderful they were not killed.

The crew, though half dead with fatigue, and steeped up to the middle in water, exerted themselves pumping and baling incessantly. Rather better weather prevailed for the next two days; but the gale freshened on the seventh, and the sea ran mountainous and horrible again. Sometimes the vessel rose to the very clouds, and then she descended into deep valleys among the waters, and amidst the darkness reigning around. The lightning darted with most vivid flashes, while the ship heeled so much that the water ran in by the gunwale.

The crew, now expecting to be every moment swallowed up, stood gazing piteously at one another, until the skipper, in the hope that she would right, resolved to cut away the masts, as the only remedy. The men flew to execute this order, and no sooner did the axe cut through a few lanyards, then over went mizen and main mast, a pitch of the vessel

* In a narrative of the loss of the Hercules, we find that " the pumps discharged fifty tons of water an hour." We, however, must allow for the circumstances under which our hero made his calculations.—*Editor of* SAILOR CRUSOE.

throwing them completely overboard without touching the deck. The barque now laboured less, and the crew occupied themselves during a dark and tempestuous night, in clearing away shrouds and riggings.

But now our skipper saw that the leak was gaining on us in such a way that left no hope of our exhausted crew being able to keep it under. He, therefore, determined to take to the boats, and this once decided on, gave everybody directions to prepare. My mother, sisters, and cousin crawled on deck, presenting a pitiable aspect. But none murmured. When they gazed at the gloomy heavens, when they looked down at the raging waters, they shuddered, and that was all. A great apathy had fallen on their souls.

The boats were the long boat and yawl. The former would hold about twenty, the latter about forty. It was decided that the crew should have the yawl, while we and the negroes would take the long boat. The captain elected to go with us, while his man kept in our track. The skipper knew, from various signs, that we were near land.

It was with awful difficulty that the boats were launched and provisioned in so heavy a sea. Then took place a rush towards the yawl, which in a few minutes was full. The captain had expected this. Now came the task of lowering the children and women into the boat, which was at last effected with great difficulty. I had devoted myself especially to this task, and found myself at last alone on the deck of the wreck with the captain. His leg was weak, and I had to watch my opportunity to aid him in his descent. At length he fell as it were, into the boat, and, by some extraordinary accident, the painter got loose from the belaying pin. Such was the force of the waves, that in an instanr the long boat was a hundred feet away. Still I felt no fear. They were already pulling back, and I at once prepared for action.

I rigged a rope to a yard that still clung to the stump of a mast, and waited. The boat came slowly up. I saw that human strength would never enable them to reach the ship. She rolled and pitched in such a way that precluded the possibility of the boat approaching her in safety.

I ran up to the yard. I saw the captain waving his hand to me ; I saw my mother gazing wistfully at me ; I saw my sister Ellen hiding her face in her hands ; I saw my cousin Polly, holding out her arms, and, swinging myself clear, made a mad and desperate leap.

Down, down, I seemed to go, to some fathomless depth, and then I lost all sense.

I suppose that I struck out mechanically, for in a few minutes I came to the surface, and gazed wildly around.

I was to leeward of the ship !

In my dive some current had carried me under the vessel's keel, and I could see no boat. But the bark was easily reached on this side, which showed that, in launching the long-boat, we had committed a fatal error.

I clambered on deck. I rushed to the other side. Nothing but the raging waters and the pitiless blast.

I fainted. Nor could I ever tell how long I lay insensible. I was suddenly aroused by a fearful shock. The vessel had struck some few strokes. As I started to my feet, I felt that she floated again, which she did for a few minutes, when she ran fast aground.

The wind was still violent, and it was very dark, so that I could see nothing. The sea broke violently over, compelling me to cling to a heavy piece of ordnance. Then I crawled into the captain's cabin where, with great difficulty, I succeeded in finding a biscuit and some rum, which revived me prodigiously.

The vessel did not now strike so often, but several of her timbers were broken, and some planks started.

Presently, day broke, and I saw land at a considerable distance ; but soon after, as it grew quite light, I saw that we were upon the shore, lying on the beach, which at times, as the surge of the sea returned, was dry.

A fearful crack suddenly announced that the bark was about to break up, and without further thought, I waited for a receding wave, jumped into the water, and running fast, never stopped until I once more found myself on dry land.

I looked around, but nothing met my view but a desolate wilderness, rude basaltic rocks, and sandy hills covered with scrubby palmetto, the stalks of which were so prickly there was no walking among them. I was very thirsty, but could see no water, but espying a deep kind of oyster shell lying among some stones, I took it up, and climbing up some rocks, gazed wearily and hopelessly around.

But nothing could I see cheering or pleasant, I was on an arid kind of sandy reef, without food or water ; *my whole worldly wealth was a clasp knife and a broken oyster shell.*

CHAPTER VI.

I AM ALONE.

Yes ! as we roamed, the sylvan earth seemed glowing
   With many a beauty, unremark'd before ;
The soul was like a deep urn overflowing
   With thoughts, a treasured store ;
The very flowers seemed born but to exhale,
As breathed the west, their fragrance to the gale.

SLOWLY I advanced a little farther, and then, seating myself upon a rock, gave myself up to painful and miserable reflections. I felt about as desolate and lost as Noah might have done, had all his family perished, and he been left alone on the face of the globe, to the companionship of wild beasts and domestic animals. I could see no hope, no one thing to cheer or revive my drooping spirits.

I was either on a bleak spur of some desolate continent, or upon a wretched and deserted island.

As this thought filled my mind, I leaped up, and, determined to satisfy myself, ran along a sort of pathway, which led upwards to higher rocks. It was a mere narrow ledge on the side of the cliff but so desperate was I, that, though in places it was scarcely wider than my hand, I clung to occasional projections, or stuck my knife into chinks and holes, until I reached the summit, when I at once knew the extent of my misery.

To my left was a bay nearly land-looked, forming a harbour, where a dozen vessels like ours might have ridden in safety. It was surrounded by hills, which, after several undulations, rose into conical peaks of naked rock broken everywhere into jagged and rude outlines. I could not even see a creeping plant to take off the harshness of the scene. Everything around had a bleak and wintry appearance, suited to the weather and time of year.

In front of me the scenery was exceeding pleasing to the eye, being bounded on all sides by undulating hills, covered by some kind of evergreen foliage. I could see, too, distant mountains capped with snow, rising in a variety of strange and variegated forms, while the nearer hills were covered by a dense mass of beech, willow, birch, and winter bark. These trees were about fifty feet high, and bent all in a north-easterly direction, from the prevalence of Sou'-westerly winds, a common circumstance in that part of the world.

From the lofty position in which I was placed, I could see most mighty impediments to my communicating with the further part of the land, growing out of the mountainous

No. 2.

THE LEAP FOR LIFE.

| PRIZE TICKET—No. 1. |

and rocky character of the country, which was intersected with inlets deep and impassable, and in most places bounded by abrupt precipices, with a soil which in some places might be called a quagmire, which I foresaw would make walking difficult. This appeared to prevail on the hills as well as valleys, while on some of the plains I could see a black coloured moss, with watery holes between.

Water—that was just then even a more imperative want than food. So, having rested my weary limbs, I hurried forward, as fast as I could, to where I could see a pool in the plain below. Reaching it, after much labour and difficulty, for I had lost my shoes in my plunge from of the deck—having them in my hand—I stooped down, filled my oyster-shell, and drank greedily.

It was brackish almost as the water of the sea.

Then I felt as if I had lost all hope, and as, all that day, with few intervals, the wind was very violent, I crawled back towards the rocks, in the hope of finding some shelter. I had scarcely done so, when a fresh storm of wind and rain fell, that it seemed as if the flood had broken in from the sea, upon the land.

I had only my trousers and jacket on, which, heaven knows, I needed much; but I took off the latter, and by dint of patience, contrived to catch a few drops to wet my parched lips and throat. After this I began to feel very hungry, and, despite the wind and rain, went forth in search of food.

There were many birds. They flew over the island in great abundance—frigate birds, boobies, and penguins. But they seemed to be very shy, nor had I even a stick with which to have knocked one down, would they have let me. And then, what rendered it more difficult, they made their nests upon distant sand-banks or reefs, which I could not reach.

After a long and weary search I found some wretched shell fish on the rocks, which, with a little wild sorrel and some berries I saw the birds peck at, made me a scanty meal. Poor as it was, however, it refreshed me much, and reflection naturally returning, my next thought was for a shelter that night. I had no doubt that the place was infested by wild beasts, against which I had no protection whatever.

Under the big rock, where I had taken refuge, I had noticed some loose stones, so I went back to them, and choosing a spot where there was a natural cavity, not much more than four or five feet square, I began to build me a wall in front. In my feeble state this was very tiresome, but at last I succeeded in making a tolerable shelter. But, as it blew violent and hard that night, I was very cold, wet, and miserable. Still, it had pleased God to save my life, and that was more than I could have expected.

My cave was a mere hole, and I do not think that any lad of my age, and I was now nearly nineteen, ever suffered more than I did that night. Now, that the first rage of hunger and thirst was appeased, I began to think of those I had lost—father, mother, brothers, sisters, and cousin, all at one blow. It was a fearful trial, and, as the thought gushed to my very heart, I wept bitterly.

Then I began to reflect on myself and on my own condition. I was on an island. I had no means of leaving, and I knew of no human being within many miles. I was shoeless, and my clothing was very scanty, while I had not the slightest chance of any fresh supply. I was apparently entirely dependent on rain for my drink, which was a terrible reflection, as I knew I was in a part of the world where not a drop would fall, in certains seasons, for many months. I was altogether destitute of provisions, nor could I have the slightest idea how my life was to be supported. This melan-

choly prospect, with the thought of all that had occurred within a few days, drew a second copious flow of tears from my eyes.

About twelve, being unable to sleep, and hearing strange noises in the distance, I pushed a stone away and peered forth. It was quite dark, but no rain fell. But nothing could be imagined more fearfully solemn than to have the natural stillness of the night broken by the terrible murmur of the surf beating on the shore, mixed with a violent roaring, of what I afterwards knew to be sea-lions, repeated all around by the echoes of hills and valleys, and blended with the incessant howlings of numberless seals. These, according to their age, made a hoarser or shriller noise, so that I listened with silent awe. I could almost fancy I heard the tones and outcries of every known species of animal upon earth mixed together.

Then came other strange noises from the hills, which at the time I could not understand. But more of this and of the sea-lions in their proper place.

After listening attentively, and perceiving that nothing came my way, I went into my hut once more, and after some difficulty, slept. When I woke in the morning, I was quite stiff with the cold. But all this time, it must be remembered that the wind was northerly, a very uncommon thing in those parts.

Indeed, I never, before or since, experienced such a storm, and such a succession of northerly winds—changing the very climate.

Before I could even move about in the morning, I was obliged to sit down, and plan something about my feet; they were so very sore, with very deep wounds, from traversing the rocks where they were covered with stones, and on the beach over sharp broken shells, that I was scarce able to walk at all. Many times afterwards, before I was able to find out how to make myself shoes, often, when treading with every possible caution, a stone or a shell on the beach, or a pointed stick in the woods, would penetrate the old wounds, and the extreme anguish would strike me to the ground.

Now I was fain, as a last resource, to cut up my only shirt, and swathe my foot in bandages, which did indifferent well for a short period.

CHAPTER VII.

I TRY TO MAKE A FIRE.

HAVING, as I hope ever to have done, prayed fervently on this day, I descended towards the beach, in a direction different from that I had come by. I found the soil here a mixture of clay, sand, and small pebbles. The sea was tolerably calm, and I was surrounded on all sides by large numbers of birds, albatross and black petrel especially, while I could see shoals of porpoises, and seals, and large patches of kelp.

I had managed, by the aid of my precious oyster-shell, to obtain from little cavities in the rocks a scanty supply of water, but this only added to my sensation, of hungers which were, perhaps, on this day the most acute I ever suffered. And I could see all around me stores of provisions, both in the air and in the sea, which were of no use to me, for want of a weapon or hook to take them with.

And then, if I could have found anything, I had no fuel; nor, had I fuel, could I hope to find the way to make a fire in that desolate place.

In this strait I suddenly perceived something moving a little ahead of me, and guessing, or rather hoping, that it might be something eatable, I snatched up a stone, and, crawling behind some jagged rocks, did witness a sight which, at any other time, would have let me laughing. A great crab was moving up in its odd, sidelong way, towards a little sandy hillock of stunted grass, which, having reached, it disturbed a whole colony of small snakes—which make their nests in such places—one of which it caught before it could escape, and walked off with it.

I thought it now time to interfere, and had just raised my stone to cast at it, when a shadow fell between myself and the creeping animal, and a great bird, swooping down, did take up both crab and snake, and fly away toward the hills ere I could make any effort to prevent my being so shamefully robbed.

I afterwards had occasion to remark that this kind of fishing, on the part of the larger birds, was very common, as well as another which occurred to me, fortunately, that very day.

I had found a piece of drift-wood, with which, after shaping it a little with my knife, I had made myself a stick, and walking along had peered about in every hole and corner for something to eat, without success. I knew that this part of the world must be very much frequented by turtle, and knowing that they bury their eggs in the sand, I had with great patience, thrust my stick, into the ground in search of them, without success.

Then, in the hope of finding some herbs, whereby to stay the craving of my stomach, I determined to move further inland. I found, as I quitted the beach in a northerly direction, that the country began gradually, but regularly, to rise. First, I found a long, thin grass sparingly scattered. As I proceeded, however, the grass became more luxuriant, and the sandy consistence of the soil seemed to improve into earth, capable of being brought to the highest state of cultivation. Clear and pellucid brooks, but all feeling the constant influence of the tide, calmly wound their way along, amidst tufts of shrubs, clustering so thickly along their banks as nearly to conceal their unruffled surfaces.

On the banks of some of these I found a kind of wild watercress, and, having no doubt of its salubrity, I ate greedily. It was while thus engaged that I made the remarkable discovery already alluded to. Before me lay about a hundred yards of soft sand, sloping down to the bank of a river or inlet. On the opposite side was a row of low cliffs. As I sat chewing my very unsatisfactory meal I saw several birds industriously engaged in scratching in the sand, after which they soared some distance into the air, and then dropped something out of their beaks on the stones; after which they again descended and took it up.

An idea flashed across my mind, and half wading, half swimming across the inlet, I watched until the birds again dropped their prey, when, rushing forward, I found it to be a hard kind of clam, which, burying itself in the soft sand, is scratched up by the birds and cunningly cracked in the way I have said. I eagerly devoured three, though they were not very palatable, and added somewhat to the uneasy sensation of thirst which tormented me.

There was, however, one matter which tormented me as much as anything, and that was the prospect of having always to live upon raw food. I tried as much as possible to think of some way of making fire, but for a long time could not do so. At last, however, I recollected what I had read in some book of voyages and travels, the study of which I had reason to be thankful for on many occasions; I recollected that some traveller had narrated very minutely how the Indians do make a fire.

They take a flat piece of wood that is pretty soft, and make a small dent in one side of it, and then they take another hard round stick, about the bigness of one's little finger, and sharpening it at one end like a pencil, they put the sharp end in the hole or dent of the flat soft piece, and then rubbing or twirling the hard piece between the palms of their hands, they drill the soft piece till it smokes and at last takes fire.

I spent a good hour in raking together sufficient fuel for a fire, and then following out of the above directions to the best of my ability, I sat down and worked hard for quite forty minutes. But whether the wood, after these heavy rains, was damp, or I was awkward, I cannot say, but I had my labour for my pains. Very much disheartened, I returned towards the rocks, and, by diligent search, found a little more water in some chinks and hollows. Then I spent the rest of the day in fortifying and enlarging my hut of stones, though I knew very well that life could never be sustained on that part of the island.

I had determined, however, to make that my head quarters until I penetrated deeper into the country, and found a place more suited to a habitation, such as my long-suffering predecessor had made unto himself.

Having enlarged my wall slightly, I retired within my hut, and began to reflect, even more seriously than I had done before, on my forlorn position. I was without fire, I was entirely dependent on the heavens for water, all the inlets and pools being perfect salt-pans. I had no shoes, almost my greatest suffering, while my scanty and miserable stock of clothes must soon wear out. The deprivation of my shirt was alone a calamity, which, while these north-easterly winds prevailed, pressed upon me with peculiar hardship.

I passed a very bad night, the noise of the sea-lions and seals being just as bad as on the previous night, while the reports from the hills continued just as frequent and inexplicable.

Weary nature, however, will at length prevail even over mental suffering, and at last I slept.

CHAPTER VIII.

HOW I TRIED TO MAKE A BOOMERANG.

THE wind still continued northerly, so, that when I went out into the open air, I felt, it is true, braced and nerved to the day's work, though I would gladly have had some more clothing. My first thought—and under the circumstances it was very natural—was for food. I recollected perfectly where I had seen the crab the day before, and took my way in that direction, casting my eyes eagerly to the right and left in search of water. Where I saw a little pool, with perhaps an eighth of an inch of rain left, I would take my oyster shell, and scooping a hole, let it all run in, when I would drink it, though very far from clean and pure.

At length I reached the spot where I had seen the crab, but could not perceive the slightest trace of one. As I afterwards found, they lay in great abundance, but completely under the rocks where the sea flowed. After much patience and diligent search, I did succeed in capturing one—a small one which I killed with a stone, and devoured raw. I afterwards found this delicacy in greater perfection, both as to size, flavour, and quantity than is perhaps to be met with in any other part of the world. But the sea craw-fish were best. Their general weight was about eight or nine pounds a piece, and they were, moreover, of a most excellent taste.

All this time the birds flew in abundance over my head,

and I thought, if I could but find some means of killing them, I might at least keep away the pangs of thirst by drinking of their blood, which, though my soul revolted from it, I knew to be the means by which many a cast away had had his life preserved.

I could see, on a kind of rocky ridge out at sea, penguins in countless numbers. I thought it strange, but it must have been their moulting season, as I could see them picking off each other's feathers. But, even if I could have swam out to them, which my state of weakness, from want of water and proper food, rendered impossible, I had no weapon with which to slay them.

I made careful search for such a stick as would serve to make a long handle to my knife, to serve as a pike in case I was attacked by wild beasts, but for a long time in vain. At length, however, when I began wholly to despair, I saw the stout branch of a tree cast on the shore by the waves, which, picking up, I saw at once was too crooked for my purpose; but the sight of it brought to my mind an idea, which I determined at once to carry out.

I had always taken deep interest in the weapons used by strange tribes, and in none more so than in the boomerang, spoken of by early and late navigators. This, I recollected, was a flat stick, three feet long, and two inches wide, by three-quarters of an inch thick, curved or crooked in the centre, forming an obtuse angle. At first sight, it might be taken for a wooden sword, very rudely and clumsily made, and I knew that some of the older travellers had described it as such. It was an implement used both in the war and the chase.

I know that in the hands of an experienced savage it was a missile very efficient for both, and was made by him to describe some extraordinary curves and movements. It was to be grasped at one end in the right hand, and thrown sickle-wise, either upwards in the air, or downwards so as to strike the ground at some distance from the thrower. In the first case, it was used to fly with a rotary motion, as its shape would indicate. After ascending to a great height in the air, it would suddenly return, in an elliptical orbit, to a spot near its starting point. The natives used it to strike objects which lay behind others, with great precision, and to reach those near, as if by a back stroke, by throwing it at a particular angle.

All this passed through my mind, as, with my knife, I was busily engaged in endeavouring to fashion myself a weapon, with all the enthusiasm of a schoolboy, and the more mature hopes of the man. I recollected that, when I was about eleven years old, my father had made me one, with which we had tried experiments. By throwing it downwards, on the ground, it rebounded, in a straight line, pursuing a ricochet motion, until it struck the object at which it was thrown. I had seen birds and rabbits killed with it, as well as ducks; but about that time I had a gun given me, and I thought no more of my curious toy.

The wood I worked upon was hard, and my knife far too precious to be recklessly used; still, the possession of some weapon was so important to me, that I worked for two hours without intermission, at the end of which time I had fashioned a very rude imitation of the boomerang, and gazed with considerable triumph at my handiwork.

I then looked around for some object on which to try my skill, and, presently, seeing a sea-bird flying at some little distance over my head, I took deliberate aim, and threw my stick. It may readily be expected that, inexperienced as I was, I did not hit the bird. But, as ill-luck would have it, I cast the boomerang into the air above

the angle of forty-five degrees, which makes it describe its most singular curve. I naturally looked up, to see the result of my first shot, but, before I knew anything about it, the boomerang, whose flight, on such occasions, is always backward, had struck me a blow on the head, and knocked me senseless to the ground.

When I came to, I was perfectly satisfied as to the form and qualities of my weapon, but determined to defer using it again until I had, at least, mastered its peculiar style of flight.

The blow I had received was a very severe one, and left a bump on my head as large as a good-sized walnut. But I had other hardships to think of, so made no more of this than bathing my head in the sea, after which, grasping my knife and sword, I continued on my way.

I found, a little way from the sea, some wild sorrel, and large patches of a sort of plant resembling spinach, which, after some time, I ventured to eat, and found it not unpleasant, even raw. Still, it only added to the cravings of my stomach for more solid food.

At this place I halted, and, finding a small pool of brackish but clear water, washed my feet, which were very sore and painful. The strips into which my shirt had been cut were almost worn away, and I felt that, on the rocks and in the woods I was rapidly approaching, I should become utterly lame, if I did not devise some plan by which to protect the soles of my feet.

I cast my eyes around, in search of something which might serve, however temporarily, as a substitute for shoes, and at last decided that some pieces of bark, tied with strips of my shirt, might serve until I reached the woods and hills. I could not hope to kill any animal whose skin might serve me as leather, though I often did entertain thoughts of digging pits and covering them with small branches of trees, in the hope of taking goats, hogs, or deer, in which it was probable the island abounded. But I wanted a shovel and every substitute for the purpose, and I was convinced that my hands were insufficient to make cavities deep enough to retain what should fall into it. As for my knife, it was too precious to be used for such a purpose.

There were a few scattered trees, such as willows, near the spinach patches, and what seemed to be an old trunk of a tree, covered with short moss, about the thickness of a man's waist, and twelve or fourteen feet long. Towards this I slowly advanced, still carrying my knife and wooden sword, when, as I came near, imagine the terrible terror and fear which came upon me.

It was a serpent.

As I approached, the hideous monster raised his head, and began to breathe forth a kind of hissing sound. Fortunately, as my after experience enabled me to discover, he had been feeding excessively, and could not move so rapidly as at other times, but this would have availed me little, as I stood stock still, terrified, horror-stricken, fascinated.

It was an awful sensation that crept over me as I gazed at the slowly-advancing beast, with my mouth open, and my eyes starting from my head. I had never before seen a serpent larger than an adder, and my fright was proportionably great. I little knew how comparatively small and harmless this one was to others I was doomed to fall in with.

At length it was not more than a dozen feet from me when, shaking off the fearful lethargy that was overcoming me, and which must have left me entirely at the animal's mercy, I roused myself, cast my newly-made weapon with all my force right at the monster's head, and took to my heels, every now and then casting fearful glances behind

But the serpent did not follow, at all events, to any distance, being, doubtless, amply gorged already, when they will lie a week or a fortnight in a state almost of atrophy.

But I was now far too exhausted to continue my journey that day, so looking out with care for a spot likely to suit my purpose, I tore up some handfuls of the wild spinach, and, after much search, found a few limpets with which to stay the cravings of hunger. Then I waded to a small rocky island, and, protected only from the wind by a bank about three feet high, lay me down to rest.

That was indeed an awful night. Though the wind changed to the southward for some hours, I felt little comfort, for it came in flaws, or sudden gusts from the mountains, that seemed ready to carry me away. But these squalls seldom lasted more than two or three minutes. I could only explain the circumstance by the hills obstructing the south gale, and the wind, being impeded by this means, suddenly forcing a passage through the narrow valleys, which, like so many funnels, both facilitate its escape and increase its force.

About the middle of the night I was alarmed by the rising of the tide, but, rightly judging from the nature of the soil I slept on that it was never overflowed, I composed myself to rest, and, exhausted and wearied, went to sleep.

CHAPTER IX.

THE ELK AND THE MYSTERIOUS ANIMAL.

WHEN I rose in the morning, a mist which hung over the distant hills seemed to promise a slight change in the weather. There was less wind, and I began to hope that I might have at last one fine day, by means of which to explore my place of exile.

I made a rather heartier meal than usual, of small shell-fish and wild sorrel and spinach, but the only water that I put inside my lips was what I shook, in about an hour, off the leaves of trees into my hand. It was the heavy dew which falls in those latitudes which afforded me this slight relief.

Then again, I had to go to work to make myself a substitute for shoes. This time I took care to make no such mistake as that of yesterday, and cut some bark off a tree, which served indifferently well. I bound it on carefully by means of a few strips of linen, and, thus accoutred, I started on my way. I soon found my hardly-wrought weapon, but not any sign remained of the serpent.

I dare say, if the truth were known, he was as frightened of me as I had been of him.

I now determined to direct my course towards the distant hills, which appeared covered by a dense mass of forest. As I advanced the country became a little more promising, but walking was arduous in the extreme. The ground was uneven and rocky, while here and there I fell in with deep inlets, which I had to swim, but still the hills appeared farther and farther off.

A large portion of the morning passed in this manner, and the sun, this day, proving a little warmer than usual, I was fain shortly after mid-day to rest myself under a wide spreading tree, something like an oak.

After an hour, a little refreshed, I continued my journey, and suddenly came upon one of the most marvellous scenes I could have imagined. I appeared to have found the extreme boundary of my part of the territory. It was indeed a picturesque, yet wild landscape. A deep, narrow valley lay at my feet, in many places not less than five hun-

dred feet in depth. A considerable stream was at the bottom, the river meandering through the narrow bottom of the vale, and at others lost among the green shrubs which clothed its banks, the resort, I could see, of several kinds of birds, which I was too far off to disturb.

On the side on which I stood the cliffs were nearly perpendicular, rendering all descent impossible. These masses of rocks, some of them from thirty to forty feet long, projected from the side of the ravine, like rudely shaped horizontal pillars. On the top of some of these rested other masses of rock, sometimes projecting as if about to fall.

I gazed in admiration, not unmixed with awe, and then I moved slowly along the top of the cliffs, watching the river, which formed a serpentine course from one side of the valley to the other. Fragments of rock thrown together in several places at once, formed a frightful bridge over the ravine, but on my side so rugged and narrow as not to admit of my attempting it.

Here, too, I could make out extensive caverns in the narrow valley beneath. But what engaged my chief attention, was the water, which I could see, but not get at.

I could tell, by the very trees on the opposite side of the valley, that there I could have enjoyed all the good things of this world; I felt sure that, having a southern aspect, when the cold season abated, I should be able to find something like a comfortable shelter, with water and food in abundance. But this was clearly denied me, as to cross that frightful ravine was utterly impossible.

I turned away in despair, for only near the sea beach on that desolate spur of land, could I hope to find such food as I, without utensils of any kind, could gather. A small wood lay before me, and this I determined to cross, in the hope of falling over some fruit, which might help me to sustain life.

It was but a narrow thicket, and I had soon crossed it. I then found myself on a narrow strip of lawn-like grass, and face to face with two animals, such I had never seen before. They were gently rubbing their heads together, and saw me not.

A second glance told me it was buck and doe of the elk species.*

The one next to me, and which I chiefly noted, was a splendid animal, surpassing all the tame deer in appearance; indeed, quite as tall as the shoulders of a horse, and not weighing less than a thousand or twelve hundred pounds.

His neck was remarkably short and strong, which detracted much from the elegant deer-like form of the family; but this formation was necessary to support the enormous palmated horns, weighing from fifty to sixty pounds.

The head was about two feet in length, narrow and clumsily shaped; the eye was small and sunken, the ears long, hairy, and asinine; the neck and withers were surmounted by an enormous mane; the throat was furnished with long coarse hair, the body round, compact, and short; the tail about four inches long; the legs long, and remarkably clean and firm.

I could not but stand and admire the animal, while I must own that my carnivorous instincts were sorely excited. I thought how much I should like a piece for my supper; but I had little time to waste in such reflections; though, it is true, its movements were rather heavy, its shoulders being higher than the croup. It was of a brownish-black colour, while its mane was fawn in hue.

It was cropping the tops of plants and low bushes, it being scarcely able to reach the grass without kneeling.

* Cervus Alces Linnæus. L'Elan - Cuvier.

Suddenly, a whistling, hissing sound, proclaimed that I was discovered. I knew all deer to be, by nature, timid, but I also knew that when called upon to defend the doe, it will fight, and is very dangerous.

I darted into the wood, and saw it turn round and rush at me with furious gestures. Then away it sped with the doe by its side, as I thought, bound on escape. I watched it with much curiosity. It did not gallop, but shuffled or ambled along, its joints cracking at every step, with a sound which could be heard at some distance. As it increased its speed its hind legs straddled to avoid treading on its fore heels, tossing the head and shoulders, like a horse about to break from a trot to a gallop. It did not leap, but stepped over any fallen tree that came in its way.

I watched it for some time with considerable interest, and thought it was about to disappear, when I perceived that it had left the doe, and was coming back at a rattling pace, with the nape up, so as to lay the horns horizontally on its back.

There was no undergowth or bushes in the wood, so that I had no protection from the enraged beast. A cold perspiration burst over me, as I, at once, took to my heels, running I knew not whither. Soon I heard the strange noise of its joints close in my rear.

I was going, at a fearful pace, up the slope of a kind of acclivity, which led, I knew not where. But all I thought of was escape. I threw away my boomerang, but my knife was stuck in its sheath, in my belt.

Closer and closer came the sound, and though I dared not look round I knew that in another instant I should be gored by the infuriated brute.

At that very moment a terrible chasm seemed to yawn beneath my feet. I was on the edge of a precipice, with another precipice at a short distance on the other side. But I had no power to check myself and leapt. I fell, how I never knew, into the yawning gulf, felt myself immersed in water, went downwards and downwards, until I lost all feeling of consciousness. Then I came to my senses, and my astonishment may be conceived.

Brief as had been the glance I had caught at the chasm into which I had fallen I was not in the same place, but in a kind of pit, surrounded by perpendicular rocks, the lowest of them not less than twenty-five feet high, while, in my cold, drenched, and exhausted state, I saw no chance of ever getting away from it.

A heavy body of water fell through a gap in the rocks into a pool below, which seethed and boiled, and then escaped, by some mysterious manner, underneath a large, projecting ledge.

But the water was pure and sweet, and lying down on the ground, so as to bring my mouth to a level with the stream, a single draught seemed to revive me so much, that selecting one place, where it seemed just possible I might climb, I began the ascent. But my feet bled, my hands were torn, my clothes reduced to rags, ere, after an hour's arduous labour, and six different attempts and failures, I succeeded in reaching the summit.

I was so exhausted that I had to lie down for a quarter o an hour, during which time I could distinctly hear the beating of my own heart. Then, rising on my hands and knees, I peered about, in search of the terrible animal which had so nearly cost me my life, but which, I made a vow, if I had to pass my life in this place, I would capture, and bend to my uses.

There he was close to me, but seeing me not. He stood sentinal over the spot where I had fallen, his horns tosse

back, his forefeet fixed firm in the ground, his little eyes fierce and fixed.

Now I understood the extraordinary nature of my escape.

I leaned over the abyss into which I had fallen and found that at its bottom was a large pool, into which fell a stream. The pool was shaped like a cauldron, while at one side was a hole, through which the water was carried into the pit where I had found myself.

I now knew that the island contained fresh water, but if situated in places like this, it was not likely to be of much use to me.

I was so sore and wearied that I dared not stir, lest the elk should gore me to death. I knew that I could not run, so I placed myself so that I could gain a ledge below in the pit, where he could scarcely follow me.

I watched him all that day, for, from some perverse instinct the brute would not move. He went a little way and browsed upon the bushes and shrubs, but he always returned to his post, ere I could make my escape. I knew very well that any attempt to run would be futile, as not only were my feet bare and bleeding, but my limbs stiff and sore.

At length, however, clutching my knife in my teeth, I began to crawl towards a clump of bushes. The night was coming on, and I knew that to remain where I was was to face certain death, whereas in a clump of bushes at some distance I might find some chance of life.

Scarcely, however, had I gone half the way, when I heard both the cracking of the beast's joints, and the hissing whistle from his thick lips. Fear lendeth strength to the weakest, and, with a cry of anguish, I rose and headed for the bushes, utterly helpless and desolate.

As I fell headlong into a brake, the elk stopped.

It was evening, which comes on with such rapidity in that region of the globe.

Instead of goring me with his ferocious horns, the elk started back, terrified and alarmed. I myself shook as with the palsy—for surely could I tell that something terrible must be within the bush to startle the elk. Next minute he pawed the ground with his feet, impatiently turned, ambled off, and was soon lost to sight in the increasing darkness.

I was left helpless, and almost bereft of sense, in the wretched shelter afforded by the bushes, while, I felt sure, some creature more terrible even than the elk was at no great distance.

How long I lay half senseless, with fatigue and fright, I know not, but in about the middle watches of the night, I was, I suppose being half asleep, disturbed by the blowing of some animal in my face. I looked up, and despite the black darkness, could make out that a large beast was standing over me.

I sat up, with a shriek torn from me by the terror which one in my weak and destitute condition would naturally feel.

CHAPTER X.

HOPE.

And we will sit in twilight's face, and see
The sweet moon glancing through the tooa tree,
The lofty accents of whose sighing bough
Shall sadly please us as we lean below.
Or climb the steep and view the surf in vain
Wrestle with rocky giants o'er the main,
Which spurn in columns back the baffled spray.
How beautiful are these! how happy they,
Who, from the toil and tumult of their lives
Steal to look down where nought but ocean strives!
Even he, too, loves at times the blue lagoon,
And smooths his ruffled mane beneath the moon.

BUT before I could in any way satisfy myself as to the

character of the animal which had so affrighted me, it had disappeared in the darkness. Still it could be heard stealthily moving about in the bushes, to my no small terror and discomfiture. In my agony I clutched my knife, and so sore, bruised, and broken-hearted did I feel, that I almost longed for a personal encounter with my enemy, whatever it might be—even if the combat did not end in my favour.

But he came back no more that night, and towards dawn I contrived to obtain a little sleep.

Awakening early, I determined, feeling still very ill after my fatigue and suffering, that I would go down to my stone hut, and rest, before making another attempt to explore the island in search of shelter, food, and water. But the journey was not so easy as I expected. While hunted by the elk, I had taken a direction which had led me out of my beaten track, and though very well knowing which way the sea lay, I spent half the day in reaching that part of the shore where I had been wrecked.

My feet were so sore and tender that I was forced to rest continually, while, had it not have been for a stick which served to support me, I should not have been able to crawl along at all.

I approached the rocks, where the wall had been erected against the little cavern, by the beach, as I was glad to exchange the ruder ground for the soft sand. Along this I moved slowly, almost convinced in my own mind that nothing was left me but to lay me down and die; I was so bruised that I knew days would elapse ere I could again go forth; and in the meantime I must surely perish from mere starvation.

Walking along, and leaning heavily on my staff, I was astonished to find it suddenly sink deeply in the sand, and when it was drawn forth, something clammy adhered thereto. I knew at once that what I had been before in search of was found.

Falling on my hands and knees, I began eagerly to remove the sand, when I soon came to a number of turtle's eggs. One or two were eagerly devoured—which gave me great relief, as they were fresh, and served the purpose both of meat and drink. I then collected as many as could be carried, and placed them inside my cave. They proved to be better for keeping a little, becoming thicker and harder. They were more palatable too. After all, they were not very savoury food, though one, who, as it were, had nothing but what fell from the trees, behoved to be content.

In my weak and miserable state, it was natural to be more timid than I should have been if well, so that no sooner were the eggs placed within my hut, than I blocked up the narrow entrance, and lay myself down. I now, indeed, felt desolate and deserted, even by hope; for, though believing, if strong and well, I could have made shift to live until such time as Providence chose to release me, yet, how could I imagine, in my present condition, that I could battle against all the dangers and difficulties that were likely to arise?

I have always thought that I must have unconsciously lost a day at this period, for I was slightly delirious, and often insensible. However this may be, on the morning of what I fancied to be the second day, finding myself a little better, and having drank off one of the eggs, I removed the stones, which barred my exit, and crawled forth.

The morning was very warm, the sky was clear, and the wind blew balmy and sweet. There had been a heavy shower in the night, but the sun was quickly drying up the little pools which remained on the rocks, and I had only just time to get one good drink, ere they had disappeared in evaporation. I then selected a position, which gave me a view of the sea, and there, my back against a stone, I passed the rest of the day, the tears often gushing down my face as I gazed out upon the vast wilderness of waters, in the desperate hope of seeing a vessel.

So true is it, that idleness is the parent of all evil. Had I have only been busily employed, such miserable and ungrateful thoughts would never have intruded themselves upon my imagination, as did that day.

Close beneath me was a small lagoon or pond, and whenever I took my eyes off the far distant horizon, I noticed that something seemed to glitter and shine in a very peculiar way. My curiosity at last being forcibly aroused, I crawled down, and found that the long continuance of northerly winds had choked up this little land-locked bay with kelp, and that what I saw at a distance were numerous fish which had been entangled in the weed, and were struggling to escape. I managed to get one or two, with which I made shift for supper, and then the wind rising, and showing signs of a fresh storm, I went back to my cavern, and again enclosed myself within its narrow limits.

I felt better that night, and, despite the wind and the rain, slept for some hours, when I was suddenly awakened with a feeling of surprise and terror. Some noise, I knew, had started me rudely from my slumbers, but what it could have been I knew not. I listened attentively for some minutes, but could distinguish nothing, save the terrible howling of the blast, it having now risen to the proportions of a tempest.

Then I heard the report of a gun at sea.

To dash down my guardian wall, to sally forth into the open air, to rush down to the sea-shore, was the work of an instant, and there I stood, with straining eye-balls, peering out upon the black night which enveloped the ocean. It was pitch dark, and the roaring of the heavy surf on the beach was something terrible.

Short as the storm had been, it had lashed the waves to positive fury.

Then I saw a sudden flash, followed after by a loud report. It was some vessel in a sore straight, indeed; for what else could induce them to try the effect of signals of distress in that part of the world? How I now longed, with deep anguish of soul, that I had discovered the means of making a fire. The vessel was in all probability foundering, and could I have guided them to my island, at all events I might have hoped for companionship.

It is no doubt true, that solitary confinement for life in a prison is a worse punishment than death; but solitary exile, even on an island, which you have all to yourself, is almost as bad.

I noticed not the storm. I scarcely was aware that the wind was apparently every moment on the increase, so wrapped was my soul in the thought of the vessel, which, for some time, continued to discharge its ordnance. Then it ceased, and I neither saw nor heard anything more of it that night.

I crept back to my cavern for a short time, but could obtain no more sleep. I thought of the vessel in distress, but I am afraid I thought more of myself. Already I began to miss the society of my fellow-creatures. What thoughts passed through my mind I cannot say; I only remember a confused idea of what might have been done, had I have found companions; how we might have built a barque in which to escape, and a thousand other things equally idle and unsatisfactory.

It was still very stormy when I went out and gazed wistfully on the disturbed waters.

But I could see nothing.

I gazed around vacantly, hoping still that as the wind

fell I might, at all events, discover something of the wreck. This reminded me that I had not examined the rocky belt in front of which my own vessel had been cast away. This great omission I made up my mind to repair at the earliest opportunity.

CHAPTER XI.

THE SANDBANK.

WITH a deep sigh I turned away to my usual morning avocation of searching for food upon the shore in which I was moderately successful. And thus passed two days, during which time the storm abated, and I found myself very much recruited in my general health.

On the morning of the third day I went out to the beach as usual. The sea was much calmer, and I gazed once more with anxiety on the distant horizon.

I rubbed my eyes with surprise as I did so.

Something which I had never before seen lay about a mile out to seaward, the waves going over it every now and then with great force. My heart beat violently with varied emotions. Surely this was the wreck of the ship which I had heard firing guns the other evening. Though I could scarcely hope to find any one alive on board, still there was little doubt I might discover something useful to myself in the ship.

I resolved at once, then, to try and make my way to the reef or sandbank on which the remains of the vessel had struck. But how was I to perform this perilous adventure? To swim that distance was out of the question, and though I might have waded a portion of the way, it would have been madness to have run so much risk.

I resolved, therefore, to make myself a raft—few and slight as were my materials.

I had noticed that wherever trees grew upon the slope of a hill, they were easily uprooted. This had explained to me the mysterious noises in the hills, which always accompanied high winds. The highest of trees were uprooted, and tumbled down into the valleys with a tremendous crash.

This arose from the fact that the soil was in these places very shallow, having its foundation upon rocks.

I at once availed myself of this knowledge, and going up some little distance into the interior, selected two trees suitable to my purpose, and by very moderate exertion of strength, contrived to drag them from the side of a hill, and to cut from them such branches as interfered with my project. I then, with much labour, and great fatigue, dragged them down to the water's edge. This work occupied me one whole day.

The next morning, I rose, full of hope and excitement, and collecting good stores of withes from a thicket close at hand, bound the trees together, laid over them some boughs, and thus made one of the rudest, and, perhaps, least, sea-worthy rafts, that ever man did manufacture.

But I was buoyed up by mysterious hopes, and did not relax in my exertions, until my piece of workmanship was finished, as well as under the circumstances could be expected. I had placed it at low water in a small lagoon, and when the tide flowed, had the satisfaction of seeing it float upon a pretty even keel.

Knowing very well that I should not be able to row this rude boat, I erected a small mast, to which I attached my jacket as a sail, and in this wise, with a broken bough for a rudder, I put off from the island on my desperate undertaking. I certainly had some misgivings as to the consequences, but, at the same time, was too anxious for success to measure all the evils that might befall me.

The wind was very light, and, as it always is with the breeze off the land, the sea was very smooth, so that all appeared to smile upon my undertaking. My raft, it is true, moved very slowly, and was very unmanageable, it not minding the rudder. Thus, though it kept pretty steadily in the direction I wished, yet it was constantly turning round, as on a pivot, and all I could do, I could not prevent it, which made me somewhat alarmed for my journey back.

The object which had roused my curiosity, and on board which I hoped to find, if not living beings, at all events, arms and ammunition, could now be distinctly made out to be over a hundred feet in length. If, however, it were a vessel, it was very low in the water, and I could scarcely hope for any advantage on board it.

But being soon at so short a distance from it as to discern the exact nature of the matter, I had no longer any illusion.

It was the trunk of a vast tree.

With bitter feelings of disappointment, I approached nearer, and found it to be a huge cotton-tree, which had been driven to this spot by the boisterous winds and waves. I climbed upon it, after fastening my raft, and found that it must have been years in the water, for it was covered all over with barnacles, mussels, and oysters.

So great and terrible were my emotions of disappointment I could have cried. But my better feelings coming to my assistance, I regained courage, and began to take from the tree, by the assistance of my knife, some of those parasitical shell fish which had proved to me its long stay in salt water. Of these I made a very hearty meal, and then at once determined to hasten back.

I could walk along the cotton tree as upon the deck of an ordinary vessel, and in my search after the somewhat succulent food which adhered to the trunk, I had left the spot where my raft had been fastened.

I now saw that it was afloat in a southerly direction, and distant about a hundred yards!

My folly was at once apparent. I ought to have known the danger of trusting wholly to the withes, which I could but tie imperfectly. What was I to do? There was, indeed, little time for consideration, as the raft was moving out to sea with considerable rapidity.

Then, without a moment's further hesitation, I plunged into the water, and made directly for my raft.

Scarcely had I got half-way—I swam much faster than the two clumsily joined trees—when I saw at no great distance, something moving rapidly through the water, which I at once recognised to be a shark. Every drop of blood in my veins became cold as ice. Wildly I struck out, knowing not which way to go, though still mechanically making for the raft.

On came the shark.

I had heard of desperate hand to hand conflicts with this redoubtable animal. I had been told that with a knife men had succeeded in defying and destroying the dreaded monster of the deep; but I believe that no one person placed in the same position with myself would have felt much relieved by this remembrance.

Still I determined to sell my life dearly. When I saw that the animal was close upon me I dived with terrific force. To take a deeper plunge, I almost leaped out of the water. When I rose to the surface I could see my fearful assailant in the act of turning. I fled towards the

No. 3.

ALFRED AND THE MONKEY.

shore, forgetting my raft in my anxiety to escape from the terror of the deep.

But it was in vain. The huge shovel-nosed shark, as if certain of its prey, moved majestically onward, until it nearly touched me; then it turned. At that moment I touched ground, and fear giving me wings, bounded on, to fall sprawling on a sandbank, the shark grounding itself from the shallowness of the water. I felt pain in my right thigh for hours after, the animal striking me with his head, violently, as it rushed on.

I lay panting for some moments ere I rose to my feet, and then found that I was on a huge sandbank, which I had observed to be nearly dry at low water. But I knew that it was now only about half flood, so that, when the tide was up, I might find the water over my head, when, if strength were left me to try and swim ashore, I should have to run the ordeal of all the sharks and alligators in the bay.

I made, then, a hasty survey of this dreary island, and found that in one place, in the middle of the bank, the water was not more than six inches deep. Here I sat down to reflect on my wretched position. I saw at once the explanation of the escape of my raft. A current was running to the southward, occasioned very likely by the flood tide.

Of course it was hopeless to expect to recover it now, while to swim to the mainland, as my supposed island now was to me, appeared out of the question. I had not yet familiarised myself with the idea of a hand to hand conflict with the sharks.

And the tide rose steadily, until it was up to my knees.

The day was declining fast, but I could see that the water was alive with my enemies. They had discovered the presence of their human prey, and were evidently preparing for a desperate and hungry tussle for his flesh.

Nearer and nearer came their ugly snouts, until I expected every minute, that they would touch me—*and still the water kept slowly rippling upwards.*

I clutched my knife, just as one monster, huger and more savage than the others, dashed headlong forward, from a considerable distance on the water, and, by the mere force of impulsion, passed close to me. I struck him with my knife, and the water was red with blood—but what saved me was that he could not swim in so little depth—and then, joy! joy! I could see that the water was going down.

At all events it came no higher, and I knew that I was safe from the sharks.

But what availed that? I was alone on a wretched, desert-reef, where I could not hope to obtain the slightest sustenance. I was half-naked, cold, and exhausted, and surrounded by ferocious monsters of the deep, which, as if aware that their prey was momentarily escaping from them, made desperate attempts to reach me, in which they all failed.

And thus the night came on.

CHAPTER XII.

SHIP ON FIRE.

As soon as darkness fell upon the deep, the wind changed and blew towards the land, while, the tide falling rapidly, I was left shortly upon the sandy reef. The only idea which suggested itself to my mind was to scoop a hole in the soft sand, and bury myself therein for the night, and this, as far as I was able, was accomplished.

In doing so I was fortunate enough to find a clam, which proved an indifferent sort of supper.

In this shallow hole, thus made by my hands, I lay down, covering myself over with sand as much as possible; and tried to sleep, ere the reflux of the tide forced me to take to my feet again. And in this, by great good fortune, I in part succeeded. But my dreams deprived my sleep of all refreshing qualities. I was surrounded by horrid faces, I could see fearful things crawling towards me, and I could hear the voices, in the distance, of monsters roaring with impatience to devour me.

Then I awoke with a start, and a great dread came upon my soul. I knew very little of the character of the sea lions and seals, but feared that, finding me on their own ground, they might attack me. My mind, however, became easier when I found myself alone upon the reef.

The water, however, now began to rise, and my whole attention was given to the enemies I knew would soon be gathering around me. For this purpose, I selected the highest part of the reef, which, fortunately, was hard, and as I afterwards found, was formed of coral. I could thus see the waters gradually rising, rippling towards my feet with a low murmuring sound, like that we hear inside a large shell.

At any other time, and under any other circumstances, I should have listened to it as I would have to music. But now it was rather as the notes of my death-knell that I regarded it.

Slowly, but surely, the tide rose towards me, until I saw once more the moment when it would reach me.

At this instant of time my attention was directed by events of a very different character.

The night, though calm and unruffled, was very dark. The clouded, starless heavens, seemed to portend another storm, in which case my fate was certain. Down to the very edge of the black waters hung the pall-like sky, so that I appeared encircled by a globe of gloom.

Suddenly I saw a cavern-like opening in the dreary, heavy sky down on the very level of the distant horizon. I had often seen the like, and could almost fancy I felt the hot and furious blast which would soon pour from that quarter. The wind seemed to be lifting the very clouds, and to be bringing with it a faint, ruddy phosphorous, light.

But no—it cannot be—it is—a fire!

I bounded to my feet. A fire! Then there must be human beings at no great distance; and could I but build a proper raft, I might hope to escape from my lonely and dreary abode. My heart beat with terrible violence, and I longed for day, when I would swim ashore, in defiance of sharks and alligators, and devote my whole energies to the engine of my future safety.

But again my heart leaped into my mouth. The fire grew in dimensions so rapidly, it could not be one built by human hands for any useful purpose; it must be the burning of a forest, or the eruption of a volcano. Beginning to fancy that my imagination had deceived me, I closed my eyes, and kept them so for some moments. When I opened them again I saw at once that the fire was much larger—no, it was much nearer.

It was afloat.

Now I knew what it was that had raised in my mind such futile hopes and dreams. It was a vessel on fire, and which, driven by the winds, was being carried in my direction. As it rapidly approached me, I could soon make out the masts and rigging, which were on fire, while I plainly saw that my hopes of companionship were at an end.

The ship was on fire from stem to stern.

I had very little doubt that this was the unfortunate vessel, the heavy ordnance of which I had heard, and been so startled with, a few days before. The wind being directly on the land, the burning mass approached so rapidly in my direction, as to make it more than of serious reflection to me.

Still I had no great cause for fear, knowing as I did that the reef I was on shoaled out to too great a distance for the vessel to approach very near to me.

Still on it came, until I could hear the cracking of the flames, the spitting of the pitch and tar, and the continual hissing sounds, as pieces of burning spars fell into the water. My eyes, ears, and every sense fascinated, I scarcely noted now the rising waters, though they reached unto my knees.

The burning mass was about a quarter of a mile from me now, and I began seriously to think of swimming towards the land, when it suddenly heeled to port; the flames seemed to start up afresh, and then the vast pile stopped. By the lurid light of the flames, now mingled with black smoke, I saw that it had struck against the cotton tree.

After a few minutes of rocking, the fierce furnace appeared to become more steady; and as it did so, I distinctly heard a cry, so awful, unearthly, and thrilling, that I involuntarily clasped my hands together, and uttered a silent prayer. Then all was still; and, except that I thought a low moaning reached my ears at intervals, I heard nothing save the roaring of the fast consuming ship.

When the vessel struck, the masts went by the board, carrying with them the rigging, so that all that now remained was the hull—and this I knew must speedily burn itself out when the water began to overflow the gunwale.

But now the quiet night began to wane, and before I was scarcely aware of the change, the sun leaped up from the eastern hills and flooded the purply ocean with its beams. To my surprise and delight I saw, at no great distance, my raft aground upon the reef. The currents, the ebb and flow, had beaten it about, and the change of wind had brought it back whence it came.

I waded to where it stood, without seeing one shark or alligator. They had all made for the neighbourhood of the burning vessel.

To clamber on my raft, to set it adrift, and to steer as well as I could towards the burning ship, was the work of a moment. I could see that it was fast aground against the cotton-tree, which itself, from the fierce contact of the heat, was beginning to smoulder. Still I made my way as fast as possible towards it, and when close under the lee of the trunk, saw a sight which seemed to freeze my soul with horror.

The starboard bow had been stove in by concussion with the cotton-tree, and the forecastle deck had thus been laid bare. The flames, which had evidently commenced aft, after devouring masts, sails, and ropes, had not as yet fastened on the solid beams and planks forward. What I saw there was this:—a dead body of a man, his clothes all charred and burnt, hung half out of the ship, while a large and powerful Newfoundland dog appeared to me to be savagely devouring it.

But, in my idea, I calumniated the faithful animal. Approaching nearer, I clearly saw that it was making frantic efforts to drag its master from the burning ship, in which it had partially succeeded. This instance of devoted affection, even after death to its owner, did not surprise me. When the dog, desisting me a moment, saw me it gave a low whine, ran wildly along the trunk of the cotton-tree, and seemed to wish me to come to its assistance.

Then it returned towards the vessel, and, making one mighty effort, it dragged the body off the deck, and dead man and dog rolled headlong into the sea. Then came a fearful rush, and the dog, uttering once more that fearful cry which had so startled me before, swam wildly towards the land.

The sight of the sharks tearing its master to pieces proved too much for the poor animal.

CHAPTER XIII.

A SEA VOYAGE.

I SAW, clearly, that to approach much nearer to the burning vessel, was to run the risk of being caught in the devouring flames. Still I crept as near as I could in the hope of making a meal off the oysters and muscles which adhered to the cotton tree. I was very careful this time as to the fastening of my raft, after which I crept upon the trunk. It was so fearfully hot that I could scarcely bear myself, and I found, as I might have expected, nearly all the shell-fish scorched. And I made a meal of the first cooked food I had tasted for many days.

What would I not have given to have carried some fire ashore! But this was out of the question. I had satisfied my hunger, but began again to feel all the awful pangs of thirst. I was fain, therefore, to hurry to my raft and make the best of my way towards the shore.

This proved to be a terrible task. The tides set along the island, there being no stream of any consequence for these to flow up and down, so that whether it were ebbing or flowing I was carried to the north or south, and not towards the land. Still, the wind being very much in my favour, I strove with might and main to reach the shore.

My raft was fearfully unmanageable. I could scarcely control its progress at all, and thus I saw myself carried along the island without appearing to approach much nearer. The coast which had been flat and low began now to rise, and cliffs approach near to the water's edge. Slightly ahead of me was a promontory, and I fancied, I scarcely knew why, that beyond it I should find a stream.

My thirst was now terrible, and but that by steeping my hands in the sea, I seemed to cool my whole body, I should have felt it still more.

Suddenly I seemed drawn by the secret influence of the current right towards the promontory ahead of me; then my raft whirled swiftly round, and I seemed to be actually sucked along by a kind of whirlpool. It was difficult to keep my balance, so fearfully did the raft sway about.

Those only who have endured a long series of thirst, and can readily recall the desire and agitation which the idea alone of springs and brooks have at the time raised in them, can judge of the emotions with which I eyed a large cascade of the most transparent water, which poured itself from a rock near a hundred feet high into the sea at a small distance from the raft.

I saw, however, that my feeble vessel was being drawn into a kind of vortex, the tremendous cascade acting in this way on the falling tide, while the water itself escaped by the undertow.

There was little time for thought. Before me, somewhat to the left was an arch, probably cut from the solid rock by the action of the waves. Towards this, I endeavoured to direct my raft; but I saw that it would not be diverted from its own course, and was about, weak as I was, to leap into the water, when, to my great relief, the rude pole used as a rudder, touched the ground. I at once pushed it in the desired direction, passed through the arch, and found myself in a totally different region.

The broken cragged precipices, which looked so unpromising at a distance, I discovered to be very far from barren, being in most places, covered with woods, and everywhere interspersed with the finest valleys, clothed in a most beautiful verdure, and watered with numerous cascades; no valley, I found, afterwards, without its proper rill.

The place looked like a paradise, and involuntarily bending my knee, as I leaped on shore, my next act was to rush where a grove appeared, by its extreme luxuriance to indicate the presence of water. Though the thunder of the cataract still rang in my ears, there were no visible means of approaching that.

About three hundred yards along a slope itself like a lawn in its softness, was the grove. I turned towards it, with fire in my veins. There were several shell-fish to be seen, but the tongue was swollen, the lips and mouth parched, so that to eat was more painful than would have been the endurance of hunger.

The cliff from which the cascade fell into the sea, from that spot trended inland, became slightly lower as it advanced towards the interior. A number of parasitical plants fell in rich abundance from its summit, and when the grove was reached, I saw that they fell in a perfect avalanche over the summit of trees, which were all strange to me, but which I afterwards became familiar with.

There was one, however, which could not be mistaken. It was the bottle-gourd. One of these I clutched with singular joy, and next minute stood enraptured with delight.

CHAPTER XIV.

THE WATER POOL.

It was a spot such as I could have conceived our first parents selecting for their bower in the peaceful abode of paradise. Trickling from the rocky cliff, which formed part of the formidable barrier between my part of the island and that which seemed so much more tempting to the view, a small stream filled a basin with clear and pellucid water, that was further shaded by the palm tree, the cocoa tree, and a vast matting of wild vines and other creepers.

I stood still a moment, and then was about to plunge into the cool and pleasant pond, when an odd kind of noise attracted my attention. Looking up, my eyes were fixed upon the strangest beast that ever natural-history book or travels had brought to my notice. It was a huge kind of baboon, but of so malicious and malignant an aspect, that I was, for for a moment, bereft of sense or motion.

But, whatever may have been the motive, or whatever may have been the inclination of the beast, he made no motion to attack me, so, without further hesitation, I advanced to the pool, and, using some discretion, slaked my thirst, nor did ever the most delicate wines that I afterwards fabricated, give me the same delight. Then, after scanning the trees carefully, and finding that the animal was gone, I sat me down, and began seriously to reflect.

Away with all weakness was my feeling. I was cast away on a desert island, not entirely bereft of resources, but doomed, with limited means, to labour hard for my existence. The time for repining was past. I had to provide myself with every absolute want of civilised man—a house, arms, utensils for use, clothes, a bed of some kind. The cold season of the year, which only lasted while north-east winds prevailed, must soon pass away, and then I should find the necessity for a hut even more pressing, to guard me against the scorching heat and the heavy night dews.

My ambition went so far, at first, as to contemplate the erection of a log-hut; but this, on reflection, was dismissed from my mind, as necessitating an axe and saw, at least. Then I thought of a cavern, but though the idea pleased me, yet would it require, also, to render such a place habitable, many things which I did not possess.

Casting my eyes about me to aid my reflections, I noticed, on the other edge of the grove, a small upright palm-tree, and at once determined to make this the foundation-column of my first hut. The pool of pure and cool water decided me on the locality, though I had no idea of abandoning my residence on the sea shore wholly, as there alone could vessels be seen, or any monument to attract attention be erected.

And no man who has been left on a desert island, lived more firmly in the hope of being taken away, than did the poor Sailor Crusoe.

There were bushes and small sprouts from larger trees in abundance about the grove. These I spent the remainder of the day in cutting, my only refreshment being some fruit, which, from its resemblance to a fig, I ate without fear. It was only when night came on that fatigue drove me to repose.

Nothing occurring to disturb my slumbers, the dawn of day saw me again at work. The stakes that I had cut, being of a soft nature, I thrust into holes made with a harder piece of wood. They were planted about four feet from the tree, and uniformly four feet high. Then cutting a quantity of wild vine, I made also some wooden pegs, which I hammered with a stone into holes bored in the palm tree. Above these, as high as the hands could reach, I then twisted a number of vine branches, thus forming a rude and primitive shelf.

On this, after some trouble, were rested some smaller sticks, which were then carried to the poles which made the outside wall of my house, where I fastened them, as best I might, with some tendrils and wooden pegs. Then came the thatch, which was a task of infinite labour, from want of a ladder; but by means of great perseverance, I covered my roof with leaves and grass by the evening of th third day.

The sight of this, my own handiwork, did wonderfully cheer me, and thoughts came into my mind, that if some few neccessaries, which a man cannot do without, could but be found, I might pass a year or two of my life in that spot without giving way to utter despair.

The third night I slept in my hut, having had nothing to disturb me all the time, though I thought, every now and then, that I could hear a jerking or rustling in the tall trees, that made me rather uneasy. Still the notion came into my head, that no animal could be very dangerous that kept at such a respectful distance.

Tired of living on fruits and berries, which, though harmless and pleasant enough as a change, were but indifferent sustenance, I determined in the morning to turn my steps towards the sea-shore in search of more substantial food. My gourd had been scooped out, and admirably served the purpose of a bottle. So having filled it with water, I took my way across some very steep rocks in the direction of my cavern in the cliff.

CHAPTER XV.

THE PLEASANT DISCOVERY.

Around she pointed to a spacious cave,
Whose only portal was the keyless wave,
A hollow archway by the sun unseen,
Save through the billow's glassy veil of green,
And some transparent ocean holiday,
And when all the finny people are at play.
　　　*　　　*　　　*
And all was darkness for a space, till day
Through clefts above let in a sober ray;
As in some old cathedral's glimmering aisle
The dusty monuments from light recoil.
　　　　　　　　　　　　　BYRON.

My journey by sea had brought me many miles, so that I

with difficulty reached *False Wild Bay*, as in my fancy the place of my shipwreck was called, some time after mid-day. The sea was now very calm. Innumerable wild fowl skimmed over its waters, while seal and sea lions disported themselves in the gentle waves in such numbers as to render any approach on my part dangerous. At least such was the impression made on my mind.

At length, however, hunger prevailed; and going down towards the beach I was fortunate enough to find a small turtle in the act of laying eggs. Quick as thought, I rushed between it and the sea, and then turned it on his back. This is the way the fishermen always do. I immediately cut its throat with my knife, and reluctantly enough began to take off slices to make a meal of. My eyes were cast at the time enviously to the spot where the wreck still smouldered.

While engaged in eating, which was performed as a task—my appetite not yet being used to raw flesh—I heard a growl close at hand, and turning quickly saw the great Newfoundland dog standing, with feet firmly set and lip drawn up so as to show his teeth, looking both savage and hungry.

At once, without a moment's hesitation, a large piece of turtle being cast to him, the beast most eagerly devoured it; and, as if re-assured, he approached nearer, and took pieces from my hand. Then the powerful animal lay down at my feet and licking my hand, looked up into my face with an anxious and grateful look, very much as a human being might have done. From that day Tiger—the name I gave him—proved my best and most faithful friend.

Having now my body-guard, I marched along the beach with considerable more courage, and felt even inclined to attack a seal, but being no longer hungry, did forbear.

Suddenly Tiger ran on ahead to where the waves broke over something heavy. The instinct of the animal was wonderful. It proved to me at once the value of my acquisition. That which the dog had discovered I should have passed unnoticed.

It was a great oblong seaman's chest, half buried in the soft and yielding sand.

It was a painted chest, of unusual size and length, but so securely fastened that I saw no chance of opening it. How my heart beat with the hope of what it might contain may readily be conceived. Every want that can befal humanity was mine. Had fortune cast me naked on that desolate shore my fate could scarcely have been worse. My clothes were torn in rags, my feet, though somewhat hardened by constant walking, were still tender and sore, while even the savage in a state of nature was, in general, able to procure that fire, to cook his food, which was denied to me.

I cast my eyes round, then, in the hope of finding something with which to force open the chest. Fortunately the tide was falling, so that I had time to make my search ere it got afloat—which ended in my finding a sharp stone, which, with another one as a hammer, served my purpose. The task was rude, as the lock was good, and the clasps many, but I persevered. The delight which filled my mind may be conceived, when, success rewarding my labour, I found it to be the well-filled chest of an officer.

It contained a small bale of cloth, intended for uniforms; a fowling piece, in its case; several gun-flints; a musket, with the stock off; shoes, of various sizes; several pounds of the yellow wax tapers which are used by the Spaniards; a small case of various intruments; a parcel of socks; some shirts; a few books, in English and French; some knives, scissors, needles, and thread; and a whole suit of attire, which, though rather large, could be made to suit me.

There was a flask of gunpowder, too, and some bullets.

There was a sword, also, which, though somewhat heavy, was still a welcome sight.

With what silent rapture I did take these up unto the rocks, out of the reach of the sea, may be conceived. Not Columbus discovering the new world, not the voyager falling on a diamond mine, could have been more delighted than I was with my treasure, which, in the situation in which Providence had placed me, was inestimable in value.

The chest once empty, it was easily dragged above high water mark, when I sat me down to recover from the state of excitement in which I had been placed by this discovery. The next thing was to avail myself of the glorious windfall which had befallen me.

I tore off my ragged things, with avidity, and proceeded to clothe myself. The treasure appeared to me inexhaustible, as, under the influence of such feelings, one rarely looks much to the future.

All that I did not require was replaced in the chest, and, from the habit of early days, secured as well as possible. Then it was that I began to realise the full force of the change. My appearance, doubtless, would have excited the risible fancies of my own countrymen; but as regards comfort, there could be scarcely anything to find fault with. I had a coat and trousers much too large, but which I intended to alter; I had a sword, the weight of which was almost a burden; and a very heavy gun, but this was a treasure which I clung to with all the more delight, that its use must soon fail me for want of gunpowder. Walking along by the seaside, with my huge companion, I, on reflection, determined to pass one more night in my cavern, where safety was now reasonably to be expected.

Then it was that a reflection came to my mind in reference to food, and I determined instantly to carry it out. The means of making a fire were now certainly in my possession, and accordingly it was my fixed idea to secure one for that night. To collect fuel it was necessary to go somewhat in the interior, but time to me was of little value if any search was rewarded.

Having brought down a goodly supply of dry boughs which, wherever there were any bushes were easily found all the old branches falling off themselves, and rolling away—I placed them in a heap, and then proceeded, in this way, to make my fire.

Some dry leaves and moss being placed on the ground between two stones, a small quantity of gunpowder was sprinkled amongst this rude kind of tinder; and then, with the back of a knife and a flint, some sparks being cast therein, a flame speedily arose. Then some withes, leaves, and small boughs being placed thereon, the whole did speedily expand into an excellent fire, which was a sight to do the heart good.

But there my task did not end, as I purposed to have the first good meal which had as yet been afforded me on the island. Having carefully put on one side a few straight pieces of wood, they were laid across from stone to stone, as soon as the fire had burnt down, so as to yield no smoke.

Upon these the remainder of my turtle steaks, and some shell fish were placed, and in a very short space of time, a meal was ready, such as an epicure might have enjoyed—so, at least, it appeared to me, who had so many days been driven to eat that which was repugnant to my habits and feelings.

My dainty repast finished, what remained was given to the dog. Then, having made up a very good fire, and night coming on, I retired to my stone hut, leaving the animal to keep guard outside.

———

CHAPTER XVI.

MY DOG MEETS WITH AN ADVENTURE.

ALL persons placed in my situation must have their thoughts almost equally divided between the necessities of the moment and the idea of escape. This latter, however, if too much indulged in, would always go far to weaken the mental and physical energies, by inducing that constant trusting to chance which is the bane of so many men's lives. I determined, therefore, as much as possible, to make my mind up to a long stay in my solitary domain, though hoping and trusting that the hour might finally come for my release.

Resignation to one's fate is the secret of happiness in every station of life, but in mine most of all. It was necessary, then, to fix on a permanent habitation, which I might prepare against every possible variation of the climate, as well as to ensure secrecy and safety in case my island—as I had made up my mind it was—were ever visited by savages or Indians, or even by lawless bucaneers. Even if I could hope to escape by means of a boat or raft, it was absolutely necessary that in the meantime I should live in comfort and safety.

Hitherto no position had presented itself anything like that near which I had discovered the pool. It had the advantage of seclusion, as well as of wood and water. A cave, it is true, to my mind would have been infinitely preferable to anything else; but a great deal of time might be lost in the search, and some temporary abode was, at all events, absolutely necessary.

It would be very wearisome to tell how many shifts I was for a long time daily put to to procure food. It will only be needful in future, therefore, to record anything extraordinary in this way. Having breakfasted as well as my means would allow, my steps were turned towards the hills. Many thoughts had come into my head as to the way in which I should improve my rude habitation. Tools and utensils were alone wanting to enable me to carry out my designs; but these I could as yet see no way of fashioning It would be necessary, then, to do without them as much as possible.

The weather since my residence on the island had been extremely unfavourable, but I knew enough of the position in which the island was placed to be abundantly aware that a change would soon take place. The home suited to my position must, therefore, be a peculiar one.

Moving with far more celerity than at any time since my residence on the island—thanks to the fortunate discovery of shoes in the sailor's chest—I was not long ere my steps were directed to the mouth of a gully by which I had left the more fertile and pleasant part of the island. My dog kept gambolling around me, with all the delight usually manifested by this creature when visiting new places. Every now and then, however, it would dash off at headlong speed, disappear, and, returning after a long absence, look up at me with an air of quiet satisfaction, the explanation of which did not occur to me at first. An examination, however, of its mouth presently elucidated the mystery.

It was red with blood.

It had found some small kind of wild beast.

At once the idea flashed across my mind that I might train the powerful animal to hunt game for me, as well as itself. How this plan was carried out will be seen in its proper place.

We had reached the gully, and advanced some small distance up its narrow depths, when Tiger halted, spread out his forefeet sniffed the air, and then gave a low, prolonged howl. Something, which instinct told him was an enemy, had clearly passed that way. How my gun was clutched with convulsive energy, as I gazed anxiously around, I need not tell. But nothing then meeting my gaze, I again advanced.

I had not proceeded above twenty yards, when Tiger gave another low, savage howl, and without paying any attention to my repeated calls, burst away at a rapid pace. Following him up as quick as I could, my eyes fell upon a scene which both disheartened and terrified me.

A huge, hairy-looking man, as I at first thought, but in reality a powerful monkey, was busily engaged in destroying the last few remnants of that house which had cost me so much labour and pains to erect. With an activity which was ludicrous in its intensity, it was taking down poles, stakes, and thatch piecemeal, examining each one thing with avidity, and then casting it disdainfully from its paws.

Suddenly it turned. It had heard the dog. A more hideous monster it is scarcely possible to conceive. My readings had told me of the size, force, and ugliness of monkeys, but never did my imagination realise anything like this. Its face, though having, as I thought, something human about it, was puffed, distorted, and fearful; its long, unwieldly arms were waved furiously aloft—and then it flew at the dog.

I fired.

Never since the creation of the world, doubtless, had the sudden explosion of a gun been heard on that spot of earth. The effect was wondrous. Reverberating echoes came pealing back from the rocks, birds of every hue and shape, from the gaudy cockatoo to the blue wood pigeon, and the ocean gull, that shrieks—not cries—rose, uttering each their peculiar shrill, piercing, or more pleasant notes; strange jabberings from amid the trees sounded alarmingly, while even from a distance came faint noises, as if the whole island had been shaken to its centre.

But the fierce animal, which I was sure I had hit, stood still, silent, amazed, and as if changed into a statue. Then it clapped its two hands upon its breast, as if searching for the wound so mysteriously inflicted, after which it gave a howl, such as sent the terrified dog back several yards in my direction.

But only for a moment. The native courage of its splendid race came to the rescue, and as I, after loading, was running up, it flew savagely at the monkey, and a desperate conflict ensued. The wounded animal, which was young, as I afterwards found, and not all full-grown, fought with his hands, or rather paws, tearing at the dog's throat, and inflicting fearful scratches. Being now very near, my gun was again levelled, and this time with even more success, for uttering once more its cry, which, though hoarse and loud, was not wholly unhuman, it tore itself away, clambered with great labour a tree close at hand, and disappeared in the rich and profuse foliage.

My house was totally destroyed, and the question now arose as to the wisdom and propriety of fixing my habitation in a place, which, though affording promise of comfort in other ways, was evidently the resort of dangerous and mischievous animals, which, if they attacked me but once now and then, would soon exhaust my stock of gunpowder in the effort to destroy them.

For that day, however, there was no help for it, but to stay in the place which had been the scene of conflict, and which in my own mind I denominated Battle-pool. After bathing my dog's neck, and giving him some food, I collected such fruits and berries as I knew were wholesome and nourishing, and made a hearty meal, during which my mind was wholly bent on remedying the defect in my habitation, which rendered it so easily the prey of my natural enemies.

While so engaged my eyes were cast upwards, and I could see above my head, at the summit of lofty trees, the cocoanut that would have been to me meat and drink, but which no effort of imagination as yet enabled me to look on as available to my uses. Other fruits there were hanging from the tall trees, while the circumstance that none were to be seen scattered on the ground was attributable to the presence of the monkey tribe, which eats and devours everything it can find.

After dinner, with much labour and pains, a rude hut was erected from the remains of the old one, just to enable me to pass the night. This done, a fire, more for my protection against animals than for the necessities of warmth, was made in front of the hut. Then, without attempting to close up its entrance, I strewed the floor with leaves and allowing the dog to bask on the ground between my door and the fire, composed myself to sleep.

But much as we may desire and covet the sweet restorer of our exhausted nerves, it will not always visit us. My thoughts were fixed anxiously on the animals which infested my favourite retreat. I also thought of those more agreeable ones, in the shape of birds, which might minister both to my pleasures and my wants. Ideas of traps, nets, and other inventions to scare away dangerous beasts and secure useful ones, flitted through my mind, and kept me for a long time awake. But fatigue and the utter silence of the night at last produced a soothing effect, and I slept.

CHAPTER XVII.
AN AWFUL DAY.

I was awakened on this, perhaps the most eventful day that could be counted among those which were passed in the island, by a sensation which much resembled suffocation. A nightmare appeared weighing on my chest. Alarmed, and instinctively clutching the gun which lay close at hand, my first thought was that I was attacked by some enemy, which seemed the more probable that the dog lay still, almost dead to all appearance, but uttering wild, monotonous, and low moans.

Rubbing my eyes, I gazed around. There was, though it was certainly long since morning, no sun, but a moist and relaxing sultriness pervaded the whole atmosphere, which was beyond all description oppressive.

The sides of my miserable hut appeared dripping with unwholesome vapours, everything with which my hands came in contact felt wet and clammy, yet burning. It was a terrible effort to breathe.

I tried to sit up a minute or two, but my nerves utterly unstrung, I cast myself panting, flushed, and terrified, on my withered couch.

What could it mean—what could it portend? Was it some great convulsion of nature, or merely the signs of a coming thunderstorm?

Although I knew myself—at all events, the night before I surely was so—in vigorous and robust health, a languor, accompanied by a sense of suffocating closeness, overcame me. Crawling after some few minutes to the mouth of the hut, it proved that there was not a breath of air abroad sufficient to have fanned a feather. The stillness which prevailed had something portentous about it. The sensation which fell upon the mind was something indescribably awful. High in the air the birds soared, evidently terrified and alarmed at coming events.

Creeping along by degrees, so utter was the sense of weakness, a draught of water at the pool, though it was tepid, insipid, and unrefreshing, seemed to revive me a little. I stood upright and, anxious to unravel the mystery, moved to where there was a look out upon the sea. It was glassy, and looked utterly stagnant. Even the throbbing, which is said never to leave it, was no longer apparent, while a low and unbroken mass of clouds, heavy, dense, and immoveable, obscured the heavens, and spread their sullen hue over earth and water.

Night, storm, and darkness appeared brooding over the face of the deep, which shone every now and then, however, with a phosphoric brightness, that made me sigh as I compared it to the light in the dark eye of woman.

With an awful crash came the thunder peal, and the whole heavens were lit up by the fierce and lurid flashes of the live lightning, which seemed to come from every corner of the heavens, while the big rain fell in dancing torrents that drenched me to the skin. Then again for a moment all was hushed, the same terrible stillness pervading all nature. A dread of I knew not what fell upon my soul. My reading had given me a fearful insight into what was coming. Before, however, I could almost shape into form that which I dreaded, a crash, such as could be imagined to be the crack of doom, stunned by every sense. Sky, water, thunder, lightning, rain, all seemed blended into one—and then the sea, just now so still, rushed away from me with a terrible violence, which portended an equally forcible return.

Rushing to the higher ground, though feeling the earth trembling under my feet, I cast myself on my knees near my dog, which was stricken and, as it were, annihilated, and had never once moved at this time, it being well known that animals are, as it were, tamed and subdued by these manifestations of Omnipotent power.

Then occurred a phenomenon before my very eyes, which filled me with amaze. The pool beneath the shady trees, and one side of which was bounded by the lichen-covered rock, had remained all this time perfectly still, but influenced doubtless by the same power which had drawn the sea with such fearful force from its bed, it now began to move, while small air bubbles rose to the surface.

This alarmed me still more, as it showed me that the earthquake had not subsided. However this might be, my eyes became, as it were, fascinated, for the water was clearly and distinctly going down, at first slowly, then quickly with a whirlpool motion, as if it had been in a funnel. Then all again was still, and the pool was empty.*

The outer edge of the hole was very shallow, while the centre might have been fifteen feet in depth, without any perceptible orifice by which the water escaped. While my eyes and thoughts were bent on examining still more carefully the scene of this strange event, I noticed that the evergreens near the rock shook somewhat, and at a glance I discovered the reason.

In case of need, I had brought with me two of the yellow Spanish tapers. Hurrying to my habitation, I revived the fire, lit a candle, and taking my gun, at once went to examine the nature of the hollow, before which the parasitical plants hung in such rich profusion. The entrance was very low, and when the water was in, could not be more than three feet high.

I listened, but nothing could be heard but the rippling fall of water; and at this moment my dog, taking courage by my actions, rushed past, nearly knocked me down, and entered first. This gave me courage, and following, a scene presented

* Such a phenomenon occurred, if we remember rightly, to all the wells at the great earthquake of Lisbon.

itself to me, which caused a temporary oblivion of the convulsion of nature which was going on.

It was a cave so admirably proportioned as to appear cut out by human hands.* It was about forty feet long, by five and twenty broad, and nearly as many high, as well as I could make out with the little light afforded by my candle. The floor was rather rough, while the roof was as usual hung with stalactites in a very curious way. Going once more into the open air, the atmosphere being rather close, I fetched a large bundle of dry leaves and boughs, which, igniting, I had a better view of the cavern, which had been destined for my head-quarters at the very first examination.

Close to the spot where I had lit my fire, I seated myself to rest and reflect; and mechanically examining the nature of the small objects strewn about the ground, I made a discovery so startling as to make me leap wildly to my feet.

The cave had been inhabited!

At first, feelings of mingled hope and dread filled my mind, though what I had found was nothing more than a few roughly-formed tools, such as hatchets and chisels made of shells and hard stones, sharpened by great labour, and which had evidently been fitted once with handles of wood. These, however, had crumbled away, so that the date of the habitation of the cavern must have been long ago.

On reflection, the probability was, that it had not been visited for ages. I looked about in the shuddering fear of finding human bones scattered in every corner, but in this was agreeably surprised to find myself disappointed. Then came the serious reflection as to the reasons to be given for and against a constant abode in that place.

In the first instance, there was to be considered safety and seclusion. I could, doubtless, defend that place against any number of wild savages, or even animals. It had a roof and walls already made, and nothing was required but a careful division into apartments. Now that I had a sword and gun, with the savage utensils which I had found, I began to be very confident, and to fancy that there was nothing I could not do. In imagination, I saw myself possessed of my parlour, bed-room, store-room, and kitchen; while wild fancies crossing my teeming brain, I even thought of stables for my domestic cattle that were to be.

But then, on the other hand, it was to be considered that, by residing in this gloomy place, I was away from the sea, by which I alone could hope to escape. The view from the beach near at hand was bounded by fantastic rocks in the shape of pillars and arches, while I knew that coral islands and reefs lay all around. Then it might, perhaps, prove less healthy than an open air residence.

Between these two views of the question, it was extremely difficult to decide; so having turned the matter over in my mind some time, I at last decided on a middle course. The cave should be my winter and wet season residence, and refuge in hours of danger; but another home should be provided elsewhere, to which I could resort in pleasant weather, and when I had nothing to fear.

Just as this decision had been come to, the earth shook under my feet, the thunder rolled more furiously than ever, the lightning flashed, as it were, right into my cave, and a sulphurous smell appeared to tinge the whole atmosphere. The roof of the cave seemed to totter, stalactites fell from it, and, my taper going out, I was left in total darkness, except where the embers of my fire faintly glowed.

In great terror lest I should be buried alive under the tumbling mountain, I made towards the entrance, but a gurgling rush of waters warned me to be cautious. Ere the low, narrow entrance was reached, the pool had been refilled, and, overflowing its usual bounds, was up to the level of the archway, leaving me a prisoner.

My dog, however, who cared little for such impediments, dived through, and, taking example by him, I was soon once more in the light of day, but very much deterred from any attempt to make the interior of a mountain a residence in a country subject to earthquakes.

Several shocks followed, always accompanied by heavy rain and thunder, but the shocks grew weaker towards evening, when, with great labour, a fire was again made, by which to warm myself and dry my things. So soaked was I, that my body was wringing wet. Having first placed my gun within reach to protect myself, I took off my garments one by one, and dried them in the flames, which gradually increased in volume until it was, as it were, a little furnace.

The dread which came over me, relative to the earthquake, alone prevented my passing the night in the cave. But it was not easy to overcome this feeling, so I passed the night under a tree, the materials of the hut having been used to feed the flames.

CHAPTER XVIII.

A JOURNEY.

A BLUE clear sky, a calm and balmy wind, a genially warm sun succeeded to the perilous storm. Still in those latitudes changes were so rapid and sudden that I could put no faith in the treacherous climate. As, however, a great many things were needed before any attempt could be made to erect such a house as was necessary for a permanency, after some reflection, and, for the sake of hearing my own voice, a little conversation with my dog, a journey to the Wild False Bay was decided on.

A secret hope entered my mind that the upheaving of the sea by the earthquake might have cast on shore some more treasure from the wreck. Behold us, then, armed with gun and sword, and preceded by our valiant body-guard, advancing through that territory, which we began with almost a glow of pride to call *ours*.

I had only to imagine myself Adam cast in a garden, utterly ignorant of the world's ways, and to reflect on all the difficulties he must have endured; how he had to learn to dig, to build houses, to make tools, to distinguish between the good and the bad fruits—and—but this made me melancholy—he had his Eve to keep him company, to advise and console him in his difficulties.

My position was better than could have been expected. All that man could ask for was before me, except the sweet companionship of my kind. I had food in abundance, by sea and by land, I had arms, and materials with which to forge others. In the exuberance of my thoughts relative to erecting a house and partitioning off my cavern, the idea of a saw, a hammer, nails, all appeared far from insuperable, still the idea of how they were to be made did not immediately suggest itself, though hope did gild the horizon with the idea that it could be done.

Devising, plotting, and thinking, the time passed quickly, so that the sea beach was reached before I was aware of it. I saw at once that a great change had taken place. The wreck and the cotton-tree had both been covered by water when I was there last, but by the upheaving of the earthquake they were now high and dry, though as fancy perhaps suggested very much farther out. The difficulty was to reach it, even with a raft, to which I was nowise inclined

---

* This is very common in caverns. Some of our readers may like to verify the statement. Let them read Mungo Park's last journal.

ALFRED AND THE SNAKE.

No. 4.—SAILOR CRUSOE.

as the memory of the last dangerous voyage had not ye departed.

Accordingly, turning away my head, to avoid temptation, I began searching along the shore, but all that rewarded my trouble, except eggs and shellfish, with a few spars, which, however, were carefully placed on one side, being chiefly such things as small stunsail yards, booms, and the like. Some of them were broken and charred, while others were studded with nails.

Then, like a flash of lightning, an idea entered into my head, which at once was put into execution; I took two pieces of wood, of fitting size, which I carried to where the great seaman's chest lay This was emptied and upset when by the aid of a few rusty nails driven with a stone, they were nailed on to the bottom.

This done, some of the thick uniform cloth, and of the canvass, which wrapped most of the things, was cut by means of a sharp knife into strips, which with much awkwardness and many slips for want of knowing better, were made into an article, the use of which my patient looker on little suspected.

Having fastened my harness as well as under the circumstances, appeared possible, the box gradually laden with goods and then the dog, after some hesitation, having suffered me to pass a collar round his neck, I set him the example by pulling hard myself, and, to my great joy, my heavy, and somewhat unwieldy cart did move. This was a great triumph, for it showed me that in time something better might be done, while by patience and ingenuity more fitting cattle might be found than my friend and companion, Tiger. To those who think of highways and roads, our journey may seem an easy one; but over a rough soil, with jagged rocks and projecting stones, the task was a weary ne indeed, nor was it concluded until night fell. This example of the toil and labour which must be endured ere things could be brought from the shore in any quantity, set me thinking of making a real cart, but after I had wearied my brains for some time the thought of wheels utterly overcame me, and the idea was put on one side, as unfeasible.

To begin the world with I had now some clothes, a small quantity of cloth, a musket, fowling-piece and sword, some knives, shoes, and a few other trifles, such as a file, a very fine saw—from a case of instruments, which were in part surgical. The sight of this last thing set me thinking, and as the sword, being a cavalry one, was unwieldy and unsuited to my wants, I at once determined to fashion it, if possible, into a good and serviceable saw.

Planks, square posts, and such like things it was not my intention to try and make; but there were many things which, if a house were to be made, would be indispensable. Little could be expected from the wreck when it finally broke up, as it was burnt so low in the water.

To make a saw would at home have appeared to me one of those things which it would have been madness to attempt, simply, I suppose, because money would have bought it. But now the task appeared one that was absolutely necessary, so it was undertaken with a calm determination which surprised myself. Food had not been forgotten as part of the load of the cart, and having been freely partaken of by both master and servant, the arduous labour was commenced. To me it was a mystery whether fire was a part necessary to the undertaking, but in doubt I stayed not, trusting to the file, which was admirably tempered. No, sooner, however, was the work entered upon than it was seen to be by no means pleasant. The file made little or no impression, and I do verily believe that of all my trials of patience this was one of the greatest.

Evening after evening was devoted to it when all else was attended to; but ere it was finished my patience was well-nigh worn out. For many days I visited the beach with exemplary regularity, picking up everything that had been cast up by the waves, and only hoping that another tempest would wash ashore another lot of treasure.

The wealth of the Indies *I would* have gladly exchanged for a box of carpenter's tools.

CHAPTER XIX.

ANOTHER DISCOVERY.

THE poor dog, after some days' practice, became quite clever at his work, and allowed me to put on the harness without the slightest hesitation. In this way a considerable quantity of materials for my great purpose were collected near the cave, which, no sign of any earthquake occurring for some time, I occasionally visited, though, until some comfort was connected with it, I did not think of sleeping there.

The water had regained its usual level, though for several days it remained brackish and unpalatable. This, however, was easily obviated, as within the cavern was the cold and pleasant spring which supplied the pool.

The weather was now gradually getting warmer, and I seemed to long for the hour to come for taking up my quarters in this pleasant summer abode. All this time, however, I was not idle, taking care every morning to carry out an idea, which it will readily be believed was not original. There was one dread in my mind, and that was being attacked by wild beasts and savages. As it would have been very disagreeable to have been confined to the cavern in case of an incursion of Indians upon the island, the idea entered my head of making the approaches to this part of the island very difficult.

In future parts of my narrative, it will be seen how extremely fortunate was my device; but such is always the impatience of the biographer, who always longs to come to his more alarming and terrible adventures. I must not anticipate, but go on by slow and natural degrees.

With my sword, not yet fashioned into a saw, and by the aid of my knives, I cut, from out the thickets and brushwood such small trees and bushes as seemed of rapid growth, and, planting them here, there, and everywhere, did, in less than two months, make such a little forest—not knowing as yet whether all would take or not—that I was sure no one would penetrate it in search of a habitation. I left a path which I could find, but I believed that no one else could. A further plot of mine was to have a pit at the end of the path, over which in the day time a bridge might be laid, which at night could be removed, and a false one substituted. All of which precautions proved useful in time to come.

After the earthquake the weather proved warm and mild, so that I was able to hunt for eggs very successfully; but my ambition was to capture a seal or sea-lion, that I might provide myself with oil; though, for that matter, as I had no jars to put it in, this was rather a vain wish. Nothing would prevail on me to use the little powder I had, except for self-defence. The idea of making more often passed through my brain, but as yet the trial had to be made.

Deer, a kind of wild goat like the chamois; rabbits, which my dog caught for his own purposes, often passed within tempting distance, but the value of the charge in my gun restrained me—for might it not be my life? One thing did me some service. Soon after the earthquake, the body of the huge monkey which I had shot fell down from the trees. It was dried up by the heat; and knowing well the value of a scarecrow, I hung it at some distance, as it were in chains, on a low tree, nor for a long time after did any monkeys show themselves in that neighbourhood.

CHAPTER XX.

PREPARATIONS FOR A RAFT.

The wild, glad mood
Of uncheck'd freedom passed.
Amid the ancient solitude
Of unshorn grass and waving wood
And waters glancing bright and fast
A softened voice was in my ear,
Sweet as those lulling sounds and fine,
The hunter lifts his head to hear,
Now far and faint, now full and near—
The murmur of the wind-swept pine.

KNOWING the value of practice—every day laying down my gun and all that encumbered me—I would exercise myself in running, particularly after goats, which, though I never could catch, still it proved right to continue, as every month the task grew more easy, until the goats had to use their utmost speed to escape me.

One day, while chasing one of these animals—my dog was taught to stop and guard my property—my steps led me to those cliffs which skirted that part of the island where my shipwreck took place. Imagine the burst of surprise which escaped from my panting breast.

There was the old ship I had been wrecked in, lifted high and dry between two rocks, at no great distance from the mainland.

I had heard my father often say that all he had read of men lost, cast away, or purposely left on a desert island, convinced him that at the first blush the sight of a vessel, even a wreck, is apt to arouse feelings of hope beyond measure, followed by equally deep despair, and the idea truly that now crossed my mind, was not as to what I might obtain out of the vessel, but as to how there might have been some hope of escape if the barque had floated.

It is related of a Dutch sailor, that having been put on shore for misconduct (he had previously been condemned to death) on a small island, with a very moderate supply of food, and with very little hope of escape, or of obtaining other victuals, the sailors, in derision, did make him a present of a good stout coffin, put together for that purpose by the carpenter. At daybreak on the following morning, just as they were about to sail, the ship's crew were astounded to see this man paddling, at the peril of his life, towards them in the coffin, making a rudder of the upper board, and begging, with piteous cries and gestures, to be allowed to come on board. The singularity of the circumstance and some small remnant of pity, did prevail on the officers to accede to his demand—and he was saved.

Now I, as I have said, instead of thinking how advantage might be derived from the wreck, was cast down with sorrow and dismay at the reflection, that not many days before that vessel had contained the precious freight of my fortune and my affections—and now where were they?

As usual whenever the subject flashed across my mind, it was my earnest endeavour to persuade myself that they too had been saved, that they too might have landed on some hospitable shore, and were yet living instances of the mercy of Providence. In the companionship of those to whom I was so attached it would have been delightful to colonise and cultivate my hard-won territories, nor would a single feeling of lonliness or desertion have been then experienced.

But thoughts of this kind were out of place and foolish. The duty of a man is to adapt himself, as best he may, to circumstances, and mine clearly was to battle for that life which had been hitherto so miraculously and singularly preserved. The discovery of the wreck was another link in the chain of mercies, and what wiser than to avail myself of it? The nature of the cargo was well known to me, and if but a small proportion of it had been preserved my riches would be incalculable. Whenever I thought of residing permanently on the island my imagination conjured up images of flocks and herds of domestic cattle, and, above all, of fertile fields of corn and other grain, though where the seed was to come from appeared more than I could say.

Now, on board the ship was store of everything I could wish for, even to the grain required for the feeding of ducks and fowls, while of other stores the quantity was, for one man, innumerable. But what availed me this, if there were no means of reaching the ship? To swim was quite possible, but then the sea was so infested with sharks of the very worst species that I dared not venture.

The conclusion, then, was, that I must make a raft capable of bearing me and any plunder of value which should be found on board the now long-deserted vessel.

This was a task requiring time and consideration; but for fear rough weather should arise and put a stop to my aspiration, the labour was undertaken with the energy of mingled hope and despair. To make a raft which should avail me anything was a matter of serious consideration. It must be strong, thick, and capable of bearing a heavy weight. To make it on the land was out of the question. My first task, then, was to search the whole beach for such four poles as would make the outer frame of the structure. In this, however, I was only partially successful, and a journey to the hills was rendered necessary. Even then my efforts would have been a failure but for the extreme thinness of the soil, which, as has before been remarked, enabled me to tear several pines from their roots, and, aided by my faithful and attached dog, to drag them down to the sea shore.

My sword, or saw, was of immense use to me under these circumstances, nor could the task have been performed at all without it. Having selected a small lagoon where the water communicated with the sea at high water, I did, when the tide was low, lay my pine trees so as to form a square, intending to place on these a layer of boughs and such wood as the ocean did cast up. It was necessary for this purpose to labour hard, even to the exclusion of everything else. Now, it was that I felt the want of a hammer and a good supply of nails, which would have facilitated my work very much.

To fasten the four trees together, and thus form a framework, it was necessary to have resort to the abundant crop of creeping plants with which the hills abounded. The means employed were frail enough, but, having nothing better, it was necessary to be satisfied with that which nature placed so copiously in my way. But one afternoon, soon after my task was commenced, a circumstance occurred which tended somewhat to lighten my labour.

I have already made several allusions to the huge quantity of seals and sea-lions which were to be seen upon the coast. They crowded the shore in such numbers as would have made the fortune of a ship's crew who should have come that way. For myself, I was very chary of attacking them, as their power and energy were well known to me. They are excessively harmless under ordinary circumstances, but when fighting for their young are not only brave, but desperate, often forcing a rash assailant to flee.

I had often watched them from the summit of the rocks

with great interest, and began to realise the stories which books had told me of them; how they do not walk, but shuffle, yet outstripping a man easily enough. The explanation of this peculiarity came to my memory afterwards. Serpents, it is known, have a progressive motion, which is sometimes sufficiently rapid. They move by bending their bodies from side to side. Seals, on the other hand, move forward by a vertical, not a lateral motion of the spine, something like caterpillars. During the progress of the seal on land it is never known to use its hind feet, while even its fore feet are not absolutely necessarily employed. This appears to arise from a peculiar formation of the spine.

The third morning, after I had collected together a good many materials for my raft, I noticed a number of these huge beasts disporting themselves on the rocks, and suckling their young, while others were feeding on the grain and plants which grew near to the water's edge. It immediately struck me that one of them would be very useful both for fat and sinews, and, perhaps urged by the impulse of a sporting race, I determined to capture at least one.

To shoot them is impossible, as, if you penetrate the skin, the blubber is impermeable. Taking a pole about twelve feet long, I succeeded, after much pains, in fastening to it a clasp knife in the shape somewhat of a hook. This done, watching an opportunity, I crawled towards one seal, which, older or more staid than the others, was looking on without joining in the play. He did not seem to notice me much at first, until I was close to him, when, with a dreadful bellowing like that of a bull, it showed its tusks, while the female seals close at hand hid their cubs under their fins. I took careful aim, and knowing the only vulnerable part of the animal, hit him on the nose, on which, with a strong, deep cry, perhaps more like a wild boar than anything else, he fell on his side, when, with some dexterity, I hit him exactly where the heart lay, after which he moved no more. It was dreadful to see the quantity of blood which poured from it, but though the sight was far from pleasant, I was well rewarded on floating it ashore by the quantity of fat and sinews which I procured, as well as by the bladder, which was at once cleansed and put on one side for use.

The number of uses to which this animal can be put proved afterwards almost endless, but that which served me most at first were the sinews and bladder, the oil and fat lying exposed to the air in a hole in the rocks.

To return to the raft.

CHAPTER XXI.

THE BAMBOO BREAD-FRUIT TREE.

As I approached the hills upon one of my frequent journeys my attention was called to a huge mound-like object at some distance, to which, being drawn by curiosity, I bent my way, little dreaming of the nature of the surprise which awaited me. It was a cluster of gigantic reeds and grasses, some nearly sixty feet in height, and presenting the appearance of an immense sheaf of wheat standing on end. My delight knew no bounds, for I was at once aware that I had discovered the valuable bamboo—the manifold uses of which were familiar to me. Its outer part, in consequence of the quantity of silex which enters into its composition, will strike fire with steel as well as a flint, while its canes split into very thin pieces are made into ropes, by the Chinese, of six hundred feet long, by which they tow their barges; houses are built of it, while every article of domestic

furniture was well known to me to be made from it, as well as the fact that it entered into the composition of paper.

But to me the means of making a raft was now of more importance than anything else, and abandoning all other considerations, I did proceed as well as I could, to avail myself of this precious discovery, one of the many which Providence cast in my way in my distress. Nor of all that fell in my way, was any more important than that which immediately followed. By means of my saw and knives, I succeeded in cutting down several of the larger bamboos, and, using the joints as my guiding point, divided them into proper lengths, which I purposed to lay across my raft in several directions, until it was thick enough to bear my weight and that of anything which I might be fortunate enough to lay my hands on on board the ship. The bamboo grove took me two days more work, and I was continually employed in cutting down, preparing them, and dragging them to the beach, where, the ends being stuffed full of clay and lard, they became exceedingly useful and valuable as part of the raft, and as a kind of flooring.

While I was steadily at work cutting down some of the bamboos, and preparing them for my purpose, my eyes were cast towards certain of those patches of cultivated ground which were scattered over the surface of the otherwise barren plain. My botanical studies made me scan every leaf and plant with avidity, expecting always to find something useful and agreeable. My mind ran continually on tobacco, for though smoking was a habit as yet to be acquired, the sense of loneliness which habitually pervaded my whole spirit, made me long to use the pipe—fancying it would be a kind of companionship for me.

But not a sign of the weed had as yet shown itself, though unconsciously almost the idea was continually in my mind. Halting in the afternoon to refresh myself, I seated myself beneath a tree which attracted my particular notice. It rose to the height of about forty feet, and was about fifteen inches in diameter; the bark was ash coloured, full of little chinks, and covered by small knobs. Cutting a small portion of it, from sheer curiosity, I found the inner bark fibrous, while the wood was of a smooth, soft, and yellow colour.

About twelve feet above where I sat, the branches came out almost horizontally, each branch becoming smaller as they neared the top. Placing one of the bamboos firmly against the tree, by great efforts I was able to reach to the first branch, and chopped it off with my sword. A suspicion which had entered my mind was at once realised; the leaves were divided into seven or eight lobes, were about eighteen inches long, and of a lively green. It bore flowers, which my botanical eye declared to be both male and female, the former among the upper leaves, the latter at the end of the twigs. But what I chiefly noted was the fruit. It was about nine inches long, heart-shaped, of a green colour, while the pulp was yellow and juicy. *

It was the wondrous bread-fruit tree.

This was a greater discovery than would have been a mine of gold, it being in some countries the sole support of the people; its fruit serving for food, its fibres making clothes, its wood being used for building houses and making boats; its male flower used for tinder, its leaves for table cloths, and the viscid milky juice of the young tree for bird lime. I collected a good supply of the fruit, intending to eat them for supper, when I found it, on being roasted until the outside was charred, to have a consistency not very unlike wheaten bread, the taste being between that and roasted

---

* *Artocarpus incisa.* There is also the *A. Integrifolia,* the fruit of which weighed thirty pounds; but this is peculiar to the Society Island

chesnut. It was for some time a great comfort to me, two or three trees being a sufficient supply for one man for a year.

Thinking gratefully over these wonderful and fortunate discoveries, my arduous task was much lightened. These interpositions, as it were, of Providence appeared to me in my situation little short of miraculous. Cast on a desert island without a friend in the wide world, save He who is the friend of all—food, clothing, arms, seemed as it were to start up before my very feet, and all the materials for building a kind of bridge to the wreck seemed equally to come in my way.

My raft was now far advanced towards completion. It was an ugly, awkward, and unwieldly construction at best, but then my education, though it had led me to love the sea, had not fitted me for boat building. Still, such as it was, I resolved to adventure myself upon it. A thin bamboo served as a kind of mast, while two others fastened to the side were to take the place of oars. And thus I started, at the turn of the tide, on my not unperilous journey.

CHAPTER XXII.

ON BOARD SHIP.

THE ship lay, as far as I could judge, about a mile and a half from the shore. I could further make out that it was on a shoal of rock and shingle extending along the land, from the way in which the long and lazy waves broke over it. To reach the wreck, I had to pursue a very tortuous course amid lagoons now bordered with rock, now with coral. My unfortunate raft was, moreover, excessively unmanageable; at one time it would sheer to the right, then to the left, and at last turning right round upon a pivot, would leave me helpless to guide it for some moments. I had the greatest difficulty in the world to keep my own equilibrium. Still, determined to persevere, the raft was steered along as well as I was able, though several times it grounded, when there was nothing for me but to wade in the water, and thrust it off by main force.

Presently, getting through the more broken water, the raft passed out into the open sea, and became slightly more manageable. There was both the wind and current in its favour, but it required the utmost nicety to prevent my being driven out beyond the vessel, though it is probable that, had such a misfortune have occurred, the shoal or reef would have brought me up. At length, when not more than twenty yards from the wreck, it grated, swung, and in a moment would have been fast. But being quickly lightened of the load, both of myself and dog, it floated again, and was quickly drawn into close propinquity to the barque. The very rope by which I had swung in my leap for life, was hanging yet, and to this I attached the mast of my raft.

The vessel lay on its side, knocked in here and there, and already beginning to exhibit tokens of breaking up. With difficulty the deck was reached by myself and the dog, and heaven knows what were the sensations which came over me when I once more trod those planks, which had been the scene of so many happy days as well as fearful and terrible trials. It was evident that any expectations which might have been entertained of great advantage were out of the question; the tremendous force of the tossing waves had pretty well swept the deck, though here and there pieces of broken wood—a material much wanted by me—lay by the lee-gunwale. A top-gallant studding-sail boom attracted my notice, and was speedily hove overboard.

My first visit was to the chief cabin, where the passengers were used to take their meals and spend their evenings. Stifling as much as possible those emotions which were natural in my situation, I determined to give my mind wholly to action. There was ample time. The tide wanted still three hours of ebb, and it would be hopeless to move the raft landward until the flood commenced. The steward's pantry and cabin, laying invitingly open, an examination of it was commenced, resulting in a discovery of some value. There was a small cask of brandy, which, as a medicine and cordial, was hailed with delight; about fifteen pounds of bacon, a piece of scarlet cloth, twenty yards of coarse linen, a few damaged towels and table cloths, some small ropes, and a locker, the hasp of which fastened well, containing broken biscuit. Of this both myself and dog made a meal, though it was mouldy and much injured by mites.

All this plunder was gradually taken on deck, after which the idea came upon me as to how the raft was to be loaded. My freight would be to me precious beyond all the wealth of the Indies, and it behoved me to be very careful. Looking warily round upon the horizon, it struck me that I might venture to pass a night on board, and this resolve being speedily come to, my task commenced. Breaking into the hold, I found, amid the dire confusion, a number of empty and broken boxes, which, with axe and hammer—I had at once searched out and found the carpenter's chest—were knocked into pieces, more or less suited to my purpose.

Having time before me, I proceeded, as soon as enough materials were found for the purpose, to board over the whole surface of the raft, which rendered it both more secure and better able to bear the burden I intended for it. Then, knowing the importance and value of everything in the shape of planks, the best that could be found were selected, and nailed firmly round the sides of the raft in the room of bulwarks, being, for further security, bound round by a long coil of rope.

The extraordinary vessel now appeared to me capable of bearing its intended burden, and being weary and exhausted, I took a glass of brandy and some more biscuit, after which my task was again pursued. My sight was not assailed by a great multitude of riches. The way in which the waves had knocked about the old hull of the barque had left little of value to be taken away. The water-casks were all stove in, and it was with great difficulty that two thoroughly watertight ones were found. Some small rum-casks and such like, however, had withstood the knocking about, and were placed on the raft.

After putting on board all that was found in the steward's pantry, and stripping the carpenter's chest—which gave me a crowbar, several axes, the several hammers, a moderate-sized saw, a plane and augur, some chisels, files, and a bag of nails—my attention was directed to the captain's cabin; but here disappointment awaited me, for except some money, a quadrant, and compass, with a telescope, my search was not rewarded. The stern of the ship had been much knocked about, and one of the cabin windows had been knocked in, giving free scope to the waves to wash through and destroy. All that was found, however, was put on board, as well as a pair of large pistols, which lay rusting in a locker.

Then came the store-room, which was fastened inside, it appeared, by a barrel rolling against it. The door had to be broken open by an axe, when a sight did present itself most painful to my feelings. Bottles of wine, jars of pickles, pots of confectionery—all the little luxuries provided more especially for the women and children—were cast to the ground, and being broken made most hideous confusion. But some barrels, containing split peas, grain for the fowls, and flour were untouched, and the contents of these I continued carrying to the raft until the sudden fall of night induced me to cease from my labours.

A very old-fashioned, half-broken lamp, with very little wick, and a small jar of oil was the result of an examination of a cupboard in the steward's pantry. A flint and steel, with some tinder, enabled me to procure a light, after which which I had again resource to my bread and brandy. But there was no time for idleness. No sooner had a slight repose removed something of the feeling of fatigue than I took up my lamp and continued my search. My uncle, whose estate had been on the extreme borders of Virginia, had provided a goodly case of arms, with much ammunition, and on this prize my mind had been intent for some time. The spot where they had been secreted was well known to me, it being a second side store room, the door of which was easily broken open. A dozen muskets, some very portable barrels of gunpowder, numerous bags of shot, and some rolls of lead, rewarded my search, and filled my mind with eager delight. But what did not less please me were some rakes, hoes, and reaping hooks, which, though I could not see how they would be useful to me, I yet did secure—as well as a wheelbarrow taken out as a model.

Loading a couple of muskets, and saying a humble prayer for guardianship and protection through that night, I now lay down in the chief cabin to rest, with my dog at my feet. But I slept little. The thought of all my riches, the reflection as to the perils that were to be passed through before, however, I could really call them my own, kept me restless and uneasy, while every puff of wind that reached my ears carried a sharp pang to my heart. Those mysterious noises which always seem to precede the breaking up of an old vessel could be heard throughout the barque, and several times I crept on deck under the impression that some one else had come on board. But the dog not sharing my uneasiness, towards midnight slumber fell upon me.

CHAPTER XXIII.

THE VOYAGE BACK.

IT was a still and lovely morn. The tide was nearly out. The raft was aground from its own weight and that of its cargo. Still, as the water rose and fell six or seven feet, this caused me no uneasiness, but rather urged me to proceed. All the contents of the private store room, which had belonged to my uncle, were in about two hours transferred to the raft, which was now so loaded that as the water rose I found its upper surface level with the water. To guard against submersion I did labour for two hours more, passing under the bottom of my unwieldy conveyance the topgallant studding sail boom, and other such spars as could be found, which being lashed by ropes, did seem to strengthen it much.

The wind was now favourable, and having attached the scarlet cloth to the masthead, and fixed one of the largest tablecloths as a sail, I pushed off with a heart full of fear, doubt, and anxiety. My rudder consisted of one of the bottom boards of an old boat, fixed as securely as possible by means of rope. On this was almost my sole dependence, and on a spar which I used to pole the raft off the shoal, my feet pressing the rudder.

Never since man first essayed, in the days before the flood, to navigate salt or fresh water, was such a lumbering, awkward, and desperate contrivance. Despite a favourable wind and the tide in my favour, it did not seem to move perceptibly, except when it was being poled. Speedily, however, the water was too deep for this to be practicable, while my terrors were more than ever excited on finding that my cargo was not evenly distributed, and menaced every moment to capsize. The wretch menaced with death, and momentarily expecting the advent of the executioner, could not endure worse pangs than I did while this was being shifted. At last, however, everything was more properly balanced, and my mind rendered a little easier by observing that the raft was level.

The expanse of open water between the ship and the first reefs and lagoons was not more than half a mile, and yet it took the whole of that tide to reach this first stage in my journey.

The utmost care and precision was required to secure a fit port for the raft, which however, more by good fortune than anything else, being obtained, the receding water left my vessel high and dry in a narrow and sinuous channel. On my right was a small island, much frequented by birds, and a diligent search was rewarded by some eggs, that had, however, to be eaten raw with bread, or rather biscuit. Several times I felt inclined to shoot a bird or two, but that they appeared to me likely to be totally inedible,—while, to my mind, powder and shot was of such inestimable value as not lightly to be expended.

In the holes left by the receding tide were several shellfish, but not of any size to be worth eating. Suddenly, however, in a clear pool my eyes lighted upon a bunch of something, the shape of which appeared to me to be very familiar. I ran towards it, and was not a little pleased to discover that my surmise was correct.

It was a whole bed of rock oysters.

This was a delightful discovery, and enabled me to pass away the time more agreeably than otherwise would have been the case.

At length, however, the evening approached, and with it a shift of wind and water. My sail was hoisted, my rudder fixed, as well as means allowed, amidships, and my pole brought into requisition to keep the raft off rocks and shoals. The breeze being stiffish and favourable, I hoped to reach the shore, and made up my mind to navigate even in the dark to attain the desired end.

Presently an open, clear and deep channel presented itself, up which I guided my frail back with all the ease imaginable, nor did any misadventure occur until, after about half an hour, the raft struck violently, heeled to port, sent the cargo all on one side, and pitched me, head foremost, on the top. Struggling to regain my equilibrium I gazed wildly round, expecting that my precious car o was totally wrecked. But not so. The raft was at the bottom of a kind of bay, with no issue on the land side, and aground. But I knew the tide was not up, so hastily trimming the steward's lantern, and lighting it, I hastened to repair the damage. But though I had really lost nothing, the reef was too high, and the tide when at full flood did not float my precious cargo. There was nothing for it but to pass the night in that spot.

But just as, after watching many hours, the tide began to fall, I bethought me of the wheelbarrow, and it being a moonlight night, did make up my mind not to try and rest, but to work. The wheelbarrow was got out, the lantern fastened at the end, and then was loaded with such a burden as suited my strength. Then with hope considerably revived, I began to make my way towards the shore, over reefs, by rocks, through pools, but not in water above my ankle.

In this way, working as it were for life, the guns, powder, lead, and such heavy things, were about mid-day landed from the raft, which at the first tide then floated, and was brought into a safe dock. Still the task of unloading continued, nor did I rest until not a thing remained on board, which, considering the greediness I had shown, in overloading the raft, was more than was deserved.

That night's rest in my store hut was sweet indeed, though early morn saw me again moving. It was to my cave that all my treasures were to be taken, nor did I feel happy or safe, until they were all beneath its welcome shelter.

CHAPTER XXIV.

THE ANACONDA.

MY dog, well fed, attached to me, and extremely powerful, was not to remain an idle spectator of those labours which were to procure us a home in the wet and dreary season, and a fortress in the hour of danger. The possession of so many guns and so much ammunition had excited ambitious thoughts, nor did it seem to me impossible to hold my own against a whole host of painted and half-naked savages, did they presume to attack me.

It did not, however, enter into my calculations to dwell as a permanency in the cavern, and for a very long time my brain was racked as to how I should connect the inner residence with that more airy and summer one, which I wished to form outside. Leaving, however, this to the future, my principal occupation consisted in dragging up on a sledge, and in the barrow, all such treasure as the visit to the ship had afforded me.

My experience of the raft had decided me against ever using any such ponderous means of transport again, and when, after a brief but rather severe gale, I did once more perform the journey, it was with a light raft made entirely of hollowed bamboos. The other being, to my mind, quite useless, was taken to pieces, and transported to Battle-pool as building materials.

With the planks and bamboos, a shed was easily constructed, by means of which to shelter my wealth, and after an arduous ten days of work they were all safely housed.

Then it was that, not to lose any of the fine weather, another voyage was made to the wreck. The light kind of conveyance now constructed was simply calculated to convey my own person. Two very long bamboos were lashed together at the end, while a plank was placed in the middle, to keep the little poles apart, at a distance of five feet. Other reeds and planks laid transversely, made an easily managed raft, which I guided along by the aid of a pole.

In this way the vessel was easily reached, and my labour resumed. With the heaviest axe of those found in the carpenter's chest, planks, beams, and everything which might be useful, were cut away and consigned to the mercies of the flood tide, which daily took them ashore at different portions of the coast, after which they were drawn up above high water mark, to dry.

At this time an hour or two a day was employed in procuring food, and one day I had the good fortune to shoot a young goat-like animal, something of the nature of the Swiss chamois. Having some bread-fruit, this determined me on having a new style of meal, being quite nauseated with the wearisome boiled meat and fish on which I had been dependent, though among the stores taken ashore, and afterwards examined, I had found several hams of very choice flavour, in canvas covers.

The compass box was quite new and of brass; so taking out the interior, the other was used for several days to boil water in, then being well scoured with sand, and made as clean and bright as human hand could render it, a portion of the kid's flesh was placed therein with some salt bacon, and boiled. Few who live at home at ease could have any idea of the pleasure which this new event caused. It was a meal that seemed homely and redolent of England, especially when some wild beans and celery proved upon trial to be a welcome addition to the meal. My dog enjoyed the bones as well as the more ordinary pieces which I afterwards boiled for him, not wishing to habituate him to raw food.

The plan which had settled itself in my mind was to build, now that I saw how quickly the stakes which I had planted were taking root, a kind of verandah in front of my cave, beneath which I might sleep in hot and close weather.

But it seemed to me that for the proper sheltering of my goods, it was more important to attend to my interior store-room than anything else; so, in the first instance, by means of the crowbar, I did enlarge and make higher the entrance to the cave; the stone at the mouth being of a soft nature. Then dragging some spars to the edge, I laid them across the pool, and, by means of transverse bamboos, withes, shrubs, and earth, soon made a bridge, which was not more than ten feet in length.

Then I marched into the cavern in state, taking with me my dog, and having a gun on my shoulders, while my belt was adorned with the pistols found on board the wreck.

A lantern, a couple of candles, and some resinous boughs and branches, tied together and placed at intervals in the rocky fissures of the cave, illumined its interior with a dim and vague resplendence. The grot was arrayed with torch-light, and its self-born canopy could be just seen, hanging in icicle-like particles above my head. It was no doubt an arch upreared by nature's architect, and to me more even than a temple fashioned by man's hand; for was it not home, shelter, fortress, church, in one?

Through the middle, following a narrow kind of crevice, flowed the tiny stream that supplied the pool, and having long since made up my mind to utilise this in the interior by by means of a trough or tub, I advanced, torch in hand, to where it trickled from the rock. The interior of the cave was at this end, which I had never before visited, jagged and rough. The water fell from a height of about fifteen feet, but as I raised my torch on high to examine its position I saw that under the fall was a hole about five feet high and two feet wide, which was evidently the entrance to another cavern.

Struck with surprise and wonder, the determination was at once come to to visit this as well. I was armed, my gun was loaded, and therefore I was a tolerable match for any wild beasts which might presume to attack me.

In the day-time several of the animals which roam at night are apt to secrete themselves in holes in the rocks or in the deep impenetrable shades of the forest, so that my caution was a reasonable one.

After a little reflection and an examination of the rough rocks, stepping places were found, and crawling quickly up, my entrance was made good without wetting either my torch or my gun. No sooner, however, was I inside—and doubtless for many ages the cavern had not been disturbed by man—

than the sight of my torch seemed to excite the astonishment and annoyance of a vast community of vampire bats, which fluttered around my light, and threatened each moment to involve me in total darkness, while the heavy flapping of their wings filled the cavern with a heavy kind of roar, like very distant thunder.

Presently one or two, more blinded than the others, flew right in my face, dashing down the lantern, and leaving me in black obscurity. My alarm at first was ludicrous, considering the character of the animals, but a moment after I saw that at no great distance the cave was lit up from the outside, and, therefore, advancing rapidly to where fissures from above admitted the welcome rays, the vampires did presently cease to annoy me. The stupendous nature of this cave now became apparent, extending as it probably did into the very heart of the mountains.

The thought struck me that, perhaps, in this way the other part of the island or continent might be reached, and so I determined to persevere. I suppose we had advanced about one hundred yards or so, in an ascending direction, when I came to a clear pool of water, that disappeared on my left, and doubtless was the source of the stream that trickled at the cavern's mouth.

Across the pool was evidently a cavern, but quite dark, and singularly damp and gloomy looking. My dog here hung back, nor did he try to cross the water, but peered over the pool with the air of one who supposed that all kinds of wild beasts and snakes might be beyond; nor was I myself without dread that such might be the case. Without being in any way a coward, a man may readily hesitate before he plunges into unknown regions enveloped in utter darkness.

While reflecting as to the desirability of returning for another torch and my lantern, my dog crouched at my feet, setting up such a piteous howling and moaning as made the very hair stand on end, knowing well that the faithful beast would not do so for any slight pretence.

The ears were laid low, the nostrils dilated, the mouth rested on the forepaws, the eyes stood out from the head, while the tongue hung out as if parched from excessive thirst.

Then the dog rose on his feet—facinated, blinded, utterly helpless to resist some fearful attraction.

I could see nothing.

At length, peering with agonised awe and dread into the darkness beyond, methought I could see within the inner cavern two bright spots, as of hot coals, savagely gleaming at the dog. Without hesitation, without reflecting on the consequences which might ensue, I levelled my gun at the two shining spots, and fired both barrels.

My God!—never shall I forget what then followed. The report of the gun for a moment appeared to deafen me, but my eyes never closed. I saw bounding across the pool an animals—heavens! a snake—not ten, not twenty, not thirty, but fifty feet long at least, which, with a horrible hiss, seemed to uncoil its huge folds preparatory to our utter destruction. It was the most awful I had ever seen. Its mouth appeared large enough to swallow me; its tongue lolled out in a hideous and threatening way; its eyes sparkled with mingled rage and terror.

For a moment I was as if turned to stone.

CHAPTER XXV.

PREPARATIONS FOR THE FUTURE.

The golden fruit of suffering's weighty power
Within the soul—like soft bells' silvery chime,
Repeat the tone, if fame may not be won,
Or if the heart, where thou shouldst find a shrine,
Breathe forth no blessing on thy lonely way,
Wait thou for Time—it hath a sorcerer's power
To dim life's mockeries that gaily shine,
To lift the veil of seeming from the real,
And raise the drooping heart from scenes ideal,
To a high purpose in the world of strife.
Yea, wait for Time; but to thy heart take Faith,
Soft beacon light upon a stormy sea;
A mantle, for the pure in heart to pass
Through a dim world untouched by living death.

THEN I dropped my gun, and amid a confusion to which any I ever saw cannot be compared, I would have fled; but the sight of the monster, the feeling of its slimy body, as it glided by, itself alarmed beyond measure, the awful din and uproar caused by the shot, the terrified flapping of the bats, of which it seemed to me that millions on millions were suddenly launched against me from all parts of the surrounding gloom, restrained me for some minutes.

The dog crouched abjectly in a corner, and then, both panic struck, we fled, but in the direction which the serpent had taken. Never will the remembrance of the delight with which I greeted daylight be effaced from my mind. It was like awakening from death to life; nor would I at that moment have re-entered the cavern for any temptation that might have been offered me.

Terror is one of those feelings which weighs heaviest and longest on the human mind. As an army after a panic is very difficult to re-organise, so were my thoughts. Reason was some time before it resumed its sway, and I sat on the ground, pale, the cold drops of perspiration dropping from my brow, and my heart beating swiftly and wildly.

There was only one source of comfort. The snake, huge, hideous, and irresistible in its might as it was, had evidently been quite as terrified as myself. The awful din made by the gun in that confined space was something new, and to the monster alarming in the extreme, so that in all probability the animal was by this time a long way off. Still, simply to know that the island was peopled by such creatures was terrible enough, for against the attacks of serpents there was no kind of prudence could guard me. I was not then aware that even the largest snake will never attack man except as a last extremity, when it is furious with hunger.

By-and-bye, however, I began to think more calmly, and the reflection then crossed my mind that for some time, at all events, the cave would be free from the visits of the anaconda. Taking, therefore, a good sip of brandy and water to give me courage, and loading two guns I re-entered the cavern, and not without fear and trembling again examined the entrance to the inner division. After eyeing it for some time a decision was come to on my part. Procuring as many stakes as I could conveniently cut, and sacrificing even some bamboos and planks, after some hours of the most assiduous labour, the hole was blocked up in such a way as few animals could have made their way through it.

Then again I went into the open air.

How little I slept that night may readily be expected. I would start with sudden affright—a kind of nightmare resting on my soul. But by degrees my mind grew calmer, and by the morning I had recovered something of my usual serenity.

My first duty was the complete removal of all my goods into the cavern, and this was executed without delay. Then

ALFRED AND THE GAZELLES.

No. 5.—SAILOR CRUSOE.

came another task. During my visits to the sea shore, I was continually noticing, chiefly from watching my dog, the recurrence of the footsteps of different animals, some of a size and nature sufficient to be alarming. Now my thicket was advancing in size and extent, a few days passed without my planting a fresh branch or stake, but the pathway which I left for myself would afford passage for all kinds of animals, so that some other safeguard was necessary.

For the space then of one hour every day after breakfast, I devoted all my energies to digging a pit at the end of my pathway, on my own side, deep enough to have rendered the escape of most animals impossible. It took some time, but when finished, it was a perfect pit-fall. A few bamboos and boughs were spread over the top, then grass and a shallow sprinkling of earth.

For my own convenience a narrow flight of steps were made, but all means of exit was cut off that way, by good stout beams being placed across with heavy stones to keep them down.

But all this time many hours every day were spent in collecting a sufficient supply of provisions to enable me to devote myself to the great task of making my house comfortable and habitable. The bread-fruit tree was visited, and the ripe fruit stored up, but what chiefly was desirable in my situation, was dried meat. There was the greatest reluctance on my part to expend any store of gunpowder, but one or two animals of the goat species coming within my reach, I could not restrain myself. A portion of the product of my spoil was consumed fresh, and the rest dried in the pungent smoke of certain boughs, which, though it did not improve the flavour, certainly preserved it.

Another care filled my mind. I had a goodly collection of dried peas, barley, oats, and others, the nature of which was not fully understood, but I was extremely anxious to make a trial of their character. To dig up such a field as would serve the purpose I had at heart, would have taken far more time than was at my disposal, but in my perigrinations an idea had struck me, which after a time was utilised.

Between two islands of timber, at no great distance from my cave, was a small level plot of ground that might have been described as a prairie. On examination, I found that the soil was a rich loam, without a stone over its whole surface. It was covered by a luxuriant crop of grasses and flowers, which were now dry and withered by the heat. One day, when I required rather amusement than work, my plan was carried out. There was now no difficulty found on my part in making a fire. The welcome discovery of some dry fungi, resembling mushrooms, on a tree had provided me with an ample supply of timber.

A line of dry leaves and twigs was placed along the narrow end of the prairie, which was something in the shape of a triangle, and this being effectually carried out, the whole was set on fire. Before many minutes a feeling of regret and alarm seemed to fill my mind as to what I had done, the grass blazing up so furiously as to fill the atmosphere with a dense volume of black and acrid smoke that canopied the heavens, while lurid and crackling flames arose on all hands.

Up rose with loud and shrill cries a dozen birds that had probably made their nests in the grass, if I might judge by the desperate way in which they hovered over the flames and smoke. Then I could see through gaps or arches of the heavy vaporous looking wall, small deer and other animals making their way desperately from the rushing and devastating fire.

The wind was, of course, from me, as this circumstance was well noted before I began my proceedings. The grass was dry and inflammable, so that it sped rapidly onward. One thing had not struck me. The edges of the two detached thickets were bordered by bushes, while from the trees hung long pieces of Spanish moss of a peculiarly dry nature.

It was thus that, ere I was aware of it, the forest was on fire!

This event struck me with dismay, as it was impossible to foresee to what extent it might proceed. Still my presence of mind did not desert me, and, snatching up one of the rakes which I had brought for another purpose, by following the advancing flames, and knocking amid the bushes, pulling down Spanish moss, I succeeded in saving the thicket—no large wood having been ignited.

Thus, by great good fortune the conflagration was confined to the grass, leaving before night, a black, smoking, desolate-looking plain, where had been a prairie rich in grass and flowers. Several snakes, some animals like rabbits, and one or two others unknown to me, perished in the flames.

But my own satisfaction was great, there being now the kind of ground that I required, which was prepared for cultivation in the following simple and original manner. A very large rake was selected, over which a heavy piece of wood was fastened; this forced the iron prongs into the earth, while a rope round my shoulder enabled me to drag it along. The grasses were burnt to the very roots, and the soil being rich, nothing was easier than to turn up a large quantity of it in one day, and soon, by perseverance, enough was thus rudely ploughed to enable me to throw in one half of all my seeds.

Two or three prickly kinds of bushes tied together were then dragged over all, to act as a harrow, and my work was done for the time being. The rest was left to the goodwill of Providence.

CHAPTER XXVI.

A VOYAGE OF DISCOVERY.

A COLLECTION of black clouds on the horizon of a morning, a dampness of the atmosphere, and the prevalence of southerly winds, began to warn me that the wet season was coming. My efforts were redoubled, and, among other things, I killed a seal, the oil and fat of which nearly filled the two water-casks. But another very satisfactory discovery was, that two smaller barrels which came ashore from the fast breaking-up ship, contained salt beef and pork. This was taken, part at a time, towards the hills, and then the barrels, empty of all but brine, dragged up and the meat returned to its old quarters.

Some very choice tea, which my uncle was taking out to his Virginia plantation, was long since safe in my stores, but the total absence of sugar almost prevented my caring much about it. Besides, as yet no substitute for a tea-kettle had presented itself.

Fish were very abundant at this season, and easily captured with hooks made after a fashion with bone. These were dried in the hot sun, a little salt brine being merely scattered over them, and placed in an empty rum cask.

Still the rain kept off, but as I did not venture far from the cave, lest I might be caught in a storm, my time was principally taken up in improving my defences, and planning work for the coming fine weather. Now, I had several times noticed, that among those trees which surrounded the pool was one magnificent cocoa-nut palm, the fruit of which continually excited my appetite. Besides, I had other uses for it.

I knew well that the cocoa-nut palm was of itself alone sufficient to build, rig, and freight a ship with bread, wine, water, oil, vinegar, sugar, and other commodities. It's advantages were innumerable. Its very aspect was imposing, its erect and lofty bearing seeming to compare with other trees as man with animals. The poor islander of the uncivilized regions reposes beneath its shade, eating and drinking of its fruit; he thatches his hut with its boughs, and weaves them in baskets to carry his food; he cools himself with a fan from its leaflets, and shelters his head with a bonnet from its leaves; with the base of the stalks he makes a taper. The large nuts furnish him with goblets, the small ones with bowls for his pipes; the dry husks kindle his fire, its fibres are twisted into fishing lines and cords for his canoes. His wounds are healed by a balsam from its nut, the dead are embalmed with its oil. The trunk serves him for timber, for paddles, for clubs and spears. Such was my continual soliloquy, ending always by the half-spoken words—why should it not be all this to me?

The one before me rose aloft, tall and slender, without a branch, with at the top some dozen nuts as big as a man's head, and over this graceful plumes, with their rich green gloss and beautiful fronds of nodding leaves.

Still no means by which they could be reached presented itself to my imagination for a long time, until at last the plan of the savage Indians and negroes recurred to my memory. It was, however, not very easy for me to carry out even this simple plan, still I determined to try.

Taking some very strong canvass, I sewed it into a long belt several times double. Then I went to the tree I had selected, which had an unusually tall and smooth trunk. Round this the belt was passed and firmly attached. Then my body was passed into the orifice, and it just left space for my limbs to have free play. The art of climbing in this way consisted in clambering up as far as the band would allow, and then hitching the belt itself upwards.

When fatigue rendered a pause necessary, it was easy to pass the legs round the tree, and, shifting the belt to just above the knees, to rest wholly thereupon.

Still, the task was no light one. It demanded great labour and a considerable expenditure of time. More than an hour had elapsed ere success rewarded my arduous labours, and then great indeed was my surprise and delight.

I looked out upon an expanse of country beyond all power of description lovely. I had, without noticing it, reached the summit of the rock that separated me from the higher land I had so long craved to see, and so close did the boughs of the cocoa palm grow to the rock, that, without thinking of the consequences, I swung myself on to a projecting ledge, and stood on the long-coveted heights.

Under my feet, spreading far away until the horizon was bounded by lofty hills, lay an interminable series of plains and valleys, covered by the richest and most variegated verdure and foliage. There was every product of the tropics in endless profusion.

Adam, when awakening to the beauties and glories of Paradise, could not have been more enraptured then was I at the marvellous view which lay before me. Green valleys, waving trees, rivulets, waterfalls that sparkled in the sun, made a kind of rapturous picture to behold, while a lawn-like sward came to the very foot of the rocks on which I stood.

An irresistible impulse came upon me to make a voyage of discovery. I was armed only with my pistols, but such is the ardour of human curiosity that my senses were wilfully blind to the danger that awaited me. In all probability, that lovely region, with its tropical climate and vegetation, was a perfect nest of wild beasts and creeping things.

But caution would be my watchword, and so, the determination once come to, all other considerations were placed on one side, and the descent of the rocks was commenced. It was now evident that this stony barrier extended from side to side of the island, or promontory, as hope whispered. Those hills must be in Africa; and once that I was on a continent, would not escape be not only practicable, but easy?

The bearings of the point whence I started were easily taken, there being a very peculiar pointed rock, which, in my own mind, I was careful to observe. Then, commending myself to the protection of Providence, my journey in this unknown region was commenced. Nothing could be imagined more delightful than the soft turf upon which, after leaving the rocks, my feet were placed. Flowers of the most delicate and varied hue sent forth a rich and balmy perfume. Then came forests, glades, and woods, at which I stood still and wondered, so lovely was the character of the vegetation. Every step discovered fresh subjects for admiration, until at last, overwhelmed with gratitude and joy at all I saw, I sat down on the edge of a wood, in perfect amazement.

The scene which lay before me was charming and fascinating in the extreme. A variegated prairie was bounded by a rock which slightly overhung the plain, its summit being surmounted by bushes and trees. To the right and left were trees of every variety known to the tropics, while the green sward was enamelled with flowers. Sinking beside the fallen trunk of a tree, I gazed upon the landscape with silent rapture, the more so that in all probability man had never since the creation trod that secluded vale.

Suddenly the scene was enlivened in a most unexpected and far from unpleasant manner. The bushes stirred, a little creature came gamboling out, which I knew at once to be a monkey cub. Its mother followed, and with an amount of fondness that might have shamed many a human creature, began to play with its young. They rolled together on the ground, they ran races, and the mother seemed to attach much satisfaction to the victories of the younger brute. Gradually they approached the rock, on the edge of the plain, while a strange jabbering sound amid the trees showed that there were many spectators of the domestic scene.

Suddenly the jabbering ceased, and the she-monkey and her cub remained for an instant stock still. Then, with horror and afright, my heart beating wildly, my hair standing on end, I saw emerge from the thicket to my right hand the terrible and hideous anaconda. It crawled slowly forward. It had been feeding, but not to the extent which produces torpor for its pace was quite sufficiently rapid for its purpose. With a shrill cry like that of a babe, the cub flew towards its mother, who cast it upon its back, and would have fled.

The anaconda, moving slowly at first, made a rapid spring at the female monkey, and fixed its fangs in its flesh. Then, with a sudden twist, it brought its folds to bear upon the wretched animals, encircling them in such a way as to render escape impossible. A powerful squeeze from the hideous brute completed the sacrifice. Mother and cub were reduced to a mere pulp. Then it began slowly to cover its prey with a kind of foam, after which its fearful jaws were opened, and the huge mouthful swallowed at once. *

The horrid scene over, the great snake was evidently satisfied, for it crawled close under the rock, and coiling itself up in a fearful pile, began the slow and disgusting process of serpent digestion. I would now gladly have fled, but to move was beyond my power. I lay in the most abject state of terror and horror.

Suddenly the jabbering in the woods and in the trees on the summit of the cliff recommenced, and my attention was directed to a whole troop of monkeys that probably had witnessed the tragedy with silent awe. Instinct, however, seemed to make them aware that all danger was over for the moment, and I could see them in clusters hanging from the boughs, and gazing below upon the recumbent monster. Then again the fearful jabbering was renewed for awhile until after a time it wholly ceased.

A pause, may be of five minutes, ensued, during which a conference seemed to take place. How monkeys explain their meaning one to the other, whether they have a language of their own or not, is one of those mysteries which I pretend not to explain, but that they act in concert is certain. In this instance, one of many witnessed by me afterwards on the island, there was a clear understanding, for I now saw several of the older males lean quietly over the precipice and examine the anaconda's position with a keen and observant eye. Then they all retired and to my utter bewilderment went to work. A stone, many hundred pounds in weight, overhung very nearly the spot where the coiled monster lay, and this the monkeys began slowly to push.

A dozen men, after a thorough understanding, could not have acted with more precision. The stone was moved bodily from its place until, on examination, it was poised right over the sleeping snake. Then an aged monkey peered down the side of the cliff and made a final survey. It seemed satisfactory, for next minute it tottered upon the edge, by the sheer upheaving force of a whole crowd of the infuriated animals, and fell with a crash upon the slumbering anaconda.

It smashed its head and several other parts of its body into a hundred pieces, while the rest writhed in horrible agonies, that lasted, it seemed to me, an almost incredible space of time, the monkeys all the time leaping along the boughs, capering, dancing, with a strange mixture of terror and delight.

It was a horrible spectacle, and one which not only detracted from all the beauties of the scenery around, but sent me back thoughtful and sad. Beautiful as was the verdure, clad portion of the land, it was evidently infested by creatures that would have made hideous an earthly paradise. At every step I started, expecting to be attacked by some other fearful animal, and glad and thankful were my feelings when, approaching the rocks, I recognised the landmark which was to guide my footsteps.

But the way by which I returned was not that which had taken me to the scene of the combat between the anaconda and the monkeys, so that I found the rocks considerably more difficult to climb, until at last my steps were stayed by a kind of yawning gulf, which, however, was easy to be descended into, to where a cool and pellucid-looking pool invited me to slake my thirst.

I accordingly descended, and at once recognized the scene of the encounter between myself and the huge anaconda.

My fatigue was by this time so great that I gladly availed myself of this short road, and soon as I began to remove the barrier between this and my own cave, was delighted to hear the barking of Tiger, who evidently had been very miserable in consequence of my prolonged absence.

CHAPTER XXVII.

A WET SEASON.

NEXT day the rain commenced falling in torrents, driving me very reluctantly to the shelter of the cave. My leap from the cocoa-nut tree had shaken down some of the fruit, so that I at once proceeded to make use of them in a way which had occupied my mind for some days. The nut was opened, the contents removed, and then, aided by saw and chisel, I was able to divide it into two. I had heard that the fibres of the bamboo made excellent candle and lamp wicks, so that, though I had as yet no time to make the former, the latter was very easily to be accomplished.

Softening the oil and lard together by the fire in a small barrel, the contents were poured into the half cocoa-nuts, in which I afterwards held the bamboo fibres, until the fat was of a consistence to hold the wicks upright of themselves. These, placed inside the cave, soon cooled, and proved to be very tolerable substitutes for better lamps.

Now I began to lay out my plans for the many days of this, my first rainy season.

Having discovered that I could communicate with the more fertile and lovely, though clearly more dangerous, part of the island, by the means of the anaconda cavern, I no longer thought of quite blocking up the entrance. A rough, strong, and serviceable door could easily be made, which would keep out most animals—and this task was determined on.

My own cave was to be divided into four. First there was my sleeping-room, next my parlour, then my kitchen, and finally my store-room. The first and third occupied my attention chiefly. The studding sail boom, which was extremely unwieldly, served, however, the purpose I had in view admirably. A careful measurement showed me that it was as long as the cave was wide. Now, the sides of the cave were rough and unpolished, so that, after preparing a kind of hollow in a shelf with my crowbar, I was able to raise the boom to the height of six feet on one side.

Then, by the assistance of planks, beams and the trunk or two of a tree, with the crowbar for a lever, the other end was raised on the opposite side, this cutting the cave exactly in two. Then, still using the iron instrument which had proved so valuable an acquisition, a rough narrow groove was made underneath in the soft rock. Planks, bamboos, and stakes were after this easily nailed to the supporting boom.

Several bamboos were now carried from the boom to the sides of the cave nearest the waterfall, and by dint of great ingenuity, in a few days I had at least one comfortable room, about ten feet square, with walls a little more than six feet high. A quantity of dried boughs and leaves formed as yet my only couch, though my ideas as to the future were more ambitious.

Passing out at a doorway into another enclosure, behold my store-room, next to which, and near the entrance was the kitchen, furnished as yet only with a fire-place made from

------

* The reason why a serpent can swallow bodies much larger than itself arises from the fact, that the branches of the jaw are not united to each other except by ligaments; nor are those of the upper jaw united to the intermaxillary bone in any other manner, so that they can be more or less separated, a conformation which gives these animals the power of dilating their mouth to such an extent as to enable them to swallow deer, dogs, and even cougars and bullocks.

loose stones. To the right of this was an apartment which was to be either my workshop or my sitting room, as occasion required, also, at present, my armoury.

As, after the fatigues of the day, sleep was very welcome, I naturally enough rose early, when an ablution in a half tub placed near the waterfall, refreshed me and prepared me for breakfast. Then I made a fire. At first I was very fearful of the smoke, but found it not incommode me at all, the roof being so high, and it in all probability escaping by fissures in the top. Some broiled fish, or on great occasions, a slice of ham or bacon, served me, with some mouldy biscuit, for my first meal, while, by placing a good hard cocoa-nut shell quite close to the embers full of water, and with a pinch or two of tea, I obtained a kind of beverage, which, though bitter and unpalateable, seemed to me more agreeable than water.

This business finished to the satisfaction of myself and Tiger, for some days there was work enough in dividing the cave into its four compartments.

About midday, my appetite, now revived by hard work, I dined on salt or dried meat, with some bread fruit, the solid food being washed down by some brandy and water of moderate strength.

Then I smoked for half an hour. Yes, smoked, though I had neither pipe or tobacco. But so solitary was I, that the indulgence in this pleasant intoxication, appeared to me something like companionship, so that having selected a small bamboo, which having been hollowed out, and being stuffed with the dried leaves and flowers of various bushes, served to while away the time, nor did I ever, during my wearisome period of solitary confinement, regret my indulgence in this, my only vice. But I was very glad not to have given way to the taste too early, its evil effects on the growth and constitution being known to me.

Work followed, and then a last meal, after which I sat down to less arduous labours, such as mending my clothes, making with rope yarn, seal sinews, and bamboo fibres, certain nets, the use of which had often occurred to me during my perigrinations. Then prayer and bed. My books were keenly examined, and turned out to be composed of a medical guide, a work on botany, a Bible, a French Testament, grammar, and dictionary. But during this season, my labour was too assiduous to leave me any time for availing myself of their contents.

Soon, too, efforts of high mechanical genius demanded my attention. A bedstead, a chair, and a table were my constant dream, and this dream I determined should prove reality. The bedstead was the first task, and was comparatively an easy one, though the question of bed furniture must remain matter for future consideration. Skins of beasts could alone supply the deficiency I laboured under.

The seaman's chest was about five feet six inches long, by about eighteen inches wide. I managed, by means of chisel and hammer, to take it apart, leaving each side with one of the ends attached to it. Then I placed the ends together, and nailing a board at the other extremity, had now a square box about three feet in width. Across this some planks, then bamboos, then boughs and leaves, were placed. The skins of the animals I had killed were useless, because they smelt fearfully, and also because they were as hard as boards. I had as yet to discover, or recollect, the art of making my skins soft and supple.

This bed may appear rude and incomplete enough, but to me it was a great luxury, simply in that it took me off the ground.

As to a table and chair, I did make something which served my turn, but the very worst carpenter who ever botched a job would have turned up his nose at them in ridicule and disgust. The table was an ill-jointed three pieces of board, supported by legs of various sizes and shapes while the chair was a rough imitation of a three-legged stool, which caused me several falls ere it served the purpose for which it was intended.

And thus, in these and a few other such jobs, the wet weather passed away.

CHAPTER XXVIII.

THE GAZELLES.

EVERY morning and evening I peered forth to examine the weather, but for a long time found that the rain poured down in torrents, making my clear and transparent pool muddy and thick, while such was the abundance of water, that it overflowed through various channels and escaped towards the sea. At length, however, the balmy atmosphere, the glad song of birds, and the hum of thousands of insects, proclaimed the advent of another summer.

Quickly arming myself, and, of course, taking my dog with me, I sallied into the open air. The scene was miraculous. Everything had changed to a bright green, the trees, shrubs, plants, and the grass beneath our feet were sparkling with drops of rain, that looked like shining pearls ; the feathered choristers sang loud minstrelsy aloft, and proclaimed that they were glad.

The shoots which I had planted had taken root, and so rapid had been their growth, that I had to cut away young boughs to make my way to the outside, after placing a plank as usual across the pitfall. My first thoughts were of my seed-field, to which I hurried with great anxiety, and indeed it was time.

Everything I had planted had come up, but to my horror and disgust, a small drove of the most delicate-looking gazelles were busily engaged in cropping my young shoots. There was a male, a female, and three graceful young ones. Their forms were light and elegant ; their necks long and slender ; their limbs slender and delicate ; but this did not prevent me from looking upon them as thieves, who were devouring my substance, and enraged beyond measure at what seemed to me a sheer act of piracy, I levelled my fowling-piece, and taking deliberate aim, shot the buck, which fell heavily to the ground. Then, running forward, I started the others off at gallop, and saw no more of them at that time.

On examination, it proved that my seed had come up, not only oats, barley, and peas, but carrots, onions, and turnips, which was to me a perfect mercy, as the constant eating of salt and animal food would, I knew, be sure to bring on scurvy. Still, it was necessary to guard against the invasion of my field by the birds of the air and the beasts of the field. In the first place, it was decided in my mind to skin and stuff the buck gazelle, which was with some difficulty executed by means of my knife and Spanish moss and grass. When the inside was filled, four sticks were inserted in the place of the bones of the legs, and by this time the whole was so stiff as to readily stand up.

This task, and the cutting up of my gazelle into joints occupied nearly the whole day, when I returned to the cave well supplied with fresh meat, of which myself and dog made a hearty and delightful meal. As, however, I sat that evening smoking my pipe, and executing some of the many tasks which never allowed time to pass wearily, I turned over certain things I had read in my mind, and came to a desision. Behold me, then, next morning, armed only with my pistols, sallying forth. By my side, in place of a cutlass, was the captain's telescope, in my hand two wands, at the end of which was fastened a few stripes of red cloth, and in a bundle a net something like a seine.

About half a mile from my corn fields was a valley, very narrow at both ends, but wide in the middle. It was skirted in all its length by precipitous rocks, and, being very fertile, with some pleasant shade, was a favourite passage of mine on my way to the sea. One end of it, that farthest from me, was no more than seven or eight feet across. This I proceeded to block up by means of stakes, bamboos, and stones, until I had contrived such a barrier as even a gazelle would not leap over. Then, using my telescope, I saw the little drove, at some distance, browsing and coming my way.

A little up the valley, where fertile tracts were like to draw them, I planted my wands, with the crimson cloth waving in the wind, and then crouched down upon my face, holding my dog firmly round the mouth. For an hour I lay in this position, behind some thick bushes. Fortunately, the wind was from the gazelles to me, so that even their keen scent could not detect my presence. My old hunting trick succeed⁶⁾ The little animals, attracted by the fluttering cloth, ₚme slowly up, their noses raised to the wind, the dᵒ first, the kids after. No sooner were they past me, then rising to my feet, I gave a loud cry, and rushing across the narrow mouth of the valley, had in a moment placed a net across their pathway, which effectually prevented all chance of return.

My raptures knew no bounds, I had a home, I had my corn fields—now had I not flocks and herds?

HAPTER XXIX.

A STARTLING EVENT.

I WELL knew that it would be useless to attempt to tame such an animal as the gazelle all at once, so I resolved to proceed by degrees. The grass of the valley would not last the drove very long, but before they could run short, I hoped to have such a crop of carrots, turnips, and even barley and oats, as to enable me to spare them some food. The gazelle feeds willingly on anything green; and in order to use them to my presence, I made a further inroad on their liberty.

By means of stakes and willow-like boughs, I made at one end of the valley a kind of enclosure, like a sheep-pen, into which I easily taught my dog to drive them every evening, when I made a point of giving them turnip-tops, carrots, and such like—in small quantities, it is true, but quite enough to make them very tame in a few weeks. In time, indeed, the younger ones would even feed out of my hand.

Such occupations were not only a relief to my mind, and a kind of amusement, as it were, but it enabled me to look forward to the future with somewhat more of calm satisfaction. I had not altogether been more than six months on this deserted island, where the foot of man appeared never to have trod, and already great mercies had been vouchsafed to me. My ammunition was to me invaluable, and any means of husbanding it peculiarly pleasing. None could be more effective than that which now seemed to offer itself in the form of domestic animals, that would supply me in time with milk and butcher's meat.

It was, however, a question of the future, and the present could not be neglected. My clothes were wearing out with singular rapidity; nor did I at present see very clearly how this deficiency was to be made up; and then my dread of wild beasts, mingled with a certain vague feeling of uneasiness with regard to the possibility of an attack from roaming savages, made me anxious to fortify my cavern residence against all comers.

My thicket was in itself a very good defence, but still both man and beast might force their way through its intricacies. Then my dependence would be solely in my own valour and the power of my weapons. With bamboos and stakes, a kind of wall was made, which, with clods of earth and turf, was raised to a very excellent consistency. Then, with thin bamboos, I made a sloping roof, over which the creeping and parasitical plants soon grew so thickly that it took me many hours every week to cut away superfluous quantities. Under this I placed about half my guns, fastened in such a way as to admit of being turned in various directions, while in a corner were three or four more, which, with my miniature battery, were always loaded.

Fishing supplied me with a very large proportion of the food necessary for my daily existence, while at the same time I was very successful in collecting eggs, and now and then fortunate enough to secure a turtle, which is, however excessively insipid eating unless it be properly cooked. But abundance of all that was necessary to sustain life did not render the certain dearth of clothes any the less dreary in contemplation.

There was everything on the island in the way of the raw material, but my recollections and experiences did not serve me as to preparing deer or other skins for use, while how to utilise the different fibres and grasses was a mystery as great to me as that of the Grecian oracles. Still I felt that, cast wholly on my own resources, there must occur to my mind some way of getting over these difficulties, and I spent many a long evening in making experiments that ended, however, for a long time in utter failure. It was not in my nature to despair, so for the present my clothes were repaired as well as might be with such materials as the seaman's chest and the wreck did afford.

Considering the really solitary position I was in, cut off from all communication with my kind, my evenings were much more agreeable than I had any right to expect. In the first place, we entered the kitchen, where all the while the necessary preliminaries were going on, my dog sat with becoming gravity, looking at me. A stew of meat, vegetables, and even of fish, was the general evening meal, especially if I was fortunate enough to have caught any fowl in certain rude traps which I was continually making. Then while this was cooking, little odd jobs—putting up shelves, improving the partitions, levelling the floor—occupied me. No sooner, however, was the supper ready than it was placed on the ground, a lamp was put on each side of my table, and with my knife, and a very awkward substitute for a spoon, made of cocoa nut, the food was ladled out into the half of a cocoa nut. Such portions as were selected for the dog, whose appetite troubled me much in the wet season, were cast to the ground and devoured with all due gravity. As rest was always very welcome this meal was prolonged for some time, but when finished, after a small space of time given to smoking, work was resumed until fatigue made sleep necessary and welcome.

One of my regular tasks was piecing and mending, which I cannot say was done much to my satisfaction; for though there was no one to see my uncouth tailoring, there is ever some remnant of pride in poor human nature, even on a desert island in the great ocean. My shoes caused me even still more trouble. I could not contrive to do anything in this way for some time, so was obliged to wear them until they dropped off my feet, as they were only kept together by rude ligatures.

Still, with knives, thread, and good needles, something, it was certain, could be done, if only the leather could be found.

After my visit to the interior of the island, and the terrible sight of the anaconda's death, there was not much inclination to explore that region; but about two months after the cessation of the rainy season, the idea entered my mind that I required some change. The monotony of my existence had not varied for some time, and accordingly, on reflection a journey through my own part of the island was, after some reflection, determined on.

The place evidently abounded with several of the deer tribe, and an addition to my herd appeared to me very desirable, especially if any of the goats, which must have been left by the Spaniards or buccaneers, could be captured. Several attempts had been made on my part to capture them by traps and pitfalls, but with no success; they were too cunning, or my engines were not properly constructed.

However this may be, after breakfast on the morning in question, I armed myself, and sallied forth for more accurate examination of a large wooded tract, which my telescope had enabled me to discover to the rght of Wild False Bay. I had seen many goats skipping about in that locality, and I determined to see if by any chance some means might not be found of capturing some of them, to place in company with my small flock of gazelles.

My first halt was at the bamboo and bread-fruit grove, where a hearty meal was made. From that spot to where the larger woods commenced might have been a mile, trees and bushes being scattered here and there over the otherwise sandy plain.

As this was to me a new locality, I was naturally anxious to explore it, as I continually expected that new and useful productions would fall in my way.

I had risen to my feet, and was leaning my back against the tree as I gazed around, half inclined to take a shot at some fat birds, which were perched on a bough close at hand, when a whizzing sound struck strangely on my startled senses.

A bird fell at my feet transfixed with an arrow.

CHAPTER XXX.

THE CANNIBAL INDIANS.

Where will-o'-the-wisps and glow-worms shine
    In bulrush and in brake;
Where waving mosses shroud the pine,
And the cedar grows, and the poisonous vine
    Is spotted like the snake.

Where hardly a human foot could pass,
    Or a human heart would dare,
On the quaking turf of the green morass,
He crouched in the rank and tangled grass
    Like a wild beast in his lair.—LONGFELLOW.

I STOOD, for a moment, transfixed with such horror and astonishment as a man might feel who had suddenly come face to face with the Evil One. My eyes were first cast hastily round in search of the hunter, but seeing nothing, I

took a hurried and frightened survey of the weapon which had slain his prey.

It was a long, slender, harmless-looking reed, but it had killed the bird, and was, of course, certainly shot by human hands. With eyes almost starting from their sockets, I remained, methinks, for a few minutes utterly unable in my confusion, to move; I felt like one in a dream—my feet, as it were, glued to the ground. My previous knowledge, acquired from that reading of which I had been so fond, told me the nature of the enemy I had to encounter. Casting my eyes hurriedly around, I quickly rushed to some bushes, and sank behind them in an agony of terror, while, letting go my hold on the gun, I clasped my two hands round the dog's nose, and by main force and signs kept him from barking.

Then I saw a man—and that, in my confusion of mind, was all I could see—advance slowly to the spot where the bird lay, and pick it up.

Then, despite my precautions, the dog gave a low, savage growl. The man, or rather the savage hunter, turned quickly, and peered with wild and restless eyes in our direction. Then he sat down upon his haunches, and applying both feet to the middle of the crossbow he carried, bent back the string to a notch. Then he took a fresh arrow, which doubtless was poisoned, and fixed it in the groove. I watched his movements so intently that, so light was the reed, he had to stick it on with gum to prevent its blowing away.

Then, rising to his feet, he listened attentively, while his eyes examined the tops of the bushes to see if they moved. For a moment he appeared inclined to come my way, in which case he would most assuredly have died. My brow was contracted, my heart beat violently, and I determined to sell my own life dearly.

He, however, changed his mind, and turned in the direction whence he came.

The relief was great, and without further hesitation, I hurried back at the top of my speed in the direction of my cave. Never did I run so fast, either before or since. No sooner was my home reached, than I saw carefully to the pit-fall, and then entering within my intrenchments, renewed the priming of my guns.

Then I entered the cave, and secured my dog in my bedroom by means of a stout cord, and there left him to himself, with a pile of bones to gnaw. I knew that did the savages hear him bark, they would recognise in him a strange animal, and probably run any risk to procure a sight of him.

My feelings, on sitting down within the shelter of the wall which I had erected, were intensely painful. The character of the Indians who inhabited the latitudes in which my island was doubtless situated, was familiar to my memory. They were savages and cannibals, delighting in nothing more than in killing, and afterwards devouring their enemies, and that they would consider a white man in that light was a certainty.

How bitterly now I felt the desolate condition in which I was placed? In the excitement of work, of discovery, or providing for the present and the future, little time was to be spared for bemoaning my hard fate, however much such sentiments might force themselves on me in my calmer hours of rest and repose. Now, however, that a danger which had appeared distant and only probable, was no near, my hard fate all but drew tears from my eyes. But sorrow and moaning could avail nothing—it was a time for calm and deliberate action.

Should I remain where I was, firmly entrenched, or should I go forth and see the real state of the case, acting then as circumstances might dictate? This matter was debated in my mind for some time, and at last curiosity and anxiety prevailed.

Returning within the cave, and passing through, my next act was to open the doorway I had manufactured, and to pass through the outer cave, after, however, a careful survey. In this way the upper rocks were gained, which, towering even over the tall trees that surrounded my pool, enabled me to examine the smaller portion of the island. As I expected, my telescope guided me to a column of smoke in the direction of the very wooded district it had been my intention fully to explore.

They were there, then, in numbers, but with what intention it was impossible for me to imagine. The only way was to creep as close to them as circumstances would allow, and examine for myself.

Slowly and thoughtfully the lower part of the island was regained. My pistols were fastened to my belt, my sword hung at my side, and two guns loaded with ball placed on my shoulders; thus accoutred and armed I sallied forth to reconnoitre.

My eyes were cast to the right and left, and then in front, at every step I took. The rustling of a tree top, the movement of a bush, the cry of a bird, made me start, affrighted and alarmed. But as I advanced, no signs of the savages being seen, my courage slowly returned, until at last I was able to walk along with something like calm and satisfaction.

At length, just as evening was falling, the first grove of trees in the wooded district was reached. Extreme caution was now more than ever used, as the savages might be lurking about. Then came a somewhat dense forest tract, through which I made my way with some difficulty, though now and then the course of a winding stream assisted me in my advance.

Suddenly an open space appeared before me, and, raising my head over a fallen trunk overhung with bushes, I could distinctly observe the intruders upon my hitherto deserted island. They were not real negroes, as I might have naturally expected, but of a tribe nearly akin to that race. They were very tall, strongly built, and well made—being nearly naked, except that round the waist was a belt, from which hung an apron of some skin of wild cat or tiger. Their teeth were filed, and in some cases blackened, which gave them a ghastly and ferocious look. Their woolly hair was drawn out into long thin plaits, to the ends of which were strung white beads of copper and iron rings.

Some had feather caps, some long queues of their own hair, mixed with tow, dyed black, which gave them a most wild and grotesque appearance. They were armed with long spears or lances, while on the left arm hung shields, which I afterwards discovered were made from elephant hide—that is, from the back of an old elephant, which, being dried and smoked, and as hard and is impenetrable as iron.

They had women with them less dressed than the men, and much uglier. They, too, had their teeth filed, and carried their younger children on their backs in slings. They as well as the men were tatooed, especially on the breast and stomach.

This sight terrified me dreadfully, as the presence of women and many captives seemed to indicate an intention to settle permanently. Besides they had already commenced collecting bamboos and stakes, for the purpose of erecting their huts, which some of the women and prisoners were doing in a very ingenious manner. They drove stakes into the ground; then to these they added split bamboos—one set

outside, and another in—while the crevices were closed up with large palm leaves.

Their canoes, too, of various sizes, were drawn up on the beach, while one of singular elegance and small size had been towed up a creek, and served the women for a ferry-boat.

All these preparations were terrible in the extreme, in my eyes, as if they were going to remain on the island, my hopes of happiness, and even of life, were gone. The thought flashed across my mind, that, perhaps, already they had discovered my small pen and flock of gazelles, in which case they would know the island to be inhabited. I determined then, as soon as safety would allow of a retreat, to destroy all signs of an enclosure, and release my tiny flock.

Then it struck me that perhaps these savages were on a hunting expedition. The island was not only fertile in parts, but full of game. Of this the tribe might be aware, and make a great periodical hunt. Should this be the case, there might yet be a hope of escaping their notice until the period should come for their departure.

With this view, I had determined to retreat, even during the darkness of the night, when some of the savages began lighting a large fire, round which soon a very large proportion of them were congregated.

Then behind me in the forest rose the shrill sound of a single conch, which was quickly answered from the camp. Next instant I distinctly heard the tramp of feet, at a great distance, which made me glide away in a lateral direction. I was not far off when a hunting party came in sight.

Strung on poles, carried on the shoulders of two men, *were three young gazelles.*

CHAPTER XXXI.

THE MANGROVE SWAMP.

MY heart sank within me, for now I felt that all was lost, so almost without using even tolerable caution, I fled in the direction of the larger and more fertile portion of the island. Whether any one followed me or not it was impossible to say, as my confusion was so great.

The idea uppermost in the mind was to place as great a distance as possible between myself and the savages, who, to my fancy, appeared to be covering the island in hundreds.

After running for about a quarter of an hour in the dark, burdened as I was with my two guns, I was compelled to lie down and rest. The night was very dark, nor could I, indeed, distinguished ten yards before me, so that I was compelled to feel my way. Presently, my eyes became more accustomed to the gloom, I saw before me a dark line like a wall, but what it was I could not make out. At that moment the sound of human voices, new to me for many weary months, fell upon my ear. They were close at hand.

I had no resource but to run for it once more, as else I should surely be discovered, so I retreated precipitately through a thicket beside which I had been lying; and, scarcely minding what I did, found myself suddenly up to my waist in water. Casting up my eyes, I saw that it was a mangrove swamp. A small rivulet, it afterwards proved, fell, pellucid and clear, from its narrow bed, to widen out at once into a large pond of muddy water, redolent of malaria and mosquitoes. It wound its way through an immense

ESCAPE OF THE INDIAN GIRL.

No. 6.—SAILOR CRUSOE.

grove of these trees, whose roots extended entirely across, and met in the middle, showing their huge rounds above the mire and water, like the many folds of some huge serpent.

The mangrove is indeed a most singular tree, a native of the East Indies and of most tropical parts, where it grows in swampy situations on the coast, and penetrates even within low water mark of the sea. It attains the height of forty or fifty feet, and is an evergreen.

The red mangrove grows commonly by the sea side, and by rivers or creeks. It always grows out in many roots, about the bigness of a man's leg, some bigger, some less, which, at about six, eight, or ten feet above the ground, join into one trunk or body, that seems to be supported by so many artificial stakes. Wherever this sort of tree grows it is impossible to march, by reason of these stakes, and it is very common, when forced to go through them, for people to go half a mile and never set foot on the ground, stepping from root to root. The timber is hard and good for many uses.

One of the great singularities of this tree is, that the seeds begin to germinate and send out roots while they are yet attached to the parent branches. This is the natural way in which the tree is propagated, by their roots descending and fixing themselves in the earth. It is this tree that gave rise to the fable of oysters growing from trees, because from its situation on the sea shore, and within tide mark, it becomes a favourite resort of these shell-fish, which cling to its branches, and thus have the appearance of growing from them. *

CHAPTER XXXII.

THE MANGROVE.

BUT all this occurred to my mind afterwards. Crawling on, by means of placing my two guns on one shoulder, I caught at the huge limb of a gnarled root, and in this way reached the huge parent stem, which was of immense size and fortunately for me, as it happened, hollow. Without reflecting that such holes are too often the resort and place of refuge of dangerous animals, while the swamp itself—that region of hopeless disorder—was the home of the alligator, the mocassin, and rattlesnake, I entered panting and exhausted. For some time I was utterly prostrated, but soon recovering, listened attentively. But not a sound of human voices could now be distinguished.

Still, it did not appear wise or prudent to return, so I took my guns and placed them against the side of the tree, after which, having in the morning provided against the contingency of stopping out all night, I unstrung the steward's lantern, and prepared to light it.

Then alone, when something like calm returned, did I become awake to the beauty of that dark and terrible scene, illumined here and there by the vivid flash of the fire-fly. The mangroves spread, I could see even by that dim light, in long vistas in every direction, roofed over by the leafy arches of this wondrous tree; while in the distance uprose other evergreens that formed dense jungles, green all the year round, and the home of numberless warbling birds, that luxuriate in the savage exuberance of vegetation. A heavy

drapery of vines and other parasitic plants, of gorgeous splendour, fell in rich folds on all hands, veiling at times the vistas of these long forest arches. Every now and then could be heard the splash of some huge animal in the water, doubtless alligators. There was, too, the croaking hum of the horned frog * and other of the animals which haunt these dismal and melancholy swamps.

After listening for some time, and hearing nothing but sounds I could explain, my lantern was lit. The tree was about five feet in diameter, and the hollow about ten feet high; and in this place, surrounded by the foul exhalations of the swamp, I was to pass the night, without food, or even water, unless I drank from the pool below. In my hurry and confusion, the necessity of refreshment during the night had never crossed my mind. There was, however, no help for it. Never, even in the early days of my captivity on that deserted and miserable spot, did I feel so unhappy as now. Just as, by great efforts, resignation had fallen on my soul— just as, with a firm reliance on Providence, I was about to act as if my destiny for life were fixed, and when house and lands were already prepared—had come this fearful blight. Home, fields, all were useless now.

Gloomy and sad, I sat within my tree, anxiously listening for any sound that might indicate the approach of my enemies. Close to my hand were my loaded weapons, and shaded as much from without as possible, my lantern was still so placed as to scare any animal that might have approached too near. Now it was that I missed my apology for a pipe. Thought was too painful, and as a natural consequence of anxiety and watching, my throat became parched with thirst, my lips dry, and my whole frame burning. I had with me a little gourd of brandy, and a half cocoa-nut, slung to my side. To drink the brandy alone was folly, as it would only have added to my feverish thirst.

Cautiously setting my foot upon the tangled roots of this extraordinary tree, I stooped low to reach the water. Just under the roots was a black mass, apparently a trunk which had fallen. On this I trod hastily. As I did so, it glided clear away from me, so that I plunged headlong into the hideous and slimy pool. It was a huge old alligator, which had taken up its quarters for the night, and which I had disturbed.

In my fright, as I caught at the arching boughs, I dropped the half cocoa nut, which served me as a cup, and clambering back into the hollow tree, hastily swallowed a dram of brandy, ere my equanimity was restored. Then a sense of fever and impatience came over me. The hideous and pallid gloom that environed my shelter, the hum of night insects, the splashing about of strange beasts, the bewildering noises that belong to tropical swamps, the acrid, memphitic vapour which rises from the dead leaves, weeds, and stagnant pools, made me feel not exactly drowsy, but torpid.

I fell into a heavy stupor.

And I dreamed a dream. It was glorious sunshine. The murky, wild, forsaken swamp, through which the wind whistled mournfully; the dolorous trees, with their black funeral palls of moss and lichens; the dark arches of that desolate impervious jungle, changed to a bright forest, all alive with birds, where the cedar, and the poplar, and the beech, with honeysuckles, vines, and laurels, made the scene exquisite and the heart glad.

But, treading softly over the fragrant sward, what cometh?

---

* *Rhizophora mangle*, or common mangrove, is found abundant on the shores of the ocean, and within the delta of the Ganges, where it grows to a considerable size. The seed of this species, which is from one to two feet long, very quickly gives rise to a young tree; and, as mentioned by Browne, in his History of Jamaica, if the apex from whence the root issues be stuck only a little way in the mud the leaves quickly unfold at the opposite [en]d. The wood is dark red, hard, and the bark is used for tanning [le]ather. The *Rhiz: gymnoriza* is resinous, while the pith, boiled, [is] used for food.

* The horned-frog is common in warm latitudes. Several may be seen in the *Jardin des Plantes*, Paris.

My heart beat wildly. It was a figure surrounded, as it were, with a glory—which, its eyes fixed on me, approached swiftly and joyously. And then I knew I was in the presence of my dear cousin, from whom I had been parted in the dread leap for life. ·

With a shriek and a start, my senses returned, and it was a long time ere the beating of my heart would again allow me any repose. ·

When I came to myself it was morning, my lamp had gone out, and a refreshing breeze that wafted away the pestilential vapours and dews of night seemed slightly to revive me. A slight opening in the green-roofed forest showed me that the sky was of a crystalline blue, that spread a broad sea of light over all nature, while the shadows of the forest aisles were themselves pierced by its purple rays. It was a morning to revel in, to make one thankful to Providence for all its bounties. But I was in too great a peril to allow calm and gentle thoughts to enter my soul. Then came the gnawing sensation of hunger. My head ached, particularly at the back, my eyes swam, so that all objects were indistinct and hazy, and I was compelled to drink brandy by way of keeping body and soul together.

A kind of stupid apathy came over me, which made me for a moment reckless of all consequences. I would have fought a tiger in his den, had there been a chance of water and food to be obtained.

Then I heard a strangely alarming noise, and the next instant I saw, in the distance, a body of about a dozen or fifteen warriors, armed with bows, shields, and spears, advancing directly towards me. I was seized with so sudden a panic that I fled, leaving my guns behind me. The direction I took was where I could make out dry land, and, despite the slime and mud I had to wade through, I succeeded in reaching the spot. But I felt it was impossible to go any further, so swiftly climbed a tree, the branches of which nearly touched the ground, and crouching where the huge boughs spread out, waited the event.

My pistols were primed and little as it was my wish to take human life, like any other desperate man, the resolve was now finally come to. But the savages appeared to me not to have any such intentions as had led me to flee, so that they passed and disappeared ere I had quite recovered myself.

My feelings were much like those of a man suddenly reprieved, and I sat on my bough, slowly recovering, until again I was forced to have recourse to my flask. Looking round, it was with some considerable surprise, that gazing upwards, a regularly thatched roof was discovered over my head. Some animal had taken advantage of the circumstance that, at knotted intervals of about six feet the boughs went straight out,—to lay a sloping roof of boughs and leaves, impervious quite to the rays of the sun. These branches were fastened to the tree in the middle of the structure by means of wild vines and creepers, which were abundant in these parts. Nothing could be more regular and artistic than the way in which the affair was managed, so that I was lost in astonishment at what it could mean.

Then glancing keenly about, without moving or even disturbing a leaf, so great was my caution, I at once discovered the meaning of what had so strangely puzzled me.

They were ape nests.

About twenty feet from me were two trees, distant from each other about five feet, and on each tree, at the same height, were two of these slanting green-thatched roofs.

They were fresher and more newly-constructed than mine, it being the practice of their architects, instead of repairing the old ones to make new nests, to protect them from the nightly rains or dews—they being quite capable of shedding water. Beneath these shelters were two monkeys, that, frightened by the hunters, had hurriedly sought their homes, and were now gravely seated with their arms round the trunk, grinning every now and then in the direction of the savages.

Then, with that ludicrous effect which is seen in no other animal, the male and female—for such were these near neighbours—began to crack some nuts, and pelt one another in the most odd kind of way, grimacing and turning up their odd little eyes at every moment. My pistols were close to my hand, and such were the sensations of hunger which gnawed my vitals, that I felt very much inclined to shoot one of the little wretches, but fear of attracting the savages restrained my impetuosity.

Half an hour had now elapsed, so I determined to crawl down, and, weak as I was, to return to my cave, where I should be safe, and obtain that proper food and rest which was so much needed by my exhausted frame. It was absolutely necessary to return and fetch my guns, as, if discovered, they might afford some clue to my presence on the island. How I succeeded is beyond my own knowledge. It was an arduous and perilous task, in which I was kept up solely by my flask of brandy, that truly on this occasion saved my life.

Never in the course of my life did my body feel the degrading influence of intoxication, that fatal vice which preys more even on the mind than the external frame, but in such perils as this the service rendered by the alcoholic drink was immense. My journey was performed by slow stages. The dreadful sensation of weariness and hunger made me continually lie down, and as often throw away my guns in reckless despair. But every now and then, by chewing a leaf, and once or twice by drinking from little rivulets I crossed, the road appeared at last to grow shorter.

But a new trouble assailed me. By tramping through the wet mud, and sitting in them so long, my shoes were in an awful state, and now that I was walking on pointed and sharp rocks, their soft and pulpy substance gave out completely, and but I tied them together with long tendrils of vine-like plants, and then with strips from my shirt, the end of my journey would never have been reached; as it was my feet bled dreadfully, and caused me most excruciating pain.

As I passed the valley of the gazelles my delight may be imagined at seeing the little animals feeding peacefully and unconcernedly. The savages had not then visited my part of the district; while the gazelles which I had seen were merely the ordinary product of the chase.

My great cause of safety was the circumstance that the savages had discovered an easy entrance to the other part of the island, so that they were not so likely to examine that which I called more peculiarly my own. When my eyes fell once more upon the spot which to me was home, my senses seemed to return, and though my feet scarce sufficed to carry me, being now bleeding, bare, and swollen, new vigour appeared to fill my soul. I literally crawled through my enclosure, crossed the pitfall, removed the plank carefully, and then entered my cavern. My dog barked furiously, but when he heard my voice began to whine with joy. But before I did anything else I eat a biscuit very slowly, soaking it in brandy-and-water. This appeared to revive me considerably. Then I let loose the dog, which nearly knocked me down in the exuberance of its joy.

The animal was very hungry; so, after feeding it with a little biscuit, I took a very good piece of meat and put it on to boil in my copper box, which, kept carefully clean, served me as a kettle. Then I bathed my feet, which were piteous to see, so sore, torn, and swollen, were they.

All this time my mind was still running on the strange and terrible visitors who were upon my island. Sometimes I fancied that, after all, is must be only a hunting expedition, and that as soon as th   had completed their object they would go away. Still,   uld Providence destine me to spend a long period on that inhospitable shore, the constant recurrence of such visits would be extremely annoying, as my flocks and herds, my cultivated fields, and anything else I might devote my time to, would certainly betray the presence of a white man in the locality.

What was to be done.

Weary, footsore, and utterly exhausted, my only resource was now to lie down and rest, which I did for some hours, with an amount of enjoyment which only those who have suffered as I had can understand. I anointed my feet copiously with grease, and did the same with my very last pair of new shoes. Then, having partaken freely of boiled meat and the liquor in which it was cooked, sharing equally with my dog, I laid down to rest.

Sleep fell upon me like a vaporous cloud, wrapping my senses in temporary oblivion. Not even a dream visited my slumbers, so complete was the power which fatigue exercised over my limbs, and when I did wake it was marvellous how restored I felt. My constitution was a good one, and youth was on my side, while hunger had not had time to produce its more disastrous and fatal effects.

Feeling no longer sleepy, I went out into my verandah—battery as I called it—and looked about. The night was still and calm, the clouds were heavy in the extreme, and not a star was visible. Stillness hung over all nature, except when now and then a tree waved under the influence of the wind. My weapons were already to hand, my pistols were in my belt, and my double-barrelled gun heavily loaded. I hoped, however, that any use for all this formidable array of guns might be needless.

Then my dog gave a low moan or howl, that startled me in   increased watchfulness.

   listened attentively, and then could distinguish at a   tance the hum of human voices.

They were coming my way.

I was calm and determined now, for the moment for action had come. Catching my dog by his rude collar of rope, my first act was to drag him into the cave and tie him up, my next to ignite a piece of rope, which burnt slowly like a fusee match. Then I returned to the verandah, opened the pans of all my guns that were tied to the wall, emptied fresh powder into them, and laid a train. My other guns were then seen to; my heart beating high, but my teeth firmly set I waited.

The cries of the savages were now very distinct. It appeared to me that they were chasing something. Then I distinctly heard something light, like an animal of slender foot and swift step enter my pathway. It was treading its way cautiously and carefully, as if fatigue were overcoming it, or the circuitous route were difficult to follow.

Then a dark vague form appeared, the shape of which I could no way make out. Next minute it fell with a shrill kind of shriek that did not betoken a very fierce animal, into the pitfall. I had, in my great confusion of mind forgotten this, my moat or ditch.

But now the clouds broke, and the treacherous moon burst forth, just as I heard the cries of the savages, as they halted outside my enclosure. Every gun was pointed straight at the opening. A dead silence ensued. They were searching for the path. A shrill kind of warwhoop proclaimed their success and my confusion. Two minutes, which seemed an hour, passed, and then half a dozen savages peered from the opening across the pitfall, as if surveying my habitation, and seeking to discover some way of crossing. My lighted rope was at once brought into requisition, and a tremendous flash that almost blinded me was followed by a tremendous report, and such a succession of shrieks and yells as seemed to re-echo from the very roof of the heavens. When the smoke cleared away nothing was to be seen, while I could hear the terror-stricken and frightened savages calling to one another in the most piteous and bewailing tones I had ever heard. In a few minutes all was still, and I was again alone.

CHAPTER XXXIII.
THE STRANGE CAPTURE.

MY knowledge of savage character and disposition made me now fully aware that I had nothing to fear from the warriors who had witnessed the effect of my volley. It was doubtless something quite new to them, and would for a long time prevent any intrusion upon my quarter of the island. The discharge had startled me, then how much more so must it have astounded beings who never before had witnessed any such sight.

It now remained to learn what was the nature of the game which the savages were pursuing.

For this purpose, seeing to the priming of my pistols, I returned into the cave and after taking some little refreshment, which I much needed, let loose the dog, which flew barking and yelling towards the pitfall. My cursory examination of the creature that had fallen into the trap, as well as its faint, shrill cry, convinced me that it was nothing that I need fear very much; still, not knowing the exact nature of any of the animals on my islands, no proper precaution was neglected.

The wood which covered the steps was slowly and cautiously removed.

Daylight was breaking, but a lantern was ready with which to explore the depths of the pit. The dog still kept barking, but did not show that alarm which was usual when in the presence of fierce or destructive animals. All this time not a sound came from within. Presently all that prevented the exit of the creature was removed, but it came not forth. I peered into the cave, thrusting back the dog, but still I could see nothing. As a last resource I took up my lantern, and clutching a pistol in my right hand began to descend the steps.

My God! on the ground, utterly insensible, was the most beautiful Indian girl I had ever dreamed of, even when devouring the "Arabian Nights Entertainments."

I set down my lantern, I cast away my pistol, and raising the girl—she was not a day more than sixteen—I carried her into the open air. Laying her down my flask was next fetched, a little brandy mingled with water poured down her throat, and with some more I bathed her forehead. She opened her eyes. Let he who in a dungeon has been confined apart from the human race, and who suddenly is restored to society imagine what were my sensations at finding myself once more in fellowship with my kind. Had the girl even been white she would have been handsome, for her features were regular in the extreme.

She gazed at me, speechless with wonder and terror. By signs I tried to make her understand that she had nothing to fear, and once more taking hold of my lantern assisted her to rise and enter my cavern. She moved as in a dream, but with what trembling grace! for doubtless the fearful volley from my guns was still ringing in her ear. The girl had no clothes save a wove petticoat of fibres, and a kind of necklace of some small shining nuts.

I spoke softly to her, but she shook with horror. Still I cared not but that with time I might tame her. Already visions of the joys of companionship flitted through my soul, and dreams of happiness I could not have hoped for flashed across my imagination. I led her to my kitchen, and well aware that she was only seeking an opportunity to fly placed her in a corner, and made Tiger lie down at her feet.

It appeared to me that the poor creature was as much afraid of the master as of the animal, so I began, pretending not to take notice of her, to broil some ham, which, with biscuit, I gave to her to eat. She shook her head, but, frowning I made signs to her that she must, and made believe that if she did not the dog should eat her. At this she forced herself to swallow, after which she became more friendly.

Then I showed her my cavern, and by signs which I fancy were plainly indicative of my delight at her presence, signified that the best furnished room, my own, would be for her use. By degrees her alarm wore off, and before night we were as good friends as any one could be who were unable to communicate by words.

She ate freely, smiled, showing her dazzling teeth, not filed like those of the savages from whom she had escaped—and studied everything with great curiosity and pleasure; so that when I placed her in my chamber for the night she appeared to be quite reconciled. It was many hours ere I composed myself to sleep. The island now seemed to me suddenly transformed into an earthly paradise. I was no longer alone, and my companion was as lovely as ever Eve could have been in the garden of Eden.

When dawn broke, having lit a fire and prepared what I thought to be a tempting breakfast, I opened the door of the inner chamber to let forth my prize. The room was empty. Wildly I dashed into the air, bounded over the pitfall, and rushed in the direction of the sea. There she was about a mile a-head of me. I shouted; she did not even turn, but continued running. Bracing up every nerve, and determined not to be left to dull and dreary solitude again, I ran at full speed, but she had disappeared in the forest in the direction of the savage camp.

I bounded through the woods; I reached the other side; I passed the abandoned site of the Indian camp; I reached the sea-shore, where the rich tropical vegetation in many places came down to the very water, and there she was just starting in the small canoe which I had seen in the narrow creek.

I rushed out into the water; I cried wildly to her to come back. I tore my hair, but she turned round only once, said something I could not understand, and then was carried to the eastward, along the island by the current—and I was alone once more.

CHAPTER XXXIV.

THE ELEPHANT.

There sat the gentle savage of the wild,
In growth a woman, though in years a child,
As childhood dates within our colder clime,
Where nought is ripened rapidly, save crime;
The infant of an infant world, as pure
From nature—lovely, warm, and premature;
Dusky like night, but night with all her stars,
Or cavern sparkling with its native spars,
With eyes that were a language and a spell,
A form like Aphrodite's in her shell,
With all her loves around her on the deep,
Voluptuous as the first approach of sleep,
Yet full of life—for through her tropic cheek
The blush would make its way, and all but speak;
The sun-born blood suffused her neck, and threw
O'er her clear nut-brown skin a lucid hue,
Like coral reddening through the darkened wave,
Which draws the diver to the crimson cave.
Such was the daughter of the Southern Seas.

My feelings can never be described, when, regaining the shore, I cast myself upon the beach. Resignation to my lot had come about by slow degrees. The necessity for work, the daily occupations which consumed so much time, the remembrance of how many had like myself been cast away and been miraculously saved, had slowly brought about a feeling of reconciliation to my lot, which had been a negative kind of happiness. So many mercies had been vouchsafed to me, that to repine at my lot would have been wicked in the extreme.

But now a vision of beauty had crossed my path; a girl evidently, from the general expression of her countenance, as amiable as she was lovely, had come to cheer my solitude. During the watches of the previous night, I had imagined myself another Adam, in Paradise, with Eve; I had laid out plans for taming and civilising my exquisite prize, I had thought how, when she could understand my language, it would be sweet to commune with her after the labours of the day. In my wildest dreams of providential succour it would have been madness to have placed such an event as this within the compass of probability; but against all probability it had come—to raise my fancy to the highest pitch—and now the bright hope had vanished.

A sense of utter and dreary loneliness fell upon me, as once again I rose to my feet. My dog was beside me. The faithful animal looked up into my face with an anxious glance, as if he reproached me for the scalding tears I was shedding.

"No, I am not alone, my brave Tiger," I said, patting him on the head, as my steps were turned once more towards the cavern, within which the whole of that day was spent in idleness. My courage was gone—work, amusement, all were distasteful to me. The night came, and as I lay looking upwards at the vast roof, I thought of the sweet companionship which imagination had told me I had lost, until, with very weariness, sleep fell upon me.

Next day I was no more reconciled to my lot than on the previous night, so after breakfast, taking with me a supply of food, I sallied forth. My appearance was grotesque enough. From my belt hung a powder-horn, shot-bag, and sword; pistols were thrust into it; to a thong were attached my flask of brandy and my gourd of water; on my head was a common cap shaded by palm leaves; while on each shoulder was a gun.

The marks of blood along my pathway, and for a considerable distance showed me that several of the pursuers had been wounded, which was certainly somewhat provoking, as the discovery of the leaden bullets might remove the supernatural aspect of the event. Still, the removal of the savages from their camp showed that it had had some very powerful effect on their imagination, and I had no doubt they were now on their way to their own country. Still, it behoved me to be careful, hence my sallying forth with such a panoply of arms. On reflection, thinking that, perhaps, my idea of their departure might be erroneous, I resolved to leave the dog at home, as he might betray me.

My preparations were made in expectation of a several days' exploring expedition. My plan was, to advance slowly and cautiously, peering carefully into woods and valleys, lest I might be surprised by the savages. The day was nearly spent when I reached the old camp they had occupied. Not a sign remained of their huts, nor could their presence have been suspected but for the mark of a fire in the centre of the place where their wigwams had been.

Wading across the creek which separated this part of the beach from the more tropical island, I found myself involved in a series of thickets and woods, which required some time to creep through. Night too was coming on, so I determined to camp, and for this purpose choose the protecting shelter of a kind of cliff, on the banks of a small stream. Here, by the assistance of a few boughs and leaves, I made myself a hut, and lay down.

My mind was ill at ease. I fancied every minute the cannibals were creeping on me—a sensation of itself of extreme horror.

Besides this source of uneasiness, nature itself influenced my feelings. Night in these tropical latitudes has a peculiar sadness for the isolated wanderer.

When the azure of the sky and the golden glow of sunshine covers those immense solitudes with their resplendent light, all is graceful, lovely, and enchanting; but when the first stars begin to twinkle, a mysterious influence glides with the darkness over forest, valley, and ravine; the long vistas of the woods become, as it were, corridors of the infernal regions; the trees take strange and lugubrious shapes, and their out-spreading boughs resemble the gigantic arms of phantoms, ready to clutch the imprudent individual who shall venture within reach.

I readily understood, as I hearkened to the thousand and one noises of the river and all but adjacent woods, and saw the shadows playing with the rippling waves, why savages should worship the sun, a visible god to them, driving away the horrors of night, and giving joy and life with the fresh smile of morn.

I had walked a great deal, and suffered much from fatigue, but the novelty of my position prevented sleep from visiting me for some time. There seemed to me to be strange noises in the woods, while lower down the river murmurs arose as if some huge animal were wallowing in the water and mud.

Still nothing came near me, so at last I slept, nor did anything occur to rouse me until the morning. Then, washing in the river, and eating sparingly of my provisions, I proceeded to descend its banks which, by occasionally wading, was tolerably practicable.

The beauty of the country, which now opened itself to my gaze, was something truly marvellous. Lovely and graceful trees, plants of the most varied hue, flowers of every colour of the rainbow; birds, whose plumage was glowing and rich beyond all powers of description, revelled in this new Elysium, of which I appeared to be the sole human tenant; birds, the different spieces of which, during my residence on the island, I counted by thousands.

There was the beautiful and delicate humming-bird swarming on the shrubs, each rapid movement giving a different dye, but in general like scales of burnished gold; there was the slender-billed sugar-eater, the splendid creeper, with its brown black wings, a bird that sings like a nightingale; the bee-eater; the hornbill; the shining cuckoo; the honey guiders, with their *cher, cher;* and many others I could not pause to gaze on. My memory, however, so vividly represented to me the circumstances that

venomous animals, that would have made Paradise itself wretched, infested this glorious spot, that I was satisfied, in my own mind, to remain in my more northerly abode.

The secret of the great difference between the temperature of the two divisions of the island was very simple. My portion was exposed to the north-westerly gales, from which the other was protected by the chain of lofty rocks which divided it into two. But despite the superior loveliness of the southern portion, I could not forget the great serpent. Still, at every step I was more charmed. I halted to admire the trees, I keenly examined the bushes, every plant and shrub was cursorily glanced at, in the hope that it might be useful. Suddenly, while thus occupied, I gave what, no doubt, was a very theatrical start, and resting my gun on the loam-like ground, more closely examined a plant, which had suddenly caught my eye.

It was familiar in some way to my eye.

I looked at it keenly, and then tore it up by the root, which was large, long, and fibrous; the stalk was erect, strong, round, hairy, branched towards the top, and rose five or six feet in height; its leaves were numerous, large, oblong, pointed, viscous, of a pale green colour, without footstalks, the branches were long, linear, and pointed; the flowers terminated the stem and branches in loose clusters. I knew it at a glance.

There was no doubt of it—it was tobacco.*

It may appear trivial, but in my forlorn condition, shut out from the outer world, separated from my kind, and suffering from a severe and startling disappointment, the discovery was supremely gratifying to my feelings. I took note of the place, and then cutting down some of the riper stalks, put them on one side to make a trial. The general routine of tobacco-growing was familiar to me, more from my uncle's description than even from reading; and it was my firm resolve to carry it out to something like perfection, as after all, my pipe was likely to be my only companion.

But my journey was not half concluded. While about it, I determined to have a thorough exploration, so pursued my journey. It was with some difficulty that I tore myself away from the delicious spot where the tobacco plant grew, in company with many others, but soon my attention was drawn to other scenes. Before me I suddenly found two rocks rise, as if to stop all progress, though next moment I became aware that an opening, very narrow and partly shaded by overhanging trees, led into an extensive valley.

But such a valley! From one end to the other, from side to side, there was not the most wretched sign of wild vegetation or verdure. Its sides were rocks, from the tops of which hung foliage in abundance. Attracted by curiosity, I descended, making however towards the more pleasant scene beyond, where rich foliage invited me to seek shelter from the sun, hot, arid, and overpowering in that valley of stones. There was not a breath of air, though above, the tall summits of palms and other trees waved gently in the breeze.

I was nearly over it, when suddenly turning a rock, I stood annihilated with surprise, terror, and astonishment. Close to me, not ten yards distant, was a huge elephant, feeding

* Tobacco *(Nicotiani tabacum).* This celebrated plant may properly find its place among those other narcotics which habit has rendered almost essential to man. The generic name *Nicotiani* is derived from John Nicot, of Nismes, in Languedoc, ambassador from the King of France to Portugal, who procured the seed from a Dutchman. Tobacco is a powerful narcotic and stimulant. A few drops of essential oil applied to a wound, is said, by Redi, to be as fatal as the bite of an adder. In moderation, its use is agreable and even beneficial; but excess produces a pallid countenance, indigestion, loss of sight, and debility of the nervous system. Boys should never be allowed to smoke under any pretence whatever.—THE EDITOR.

upon the green branches of trees that bent down from several rocks. It was an opening in the forest, but so overgrown by trees and creepers as to be quite dark. I would have turned and fled, but the elephant had seen me. He turned and came towards me, but without any evidence of haste or rage. The vast brute was in a good humour, and probably not at all afraid of so insignificant-looking a being as myself. After looking at me some time with its little eyes, it slowly bent its tremendous limbs and lay down. My state of mind was such as left me little discrimination. I was in the animal's power, but I had often heard that when not attacked, the animal, as if conscious of its own might, will permit the presence of man, and therefore I had some slight hope of safety.

It was the first elephant I had ever seen, and I gazed at it with awe, though not forgetting the placid character of the animal, which—

> "Calm, amid scenes of havoc, in his own
> Huge strength impregnable
> Offendeth none, but leads a quiet life
> Among his own cotemporary trees."

These stupendous creatures live in troops or herds, in a state of inoffensive quiet, unless when attacked by some of their larger and stronger animal assailants, or their powerful and more relentless enemy—man. They delight in the boundless forest, and in the vicinity of water, where a more gorgeous and efficient shade is afforded, and they can enjoy the luxury of a cold bath and wallow, covered at once from the influence of the sun and the torment of insects. Here, the herd, led by some monstrous male, long standing in years, spend the forenoon heat; at evening or morning venturing to the outskirts or open glades, to feed on the tender foliage, which they can reach, and are able to pluck from a great height by means of their trunks.

They are easily alarmed and retreat to cover, unless when attacked or wounded, when they turn upon their assailant with the utmost fury.

The one before me was unwieldy in appearance, but I knew that its activity and speed were very great, so as to outstrip a horse. The skin was thick and hard, dry like, and wrinkled into folds about the setting on of the legs, and on the neck and breast. It was a brownish grey colour, mottled with flesh colour. Its tusks were of enormous size, while its trunk was very long.

It was over ten feet in height and proportionably stout, which made it look smaller than it really was. I could not but admire the skill with which the intelligent beast used the trunk, which to it was hand, nose, and, as far as breathing is concerned, mouth also. It tore off the tender boughs and placed them in its mouth, where, all the while, the process of chewing was going on. Its trunk occupied my attention particularly. I now understood that it was a mere elongation of the nose, but which it used with as much delicacy as we do the hand. But my chief thought, after a few minutes, was—how to get away?

It was, however, out of my power to flee. My knees refused their office, and I sank on the ground, helpless and yet watchful. The elephant gave vent to a kind of friendly grunt, which slightly reassured me—as, did he intend mischief, he would not have suffered my presence so long. Then I saw a sudden change in its demeanour. Its huge ears were raised on end, its trunk seemed to sniff the air, its eyes gave forth uneasy glances, while a sullen sound emanated from its throat, like the dull roar of a torrent in some deep cave. I retreated before this warlike demonstration.

It was time, for just as I reached the shelter of a huge block of stone, and crouched beside it, the animal rose to its feet. As it did so, a fearful series of yells warned me of a

new and most unexpected danger; while the elephant was literally riddled first with arrows, then with javelins and spears, until he looked like a huge porcupine. I now understood the visit of the savages. They had come to my island in search of ivory.

The elephant would in all probability have not suffered much from the weapons poured upon him, but that, as I felt convinced, they were poisoned, so that, after one fearful cry and wild rush at his enemies, who kept behind the trees of the forest, he fell, a heavy inert mass, to the ground, and expired in tremendous agonies.

The savages uttered loud cries of congratulation, and then withdrawing their spears and arrows, moved away through the forest without even casting a glance in my direction. I had remained under cover. Without reflecting on the danger which might befall me, I hurried after them—for now I began to have a faint key to the motives of the young girl who had so abruptly left me.

CHAPTER XXXV.

THE SAVAGE HUNTERS.

In a grassy plain, the centre of which was adorned by a tall and handsome tree, the savages had erected a few huts, but in such a hasty and evidently temporary way, as to convince me that the search for ivory was the motive which had brought them in such unpleasant proximity with myself. The plain, in addition to being itself lovely, was skirted by trees of a pale green hue, while bushes of a kind of wild nut, very oily and nutritious, abounded.

Despite my anxieties and excitement I could not forbear one glance at the tree. The Boabab* is believed to be the largest tree in the world, and this was a gigantic specimen, nearly twenty feet in diameter. The height by no means corresponds with the thickness to which it attains. At one year old its diameter is one inch, its height five; at thirty its diameter is two feet, while its height is only twenty-two. There was one which I remembered reading of that was believed to be five thousand years old. It was thirty feet in diameter and only seventy-three high.

The roots are of most extraordinary length, so that in a tree with a stem seventy-seven feet round the main branch, or top root, they measure a hundred and ten feet in length.

The tree before me had such a profusion of leaves and drooping boughs as almost to hide the stem, and the whole formed a hemispherical mass of vendure, about a hundred and thirty feet in the diameter. The wood is pale coloured, light and soft, so that the wild bees perforate it, and lodge their honey in the hollow, and such honey is considered the best. The negroes apply their trunks to a very extraordinary purpose. The tree is liable to be attacked by a fungus, which, vegetating in the woody part without changing the colour, or appearance, destroys life and renders the part so attacked as soft as the pith of trees in general.

Such trunks are then hollowed into chambers, and within these are suspended the dead bodies of those to whom are refused the honour of burial. There they become mummies, perfectly dry, without further preparation or embalming, and are known by the name of Qiuriots.

But of this tree, at a future time—all its qualities and appearance not being taken in at a glance. My eyes were now directed to the plain.

---

* *Adansonia digitata; monodelphia, polyandria* of Linnæus

Here the Indians had located themselves, evidently with the intention of making it their camping ground. The prisoners, or slaves as I afterwards found they were, were engaged in packing several parcels of ivory, which they had already succeeded in obtaining during their stay on the island. There were also bales of furs, and other products of the chase. The warriors and their wives were now all congregated together in waiting for the meal, for which the hunt had given them an appetite.

The captives were half concealed from the savages by one or two of the tufted bushes, and I could remark from where I was their melancholy and sad state of being. They worked bitterly and slowly, as do all slaves. They were a much more comely race than those who had succeeded in conquering them, and it was a great puzzle to me, how it was that beings so far superior were subjected to a savage and brutal race.

But all my conjectures were now driven out of my head by the next event that occurred. About thirty or forty feet from the spot occupied by the captives was a beautiful opening in the forest, where a perfect festoon of creeping thing fell over the boughs to the ground. It was, as it were, the mouth of a cave, and led probably into some lovely forest glade.

While I was glancing my eye keenly around I saw something move in that direction, and next minute my lost Indian girl, the prize of the night before, crept slowly to the edge of the thicket. A quick, restless, rapid glance showed me that I too was observed.

Then with a smile, followed by a look of great anxiety, she placed her finger on her lips and pointed slowly towards the prisoners. Now the reason of her flight appeared to me explained. She had friends, perhaps relatives, among the captives, and she wished them to share in the good fortune which had befallen herself.

Here then, was a chance of escaping from my state of solitary and miserable exile. If this girl had friends there would probably be amongst them those who would be able to assist me in building such a boat as might enable us to escape from the desert island. It was my duty, then, as well as my inclination to assist her as far as was in my power in her self-imposed task.

I made cautious signs to her, and she for a moment stood irresolute. Then taking courage, probably from my pacific exterior, she disappeared in the darkness of the forest, and soon could be heard cautiously gliding through the wood. I myself hurried to meet her.

Next moment we stood within a couple of yards of each other. There was still considerable remains about her of timidity, which it was not easy to see how to eradicate. She, however, was the first to decide the matter. Clasping her hands, and casting towards me the entreating glance of her really beautiful eyes, she kneeled at my feet imploringly and humbly. I smiled, and leaning one of my guns against a tree, smoothed her glossy black hair with my right hand, and otherwise caressed her as I would a timid animal I should have desired to tame.

The girl then, at a sign from me, rose to her feet. All her fear had vanished. The tenderness of my manner had completely reassured her. There is no mistake in the human eye, and we had exchanged affectionate glances. She then took me by the hand, and peering forth from the leafy arches of the forest, pointed to where a man and woman stood, whom I guessed, from their age to be her father and mother. Then she made signs to me that she would go and

fetch them. I laid down my other gun, and, taking her two hands in mine shook my head.

She stamped her little foot impatiently, and made signs as if she would run away. I pointed to the savages, and again signified that she would be taken. But she energetically repudiated any fear, and pointed to me, making unmistakable motions that I should kill them. Again I tried to make her understand that they were too many in number. She would not be persuaded. Then it came into my head to try the powers of my seductions against her filial devotion. I pointed to my cave; I bent low to intimate that I would serve her; I pointed to my own clothes, and made signs which she could not misunderstand, that I would clothe her sumptuously—then I drew her beautiful head towards me, and pressing her to my heart, kissed her lips.

She made no resistance, even by her soft and gentle glances intimating that she would be happy enough to be my companion and helpmate—but then with an expression of intense love and affection which I had never seen on human face, she pointed to her father and mother. It was impossible to resist this appeal. I let her go with a deep sigh, after motioning her to be cautious of her own life and liberty. When the heart is full it is easy to be eloquent. Now it must not be understood that I was what is called in love with this girl. It was no such distinct feeling that actuated me, but shut out for so long from all society, I looked with ravishment to the luxury of companionship, nor did I seek to conceal from myself that I infinitely preferred the prospect of a Miss to a Man Friday.

A thousand schemes for teaching her to talk English floated through my excited brain, of civilising her, and eventually, by her aid and those of her friends, returning to my native country. But this was no time for any such considerations. My whole soul was wrapped up in the thought of how she was about to proceed.

The slaves were about twenty in number, and engaged in various occupations. The hunt had been prosperous, and some were, as I have said before, making packages of ivory, others were working at skins of deer and other beasts, while some were engaged in cooking. A good-sized fire had been made, beside of which two stakes had been planted across; and another stake, placed from one to the other, on which was fastened the food they were cooking. It looked strange enough to my eyes, nor could I for some time form any idea of what it was.

But my whole thoughts were now centred on the girl who had crouched down upon the ground, and, taking advantage of the abundant prairie grasses, the papyrus, and the rush, had began to crawl slowly towards her old companions. I noticed that the couple to whom she had pointed were in grave and earnest conversation. They were probably speculating on the flight and escape of their child. She meanwhile, with a slow motion like that of the snake, advanced straight towards them until she was within ten feet, when I saw the two start as a faint sound fell on my ear.

Next instant she was being clasped in their arms, while all the captives crowded round in evident astonishment and wonder. But the girl appeared to wish to lose no time. I saw at once that she proposed to bring over the whole party to her views. This was startling enough at first sight, but when the reflection came to my mind that they were evidently of a quiet and inoffensive race, while she was my friend, the one great idea of escape flashed across my mind. The young woman pointed to the forest, and appeared to be addressing the excited captives in a regular speech. They uttered a cry of wonder.

It was fatal.

THE CROW'S NEST.

No. 7.—SAILOR CRUSOE.

Half-a-dozen armed savages, waving their war clubs, came bounding towards them; the girl ran; a huge fellow, with a yell of mingled delight and rage, flew towards her. She stood motionless with horror and affright. The club was waved over her head. Quick as lightning my gun was levelled, and the tall savage fell back upon the sward. Firing my second musket, I then sallied towards them, a pistol in one hand, my sword in the other, a very mad proceeding certainly, but warranted by the occasion, as they fled helter skelter, savages and captives all, except one who lay stark-staring dead upon the grassy plain.

They all made towards the water, and so swift of foot were they, that when bounding along at my quickest pace, I came within two hundred yards of the shore, they were already pushing out to sea in their canoes. I caught one glimpse of the ill-fated girl and that was all. She was thrust ignominiously to the bottom of a perigua, and I saw her no more.

CHAPTER XXXVI.

THE DEVASTATION.

THIS was double sadness for me now. It was clear that the unfortunate and beautiful Indian captive had become reconciled to the prospect of the home which I had offered her, and would, but for her filial duty and affection, have remained. But it would be wearisome to relate all my bemoanings and sorrowings, nor how madly I complained to heaven of this, my now hopeless bereavement. My soul was cruel, and when I returned to the scene of the engagement, I spurned the dead Indian with my foot, while I freely availed myself of the skins and other things which they had left behind them.

Being faint and hungry, I seated myself, and with the idea of adding to my meal, examined the somewhat nicelooking roast which the captives had been preparing. It was, however, a roast monkey, at which my stomach revolted. Making a hasty meal of what I had myself, I picked up my guns and slowly returned towards my home. I may truly say, that for several days my mind was not in a fit state for any consecutive work. But it is the province of youth to be elastic, and at length I contrived to throw off the apathy which availed nothing, and to continue my duties. My first visit was to the valley of the gazelles. I found the little animals lying under a palm tree, exhausted with heat. The chief part of the valley was an open prairie, except where some trees grew round a rather brackish pool, and where one or two palm trees lent their shade. The grass was burnt up, and evidently afforded but very little nourishment. Throwing over the net a quantity of grass which I immediately cut and which the gazelles hastened to consume with evident delight, I hurried away to my fields, which were close at hand, with the intention of pulling up some carrots and turnips for their use.

The weather had been very warm for some time, and my corn was necessarily nearly ripe, so that my thoughts were much bent upon reaping it and putting it away. Thinking of how this was to be done I reached the edge of the field when my heart fell within me as I heard a rush through the corn, and saw that some animal or other had been devastating my unripe harvest, eating the corn, pulling up carrots and turnips, and doing considerable damage.

This was very disheartening, and in the first moment of annoyance and rage I fired. Again I heard a rush, but could not make out what kind of animal it was that had been so mischievously at work. I determined, however, to be

even with them, should I be compelled to watch until the whole of my crop was taken in. First, however, a load of turnips and carrots was taken, by means of my wheelbarrow, to the pen in the valley, into which, aided by Tiger, I drove the gazelles; then a visit being paid to my home, I brought with me four guns and an ample supply of powder and shot.

How to pass the night now became the difficulty. After some time, however, casting my eyes about, I espied a tree, in which, by some exertion and ingenuity, it was possible to ensconce myself. Taking example by the apes a roof was easily constructed capable of keeping off the dew. By lifting some boughs, vine branches, and a plank or two, a flooring was made, with an apology for sides, and in this kind of crow's nest I determined to pass the night.

My mind was racked with sorrow and disappointment, and though the attack on my green fields appeared to be a minor evil, it irritated me more than it would have done at any other period. I felt savage and revengeful. Trying all the time to think of the pilfering thieves, who had devastated my corn fields, my thoughts reverted in spite of myself to the young Indian girl, whose presence would have lightened even the wearisome task of watching. My dog was my only companion, and he was fastened to the trunk of the tree below.

At length I slept.

When I awoke it was not yet dawn. A vast and half luminous fog overspread all nature, scarcely enabling me to see the nearest tree; while, in the stillness of that starless night, sounds of rivulets, and even the far-off murmur of the sea, could be distinguished amid those distant and vague murmurs, which invariably accompany the approach of day in the woods. Then a soft breeze, wafting perfumes from the distant forests, raised the veil of mist, and a faint light from the stars illumined the scene.

On each side of me were the two woods that skirted my fields. They were, though small, thick and impenetrable to the rays of the sun, which now rose suddenly in all its glory. It burst from the distant sea like an isle of fire, and flooded the whole scene with life and light.

Then, in the distance, I saw a sight which filled me with indignation and terror. A whole army of apes, guided, doubtless, by some marauder whom I had surprised the day before, came in view. They were marching directly for my plantation. An aged monkey marched at their head, like the general of those hords of savages who, so many years ago, pounced upon civilized Europe, to kill and destroy. By means of my telescope, I could make out that the leader was tall and strong, while, though bowed by age, he was ferocious and thoughtful. He seemed to know the country well, and did not hesitate one moment in his march.

He was making in a straight line for my corn-fields.

The true and natural abode of the monkey is the trackless forests, which so richly clothe the country under the Tropics, and which alike supply them with food, and protect them from the heat of those scorching climes. During the middle part of the day, these forests are filled with the animal world, courting their grateful shades, silent and resting; and it is only in some deep glade, that the scream of an awakened parrot, or gambols of a monkey, disturb the universal solitude. As soon as a declining sun and the evening breezes reduce the overpowering heat, these vast nurseries resume their daily routine.

The more timorous attract the observer's attention by their endeavours at concealment, and the protrusion of numerous little heads, with bright and searching eyes, from behind the thick boughs and foliage plainly tells that curiosity almost overbalances fear. Others force attention by showers of rotten branches, fruits, flowers, and nuts. This interval of activity in the tropical forests lasts for a comparatively short time, a few morning and evening hours of milder heat are sufficient to satisfy all their wants ; the blaze of a vertical sun, or a short twilight, again obliges them to seek a covering from its beams, as a place of rest and security.

Others reverse this order, and are nocturnal in their habits ; some of the larger species, remaining in complete inactivity during daylight, come forth at night and make the forest resound with their yells and howlings. Nothing can sound more dreadful than the nocturnal howlings of the Red Howler you hear in these gloomy and immeasurable wilds from eve till morn. You might fancy that half the wild beasts of the forests were collecting for the work of carnage. Now it is the tremendous roar of the jagur as he springs on his prey, now it changes to its terrible deep-toned growlings, as he is pressed on all sides by a superior force, and now you hear his last dying moan beneath a mortal wound.

A deep and dark evergreen, or the hollow of some decaying tree, are the abodes of other species. But, to my fancy, the army which was advancing was composed of every known variety of this mischievous and malicious race of animals.

The monkeys followed their venerable guide with blind confidence, like careless and thoughtless soldiers, who think of nothing when they have once given up their individuality to their chief. These atrocious immigrants came in groups of families, the mothers holding their very young ones at the breast, while they led the elder cubs by the hand ; while the fathers were armed with sticks, with which they guided the others' steps. Older monkeys, who were deprived of such domestic felicity, mingled with groups of antique females, the whole intent upon the great object of the day.

I was annihilated with a mixture of curiosity and admiration. Now and then the chief of the expedition halted and looked around, all did the same, save that, instead of being silent, they put their heads together and began to jabber audibly. Then on they came like a flood, the chief marching now with great strides. Suddenly he halted again, and leaping into the branches of a beautiful magnolia, peered cautiously and keenly around. I kept strictly in the background, and moved not even a muscle.

Then he gave the signal, and the whole furious troop rushed upon my cornfields. They absolutely revelled with delight, leaping, jumping, and picking the ears from the stalk, began to rub it in their hands with rapturous delight. The little ones rolled on the prairie, while the mothers fed them. I could not bear it any longer. I fired gun after gun, loosened the dog, and started with one loaded musket in chase.

Never shall I forget the rush, the yells, the cries, the screams, with which the monkeys fled across the plain. They were panic-stricken. But I had no mercy. Reaching the edge of my turnip-field, I fired my double-barrelled gun. This completed the flight, except that I found myself face to face with the great monkey who had been the leader of all this devastation.

To my surprise this was a perfect monster, one of the dreadful tribe of gorillas. Could I have escaped I would have done so, as this beast was at least half a foot taller than myself, and much more powerful. He was stout in proportion, and, except that it seemed painful to him to stand up, there was a terrible likeness to man about him, which was bewildering and alarming. He was old ; that I saw was my only hope.

He gave a fearful growl as he raised his stick, while I had recourse to my sword-saw, having that very minute fired my gun. He showed his teeth very savagely and rushed at me. I cut him sharply across the face, which made him yell in a still more horrible way.

But next instant the monster wrenched my sword from me, threw it on one side, and at the same moment tripped me up.

Mechanically I placed my hand in my belt, and drawing forth a pistol fired. The animal started back, awe-stricken, and prepared to fly. But at that moment Tiger, who had been chasing the flying monkeys, caught the unfortunate gorilla by the tail. The wounded animal, frantic with pain, turned upon him, and I verily believe would have killed him in his fury, but that I shot him at the same moment through the head with my remaining pistol.

The huge creature gave one horrid scream, and fell dead.

I was the master of the field of battle.

Picking up my gun and sword, I now scoured the plain in search of any other marauders who might have stopped behind. But the report of my artillery had been too much for them. They had all fled. Still I fired once more in the air, to warn any of the animals who might be lurking in the skirts of the forest.

This done, I returned to my field, called away my dog, and surveyed the damage done.

The next and following days, though nothing was quite ripe, I cut down everything, and wheeled it all into my cave in my wheelbarrow.

I was determined that the monkeys should have no more of my corn or vegetables.

CHAPTER XXXVII.

MEMORIES.

I AM monarch of all I survey,
My right there is none to dispute,
From the centre all round to the sea,
I am lord of the fowl and the brute.

Oh, solitude! where are thy charms
That sages have seen in thy face?
Better dwell in the midst of alarms,
Then reign in this horrible place.

Society, friendship, and love,
Divinely bestowed upon man;
Oh, had I the wings of a dove,
How soon would I taste you again

COWPER.

IN my boyhood's days I had often dreamed of the joys of solitude, and had, while reading both the works of poets and prose writers, fancied that I too could understand its mysterious and entrancing charms. But then, this solitude must be one of your own selection—it must not be involuntary. Houses and people must be at such a convenient distance that they could be reached at will. Then it is possible that man might consent to live alone for a time. But let anybody be placed in my situation, and he longs at once, and above all, for the luxury of society.

As a boy, I had read the story of every castaway recorded in the pages of voyages and travels. In days gone by when law was less stringent and the buccaneering spirit more rife, nothing was more common than for many to be set ashore on a desert island as a punishment, and I could not remember one who had ever said one word in favour of that solitude which poets, philosophers, and dreamers seem to think so conducive to happiness and a fitting state of mind. There was not one of them who would have been pleased to try the experiment in person.

There was first one whose name is not recorded, who, quite two centuries ago, relates how a certain ship was cast away upon an island, and he the only one man saved; and he lived alone upon the island five years before any ship came that way to take him off. For this deliverance, he said, he blessed and praised Almighty God. Nor would he ever, to his dearest friends, tell of his sufferings during his solitude, such great horror did they inspire.

There was Williams, a Musquito Indian, left years on Juan Fernandez, but when a ship came that way and some English landed, he threw himself flat on his face at their feet, and embraced them for joy to be released from his ruler-ship over that beautiful island—so repugnant is solitude.

There was Selkirk, who voluntarily secluded himself, but who on the very first night found his resolution fail him, so that he would have fain been taken on board again. When he found himself really alone, he had much ado to bear up against his dejection; desire for society was a strong call upon him, and though the support of his body was easily attained, his eager longings for seeing again the face of man, made him grow dejected, languid, and melancholy. There were many other castaways, whose utter despair at being alone it would be too painful to record.

I would sit for hours speculating on these memories, which came over me like a vision of the past, and the more I thought the more I worried and discomforted myself. Fortunately for me I was too busily employed wholly to give way to idle regrets and vain repining. I had stacked my corn close to my cave and I had piled up my vegetables under the cover of palm and bamboo roots, but the corn had to be removed from the ear, which as I knew no way of doing except by hand, took me a considerable time.

Then it was garnered in my store-room, though I foresaw that the time would soon come when I should require further space, while also my store-room must be protected against the rats and other vermin, which are sure to swarm wherever there is grain. I laboured very hard to secure this division of my cave by means of planks and bamboos, but knew that all such precautions are vain whenever these animals scent their prey.

In my walks a kind of rat had come under my notice, which appeared to infest all water-side places, and this it was that had made me uneasy about my property. For the present my only course was to let my dog sleep in the store by night, which did for a time keep away these worst plagues of the agriculturist.

During my wars and adventures my clothes had not improved in case, so that I was now compelled to think of a complete change of costume. It was with considerable regret that I gave up the idea of wearing the costume of civilised ife, but it was useless to resist. The cloth which I had found in the seaman's chest was not fit for the brakes, thickets and rocks I had to climb. Lucky it was for me that the savages had in their hurried flight left behind them certain skins, but rather would I have had them left me the knowledge of how they had made them so soft and pliable, as in my own mind I had already made up my mind that I would always find the raw material in plenty without having recourse to my gun.

A voyage was undertaken to the scene of the late contest, and on my way the spot where the elephant had fallen a victim to the poisoned shafts of the savages, was visited. I entered the valley with considerable exercise of caution, as it was impossible to say but that the place was the general resort of elephants, animals which, despite my belief in their gentleness and playfulness, I had no wish to affront too

often, especially should they happen to be in anything like droves.

Gazing around with extreme caution, however, I could see nothing, and so boldly advanced towards the spot where the huge animal had succumbed to his enemies. Lucky was it for me that I stopped in time, or else I know not what the consequences might have been. A legion of ants had left their hills, and were busy devouring the vast carcase of the beast, which they had already eaten and removed so completely as to lay its bones quite bare.

These animals are well-known to all for their extraordinary industry and singular economy. A community of ants contains males which have four wings, females which have wings only at certain times, and other females, or workers, which have no wings. Between midsummer and autumn, on examining an ant hill, a number of males and females with white glittering wings may be noticed. These are strictly guarded by the workers, and if they leave the boundaries unawares, are brought back by force.

Nothing more singular than the process of colonization can be imagined, while their industry is perfectly wonderful. The material of their building is hollowed out of the soil. Some will only eat honey, but in general they are fond of animal food and vegetables.

Those which were at work on the elephant had probably migrated from a distance, which will often take place on the part of these animals, in search of more convenient forage. Some of these immense swarms, I remembered to have read of as of such prodigious density and magnitude, as to darken the air like a thick cloud, and to cover the ground to a considerable distance where they settled. Many years ago shoals of a small black ant appeared in Germany, and formed high columns in the air, rising to a vast height, and agitated with a curious intestine motion, somewhat resembling the Aurora Borealis.

Man himself is not safe from them. When they enter a house, during their fearful migrations, they are not to be stopped. Before a sleeper is aware of it, they swarm over his body, and bite furiously, especially the *bashsikouay* ants of Africa. Travellers tell stories of whole villages being attacked, and being compelled to build corridors outside, to protect themselves, while the devastating little brutes eat and devour everything comeatable. The vast number, the sudden appearance, the ferocity and voracity of the frightful animals were described as all but incredible, while the numbers were said to be millions and billions.

I was lost in admiration, nor could I, but for my previous studies in natural history, have believed anything of the kind possible. And yet there is nothing, when we thoroughly understand the subject, which ought to surprise us on the part of the lower orders of creation. Aware of the danger of lingering near the column of these animals, I hurried away, calling my dog to my side, and not without feelings of deep grief and pain did I revisit the spot where I had last parted with the companion so mercifully, it appeared, given to me in my days of solitude and affliction.

The horrid flapping of some vultures, those scavengers of the wilds, startled me, and reminded me that death had passed that way. The skeleton of the savage was bare, and there sat on the distant boughs several of the monsters waiting, one would fancy, for some fresh tragedy to fill their never-wearied maws. On several occasions, when I had left the remains of my prey, it always surprised me to behold how swift these birds were to scent the carrion. In hot countries they are decidedly a blessing, and I recollected that in India they are regarded as the privileged scavengers of the land. They are birds which may truly be called voracious, cowardly, and filthy. They prefer carrion to live animals. They will never fight except when driven to it by extreme hunger, and then only attack their prey in great numbers. No corruption can affect them in any way. They seem to revel in horrible places. Their look is dull and stupid. A horrible odour exhales from their bodies.

But this taste of the vulture for filth, for dead bodies of all kinds, is greatly advantageous to man, for it is quite certain that in hot countries, where indolence and folly allow everything vile to accumulate even in the towns, they are extremely useful.

The vulture is said to have a keen scent, so much so, that whole droves of them crossed from Africa and Asia to Europe, after the battle of Pharsalia to devour the carcasses. The huge condor, eternally a sentinel on the heights of the Andes, swoops down wherever human or other prey is to be found, though hundreds of miles off. Their sight, too, is exceedingly sharp.

My skins were untouched, as was the ivory, which, however, was to me of no value. The first, however, were divided into four bundles. Over two a fallen tree was placed, while I carried one myself and tied the other on the dog, which had now grown extremely docile and willing. In this trim we returned by slow degrees to my house, not however without a good supply of tobacco. It was crude, rough stuff, but there were plenty of seeds, and it was my fixed resolve to cultivate this weed in sufficient quantities to satisfy my wants as soon as I could find leisure.

CHAPTER XXXVIII.

TAILORING.

THE skins had to be manufactured into clothes; there were shoes to make; a hat; I did even dream of an umbrella, so oppressive was the heat at times, and it seemed to me that while I was at work a pipe would be very agreeable and pleasant. To effect this purpose a very small cocoa-nut was selected, from which, cutting off the top, the inside was scraped, after which it was not much larger than the Dutch bowls which I had seen the sailors smoke. This part being done, by much patience a small hole was bored in the bottom of the nut, through which I passed a slender reed, a supply of which had been provided for the special purpose. The tobacco leaves were simply dried over hot embers and put up to hang, which served very well at first, though such was not the proper way of preparing them. But this was left as a matter of future consideration.

As it was the tobacco smoked very well, and was a great relief to me during my arduous labours, for such, above all others, proved to me the task of tailoring.

But I did not give up my whole time to this. Another short wet season was soon to be expected, and I had very great plans with regard to the valley of the gazelles, a very large part of which was inclined to be damp. This part of the soil, however, was covered by reeds, which, being now excessively dry, I did purpose to destroy by fire. The extent they covered was about four acres, and not a tree near them except one large one in the centre, the character of which I did not comprehend. It was straight for some little way up, and then became very tufted.

To fire this expanse of reed was comparatively easy, and I hoped to do it so effectually as to destroy even the roots. The reeds were six or seven feet high, a kind of jungle and as dry as tinder. A number of pine knots and other combustibles were collected first, and then a pile was made at one end, and

no sooner was it set fire to than the clamour became something really fearful. The cracking of the reeds alone was something frightful, but for a moment above this rose the clang, shriek, and clamour of sand-hill cranes, herons, and other birds, which rose wildly on the wing, while the croaking of the frogs was fearful.

But nothing checked me. Taking blazing pine knots from the burning pile I cast them into the jungle, which hissed and cracked and spurted as it yielded to the influence of the fierce and rapid element. For an hour this conflagration lasted, during which time I feasted my eyes on my own work. Then a shower of rain, as sudden and heavy as unexpected helped to put it out.

Then I went away, after driving the gazelles, now very tame, into the pen, where they fed from my hand, when I offered them luxuries, such as carrots and turnips. These animals generally feed upon grass and the young sprouts of trees and plants, but they soon learn to consume any kind of vegetable.

It was now approaching to dinner time, and as Tiger manifested considerable impatience, I thought it but right to indulge him as well as myself, so, putting my gun on my shoulder, marched off; as usual, however, sauntering along slowly, and examining carefully everything that came in my way. Suddenly, as we approached a small thicket, Tiger gave a low growl and dashed forward. Then came to my ears a concert of hideous sounds, such as had not greeted me for some time, and, rushing forward, I found the brave animal face to face with a huge sow, behind which were congregated some dozen small ones.

There was no mistaking the race. It was low set, its body nearly cylindrical, its head in the same line with its trunk. Its skin was thick, covered with strong thick hair. Its tail was short and twisted. As most persons know, these animals feed mostly on roots and vegetables, with worms and insects, to procure which they are furnished with an elongated nose, supplied with a strong cartilage at the extremity, and with powerful muscles, which render this flexible, and enables them to turn up the soft and moist ground in search of roots and worms and insects.

Acorns, beech-marl, chestnuts, are also favourite and fattening food. But when hard pressed, swine are a race that can subsist on almost anything placed within their reach. Their sense of smell is extremely acute, and they have been taught to hunt, quarter the ground, and back the other pointers. One pig was known to stand at snipes. The wild boar, when at bay, is a very savage animal, and will hurt or kill both man and beast.

It was a pig of a curious breed, mixed, but partly, no doubt, descended from those which were so widely left about in scattered islands, and on continents, by the buccaneers, in the hope of their turning up some rainy day, but which generally became wilder than those which had always been living in a state of nature. Its appearance was more that of a Pupuan than anything else.

It was a huge animal, very strong and savage, and I was afraid Tiger would be no match for it unless I came to its assistance, and was about to wound it by means of a shot, when the noble dog flew at the beast, caught hold of its ear between its teeth, and held it fast.

Quick as lightning, a wild thought flashing through my brain, I took from my girdle a long piece of cord, and, using it as a lasso, threw it round the animal's legs—then with a jerk, I cast him to the ground.

The sow was now powerless, and I at once, despite its furious squalling, proceeded in my design. Tying the feet together, just to admit of the animal's walking, I next fastened my lasso to one of its forepaws, and then let it loose. Staggering to its feet, it made at the barking dog, but stumbled—on which I drew it onward, calling the dog to my side.

The pig was obstinate but helpless — while its litter running after it, with shrill cries, took up half its attention. I looked at the thicket. It was not very large, but one mass of nut trees, and a kind of oak, which accounted for the presence of the sow in part, though I saw by the ground turned up, near where the capture had taken place, that she had been rooting.

Curious to see what was the nature of its food, with a knife I turned up the ground, and to my astonishment and amazement, found that the pig had enabled me to make a most agreeable discovery. The esculent which the pig had been disturbed in the search of was the truffle, in the hunting up of which it is used over all Europe most effectually.

But it behoved me to look to my prize. With this view I skirted the thicket, and found that, except in about a dozen places, its edge was impassable, even by a pig, and everywhere the addition of stakes, bamboos, and other such wood as I could procure, would soon confine the animals within the range which I intended to give them. The pig was then dragged within the thicket, tied to a tree, and left to it meditations and its litter.

After dinner the business of enclosure commenced, and by the next night was carried out so effectually that it became a perfect pound. To make rails and barriers on the outside, I cut down many trees on the inside, and by this means—in the centre of the thicket, accounting for its fertility and exuberant vegetation—came upon a small pool fed by a spring.

The sow was now let loose, and from that day I never wanted fresh meat. All my refuse was wheeled in the wheelbarrow and thrown over a kind of gate, while the moment the young ones began to feed I shot the mother, and, by judicious thinning, contrived that they never grew too many for their enclosure. I thus had an ample supply of fresh pork and bacon, which, having salt in abundance, as will be seen anon, I easily made.

As soon as the sudden dusk of a tropical climate had fallen on the island my lamps were lit, and my evening meal —on the first occasion composed of stewed truffles and a bird I had shot—on the fire, than I began my ungrateful task of tailoring. How to cut out a garment was that of which I had not the slightest notion, but taking my own ragged things for a pattern, I to a certain extent, with a sharp knife, cut out from the skins I had captured something that bore a resemblance to a coat and waistcoat. Then began the sewing, of which I had not the slightest idea. My needle was a small kind of sailmaker's, used in the manufacture of coarse canvas trousers, my thread, fibres of vegetables and sinews of seals; so that when, after a week, I turned out in my new garb, my appearance was indeed ludicrous.

I had put the hairy side out. My coat, very much like a sail ripped up in front, was fastened by strings of leather; my trousers hung like two ill-shaped bags; my feet were encased in pieces of skin drawn together by a thong, a kind of bad imitation of a mocassin; while my hat was a thatch of fur and leaves stretched above a withe, which had been bent by way of a frame.

My very dog did not know me, I thought.

CHAPTER XL.

THE INLAND LAKE.

I WAS comfortable, however, and sheltered from the heat and rain both. Having overcome this difficulty, and then spent a week in collecting all I possibly could in the way of provisions that would keep, I attended to some other duties. Among the prizes which I had captured from on board the wreck, were some seeds of grasses of various kinds, and these I determined to scatter over the damp field, left after the burning of the reeds.

The ground was no longer soppy as before, but was gradually being dried up, though still some moisture did remain. Two days were occupied in scattering the seeds, after which I devoted a whole week to my cornfields, around which I determined to lay scarecrows enough before the next crop. Again the earth was painfully torn up by a rake, making me long anxiously for some animal which would do this arduous work for me. Again the seed was cast, and then, feeling a strange desire for a holiday, I again started on a journey of exploration.

This time my path was through my hidden cavern. I was in full dress with pistols and gun, a knife, a small axe, a coil of cord, some nails which were to aid me in climbing trees, with a small supply of brandy and provisions.

My way was different to any I had hitherto followed. I took more to the left, towards the higher ground or mountainous district. I was anxious to discover whether or no we were on a desert island, which I could only do by ascending to the very summit of the distant hills and taking a survey with my telescope, without which I never left my abode.

The country, as I passed along, was superlatively beautiful. Every tropical plant and flower rose before me. There was the tamarind with its beautiful and variegated flowers, the flowering prickly pear, the melon thistle like a large fresh green melon, the night-flowering cactus, the Indian thistle, and a hundred others, of which I shall speak in their place.

I could not get along very quickly for simply admiration at what I saw. Several times the idea entered my head that here it was I should have located myself. At all events it would be pleasant to have a summer-house on this side, which I could make my residence when I wished to hunt, shoot, or fish. While speculating on this and other things, never without reverting with regret to the loss of my companion, I began to descend, through scattered trees and bushes, towards what appeared to me to be a valley covered by trees. Presently I came to a grove of evergreen pines, and, passing through in stooping attitude, saw beyond a sheet of placid water.

I ran forward, and found that I was on the borders of a placid and beautiful lake, surrounded by hills that rose sheer from the water's edge, covered with the richest and most exuberant vegetation. There were trees without end which I know not, and many that I knew. Afterwards, I found that the place abounded in pineapples and guavas. Birds— parrots, birds of paradise with their lovely plumage and peculiar cry, the ever-flickering and noisy humming-bird, were on every branch.

The water was smooth and unruffled. On one side it was bright blue and pellucid, while on the other, where fell the dark shadow of the hills, all was dark. How I longed for a fairy-like canoe to float, as it were, through that clear element. But it could not be. One of those arts which I had yet to learn was that of boat building. But time and patience will do anything, and, as it will be seen in its proper place, I became a very good hand even at this in time.

Gazing at the softly-slumbering lake, I suddenly became aware of a fact which considerably raised and heightened my curiosity. Exactly facing me was a promontory as I thought, but on closer examination it proved to be an island. This roused my feelings to a very high pitch, and disencumbering myself of my gun, I determined at once to make a raft. The pine trees were light and easily cut; I had with me my axe and saw; so that the labour would not be very great.

I cut down several and floated them on the water. They were fastened together in the usual way by means of lichens and fibrous plants, with here and there some wooden nail-like pieces knocked in. It was a very rude and unwieldy-looking thing, and took me so long that I was compelled to give over at night-fall without having quite finished. A supper of dried meat and biscuit followed, after which a shelter was made of pine boughs, under which my dog and I crept, and passed a calm and undisturbed night.

At dawn of day my raft was perfected, two rude oars fastened to its side, and then pushed off by a long pole. My dog, who never, when he could help it, allowed me to leave him a moment, leaped upon it, and we set out upon our somewhat perilous journey. The floating machine which bore my fortunes and those of my faithful follower was very unmanageable, and my two oars were so situated as to scarcely admit of being used at once.

At first, however, the shallowness of the water admitted of my poleing myself along, which it was necessary to do on my knees to preserve my equilibrium. I had a valuable freight on the raft, such as a gun, an axe, a saw; things which were not easily to be replaced in the circumstances in which we were placed.

Several times I paused, however, to gaze round at the beauties of that marvellous little inland sea, of which as yet I could not see the outlet. It was a fact familiar to me that lakes do exist which have no visible means of escape for their waters, but I had no reason for believing this to be the case here.

But I was determined to explore it thoroughly, and to take my time about it. The lake, to all appearance was as circular as a cart-wheel, with the island in the centre for an axletree. The vegetation rose on all sides to the summits of the glorious hills, the bottom branches in almost every place bending low into the water, and concealing every vesige of shore. The variegated foliage flashed, pregnant with beauty, in the morning sun, while here, there, and everywhere, could be seen the glad songsters, unconscious of any danger from the presence of a being to whom they were unaccustomed.

The waters, too, swarmed with fish, which peered up at me, as it were, curiously, while others leapt eagerly after the flies and other living things which skimmed or floated on the waters. In the distance loomed the graceful forms of ducks and swans, while on a spur of the island which I was fast approaching stood a number of flamingos that, rather passive in their movements, look like weeds or jungle rather than live animals.

There was not in that earthly Paradise a want which might not have been satisfied, save that of society. So lovely, indeed, was nature in its every phase—sky, water, trees, and animated beings—that it seemed possible to live there for ever, if only a companion were present, with whom to expatiate on the beauties which presented themselves to my notice.

As I proceeded and began to speculate with how much ease fish might be caught, birds snared, and every necessary procured, the thought flashed across my mind, that here might be a much more charming residence than my cave. But it was away from the sea, and away from all hope of that escape from which I now so eagerly longed.

My progress was very slow indeed, though I toiled with all my power, but presently a slight, favourable breeze sprang up, which aided me a little, and then, with a shrill cry the flamingos rose on the wing and disappeared. My raft now kept grating on the bottom of the lake, so that both I and my dog were fain to leap out and tow it on shore.

Poets and others have sung and talked of the loveliness of a tropical forest, but none, in the wildest flight of their errant fancy, could have conceived anything like this. I could not make it out at first. Fastening my raft to a small rock on the shore, I walked along the spar of stone and sand into the interior, which I gained by crawling on my hands and knees beneath the rich festoons of vines and other falling things that impeded my progress.

I had seen a water-colour drawing representing, in what I thought an exaggerated way, the beauty of a tropical scene. Every colour of the rainbow was brought into play. In the centre of the island was an open glade, sparkling with flowers that looked like myriad eyes of every size.

The grass had been cropped by some huge animal, leaving only the flowers.

A rich perfume pervaded all nature, while above a marvellous effect was produced by trees, which rising to a vast and prodigious height, crossed and interlaced their topmost boughs, and formed a huge green and endless summer-house. A soft and entrancing shade kept up a balmy and perfumed freshness. Here and there the roof opened and showed the blue and hot sky. The rich nature of those latitudes seemed to have adorned itself with all its graces to win the admiration of man. Cactus and aloes grew around in rich abundance.

I cast myself on the ground, unmindful of the danger of snakes and scorpions, and as I gazed about on every side thought that it was heaven itself, I determined on the spot to erect a summer-house, which in hot and sultry weather I could visit, or when I was tired of the vicinity of the sea.

Like the ant and every other building animal, I was resolved to avail myself of every advantage given me by nature. I therefore selected one or two trunks of trees and determined to make them the supports of my summer-house. But first it was necessary to provide for existence. My ingenuity had enabled me to make a few hooks, which I baited with small strips of meat and put out into the water, while in a distant corner of the prairie I set one or two rather awkward traps, but which had served me on occasion to capture small animals like wild hares.

Then I cut branches, small trunks, strong reeds, and other useful materials, with which I made me in the course of the day a very comfortable and secure hut, as far as the wind and weather was concerned. My trap did not yield me anything, but the hooks were eagerly caught at by several very good-sized fish. But I could not of course, catch any of the large fine ones which I could see leaping out of the water. This, however, did the less annoy me that I had another very excellent idea in my head with regard to this part of the matter.

A fire was now lit on the spar of sand rock, by which what food I had was cooked, and a supper being made I took refuge in my tent, after commending myself to the guardianship of heaven, My dog lay close to me, and I was soon fast asleep. A low growl awoke me, I started, sat up and listened. A terribly heavy footstep was marching heavily through the bushes, while an odd kind of snorting preceded the advance of some kind of animal. That it was big I could hear, but what it was never entered into my mind to conceive. Fright had taken possession of me. I momentarily expected the vast beast to fly at me.

It was light. The moon fell in deep, translucent beams upon the flowery plain, when an animal, tall as an elephant but more unwieldy, came forth from the wood, and without taking any notice of the furious barking of the dog, proceeded to crop the high grass near the edge of the plain.

This continued for some time, until my eyes became slowly accustomed to the scene, when it turned away slowly, took its way to the water, where a huge plunge gave me notice it had left the island.

No sooner did that plunge reach my ears, than I again resigned myself to sleep, nor woke until dawn.

Before thinking of anything else, the water's edge was sought, and my clothes cast off for a bathe in those translucent waters.

But where was my raft?

It had got loose, and was careering down the lake as if carried away by a swift current. I never reflected on the consequences, but swam after it with all the strength which I could master. The raft being heavy did not make very rapid progress. But then I soon found that I was on the end rift of a current. Its power was so great that I knew it could only be caused by the suck of a waterfall. I gazed hopelessly along the waters. I saw the thrashing of the low-bent boughs on what seemed the shore ; I heard the heavy, sullen roar of a mighty waterfall, and, after one or two desperate efforts, I became aware that all resistance to the terrible power of that current was vain.

Death stared me in the face in that Eden-like spot, and casting up my eyes, I took one long, lingering look at life and——

Heavens! I was sucked in the mouth of a kind of cavernous hollow, when, like any other dying wretch, I grasped at the boughs, which overhung the yawning gulph, and by a superhuman effort, raised myself out of the fearful power of the stream.

But when my breath returned, I was hardly better off. I was simply supported by the lower boughs of some trees, through which I could see that the whole body of water that entered the lake by some secret orifice, was carried bodily into this luminous cavern, into which it fell with a terrible and deafening roar.

CHAPTER XLI.

FIRE FISHING.

The nightingale, their only vesper-bell,
Sung sweetly to the rose the day's farewell ;
The broad sun set, but not with lingering sweep,
As in the North he mellows o'er the deep ;
But fiery, full, and fierce, as if he left
The world for ever, earth of light bereft,
Plunged with red forehead down along the wave,
As dives a hero headlong to his grave.
Then rose they, looking first along the skies,
And then for light into each other's eyes,
Wondering that summer showed so brief a sun,
And asking if indeed the day were done ?
                                    BYRON.

By dint of efforts which were, in my terror-stricken state, almost superhuman, I contrived to crawl upwards, and to obtain a seat on a bough far out of the reach of that swift and devastating current, which had so nearly been my destruction. Then I had leisure to contemplate the nature of the extreme danger which I had escaped.

Instead of the lake being wholly surrounded by hills, as I imagined, there was at this spot a gap, but so narrow as to be all but imperceptible. It was a kind of slit, across the face of which the trees grew so as to conceal it altogether. So fertile was the soil, and so tenacious of life the trees which took root thereabouts, as to plainly account for their hanging even to the water's edge, and being continually whipping, as it were, the otherwise calmly flowing waters.

I sat looking at the cataract for some time with a listless stare. I could scarcely recover the shock which I had received. My heart throbbed and beat within my bosom as it never had throbbed or beat before. The danger I had escaped was something terrible, and it was not easy to realize the fact of my having avoided it.

Below, as could be made out through the trees, the country was arid and hilly, while at no great distance was the sea.

The question now, however, was how to return to the island. There was I, naked as the first man who walked in Eden, perched like a bird upon a tree. Below me was a roaring waterfall. Above, trees and shrubs of a character not to be affronted in my peculiar state of costume.

There was nothing to do but to swim for it.

But how was the swift and overpowering current to be passed? I was now a good and powerful swimmer. Still, that would not enable me to contend against such a rush of waters as came round the southern side of the small island, and swept with such impetuous wild fury over the rocks. To crawl from tree to tree, and bough to bough, like the chattering monkeys I could hear at no great distance, was neither easy nor pleasant. Nor should I probably have discovered a plan but for a peculiarity I noticed when my senses were slowly returning to me.

The raft had not been carried over the falls at the same time as myself.

I watched with a vacant eye at first, and then with a considerable amount of curiosity. The raft, which moved much more slowly than I did, appeared to be on the very edge of the stream that was impelled by its own weight towards the gulf. Presently it seemed to ground upon a rock until it was wholly checked in its progress, when it swung round and slowly turned in the contrary direction from that which it had been following.

There was a back water or undertow on the very brink of the terrible stream, which carried the raft slowly but surely back. The trees were fortunately so interwoven and interlaced that to crawl from one to the other was easy enough, though I was continually alarmed lest snakes or other vermin should take advantage of my defenceless position to attack me. By using, however, extreme caution the effort proved successful, and I at length stood on the shore beyond where the eddies and bubbles showed that the current extended.

I was now faint enough, but there was no help for it. To regain my clothes, arms, and provisions, it was necessary once more to swim the lake. Fortunately the water proved to be so shallow—one cause of the backward stream—that the raft was almost reached without swimming. Then, by great exertions, this somewhat unwieldy contrivance was clambered upon, and pushed, by means of the pole and oars, to such a distance from the current as to render any danger of its being sucked in out of the question.

The joy of my dog, which, with the marvellous instincts of its race, had swam about without being drawn into the

FIRE FISHING.

No. 3.—Sailor Crusoe.

current, was indeed pleasing, as in my state of solitude the presence even of a dumb animal was some kind of consolation to my mind.

On reaching the island I hastily dressed myself, and, only too glad to take repose, made a good fire and cooked my reakfast. After this nearly the whole of the day was consumed in improving my hut, as well as in manufacturing a kind of spear, for which I had a very special use, as will presently be seen. This cost me much labour, as I was as yet but a poor workman, and during the whole of my career I found nothing more difficult than to teach myself any mechanical trade whatever.

Towards evening I collected together a quantity of resinous knots, of which there was a goodly supply on the island, and then made a little platform of sticks, raised upon small poles not more than two feet from the ground. Then I fastened my raft very near the shore, deep water being between myself and the intended fire, which was lit as soon as ever the darkness was complete. Evening always falls very suddenly in these latitudes, so that it is almost impossible to discover the transition from light to darkness. Before we are aware of it, dusky shadows fall upon all nature; the song of birds is suddenly stilled, while the hooting of owls, croaking of frogs, and the rustling of the other night-prowling animals commences.

The fire once fanned into a flame, I stood still upon my raft. The blaze soon became clear and defined, falling upon the water with a brilliancy that revealed the sand at the bottom, and showed how clear and pellucid the water was itself.

I had not long to wait. How fish in general pass their nights is more than my reading has taught me, but this at once became apparent, that either the inhabitants of the deep are actuated by a singular amount of curiosity, or imagined the presence of the fire to be the harbinger of light, when insects and flies do abound in the air and in the floating *debris* of the trees and boughs.

They came in droves, and there was so little difficulty in capturing them that I was careful not to waste my time over any but large and plump fish, that promised to be good eating.

Such, however, is the natural taste of man for sport, that when I saw the crowded masses of fish rushing past sniffing the air in the direction of the fire, and wriggling in serried crowds in the water, I could not prevent myself from spearing a great many more than could be of any use.

At length, however, somewhat fatigued and, indeed, a little ashamed of myself, I desisted, and removing my fire more inland proceeded to broil some of the rich prizes I had taken, my appetite considerably whetted by the exertions I had undergone.

The effect of a life spent in a natural way, of early rising and regular rest, of abstinence from all evil habits and indulgences, was visible on me in every way. I was extremely powerful, could run with the fleetness of a dog, while my natural appetite was very different from that which is nourished by artificial excitement and destructive sauces.

Hunger was, truly, my only sauce, and a most satisfactory one it was too, nothing eatable coming amiss either to myself or to my dog.

The presence of this animal was to me a consolation and a cause of regret, for it could not be but that he must die, as at any moment he might be killed in combat with some of the fierce and terrible animals with which my island abounded.

Supper over, my gun was examined, the priming of my pistols looked to, and then once more I lay me down in my bower or summer-house, as I resolved to call it. The night was lovely in the extreme; a balmy air fanned the cheek and cooled the brow pleasantly, as no dew could penetrate the vast roof of verdure that extended over my cabin roof. I could now hear the murmur of the waterfall, while now and then the cry of prowlers on the distant shore would excite my curiosity.

I never slept under such circumstances without a fire, as I knew that it is that which chiefly alarms the wild beasts, and so strong was the habit that no sooner did my watch-fire burn low than I would instinctively awake, and replenish my supply of wood. On this occasion a strange sleeplessness was upon me. The only explanation that suggested itself was the heartiness of my supper, and yet this could scarcely be, as fish is notoriously the lightest and most wholesome food man can eat.

A kind of shadow of coming ill was upon my soul. This is common to all ardent and excitable minds; and though I could scarcely realise to myself the event which could occur to damp my hopes, which were once more restricting themselves to my island, I felt myself yielding to the nightmare influence. Sleep did several times visit my eyelids, but I invariably woke with a start. Presently I noticed that my dog had left my side, not barking, yelping, or even moaning in low warning tones, as he would sometimes do, but cautiously, and as if by stealth.

I called him loudly, coaxingly, and then threateningly; but in vain.

My dog had deserted me.

This, then, was the inconceivable misfortune which, by a kind of prescience, had so darkened my spirit. Now, everybody has had a pet animal of some kind, and I am sure shall have the sympathy of my young readers, both male and female, when I confess that this inexplicable abandonment of its master on the part of a dog was to me a blow which seemed for a moment to annihilate my energies.

I sank back in my couch after taking a small quantity of brandy, and prepared to sleep, when I heard, at no great distance, something rustling in the woods. I sat up and mechanically seized my gun. Then I felt, or rather saw, that I was in the presence of something awful. It was there on the other side of the fire. I knew it well, but I could not see it. I felt it glaring at me. Not in the horrors of the hideous nightmare does man suffer such a spell as came upon me then. I could not move. My hand refused to obey my will, until at length, by a mechanical motion, I snatched up a handful of dry leaves and cast them on the all but expiring embers.

As I did so I started to my feet, and as the flames rose quickly on high, found myself face to face with something, of which, however, I could make out only two glaring eyeballs that shone across the fire like nothing I had ever seen before. Then it vanished, so that the pistol I fired hurriedly was discharged at empty air.

But all this time my dog returned not, nor could I in my own mind conceive any possible reason for a desertion in the hour of danger, so sudden, stealthy, and inconceivable. No sleep came to my eyes that night, and in the morning I hurried on my return journey, after duly fastening my raft to the shore, nor stopped once, except for needful rest, until my cave was reached, where everything was found in order as it had been left.

————

CHAPTER XLII.

A FIRE.

I HAD now been nearly one year upon that deserted spot of earth, and though my dangers and tribulations had been many, though I had escaped, by a miracle as it were, from savage animals and still more savage men, I had much to rejoice at and be thankful for. The island was well supplied with provisions, the sea and lake also, my herd of gazelles promised the luxury of milk; my savage Papuan sow was mother to a progeny that would be useful, especially as any superabundance of population in that quarter could easily be obviated. My fields of corn and vegetables, despite the devastations of birds and monkeys, had yielded manifold, while no monarch had more choice of residences and sport than myself.

What was wanted beside companionship was a supply of tools, that I might improve my furniture, make a cart of some kind; and the presence round my residence of domestic animals. My dog having left me in this strange and singular manner, it was my constant idea to find some other companion. Nothing would have been easier than to have tamed one or more of the gazelles, but these delicate little animals were not likely to prove of any use, my ideas always running on animals which might prove of value and importance to me in other ways.

I went so far as to meditate on the probability of having some animal which might serve me a steed. But this was only in very romantic moments; and when smoking my pipe after dinner, I built such castles in the air as men do who have no one to commune with on real and positive interests. Still, my occupations were varied, and sometimes arduous. Sowing and tilling the ground, even in my rude way, was a very laborious part of my duties, which, however, I never neglected, as habit made all these products of cultivation necessary to my comfort and existence.

Still I continued to explore the island, though something like a fear of the vision—more, I thought, like an emissary of the Demon than anything else—did restrain me from returning to the lake for some time. But as the spot was very beautiful, and also was in the centre of hills, where alone I had seen wood suited to a large raft, which I was always contemplating as a means of escape, I at length determined just before the rainy season, to explore that neighbourhood once more.

But pass a night in my bower I would not, as the memory of that startling interruption was too much for me. My gun, sword and pistols, were all I took except provisions. I was in no hurry. My planting was all over. A very large supply of refuse, coarse large carrots and turnips, had been carted both to my gazelles and pigs, which, except the mother, would come and grunt at the narrow palisade I had made, in a most friendly and even greedy manner.

But I had no need to trouble myself, as this was the season when the nuts and acorns fell in such abundance as to satisfy their wants without any attention on my part. Still, it seemed slightly to domesticate them, and in my position the tameness of even so lowly an animal as the pig was a matter of considerable interest.

My course was taken this time again through my large cavern, where, as usual, I disturbed vast numbers of bats, but met no more serpents to alarm and terrify me. When once the kind of shaft was reached, and I had climbed to the summit of the rocks, I paused, as usual, to gaze around. The sea was of a translucent blue, and calm as a lake. Not a breeze ruffled its surface in the slightest way. But still

nature was not; for when I neared the woods—I kept this time in sight of the sea—a concert of a thousand sweet singers arose. Perched on the branches of the stately trees, amid a world of leaves, all dancing in the light, were the feathered minstrels, singing as if in thanks for the glorious and magnificent weather.

Myriads of insects floated in unnumbered clouds above my head, and a thrill of pleasure seemed to reach my heart as I walked along bathed in the flood of light. Suddenly I gave a start, rubbed my eyes, and stood still in most extreme and unqualified astonishment; I could not believe that which I saw to be true. It was so unexpected, so sudden, and at the same time so inexplicable.

But it was true. Yes! there out in the far distance, as it were on the edge of the horizon, rose high towards the heavens a vast column of smoke. Being undriven by wind, it tapered upward slowly until it seemed to disappear in infinite space.

What could it be? where could it be? and what did it portend? A thousand wild ideas flashed through my brain. Was it a continent? was it a burning mountain? or was it a fire which had sprung up accidentally, as is often the case in hot countries? I gazed with absorbing interest at the blue-black column, nor could I for many hours think of anything else. In my anxiety to make out more with regard to this mystery, I spent the whole day on the spot.

Then, when darkness came on I was enabled to make out that it was a large stationary fire on the side of a very distant hill. This I could see by means of my telescope, which was very powerful. My curiosity had now arrived to the highest pitch. It would not be likely that such a fire as that would be made for any necessary purpose. What was it, then, but a beacon lit up by some one like myself, who had been cast away on some deserted shore, and who was anxious in this way to attract the attention of any passing vessel?

The moment this idea took possession of my mind, the wildest hopes and fancies filled my brain, and, utterly mindless of the folly of what I was about, I spent the whole night in cutting down trees and bushes, and so arranging them as to insure the burning of a large and inflammable thicket. Though the operation exhausted me with fatigue, I thought nothing of that, so eagerly does the mind fasten on a new idea when connected with the hope of escape.

My belief was that on some island at no great distance—say, perhaps, twenty miles from me—were other unfortunates in the same position as myself; that it was my duty as well as my interest to communicate with them, which could only be done by a huge bonfire. The post I occupied was sufficiently lofty to be seen a long way off, and when just as day broke, the huge mass of wet and dry timber began to crackle, spirt, and flame, while a ponderous cloud of smoke rose slowly to the heavens, then I became satisfied that my convictions were right in the main. Some watcher near the beacon had evidently seen my answering one, and had hastily cast on a pile of damp wood, which rose in clouds of black smoke to the heavens. Here was hope. That the others were white people I could now no longer doubt.

My joy was so excessive for a short time that the difficulty of any personal communication with the supposed fellow-sufferers was forgotten. Then, when I came to think of the dangers and uncertainties of the sea, the mighty undertaking it would be to build a raft of sufficient size, and the perils of navigation, my spirits fell, and I had rather to trust to the idea that if they were many they might finally visit my island, and take me away in any vessel they might construct.

Thus were the wild hopes of two whole days dashed to the ground by one glimpse of reason; so, tearing myself away from the idle and delusive prospect, I again proceeded on my journey, having wasted two days in a kind of fool's paradise.

But could I only have suspected the truth what would have been my feelings?

I found my raft on the inland lake untouched. Even the mischievous monkeys had not ventured to assail it. I believe that my attack on them had taught them a certain amount of good manners. The lake was as beautiful as ever, though the heat had dried up vegetation to a great degree.

Again I gazed with rapture on the terrestial paradise which had so nearly cost me my life, and which, but for the distance from the sea, would still have been my dwelling-place. As I sat on my raft, bathing my chafed hot feet in the water, I could see a sleek opossum peering at me from his hiding-place in a hollow tree; then a snake would rustle through the tangled grass, while here and there a grave old cockatoo stood sentinel on the high tree tops, while parrots, black and white, and blue and grey, flew about in admirable disorder.

It was a heavenly place; but what chance was there, if I remained on that spot, of ever seeing any one to take me away from that enchanted spot, where nature seemed to revel in delights, where flowers, fruits, and birds vied with each other in varied loveliness?

But now I am again afloat upon the lake, and making straight for the island.

What sound is that? Surely it is the barking of a dog. My heart bounded with pleasure at the idea of finding old Tiger again. Several vigorous shoves of my pole brought me very near, and then I clearly saw the splendid fellow bound into the water and swim towards me, leaving a companion standing watching him from the shore.

I was forced to lie down to receive the attached brute's caresses. He then swam away and rejoined his companion, which stood still and noiselessly watching my approach.

I really had no right to be angry with Tiger for what he had done. He had obeyed the universal law, and preferred love to friendship; and the object of his affections was a most beautiful little black she-wolf, as it appeared, though there was an absolute canine mixture in her, which puzzled me much.

The animal looked shyly at me at first, but soon perceiving that I and Tiger were great friends, it seemed to shake off its timidity, and by degrees became, not only tractable, but very tame, and at last fond of me. I gave them soon after a hearty meal of fish and flesh, for which, poor creatures, they were very thankful. Nor could I ever make out how they had contrived on that island to feed themselves so long. I saw, however, bones of hares, rabbits, and monkeys, about the flowering prairie, which satisfied me that they had hunted with considerable success.

But this life would, I knew, make Tiger far too savage; so I determined, after one night spent in the place, to take them home, and to domesticate as much as possible his companion. There is no animal more easily tamed, nor which assimilates itself to the dog as the wolf before age has made it savage, and when hunger does not act upon it with its imperative and imperious demands.

That night I received no interruption from the animal, whatever it may have been, which had so alarmed me on a previous occasion. This, in all probability, was owing to the presence of my faithful watch dog; which, by his affectionate manner and caresses, seemed to implore pardon for himself for having so long deserted my service.

In the course of my life I have been served by many animals, but never by any which showed such depth of intelligence and unchanging fidelity as the dog, and glad was I now to see his portly bearing, his black shaggy hair, his long bushy tail, and dangling ears.

At early dawn I amused myself with fishing, and soon, in that richly-supplied water, found sufficient for myself and companions; after which, I fastened a cord round the wolf's neck—the gentle thing making no resistance—and led it on to the raft, from which I drove Tiger into the water, his gambols being of a nature which threatened to upset my unwieldy craft.

CHAPTER XLIII.

A GREAT MYSTERY.

IT is certain that the discovery of my dog, and of his interesting companion, withdrew my mind from too great contemplation as to the fact that human beings, probably of my own race and colour, were at no great distance from me. I had a faint idea of my whereabouts; but now I determined to endeavour and find out more exactly the spot on which I stood. I had nautical instruments and books, but I wanted the necessary knowledge. This, however, it would be easy to master during the rainy season; the simple elements of navigation, such as finding the latitude, and so on being extremely facile.

Certainty was out of the question, as I did not know the time of the year, nor the day of the month, an omission of great culpability on my part, but which I was not without hope of repairing. As it was, however, it was necessary to give up all theories, and spend the few days which would elapse ere the rain began to fall, in completing my arrangements for the period of confinement, which must necessarily be endured.

Mechanically I made for the seaboard, where high and massive cliffs enabled me to gaze out upon the vast expanse of the ocean. My dog trotted on before me, while I, as a matter of precaution, led the little wolf, which was, however, singularly tame, with the end of my lasso round its neck. For a long time I could not understand how it was that brave old Tiger had made this singular capture; but one day, when exploring the little island on the lake, I found the remains of a huge she-wolf, and the very look of Tiger, as he turned from the disgusting remains, explained the story. He had killed the dam and then taken the helpless young creature under his noble protection.

Tiger would not march steadily on in any one direction, but ran on a-head, wheeled round in circles, snuffed the ground, and came back, as if to say that the passage was safe. Suddenly he stood still, an animal of some kind darted from amid a tuft of grass, and fled, followed by the dog. The wolf, which was held by a loop of rope passed round its neck, gave a jerk, got free, and followed.

There is a fascination, wild and strong, in the chase which more or less affects every man. Though I had not the slightest idea what the animal was they were in pursuit of, I cast my gun on my shoulder, and taking to my heels ran after them as fast as it was in my power to do. The ascent towards the rocks was somewhat steep, yet from practice I ran up it with such uncommon swiftness that few animals could have outstripped me.

Still, though I could see to the summit of the rocks not a

trace of pursuers or pursued was visible. Presently, however, I heard the low growl of my dog, and hastening to the edge of the cliff, looked down. My heart fell within me, for how the dog and myself were ever to be reunited was a mystery which I really could not solve.

The animal of which Tiger had started in pursuit was evidently small, swift, and cunning, probably some kind of fox. It was evidently flying to some well-known lair, and in its desperate effort to escape had rolled over the cliff, alighted on a ledge ten feet below, and escaped by a small narrow hole, against which Tiger was now furiously sniffing. But how he had contrived to save himself on that ledge, after in all probability falling over the cliff was inexplicable. But there he was, scratching, sniffing, and whining without any thought of his own danger.

But where was the wolf?

For a moment I gazed hopelessly down the dizzy height, upon the glassy water, upon which the sun's rays danced gloriously. I saw the disturbed sea fowl sailing round in rude eddies, and then my attention was attracted once more to the dog. The animal, whatever it was which it had pursued, had taken refuge in a hole which Tiger was seeking to enlarge by that peculiar quick scratching motion of the paws which dogs always use on such occasions. But it was quite clear that he did not succeed in enlarging it. There was no soft yielding soil, but hard rock to be contended with, so that it was not doubtful that the dog must fail.

My mind misgave me. I had, it is true, a strong cord with me, which I used as a lasso; but would it bear my weight, and, if so, would it bear the additional weight of my dog too, if I succeeded in descending to him? While this thought was passing through my mind a shrill cry or two called my attention to other things. I turned round and saw the little wolf coming towards me, as if frightened at a fox which had just escaped from a hole.

This explained the position of the dog. The cunning fox, in his desperate hope of escape, had entered his lair by the wrong end. He had leaped, at the risk of killing himself, but, alighting on the ledge, had been immediately followed by the dog. Running rapidly through the hole, it met the wolf, which fled before it. Now I knew why it was the little animal had so mysteriously disappeared.

Still the dog kept scratching furiously, but without making any impression, so that I had to devise in my own mind the best way of aiding in his escape. To descend the face of the rock, which was perfectly perpendicular, was extremely dangerous. It might be easier to climb to him through the cavernous way, and by means of my broadsword open up the narrow gap at which he was striving.

Descending to the place I had seen the fox make his exit, the entrance to his wild lair proved to be a tall and narrow fissure. It was very dark, and being assailed by a natural feeling of dread, I hesitated. Presently, peering into the gloom, my eyes became gradually accustomed to the darkness.

The hole, or fox's lair, trended upwards. But I resolved not to venture without a light, so returning towards a thicket, still hearing the moaning and whining of the wolf, which had run on before, I cut myself some large pine boughs, to which I fastened a number of cones and pine knots. This being fired, made a tremendous torch, which, having duly lit, I began my ascent of the cavernous slit.

Heavens! My feelings may be conceived when I clearly distinguished a flight of steps before me, steps as undoubtedly made by human hands as were the pyramids of Egypt. In my astonishment I nearly fainted. Somebody, then, had been here before me—some other being had visited this island of desolation, and made his residence in this wild cavernous fissure of the rocks. Could it be possible that this other hermit of the wilds still lived and dwelt within this dark and gloomy place?

I advanced upwards, with awe intermingled with hope. I had my saw-sword by my side, and my large horse-pistols in my belt. But I did not feel to need them. Of whatever nation or race the Solitary might be, we could not be enemies. Nothing could turn two human beings against one another, when society was the one blessed thing coveted by both.

The ascent was very narrow and winding, and the steps were only cut where they were really useful in aiding the advance of the explorer. At length the cavern widened, just as a kind of platform was reached, and the whole mystery of the place was revealed.

It was a square room, which by art had been made tolerably comfortable. It was lighted from several small fissures in the rock, while round were shelves, a rude cupboard, a bedstead, chairs, a table, and several other articles of furniture. But that which chiefly astonished me—nay, thrilled me for a moment with horror—was the ghastly story revealed by the sight which presented itself to my eyes, in an arm chair, beside a rude fireplace, on which still stood the ashes and embers of a long extinct fire.

But in the arm-chair, with its head leaning back in the attitude in which death had fixed its living owner, was a skeleton. Not a trace of flesh or skin remained, not even a shred of the clothes which must necessarily have once covered this human form.

At the feet of this ghastly memorial of the past was a shapeless heap of bones, that a hasty glance told me were those of a dog, the presence of which on the island in part explained the somewhat mixed breed of the little wolf, which I had at once remarked when that animal first came under my notice.

In a large wicker cage, itself mouldering to the dust, was a mass of bones and feathers, which clearly belonged to the parrot tribe.

On the table was a rusty knife beside a platter, on which was rudely cut a date. I read it; it evidently had been cut by the trembling hand of a dying man. It preceded my arrival by twenty years. A rusty old gun, a horn empty of powder, a rude shot-bag hung on a large hook near the fire; while a very old harpoon, some ancient fish-hooks, and rotten nets showed the habits of the Solitary.

How my heart beat at this startling picture of man's nothingness, and how deeply the conviction reached to my heart, that such must, at a later or an earlier period be my fate also! How deeply I regretted that we had not met! In that case how easy it would have been for two of us to have constructed such a boat or raft as to have enabled us to escape from the island.

But regrets were useless. I had other thoughts to occupy my mind. I looked at the whole scene with a kind of solemn reverence. I felt, as it were, in the presence of a great mystery. What had this man not undergone? What had been his life, his adventures, his thoughts? Had he died from misery and starvation, abandoned by all save the faithful beast which crouched at his feet? or had he lived to a good serene old age, and died calmly and happily?

But here all speculation was vain, and sadly and mournfully I went on my way, still ascending in the direction where the dog was hard at work. It was not far off. To my astonishment the ascent ended in another chamber, a kind of store-house, as could be seen from mouldy jars, broken wicker baskets, and little piles of what had evidently been in days gone by grain, hams, and other provisions, but of which nothing now remained but mildewed bones, that turned to dust when touched, and a nasty soddened soil.

The hole which my dog was vainly striving to enlarge, was a kind of window to admit air and light. I, however, by means of my sword, was able to displace a stone or two, when the delighted animal came tumbling in, and was greeted with great delight by his female companion. They were then about to follow the scent of the fox, when I literally called them back, and slowly descended that extraordinary cavern, where this strange and bewildering discovery had befallen me.

I do not believe that the adventure with the Indian girl excited in my mind more feelings of regret than did the circumstance of this being having lived and died in this miserable and obscure place, abandoned wholly, except by a faithful animal and his God. Doubtless, his sojourn on the island had been long—and not once, probably, had even the sight of one of his race greeted his eager eyes.

I passed through that solemn chamber of death with a kind of awe—such as one feels before the veil of a temple. My eyes involuntarily, however, took in the whole scene once more, and then an idea flashed across my mind. I would bury the remains of my unfortunate predecessor. On the bed was a large and coarse blanket. This determined me. I went down to the foot of the cavernous hollow, and there, by sheer hard work, I did, by means of my sword, dig a shallow grave. I then ascended to the room again, and carried down, not only the bones of the man, but those of the animals, which I laid reverently in the pit.

I then took an inventory of the goods. There was scarcely anything of the remotest use to me. The gun was rusty; the knife was worn out; but, on removing a kind of kin wrapper, which lay u on a shelf covered by a coating of dust I found—imagine it, oh Heavens!—a pile of manuscript, written on some peculiar kind of paper, the material of which I could not make out. The colour of the ink was faded and indistinct, but I had no doubt that, by perseverance it might be decyphered.

Delighted with this most wonderful discovery, I wrapped it up with extreme care, and once more returned to the open air. Then I reverentially placed a cross over the last remains of the unfortunate being, and after promising to myself to visit the place again, I went my way.

Home, be it even a cavern fashioned by nature, is dear from association to the heart of every man, and I was glad to reach mine. Nor did I leave it again for some time, as the wet season set in immediately. But I cared not, my provisions were in abundance; I had the companionship of my dog and wolf, which I found every day more canine than I at first expected; and then I had my manuscript to decypher.

This was my occupation of an evening, and never, during the whole course of my chequered career, did evenings pass so swiftly, or so agreeably. It was a narrative such as never I had read before. The first line made me literally turn pale, and a sense of choking came over me, which will not be easily forgotten. But I had no leisure to give to the unheard of sorrows of one who had preceded me on my island, and who, in the course of a singularly versatile career, had passed through trials, to which mine were as nought, and who, from the hour of leaving home to that on which the pen fell from the trembling hand, encountere

adventures such as man or woman could scarcely have conceived to be possible. *

My rainy season was unusually short. It passed with considerable rapidity. My store-rooms were improved, my bed and sitting-rooms made as comfortable as possible, my clothes mended and patched, and everything, in fact, done to prepare for another campaign. My mind, too, was stored with many a useful hint from the notes of the unfortunate being whose death was so much to be deplored. Besides that, my books of navigation were keenly studied, that I might carry out my great idea of not only finding the latitude, but arriving at a correct solution of the day of the month.

When the warm sun broke forth—when the birds began to sing—when the waters ceased their rise, and the heavy dew-drops dried upon every tree—I sallied forth. My first visit was to my plantation. It was progressing favourably; the young shoots were already up, and everything looked bright and promising. My pigs were ravenous; so, without more ado, I shot the old sow; and, bad in a human point of view as it may appear, she was incontinently devoured by her own young.

I had confined my dogs at home, as there was a probability of an addition to my establishment; so advanced alone towards the valley of the gazelles. Three delicate little creatures had been added to my herd, the tame ones of which seemed to hail my advent with joy. I fed them as well as I could, and was delighted to see that the plain where the reeds had been cut down was now covered by a rich crop of nutritious grasses.

Every day it became more and more clear that my physical nutriment was provided for, while now was before me the prospect of two delicious luxuries to any one in my condition—milk and butter. But my natural studies had enlightened me enough to make me aware that there were animals on the island far more likely to suit my purpose in this way than the little gazelles.

I had seen their footsteps.

The gazelles examined, I slowly advanced towards the sea. My telescope was slung by my side. My thoughts were bent on that column of smoke which had so startled me six weeks before, and the presence of which seemed to speak of the residence of other white people—perhaps, my own family, my sister, father, cousins—on an island at no great distance.

I went slowly up the bank towards the edge of the cliff. What is that that tapers yonder within a quarter of a mile of the shore?

The masts and half-furled sails of a large and splendid built brigantine. I sank on the sward in utter astonishment and surprise, utterly unable to overcome the wild sensations which bounded through my heart.

Then I took my telescope, and peered down upon the waters below.

CHAPTER XLIV.

THE FUGITIVE.

Beside the jutting rock the few appeared
Like the last remnant of the red deer's herd;
Their eyes were feverish, and their aspect worn,
But still the hunter's blood was on their horn.—BYRON.

A CRIMINAL reprieved from the scaffold, a sinking, dying wretch, dragged from the depths of the sea by some kind and helping hand, could neither of them feel more relieved,

* The MSS. came into our hands with that of THE SAILOR CRUSOE.—ED.

rejoiced, or delighted, than I did for some few minutes. The telescope shook in my hand, nor could I, for a considerable period, so steady it as to be able to distinguish anything.

The vessel was of that mixed sort which appertains both to the brig and schooner, built in this way for the sake of swiftness, as being suitable both for sailing before and on a wind, and in fact, for running almost in the wind's eye, as might a taut and perfect schooner.

Everything about her was evidently calculated to promote speed. Her spars were tapering and elegant, with the slightest rake in the world aft; her running gear and standing rigging were in perfect order, not a rope being out of place, while her canvas, white and unpatched, had been renewed regardless of expense.

She had just anchored; for as I gazed through my telescope, I saw that there were men aloft, occupied in fastening the reef points and gaskets, while the vessel itself was swinging round on a spring cable, to face the tidal current. There were a great number of persons on her deck, and my telescope indicated that, though whites predominated, there were still some very dark and swarthy, probably Brazilians, Portuguese, Spaniards, though others were unmistakably black.

Now I saw they were hoisting out boats. In the first place there was the long boat, which was quickly loaded with casks.

Now I knew they had come to my island to water.

A strange suspicion flashed through my mind.

All this time I had been so deeply engaged in viewing their movements, as if they had been a set of play-actors, that I scarcely allowed myself to think.

The sight of fellow creatures of an European ship absorbed every faculty.

Nobody ever watched the varied scenes of a tragedy with more intense, more absorbing interest.

I never asked myself what those men in loose cotton jackets, in broad Panama hats, in striped trousers, might be. They seemed to be Christians and white men—what more could I wish or desire?

The long boat once out and moored to the ship's side with a painter, then I saw they were hauling out two cutters to accompany the other, they no doubt fancying the island to be inhabited by ferocious natives, instead of by a harmless and hopeful white man.

Then—oh, how wildly my heart did beat at the sight!— I saw three men, naked and perfectly black, plunge headlong into the water, sink, rise again, and strike out for the shore.

Now I knew what had previously been a suspicion—it was a slave ship.

A loud cry, which reached even to the top of that lofty cliff, resounded through the air, and then four or five musket-shots were fired in succession, but without doing any execution. The shore was so near that escape seemed now easy, as once the dense tropical thickets reached, nothing could be easier than for men trained to hardships to conceal themselves from less active and acclimated white men.

The shore towards which the negroes were swimming was about a quarter of a mile to my left, where the rocks ceased and a small bay was wholly lined by trees, several of which were *baobabs*, while below rose bushes in great profusion, of

a smaller character. There were prickly shrubs too, through which it is by no means easy to penetrate.

Meanwhile, the swimmers were advancing without the slightest interference on the part of the crew of the vessel. They were, however, slowly but surely getting ready their boats, into which many armed men descended.

Then I saw a tall man jump down the gangway, followed by two huge black hounds fastened together.

I shuddered. All my visions of delight at the sight of white men vanished; for I knew that, instead of falling upon peaceful traders, or even upon privateers, my island had been invaded by men, who, born and bred to an iniquitous and foul traffic, were utterly beyond all remorse, good feeling, or generosity of purpose. It may be said that the savage tribes of the interior of Africa are inhuman canibals, but then, those who trade in human flesh are immeasurably worse, being more degraded than the blacks whom a stupid prejudice of colour leads them to detest.

But why that shout—that loud, uproarious cry?

I moved my telescope, and at once understood that fearful, that rejoicing cry. But two swimmers were now contending with the sea, breasting the waves, in the hope of freedom, of any fate but slavery. The third I caught one glimpse of in the empurpled water, as he was drawn down by a huge shark.

Horrible is the fascination of such fearful tragedies. I could not take my eyes from the scene, and when the two swimmers, panting for breath, seemed just about to reach the shore, I believe a shout escaped my lips. Alas! they were again quickly silent, for at that instant a second negro, on the very threshold, as it were, of life and liberty, was caught by another hideous monster of the deep, and greedily devoured.

The third rolled insensible on the strand, out of the reach of the fierce animals, and there lay some minutes. Then he rose, glanced at his rapidly approaching masters, gazed upwards at the rocks, and plunged into a deep thicket overswept by the huge boughs of a circular *baobab*.

Now many strange thoughts entered my mind. To discover myself to these inhuman monsters—these dealers in human flesh—was abhorrent to my feelings. It would be necessary to join in their monstrous views, or else to perish by their hands. It often afterwards occurred to me how it was possible that men could be so cruel to others, simply because they were of a different colour? as I had often read of slave-owners being good fathers and husbands, who, after loading their own wives and children with affectionate caresses, would go forth to slay, murder, and destroy the men, women, and children of another section of humanity.

Such anomalies were not to be explained.

What, then, was the course to be pursued? Every impulse of my nature decided me on saving the poor black if it were in my power, though how it was to be done was another question, not easily to be decided. It would be fatal on my part to draw either the black or the whites to my part of the island, where they would easily discover signs of cultivation.

There could be no doubt that a general search of the island would take place, which could scarcely fail to be fatal to me. I knew that such men were not to be trusted if I voluntarily gave myself up, still less so if I were captured after playing hide and seek.

It was fortunate, then, that they had not landed on the old part of the island, on which was my cave, my gazelle preserve, and the pen in which I kept my pigs. All my hopes would have been annihilated in a moment, and myself reduced to the same miserable condition which had been mine on first my shipwreck on that apparently desolate spot.

While communing with myself I turned in the direction taken by the black. My mind was made up. The dogs, if I kept out of sight, would not take notice of me, they being only taught to track the blacks, while, should they by any accident do so, my gun would soon bring them to reason. As a matter of course, I knew that the negro would be as frightened of me as of his captors, but that was a feeling which I had to overcome. This was best to be done by showing myself his friend.

I turned rapidly towards the plain across which I had reason to believe he would start on his way to the hills, where alone, in almost inaccessible caverns or on lofty and precipitous rocks, he could hope to be out of reach of his enemies.

Using my telescope as soon as I was at the foot of the rocks, I saw him plainly. He was resting, as if to prepare for the terrible encounter he was fully aware he had to go through.

He was a tall and very powerful negro. It was a question if, but for the possession of fire-arms, I should have even thought of subjugating him.

My theory was to subdue him by force first and then to tame him by great and continued kindness.

He held a small tree in his hand—a kind of hickory, which he had torn up by the roots, and from which he was breaking the branches and roots. I put down my telescope, and cautiously advanced on my way.

Then I saw the negro turn in the direction of the sea, and swing his club, with intense hatred in his looks. He was close to a small stream, in which he had been bathing his feet.

Now he stopped, and took a long draught, which probably he had not done for some time, water being, on board these fearful slave ships, the greatest of luxuries. From the want of it, with the absence of ventilation, they become truly pest-houses.

My own sufferings alone on that deserted island had made me sensitive to those of others, and I looked with intense pity on this denizen of the free wilds of the African interior, torn away from home and family, to serve the cruel and unfeeling planters of the New World.

I remembered my father's stories of these magnificent savages, dwelling round some treasured well in the desert, satisfied with the possession of a cow, but too willing to barter ivory and gold dust for the meanest of manufactured baubles.

The negro had laid himself flat on the ground to drink, and as he lay in this position, I saw him suddenly start, listen with his ear to the ground, then rise, and again shaking his club at the pursuers, dart away from them at a rapid pace.

Then I heard the deep baying of those horrible hounds, which is of itself enough to terrify the bravest and stoutest heart. The spot selected by the negro, by which to make head for the mountains, was a desert on a small scale, but like most of the deserts spoken of by travellers, not wholly devoid of vegetation. It was simply badly watered, and somewhat dry, being covered with grass and a great variety of creeping plants, with here and there a bush, and sometimes a tree.

It was very flat for about three miles, when the slope of a hill commenced, covered by a rich mass of verdure.

To the left of the negro he might have seen a small drove of antelopes, feeding upon the extraordinary thick grass which grew on that plain. It rose in tufts, with bare spaces between.

I noticed that the negro took prodigious strides over the grass, alighting as much as possible on the bare soil, as if he thought the dogs would find it more difficult to follow him.

Now I saw the chase coming up.

There were two huge dogs, which lugged, tugged, and tore frantically at the leashes by which they were held, lest their rapid pace should take them out of sight.

A more motley set of ruffians I had never seen, and not a feeling of sympathy towards my kind was awakened in my bosom when I saw them pass me, and heard execrations in my native tongue.

The men who held the dogs in leash were not sailors. Their broad Panama hats, red flannel shirts, loose striped trousers, with the long lasso whip they carried, indicated their being supercargoes or overseers of the slaves—perhaps planters on their own account.

The rest were Portuguese, Brazilian, and English; these I heard anathematising the negro's limbs in the most energetic manner.

Strange, but not a single sentiment of sympathy did I feel for them. It was all given to the unfortunate black, whose destruction they had determined on.

CHAPTER XLV.

THE CHASE.

THE negro saw them. He paused, as if to measure the force that was arrayed against him, and, as he did so, raised a loud shout of defiance.

He knew the white man well. He had nothing to expect from him but cruelty.

Nothing he could do would make the pale face more exasperated against his colour and race than what he had done.

He seemed, indeed, by his manner to nerve himself to the stern alternative—escape or death.

The sailors fired a musket or two in pure recklessness, for they could not reach him. I believe that had I have been armed to the teeth—that is, with several guns and my pistols—I should have tried to destroy the whole party; but my very natural impulse was restrained by prudence.

The dogs still dragged furiously as the pursuing party, with a wild and savage hallo, started off in chase. They were nearly a dozen powerful men, armed with whips, knives, guns, and pistols, after one poor naked, unarmed savage.

But these wretches hunt a black man as they would a noxious animal, and hound on the savage beasts that are taught to chase them as we would a pack to the pursuit of a fox.

The plain was dotted, I have said, here and there with trees. This enabled me, as soon as the party of hunters had passed to follow without much danger of discovery.

Nor did I much seem to care if found, for I was fleeter of foot, I knew, than any of them, while, even if the hounds could be persuaded and coaxed to track me, my gun, sword, and pistol would soon bring them to bay.

I started off in the track of the men hunters as soon as they disappeared behind a grove of trees.

My movements were so quick that when I halted at this thicket, and took up the telescope, I saw the negro just dashing into the woods, while the slavers were with diffi-

THE CHASE.

No. 9.—SAILOR CRUSOE.

culty keeping the hounds from turning aside after the small drove of flying antelopes, their appetites being, in all probability, whetted by spare diet on ship-board.

A lash from the long whips of the supercargoes brought them back to the trail, which they again followed with their unerring and wondrous instinct.

In five minutes more they, too, were concealed beneath the leafy arches of the forest.

I waited a few minutes ere I attempted to follow, as I knew not but some of the pursuers might halt.

Seeing, however, that they did not, I once more started at a rapid pace, easily following the fresh footsteps of a dozen men upon the plain.

The woods were so strewed with leaves as to leave a marked track, which, with the howling of the dogs, enabled me to follow easily.

The ascent was steep in the extreme. Here and there the undergrowth was thick and tangled ; in other places only a few creeping plants surrounded the trees ; but everywhere its was difficult to advance.

At length, however, I reached a comparatively level plateau, and stood appalled at the scene before me.

The negro, in his utter ignorance of the country, had placed himself in a most terrible position.

He had, on reaching the edge of the plateau, at one higher end of which I stood, run forward, probably as is much their habit, with his head downward.

There was for a few minutes a trifling descent, and then a rise. Then the grassy plain continued sloping gently upward, until he was suddenly brought up on the edge of one of those singular fissures which seem to yawn beneath the feet of the traveller, and into which many have stopped ere they were aware of their danger.

It was, indeed, a fatal mistake, for the dogs, and their still more savage masters, were not a hundred yards behind him.

What, then, was to be done?

He looked slowly round, saw his yelling, shouting enemies, and then glanced below at the awful chasm, at least twelve or thirteen feet across.

His mind seemed made up. Slowly he walked towards his captors, as if, by quiet surrender, to propitiate their mercy. I was almost angry with the man.

Then, with a terrific cry, like to the wild whoop of the American Redskins, he flew rather than ran, gathered himself strangely up and leaped high into the air. Great God ! he totters on the brink, he is fallen headlong into the pit below—but no!—with a mighty effort, he cast himself forward on his face, and when the howling dogs and yelling pursuers came up, they could not see him. I could. Scarcely taking time to recover his breath, he was rolling himself along the slope towards a grand-looking forest.

Loud and furious were the execrations of the infuriated slave-hunters. They looked up, they looked down. There seemed to be an easy passage upward, and away they started, while I, skirting the trees, rapidly turned the lower end of the fissure. When I did get round, the negro was nowhere to be seen, while the pursuing party were slowly following the edge of the chasm ; the men talking, the dogs sniffing the air, casting their bleared eyes round, lolling out their tongues, as if considerably fatigued.

They every now then stopped to smell the ground, and then suddenly set up a terrible but joyful whine ; they were upon his track. The pursuers chuckled loudly. They cared not for a little trouble, so they wreaked their vengeance—

and well they knew that, sooner or later, they must come up with the hunted wretch.

Again making use of the skirts of the wood, I followed, in several instances finding the assistance of my telescope extremely valuable in saving myself from the windings and detours the dogs were forced to make by the wily negro. Presently the chase again came out upon an open plain, and I saw that the black was becoming slightly wearied. He dragged his legs, he glanced every now and then over his shoulder, and when I saw the fierce and savage dogs let loose from their leash, I felt that all was over.

With a savage roar, or rather howl, away they flew like arrows from the hunter's bow, nor could I imagine how in any way the poor man could hope to defend himself.

On the other side of the plain, and near to the dense forest, was a vast *mowana* or *baobab*, surrounded by *euphorbias*. This was, perhaps, the most mighty specimen of this huge tree I had ever seen. It must have been eighty or ninety feet in circumference. On sped the negro, the dogs close behind him—aye, not twelve yards in his rear —when suddenly he disappeared, and they came to a standstill.

The prodigious tree projected its vast limbs out on all sides, and some of these seemed, so extensive had been the growth of both, to be supported by the *euphorbias*. At the foot of one of these the dogs halted. The negro, aided by the hanging creepers, had vaulted aloft, and disappeared in the leafy masses of the huge and mighty *baobab*.

Again were the dogs at fault, and so vast is the size of these trees, and so dark is their shade, I fancied now that unless the negro were starved out, he might escape. But the slave hunters knew better.

No sooner did they come up, than they drove the dogs from the foot of the smaller tree, and made them go round the *baobab* in a circle.

The dogs were well trained to this ; and soon giving mouth, I knew they were on the trail again.

I had rapidly skirted the plain, and could see the negro crouching on the ground, and yet moving at a rapid pace. No sooner, however, did the dogs make him out, than up he leaped, darted into the air, waved his club, and again trusted wholly to his great power of endurance, which had, however, been tolerably tried by his wondrous leap over the chasm.

All this time I had followed the chase with a wild kind of interest, which carried me forward, without me being aware of how much I was fatigued.

My limbs, however, were now stiff, my lips were parched, and my senses all weak and exhausted.

I would not give up yet, but taking a good draught of weak brandy and water, and eating a bit of such cake as I had manufactured myself, again hurried forward.

The negro, I could see through my telescope, had turned my way.

The forest towards the more distant hills was evidently too tangled.

I hastily hid behind a tree, overhung by the rich, wild vine, and unslung my gun, looked to the priming of my pistols, and waited.

The negro might have been a hundred yards from me, the dogs not twenty more, some of the men in sight—when the poor hunted wretch turned at bay.

An awful howl showed what a terrible blow he had dealt to the first savage beast. But vain was his courage and resistance.

They soon had him down, and before the inhuman

wretches in pursuit could come up, his life was ebbing through his ghastly wounds. Wounded, dying almost, the negro looked up at the cruel, white tormentors of his race. I crept nearer. They pulled off the dogs and examined him.

"He'll never see the ship again," said one fellow, with a strong Virginian twang.

The supercargo scowled at him, and raising his whip, began to lash the dying wretch, who had thus escaped the degradation and suffering of slavery.

The negro gave one awful groan, and then was silent, nor could all the execrations or lashes obtain from him another word.

The horrible cruelty of this man, however, exasperated me beyond all measure, so that, losing all discretion, I fired both my barrels of heavy shot, and then took to my heels, nor did I stop until I had put many miles between myself and the spot where this frightful tragedy had occurred.

It was night when I halted on the summit of a hill that was thickly wooded nearly all the way up, and partially so at the top. Here I lay down, thoroughly wearied and exhausted.

My fatigue was so great that I could scarcely eat a mouthful, but quenching my thirst, very imprudently, with the whole of my gourd of brandy and water, fell asleep, to dream of fierce and savage dogs, of hunted negroes, and of murder done by a white man on white man like himself.

I was under the influence of a fearful nightmare. But to resume my narrative.

CHAPTER XLVI.

DELIRIUM.

I FLED, as Cain might have done when his hands were hot with the blood of Abel.

My abhorrence of the crime perpetrated on the poor black did not disguise from me the fact that I had no right to be the avenger.

Hence the terrible sensation which seemed to pursue me as dashing wildly away into the hills, I felt pursued, not by living men, not by hounds in mortal shape, but by some mighty Nemesis that lowered on me from the heavens above, and glared at me from every hollow and abyss I passed.

Sleep was worse than waking. A nightmare of fear and awe was on my soul.

It was no longer one negro chased by one savage hound, but a hundred thousand negroes pursued by a myriad of blear-eyed and red-tongued brutes, that made the very welkin resound with their yells and howls.

When I awoke, as the grey dawn fell upon me, my throat was parched, my lips were dry, my tongue swollen, while, though my skin was scorching to the feel, my whole frame was taken with a quivering and shivering, which at once told me I was in a burning fever.

Then I remembered no more, until at last my returning senses enabled me to appreciate the full peril of my situation.

I had evidently been ill some days, for I was prostrate from weakness and exhaustion.

I lay on a shelf of rock, beneath an overhanging cliff, but where, I had not the most remote idea or conception.

I was in the midst of arid hills and places almost devoid of vegetation.

I had no gun, pistols, or telescope, nor could I, in my weak and feeble state, tell whether I was to take my way back to the right or the left.

There was no pain about me.

I had not cut or bruised myself, but my sensation of thirst was dreadful, while gradually I became aware of a feeling of intense hunger.

During my delirium I must have found water; indeed, the state of my garments proved that I had plunged into streams in my burning fever.

How I escaped death during that terrible trial it is impossible for me to say.

The only kind of vegetation which the eye could perceive, were some creeping plants, which, having their roots buried far beneath the soil, feel little the effects of the scorching sun.

The number of these which have tuberous roots is very great, and naturalists have proved that their structure is intended to supply nutriment and moisture, when during the long drought they can be produced nowhere else.

As I reflected on this, my mind, naturally bent under the circumstances to appreciate the mighty Artificer of the world, was struck with wonder.

Here was a plant not generally tuber-bearing, which became so under circumstances where that appendage was necessary to produce a reservoir for preserving its life.

I subsequently found, in my exploration of the island, the same happened to a grape-bearing vine.

The plant, which grew in the shadow of the cliff, bore a scarlet-coloured eatable cucumber when quite ripe, but what I now desired was the root, at which I dug with an energy and perseverance, which, in my weak state, astonished myself.

I had a knife.

At my feet was a plant with linear leaves, and a stalk not bigger than a crow's quill.

I dug perseveringly, and though I was a long time about it, and was forced to pause several times, the feeling that I was battling for life kept my courage up.

At length I came to a tuber, which was almost as large as the head of a child, of which I hastily removed the rind, and found a soft pulp, with a liquor in its cellular tissues, which I hastily and thankfully swallowed. It was indeed delightfully cool and refreshing, and doubtless contributed more than anything else to save my life.

Resting a little after this, to me, terrible exertion, I crawled to my feet.

Desolate, indeed, was the spot, which in my delirium I had chosen for my resting-place.

In what part, how far from my home, and in what direction that lay I knew not, but presently a careful examination of the sun's position determined me in my course.

How I had crossed those pitiless rocks, how I had found those bleak and narrow passes, while flying doubtless before my own panic-stricken thoughts, I could not say. There is a Providence for the madman, and mad I was, to all intents and purposes.

But now it was different.

Weak, tottering, and ill I crawled instead of ran. Frightful precipices, steep hills, cavernous holes, met me at every step, but not one rill, one brook, one single drop of water—that most blessed of all things to man in a state of nature.

As I crawled along I cast my eyes on every side with deep and earnest longing.

Nothing, however, met my gaze, but sand and stunted trees, except a little ahead of me a grove of mopana trees. Towards these I made my way. They formed a thick belt.

Suddenly I felt a sensation of delight fill my soul, for the setting sun, casting a beautiful blue haze over what appeared to be a small and lovely lake, I roused myself, and after unheard-of exertions, contrived to get through the belt.

Then I saw that I had made a discovery which would have delighted me at any other time.

It was a salt pan, over which hovered one of these mirages which so deceive and inveigle the weary traveller.

This mirage was marvellous. It was perfection. Not a particle of imagination was necessary for realizing the exact picture of large collections of water; the waves danced along, and the shadows of the trees were vividly reflected beneath the surface.

I turned away in mortal agony.

My sufferings on my first arrival on the island were intense indeed, but not like these. The wind came, warm and scorching, on my weakened frame, from hot sandy plains and bare rocks, so that I could scarcely breathe.

Then, at last, I descended slowly towards a plain. At the foot of the rocks there was what looked to me to be an old river bed, with here and there tufts of reeds, nearly concealed by sand. Now, I was quite aware that reeds will not grow except in the vicinity of water, so, kneeling down began to scrape out the sand beside the reeds with my hands.

I had not far to go. At a very little distance from the surface was a hard stratum of incipient sandstone, along which flowed a small quantity of clear, cool, and refreshing water.

This is the way that water is found in the desert, either the result of rain, checked in its descent by the sandy stratum, or flowing underground from springs in the hills.

My thirst quenched, every nerve in my body was brought into requisition, to enable me to reach the skirt of a small forest, where it was my resolve to pass the night.

I was completely defenceless, weak from hunger, prostrated by fever, so that, even with fire-arms, I could scarcely have defended myself against the beasts of the field.

My hope was wholly in Providence, in which humbly I did put my trust, especially after my late miraculous preservation.

The wood was small, and skirted by a rich fall of vines. These grew round the trunks of the trees, their tendrils clinging to the branches until, from their great weight, they fell over.

To my great delight this was a genuine grape vine, and covered by rich and delightful fruit.

As I knew this to be an excellent restorative against debility produced by heat and exhaustion, I ate tolerably freely, and then, without care for the dangers which might attend my doing so, crept under the rich foliage, and slept.

The thickly-leaved trees and creeping plants kept the dew off me, so that I awoke much improved in feeling. My whole frame seemed imbued with additional energy. I could walk erect.

The first use I made of my strength was to cut a stick with which to assist my progress and defend myself against the lesser animals.

After a breakfast of grapes which, though not sufficiently restorative, were pleasant to the palate, I hurried, as fast as my steps would carry me, through the wood, which was more scattered and torn down than in my part of the island. Gradually, too, it became thinner and thinner, until through the trees I could discover that I was coming out upon a somewhat extensive plain.

As the day advanced, the heat became overpowering, my pulse beat with amazing force, and my brain felt as if thumping against the crown of my head.

The trees and long grass excluded the air, so that not a breath reached me.

I halted and rested against a tree, gazing upwards to see if a breath moved the tops of the taller trees. Not a branch, not a leaf shook.

Then, oh heavens! I heard, distinctly heard, close to me a loud and maniacal laugh. It was a fierce, quick, angry laugh, but still a laugh.

I turned wildly round, and gazed frantically in every direction, but could see nothing. I clutched my stick, loosened my knife in my sheath, and stood ready.

I had not the remotest doubt that some of the slavers, with the infernal patience of their race, had waited to wreak their vengeance on my head, and were now enjoying the luxury of revenge.

"Ha! ha! ha!"

Again that awful laugh, but this time with repeated echoes, and much nearer to me.

In my great alarm, I shouted to them to come on, and not conceal themselves behind trees like cowards. No sooner was my voice raised, than swiftly rushing past me, came several animals of the size of wolves, uttering their doleful cry as they fled.

It was a pack of laughing hyenas, animals which imitate that one inflection of the human voice so admirably as to deceive any but the most practised ear.

But before I recovered my astonishment, I was more than ever bewildered, as I gazed right and left, to behold the whole forest as it were in motion.

Usually, during the fierce tropical heats of the day, all animals conceal themselves, coming forth only night and morn.

But now this sudden dry, hot, scorching wind had roused them. Some influence, which I could not understand, was taking them all in one direction.

As I stood on a small hillock, sheltered by several thick trees, and gazed at the scene before me, I rubbed my eyes several times, to convince myself I was awake.

From my post of observation I could see lions, hyenas, jackals, antelopes, large deer, and other animals, coursing past like the phantasmagoria of a dream.

They took no notice of each other. But this was no wonder. I soon found that, tormented by the furnace-like heat of the day, the whole were under the influence of burning, parching thirst.

I have seen a *stampede*, where every variety of animal of the mountain, plain, and forest, has under the influence of a panic, rushed in one furious troop together; but I never saw the animal creation proceed so steadily towards one point as did these many varieties—mostly inimical to one another.

I, myself, caught the contagion, and hastened to the skirt of the forest and to the edge of the plain.

The first glance told me what the mystery was. There is an instinct in animals, which I do not attempt to explain, but which I know to be. These varied and incongruous beasts, roused in their lairs by the fierce noontide heat, had one and all taken their way in the only direction where, in the absence of water, they could quench their angry thirst.

The whole plain was covered by the *cucumus caffer*, or water-melon. This extraordinary plant literally hid the ground, as it does vast regions in the interior of Africa. Animals of every sort and name, including man, rejoice in the rich supply. The elephant, that mighty lord of the forest, revels in this fruit, and so even do the different species of rhinoceros. But those which I could see were, in this instance, the hideous hyena, several antelopes and jackals, with, in the corner of the plain, one small lion.

But none took notice of me. Thirst is almost as great a means of taming the animal creation as hunger, and when I advanced into the plain, and took one or two for my own use, none of the eager animals even turned their heads. I found the melons delicious. Their fragrant and wholesome juice spread like a balm through my frame. My tongue seemed to return to its proper size, my lips recovered their moistness, even a sense of renewned vigour appeared to pervade me.

It may readily be believed that, once my appetite satisfied, I did not remain in the neighbourhood. There were two many hungry beasts about, and it occurred to me that their thirst satisfied, they might discover they had another form of appetite.

The chief drawback to my progress now was my sore feet. My shoes were torn to atoms, but I was too eager to get away from the dangerous proximity of that plain to feel much pain.

The lion I had seen was was a small one, one of those insignificant animals such as I had seen seen in shows, but this did not make an encounter desirable to my mind.

Late in the evening I contrived to crawl into the boughs of a thick tree at no great distance from the ground, where I contrived somehow to obtain a night's sleep.

Some berries, a red cucumber about four inches long and an inch and a-half in diameter, was all my breakfast. It was of a bright scarlet colour, and, strangely enough, quite ripe.

But I never could account for the strange variety of climates which soil, trees, and in other places the absence of trees made on my island.

That evening, after moving all day at almost a snail's pace, I came in sight of the spot where I had left my gun, telescope, and other articles.

No sooner did I obtain possession of firearms than I looked around me in search of game.

There were many birds upon the trees, but not temptinglooking ones, a squirrel or two played about on the boughs, but these were not worth throwing away powder on. Presently I saw something move in the branches of a thick tree.

It was still hot, dry weather, but as the evening drew in it became cooler.

Impatient of delay I fired into the thick foliage, when half a dozen birds very much resembling turtle-doves came fluttering to the ground.

I sprang towards them, killed those which were only wounded, and then, rejoiced at the prospect of a broil, hastened to make a fire.

This was not a very long operation, and in a quarter of an hour my birds were plucked, split open, and being turned on my ramrod before the fire.

When I fired my gun the sound seemed to me strange. The echoes reverberated through the hills, first loudly, and then dying away in faint murmurs.

But what is this?

Scarcely had I put everything ready for my evening meal, when a deep, loud bark fell upon my ear, coming nearer and nearer every moment until just as I was about to secrete myself, Tiger bounded upon me, as usual, nearly smothering me with his caresses.

When I was able to calm him a bit my thoughts took a fresh turn.

My dog had been left in a room in my cave, carefully fastened in with a tolerable supply of food for several days— and now I found him outside.

How he had found me, except by hearing the report of the gun, I could not say. Then came the question as to how he got loose.

Had those ruffians, upon whom in a moment of impulse and passion I had fired, found my cave and devastated it? If so, sad indeed was my fate, and dismal the prospect of the future.

But reflection was useless, so I resolved to wait till the next day, and content myself with what fortune had provided for my present use.

Having shared my supper with my dog I fell asleep nor woke till sometime after day.

A hurried meal ensued, and then I started, full of anxiety, to learn the truth. Tiger seemed as impatient as myself.

A slight shower fell at sunrise, which partly cooled the air, and in this way a forced march brought us, by nightfall, within sight of my cave.

Then Tiger started off at a gallop, leaving me to follow at my leisure.

CHAPTER XLVII.

THE LAND TORTOISE.

The horse was brought,
In truth he was a noble steed,
A Tartar of the Ukraine breed,
Who looked as though the speed of thought
Were in his limbs; but he was wild,
Wild as the wild deer, and untaught,
With spur and bridle undefiled——
'Twas but a day he had been caught;
And snorting, with erected mane,
And struggling fiercely, but in vain,
In the full foam of wrath and dread,
To me the desert-born was led.

BYRON.

WHEN I came to my cave, I found that Tiger had contrived himself to escape in a most ingenious manner. The food that I had left him being utterly exhausted, and the half-canine she-wolf having by this time a litter of most beautiful puppies, he had succeeded, by scratching and biting, in further undermining the room, so as, when he got a purchase below, to remove a bamboo, and thus reach the much-coveted open air.

He had then, as I could judge from the bones about, amused himself by hunting down animals, such as hares, rabbits, and others, with which to supply the she-wolf in her trouble.

Water was abundant, as they had access to the stream which filled my fountain or pool. In this way the brood had been brought up admirably. They were still blind, but rather fat.

Tiger looked up at me when I came in, with a pride which I readily understood. He had been clearly the means of saving them from that worst of deaths, starvation, and thought not a little of himself for so doing.

I have very great reason to speak highly of the instinct of animals, having seen much of their extraordinary acuteness, but there is none which so nearly approaches to reason as man's faithful companion—the dog.

How my life was saved by this faithful creature will be seen on a subsequent occasion.

My first care now was to restore myself to health, as my body had been terribly shaken by the ups and downs of those terrible hills, while my constitution bore great tokens of the fever.

My work on medicine was carefully consulted, and its advice followed as much as possible.

I then made up my mind to rest wholly from arduous labour for some time, nurse myself, and thus restore my energies and muscular strength.

I visited my valley of the gazelles, and brought away with me one of those animals, which I caught with the lasso after chasing it into the pen.

This I killed, though not without reluctance. But I required broth and fresh meat, which could just then be procured in no other way. Besides, my dogs had to be thought of.

Indeed, they were calculated to be a very great trouble to me, as this animal, when domesticated, cannot be allowed to provide itself wholly with food, or else it would become as savage, emaciated, and gaunt, as those of the continent; I was compelled, then, in self-defence, to provide them, as well as possible, with proper food.

Determined not to be idle, though I could do no really hard work, I got as many cocoa-nuts and gourds as I could, which, sitting under my leafy shelter beside the pool, I fashioned into cups, dishes, platters, and bottles.

My convalescence proceeded slowly, which I regretted the more as I had resolved to return with Tiger to the salt pan, and procure a goodly supply of that useful and agreeable article.

I had not lost my taste for this most wholesome relish, but my chief desire was to preserve as much pork as possible, my pigs increasing in size and weight almost every day. Their numbers, too, were far too great for the space they occupied.

This, too, necessitated a gradual thinning out, which was an occupation which I was not butcher enough to take much fancy in; but while on my island I was compelled to do many things abhorrent to my nature.

While sitting at my work, or while smoking my pipe of an evening, I turned over more and more, the idea of capturing some animal which should enable me to explore my seat of habitation more narrowly, and which would draw some rude kind of car, that would transport me and some part of my effects to different places.

I had made up my mind to catch the elk, but I had never seen him since, nor could I imagine, very well, how he could be caught.

I knew well how the inhabitants of the African continent managed, but that plan would, doubtless, be beyond my means. Besides, it was a cruel and useless waste of animal life.

To have carried out this mode of capture, I must have constructed two long high hedges, very far apart at one end, and close together at the other, as if they made the letter V. Where they met, a narrow lane would have led to a deep pit, seven or eight feet wide and many feet longer, with another hedge round to prevent escape. Then, by means of my dogs, I must have driven such game or large animals as I wished to capture into the trap.

The Africans, who utterly disregard animal life, and who are never so happy as when destroying it, drive the poor beasts up to the narrow part of the hope, shouting, yelling, and casting javelins, until they have a complete pitfull. It must have always been a frightful scene.

Still, though I could not attempt anything on so large a scale, and would not if I could, something similar might be invented, except that, as a rule, it would be extremely difficult to dig a pit.

A large portion of my time, during my convalescence, was spent in making rope and cord.

Particularly I contrived a lasso, the use of which I was well acquainted with. Then I made several halters and good strong leashes, by which to hold my dogs when necessary.

These animals, when not trained to hunting, are very difficult to restrain. They consider everything wild which comes within their reach as fair game. Now, there were very many animals and birds which I was desirous of capturing, which never could be, if they were in the first instance terrified by my own dogs.

Every day my strength seemed to return, and I felt at the end of ten days quite another man. Advantage of this would speedily have been taken to again make a tour, and collect some salt, but that a very hot wind blew from north to south for three days.

The air was deeply charged with electricity, and everything wooden became dry and warped, and in some cases useless.

During this time I remained still, reclining nearly all day under the deep shadow of a mimosa outside my enclosure, where, if a change took place, I might expect to feel the first effect of a cooling breeze.

In this way I made a discovery which proved of very much greater importance than at first sight it appeared to be.

During my residence on the island, I often wondered at not having met with an animal almost always found in tropical climates.

All students of natural history will be aware how agreeable a dish it makes with its unlaid eggs.

I mean the land tortoise.

Several times I thought I had seen its trails near the fountains, but could never catch one.

On this day, however, I distinctly saw something moving slowly along, at no great distance, which I at once recognised.

Despite the great heat and the warm dry wind, my curiosity overcame my languor, and I rose to my feet, looked around to find something which should protect me from the heat, and saw what I had not observed before—a fan palm, close to me.

The fan palm is very tall and graceful, each branch having the appearance of a beautiful fan; and when gently waved by the wind, the effect produced was indescribably pleasing. This species of palm is very rare.

It produces fruit about the size of an apple, of a deep-brown colour, with a kernel as hard as a stone, and not unlike vegetable ivory. This fruit I afterwards found had a bitter taste; but, farther south (where, as will be presently seen, I found the tree very plentiful) I found that it was exceedingly palatable. On account of the great height and straightness of the trunk, the trunk was very difficult of access.

Hastily plucking several boughs, I held them over my head which was thus protected from the extreme heat, and keeping in the background, followed my slow discovery through the grass and jungle.

What could make him travel on such a terrible hot day as this, was a question which I had asked myself and been unable to answer, until, using my retentive memory and recollecting my reading, I determined to verify a faint suspicion which had flashed through my mind.

It skirted the rocks in which was my cavern, but in a way I had never noticed.

It kept, fortunately for me, nearly all the time under trees, and though its space was very slow on a day like this, there was no disposition on my part to complain.

At length, it came to were the trees were less verdant, and even many of them dead.

They were in a circle around a small pool-like spot. I was right in my suspicions.

The land tortoise had led me to a salt pan.

The trails of these animals may always be seen about salt pans or fountains, and they will travel many, many miles in search of this necessary and health-giving article, in lieu of which they will often devour wood ashes.

They are generally found where they can find the effloresence of nitrates which contain salt.

And yet it is wonderful where man exists that this animal can exist also, for he is no sooner seen than taken.

The young are taken for the sake of their shells, which the natives of Africa, especially, make into boxes, which, when filled by sweet-smelling roots and herbs, are hung round the persons of women.

When full grown it is made an article of food, while its shell is turned to various uses, such as to hold water or serve as a dish.

Everybody who has seen one must be aware that it can owe its perpetuity in the land neither to speed nor cunning, but it has been often remarked that its colour, yellow and dark brown, is admirably adapted, by its similarity to the grass and brushwood, to render it invisible.

It will, however, when man pursues it, make a faint and miserable attempt at flight, but its real defence against animals is its armour, its thick long shell.

In this way it often defeats the hungry propensities of the hyena, the jackal, and its other enemies. They are, when not disturbed, very long lived.

I subsequently found many of them, and watched them intently.

I remarked that when it was about to deposit its eggs, it scratched a hole, threw up the earth round the shell, and almost buried itself.

This done, it covered its eggs up, and went away.

This was generally before the rainy season, after which the little ones would crawl out, in their perfectly soft shells, and cropping the fresh herbage shifted for themselves.

Having caught the one which had so opportunely discovered the salt pan I carried it home, made an inclosure for it, and placed it within.

By keeping it well supplied with leaves, grass, and certain plants which I remarked it was fond of, with a proper supply of salt and ashes, it became very tame, and soon knew me when I called it.

In future, however, I never allowed one to escape, as the eggs were agreeable, nourishing, and wholesome. But gratitude made me keep the first one.

CHAPTER XLVIII.

THE HYENA.

HAVING, as soon as the hot weather was over, killed and salted as many pigs as I thought were useful, I did a little carpentering, improved my table and chairs, and took in such vegetables and grains as were ripe.

All this was fearfully laborious, and made me long more and more for some animal I could make a beast of burden

of, and harness to my plough—for such a thing I intended to make, however rude and imperfect.

It was one of those things which were absolutely necessary, and which, if the proper animal were discovered and captured, would ease my labours very much.

But there was no chance of meeting anything of the kind in my part of the island, which made me resolve, at no distant date to start upon a thorough exploration of the interior.

It was not my intention to venture into the arid hills, those bare and pine-clad mountains, where I had endured sufferings I never could forget, but to strike along the shore, where, at all events, if several days out, I could add fish to my other resources.

The destruction of so many pigs, and the quantity of offal, fat, and other parts which I disdained, had made my dogs rather dainty, especially as I took many birds with nets which I placed in different trees and bushes.

All this refuse I threw without my fort, a very necessary precaution in a hot country.

But as sure as I threw anything out in the evening, had disappeared, every scrap, bones and all, before the morning.

This made me aware that some animal had been attracted to my neighboured by the smell.

Now, one evening the dogs, having been out hunting for themselves—which they often did—had come home very tired and betaken themselves to the interior of the cave, while I sat in my verandah.

The little ones were, as I thought, safe under their mother's guard.

Had the pupppies have come into the world during my presence, two out of the four would have been sacrificed; but as it was I had not the heart to kill them.

On this night I remarked that the she wolf was very restless, came running out, hunted about, but strangely enough, did not particularly attract my attention.

Then I heard a sudden rush, a squall, and a fearful growl from Tiger and the mother, when both darted off in pursuit, but returned some hours after utterly exhausted and chop-fallen.

It was only in the morning I found that the animal, whatever it was, had carried off one of the puppies, and as the intruder was so excessively daring, I now became personally interested, and determined to put a summary end to his rapacity.

My own suspicion led me to suspect the relatives of Tiger's mate.

But whatever was the fact, my ingenuity, or rather my memory, was taxed to provide a remedy.

Pits are usually made use of to destroy wolves, but that was too laborious, so I resolved to try a plan, of which I had often heard, as practised in Switzerland.

Selecting a spot at some distance from my fort, I chose two young trees, which I completely divested of their branches.

To these I lashed a gun firmly, in a horizontal position, with the muzzle pointing slightly upwards.

A piece of wood, about six inches long, was then tied to the side of the gunstock, in such a way as to be free to move forwards and backwards. This was to act as a kind of lever.

A piece of my bamboo-string connected the trigger with the lower end of the lever.

A longer piece of cord was then attached to the upper extremity of the latter. This cord, having been passed through the bands of the ramrod, itself removed, a lump of flesh was fastened on, hanging over the muzzle of the gun.

Bushes and boughs were then piled around, so has to conceal all but the meat.

This done, I retired, and when night came, fastened my dogs inside, and laid myself down in the verandah, where I burnt a light, while I worked at different things.

My fancy had gone so far as to desire the possession of a hammock, and this I had begun to manufacture out of grass and such strong fibres as I could procure.

To anyone who has ever enjoyed the luxury of a swing in this delightful convenience, the habit becomes second nature.

My plan was to select two of my very best ropes, which I fastened together, so as to allow the end of each to be about six feet beyond the intended hammock.

These were the clue lines or ends by which the hammock was to be strung to supports. Between the two cords which were to constitute its sides, I lashed thinner ones, more like twine than rope, and then from end to end, I carried a kind of grass.

This luxurious couch was intended for my summer-house in the lake.

I do not know at what hour it was, but certainly late, when I heard the gun go off, followed by a shrill and piercing cry. Satisfied that something had been done, I retired to rest, determined not to visit the scene of action until morning.

I did so at an early hour, accompanied by my dogs, and found that the trap had succeeded.

A magnificent hyena lay dead by the muzzle of the gun.

It was a very handsome animal, of the tiger wolf, or spotted hyena breed.

With much difficulty I kept the dogs off, as I wanted to preserve her skin, which I at once removed from the body, and, for further safety, before I thought of breakfast, deposited in my pool, with a number of stones to keep it down. My dogs were so dainty, they would not touch the flesh, which became the prey of the carrion vulture.

I have already alluded to my traps and nets for catching birds. About this time it was that, by means of some very coarse bird-lime, I became possessed of a parrot and a bird of paradise, which I contrived, after some starvation and considerable coaxing, to tame, and even in time to render docile.

At last, they both became exceedingly fond of me. These details about animals take the place, in my history, of discoveries and meeting with strange men and stranger civilisation, with other travellers.

From events that soon occurred, I was almost inclined to say, I wish my records had never again been of anything but animals. Before my narrative is concluded, my grievances against man, and woman, too, will be considerable.

As soon as my harvest was over, feeling myself perfectly recovered, an exploring expedition was determined on in my own mind.

My animals were seen to, my birds fed, and provided with food during my absence, the puppies fastened up, with meat and bones, and then my dogs and I started.

My summer-house was my final destination, but I took first my way along the shore.

CHAPTER XLIX.

THE SALT LICK.

A LOVELY day, a light and pleasant wind, a sun shaded from my sight by a few clouds, and away we went. Again I followed that part of the coast which had brought me to the rock whence I had seen the slave-ship. But I sought for no more such discoveries, hurrying on rather for three days, until I came to regions which surpassed in beauty anything I had seen. Once or twice, in the distance, I fancied I saw giraffes, and animals resembling mules or horses.

Several times I discovered ostriches, but never near enough to attempt their capture. The sight of them, however, excited singular hopes in my mind, as I had often dreamed of taming these creatures.

The scenery was both interesting and novel. Now we passed through meadows, or prairies, where the grass grew so high it would have concealed a horseman; at others, we passed through forests of straight-stemmed and dark-foliaged timber trees, which seemed like the abodes of gigantic animals of every class.

Beneath one of these, on the third afternoon, I pitched my tent, and fastened the dogs, so that they might guard my slender luggage, and guide me back to my temporary abiding place by their barking.

Lucky it was I left them.

Roaming about as usual in search of plants and bushes, I discovered a salt lick, which I at once knew, by the marks around it, to be much frequented by large and dangerous animals, such as rhinoceros, elephants, and giraffes.

Though I had seen none of them I could not mistake their marks.

No one who has once seen them will ever forget the effect produced on his mind by the gigantic footprints or tracks of elephants. All others appear puny alongside of them.

But what delighted me most was the undoubted presence of some animal of the horse species.

Determined to discover what it was, I resolved to watch. Beyond the salt lick, and separated from it by a neck of land, was a pool where, doubtless, the same animals came to drink. Here, at the northern extremity, I dug a small hole, and covering it with branches, crawled into it, my double-barrelled fowling-piece being loaded on one side with swan shot, on the other with several balls.

I had a spare gun, too, which on this journey I had strapped on the back of Tiger.

The larger animals of the creation generally like to roam at night, so that until darkness came on I was glad to rest beneath a tree, and give my mind to thoughts of the past and future.

It was only at nightfall I sought my pit.

It was one of those gloriously magnificent and serene tropical moonlight nights, when an indescribably soft and enchanting light is diffused over the slumbering landscape, from which ascended on all hands the most odoriferous scents that grass or flowers could emit; the moon was so bright and clear that I could have discerned even the smallest animal at a considerable distance from where I lay.

The fatigues of the day, the quiet, the indescribable charm of the scene, all tended to make me drowsy. But I contended against this feeling as much as possible! Once or twice I thought the desired game had come, but it proved to be only my old acquaintances, the hyenas, which I drove away by the power of the human voice.

Then I fell asleep. When I awoke it was very dark, and that darkness was deepened by the foliage close at hand. I could not see the end of my gun. Presently, however, my yes becoming used to the gloom, and the clouds breaking somewhat, I saw that I was not alone.

Several giraffes and zebras were drinking from the pool;

CAPTURING A ZEBRA.

No. 10.—SAILOR CRUSOE,

while peering out of the water I could see the heavy shape of some animal which I did not recognise.

I at once determined to shoot one of the former.

I had just completed my preparations, however, when a noise, that I can compare to nothing but the passage of a train of artillery, broke the stillness of the night air; it evidently came from the direction of one of the numerous paths, or rather tracks, leading to the water, and I knew not what to think.

Raising myself cautiously from my recumbent position in the pit, I fixed my eyes steadily on the part of the bank whence the strange sounds proceeded; but for some time I was unable to make out the cause, though I remarked that the game I had previously seen had all fled.

All at once, however, the strange mystery was explained by the slow appearance of an immense bull elephant, followed immediately after by others, amounting to seven or eight.

Their towering forms at once seemed to warn me, at a glance, that they were all males.

It was a magnificent sight to behold so many of these vast creatures approaching with a free, sweeping, unsuspecting, and stately step.

The somewhat elevated ground whence they emerged, and which gradually sloped towards the pool and salt lick, together with the misty night air, gave an increased appearance of bulk and height to their naturally giant structures.

Crouching down as low as possible in the pit, I waited with a wildly beating heart and ready gun the approach of the leading bull, who, utterly unconscious of peril, was making straight for my hiding-place.

The position of his body, however, was not suitable for a shot, and, knowing well that I had little chance of obtaining more than a single good one, I waited anxiously for an opportunity to fire at his shoulder, which it is always said, is preferable to any other part when shooting at night.

But this opportunity, unfortunately for me, was not afforded till the enormous bulk of his whole body towered just above my head.

The consequence was, that, while in the act of raising the muzzle of my gun over the pit, my form caught his before unobservant eye, and before I could place the piece to my shoulder, he swung himself round, and with trunk elevated, and ears spread, as is the elephant's wont, he desperately charged me.

There was now no time to think of flight, much less of slaying the savage beast.

My own life was in imminent jeopardy; and seeing that, if I remained partially erect, he would inevitably seize me with his proboscis, I threw myself on my back with some violence, in which position, and without shouldering the fowling-piece, I fired upwards at random towards his chest, uttering, at the same time, the most piercing shouts and cries.

The change of position, in all human probability, was the means of saving my life; for, at the same time, the trunk of the infuriated animal descended precisely on the spot where I had been previously lying, sweeping away the bushes (many of a large size) that formed the fore-part of my hiding-place.

In another moment, his broad fore-feet passed directly over my face.

I now had no reason to expect anything short of being crushed to death.

But my relief may be conceived when, instead of renewing the charge, he swerved to the left, and moved off with considerable rapidity, most happily without my having received other injuries than a few bruises.

There is no doubt that, apart from a guiding Providence, I had to attribute my extraordinary escape to the astonishment of the animal by the wound I had inflicted on him, to the report of my gun, and to the outcries drawn from me when in my utmost peril.

Immediately after the elephant had left me I was on my legs; and snatching up the spare gun, which lay close at hand, I pointed at him as he was retreating, and pulled the trigger, but to my intense mortification the piece missed fire.

It was matter of thankfulness to me, however, that a similar mishap had not occurred when the animal charged, for had my gun not then exploded, nothing could have saved me from destruction.

During these events the rest of the elephants retreated into the bush; but by the time I had recovered myself they reappeared with stealthy and cautious steps on the opposite side of the pool, though so distant that I could not fire with any prospect of success.

I made up my mind to watch at that pool no more in the night-time, though when my spirits had recovered their tone, I was none the less resolved to capture one of the zebras.

With these feelings it was I returned at daylight to my camp, after experiencing one of the most terrible nights I ever remembered to have endured.

CHAPTER L.

THE ZEBRA.

MY young readers are many of them, doubtless, aware that the horse, mule, onager, ass, and zebra, are all of one family; and though only three of these are usually tamed for domestic purposes, yet both onager and zebra have been brought under the command of man.

The quagga, a species of zebra, is used by the natives of Africa for the purposes of draught.

Another species of zebra was even exposed for sale with a rider on his back to show its semi-domesticity.

The Hippotigrine group, or zebras, was not known to the ancients, except in a circus.

It stands between the horse and the ass.

The head is of intermediate length, the neck naturally fuller and more arched; the mane vertical, forming a standing crest.

There is more girth, muscle, and compactness than in the others; the shoulder is more oblique, and the withers more elevated than in asses; the hoofs higher, and, as in the horse, they are round and flat; in the ass, oval and hollow; and in the species of hippotigris they are oval at the toe.

I was perfectly aware that nothing could be more difficult than to catch one of these animals, and having caught it I was aware that it would be extremely hard work to tame its unsubduable nature. But I knew that it had been done, and saw no reason why it might not be done again, with perseverance and ingenuity.

This idea kept the more complete possession of my head, that doubts often flashed through my mind whether or no I was on an island at all.

This was all the more readily believed when I discovered the presence of so many elephants, cameleopards, and other large animals, which must necessarily have a large space of ground to range over.

There is, it is true an island which contains all the largest specimens of animal creation known to man, but then the island itself is large.

Now, if I could conquer the stubborn spirit of one or more of these animals, this suspicion of mine might be made a certainty.

But the affair was not an easy one. Traps at the salt lick, pitfalls, and other strange devices, entered my head, but nothing would I entertain which involved a visit to the salt lick and pool at night.

Then I determined to watch and see, if possible, what were the habits of the zebra, and thus solve the difficulty as to his capture.

I again fastened my dogs in their leash, and taking with me my fowling-piece, which doubtless had been the means of saving my life, I walked towards some high trees, by ascending which I could overlook the salt lick and pool.

Ascending, not without difficulty, into the topmost boughs, I directed my telescope in search of the animals, but for a long time could not make any out.

At length, however, when I had some time been admiring the glorious landscape, I caught a glimpse of a drove of pretty striped creatures, feeding in a natural clearing, which seemed to be covered by a deep green grass, that probably they were particularly fond of.

Descending cautiously from the tree, and peering about in search of more savage animals—I had seen marks which looked like the marks of lions—I made my way in the direction of the little prairie, taking care as I went to note such landmarks as might aid me in my return.

Skirting the pool above which had befallen me my never-to-be-forgotten adventure, I entered the leafy arches of the forest, and at length reached a spot where I could see the drove of beautiful creatures, which were, indeed, zebras.

After feasting my eyes for some time on their lovely forms, keeping all the time carefully concealed, I examined the prairie.

It was surrounded by such a dense mass of undergrowth, that I could not see how the zebras could ever leave it to go, as they must periodically have done, both to the salt lick and the water. Keeping within the trees, and moving slowly round, I soon, however, became aware of a beaten path through the forest, which, had I come upon it unprepared, I should have taken for one left by man.

Now I saw my way clear enough, as I thought, to the capture of one of them, but not being thoroughly prepared, determined to adjourn any action until the next day, particularly as it was getting dark.

Anxious not to miss my camp, I followed the zebra trail, walking very slowly to avoid losing my way, when suddenly my startled senses were assailed by sounds of the most horrible and painful description, resembling nothing more than the groanings of a human being who is on the point of drowning.

I stood still, my gun pointed instinctively before me, and listened.

Still the groans, sighs, and stifling sounds, were heard, but fainter and fainter every moment.

Advancing hurriedly—the darkness was almost impenetrable—I next minute stood upon the edge of the forest, and saw on the slope towards the pool a huge beast, with something in its mouth, which now moaned in a low and almost extinct voice.

The coming into the open air from the gloomy shelter of the forest was like coming from darkness to light, and I saw it was a lion carrying off at a zebra.

I subsequently became fully aware that the dying groans of this animal always resemble the faint gasps and ejaculations of a drowning man, while even their subdued neighing is of a melancholy nature.

But it formed no part of my project to attempt to rescue the unfortunate beast.

I had too much respect for the mighty monster which had captured him to attempt to interfere.

I had yet to learn how great is the dread of the lion for man. My knowledge of natural history, derived in great part from that great French romancer, Buffon, led me to believe the king of the forest a noble and daring adversary, whereas there is none of the feline race more averse to an encounter with the human species.

The fiercest pangs of hunger will not always rouse them to such a state of boldness.

The younger lions are generally pretty well provided with game; but then they will not attack a cameleopard or buffalo, except in droves.

It is when the lion is old and toothless that he prowls round villages, killing goats, women, and children.

Hunters have always remarked that "man-eaters" are very old animals, who, finding themselves weak and ill, first strive to live on mice, rats, and even grass, before they venture, in agonies of hunger, to prowl near the habitations of man.

But not being aware of this at the time I remained still, and allowed the animal to walk off with his prey.[*]

No sooner was he out of sight, than hurrying across the neck of land which divided the pool from the salt lick, I hastened to rejoin my dogs, nor did I consider myself safe until I was ensconced by a very large and roaring fire. But nothing occurred to disturb us, and when the hungry animals roused me, the sun had been up some time.

A few birds, trapped in the usual way, a couple of land tortoises, over which I had fallen the day before, served, with the eggs of the latter, for a hearty meal. Then, to the delight of Tiger and his companion, I started with them to the prairie of the zebras.

My attention was kept alive by the thoughts of the lion, but not a sign of him appeared, so that we reached the desired spot without molestation.

After fastening my dogs to a tree, my first duty was to tie a rope across the zebra trail, just about as high as the breast of the animal.

Then I let Tiger and Pet loose. They had been tied up for two days, and, as I expected, made a furious dash into the prairie.

The zebras rushed together instinctively, and then with

---

[*] As very erroneous opinions are entertained of this animal, and as our desire is to instruct as well as amuse our readers, the following, from Livingstone, will be read with interest:—"When a lion is met in the day-time—a circumstance by no means unfrequent to travellers in these parts—if preconceived notions do not lead them to expect something very 'noble' or 'majestic,' they will see merely an animal somewhat larger than the biggest dog they ever saw, and partaking very strongly of the canine features; the face is not much like the usual drawings of a lion, the nose being prolonged like a dog's; not exactly such as our painters make it, though they might learn better at the Zoological Gardens; their ideas of majesty being usually shown by making their lions' faces like old women in nightcaps. When encountered in the day-time, the lion stands a second or two gazing, then turns slowly round and walks as slowly away for a dozen paces, looking over his shoulder; then begins to trot, and, when he thinks himself out of sight, bounds off like a greyhound. By day there is not, as a rule, the smallest danger of lions, which are not molested, attacking man, nor even on a clear moonlight night."

one accord made a wild dash for their hard and beaten trail.

The cord checked them, and they passed me like the wind.

But the dogs, barking and yelling, kept up the chase; and here they come again, their heads up, their tails in the air, their eyes darting fire.

It is a magnificent sight; but I have no eyes but for one, a lovely creature.

Out into the air flies the noose of my lasso, which falls with unerring nicety over the animal's head. A sharp turn round a tree, and the zebra is sprawling, choked and suffocating, on the plain.

With a rush, I was by its side, and at once, having made fast its legs, loosened the rope.

It was time.

The poor creature's tongue was lolling out of its mouth, from the frightful jerk of the lasso. Another minute, and it would have been choked.

As I rose to my feet in triumph, I found I was not alone; a little zebra foal was standing, looking pitifully at its mother.

It was beautiful to see the elegant and almost helpless little creature looking with affectionate solicitude at its dam, while now and then its eyes were cast upon me, as if reproachfully and imploringly.

I never saw such tenderness in any eye, save that of the deer, though I was accustomed to see evidences of intense love in the animal creation; love—one's being's awaked bliss—that would not have disgraced manhood.

Securing it, and driving away the dogs, which would have made short work with it, my delight knew no bounds. I was now quite certain of having gained my object.

If I could not tame the old one, I could the young; well knowing, as I did, that when taken in time, firmness and kindness combined will conquer most animals.

The old one, as soon as it recovered its senses, bit furiously at me, so that I saw severe measures were necessary.

My dog Tiger was excessively intelligent, so that I had not much difficulty in making him understand what to do.

At a sudden signal from me he bit the zebra by the ear, when that animal began to emit the horrid sounds I have already alluded to, bringing one of the beautiful animals of the herd very near.

Doubtless it was its mate, which knew the voice of the mother of the foal.

Taking no notice, however, of this episode, I muzzled the zebra effectually, and then took off the dog.

Then, having so attached its legs together that it could just walk, I loosened the lighter cords, and allowed it to rise on its legs.

It trembled all over, as with the palsy, as I believe with rage, nor would it move when I pulled the halter, until I set the dogs on it, and made as if I would lead the foal away.

But I had a remedy for this.

The dogs were there and quite ready. Nothing delighted these animals more than to be allowed to bark and jump about, which they did at a signal from me.

Still the beast was obstinate, and stood its ground bravely for some time to my infinite chagrin.

But when it did move my pride was great. My plan was to take it to the borders of the lake, on which was my summer-house, and there tame the savage creature.

As we proceeded I began by keeping it very short of food.

When we camped at night I loosened its muzzle, after securely fastening it to a tree, and then allowed the poor little hungry foal to obtain its natural sustenance, of which it evidently was very much in need.

It was the evening of the third day when we reached the borders of the lake.

Another whole day was then occupied in cutting down trees, and clearing a small space about a dozen feet square, as a stable.

This I did, however, tolerably easy, as I left the natural supports, only requiring the addition of cross beams.

But we did not reach the lake without incident or adventure, while an event was now about to occur which, while it expelled every other thought from my mind, nearly drove me mad.

About every six months I seemed to grow reconciled to my position, when something would occur to destroy all my serenity of mind, and cast me back into the great slough of despond and despair.

What I endured on those occasions it would be painful to record.

But let me not anticipate, but record the two adventures to which I have alluded.

CHAPTER LI.

THE OSTRICH.

And down the cliff the island virgin came,
  And near the cave her quick, light footsteps drew,
While the sun smiled on her with his first flame,
  And young Aurora kissed her lips with dew,
Taking her for a sister; just the same
  Mistake you would have made on seeing the two,
Although the mortal, quite as fresh and fair,
Had all the advantage, too, of not being air.
                                        DON JUAN.

OUR daily march was sufficiently amusing. The zebra was fearfully obstinate and slow. Every now and then she would make desperate efforts to escape from her custodians; but, as her legs were so hoppled she could not kick, the dogs soon brought her to reason. They would bark, and not unfrequently bite, at her heels, in a way that must have been anything but pleasant.

My plan of keeping her all day without eating did, however, make her a little tamer; and she was so glad to get food at night, that she would even accept it from my hand. But her hunger once satisfied, she was as savage, turbulent and sullen as ever.

Still, I cared not so much since the young one was evidently disposed, from the first, to be tame and friendly.

But I would not give up, on that ground, attempting to tame the mother, as I could not afford to wait while the foal was growing.

My constant practice was to stand beside the zebra of an evening while it was eating, and stroke its neck, play with its ears, and in every way make friendly manifestations. As I did so, it seemed strange to me that an animal so very much like the common ass, only taller, and with more beautiful skin, should be so exceedingly fierce, while the other was the meekest of beasts of burden. But, then, the wild ass is as savage as any.

The zebra would glare at me from her eye, curl her lip from off her teeth, snarl, and even, despite her muzzle, try to bite.

Several times I felt inclined to use a switch rather severely, but forbore, as it might make her more inveterate against me.

I was, indeed, sorely puzzled to know how to begin, as not even the presence of her young would restrain her from flight, if I let her loose.

But it was of no use worrying my head until I had her in safe custody, so, as I have already said, I hastened on my journey as fast as her hoppled legs would allow.

It was the second morning, and our breakfast being scanty, I thought I would scour the neighbourhood in search of extra provisions, such as fruit, a nut or two, and, perhaps, a land tortoise or so. With this view I advanced towards a row of cotton trees, that indicated the presence of a small stream, and, wading through, prepared to scour the fertile grassy plain beyond.

At that instant a roar—such a one as books had told me usually came from the lion's throat—burst on my ear, and sent me crouching in the grass, while my dogs slunk behind.

It was very far less majestic than I expected, but it was certainly startling.

When, however, I became accustomed to the lion's voice, I was at a loss to explain the poetical license which has invested it with so much terror, unless, indeed, we fancy a benighted traveller hearing it for the first time, with the loud thunder roaring above, and the intensely vivid lightning bursting on him through the pitchy darkness, while rain swept down in sluicy torrents.

However this may be, not hearing the cry repeated, I crept through the low jungle, keeping my dogs down until I advanced about a hundred feet, when up jumped a whole covey of ostriches, two old ones and a young one.

It then occurred to me that I had heard the singular fact stated that though the lion's voice seems to come deeper from the chest than that of the ostrich, it is impossible, at a moderate distance, to tell one from the other.

Away darted the dogs before I could stop them, sending the whole brood rushing over the plain, on which, in the distance, I could see many other of the same birds.

Now, in ordinary instances, to pursue an ostrich on horseback is folly.

Its pace, when feeding, is from twenty to twenty-two inches; when walking, without feeding, twenty-six inches, but when startled or alarmed it takes strides of twelve or fourteen feet long; and of these it would take thirty in ten seconds.

In fact their speed is calculated by naturalists at twenty-six miles an hour, a rate beyond which nothing can ever go. *

The only means by which they are ever shot is that knowing they never swerve from a course once taken, the hunters intercept them.

But in this instance there was another thing in our favour. The ostrich, contrary to popular theory, is extremely fond of its young.

When, therefore, the callow brood, not larger in size than bantam cocks, took to their heels, the female led the way, while the cock hung behind to protect the rear.

Their evident anxiety was to save their progeny, some sixteen in number, at any cost; while mine was to capture

them, as I knew the prodigious value of such a commencement to my farm-yard.

Imagine eggs, which each give twenty-four times as much meat as a common hen's.

The dogs were with difficulty called away from the chicks, more, however, by the cunning of the cock, which, after attacking them with his heels, led them away from the brood, thus giving time, as he thought, for the mother and young to escape.

As he went, not using his speed, but making circles around, he kicked out behind; but the dogs kept out of reach, fortunately for them, as a single blow from its gigantic foot is sufficient to prostrate and even to kill hyenas, panthers, and wild dogs.

Then, thinking his trick successful, and not seeming much to notice me, he darted off in an opposite direction.

The young ones were not very easy to catch, but at length I succeeded in capturing the whole brood, which I tied two and two by the legs.

When my task was completed, to my great regret I was obliged to shoot the mother, which attacked me.

It was between seven and eight feet high, and I have no doubt weighed nearly three hundred-weight.

My dogs having started one or two other birds, I was fortunate enough to find a nest of fresh eggs. But how was all this prey to be taken to the camp? Fortunately, I always had with me a ball of twine of my own manufacture.

With this I tied the feet of the juvenile ostriches—which naturally ran very quickly—so close together, that they could only waddle, and this way I and the dogs drove them into the camp.

I was excessively proud of my capture, as I knew that they would thrive in my gazelle valley, and, by judicious clipping of their wings, and severing a particular tendon in the leg, be unable to get away.

My experience of the breakfast which I had earned did not decrease my pleasure.

I opened one end of the egg, put in salt and pepper, of which latter I had found plenty of the black sort, and then shook the whole up.

It was then placed on the hot ashes, and baked. Nor did I feel one too much, such is the appetite produced by the kind of life I led. *

I love to dwell on these remembrances of my youth, and at the risk of being called a garrulous old man, will say a little about the animal which had so fortunately come in my way. The ostrich lays its eggs in simple hollows in the sand, not more than a few inches deep. It lays about twenty.

Some contain small concretion of the matter which forms the shell, as in the egg of the common fowl, which made old naturalists speak of stones in the egg.

As the cock has many wives two often sit on one nest, taking care to have a number of eggs outside on which to feed the young brood as soon as hatched.

They soon, however, run after the old cock, who teaches them all manner of tricks to escape pursuers.

---

* In those days, locomotives had not been invented. If we are to credit the testimony of Mr. Adanson, who says he witnessed the fact in Senegal, such is the rapidity and muscular power of the ostrich, that, even with two mounted on his back, he will outstrip an English horse in speed.—Burron.

* The ostrich (which, from possessing the rudiments of a gall-bladder, and the absence of wings fit for flight, seems to form a kind of connecting link between the two great families of mammalia and aves) is an inhabitant of a large portion of Africa, but rarely extends farther east than the deserts of Arabia. Throughout the Indian Archipelago, the family of birds of which the ostrich is the leading type is represented by the cassowary; in Australia, by the emu; in the southern extremity of the western hemisphere, by the rhea; and even in Europe, though somewhat departing from the type, it has its representative in the stately bustard.

The food of the ostrich consists of pods, seeds, and the top buds and leaves of several plants.

When feeding, it is that the bushmen and others stalk them, and they must do so to a large extent, as for many years the supply of feathers has been considerable.

The male bird is of a glossy jet black with the exception of the few white feathers which form an article of trade.

It is said to live thirty years.

Its flesh when young is not unpalatable, resembling in part turkey; but that of the old bird is very tough and rank.

The ancients, however, thought it a great luxury. The shell of the egg is both ornamental and useful.

It is in some parts of Africa the only vessel the natives have for carrying water.

In a domestic state the ostrich is a quiet, dull, heavy-looking bird, but when wild it is reckless, wary, and difficult of approach.

Its sight is wonderful.

I have mentioned what it eats in a wild state. I daresay it devours many other things; but in confinement it has no discrimination, swallowing with avidity, wood, iron, spoons, knives, and other articles. One some years ago, in England, swallowed a street-door key, while another, which had been placed in a large yard, did worse.

A Muscovy duck one day brought a promising brood of ducklings into the world, and with maternal pride conducted them forth into the yard.

With solemn and measured stride up walked the ostrich, and wearing the most mild, benignant cast of face, swallowed them all one after the other, like so many oysters, regarding the indignant hissings and bristling plumage of the unfortunate mother with stoical indifference.

They collect together in troops, and will associate with the zebra, the spring-bok, and the gnoo, but never with birds.

It was with no small pride that I viewed my flock as they were driven forward that day.

The lake reached, a rude pen was easily constructed, in which they were placed, with such food as the neighbourhood afforded, and there left.

———

CHAPTER LII.

A HALT BY THE WAY.

I HAD now the elements of a farm-yard in my possession, the hope of a beast of burden, if not of a steed, and many other increasing blessings.

But a great deal had to be done before any of these things could be brought to perfection.

In the meantime a journey to my cave had become necessary, as I intended remaining at my summer-house for some time, and the puppies, ample as had been the supply of food, would by this time be half-starved.

Then there were my birds, which would grow wild, and neglect me, if I were too long away.

All things considered, then, I determined to make a rapid journey to the cave, to perform which I took with me one gun and a light load, followed by the dogs.

I cut down a good supply of grass for the zebras, while the little ostriches were supplied as well as I could.

Then away I started at a rapid pace, which I was able to keep up with ease, it being a moderately cool day.

I found that no visitors had been within my domain, but it was a sight to behold the delight of the puppies which were,

I believe, pretty nearly turning upon one another when we arrived.

A lot of dead birds in my nets and on the bird-limed branches soon satisfied them, the more easily that they had plenty of water.

The bird of paradise and the parrot were famished, and much tamer than they had ever been before.

As soon as I had put things to rights I passed right through the cave to the summit of the rocks, and there began the construction of a sledge, which was to serve my purpose.

On this I placed tools, some gourds of brandy, salt food, and everything else wanted at my summer-house, not omitting ammunition and rakes and hoes, as it was my intention to take advantage of the fertility of the soil to make my tobacco plantation.

In my solitary condition it was a necessity; but wild, it was coarse and hot. The leaves were three feet by two.

It was that peculiar kind which the natives of the interior of Africa smoke—stalks and leaves—in a hollow piece of wood.

But no one able to obtain the finer leaf would smoke it.

The sledge, which was built as lightly as might be with due regard to strength, being loaded, my next task did not promise to be so easy.

But I was agreeably disappointed.

Tiger allowed himself to be harnessed without difficulty, and Pet, when placed side by side to him, made little more resistance.

The puppies followed, yelping with delight, though I was compelled to keep them in order with my whip when they persecuted their mother too much.

The bird of paradise and parrot perched on the sledge, though as we halted frequently they often found an opportunity to feed.

It was curious to see how much more easily they found food here than on the more arid part of my island.

Nature in this rich and moist soil teemed with life; the greater quadrupeds I knew were not far off; the forest echoed with the notes of birds; while myriads of insects were supported by a luxurious vegetation.

It was now I saw for the first time the beautiful sun-bird, the elegant bee-eater, and the plantain-eater, the size of a crow, with wings of the most lovely crimson, glossed with purple.

I heard, too, with deep satisfaction, the cry of the guinea fowl as we passed the morass. I at once made up my mind to add it to my menagerie.

But just then I could not leave my caravan, or the dogs would have soon run over their traces. Indeed I was obliged to be very cautious, to assist them in all difficult places, and to take up my turn at pulling.

Every half-hour or so we halted, and then it was the birds enjoyed themselves. There were many locusts and cicadas about.

In some places, sandy spots thinly covered with grass, they appeared almost innumerable, while their chirping was deafening. They were of various sizes, kinds, and colours.

The presence of locusts alarmed me, as I knew that the fearful swarms, the horrid clouds of locusts mentioned in history as astonishing and frightening mankind at remote intervals, all took their flight from the continent near which I was. But I hoped for the best.

Nor did I like much more the termites or ants, which I found at intervals. I knew the danger, those of Africa being a numerous species, intent apparently on removing from the face of nature every animal or vegetable substance no longer necessary or useful.

Like the Destroying Angel, they walk steadily forward in the path ordained them, sparing neither magnitude or beauty, neither the living or the dead.

One species, which seems at times to have no fixed habitation, ranges about in vast armies, and being furnished with very strong jaws, can attack whatever animal impedes their progress. There is no escape but flight or a retreat to water.

I had much difficulty in avoiding those which I had continually noted, and for this purpose was compelled to unload and carry everything over a stream.

While so doing the dog started a most beautiful spring bok, of the blue antelope variety, which sprang to a height of about five feet, and cleared the stream, twelve feet wide, at a bound.

I was sorry to do so, but I could not help shooting it, food being a consideration, especially with my ravenous attendants.

Soon after, a halt was declared, the beast flayed, and a goodly meal furnished to my dogs. I myself cut off the choicest parts, and immensely enjoyed a broil.

As I sat after supper smoking a pipe with all my servants about me, I felt very much like one of the ancient patriarchs.

A fire burnt, crackled, and sparkled at my feet, my dogs slept with one eye open, a cockatoo and bird of paradise perched on a bush; while I, having made a kind of hut of my sledge and its contents, beneath the shelter of a large outspreading tree, enjoyed the luxury of a smoke.

I cannot say that I was unhappy. Certainly the hope of escape from that solitary dwelling-place was often present to my mind, but my avocations were so many and so varied, my blessings so numerous, my companions so faithful and attached, that I had scarcely time to give to that most dismal of all maladies, mental despondency.

Besides, before I could devote any time to plans for escape, it was only proper that I should provide for the present, and think also of the necessities of the future.

During the whole period of my captivity I enjoyed, with rare exceptions, excellent health, and this I owed almost wholly to early rising, and temperance in eating and drinking.

I stinted myself in nothing, and once in a way enjoyed a feast, but as a rule moderation was my law. There can be no doubt, and my experience was great, that the air of the early morn has a refreshing and soothing effect, which this pure genial breath of heaven does not possess at any other time of the day.

Besides, what beauties are not then revealed of which the sluggard never dreams! It is in the calm and silent grandeur of the morn that man is deeply impressed with the power of his Creator, and feels the sweet balm of his works.

I invariably when I slept in the open air, having retired to rest early, awoke before the sweet song of the bird rose aloft to proclaim the beauties of the coming day.

I slept soon after dark, and awoke at the first approach of the morning light, as it broke over the hills and trembled on their tops; the light clouds were skimming along the grey vault of heaven—light and feathery messengers, borne by the gentle and noiseless breeze, scarce trembling among the trees to announce the silent and magnificent approach of the orb of day.

On the edge nearest the dawn, heavy masses of grey clouds blushed deep red, and soon the whole firmament glowed with a rich golden light, which tinted with brilliant lustre the distant mountains' brow, leaving the sides and the valleys clothed in deep and misty shadows.

Then came the soft morning breeze, and the splendid rays of the sun, as it rolled away the wreathy vapours from the tall trees, touched with diamond brightness the delicious green of their elegant tops, reeking with dewy freshness.

And then outburst the mingled chorus of shrikes, quails, orioles, and rollers; while on the bough close at hand, perched the long-shafted goat-sucker* one of the most curious birds I had ever seen.

It was no bigger than a thrush, but from each wing projected a feather nearly twenty inches in length, with the shaft naked except at the tip.

But leaping to my feet, and casting from me the languor which seemed to pervade me in the presence of nature's beauties, I proceeded to provide for my necessities.

I had now a very good supply of lines and hooks, so that baiting them with strips of meat, I cast them into the water.

This done, I made my fire, cut some steaks from the springbok, threw a few grains to my birds, which, however, were busily engaged in scratching the ground and eating food, which at first I paid little attention to.

They had found some caterpillars of the beetles which live on decayed wood, which I knew to be delicious eating; also the parrot was scratching out of the ground, what turned out to be the females of a particular kind of cricket, which were full of eggs enclosed in a bag, so as to resemble the roe of a large fish. I was perfectly well aware that travellers had extolled even these as delicious eating, but I felt no inclination to dispute with my birds.

My antelope venison, with the produce of my fishing—which was excellent, several large eels rewarding my exertions—satisfied me with a drink from the stream, to which in general on my voyages I restricted myself.

This done, the word was "start;" my animals were buckled to; I took a cord, which I passed over my shoulder and pulled away, and one hour before sundown we reached the borders of the lake.

The old zebra was hungry and tolerably tame; while the young ostriches were very noisy. I had collected such food during the last hour as suited them, which I gave them freely.

When my means allowed me my usual treat to them once a day—they finding their own during the rest—was a mixture in the proportion of one pint of oats, one pint of coarse rice, half-a-gallon of chaff, and four pounds of cabbage. But I must not anticipate.

That night I reposed on the shore, but early next morning, eager to begin working at my summer-house, I prepared to undertake the journey across the lake.

My raft was no longer to be seen, so being in a hurry, I determined to construct one solely of reeds; the most original and easily-constructed of all means of water conveyance, and of which I had even made experience as a boy. I now, however, cut a lot of reeds, which grew out in the shallow part of the lake—they were the buoyant palms—just above the water, and threw in layers crosswise, until the heap appeared to me sufficient.

The raft was made.

No binding of any kind is requisite, but fresh layers of reeds must occasionally be added to the raft, as from the

---

* *Macrodipterix Africanus.* Swainson.

constant pressure at the top, the reeds get soaked, and the air contained in them displaced by water.

The greatest recommendation of this raft is its buoyancy and the ease with which it is constructed.

I made it unusually large, as I wished to take across as much as I could at once. My birds perched upon the different articles of furniture, and to the parrot and bird of paradise I added a male and female ostrich, of which I determined to make pets, despite the multitudinous stories of their ferocity and wickedness I had read.

CHAPTER LIII.

TAMING A SHREW.

I POLING, my dogs swimming round in delight, I reached the island without any accident. I drew the raft as close as I could to the shore, and landed all my goods. My island did not appear to have been visited during my absence, which encouraged me still further in my intention of establishing there my summer quarters.

The island was skirted by the celebrated cameldorn tree, which is of such slow growth as to take many hundred years to arrive at maturity.

Its grain is very close, and after being dried for years it will sink when thrown into the water.

It is harder and more durable than oak, and excellent for building. But within were trees more suitable to me, while vines, red eatable berries, and a gigantic fig-tree, promised both pleasure and utility.

I did not fix my habitation exactly in the place selected before, but patiently seeking out a spot where the trees would aid my plans, then began my labours.

In the first place the ground was cleared of decayed wood, bushes, and stones.

My first essay induced me to act with extreme caution, as on lifting a fallen trunk of a tree which was quite rotten, there issued forth a whole swarm of scorpions, which gave me a start I did not easily forget.

These animals lie dormant in the hottest weather, but when the air is damp, come forth.

No sooner does the scorpion feel himself in contact with any part of the body of a man or beast, than he lifts his tail, and with his horny sting, inflicts a wound, which, though rarely fatal, is still of a very painful character.

I at once was careful to use a rake for the future; and no sooner was the ground clear and level than I made a great fire, which, as soon as it was burnt to cinders and ashes, I spread over the whole surface of my future summer-house.

Then a number of poles were cut, which were planted at intervals between the trees, to encourage the growth of creeping plants, while others were crossed overhead, and thickly thatched with palm leaves and other branches.

Beneath this I swung my hammock, but not before, with great patience, I had made myself a ladder.

Fortunate was it that I had brought my tools ; this machine, which in my eyes was a master-piece, being absolutely necessary to my arrangement.

Without the house, indeed at some little distance, was erected the kitchen, which was simply a shed open an all sides, but roofed over.

My utensils for boiling were not efficient, though I did slowly make broth in the half of a large gourd, by means of hot ashes ; therefore my diet was chiefly restricted to roast and broiled meat, with fish and such fruits and vegetables as I could venture to make use of.

Man is never satisfied.

With all the good things that my island provided me with, with all the treasures of food that I possessed, I often found myself longing for the homely potatoe of my native isle. Still I never degraded my manhood by foolishly pining for anything, especially as I had so much occupation.

Every day I crossed over the lake to my zebras and ostriches, which were growing wonderfully quick.

Several times I approached the old zebra, with the intention of vaulting on its back, but its savage manner prevented me.

It was absolutely necessary to have a saddle, bridle, and spurs, before I could subdue his untamed nature.

On the other hand the foal was very gentle, fed from my hand freely, and soon began to prefer grass and herbs to its mother's milk.

Still it was not quite old enough to be weaned, so I determined to wait for that interesting period ere I made the final attempt.

This made me determine to transfer my ostriches to the valley of the gazelles, as the trouble of feeding them was considerably too great.

I was not sorry, too, to visit those interesting animals, in number over a dozen, and see if the valley still afforded them sufficient food.

This proved to be the case, fortunately, owing to my having burned down the large reed morass, which had dried up, and furnished excellent grass.

From another reason, I remarked that here and there places which had been arid were becoming grassy and rich in verdure.

The most fortunate part of the whole affair was this. Close to the large tree, which had been in the centre of the morass, was a fountain, or spring, which before had filtered over the plain and been lost amid the reeds.

When, however, the reeds were burned up, by a very slight and judicious turning up of a very small bank, the spring first made a pool, and then trickled away in a rivulet across the plain, the promised abode of future rich undergrowth.

An English park could not have been more delightful or more useful.

But sometimes, when in hypochondriacal moods, how I trembled lest some sudden eruption of savages should deprive me of the result of all my hard labour.

I would tremble at the faintest breath of wind—at the rustle of a leaf—at the creations of my own excited and vagrant imagination.

These lengthened journeys between my cave and the summer-house made me all the more anxious to tame some animal which should endure the fatigue of carrying me, and which might be swift in its course.

But the more I thought, and the more I worried myself, the less did any rational mode of proceeding suggest itself to my imagination.

At length, however, a very cruel and somewhat savage mode of proceeding came to my recollection, which, after considerable hesitation, I resolved to put in practice.

It required, however, all my powers of mental reasoning to bring myself to try an experiment from which my soul, under any other circumstances, would have revolted. All the way returning I turned it over until I logically came to the conclusion that what I was about to do was right.

As soon as I had placed the birds within the enclosure, and seen them apparently happy and contented in their new home, I started on my way back.

A MIDNIGHT ENCOUNTER.

No. 11.—SAILOR CRUSOE.

I was anxious to get over the severe trial which I knew awaited me.

I hurried along, with a feeling almost of anger against myself, but of serious determination.

The zebras had been left in possession of so much food that the mother was more savage than ever, which made me determined to have no further mercy.

No sooner, therefore, was I rested from my journey, than I began my preparations.

In the first place, the zebra was tied more tightly than before, and its muzzle drawn so tight that it could not breathe, except through its notrils.

Then, by means of my lasso, I again threw it to the ground.

This done, from skins, cloth, and fibre rope, I manufactured a rude kind of saddle, which, despite its kicking and other forms of resistance, I managed to pass round its body. I had seen oxen saddled to be ridden, and had witnessed a struggle on their part, but it was as nothing to the untamed ass of the desert isle.

A stick, thin but very strong, of a hard and well-seasoned wood, was then prepared; through each end of which was bored a small hole.

Then an iron ramrod, which I had ground to a point, was heated to a white heat; after which, holding on firmly to the head, I did deliberately thrust it through the animal's nostrils, so that after a moment's struggle it became, as it were, stupefied and insensible from pain.

I hastened to thrust the wooden kind of bit through the hole and then let go.

The animal, as soon as I let him free, rose humble and cowed.

Its eyes glared at me with abject terror, and when I vaulted on its back, it made not the least effort to throw me. I gave a slight touch to the wooden bit, and it reared. There was no difficulty now in guiding it. It was my servant. It went the way that I liked obediently as a well-trained horse.

I did not, however, carry my triumph too far, but satisfied myself with walking the poor animal round the neighbourhood slowly, and so as not to irritate him.

Then I led it back into its stable, washed its mouth and nose, and gave it not only a feed of its own fresh meat, but of corn and barley, to which, after some general show of repugnance, it took kindly.

Here was, indeed, a triumph, on which I gloried myself with some show of reason. I was, indeed, delighted, and looked to the day when I should gallop over the beautiful hills and vales of my desert home with pride and joy. Now no animal seemed beyond my reach, and as I lay on my couch that evening, I firmly believe I entertained serious projects for taming young elephants, and adding them to my already somewhat varied menagerie of useful beasts and pets.

CHAPTER LIV.

MY SUMMER-HOUSE.

DETERMINED to let the painful and disagreeable wound of the zebra heal before I put it on its mettle again, I once more ferried myself over to my island on the reed raft, though I began to feel dissatisfied with such a slow and unsatisfactory mode of progression, so apt is man to crave for more the more he has.

Besides, the shores of the island were lined with numerous trees which were suitable for canoes of the fashion made by the savages, and I determined to lose no time in constructing such a one as at all events would suit the navigation of that small lake.

But what was my surprise on reaching my summer-house to find my parrot, bird of paradise, and two little ostriches, crouched in a corner, while the puppies were barking away furiously at some animal which had evidently frightened the birds.

With a bark and a howl, the dog and she-wolf darted away.

The animal, whatever it was, had flown up a tree, however, and before they could interfere was out of sight.

This did not suit my view of things, as I had no wish to have my bower haunted by animals inimical to my feathered pets, as now they were tame and friendly it would be exceedingly difficult to replace them.

But what could I do with a beast which clambered so quickly into a tree, and which none of my guardians could follow?

The day following was tolerably cool, so that having now the advantage of tools and a ladder, I proceeded to make certain additions to my hut which were much wanted. One of these was an exceedingly pleasing one for myself and animals.

About fifteen yards from the place where I had fixed my abode, I noticed a little hillock on which the grass grew unusually luxuriant, on which the dead leaves lay damp and thick.

It is true that the shadow of tall and bushy trees made pleasant shelter in that spot, but this did not account for the extreme dampness of the soil.

My fancy being excited, I kneeled down and cautiously removed the leaves, then the soft and half mucky soil, until I came to a mixture of blue clay and gravel, through which I poked a stick.

At first there came bubbling up a quantity of silt puddled with water, then a clayey coloured mixture, and lastly a tiny stream of sparkling fluid, that was indeed pleasant and refreshing to the mouth.

I at once set to work to improve this discovery.

In the first place a depth of soil was removed sufficient to take in a tortoiseshell, over which, to keep away animals, I made a kind of cage of bent wicker, while below a ruder trough was scooped out for the use of the beasts, which always afterwards preferred it to the water of the lake, as being cooler and more refreshing. I did so myself as a drink, but the other was best for cooking purposes.

The discovery of a rich pure clay made me eager to try my hand at the potter's art; but I must confess that here I was at fault, though I had a rude, general notion, as to which was the way to proceed.

I would have given much to have made even the rudest attempt at an earthen pot, being always particularly fond of broth, stews, and boiled meat, which I could but very seldom enjoy.

Then I made a kind of hedge round my summer-house, so as in my absence to enclose my birds, and render them less liable to an attack from small but destructive animals.

Towards evening, I was standing motionless, contemplating some piece of work which occupied my thoughts, and speculating how it might be improved, when another commotion among my pets attracted my attention.

Casting my eye quickly in that direction, I at first could not comprehend the strange disturbance.

The birds crowded together once more, but this time without any defence, as the dogs had run away probably in search of game.

I gazed around anxiously, and then saw on the bough of a tree a small but handsome furred animal, approaching with a slow and cautious step, its eyes all the time fixed on the ground, where cowered its prey.

I knew it at once, and for a dangerous and greedy animal, which could not be too soon destroyed. I fired, therefore, and down it fell in the agonies of death.

It was the caracal (*Felis caracal*), or wild cat; perhaps as beautiful an animal as any in creation; but in its savage state, as cruel and mischievous as it is sometimes pleasing and faithful as a domestic.

But I was not at all anxious to tame one, being quite satisfied with the attendants I had already.

Its fur, however, made me an excellent cap, while that of the hyena formed a splendid coat.

And thus apparelled it was, that four days after I mounted my zebra, and gave her the reins.

No sooner was she out in the open air, than she stood stock still.

The wound in its nose was nearly healed, and at first it did not seem to heed it.

I had passed thongs through the holes, and held it firm. Then I cut the beast a severe lash over the ears, dug my knees into her ribs, and hauled on the rude bridle.

Had my father not have taught me how to ride like a centaur, I should have rued the day.

Away, like an arrow from a bow, sped the zebra, taking no more account of my weight than of a feather; away—over hills, through plains, underneath trees, until I was obliged to bow down to avoid the fate of Absolom.

Then she darted to the right, to the left, over arid plains, into streams of water, while all this time, instead of restraining her, I let her go.

Gradually, however, as her wind became less, I cautiously caught up the leather bridle in my left hand, clutched the mane with my right, pressed my knees firm, and stooping, caught her ear in my mouth, and bit it sharply.

Instantly the zebra stood stock still, as if utterly astonished.

Then she uttered the old moaning cry which once before had startled me.

I let the ear go, and then tried the effect of the bridle. The beast was at once as quiet as a lamb.

From that moment the animal was completely under my control.

I led her into her stable, gave her some fresh grass, washed her mouth and legs, and then left her, conquered, subdued, mastered,—another specimen of the power of man over the inferior animals.

I was glad myself about midday to return to my summerhouse, the economy of which was now tolerably complete.

My hammock, lined with fresh Spanish moss and grass, which I renewed every morning, served me as a bed at night and a sofa by day.

Close at hand was a shelf, on which rested my pipe, my tobacco gourd, and my flint and steel; again within reach was a large calabash full of water; beside this was a bench and a rough table, such as I had seen in front of road-side inns; then above this were two perches for my birds; when they were not foraging after locust, larvæ, or ordinary insects, they would perch themselves and feed from my hands.

At my feet were my dogs, anxiously looking up in my face for a chance morsel or a bone, which I verily believe these animals like better than a hearty meal in the ordinary way;

while, lord and monarch of all I surveyed, I was, on these occasions, peculiarly happy.

It must have been half-past twelve—I knew midday by the sun—or, may be, a quarter to one.

My violent journey had fatigued me, but it had also given me an appetite, and I had thoroughly enjoyed a broil of a sort of wild turkey my vigilance had trapped, and of fish from the abundant stores of the lake. I had, by way of a treat, made myself a glass of brandy-and-water, which, when used temperately and moderately, is indeed a luxury.

Then, like any other lord of the creation, having loaded my pipe, I laid me down in my hammock to smoke, and as I smoked, lo and behold I had a dream !

At least, such was my belief.

The pipe, acting on me with its usual narcotic power, had sent me off into a short doze, from which I seemed to awake by the simple fact of letting it fall.

I turned in my hammock and gazed around.

I was in my bower, for there were my dogs at my feet, while I could hear the call of my merry cockatoo, and saw the bird of paradise asking eagerly for her caress.

Nature itself seemed in a doze, for not a blade of grass shook, not a branch moved, not a sound could be heard, when a light footfall fell upon my ear.

I sat up in my hammock, and then, persuaded still more that I dreamt, passed my hands over my eyes, and then looked again.

It was gone !

What ?

The Indian girl—that vision of beauty which once before had so gratified me, only to make my loneliness more lonely, my sense of the loss of human society more keen—had flitted before my eyes in the waving bushes that surrounded the summer-house.

It was the same face, the same features, the same expression, even the same dress.

And yet if it were real, why had not my dogs barked ?

But surely I could not be the victim of an hallucination, nor did it seem reasonable for a sane man to be sitting up in a hammock and asking himself, *is it a dreem ?*

CHAPTER LV.

THE TRAIL.

A wif is Goddes yefte verally ;
All other manner yeftes hardely,
As londes, rentes, pasture, or commune,
Or mebles, all ben yaftes of Fortune,
That passen as a shadow on the wall ;
But drede thou not if plainly speke I shall ;
A wif wol last and in thin hous endure
Wel lenger than thee list—paraventure.
A wif ? A ! Seinte Marie, benedicite !
How might a man have any adversite
That hath a wif !—CHAUCER.

LEAPING from my hammock, and passing my feet quickly into my rude moccasins—my shoes were all worn out, and how I made moccasins will be presently seen—I darted into the bush, followed by my dogs, but not a trace of anyone or anything could I see.

I stooped to examine the soil, in the hope that there would be some sign of footsteps, of a trail, which I might follow.

But there was nothing to guide me, and strangely enough, my dogs did not bark, or run up in the way these animals do when something strange has passed that way. They roamed about in their usual frisky manner, but not in any particular direction.

But my eyes could not have deceived me. It is true, I had been asleep, I had dozed, at all events; but then I had sat up, I had heard the step on the cracking wood, and I had seen that face, which, since I first gazed on it, had never faded from my memory; the one joyful and painful memory of the past, since I had established myself upon the island.

But I would not give up the idea that somebody had been there, so I rushed towards the beach—fool that I was, it was what I should have done before—and there, on the sandy soil which covered my landing-place, I saw the print of a naked foot.

A small, pretty, feminine naked foot.

I thought I should have gone mad with vexation, annoyance, and a kind of savage despair.

Once before I had found a companion, secured a friend, as I thought, and had lost her.

Again, I was certain of it, the same person had come within my reach, and I had allowed her to escape.

But how had she returned to the island, and why? This was a question which bothered my brain for some time, during which I was deciding on my course of action.

It flashed through my mind that the second apparition of the Indian girl had something to do with the fire on the distant island.

My responding signal had been seen, and she, knowing of my presence, had come to spy out the nakedness of the land.

And yet she was not unfriendly; but still, if not, why had she been so anxious to make her escape?

All this time I had been making my preparations. It was my fixed determination not to allow her to leave the island again without, at least, an interview.

Now, my dogs would, if they accompanied me, materially prevent any approach to her by their barking and playing.

Taking my best gun, loaded with heavy slugs and one ball —in case of savage comrades of hers—putting my pistols and knife in my belt, providing myself with brandy, some cakes, and my telescope, I hastily repaired my raft, and motioning to the dogs to stay where they were, put off on my extraordinary chase.

I had entered with enthusiasm on many an adventure, but this was that which filled me with the most intense desire and hope of success.

Companions I had in plenty, all that I needed now I had to my hand; but what was this in comparison with the hope of enjoying again the society of my own race, of gazing on the human face divine, which, except reflected in a pool, I had not seen for such a length of time?

I determined to be wary and cautious.

I would reflect on all I had heard of the ingenuity of savage races, which are said to follow up the track of men and animals with such surprising ingenuity and patience.

But how could a tyro like myself, how could one who had no practice or experience, hope to imitate the natural born gift—improved by daily study—of the Redskin and other savages?

Besides, could I be a match in endurance for men who will go days without food or water, drawing their belts tighter every day, or who can, at a pinch, subsist on anything, from grass, seed, nuts, roots, grasshoppers, lizards, and rattlesnakes, to antelopes, elk, bear, and buffalo?

Still, I determined to try.

Impelling my raft to my usual landing-place I soon reached the other side, and peered about once more, the more eagerly that I at once distinguished on the water a small raft of the same material as my own, which had been cast adrift, and was floating in the current on the right side of my island towards the fall.

My emotions now were beyond control.

There could be no reasonable doubt now. But having determined to follow the trail, and on foot, I peered about, and at once discovered the spot where my dear fugitive had landed.

Again I saw the mark of two small naked feet, for quite four or five steps, when the party had halted, seated herself and put on—what! have my senses left me, that I fancy such things?—a manufactured shoe, the mark of which, with its high heel and elegant foot, is clear upon the sand.

This was too much for me, and I was about to rush blindly forward, when again the reflection came to my mind, that in this way I should lose the trail.

Determined to put a check on my native impulses, I cautiously examined the tracks, and soon found that my stable had been visited.

There were footmarks all round it; and more than that, a number of fresh branches of trees loved by the zebra had been thrown in.

Everything seemed friendly and kind. Why, then, fly from me with such pertinacity? However, this could only be cleared up by capture, so I soon found myself following the track.

It was easy enough to do, as the high-heeled shoe, or rather, boot, left marks even on the grass.

But it was slow work. Every now and then the track diverged, or the ground was bare and hard, or I accidently missed a sign.

But still, if I did go back several times, I never lost it.

One thing I soon discovered. It was in the direction of the sea—in the direction of the distant island.

While my heart fell within me at the prospect of losing her again, I was still more distraught and worried to find a motive for what appeared to me strange and inconsistent conduct.

It was quite clear that she had escaped from her former savage, inhuman, and cannibal captors; but how or why had she returned to my island, and having returned, why had she fled again so swiftly, so eagerly?

With all the ingenuity of my mind, and it had been pretty well exercised, I did not come anywhere near the truth. Indeed, simple as it was, the bare thought of it to me would have been incredible, absurd beyond all reasonable belief.

And yet I, who had been so miraculously saved, who had found bread and manna in the wilderness, should have been surprised, been astonished, at nothing.

When I became firmly convinced that she was taking her way as quickly as possible towards the sea, I used far less caution in my proceedings.

But still, it was necessary not to lose the trail, that involving a return journey. I used, however, one precaution, that of barking the trees I passed, so as to be sure to find the return track.

But soon there was no further caution required. The arid rocks of the coast lay before me, and the ground was too hard to leave any trail.

She might have taken to the right or to the left; but it was more likely that, after keeping so long in this direction, she had sought the water's edge, than have entered the thicket to the right, or the gloomy forest to the left.

With considerable hope still of overtaking her, I took a clump of bushes, shaded by a live oak, for guide, and made straight for the cliffs.

They were soon gained. I looked wildly down upon the shore—nothing was to be seen.

All this seemed to me so much like magic that I knew not what to think.

There was one thing, however, to be said, she had many hours' start of me, as, following the trail so minutely I had been six hours on my way, and it was nearly the dusk of evening.

I put my gun down, and laying myself flat upon the cliff's edge, drew forth my telescope, with which I swept the whole range of vision—nothing, nothing, nothing!

Night was now rapidly falling. In a few minutes it would be dark.

The position was by no means an agreeable one; so far from home, so utterly disappointed, so weary and desolate.

To add to the gloominess of my solitude, as the day cease I could hear the occasional " qua !" of the night heron which made the succeeding hush more dreary, during which even the falling of leaves and rustling of insects upon dry grass was hailed as a relief to the oppressive silence.

I was overwhelmed with grief, and never felt in that savage wilderness how inexpressibly solemn was utter silence combined with the deprivation of light.

CHAPTER LVI.

A MIDNIGHT ENCOUNTER.

THEN suddenly I thought I heard the purr and breathing of some animal close behind me. I wheeled slowly round, and could see nothing.

Next instant I became aware, as the moon burst forth in all its rich beauty, that but a few yards distant from me was a huge lion.

Mechanically I felt for my gun. No sooner did my hand move than a low and fearful growl warned me to be cautious.

The beast, which was perhaps the largest I ever saw, impressed me at the moment with the feeling that it was a grand and imposing sight to gaze upon the king of animals in his native wilds, especially when he assumes an attitude of surprise or defiance.

I had yet to learn how little is his inclination to cope with civilized man.

But on this occasion, though my imagination was in a heated and excited state, I considered it best to act with extreme caution.

When wounded they will often spring furiously at their assailant, and then, in most cases, woe betide him, as their muscular strength is very great.

Suddenly I saw the animal turn slowly round and gaze in a direction different to mine; and following the direction of his eyes I saw a troop of some kind of deer with short horns, passing over the plain below at no great distance.

So intent was my gaze for a moment that I forgot the lion, but suddenly there was a low stifled growl, and then the faint cry as of some dying animal.

Then, again, all was silent and still.

I strained my eyes in vain, a cloud having passed over the moon, to catch sight of what was going on, but I could hear the crunching of the victim's bones.

I held my breath in fearful suspense, not knowing when I might be attacked, or whence. But for some time I made nothing out, and, weary and exhausted, allowed myself to dose off a little, imagining the beast would be satisfied with his prey.

But I have no doubt my sleep, under the circumstances, was a half waking, for I never seemed to lose entire consciousness. This is carried to a great extent in the hunter, who has much of night watching, and to this remarkable faculty he often owes the preservation of his life.

Be this as it may, something on this occasion seemed to tell me that I was in danger, and I moved uneasily in my sleep, gradually, but surely waking to consciousness.

Then, as my senses came to me, scattered and confused from the events of the day, I heard close to my face, though the darkness was so great I could see nothing, the slow breathing of some large animal, followed by what appeared to me the good-humoured purring of a great cat.

But I knew it was a lion.

He could not have been more than two yards from me, if so much; indeed, he appeared to be actually stooping over me. For a moment my senses were stupefied. I gave myself up for dead, and, indeed, there can be no doubt that few men ever had more serious cause for dread than I had on this occasion. I knew not what to do. My first impulse was to rise and fly, but this would, in all probability, have proved fatal, so I determined to get possession of my gun, which was lying at full cock close to my hand somewhere.

But I could not remember exactly; so slowly, and with a fearful sinking of the heart, accompanied by a humble prayer, I began to raise myself to a sitting posture.

Naturally I endeavoured to attract the animal as little as possible, so made no perceptible noise. But its hearing was terribly keen, for, faint as was the sound, it was heard by the savage beast, which gave a growl which I could not mistake.

It appeared to me to be about to spring, though for half a minute I could not see it. Then, indeed, I made out a dark lump, like a rock, and at once, after commending my soul to God, pulled the trigger. I never shall forget the double effect of the reverberating echoes of the report and the roars of the wild and savage beast, which was however in the agonies of death. His fearful growls, however, as he rolled and tore up the grass and stones, induced me to decamp to a distance; nor did I sleep much that night.

When morning broke, I found the animal to be a very large one, but quite dead. At any other time I would have skinned him, but my thoughts were now bent other ways. I knew not, however, what to do. Had she escaped by the sea, or was she still concealed on the island ? I determined to satisfy myself on this point, at any cost, so took to the right of my night encampment, and made towards the woods. No sooner had I descended from the rocks, than I came upon a plain somewhat like a meadow, though in places it was swampy as a morass, and here I made the looked-for aid, in part, most valuable discovery.

I stood still in perfect awe and trembling, for there, before my face, were the steps of the flying girl turned clearly from the sea, and there, aside and around, were the great splay naked feet of other savages in hot pursuit.

Either she was hiding from the fierce blacks whom I had seen on a former occasion, or she was once more their unfortunate prisoner.

My rage and indignation knew no bounds, for, though I knew nothing of the girl, I felt convinced her intentions were kindly towards me, while, could I have succeeded in calming my apprehension, what a helpmate she would have been to me in my solitude.

But I was well armed; the savages had only bows and spears; and, mad as the idea was, I did resolve to follow up and rescue her.

Then I thought of returning to my home, and fetching the zebra, but the reflection that they might in this way get off the island before I got up with them, determined me to risk everything and start at once.

The trail was now easy enough to follow, and I had not tracked it many hundred yards, when it became clearly apparent that the girl was a prisoner.

She had tripped, fallen, and been instantly captured by the savages.

I then remarked that they made straight for the forest, not turning towards the sea, as I had expected.

This made me hopeful that they were still on the island.

It was of course very difficult to follow them beneath the foliage of an African forest, but with courage and perseverance one can do anything.

My solitary residence on the island had sharpened my wits, so that many things were easy to me which in a state of civilization would have been impossible.

I saw that they entered the forest where the trees were very lofty and the undergrowth scanty and thin, so that, moving as they did in a scattered way, nothing was easier than to follow their track.

The girl walked in the middle, guarded by at least a dozen, so that there could be no chance of escape.

Poor thing, I thought to myself, and perhaps never did man more sincerely pity another human being than did I this girl—so true it is that we are affected most deeply where our own interests and affections are concerned.

About two miles farther there was a very beautiful spot, which, however, I had avoided as being too much frequented by wild beasts.

It was an open glade, with a fountain or pool in the middle at which the animals came to drink.

Here the savages had slept, and here the cruel monsters had inflicted on that vision of beauty and of love the most abominable torture.

They had made a fire for themselves, which is never unwelcome at night in any country, as keeping off both damp and vermin, while at some little distance they had bound the Indian girl to a tree, as I could see by the withes, cut with some sharp instrument, on their departure.

But this proved that they were not far off.

I drank at the fountain, I ate some fruit and berries, and then once more began my pursuit.

Their straggling footsteps were easily followed for a short time, when they suddenly became invisible.

I had reached a chain of small stony hills, on which nothing was visible but a wretched stunted vegetation, that scarcely left a mark.

I looked to the right, to the left, on all sides, but could not discover a sign.

Then my reasoning faculties were brought to bear, as I judged it most likely that they would follow in the direction they had already been going, and in which I feared the great continent lay.

I accordingly mounted to the summit of the hills, and looked down upon the opposite side.

I was now somewhat weary and very much in want of food, my breakfast having been but scanty, but could make out nothing that would serve my purpose until I descended

towards the level country, which was very beautiful. It was a mixture of wood and prairie; thickets, clumps, and small woods being scattered over an extensive plain, which rose and fell in waves as high as the great billows of the ocean.

But the plain had other sources of interest.

Taking out my telescope to scan its surface in search of the fugitives, I saw here and there the huge heads of elephants, feeding, while in other parts were groups of graceful giraffes that cropped the lofty boughs of trees in peace and quietness.

Then I saw a disturbance amongst the animals, both elephants and giraffes; and, as I knew that the lion does not hunt in the day, it flashed across my mind that the savages were again hunting, and that the search for ivory and skins was the proximate cause of their presence on my island.

But if their minds were given to the chase, the prisoner would in all probability be left under a small guard, and in this way might, perhaps, fall into the powers of a gentler and kindlier taskmaster.

Taking a careful observation of the direction in which I believed the savages were hunting, I descended with all due caution towards the plain.

As was to be expected, when the ground became soft once more, the track of the savages became clear; though now, as if they expected to start game, they kept close together, in a double kind of Indian file.

At length I came in sight of the whole party, or at least a great many of them, as nowhere could I see the girl. The men were engaged in a way that was incomprehensible to me, though afterwards it was clear enough.

The whole plain was dotted with elephants quietly feeding, and, as usual with these great animals, though they stray great distances in search of food, had evidently spent some time in cropping the herbage.

Round the plain, which was scattered with clumps of trees and bushes, were very tall trees, from which the savages were tearing down rough, strong, climbing plants, or rather vines.

Others below, were twining these together into a sort of strong fence.

It was quite clear that this obstruction was not sufficient to hold the elephant, but it might very likely check him in his flight, and entangle him in the meshes till the hunters had time to kill him.

This done, a number of the savages, and, to my horror, they were altogether over a hundred, made a large circuit, and soon after, making a horrid sound of blowing horns, and yells more maniacal than human, drove many of the herd in the desired direction.

I could see, by means of my telescope, the dusky bodies of the savages crawling at full length on the ground, just like snakes, and quite as swiftly.

Away sped several of the huge animals, and rushing forward with headlong speed, were soon brought up in the tangle of wild vines.

Then enraged, and even terrified, they began to tear everything with their trunks and feet, but the tough vines and other creeping plants gave way at every blow, and the more they laboured the more they were held.

Then came up the hunters, some staying on the ground, others climbing trees, and by swift discharges of their arrows and spears, soon finished the giant beast, amid loud cries and yells.

The hunters were all very cautious, approaching the

elephant from behind, or climbing into the loftier branches.

As soon as the savage hunters were satisfied, they began some to cut off the feet, particularly choosing the hind feet, while others were engaged in getting out the ivory.

As soon as this horrid scene of butchery was over they moved away, leaving all they could not carry a prey for the cowardly jackalls, prowling hyenas, and devouring termite ants.

I followed them, keeping carefully in the background until I reached their halting place.

It was on a gentle slope beneath certain trees where some rude huts had been erected by a small party of youths, but nowhere could I see the Indian girl. Probably she was within the huts.

Now began one of those scenes of actual gorging which appear to be the delight of the savage, whether it be the Esquimaux, devouring thirty pounds of blubber, the Nubian eating a whole sheep, or the Red Indian swallowing all that is set before him.*

The feet of the elephant being the choice part, were first, however, prepared quite in an epicurean manner.

Holes were dug in the earth and filled with blazing fires; as soon as the wood was quite charred, the feet were placed in their extempore ovens, and other fires were made over them.

Before these long strips of elephant meat were warmed, nothing more, and then were consumed.

And thus the day wore away with them and with me.

CHAPTER LVII.

THE CAMP.

I WAS hungry, sick, and hopeless. What could I do against such a band, and yet it never occurred to my mind to depart.

There was a chain which linked me forcibly to the spot. I hid myself, therefore, in the bushes at no great distance from the pool, whence the hunters took their water, which necessarily they consumed in great abundance. I felt no fear.

I would have faced them for the remotest chance of saving that girl, but how to commence I knew not.

Gradually night fell, very clear and chilly for that part of the country. The savages had made huge fires, round which they had been carousing. It seemed to me some liquor had been added to their other articles of luxury.

Seeing that they were so engaged as not to notice me, I crept nearer.

They had made a huge fire now in the centre of the camp, and were busy digging up the ground for the baked feet.

They certainly smelt very delicious, and in my hungry state, it was a great wonder that I did not crawl in and try and take my share.

Suddenly, however, my attention became wrapped on something else. Gazing across the group, my eyes presently were able to penetrate the gloom, and I saw, seated within a small pent-house like hut, the Indian girl, gazing mournfully at the scene.

Her feet and arms were securely bound, so that she could not move at all from the half-reclining posture which she had assumed.

My blood boiled with indignation, that one so beautiful and different from these painted savages, should be thus severely used, and I began to devise the wildest and most absurd plan for her escape.

However, before I did anything rash, I saw the over-fed savages gradually lying down with their heads to the fire, to sleep off the stupefying effect of the feast.

At the same time the odour of elephant meat again assailed my nostrils, and I felt how absolutely necessary to enable me to enter upon my arduous undertaking was the refreshing influence of food.

I crawled towards a spot where I perceived a whole elephant's foot placed on one side, probably in reserve for the morning's meal, and after assuring myself of the savages near it being fast asleep, cut off some portions and devoured them greedily.

It was, without exception, the toughest and most disagreeable meat I had ever tasted. It is impossible to describe or explain its taste, because there is no other flesh which in any way tastes like it. It seemed to be one mass of muscular fibre or gristle.

It was not that it was exactly disagreeable or unpleasant in flavour, but it seemed, no matter what amount of cooking it endured, to be still tough and hard.

But it seemed to renew my energies, and I now determined to effect my great purpose. I had some rum with me, of which I drank rather freely, and then crawling away made a large circuit in the direction of the hut occupied by the Indian girl.

It was now a starlight night, the moon having not yet risen; but beneath the arches of the forest the light was very sombre, while every now and then voices disturbed me.

It was the night life of the woods.

Now and then the crackling of twigs, and an eloquent grunt, told of some perambulating pig; then a whole herd of gazelles, heedless of my presence, swept by chased by wolves; then came the call of the grey partridge to its mate; these birds sleeping always side by side on one particular branch of a tree, the first home calling incessantly until the other arrives; then might be distinguished the gambols of monkeys in the trees; and then I stood erect, beside the hut, in view of the whole camp.

As a rule, these savages lie about their fires nearly all night, smoking and telling stories; but the unusual quantity of animal food had deadened their perceptions, so that they slept soundly.

Then I peered into the hut.

She was awake. Placing my finger on my lips I came in front of her, and raised my other hand warningly. She uttered a shrill but pleasant cry, and again I had vanished into the darkness.

My precaution was wise, for several heads were lazily lifted off the ground, and a-dozen pair of eyes peered into the skirts of the camp.

Then, as if satisfied that it was but the cry of some animal, they curled themselves up, and again gave unmistakeable evidence of slumber.

This time I approached the hut gently, and whispered low a gentle hush.

Then I drew my knife, and cut her bonds, after which, seeing that the ligatures had hurt her, I lifted her in my

----

* There is a great deal to be said about this matter in the way of extenuation. An open-air life has marvellous effect on the appetite. When the editor was in the war between Texas and Mexico, officers and men had ten pounds of meat served out to them. Most ate it. Vegetables and bread, however, were rare articles.—EDITOR.

arms and carried her unresisting form to a tree, where I had left my gun.

As soon as I had deposited her on the ground, my next duty was to chafe her wrists and ancles, during which operation she looked at me with a tender and grateful glance which went to my heart.

As soon as she seemed able to move I made signs to her to rise and fly, which she did nothing loth. Clutching my gun with calm determination I led the way, which was in the direction of my own residence.

CHAPTER LVIII.

THE FLIGHT.

OF course we did not speak. We neither understood a word of the other's language; at least, I never thought of trying, but I held her hand in mine, and saw that she was pleased at my attention.

Never did man feel more valiant or more timorous. My determination was great to fight the whole tribe, while great dread was on my soul, lest I should lose that which would make life at least endurable in that desolate place.

When I was cast away, female society was dear to me in the extreme, but it never entered my mind to believe that the absence of it would be felt by any one so acutely as it was by me.

The longing was irrepressible, and now that I found such a companion, my life appeared to have become more valuable.

We moved for a considerable period at a rapid pace, until, to my great surprise, I found we must have turned the wrong way, as the distant boom of the surf could be distinctly heard.

Then the sky, before so clear and bright, became suddenly overcast. It was clear that we were about to have a storm, if not a tornado.

Looking quickly round, a clump of thick vines falling from a boabab tree, seemed to promise ample shelter, and beneath this we hastily crept.

It was a very dangerous thing to do, as it thundered and lightened violently soon after and rained as it only can rain in the tropics.

But I thought not of danger.

My new-found companion was by my side, and, wholly occupied by her, the danger did not alarm me. Every now and then, as the lightning was more than usually vivid, I saw her bright little eyes fixed upon me with a curious expression—half wonder, half doubt.

But, by signs and gentle caresses, I endeavoured to reassure her; and when the storm was over, which it was in less than an hour, she was sleeping soundly, with her head upon my shoulder, and my arm supporting her.

As soon as it was thoroughly light, she awoke and looked round timidly, while a rosy hue burst forth upon her cheek. She then hastily rose, and listened.

After a moment, she lay lay down with her ear to the ground, and making signs to me, jumped up and fled.

The savages were clearly on our track.

We were now crossing a little prairie, about a mile long by half a mile wide, quite clear, and covered by luxuriant grass, the abode of snakes, no doubt.

But no thought of the beasts or reptiles of the field moved us, as we made for the skirts of trees.

Passing through these, we soon saw that we were close to a somewhat remarkable river.

It had no banks, but the mangroves grew down into the water, while for a hundred feet on each side was a huge unhealthy and unpleasant swamp, the odour from which was exceedingly bad.

But there was no time for hesitation. The girl made signs that the savages were quickly coming up, and it was not for me to dispute her experience. With an elasticity of step, which was marvellous for one so frail and young, she leaped on to some of the huge stumps of trees, and darted from root to root with a light and even bound I could scarcely imitate.

She was guide now.

Every two minutes she paused, listened again, and then, if she noticed a dead leaf had been trod on, or that our feet had made a mark on the decayed wood, paused to efface it. Very soon we were close to the river, into the turbid and muddy water of which she leaped unhesitatingly.

I followed, wading a little above my knees, and hurrying so rapidly, that I scarcely understood her motive.

It was to turn a bend in the river before the savages came up.

The whole shore, several mud islands, and the waters, were alive with birds.

Sometimes a flock of pelicans swam by, giving us a wide berth, while at others, a long string of flamingoes stretched along the muddy shore, looking like a line of fire in the morning sun.

There were herons, too, and cranes and gulls.

But this occupied us little, as I had eyes only for the graceful form of my Indian girl, while she was intent on her duties as a leader.

Down the stream we moved, turning back every moment to look over our shoulders, in fear of pursuit.

For some time we saw nothing of the *Fans*, for such, I afterwards found, was the name of the tribe.

Then, however, the girl clutched me by the arm just as a shrill cry of triumph warned me that we were discovered.

Quick as thought, she drew me beneath the roots of a mangrove up to our waists in slimy mud.

Then she took a log that was floating on the water, but attached to the roots by some creeping plants, which, having severed, she thrust it out into the stream.

For a moment I did not understand her meaning, but when I saw that her quick eye had noticed a branch dipping in the water, that drew up precisely the same mud and bubbles that our steps did, I comprehended the keen wit of the Indian girl.

Ten minutes passed, during which we very cautiously drew ourselves back in the swamp, the abode of alligators and snakes, until we were in a dark and noisome recess, perfectly pestilential in its odours.

But to me it was delightful, as in my enthusiasm at her ready wit, I clasped her in my arms, and even received from the dear and affectionate creature a most expressive kiss.

But this was no time for ecstacies, as we could now hear the guttural cries of the *cannibals* at no great distance.

Then we saw a body of them pass.

They had secured a huge log on which some twenty of them sat astride, using sticks for paddles.

About four guided the clumsy construction, which, however, moved rapidly enough with the tide, while the rest, armed with spears, bows, and war-hatchets—terrible weapons—

ESCAPE FROM THE FAN VILLAGE.

No. 12.—SAILOR CRUSOE.

cered about in search of the fugitive, or rather fugitives, for, doubtless, the footmarks had betrayed my presence.

Our hole, however, sheltered us, and I was about to step out and look after them, when the girl checked me.

She knew the cunning of these ferocious savages (who cook and eat human flesh without compunction) better than I did.

The raft was only a blind, for soon there appeared several scattered savages peering at both shores, sounding the roofed and arched roots of the mangroves with their lances, and examining every possible hiding-place with keen and savage scrutiny.

I made ready.

My double-barrelled gun was cocked, my pistols were in my belt out of the reach of the water, and with these I felt a match for a half-a-dozen.

They all carried spears, huge shields of buffalo hide, and tomahawks, slung in their belts about the extent of their garb.

They passed in dozens close to us, but the mangrove root on the side of the water appeared too low, probably, for the entrance to a hiding-place.

Then there was a great stillness in the air, and I thought all was over.

Still I paused, and allowed some minutes to elapse ere venturing to sally forth.

It appeared, then, well that I did so, for next instant I saw at some distance from the opening a very tall and grizzled-looking old warrior, who was slowly and carefully examining every faintest sign by which to trace us.

Suddenly I saw an infernal grin on his face as he looked at our opening, towards which he next instant made his way.

By the way that he poised his spear it was clear he meant mischief, so taking deliberate aim, I fired.

I felt my companion shudder intensely—in her fright she had clung to me—but when the smoke cleared away the Fan warrior was nowhere to be seen.

Drawing my half-fainting companion into the open air, I retreated through the swamp until we stood once more on dry land.

I could see some high rocks in the distance, and towards this directed my way, after loading my gun in presence of the girl, who, however, to my utter amazement, appeared quite familiar with the process.

Then on we started in the direction of some huge boulders on an elevated *plateau*, some of them thirty or forty feet high, by one hundred long.

Above there were some steep rocks, from which depended the India-rubber vine, from which—and not from a tree—the caoutchouc of commerce is obtained in Africa.

It is a vine of immense length, with singularly few leaves, and those only at the end.

These leaves are broad, dark-green, and lance-shaped.

The bark is rough, and of a brownish hue, while a large vine is often five inches in diameter at the base.

Towards this part of the rocks I made, and having reached their foot, made signs to Pablina—such was the girl's name—that I would ascend.

She looked wistfully up, and shook her head.

Then I recollected my lasso, which I showed her, and then hurriedly began to climb.

The vines were so thickly intertwined, that it was no easy task.

I soon, however, found myself at the summit.

The rock was quite perpendicular, and I was concealed in a thicket of low prickly trees.

To one of these I fastened my long lasso, and, lying flat on my face, proceeded to cast it down to where the girl stood.

Then I heard a shriek which rang to the very welkin, followed by an angry and savage cry like nothing I had ever heard before.

I bent over just in time to behold Pablina caught in the arms of a huge being whose features I could not distinguish.

Then, having secured its prize, it fled precipitately.

The girl was in the hands of the terrible and ferocious being whom some have dared to compare with man.

She had been carried off by a gorilla.

I descended from my eminence in utter horror of spirit, and, just as I alighted on the ground below, saw some twenty of the Fan savages debouch upon the plain.

They, too, had seen the rapt, and instantly gave chase.

With a weary, almost a broken heart, I followed.

CHAPTER LIX.

A FEARFUL SCENE.

Her feet beneath her petticoat,
Like little mice, stole in and out
    As if they feared the light;
But oh! she dances such a way,
No sun upon an Easter day
    Is half so fine a sight.
Her cheeks so rare a white was on,
No daisy bears comparison,
    (Who sees them is undone),
For streaks of red were mingled there,
Such as are on a Katherine pear,
    The side that's next the sun.—SUCKLING.

I HAD read in story books of monkeys stealing away girls and then returning them home unscathed, but I had no such belief in the amenity of the gorilla, which was, without exception, the most hideous and unsightly monster which ever had crossed my path.

Its immense and fearful muscular power was something awful, it carrying the unfortunate girl like I should have carried an infant.

My feelings of grief and rage were such as almost to put me beside myself.

I however hurried on the track of the savages in a state of double terror.

It was very probable that they would kill the beast, but in what way could this advantage me? They would become the possessors of the person of the rescued captive, and thus in either way she was lost to me.

The track, or trail, of the Fan Indians was easily followed, and presently some drops of blood indicated that, by means of their bows-and-arrows or spears, they had wounded the animal.

Then I heard, first, a most singular and awful noise. It began with a sharp bark like that of an angry dog, then glided into a deep bass growl, not at all unlike the roll of very distant thunder, followed by a great shout, as of rejoicing, which was again succeeded by complete silence.

Again hurrying on, the explanation of this rejoicing was luckily found.

On a bank, underneath a tree, was the gorilla riddled with arrows and spears, which he was endeavouring to tear forth. But he was fast going.

Death had set its seal upon him, and when I came close up

he could only gnash his teeth and make a faint moan of mingled ferocity and anguish.

Despite my own sorrow and affliction, I stood still a moment to gaze with affright, mingled with admiration, at this wonderful animal.

This one was quite six feet high, with an immense body, a vast chest, great muscular arms, fiercely glowing, large, deep grey eyes, and a hellish expression of countenance, that reminded me of some terrible nightmare vision.

The beast, weak and ill as it was, glared at me from beneath the penthouse of its eyes with intense ferocity; its eyes flashed and rolled, while its huge and powerful fangs were clenched in impotent rage

I believe no man in his sober senses, gazing at that fearful dream-like creature—at that hideous caricature of humanity —could have ventured to compare it to the noblest and greatest of God's works.

Its four paws, its fearful ugliness, its howl, were of the very lowest order of the brute creation.

It may suit the purpose of men who wish to make out that we are mere animals, with nothing but a superior instinct, to compare the man-like apes to human beings, but during my residence on the island, though every kind of African monkey passed in review before me, they were, though artful, cunning, cute, and clever, very inferior in so-called intellect to the dog, the horse, and elephant.

Still, when I saw them running at a distance I could understand that ignorant people in early ages may have been misled by the glance, and thus have originated those stories of pigmies and hairy men, of which my reading had given me so many instances.

But the chimpanzee, the ourang-outang, and others, all come up to this peculiar standard—though perhaps less than the gorilla.

This animal is without exception the most ferocious animal in existence, and cannot, except when very young, be taken alive, in which case it always dies.

The males are very fond of the females, and always allow them to retreat before they themselves retire.

Their bodies are completely covered by hair, and the young sleep in trees.

They eat vast quantities of vegetables, particularly nuts, but touch no flesh.

It dwells in the loneliest and darkest parts of the forest or jungle, preferring deep wooded valleys, or rugged heights.

It, however, is careful to keep near water; but is compelled, by the fact of its dislike to animal food, to wander over vast tracts of country in search of food.

This is chiefly composed of berries, pine-apple leaves, and other vegetable matter.

It is a tremendous eater, and it often struck me that its great power and strength was a kind of apology for those who would have us all feed on vegetables. The wild sugar-cane and nuts are its choicest food.

But enough of this beast.

The one before me was fast sinking, and I had a great mind to finish its sufferings by one shot in its breast, when recollection came to me, and the danger of such a proceeding was made manifest.

Turning away, then, from the horrible sight, I again looked down upon the ground in search of the trail of the savages.

In the kind of open clearing, where the huge ape had fallen a victim to his rapacity and greediness the mark of their steps was obvious; and, determined now more than ever to brave every danger rather than lose her, I again, after seeing with fearful care to the priming of my gun, hurried on my way, though scarcely hoping for an advantageous result.

The forest was, for a little way, dark and almost impenetrable, so that my movements were very slow, until suddenly the undergrowth disappeared, and once more the savages were in sight.

They had halted in a small circular spot quite devoid of vegetation.

The ground was bare rock, while all around were huge trees with waving and projecting branches, whence depended vast curling vines, that in many cases hung to the ground.

Tied to a small tree was the Indian girl.

She was weeping.

They had fastened her wrists behind her back, and herself to the sapling, while they were seated round in a circle debating earnestly upon some question of vital interest.

That it regarded the girl I could tell from her frightened and averted looks, and those glances which she cast every now and then towards heaven, as if appealing to it for mercy.

In the hour of tribulation and of trouble, the wildest nature learns to appeal to One who alone can guard and save.

The debate was very hot.

Some were for one thing, some for another, but all pointed to the girl.

Then I saw a shadow of nameless horror fall upon the countenance of the girl who, having been long a prisoner with some of the tribe, had learned their hideous and guttural language.

A terrible and fearful dread went to my heart.

These wretches, who are all cannibals, and who delight in nothing so much as in human flesh, were about to immolate the poor trembling victim and eat her.

Once this awful idea had taken possession of my soul my mind was made up.

Most of the trees were covered by dense foliage, so that once having climbed up there was no difficulty about my creeping slowly from tree to tree until I was not fifteen feet from the girl, less than thirty from the savages.

My two barrels were loaded, and I had made up my mind to run every risk in the defence of youth, innocence, and surpassing beauty.

Then the whole party rose, and joining hands in a circle began to move slowly round; in a few minutes the speed was increased, until in less than twenty minutes they were whirling round like mad witches round a cauldron.

After this they halted, gave a loud cry, and the majority seated themselves.

Then a very powerful man, a perfect giant, stood out.

He appeared to me to be a chief, for he was attired in a feather head-dress of glowing colours, his body had been oiled that morning, his teeth were black and polished as ebony, while a huge knife hung at his side.

This he slowly drew and flourished before the eyes of the girl.

Then he began speaking.

I listened with intense interest, as the tone might tell me something.

It was, however, a monotonous song that sounded very much like O! O! O! repeated a hundred times.

Then he pointed his left hand at the girl, looked on high, and raised his arm, in which was the fearful instrument of execution.

The girl hung almost dead from the tree.

The savage stepped back to make a kind of spring; his breast was full in view.

Without caring for, or reflecting on the consequences, I fired both barrels.

CHAPTER LX.

CANOE TRAVELLING.

THE concussion would have knocked me off my bough, had not my back been to the trunk, while my feet were firmly implanted on another branch.

With eager haste I looked down.

The wretched cannibal who had been appointed to the office of executioner, lay flat on his face, while not one of the others had moved.

They were still seated in a circle as if changed to stone.

They appeared momentarily in expectation of being punished in the same way.

Then one looked at the other eagerly, and each, seeing that no harm had occurred, began to examine their own persons.

As soon as they became persuaded that only the intended murderer had perished, a conversation in a low hushed voice ensued.

During this time the girl had roused herself, and I became aware that she had some faint suspicion of the truth. A quick motion of her head in my direction made me suspect this.

But I kept as still as death, except that I cautiously and noiselessly loaded my gun.

Then, to my amazement, the Fan Indians rose to their feet in a slow, quiet, humble way, and with many an obeisance and bow, approached the girl.

They halted several times, singing in a chanting and monotonous way some deprecatory song, and casting fearful glances at the motionless dead body, for this man had died without a struggle.

Then one or two of the number advanced and loosened the young girl, who appeared to take this treatment as a matter of course.

These savages have a great belief in witches and sorcerers, a kind of medicine men.

They have no mercy upon the former, and whenever an apparently healthy person dies, are sure to search out the evil-doer.

The doctor, or sorcerer, is generally selected to nominate the guilty, which he no sooner does than the whole tribe is rapt in an indescribable fury and horrid thirst for human blood.

No sooner are the wretched women, generally young and pretty ones, pointed out, than they are dragged down to a river, placed in a canoe, hacked to pieces, and cast into the river.

But not so the sorcerer.

He is looked up to, feared, and respected. No doubt, despite the fact that in this case it was a woman, the marvellous display of power on the part of one so young and fair, had gone far to convince the ignorant and savage cannibals that they were in the power of a great Medicine.

They led her into the midst, quite free now from all shackle, their air being one of singular admiration and awe. She stood evidently half amused and half frightened, but quite anxious, I am sure, to escape their clutches.

But this was out of the question, as they were evidently resolved to treat her now with as much deference and respect as hitherto they had been cruel.

For myself nothing had been gained, but on the other hand, her dear life was safe, and that was worthy anything else.

After a while, not one having dared to touch or raise the body, they seemed to take counsel of her, but she shook her head and turned away with disgust.

Had the wretches proposed to eat him?

The savages, who were quite humbled now, bowed their assent, and when she made signs that they should return to the camp, readily obeyed.

But they now walked slowly and gravely, with measured step, allowing her precedence, which she accepted in a very pretty and taking way.

As soon as it was safe, I slid from the tree, and though the wear and tear of the last three days had nearly exhausted my physical energies, made after them again.

They were now evidently thoughtful.

These twenty warriors had seen the effect and heard the report of my gun—but how were they to explain the matter to their fellows?

Probably they were familiar enough with words that expressed such meanings as thunder, lightning, and thunderbolts, but what credit could they expect to obtain from those to whom they asserted that such was the agency which had been miraculously employed to save her?

Besides, there were the deaths of two warriors to account for, and should any of the party have seen me, their suspicions would be aroused, and my supernatural character would not stand the least examination.

Savages may duped to a certain extent, but their natural cunning and intelligence soon comes to their assistance.

My appearance and costume must soon have opened their eyes.

Soon the savages, behind whom I kept at a safe and cautious distance, came within sight of their camp, and up rose the whole of the rest of the party to meet them.

They were struck dumb with mingled astonishment and rage when they saw the girl walking freely in the midst of the others, and some even poised their spears and felt for their arrows, preparatory to executing summary vengeance on the runaway.

But the returning warriors gravely interfered, and began an explanation of what had happened.

Young and old, warriors and chiefs, had been crowding round the girl with terrible and menacing looks, when the narrative began.

One of the warriors spoke energetically and loudly.

Some of the listeners shook their heads with an incredulous smile, and I could see that two parties were forming, one in favour of the girl, the other against her, in which case the matter would finally be settled by an appeal to arms.

I again, in my impetuous way, had forced myself up as near to the camp as I dared, screening myself behind bushes.

The Fan Indians had their backs turned to me.

On a bough of a tree, above where she stood, sat an old vulture watching the scene.

Evidently the savages had been feasting, and this unclean beast was waiting to clear up the offal and other remains of their meal.

Keeping my eye steadily for a moment on the whole group, and taking exactly the right opportunity, I fired, and shot the bird, which fell at the feet of the young girl.

The whole terrified and affrighted group at once fell upon their knees, and the triumph of the former prisoner was again complete.

The savages were, however, not blind to their own interests, nor were they inclined to part with one whose power was so great.

Little did I imagine the use they would require her to put it to.

After some hasty refreshment of meat and what I afterwards found to be palm wine, the whole body started in an easterly direction.

It was clear that she made a faint resistance.

But this they would not listen to, for though their awe still continued, it did not make them any the less taskmasters or tyrants.

Again the greater part of them availed themselves of certain logs of wood, of a nature peculiarly fitted for canoe building, to make their way up the river.

It was clear that this was done for the sake of the wood itself partly, and then to avoid the jungle and forest on its banks.

I was compelled, to keep them in sight, to use my utmost vigilance, especially while the banks were composed of the usual mangrove swamps.

Then the bank became higher and clearer, until it spread out into a kind of lake with very low marshy banks and no wood.

As far as the eye could reach, the country was composed of vast fields of reeds and other water weeds, while there was scarcely any current, and the water was turbid and unpleasant to the smell.

Here the savages halted so suddenly that I had scarcely time to bob down into the water and conceal myself behind a log, to escape detection.

CHAPTER LXI.

WATER-HUNT.

It was now night.

The fire-fly began to sparkle in the gloom, the musquito to buzz and bite, and the thousand and one mysterious noises of the shore and water to rise on all sides.

It was a faint crepuscular light, such as in the tropics is apt immediately to succeed day, during which the landscape assumes an aspect of most enchanting but somewhat cold beauty.

The grey hard granite sky, the turbid water, the waving reeds, and here and there a stunted tree, made up a landscape of wild and mysterious beauty.

The negroes, who probably were acquainted with this river, selected a narrow slip of land, not above a foot out of the water, for their camp, and proceeded to erect some sort of hut for the girl, whom I could see walking about and casting her eyes into the gloom.

She was doubtless looking for me, and hoping yet that I might save her from a degrading slavery, which would probably end in her being sent to a barracoon and transferred to the Western Plantations.

Now, my wish was nothing more than to aid in her escape, but how it was to be brought about, it was more difficult than ever to say.

The Fans were fully aware that she would escape if she could, so kept a strict watch over her.

She appeared to me like some kings and queens of savage nations, which are petted up and kept in splendid palaces, but never allowed to come forth in the light of day, or see the blessed sun.

Communicate with her I could not without showing myself to the savages.

At least, such was my fear and dread at the moment.

Where I had halted in my mad pursuit of the poor girl, I was about up to my middle in thick muddy water, while a log that had floated and then become fixed, formed a breastwork.

The log, or snag, as such impediments to navigation are technically called, was indeed a miserable place to pass a night on.

But there was no help for it.

On every side but that on which the negroes had pitched their tents, I could see nothing but reeds and water—the abode, to a certainty, of crocodiles, of which animals I had a most abhorrent aversion.

During the great heats of the day these hideous animals are accustomed to retire to the reeds, or to lie sleeping under deep banks, where they are sheltered from the sun.

It is only just about daybreak and after nightfall that they sally forth in search of their prey.

Nothing can equal the stealth with which they move, scarcely raising the faintest ripple on the water.

They swim something like a dog, the paws moving over and over; but they can lie like a log on the water, staring about with their dull, wicked little eyes.

Often have I trod upon them by mistake for a piece of wood, and been frightfully terrified.

They sleep about anywhere during the heat, laying their eggs on the sand, and, covering them over, leave them.

Where fish is large and abundant, they increase wonderfully, and their large carcases, slimy and loathsome, may be seen on every side.

Crawling on to the log, which, in its highest part was not a foot out of the water, I lay at full length, hiding my gun lest a flash of the coming moonbeams might betray me. In this position, as my eyes grew accustomed to the gloom, I could see the negroes were busy at some preparation, but for some time I could not tell what it meant.

Then some men began wading into the water in my direction, with great harpoons in their hands, and I knew that they were going to harpoon the crocodiles, the flesh of which all these coarse and powerful races much admire.

My heart beat wildly.

I was not more than thirty yards from the sandbank on which they were encamped, so that, did they make a move close to my log, I must be discovered.

I had two pistols and my gun, so determined, if it came to a tussle, to make a dash for the bank, firing right and left, and thus inducing the savages to flee while I gained possession of the Indian girl.

The savages moved slowly, some with lances, others with harpoons.

Then came a whizzing sound, and a prodigious fellow began kicking and plunging to gain deep water, where he would have been inevitably lost.

But the negroes were too much for him, and after a few final kicks it was drawn ashore, dead.

A loud shout proclaimed their success, after which, in a few minutes, a bright blaze, ascending to the heavens, indicated that they were about to have a feast. Never, anywhere, on land or sea, had I witnessed a more picturesque grouping than that of those black savages in the midst of that watery plain.

The moment the fire blazed up all the surrounding landscape fell into a darkness that resembled ebony, except that I, at a distance from the fire, could see glimpses of light on the edge of the horizon, as if the moon were sending forth harbingers of its arrival.

Then, for a space of some twenty yards or so, the atmosphere glowed with a ruddy and lurid glare, just as the smoke and flame got the mastery.

By the warm and not unwelcome blaze—fire is always a companion—the figures of the half-naked savages looked gigantic, while she, who only occasionally appeared, looked a form of fairy-like proportion alongside their huge painted bodies.

Presently several of the savages started up. I was very nearly doing the same, for close to me I heard a snorting and splashing.

My good genius, however, enabled me to lay still, for I at once knew that I was in the very midst of a herd of hippopotami, having before heard their snort-like roars breaking the still night air.

I peered round and found that they were to windward of me, standing on the shallows, and looking like so many old weather-beaten logs, stranded on a sandbar.

Very little more could be seen save their ugly noses. I lay myself with a clutched and cocked pistol in my hand, for the savages were up, and evidently prepared for sport, though it was almost impossible for them ever to catch these animals, even in pitfalls.

It is a most clumsy-built, unwieldly animal, remarkable chiefly for its enormous head, and disproportionately short legs. Its feet are constructed so as to facilitate their walking among the reeds and mud as well as for swimming. The hoof is divided into four short, apparently clumsy, and unconnected toes, by means of which they walk rapidly, even on mud. They have huge crooked tusks, with which to hook up the long river grasses. They go in droves in places where their bodies are submerged, and yet they can touch the ground. Their food is entirely vegetable.

Presently the negroes came down to the water's edge, just as a sudden groan was heard close to me, and peering into the half-light, I saw, dimly, a huge animal, looking doubly monstrous in the uncertain light.

Some fifty negroes now advanced, brandishing their spears, and when they were close enough, actually throwing them at the beast, which, except that it annoyed him, felt no more than I should the prick of a pin.

But he was irritated, and suddenly putting out his great speed, he flew at the negroes in a savage and angry way, which boded no good.

With loud and hideous yells, the savages fled, for they knew the danger; this animal, when savage, often killing his persecutors. His bulk causes neither rocks, nor bushes, nor swamps, to be any impediment to him, so that in this case, he went direct at the island.

Then I saw her stand alone—after every negro had disappeared, hiding in the water, or lying down, or skulking somewhere—in front of the fire right in the brute's way.

My hand shook convulsively as I caught up my gun, leaped into the water, took aim at the ear of the huge brute and fired. With a hoarse groan, or rather grunt, it stood still and then fell down dead.

I stooped low, but still in a position to see all. She had not moved. There she was with clasped hands and upraised eyes, perfectly certain—it must be so—who had saved her.

So completely had the negroes vanished, that my impulse was to make a push for her.

Luckily the resolution was not carried out, for in another moment heads peered up on all sides, until perceiving the hippopotamus motionless, they ventured to approach it.

Their astonishment and delight seemed to know no bounds, as probably they never had seen any killed, save some little thing with a harpoon, though some of the savages do kill them by means of great heavy weights attached to cords in trees.

It is no wonder that the negroes should be anxious to capture them, as the meat, though coarse-grained, and not fat, does not taste unlike beef, and is to the hunter a most welcome and wholesome dish.

But the way in which the negroes danced, capered, and yet every now and then glanced round with awe and terror was perfectly ludicrous.

They did not actually know whether to give way to joy or sorrow; while every now and then they would turn and worship the Indian girl in the most absurd manner, clasping their hands, kneeling, and offering her tit-bits.

But at length pleasure carried the day, and setting to work, they skinned their prize and began to eat.

This is always a serious business with savages, but no sooner had they satisfied their somewhat inordinate appetite, than silence ceased, and by the laughter, singing, and story-telling that ensued, it is probable they were not ill-supplied with palm wine.

I, all the while, lay ahungered and athirst on a log, daring not to move, scarcely even venturing to breathe.

––––––

CHAPTER LXII.

THE WATER TRAIL.

WHEN the first streak of dawn was in the sky, and while the savages still slept, it was my resolve to gain a more safe place of concealment, which I did at the risk of meeting an alligator in the tall reeds.

Some of those Fans might by chance have heard of white men and fire-arms, and when broad daylight appeared would perhaps pluck up courage and search for me.

So it was the wiser plan to keep strictly concealed until they left, which they did considerably earlier than I expected.

About two hours after sunrise not a soul was to be seen, while I arrived in time to drive away the filthy vultures and take a meal from some stray and inferior part of the beast. But I was glad of it. This and a draught of muddy water served me for breakfast.

Now a feeling and hopelessness of despair came over me. What could I do against such an overwhelming force, and yet, having once succeeded in emancipating her from their clutches, why not again?

Then the reflection occurred to my mind that these savages, who belonged certainly not only to the continent but to the interior, were about to return to their homes on that vast continent on which, if I ventured, every suffering from hunger, thirst, and slavery, might be my lot.

I was turning my back on that little earthly paradise which I had created for myself, and how could I be certain, under any circumstances, that I could ever see it again?

Little do we know the value of anything until we have lost it, neither in the case of human beings or anything animal or material, which one has loved.

How miserable seemed my state when first I was cast away on that deserted spot, and how rapidly had I learned to know what any man, however lonely, may do for himself if so much inclined.

After two years and more, though still longing to see once more the country of my birth, the island had become a sort of home.

I was reconciled to it—I was used to it.

There were my horses, dogs, gazelles, ostriches, and other animals—what a state they must be in.

It seemed another shipwreck to have fallen upon such evil days, to be lost upon a part of my supposed island which was so far away from home, and across which it would cost me so many weary hours to penetrate.

But would it be right, would it be manly, would it be proper, to desert that girl who had won for herself such a place in my affections?

I could not do it—so having made the heartiest meal I could out of what offered itself, again proceeded in pursuit.

It was a water-trail now, for the savages, some sticking to their logs, some wading, everywhere left their mark.

But now to my utter surprise, this muddy lagoon, or lake as it may be called, had no outlet, at least in appearance, until at last a narrow opening was found completely overhung with trees, through which the negroes had forced their way.

The bank was lined with palm trees of an immense height.

But everywhere on the slimy bank were huge, fat crocodiles, pelicans, herons, and ducks, and other water-birds, fed indiscriminately.

But as I had no desire to be food for crocodiles, I left the stream, and only keeping it occasionally in sight, contrived to still follow the trail, for before an hour had expired I saw the troop of negroes hurrying forward with the utmost speed.

But what else did I see?

A channel some five or six miles wide, separating my island, as now I knew it to be, from a vast mainland, on which I saw rising, in the far-off distance, certainly lofty mountains that towered to the very skies.

But grand as was the sight, even to the arid rocky shore of the continent—stony, dry, and without vegetation—it could not occupy my attention a moment.

At my feet, not half a mile distant, was a very large village, or rather town, while dispersed over the plain below were animals of some kind that looked like oxen, cows, and horses.

Then I thoroughly understood the character of something which I had caught sight of on the opposite shore, and which had at first, when I examined it through my telescope, made my heart beat with joy.

It was an immense enclosure protected by a fence of palisades.

I knew it to be a great Portuguese barracoon or slave pen, and knew also that a stranger had better fall into the hands of the cannibals, than an Englishman into the hands of these jealous ruffians.

The Fan village, which lay at my feet, was, I thought, in league of course with the slavers.

But—it may as well be known at once—the barracoon was deserted.

It had been so long since, a fever having carried off a few old watchers who were left in charge, and the savages having been tempted to pillage and take the few cattle that remained, in consequence.

I followed the savages at a distance, and saw the women and children come forth in droves to meet them.

I crept from tree to tree, and bush to bush, until I got where I could have a complete view of all that passed.

The village was composed of huts and tents mixed together, but, with few exceptions, ranged round a semi-circle, outside of which was a species of stockade.

I saw the Indian girl in their midst, receiving all the honour which the wonderful story the savages had to tell could entitle her to.

She bore herself with an uneasy and half-amused dignity, which under any other circumstances would have been comic, but which now went to my heart.

Everything conspired to make her loss to me greater and more painful.

Following a circle of palm trees that grew at no great distance from the stockade, I worked round towards the sea-shore, whence I could get a better view of the whole scene.

It was indeed very beautiful; to my right was the rolling sea, sending up its surf to wash that sand-bound coast eternally, while nearly everywhere else, but where the village stood, were dark green forests coming down in impenetrable masses to the very water's edge.

Before me lay the vast and mighty African continent, naked, bare, deserted, save where I could just make out the abandoned barracoon.

A number of the largest sized canoes, with a huge raft, made, as I could judge, from beams cut in other days by the Portuguese slavers, and covered by lighter wood, were drawn into the mouth of a creek which, canal-like, wound up to the front of the village, and then disappeared amid a mass of dark green foliage.

Everything was clearly ready for a start.

These savages would in all probability not delay long their departure.

They had store of ivory; they had some cattle; they had, more wonderful still, horses of a stunted European breed; and they had their fairy queen.

I sat still, planning, plotting, trying to invent some plan, however wild and dangerous, by which to attain my wishes, until gradually night fell, and the sound of music recalled me to myself.

I crept round as close as I dared, and peering over the stockade, saw that the girls were dancing, while the men sat round in a half-circle.

The music consisted of a drum made of wood and goat skins, while the dancing was indescribable.

It was a mixture of wild energy and deliberate indecency.

As *she* was nowhere to be seen, I leaned moodily against a tree, and scarcely noticing what was going on, still mused and mused and thought, until a cessation of the dancing again aroused me.

Then the men crowded round the camp fires, while the women stood apart conversing in low, hushed whispers.

Their voices were merry enough, sometimes even their laughter were musical and pleasant.

They were talking about her.

This I could make out by their pointing towards a large tent, which, closed and apparently without any ordinary door, stood on the edge of the village.

Near it was a kind of pound, in which they had placed a mare and colt, that, as if in want of fresh food, were rubbing their noses against the palings, and whinnying every now and then in a mournful manner.

It was quite clear that these Indians did not understand the nature of the animals they had captured, and kept them more for ornament than use.

How I gazed at them, with what burning longing, with what deep anxiety! What projects the sight of them roused within my mind.

It was a good omen to my fancy that these savages had not brought with them any of their cur-like dogs, so that is might be possible for me to carry out an idea of rescue which had now occurred to me.

She was in that tent.

The mare was strong, the colt above two years, I thought.

At all events it would bear her.

Then, as soon as the savages were asleep, which, unfortunately, they were not likely to be for some time, I would boldly enter the village, visit the tent, lead her to where the horses stood, and then, armed as I was, escape was easy.

My very heart once more thrilled with joy at the thought.

But at this moment I was compelled to bury myself deeper in the bushes, as I saw two girls coming towards me loaded with gourds and calabashes.

My impulse of thankfulness was great, for I was perishing with thirst.

They walked slowly, chatting and laughing until they came within ten yards of me.

One turned towards a little hollow, whence she returned with several gourds of water, but the other stood still under a palm tree.

What could she be going to do?

Had she obtained some inkling of my presence?

It was possible, for their hearing is very keen.

I was soon undeceived.

With an instrument something in the shape of a gimlet she bored a hole in the palm tree, after which a tube was inserted and the calabash fastened on.

This she did in several places and went away, leaving the juice to run till morning.

I was, I knew now, about to be amply supplied with palm wine.

Knowing, however, that the process was slow, water was my first requisite, and, descending to the pool, I drank freely.

I came up and again took up my post of observation.

The savages were still laughing, talking, and telling stories.

The girls and women were, however, gradually moving off to their several huts and tents.

Then I rubbed my eyes, fancying that I was in a dream.

The skins of the tent—that of a great chief—were raised, and the Indian girl came forth.

Her step was cautious and slow for a few minutes, when she sank down upon the soft sward.

What was she doing?

Something with her hands I could make out, but not what she was doing.

This lasted some minutes, when she rose, with a good bundle of fresh green grass.

My heart leaped within me, from mingled joy and fear.

Then she moved slowly, casting stealthy glances every now and then towards the camp fire, round which the savages were collected, until at last she reached the enclosure.

The mare whined loudly, and at once the girl cast the grass orward.

The two animals began at once to eat eagerly, as if they needed such refreshment.

Then she climbed over the palings, and stood in the enlosure herself.

In her hand was a strip of something—it was—yes—it was a halter.

Then she was about to escape without me.

This was not utterly disheartening, but still the chances were against her alone; whereas, aided by me, she might have made it a certainty.

Still, I prepared to join her.

It was a matter of certainty she would not be frightened if she saw me, so I prepared to head her off in the direction which she must necessarily take.

Then imagine my dismay and surprise, when removing two or three palings, she led forth the mare coaxingly; then, with a bound, leaping on its back, urged it at once to a trot.

The savages were silent a moment.

Then, at a cry from one of their body, they darted to their feet, yelling, shrieking, and making such hideous noises as made me stand transfixed to the spot.

She, however, neither swerved nor hesitated.

In her hand was a thong, with which, and the heel of her little boot, she urged the stout and active mare forward across the plain and towards the rocks.

Still, several of the fastest runners of the tribe dashed off in pursuit, though evidently, from the glances I could make out, reluctantly.

They looked at her now with more awe than ever, having probably never seen the horse or its use before.

But I was annihilated.

To show myself was impossible under the circumstances; so just as I lost sight of the pursuers and pursued, I sank down on the ground in a state of mind not to be described.

It was a sort of trance, for it was nearly daylight ere I roused myself, and took precautions for my own safety.

Snatching away no less than three of the calabashes of the palm wine, I hurriedly retreated towards a thicket, looking around for a place of safety.

The only thing that presented itself to me was a half-dead tree, covered by masses of the India-rubber vine.

Into this I ascended by the assistance of the creeping plants, and climbed up to where its branches were thickest.

It was a very large tree I now noticed, with green boughs on one side, and rotting ones on the other.

The vine, however, was thick and shady, so that there was little danger of my being seen.

CHAPTER LXIII.

SMOKED OUT.

It was the cooling hour, just when the rounded
Red sun sinks down behind the azure hill,
Which then seems as if the whole earth is bounded,
Circling all nature, hush'd, and dim, and still,
With the fair mountain-crescent half surrounded
On one side, and the deep sea calm and chill
Upon the other, and the rosy sky
With one star sparkling through it like an eye.
                                        BYRON.

Now, beginning to collect my scattered thoughts, after taking a large draught of the palm wine, various plans suggested themselves to me.

Hope told to me the flattering promise that she would go at once, and with the least delay possible, to my summer-house, in which case I knew that the poor suffering starved beasts would be attended to.

There in all probability she would wait for my return, as she knew that I had followed her.

All my fatigues, all my dangers, all my sufferings, past,

No. 13.—SAILOR CRUSOE.

ALFRED ON THE STONY PLAIN.

present, and to come, at once seemed to vanish at the mere thought of such a prospect.

It was very unlikely that the savages would again venture into those parts of the island where I had made my power manifest, so that could I evade them here all would be well.

I had my pistols, gun, telescope, and all my other traps safe, but I had no food of any kind whatever.

This was certainly a terrible reflection, but, at all events, there was nourishment in the palm wine, of which, however, it was necessary to partake sparingly, as in my state of stomach it would prove unusually heady.

The day was hot, and soon I began to feel its torrid influence.

The immense palm trees all round kept off the breeze, and then, despite my efforts to repel it, the feeling of hunger predominated over everything else.

It is a horrid sensation.

But almost close to my hand hung the bough of a certain palm on which grew some nuts.

It was shaped like an egg with rounded ends.

With the butt end of my pistol I broke off the husk of one or two, and then eat the inside.

It was bitter as gall, very disagreeable, and hard; but it was a momentary relief, and had any more been within reach, I would have gladly ate them.

My hope was to exist through that day as well as I could, then crawling through the wood, ascend the rocky hills and wait until morning, when it would be easy to follow the trail of the adventurous and noble Indian girl.

Thinking, waiting, the weary hours seemed not to move, until again nature asserted her rights, and hunger came upon me. It began by a dimness of sight, followed by a faintness I could not control, so that I lay back against the trunk helpless and exhausted.

I often have since believed that I must have fainted, but could never tell how long I remained insensible to what was passing around me.

I could see the blue sky, and floating in it, as it were, the birds; I watched, with keen and eager eye, the gambols of a squirrel on a neighbouring bough; I could see some of the lesser order of snakes crawling amid the leaves; a vulture almost dared to come near me, so certain was he of my approaching death, and only was induced to leave by my stern and savage look.

Many and varied were the sounds in the air, and none of them did I hope to hear again, for I felt that I was dying of starvation.

An eager pull at the intoxicating palm wine revived me just as I heard loud shrill cries from near the water pool, cries of women, soon re-echoed by men.

They had, doubtless, just discovered the abstraction of the palm wine calabashes, and these were cries of rage and wonder.

Now knowing, as I did, the energy of these men, and being aware that, though these negroes have not the ability in tracking which characterises the North American Indian, still I could not doubt they would make some search for the audacious intruder, who had deprived them of a luxury which they prize so much as to steal into the woods over night, and place calabashes under the tap, going there in the morning and drinking it on the spot, lest any of their comrades should require a taste.

The cries continued, and then I could hear the savages running through the woods, shrieking, yelling, and uttering their jabbering war cry with perfect frenzy.

I heard, too, another thing which alarmed me considerably.

They were shooting arrows up in the trees, and uttering angry execrations all the time.

Now, though this made me fully aware that they suspected the monkeys of having been the culprits, still a chance shot might prove fatal, especially as their arrows are nearly always poisoned.

A little while before, and the thought of death seemed to me to be quite natural. I had all but resigned myself to it, and believed that I never should descend from that tree again, until I dropped off a corpse.

Now, at the idea of a conflict with the savages, I roused myself, and looked to my weapons, determined to sell my life dearly.

I crouched, however, quite out of sight, and, gazing straight down, saw clearly that in this way they would never succeed in finding me.

Presently I heard them come to the tree with fierce and horrid cries, that resounded through the woods.

Then, to my great astonishment, they joined hands and danced around, still hollowing and yelling fearfully.

Had they discovered me, and were they rejoicing at the fact, or what was the reason of their outcries?

I could not, for the life of me, make out; but when the whole village seemed to be congregating on the spot to join in the fun, whatever it was, the idea crossed my mind that my track had led them to the foot of the huge and half-dead trunk round which they were laying siege.

I was treed like a coon.

What to do I did not know.

My powder-horn was well-supplied, my bullets were not out, and there would be no difficulty in picking off half-a-dozen of them, if so inclined.

But there were two very serious objections to this course of proceeding.

In the first place, it was cruel to slay, almost without motive, a number of ignorant savages, and then, common sense whispered to me that the startling effect of fire-arms might wear out, and its constant repetition induce the negroes to think, and perhaps penetrate a part of the mystery.

But what are they about?

Several of the negroes, after carefully examining the tree, are collecting dry boughs, green boughs, and leaves, and piling them in and around the hollow trunk in great quantities, and so arranged as to burn quickly and smoke as much as possible.

The horrid conviction flashed across my mind that they were about to put me to the ordeal by fire.

My limbs began to tremble, my teeth to chatter, as I reflected how, in a very little time, the powder which hitherto I had regarded as a friend, would soon prove my bitterest enemy.

What was to be done?

I glanced around at the neighbouring trees, to see if I could reach them, but no branch firm enough presented itself to my view.

Then I heard the crackle of the flames, and the smoke rose in a dense cloud, which appeared to exclude all nature from my view.

This lasted but an instant when it became a steady and solid column.

I sat shivering on my bough.

There was no chance of safety, unless I fired at the savages, and descending the tree in the confusion, escape without being seen.

But what is this?

The smoke is stealing up now through the hollow trunk, and escaping by numerous holes just where the branches fork.

But what is escaping with them?

Surely, I am not mistaken.

They are wild bees, and the cannibal negroes are smoking them out in search of their most delicious luxury—honey.

This was a relief.

They had not discovered me, but while wandering in the wood had fallen over the signs which indicate the presence of honey.

It was, indeed, a piece of good fortune, that ascending, as I did, by the assistance of the india-rubber vine, I kept clear of the hive, and did not disturb the little animals—by no means, when in a passion, to be despised.

But now, what was to be done?

In my faint and hungry state a meal of honey, washed down by palm wine, would be delightful, and I resolved to obtain it at any price.

But how?

Instantly a plan flashed through my mind, daring, audacious, and dangerous, but which, in my half lunatic state, appeared to me both ludicrous and feasible.

No one who has not tried it can tell the state of mind produced by hunger.

It is painful at first, but before it reaches the point of agony, it becomes dreamy—it puts you into a kind of torpor, from which you wake with wild and strange notions floating through your brain.

Placing my gun on a bough, I looked down and saw that the hottest part of the fire was close under me.

This observed, I poured half of my gunpowder into a small shot-pouch, which I then stuffed into one of the palm calabashes, and corked up tightly by means of a palm-nut husk—so tightly, indeed, that I could not have taken it out again.

Taking careful aim, and marking where the fire was deepest and hottest, I poised it over the fire, and it dropped with a whirr and a rush into the flames.

The savages started back in amazement, looked up at the tree, glanced at one another, and began jabbering and pointing upward.

It was a very anxious moment.

They, doubtless, believed that some animal was in the tree, perhaps a monkey, and a shower of arrows shot from such a body would be almost certain not to fail in their mark.

The conference lasted, perhaps, two minutes, when I saw one of the Indians poise his spear and then cautiously approach the fire.

He was about to examine into the nature of the object which had fallen.

Of course the palm wine calabash would be recognised.

What then?

The savage stirred the fire with the end of his lance, and seemed pondering on the round bullet-shaped mass.

But his stirring agitated the flames, and, for a moment, concealed the thing from view.

Then, as if to roll it out, he pushed it—it fell to pieces, and, with a loud and startling explosion, the fire was scattered right and left over the wonder-stricken and yelling band.

Before the smoke had cleared away, and I could peer down upon the scene below, not a sign of savage, male or female, was to be discovered.

There was no time to be lost; so, securing everything firmly to my person, I slid down, and, the bees having by this time taken their departure, at once cut through the soft bark, and made an incision which laid bare the most magnificent hive I ever saw.

I devoured it greedily, all the while pouring as much as I could into one of the gourds, as part provision for my journey.

Then having—using caution—filled the other with water, I turned my back on the Fan village, and struck for the hills, keeping myself carefully concealed by means of bushes and trees.

As soon as I was at the foot of the rocks, I sought a sufficient shelter, and lying down, enjoyed something like a pleasant sleep.

As soon as night fell I awoke, and moving slowly and deliberately, gained the narrow cavern or gully which led upward from that sea-girt spot into the interior of the island.

I travelled a mile or two more by the faint light of a moon that was continually obscured by clouds, and then again halted to wait for morning.

—— ——

CHAPTER LXIV.

THE RETURN TRAIL.

IT broke glorious and warm. I had, deluded by the darkness, left the proper path and taken too much to the left for the track which I intended to follow.

My goal now was my lake home, my summer-house, and my animals, to which I hoped to find added that one charming companion to whom all the rest were dross—something better and more delightful than gold.

The place were I had halted was a charming spot.

There was, at no great distance, a small lake or pond, in which wild ducks were bathing and fishing, while I could see fishing hawks and eagles watching them from aloft.

Some graceful palm trees hung over the water, and what added a charm to the scene were a number of bright-feathered parrots and other beautiful birds, with squirrels of all shapes and sizes* running up into the palm-tree and feeding on its bunches of yellow nuts.

It was a spot, one of many in my island, that made me in after days give it the name of a smaller one near the Gaboon river—Corisco the Beautiful.

I found many such lakes, and all begirt with a broad green belt of grass, dotted with flowers of every hue.

There were trees loaded with nests like little conches, of an azure tint, in which birds deposited eggs of a pale golden colour; there were butterflies of topaz and emerald, on every blooming bush; there were beetles with breasts of sapphire, and humming-birds, and little parrots, which balanced themselves carelessly, rocked by the faint breath of the breeze over the bosom of flowers tinted like the bright rays of the setting sun.

The flowers were many and varied; long lines of rose-bushes were shaded by Chinese lilacs; and the chorus of birds was deafening.

The widow bird and the dove sent forth their notes from

---

* Du Chaillu discovered a squirrel the size of a mouse.

among the trees, and the mocking-bird whistled his eccentric song.

I thought of the poet who said that their sweet strains, sad and harmoniously lost in the silence of the desert, reached his ears like the last sighs of a dying virgin, and filled his heart with melancholy.

But I must confess just then I regarded everything living with any but poetical feelings. *I was hungry!*

But though I longed to make the rocks ring with the echoes of my gun, and thus procure some food, I did not dare shoot, I was still too near the Fan village, whose warriors might, indeed, be close to me, on the track of the Indian girl.

I descended, however, to the lake and bathed my feet, which both restored me and caused me to make a discovery, that of some stray ducks' eggs, which were of course greedily devoured.

This done, I rose and skirting the little lake, turned in the direction of the way by which I had followed the savages, and which I believed to be the direct road to my summer-house.

But here again I met with a surprise, for close to the lake, in a very different direction from that which I expected she would have taken, were the tracks of the horse by means of which she had escaped.

I paused. What was now the right plan for me to follow? Doubtless, whatever devious course she might pursue, her aim was to return to my habitation, or why had she visited it at all?

At the same time, there were very mysterious incidents connected with her, which I could not satisfactorily explain, and which left me in a cloud of doubt and perplexity.

Still, it was more prudent to follow, and upon this course I determined.

The track of the horse, whose marks were those of one used to be ridden, led me for some time across the prairie and then through a thick wood, where I observed the rider had alighted, walked, and led the mare.

Then came an open space, half trees, half bushes, where she had mounted again and pursued her way.

It was easy enough to follow, but my strength, it was apparent, was quite spent.

The fatigue, the worry, anxiety and trouble, the hours I had passed wading in water and then sleeping in my clothes were telling on me.

I was ill. A severe cough hacked and tore my chest, so that I could scarcely make any way. But heavens! what do I see? A column of smoke rising from a wood at no great distance.

Then the girl had halted, made a fire, and awaited my approach.

Roused to new exertion by this circumstance, I rallied and started on. It was a grove of moderate-sized trees to which I was advancing, and in another minute I was close to the fire.

I stepped lightly and warily not to alarm her. I might have saved myself the trouble. She had been there, it is true, for there was the fire, there were the signs of the horse; and a number of feathers and bones showed that she had succeeded in trapping some kind of game. It was a disappointment, but I was so used to them, that it did not move me. On the contrary, the remains of a very fat bird, ready roasted and placed near the embers, served to revive me.

But why was it left?—she must be under the impression that I was following in her wake, and had left this as a sign.

My heart beat with grateful emotions and pleasant sensations, so that after a meal of roast bird, honey and water, I arose with a feeling of refreshment such as I had not had for some days.

A small stream close at hand enabled me to refill my calabash and then on again, always following the horse's track.

That night I slept under the shelter of a palm tree.

When I awoke my limbs were stiff, my feet sore and bleeding.

I had been walking without mocassins for a whole day over stones and amid briars and thorns.

It was a fearfully still morning, portending heat and storm.

Not a sign of life was to be seen, save insect life.

I could see a spider's web or two. The gloom, indeed, was something quite appalling.

I lay under a palm, but round about were ebony trees, some bar-wood and other hard timber, while at my feet were a lot of pulpy pear-shaped fruit, which should have alarmed me, but which, on the contrary, I ate eagerly, knowing how pleasant was its subdued and grateful acid.

I was not then aware that it was the favourite food of the gorilla as well as of the negroes, or I should have hastened from the spot, which seemed a fit haunt for some sylvan monster, delighting in silence and the shades of night.

As soon as my body felt refreshed I rose, but was obliged to cut a thick stick to aid me in my walk.

I was half inclined to throw away my gun, but forbore, as at any moment I might meet animals, against which it would prove my only chance of safety.

About a quarter of a mile from my resting-place, I came to the edge of a plain, at the end of which I could make out the hills which doubtless surrounded my beloved home, for which I sighed now with an ardour such as never had overwhelmed me before.

I could see the green verdure that clothed them from top to bottom, and so started across, after one heartfelt and fervent prayer to God.

What decided me may as well be confessed—she had gone that way.

The sun was hot, the sky was blue, not a breath of air agitated the scanty grass that grew upon that stony plain.

My feet were in a dreadful state, so that at every step I took, leaning on my staff, I groaned aloud.

In my agony I felt almost inclined to shriek with despair, but forbore for shame for my manhood.

Luckily I had water, or I must then and there have died.

Several times I sat down, and looked around at the arid soil, gave one glance at the heavens above, and while listening to the " cri-cri " of the grasshopper, envied their power of locomotion.

Oh! but for a breath of good wholesome wind. That would have roused, revived me.

But it came not, and fearful that if I gave way too much I should die, I hurried on as fast as my tottering limbs would carry me.

Slow as was the progress I made, still hours will show some result, and very soon the distant hills seemed to become more distinct, the trees more sharply defined, the verdure more sparkling and real.

Then I tottered.

The heat seemed to scorch me, and with one wild, last despairing cry, I fell flat on my face—to die.

———

CHAPTER LXV.

HOME.

IT would be difficult to say how long my senses remained in this state of utter unconsciousness, but at all events it was some time, for when my hearing returned it was growing dark.

A grateful shower had conduced to the saving of my life, by cooling the atmosphere.

But I was, though hearing distinctly, and looking out on the vast plain, unable to move my head, so fearfully did it ache.

Then came wafted to me some singular sound, and I saw afar off, as I thought, something circling round.

It was a wild beast. Now it halts, now it gazes about—and now——

My God!—it is, it is my own friend and companion, my dog! Again I sank fainting in something like a delirium of joy. When, after about five minutes, my senses once more returned, there were bending over me, on that desolate plain, my dog, my wolf, the puppies, and my zebra, which smelt at my seeming dead body, with an interest which it was hard to believe.

Hark!

What comes, with clattering hoof and quick step? This must rouse me.

I glanced upward.

It is the Indian girl, who reins in her stunted pony, and gliding to the ground, raises my burning head on to her knees, and chafes my temples with some alcoholic mixture. Then noticing my parched tongue, she squeezed some into it, which enabled me to speak.

"God bless you!" I murmured, unconscious that she understood me not.

She made some indistinct reply, and then a tear, a tear of womanly sympathy and tenderness, fell upon my burning cheek.

I could but press my lips to her hand, for I had no power to do else, and then once more my weakness overcame me, and I became insensible.

I can never ascertain now what time elapsed ere this fainting fit was over, but when it did subside, the sight that met my view was indeed gratifying.

I was seated astride on the zebra, while she walked beside, supporting me with her left hand, while her right guided her own horse.

My dogs were close at hand, and then we were under the shade of deep green trees that shaded out that hot and burning sun, which had been one of the causes of my severe illness.

I did not attempt to speak.

It would have been useless, for though we were both human, our tongues were different, and we did not understand one another.

The caravan soon halted, and being assisted to alight—how I had held on was a mystery—my island home was before me.

She had travelled thither in search of me, and finding, from the state of my animals, how long I had been absent, had fed them and let them loose.

But her own kindness to them induced them not to stray, so that when she took the return trail to search for me, they all remained with her, and thus were instrumental in finding me.

The horse and zebra were placed in their enclosure, and were welcomed by the younger animal with great delight.

Then the old plan of a raft was resorted to, and in half an hour I was within the walls of my old hut.

My birds screamed with delight, and were rewarded by a plentiful supply of grain.

But my illness was too much for me.

Despite every effort that I made to resist nature, I was compelled to retire to my bed, after ridding myself of those clothes which had been a burden to me for so many weary days.

Now came a time of suffering which will not readily be forgotten.

I was in a raging fever, but never completely lost my consciousness.

I was always athirst, and every minute wanted some attention.

Never, were my being to outlast the world, shall memory fade so far as to forget her kindness, her devotion.

She nursed me as if I had been her own child.

Not only were her ways winning in the extreme, but her handiness was wonderful.

Nothing that could do me good was omitted.

She never seemed to take any rest, for no matter when I awoke, with feverish tongue and haggard eye, there she was with broth or lime juice, or something to refresh and cool me.

Then came the convalesence. It was long but it was delightful.

As soon as my strength allowed me I shifted from my bed on the floor to my hammock, beside which she would stand for hours.

Her glance was tender, pitying, and affectionate; but at last, when I began to teach her words in English, she would smile, but very, very softly, I thought sadly.

Ah, me! the meaning is quite clear now, but it was not then.

I taught her the name of everything within sight, and she was wonderfully quick to learn, quicker than I had ever seen any one before; but then I was certainly a very patient and devoted master.

At the end of a month, not before, I found myself up to breakfast.

All this time she had nursed me, fed my animals, fished, hunted, and snared, and yet never seemed to be away.

But, then, my hours of apathy were many.

I made her sit down now, and enjoy her meal, while I waited on her. There were eggs and broiled meat, but nothing but water to drink, and yet was the meat delightful, for we were now two instead of one.

What plans for the future, what hopes, what ideas of happiness here, and of ultimate escape, flashed though my mind, it would be futile to record.

We were seated side by side upon a rude bench near a ruder table. I was so placed that I could see into her eyes, which danced with fun as she pronounced some new word that I had taught her.

She was now able to say all such words as *water, meat, cook, come here*, and the like, with the names of all my animals, as well as many small sentences necessary to our constant intercourse.

But there was a language she could speak as well as myself, which I was now desirous of interpreting in my favour. This was the language of the eyes.

Breakfast was over. She had rejected the last morsel I had offered her, and was, I saw, ready to rise.

I felt a kind of tremor over my whole frame. Never in

any encounter with animals or savages had I experienced such a sensation of genuine timidity.

But it was of no use hesitating. It could not last for ever this way.

What I wanted was a companion who could converse with me, who could comprehend feelings, understand sentiments, and sympathise with me. It is truly my belief that what I desired and coveted was a wife.

I took her hand in mine, and pressed it to my lips respectfully, but with sufficient warmth to denote my real devotion and affection.

She bent her eyes upon the ground, and blushed through her dusky skin.

I now drew nearer, and passing my arm round her slender waist, whispered, in low accents, words which, of course, she did not understand, and yet which must have conveyed some meaning to her mind.

She raised her head and looked me full in the face. There was a heavenly smile upon.

She took my two hands in hers, bent low her forehead, and kissed my hands with deep respect.

Then she rose, and by signs described the occasions on which I had saved her life.

Her action was so dramatic I could not fail to understand. I smiled and held out my arms.

Then she came and kneeled at my feet, placed my hands upon her head, and intimated that she was my slave for ever.

I raised her up, pulled her to me, and by every sign I could think of intimated my wish that she should consider herself my equal, my companion, my wife.

I would fain have kissed her lips and clasped her to my heart; but a tear trickled from beneath her eyelid, she shook her head, and, rising to her feet, spoke in low hurried accents some words which myself had taught her—sweet, beautiful child of nature.

" Come—show—cave."

I smiled. It was charming even to hear her broken English; but, rising to my feet, I showed her that my strength was not yet sufficiently great to enable me to walk, and so went and lay me in my hammock, where I soon fell asleep.

When I awoke I was alone. This, however, gave me no uneasiness, for she had many duties to perform.

Before rising to take a stroll, I communed with myself.

We were alone.

We were all in all to one another.

Like the first man and Eve his companion, we had none to give us in marriage; but the contract could be for ever made by both our hearts—if we really loved.

CHAPTER XLVI.

ALONE.

She did not reappear, so, desirous of taking as much gentle exercise as possible, I went down to the landing to watch for her. Yes, there she was crossing the lake from the direction of the zebra's stable, but not as I had done on a rude raft of reeds, but on one made with poles and bamboos, quite elegant in form.

I hastened to hand her ashore, but she was too quick and too light for me.

She had been feeding my animals, and had also snared a large animal like a hare, which, carrying up to the house, she hastened to skin, prepare, and cook.

Then she sat down, and while the dinner was under way took her usual lesson, during which she asked me over and over again the meaning of such things as she had forgotten.

By great trouble I got her to understand the meaning of the word " pretty." At first she fancied that it was a part of some animal, especially as I selected the bird of Paradise's tail as my first illustration. But when I also picked a beautiful flower, and taking her soft hand in mine, pointed to her eyes, mouth, and chin, she blushed and laughed outright.

Then wishing to reward my pupil I kissed her eyes, chin, and mouth several times, she being, I thought, as pleased as myself, until at last she jumped up and hurried to see to the dinner.

" No, no," were her words, " not good."

Now I had never, that I remembered, taught her this word; so I stared with surprise, at which she only laughed. The truth is I felt very awkward and foolish.

It was my fervent desire to explain to her the state of my affections, and my wish to detain her perpetually on my island by making her my wife.

But how could this be done to one so modest, innocent, and simple until I knew her language or she understood mine?

Then I made a stern resolve to study together without thought of anything else, until I could say to her, in words that she could understand, " I love you."

That evening, after smoking my first pipe for a long time, I retired early to my hammock.

I felt much better, and knew that a calm night's rest would enable me, perhaps, to carry out my promise to show the whole of my territory.

I had been easily able to speak of my cave, as that she had seen already.

Her wonder at what I had done seemed great, as she regarded everything with admiration.

The girl, who told me her name was Pablina, having set the dogs to their watch, and made the whole interior of the hut neat and clean, came and wished me " good night." I was half dozing as she stooped over my hammock and kissed my forehead.

I awoke and held up my lips. She shook her head, raised her finger, but ended by kissing me.

I would have detained her, but two hot tears fell upon my cheeks, and I loosened her hands.

She retired to the other side of the hut and sat down upon a mat of her own making.

Soon the hut was hushed in all the silence of night, save that I lay awake for a long time, gazing fondly at the gentle being opposite, as now and then the waving of the wind opened up the trees, and the moving of the leaves enabled a stray moonbeam to fall upon her exquisite and rounded limbs.

It was late when I awoke, but I was indeed very much refreshed, and felt better than I had for a very long time. I was afoot early, and assisted her in those duties she had voluntarily undertaken for so long a time.

She lingered, I thought, a long time over the morning meal, was peculiarly affectionate to my birds, fed my dogs, and patted them on the head in an unusually kind way.

She scarcely looked at me, and, what puzzled me more than anything, seemed suddenly to have lost her appetite. This, in a child of nature like her, seemed strange.

Then she bustled about and saw to the raft, which required some addition to make it bear us both.

At length we started, and crossing over to the shore mounted our several nags—riding, of course, without saddle or bridle.

Our dogs followed, and in this way my long abandoned cave was again reached. It was much in the same state that I had left it, except that some ferocious rats had eat up nearly all my grain. They, however, made a rapid exit when my dogs entered the cavern.

Lighting a lamp or two, I visited my cave with considerable satisfaction. It no longer appeared in the least lonely.

Hand in hand, like Adam and Eve in Paradise, we roamed about, putting everything in order, while, as the wet season was approaching, I explained by signs that we must remove our habitation.

A sudden look of sadness overspread her face. A struggle of some kind was evidently going on in her mind—a great and terrible struggle, as I afterwards knew.

Now she would cling to me tenderly, when, in a moment of exulting fondness, I pressed her to my heart, and vowed to love her all my life.

She would look at me with those deep blue eyes of hers, as if her love had been unfathomable; and then she would shrink from me with an air almost of loathing—but no, it was not that—but of fear.

That this beauteous child of nature loved me was certain. How, then, was this strange conduct of hers to be explained?

We dined by the pool, beneath the shade of the glorious palms, and we then wandered towards the sea-shore. She had began to prattle English like a child, never resting a moment hardly without asking questions. She appeared deeply anxious to learn.

It was hot, and Pablina made signs that she would go into a thicket that skirted a small lagoon, and there bathe. I smiled, and indicated that I would do the same in a pool close at hand.

But first I insisted on clasping her in my arms, and taking a kiss. She returned it wildly, passionately, fondly—and then walked slowly in the direction which she had previously indicated.

I sat me down on the shore, and gazed out on the sea. A melancholy sensation crept over me, a sense of loneliness and sadness quite unaccountable to my senses.

But do not coming ills cast their shadows before, and hint to us that something terrible is coming?

Then I rose and advanced towards the shore to bathe. Out on the open sea, in her bark canoe, was Pablina. Her face was turned towards me. She knelt up in the boat and clasped her hands as if in prayer. Tears were streaming from her eyes, while her glance was imploring and beseeching—as much as to say, "Forgive me, but go I must."

I rushed into the water. A stroke of the paddle sent the canoe out of my reach.

"Come back!" I screamed, rather than said.

She shook her head mournfully, sadly, but she gave no signs of yielding.

I cast myself on my knees, and cried to her frantically not to go.

"Must—no good stop," she said, in a clear distinct voice, that came to me like the echo of a dream.

Then, as if afraid of her own self, she paddled away, without once looking-back; and I stood once more alone on that desolate and naked shore—worse than alone, for she had taken my heart with her.

And I blasphemed, for I cursed her—noble, generous, true-hearted child of the sunny South, the angel of my chequered and terrible life.

But let any one place themselves in my situation, let them picture Adam in his glorious Paradise alone, and they will forgive me—for happiness was born a twin.

CHAPTER LXVII.

The soil untill'd
Pour'd forth spontaneous and abundant harvests;
The forests cast their fruits, in husks or rind,
Yielding sweet kernels or delicious pulp,
Smooth oil, cool milk, and unfermented wine
In rich and exquisite variety;
On these the indolent inhabitants
Fed without care or forethought.

ANON.

He sat and talk'd
With winged messengers, who daily brought
To his small island in the ethereal deep,
Tidings of joy and love.

WORDSWORTH.

THERE is no more terrible affliction than one of those unexpected losses which come upon us with the stunning effect of a thunderbolt. It is dreadful to note the slow wasting away of the being we most love, until that dread hour comes, when the spirit departs, and we are left solitary and alone on the bleak shore of life. But then we are prepared. Far different is the suffering of a mother, whose child is struck down by some fatal accident in the pride of his youth and beauty, to whom she has at least had the consolation of devoting her self-denying and earnest love to smooth the awful passage from this world to the next.

While recovering from my illness, it never entered into my calculations to think of the time when I should be separated from this fair being who had been sent unto me, as Eve unto Adam in Eden, for a consolation and a comfort. All my speculative arrangements for the future were based on the supposition that she was to be my companion. And now I was again not only alone, but alone in a desperate and unhappy mood of mind.

How far my feelings had overcome me, may be judged from the fact that I could not even pray for consolation in my affliction. My soul was in arms against all and everything.

I rose from my knees sullen, angry, full of evil thoughts and designs, to say nothing of regrets.

Thank Heaven, I lived to repent in days far away those wicked suggestions of the enemy of man which assailed me now, as well as to understand the motive of much that now was mysterious!

That her resolve was no momentary impulse was quite evident, for, from the moment that she started, she never once turned back, but paddled steadily for that distant island which I could see rising like a cloud from the sea, and whence had ascended that column of smoke which so much puzzled my ideas.

Unable to bear the sight of the fast fading canoe—oh, had I but known of its existence!—I turned away to return towards my cave, communing with myself as I went, in silent and speechless agony.

Why had she come a second time to seek me out, and to fill my imagination with hope and joy, if she had no special object? And why, having come evidently on purpose across that large expanse of water, had she returned, leaving me abandoned and alone? There must have been some motive for all this which no suppositions of mine could fathom, or she must be guided by that feminine failing, caprice, a fault of which, even in my anger, I scarcely felt inclined to charge her, of all created beings.

My cave once reached, my anger was vented on the faithful dogs, who had remained behind rat-hunting. I drove them from me with rage, unable to bear the sight of any living thing.

Then I went to my brandy keg, and took a large quantity of the spirit, though now it was nearly exhausted; which, however, instead of filling me with consolation, only added to my misery by inflaming my already too ardent imagination.

Presently, however, it procured me sleep, which did certainly refresh me much.

When I awoke with something of an aching brow, it was my first endeavour to arrange and calm my thoughts. My poor father used to say that there is only one remedy for sorrow, only one means by which grief can be allayed, and that is, an occupation both of the body and the mind; and I lived to know that my father was right.

Now during my wild-goose chase after the Indian girl, and during my illness, my domestic animals had been neglected.

I had also forgotten to garner my harvest. Rousing myself to a conviction of the necessity for action, I rose from the ground, whistled to my dogs, which came bounding to me as if nothing had happened, and took my way towards the valley of the gazelles.

Everything there was in proper order.

The gazelles, however, were very wild, while the ostriches stalked about with an air of ludicrous gravity most amusing to behold.

Entering within the enclosure, which required some slight repairs, the cause of the wildness of the gazelles became at once evident to me.

Some savage beast had been there. A large gazelle, the mother of the whole party, lay panting on the ground in the agonies of death.

I clutched my gun, and looked around. But nothing was to be seen. No doubt the beast, whatever it was, had been scared away by the barking of my dogs.

What was to be done? I could not allow my pen to be destroyed in this way.

Besides, my mind was in such a mood, that action was above all things necessary to me, and no action could be of a more exciting nature than the destruction of the savage prowler which had dared to attack my flocks.

Looking around, a plan occurred to me, which at once was put into operation. Close to the fold into which, by the aid of my dogs, the gazelles had been driven, was a steep and rugged ascent, leading to the summit of a sort of cliff. But it was evident that on that side it could not be climbed. I at once, after dragging the dead gazelle close to the fold, left the valley with my dogs.

The way I took was one which had never been followed by me before.

Generally, my road lay through the valley, or to its right. Now I took to the left, and after considerable toil and difficulty, ascended to the summit of the cliff. More and more was I surprised at the difference exhibited by the two extremities of my island.

Here were blackened and bare lava rocks, steep volcanic ridges, gorges, and irregular truncated cones, the work of old out-breaking fires; these, with abrupt jagged precipices, grizzly or grass rown, faced the sea, while directly in the shore were a few lank cocoa-nut trees, with crowns of scanty fan-like branches.

I hurried along, however, without much close remark, until I found myself in such a position as to command a view of the pen, in which my gazelles were huddled in a corner, evidently not yet recovered from their fright.

Placing my dogs behind me, and motioning to the faithful animals to be quiet, I laid down flat on my face, and watched.

As I did so, my eyes fell upon the valley generally, which appeared to me somewhat less fertile than I could have wished.

This set me thinking, and combined with the somewhat lean appearance of the gazelles, determined me to endeavour to make it more productive.

A very large patch was almost without grass, but it seemed to me, that if the soil were turned up just before the rainy season, and some of the numerous grass seeds which abounded on the island cast therein, the result would be satisfactory.

But this was a matter for future consideration. What was now to be done was, to destroy the enemy of my flock. A movement of terror from my gazelles warned me to be ready.

A hasty glance from the summit of the cliff at once revealed the mystery.

About fifty yards from the pen, a number of rocks, falling by accident in a fantastic and odd manner, had made a small cave, from which now issued with stealthy and slow step, a very large specimen of the hyena tribe.

Its eyes were cast about in all directions except upwards. It glanced to the right and left, then behind, then forward, until it seemed convinced that the coast was clear.

Then it came on, not boldly, not with a spring, but in the same sneaking and cautious way it had commenced its approaches.

In two minutes, however, it was close to the still warm body of the gazelle.

I had long been ready, and just as the marauder thought himself sure of this prey, fired.

It was impossible to restrain my dogs after this, so leaping to my feet, I prepared to support them. Down the almost perpendicular rocks they bounded in pursuit. They had not far to go.

The hyena had received his death wound; for instead of fleeing, as is the nature of the beast, he turned to fight.

But the contest was short.

The bullet had gone right through him just by the joint of his hind leg, and when the dog and she-wolf flew at his neck, he fell over helpless and overcome.

Not caring to witness the clusion of a combat which was already decided, I turned away to explore the neighbourhood.

It was new to me, and in my present mood, novelty was one of those things which I chiefly coveted. Anything to drive away thought, to make me forget the terrible loss I had experienced, the blank which filled my heart.

Probably Adam in Paradise might have been happy alone had the woman not have been created, but once having seen her, solitude must have been too awful to bear.

For myself, I doubt if solitude is to be endured under any circumstances whatever.

No. 14.—Sailor Crusoe

MAKING A CANOE.

CHAPTER LXVIII.

THE ALBATROSS.

TAKING my way down towards the shore, I soon found myself near the sea, in a spot which was not familiar to me. Standing on the summit of a cliff, about twenty feet above the level of the raging sea, which on this side always was in motion, boiling and seething probably since time was, I was able to take a fair view of the shore for a considerable distance to my right and left.

There was at all events one subject of attraction, and that was a number of albatrosses, variously occupied.

Some were flying about; others engaged in fishing; others sitting on small solitary rocks alone, evidently hatching.

I watched these birds with interest, and bethought me of all I could remember hearing of them. As my father had told me, their motion through space was most easy and graceful. In storms or calms, once raised upon their broad pinions, you never see them flutter, but away they sail, self-propelled, as naturally as we breathe. A motion of the head or the slight curl of a wing served to turn them. It was just like that motion through space which we sometimes conceive in dreams.

Men call the eagle the king of birds, but surely this is the queen—for queenly like and stately is her course upon the wing, and dignified, mild, and unfearing her expression when captured (as she often is, with a hook baited with pork and blubber, and a piece of wood for a float). But I never did, for a reason presently to be explained. Yes; from that hour I could have cried with the poet—

> " We had done a hellish thing,
> And it would work us woe.
> Stout they averred we had killed the bird
> That made the breeze to blow.
> 'Ah, wretch!' said they, ' the bird to slay,
> That made the breeze to blow.' "

The eye of the albatross is full, bright, and expressive, like that of the gazelle; the head and neck large, but admirably proportioned; the feathers either a pure white or delicately pencilled and speckled, except on the upper side of the wings, which are mostly black.

There is, too, an expression of pathos and intelligence about the eye which is singularly attractive. They sometimes weigh twenty pounds, and have twelve feet stretch of wing.

It sits on the water light and graceful as a swan, and will dive under, like a hawk or pelican, for something discovered by its keen eye beneath the surface. When it is about to rise on the wing, it has positively to tread the water for a long way, like a running ostrich, before it can get the proper momentum and soar aloft; but once it is fairly up, and its pinions quite free, it cleaves the air with exceeding swiftness, and skims the waves, like the smallest swallow, with perfect ease and grace.

It flies against as well as before the wind. It enjoys the calm, and sports in the sunbeams on the glassy wave; but its revel is the storm, when it darts its arrowy way before the fury of the tempest. It is now in its proper element, and seems to delight in breasting an mocking the surges of the mighty sea.

It feeds on small marine animals, mucilaginous zoophytes, the spawn of fish; but its chief delight is whales' blubber. When breeding, the female flies to some inaccessible rock or lonely spot of ground, lays seldom more than one egg, and builds a nest around that. All this time the male watches and tends her with great assiduity, bringing her the daintiest morsels from the deep.*

From its often choosing the same place of breeding as the penguin, the albatross is thought to have a peculiar affection for that amphibious creature, and is supposed to take pleasure in its society. Their nests are continually to be seen together on rocks and small uninhabited island.

The albatross generally raises its nest on a hillock of heath, sticks, and long grass, about two feet high, and round this the penguins, in a circle, make their lower settlements in burrowed holes in the ground, commonly eight penguins to one albatross.

But it is useless putting off the narration of one of the most wonderful adventures which ever happened to me during the whole of my adventurous career—a circumstance almost without parallel, I should think, in the history of any man.

The sea came, I have said, to the very foot of the cliff on which I was now reclining.

Somewhat tired with my day's journey, my gun had been laid on one side, with everything which was a burden and a restraint.

After gazing for some time at the scene below, at the tossing waves, the grand horizon, and watching with interest the movements of the birds, a feverish thirst came upon me. Now I was well aware that no water could be found nearer than the valley.

I was not inclined to walk through the burning sun in search of a drink, but thought I would quench my thirst with a few raw eggs.

To reach these much-coveted dainties it was necessary to make a long circuit, or to descend the steep cliff, and swim a few yards to where there was a slanting piece of ground, with many albatrosses and penguins.

The cliff was steep, but there were many projections as well as holes to plant my feet; so the determination was no sooner come to than it was carried into effect.

Planting my feet firmly on a small ledge, I began crawling down the side of the rock. It was no easy task, but my many feats made things easy to me now, which, in days gone by, would have been simply impossible.

I was about half way down, when suddenly I found that the face of the cliff was giving way under my weight, and before I could cling to the rock above, I glided down, and fell into the boiling waves. In an instant I was carried out by the tide and the receding waves.

I knew that my strength was not equal to any long battling with the raging waters, so at once hurriedly glanced round to measure the distance I had to go.

The rock was already more than twenty feet distant. But it was useless to make any efforts in that direction. My only chance of safety was to swim as rapidly as I could for the low beach to the right.

It was a fearful task. The waves hissed, boiled, and roared in my ears with a fearful din, the current swept against my legs and impeded my advance, and then—

---

* In the classification of Linnæus, the albatross is the *Diomedea exulans*, a genus which is described as having the bill very long, stout, edged, compressed, straight, suddenly curved; upper mandible channelled on the sides, and much hooked at the point; the under, smooth and truncated at the extremity; nostrils lateral, remote from the base, tubular, covered on the sides, and open in front; legs short, with only three very long toes entirely webbed; the lateral ones are margined; wings very long and narrow, with the primary quills short, and the secondaries long.

horrible to relate—I felt a sinking faintness come over me of the most horrible description.

Besides, there was a despairing sensation as of coming inevitable death.

Behind me was a small rock which I might reach—but what then?

It would be harder to swim ashore from that spot than from where I was.

Again my feet were brought into play, again my arms were exerted with what little strength remained, but in vain. Not a step was made in advance.

The sea ran stronger and stronger every minute, and there was nothing to be done but yield to the boiling waves and die.

So young! That morning so full of hope, of happiness, and life—in sight of the shore—within a short distance of home—with a blue smiling sky above, and an element beneath which usually was easy enough to control.

At this moment a cloud passed over my head, and a huge albatross—evidently suspecting me of some improper intentions with regard to its mate, which was sitting on a nest close at hand—coming like magic, with an almost imperceptible motion, approached, and made a swoop at me to strike my head.

I raised my hands mechanically, and in my desperate strait seized the bird, which began struggling violently to get free.

But I held fast, determined, like any other dying man, to catch at a straw rather than nothing.

Next minute my feet touched ground—the next I was rolling on the soft and sandy slope by the sea—saved by an albatross.

My astonishment, bewilderment, and gratitude, may be conceived.

The fact is that in my struggles I had made for the slanting beach in a kind of sideway, so that at the moment of my clutching the huge bird in my agony I was not more than a few feet out of my depth.

However this may be it was the albatross that saved me, and from that hour until the day of my death never did the thought of killing one enter my head.

The fatigue and exhaustion of my terrible struggle was such that I lay exhausted quite half an hour.

My frame had received a great shock, and when I rose to my feet, it was with the firm conviction that another fit of illness was about to visit me when I was alone.

This reflection made me feel doubly the departure of Pablina, my comfort, my consolation, my nurse.

Then, as in my desolation I strolled towards the interior of the island, after wetting my parched and feverish lips with the yolk of an egg, the idea flashed across my mind that she had only left me to communicate with her friends, and that she would shortly return in their company.

This idea so affected me that I was compelled to sit down in order to recover myself.

In this way the valley was regained, after a long detour to fetch my gun.

Then calling off my dogs from their feast on the gazelle I slowly returned to my solitary cavern, there to spend the night.

CHAPTER LXIX.

I TURN PLANTER.

IT might have been from a sense of gratitude for my narrow escape from death—it might be something like reaction on my mind, after so much excitement and anxiety; but when I awoke in the morning, after a long and refreshing sleep, I felt more resigned to Providence, and in a better humour to contend with the ills and sorrows of life.

Not that I abated one jot of my regrets—not that I ceased to be sorry that I had lost her—but my nerves seemed braced, my energy revived, and my whole being, as it were, renovated and restored.

There was much to be done.

My fields had to be garnered and sown again, and then it was my earnest resolve to improve the state of my gazelle pen, so as to admit of its containing a greater number of animals, in expectation of the day when I should be without gunpowder.

Another idea struck me, and that was, as my young dogs grew up, I would arm them with spikes and chain them, or rather fasten with a long lariat, in such a way as to frighten away such sneaking animals as wolves and hyenas.

Lions, and such like beasts, were not likely to visit this part of the island, which was without forests in which they could take shelter.

But the prowling beasts, to which I allude were here, there, and everywhere.

My plan of ploughing up the field already indicated was to fasten an iron spade, in a kind of slanting direction to a good stout piece of wood, to which, with great labour, the horse and zebra were harnessed.

Then, seating myself on this, I urged the animals forward with the whip until a very large space was turned up.

This was sown with the seeds of several rich natural grasses as thickly as appeared advisable.

Then a large rake was dragged over the whole much in the same way, and nature and the climate was left to do the rest.

Another idea, however, suggested itself, while engaged in this task, and that was simply enough carried out.

The properties of the cocoa-nut-palm have been already alluded to.

Near my cave were several, which were profusely covered with ripe nuts, some trees producing more than two hundred.

A number of these were collected and carted down to the valley.

The stream, which ran through it has already been alluded to. Along the banks of this a number of holes were made, and into these a fully ripe nut was dropped.

Those who only know the nut as an esculent would marvel at its growth.

In a few days after being planted a thin lance-like shoot forces itself through a minute hole in the shell, pierces the coarse outside husk, and soon unfolds three pale green shoots to the air.

Then originating in the same soft white sponge, which now completely fills the nut, a pair of fibrous roots, pushing away the stoppers that close two holes in an opposite direction, penetrate the shell, and strike vertically into the ground.

A day or two after this, so rapid is growth in this climate, the shell and husk which, in the last and germinating stage of the nut, are so hard that a knife will scarcely make any impression, spontaneously bursts by some inner force.

Then the hardy young plant thrives apace, and needing no culture, pruning, or attention of any kind, rapidly advances to maturity.

In four or five years it bears; in twice as many more, it lifts its head among the groves, where, waxing strong, it flourishes for nearly a century.

Such are some of the wonders of the great vegetable creation.

This somewhat laborious task executed, my steps were directed to my plantation, which was in sad disorder, and took me more than a week ere it was in order, and fully started for another crop.

At length, however, all was housed, and then, listening to the dictates of my own feelings, I started on a gallop to the summer-house on the island, where my animals were all found prosperous enough.

The birds were so tame that even my absence did not frighten them. The house served them as shelter and the woods provided them with food.

Having taken one long, lingering survey of the place, a secret presentiment appearing to fill my soul, that never more would my footsteps tend that way, I again crossed the lake and returned towards the cave.

The wet season had again commenced.

During this time it would be utterly impossible to feed my cattle. It was necessary therefore, to devise some way of enabling them to earn their own living. Still I could not bear to lose them.

Selecting, therefore, a spot as near to me as possible, they were both hoppled, that is to say, their legs were tied in such fashion that they could not run, but still could walk about freely and crop the pleasant grass. But there was one source of satisfaction, which little struck me.

The two animals were singularly attached to each other, and thus were kept together.

The young zebra, which was very tame indeed, was allowed to run loose, trusting to its instinct to keep it from straying away. This done, my duty was over, and my mind could be given to the one idea, which had never been absent from my thoughts since the first moment of the escape of the Indian girl.

With this view I had laid in a large stock of cocoa-nut fibres, cocoa-nut wood, and other things, devoting one spare hour every day to the task.

Besides these things, I had cut down several straight trees, a goodly pine among the others.

What I was about to do will shortly be seen.

I had for weeks been planning a great, and at the same time, a marvellous deed.

CHAPTER LXX.

WINTER QUARTERS.

I WAS about to make a canoe, with which to attempt a voyage of discovery to that island which, it was my impression, contained the person of the fugitive from my shores.

While devoting myself earnestly to those tasks which were necessary to the prolongation of my existence, my thoughts had never swerved from the one great idea of the girl I had hoped was to share my involuntary exile, and the result had been, that as she had run away from me, I would go in search of her.

But as the navigation was perilous and unknown to me, it was necessary to be provided against all contingencies. It was of importance to have food in abundance, water, and arms. Now an ordinary canoe like that which Pablino had fled with was all very well for one who knew the land-marks, and was able to go straight to a certain point, but it would not have been advisable for me to attempt anything of the kind.

Mine was to be a kind of voyage of discovery, and therefore I required a vessel which would do service both in fair weather and foul; the former of which had always been selected by Pablina for her journeys.

But while it was my fixed determination to make some kind of vessel, my mind was not quite so satisfied as to the nature of the thing to be done.

My youthful studies had made me familiar from mere boyhood with every style of water conveyance, from Noah's ark to a Welsh coracle, including junks, prahus, canoes, duggouts, periguas, sampans, and the like.

But there is a great difference between knowing the shape of a thing, and being able to make it.

Still it was my solemn resolve to try.

My first thoughts ran on a double canoe, which is composed of two single ones of the same size, placed parallel to each other, three or four feet apart, and secured in their places by four or five cross pieces of wood, curved just in the shape of a bit-stock.

These are lashed to both the canoes, with the strongest sinnet, made of cocoa-nut fibre.

A flattened arch is in this way made by the bow-like cross pieces over the space between the canoes, upon which a board or a couple of stout poles, laid lengthwise, constitute an elevated platform, for passengers and freight, while those who are to paddle and steer sit on the bodies of the canoe at the sides.

A slender mast often rose from the middle of the platform, giving support to a very simple sail made from matting.

But there was an objecion to this plan which was this:—To make two canoes was to undergo double labour, and if they were replaced by beams of wood, the raft would be unmanageable.

Still, no rational or feasible idea suggested itself to me. It was at last decided in my mind to leave the decision of the matter somewhat to fortune, while in the meantime I prepared such parts of a canoe as could be constructed in my cave.

There were indeed many things which would have been far more useful, and the devotion of time to which would have been decidedly more rational, but my mind was made up, and nothing could move me from the contemplation of my hobby.

As my vessel was to be a sailing vessel, a mast, a rudder, a yard, and a pair of sweeps were absolute necessities, after which there came the important item of sail and rigging.

People talk of a labour of love.

With me, this was the right epithet to apply to the task which I had undertaken.

I was goaded on by the sweetest of hopes, that of finding a companion to share my solitude and lighten my cares.

I worked like a slave, and often was compelled to own to myself that I had overdone it.

First, the pole, which had been selected for a mast, had to rounded and smoothed, to admit of its being placed upright without toppling over, as the vessel, which I could hope to make, must be somewhat light.

Still it must have strength to support my sail.

My anxiety was great, as using my small axe with great caution the pole was rounded, the asperities clipped off, and the whole made to taper off gradually to the trunk.

This done, it had to be scraped with a piece of old iron hoop, that there might not be the slightest chance of a hitch in drawing up and lowering the sail.

As my ingenuity did not admit of my constructing a block, through which the halyards, or rope that pulls up or lets down the sail, I was compelled to weave a kind of ring of rope, so well-oiled and smoothed as to admit of the other being dragged through it, in order to give it as much of a round shape as possible, the inside was a stout piece of old rope, round which was entwined some fine twine of my own making.

This took me four days of excessive labour.

In the evening, while enjoying my pipe, my fingers were diligently engaged in weaving cordage from fibre, and during the winter season the quantity which was made appeared to my mind to be very great.

But it was poor stuff, as having no one to turn a handle for me, it was necessary to plait it rather than twine it.

There is no doubt that with assistance I could have made as good rope as could have been required, as watching the rope makers was one of my amusements when visiting the fishing town of Yarmouth in Norfolk, near which place, as has been already indicated, I was born.

The rudder was no easy matter.

The shape was familiar to me, but how to fashion it was a mystery that I could not easily fathom.

Besides, there were no iron rings and hooks to hang it by, so I determined at last to use a wide paddle, fastened in a rollock by means of some good strong cord.

Had my saw have been a really serviceable article, my progress would have been swifter.

To make a wide paddle and two long sweeps or oars—the former being the right name for all over a certain size, as those of a barge—it was necessary to take three distinct trees, and to fashion them out by means of my axe, leaving one end wide, and the other such as could be clasped by the hand.

When they were finished, no boat-builder in Europe would have allowed them a place in his yard.

But everything must have a beginning.

The Chinese assert that the first idea of a boat was taken some two thousand years ago from a woman's slipper, and they do not seem to have improved much upon it.

Still, others have, and boat-building is now quite a science.

When everything necessary to a boat itself was constructed, except the body, there remained preparations against hunger and thirst.

Calabashes, gourds, and a small keg, were provided against the latter; while meat was smoked, biscuit packed, and vegetables put aside for the former purpose.

When ready to depart, fruits and other necessaries could be added.

At length, just as, from having nothing more to do, my spirits began to fall, the rainy season ended, and the warm, glad sun, the clear blue sky, and the song of birds, invited me to sally forth.

With what delight I did so may well be imagined.

Having hastily visited my gazelles, and killed a pig or two, both for my own use and those of my animals, my preparations were made for a journey into the interior. My horse and zebra I found fat and rather shy, but a little corn and salt soon got over that.

Then they were loaded; and, armed with gun and sword, and all the tools I could carry, I sallied forth into the interior, as proud, in all probability, as Noah was when he first began to build the ark.

The spot which in my mind's eye had been selected for the purpose of trying my hand at boat-building, was three miles from the sea, but close to a stream that ran to the shore, and was navigable all the way.

There I had observed some trees, which were likely to suit my purpose.

My recollections of the misfortunes of my great predecessor prevented me from making a similar mistake.

There were much better trees, and much better suited to my purpose, on other parts of the island, but then they were far away from water.

The spot chosen by me was a small glade, close to a narrow bayou that ran into the river.

Beside this was just such a tree as I wanted, though not long enough; but it was wide and straight.

My first task, after fixing my camp, was to dig round the roots, at which I then began to cut with the energy of one whose life is at stake.

This took me a whole day, and then the tree did not fall; but at early dawn again my axe awoke the echoes of the forest, and about mid-day it fell.

The trunk part, which would have been of use to me, was about fourteen feet long; and though my boat would have to be much larger, yet still I did not despair.

My brains were at work, both remembering and inventing. The trunk once on the ground, the whole of the superfluous branches and wood had to be hacked off with my axe.

Then the want of a good saw became visible.

But to cut a very long and wearisome story short, at the end of a week I had before me a solid trunk nearly fifteen feet long by four wide, and as many deep, on which to commence my arduous proceedings.

The labour was fearful, but I never flinched. My meals were hurried over as much as possible.

There stood the log, and I could neither eat, drink, nor sleep in peace until it was turned into a canoe.

The hardest part of all proved to be flattening the upper side.

This took me four days hard consecutive work, taking off my coat, too, in earnest.

Then I began to make way.

A good fire was lit at some little distance, from which I every now and then took the live coals, and so placed them on the wood of my future canoe as to burn away the interior while I fashioned the outside.

In this way nearly all savage duggouts are made. For several days, while I was cutting away with extreme care and nicety the asperities and superabundant wood, the fire process continued until the trunk was hollowed out in a satisfactory way.

But this was only in the rough, as my axe had again to come into play to make the rude thing level.

Then by the assistance of my horse and zebra the trunk was turned half over and supported by two thick branches, while I fashioned something of a keel.

This done, my boat being quite water-tight, though the ends were somewhat slight, my resolution was to put it on a gridiron.

This is a thing used in dockyards to clean the bottoms of vessels.

My way of making it was thus—a number of poles and bamboos were cut and laid across the bayou or creek, just about four inches above the water, and on to this the boat was dragged by my cattle, while I guided the progress of my precious treasure with a kind of rude handspike.

My object in placing it in this position was to lengthen it, both at the bow and at the stern.

For this purpose the thick bark of similar trees was cut off in one solid mass, and by judicious management and coaxing made to assume the required shape.

It was then fastened to the trunk by means of bamboo dowel-pins, or wooden nails, which were let in by means of a red hot ramrod being used for an auger.

Across the bow was placed a small deck of bamboo, to consolidate the structure, other bamboos and bamboo cords being bent round outside.

Two powerful stretchers were placed above the hole in which the mast was to be stepped; these also were secured by strong bamboo dowel-pins.

A seat in the stern sheet, and a small plank to place my feet on, and my boat was complete.

No; the master-piece of my cunning was yet to be developed. The presence of a large quantity of India-rubber vines had been one object of my selecting this spot.

My gourds were now prepared and the proper incision being made a good supply of the milky juice was procured, with which, by the exercise of great patience, every seam, every join, every dowel-pin, was duly payed and caulked.

My triumph was complete. I had a boat.

But now came the launch. With a view to the proper and due observance of the ceremony I placed on board my craft some large pieces of meat cut from a deer I had killed that morning, some corn, and a gourd of brandy and water.

Then a loaded gun was put in the stern sheets, and I cleared for action.

With my axe the centre supports were cut away, leaving only one at each end.

Then the weight of the boat brought the keel to the water's edge, after which I cut away the stern end, and the canoe was in the water on a level keel.

Frantic with joy I cast the food to my dogs, zebra, and horse, drank a good draught of brandy and water, and leaped into the canoe.

I was afloat!

————

CHAPTER LXXI.

PREPARATIONS FOR MY JOURNEY.

I had a dream which was not all a dream.
The bright sun was extinguish'd, and the stars
Did wander darkling in the eternal space,
Rayless and pathless; and the icy earth
Swung blind and blackening in the moonless air.
Morn came and went—and came, and brought no day,
And men forgot their passions in the dread
Of this their desolation; and all hearts
Were chill'd into a selfish prayer for light.
And they did live by watchfires—and the thrones—
The palaces of crowned kings—the huts,—
The habitations of all things which dwell,
Were burnt for beacons; cities were consumed—
And men were gather'd round their blazing homes
To look once more into each other's face;
Happy were those who dwelt within the eye
Of the volcanoes, and their mountain-torch.
                                        BYRON.

A CHILD with its first toy, a young mother dandling her first child, a lawyer with a long expected brief, are usually quoted as instances of perfect happiness; but who so happy and proud as I?

Here on this desert island, with but a few old tools saved from the wreck of a ship, with but scanty knowledge of the way to proceed—thank Heaven, that my youth had been spent in reading—I had succeeded in building myself, without the remotest assistance, a canoe, able to bear at least six or seven people, and it appeared to me that with the cargo

which one man could take with him, this admitted of my sailing round the world.

In the early days of voyage and discovery, men had travelled wondrous distances in small, rickety and frail open boats, and had thus arrived in safety at their destination.

Thus had the six hundred islands of the Pacific been peopled, that island world, embosomed in a vast ocean, sweeping in latitude from pole to pole, rolling in longitude over a whole hemisphere, and exceeding in area all the continents and islands of the globe, by ten millions of miles.

Many years before any record that we have, these islands rose from the deep, and were peopled by stray Malay and other boats being carried thousands of miles out of their course.

Chinese junks were known to land their human freight after being tossed a whole year on the angry billows; and then, too, I was well aware that Columbus himself had made his voyage to America in a caracal not much bigger than a barge.

How proud then I was of this my vehicle for locomotion may be imagined.

Now, however, came the reflection, that my boat had to be got down to the sea, which, without oars or rudder, was no easy matter. My animals, too, had to be taken back to the place whence they came, so that they might provide themselves with food during my absence, which might—who knows what may or may not happen when he starts upon a journey?—be eternal.

The precious canoe was then docked in the bayou; after which, mounting my zebra, and leading my horse, which was more obedient to the yoke, and therefore employed as a beast of burthen, I started for home, followed by my animals. The journey was delightful, but was not completed in one day, as I wished to select the proper place at the mouth of the river for fitting out my vessel finally.

The mouth of the river was wide, with a shallow bar, over which at times the waves dash furiously. These bars are occasioned by the action of the wind against the natural course of the river, causing the sediment to be deposited at their entrances instead of being carried out into the deeper parts of the sea.

When the wind blows strongly—and it generally blows in one direction—the water, struggling to ooze forth, causes a terrible wave, which is by sailors technically called a "bore."

It was necessary for me to fit out my boat, provision it, and then select a calm day for my departure. But even with a stiff breeze, the sea here was scarcely ruffled. The spot was not one I should have selected as a residence, but it did very well for a port.

Broad mudbanks extended on either side when the tide was low, while birds and reptiles covered its banks. There were alligators, too. Indeed, the number of these loathsome brutes was very great, either swimming, or lying sprawling on the mud in wait for their prey.

My camp was on a rising knoll, whence I looked out upon the distant and promised land, which loomed grey and indistinct in the distance. Here my poles were erected and a bush hut hastily erected for the night. Here I sat after supper gazing out at the scene before me, on the soft unruffled sea, on the wild and furious bore, on the flat sea-coast, on the distant hills; until slowly the setting sun tinged their peaks with rosy and purple tints, when they gradually sank into darkness as the evening mists gathered strength on the seaward edge of the jungle-like prairie, and, moved by the evening breeze, sailed along like huge phantoms. Then come night itself, with its dew-laden atmosphere—against which I had guarded by means of my hut—and soon a starlit sky.

And then began the busy hum which is ever attendant on tropical nights, when the insects, and monkeys, and other restless beasts come forth in search of prey. But, guarded by my dogs, my gun near at hand, and my fire blazing cheerily, I cared not, but slept soundly through the long watches of the night.

Up at dawn of day, with a stiff squall just ending. While getting my breakfast and loading my patient cattle, I noticed how the gust seemed to have cleared the atmosphere.

The distant island seemed nearer, everything appeared to have fresh life, the very sea glittered in the sunlight with a brighter and a deeper blue, and the forest-clad slopes of this land looked more gorgeous, as they sparkled in the sun's rays, in all their varied panoply of gold and green. The whole scene was as of a "summer isle of Eden lying in dark purple spheres of sea."

Away with all speed to the cave, where necessarily two days were spent in final preparations. My provender consisted of one rum keg of water, six gourds and calabashes ditto, one gourd of rum and water, one ditto of brandy neat; a fair supply of tobacco and sundry pipes.

Then came one keg of half-salted pork raw, two joints of ditto roasted, much jerked or dried meat, some carrots, turnips, yams, and cocoanuts; also a small quantity of corn, with two guns, a powder horn and some bullets.

In addition to the clothing that I wore a number of furs were taken down to the beach, where my store was established.

The mast, sail, oars, and rudder, were next transported, with due care, to the water's edge. A rough hut was erected over them, and then, with an ample supply of provender and bones, two dogs were tied up to guard them.

My gazelle valley was visited the first day, and the gazelles driven into the pen, with a quantity of green meat. This done, on my return I was able to notice with pleasure the rich grass that was everywhere covering the valley, and which had hitherto kept these little creatures from attacking my cocoa palms, which were rising in a most astounding manner.

I killed two pigs, these animals breeding very fast, which I placed in an out-of-the-way place, for my dogs to find in case they were unsuccessful in hunting.

A few additional scarecrows, in the shape of a stuffed monkey or so, were added to my plantation, and then, having acted like a prudent man, I thought it was time that I should give way to my feelings, and start on my voyage of discovery.

This time I took my solitary way towards the spot where lay my bark canoe. I had to bring the precious treasure down the river, and wanted no animals with me. Besides, I wanted to be alone, to dance, to jump, to expand my chest, to breathe freely, as the thought filled my soul of what might be the ultimate result of my voyage.

Mine was not hope—that told me no flattering tale. It was a certainty. Methought I saw her, as I walked, already my companion in this new garden of Eden.

My way lay through dense forests, open glades, across streams; and, as I was on foot, the way was long, so that it was evening before the camp was reached; and the thousand stars that strewed the sky peered knowingly down upon me, through openings in the forest, and the tall trees waved their sable plumes over my head, and the firefly and other luminous insects lit up, first one tree and then the other, as if sparks of liquid gold were being emitted from the rustling and trembling leaves.

But my boat was safe, and I lay down that night within it with rare satisfaction, wrapped in a huge rug, made from two lions' skins sewn together. I made no fire.

My surprise may be conceived, when, towards dawn, I discovered how cold it could be at so short a distance from the equator. I found, however, that the night dew struck a chill to my very bones, so that when I crawled on shore, to illuminate the scene, my limbs were quite stiff.

A roaring fire I made of many a huge bough and many a branch, with chips that had been left, and Spanish moss, soon relieved me, and I returned to my couch, drawing it close in shore with something of a feeling of satisfaction.

But sleep not being so easily wooed as I could wish, I was again on foot, and partaking of a hearty breakfast; after which I hastened to make up my fire cheerily, and then proceeded to cut down the pole which was to serve me to guide my boat down the river.

A long and straight one being found, it was cut down, its branches lopped off, and the whole ready for use in little more than an hour. Then my canoe was entered, and one thrust of the pole sent it gliding gracefully and swiftly into the clear open water.

Above the dock where she had lain was an open lake-like space, where it took my fancy to give her a trial, for which purpose the pole was rigged up for a mast, and my lion skin hooked on for a sail. A stout bough of a tree served for a temporary rudder or scull.

She behaved beautifully.

But before I give any account of the Stormy Petrel, as my canoe was christened, let me make one remark.

I left a roaring fire on the beach, close to a large tree, which was thickly over-grown by creeping plants and Spanish moss, that hung down in graceful festoons to within a few feet of the fire.

CHAPTER LXXII.

TRIAL OF MY BOAT.

THE lion skin was rather heavy and awkward as a sail, but this only proved the tautness and excellence of my canoe. As I turned her to the wind, the boat tilted a little, and lay down to leeward, but she kept her own, and, to my infinite delight, it was evident that, properly managed, she would beat to windward.

This was a most soothing discovery, as on this coast the wind appeared to blow periodically in one direction, except that it often shifted at evening and morning.

So transported with joy was I with my discovery, that, like a school-boy, I could not sufficiently glut myself with trials, until the sun, rising hot and sultry, warned me to start on my way.

Still, such was my infatuation, that I still continued disporting myself for some hours, until I was so fatigued that I was obliged to bathe to restore my exhausted faculties.

Then, however, the lengthening shadows warned me to make haste. The river below my dock was narrow, and overhung with trees, while the jungle reeds grew right into the water, so that a night journey would be both dangerous and difficult.

This necessitated my pole being taken down, as it would be as much as I could do to navigate by means of my boat-hook, keeping the canoe in the middle, and especially avoiding the peril of snags and fallen trees, so often fatal to the traveller in undiscovered regions.

I feared not for myself, though alligators and hippopotami are no mean enemies; but my anxiety was for my own darling boat—to me, worth all the other treasures I possessed.

Hark! what do I hear? The roar of artillery, the report of ten thousand muskets, or the fearful outbreak of a thunder-storm.

No—it is the forest on fire.

Up high into the heavens rises the dark and pungent smoke, while the fierce element, burning up the reeds and jungle, causes them to send forth an intermittent roar, which, at times, was deafening; at others, a series of loud and rapid cracklings, which I had mistaken for musketry.

It was a fearful scene, and what was I to do?

There was the choice of waiting until the terrible conflagration was over—until the furious element had expended itself on the dry trees, moss and reeds, when a way through the blackened mass could easily be made; or I could run the gauntlet, and descend the river in spite of the flames, smoke, and falling masses of fire and flame. In my peculiar frame of mind, it could not be difficult to decide on which course to pursue.

I would risk the trial by fire.

I was now about twenty yards from my dock, the aspect of which was so changed that I scarcely could recognize it at all. The half-dead tree, from which the dry moss and creeping plants had depended, had caught fire.

The heat of the burning pile had been so great as to scorch the plants and trunk, until they were as dry as tinder, when they flamed up in a hot and massive column, that seemed to reach the very sky.

For now more than six weeks had all this tropical vegetation been under the influence of a broiling sun, that penetrated to the very sap. Grass, leaves, trunks, were all equally affected by the scorching sun, so that in a few minutes one broad sheet of flame enveloped the whole of the woods within sight.

But one side of the river was free, and I determined, despite the smoke, which was blown *across* the stream, to attempt the passage, as if the fire were to be general, the journey would be perilous in the extreme. Fortunately, my canoe was extremely manageable.

So great was the necessity for extreme caution, that I allowed the boat to go down with the current, only being careful to keep her off from the other side by means of my invaluable pole. In this way I made some slight advance when, lo! another danger, on which I had not calculated, faced me.

Both sides of the river were on fire.

This is how it happened. I have said that large trees, mangroves, and others, grew close to the water's edge, the branches of which overlapped each other. But just facing me the narrow gap of the river was lined with cocoa-nut palms. The trunks had been entirely hidden when I saw them last by dependent vines. These had been caught by the swift march of the terrible element, and now the trees themselves were on fire.

It was grand. It was now dark. The felt-like substance between the roots of the trees, as well as the leaves themselves, catching fire, and communicating from one to the other, the falling, scorching branches made firework-like descents, and the banks of the river on both sides resembled a row of gigantic torches flaming and waving in the air.

It was awful, for how to pass I knew not, as the fierce rapidity of the flames could scarcely be described. The fire leaped from tree to tree, from bush to bush, ere you thought one, and licked up with its fiery tongue everything within reach—grasses, vines, leaves, and then the trees themselves. I looked behind.

The huge, massive trees, baobabs, and others, which interlaced their boughs, were one sheet of flame, while the falling flakes had set fire to the reeds, which crackled, spurted, and burnt with the intensity of turpentine.

It was one vast bonfire. The aspect of the heavens was infernal. Just above the line of flames, themselves bright and clear, there was a lurid yellow glitter, gradually tapering down to the faintest of light. Above this was a dense black canopy of smoke, which hung like a funeral pall over the whole island.

The effect was of the most oppressive character, as, to gaze around, the last hours of the earth seemed to have been counted; while that the beautiful vegetation of the island was to be destroyed, scarce admitted of a doubt.

But this was not an hour for action, but reflection. Escape from my post seemed impossible. My position was awkward and peculiar.

I was in a bend in the stream, where the width of the river was nearly double what it was both above and below. The shore was away some fifty feet on both sides, the trees to which I was tolerably near growing right in the water. To escape was easy, for I could note that the forest was still unscathed at the back. But then, what was to become of my canoe?

This thought roused my latent energies. I grasped my pole, stood up, and proceeded to guide my way. The noises were hideous. I could hear, amidst the roar of the flames, the hiss of the dying serpent, and I could see huge crocodiles, which at first had taken the fire for the beaming of an unusually hot day, gliding their slimy bodies through the water to escape the fire.

Hundreds of fish floated on the surface, killed by the fearful stench that rose from the river as vast blazing masses fell into the channel. Eels of a huge and strange species came crawling, half dead, out of the reeds, while toads and other reptiles skipped about with unusual activity.

It was a regular scene for Pandemonium, through which I passed with a beating and anxious heart. My lion-skin mantle was cast over my shoulders to ward off the falling flakes of fire, burning trees, and wood, and thus I steered as rapidly as I could through the ordeal by fire.

The heat was intense, the smoke came wafted in clouds to my nostrils, bringing on violent fits of coughing, which caused me several times nearly to upset the boat.

Still the awful conflagration seemed not to decrease, the heavens looked angry and red, when my thoughts and fears were nearly brought to an end for ever by my canoe running against something that looked like a rock, which, however, as it was touched, seemed to rise out of the water and lift my canoe bodily from its own element.

I fell flat on my face, with a rapidity which did my presence of mind great credit, and next minute was again afloat. Then peering over the side, it became clear, as I suspected, that the canoe had gone full tilt against one of a herd of hippopotami, escaping from some favourite feeding ground, driven forth by the fire and smoke.

It was fortunate that the animal had been satisfied with just lifting himself out of the water, as, when enraged, it has been known to lift a boat full of men, and send them all sprawling into the river for caymans, sharks, and alligators to prey upon them.

When the first effect of my startling rencontre was over, I became aware that the fire was behind me, and having had quite enough danger for one day, the canoe was cautiously

THE START.

No. 15.—Sailor Crusoe.

mpelled up a little creek, where, should the fire not reach me, I resolved to pass the night.

My sleep was very sound, and when morning broke, to my amazement, the strength of the fire was broken. In some mysterious way it had gone out, and nothing could be seen but huge columns of black smoke that soiled and obscured the heavens, while high in the air soared the vulture,* and high on the tree branch croaked the turkey-buzzard.

I looked with regret at the desolation around, but soon the reflection came to my mind that nothing in the world can equal the growth of tropical vegetation, the action of which can be compared to nothing but that of the ocean, which bears but the impress of the track of a ship a minute, and then rolls on, the same as ever. One rainy season would restore all that rank growth of creepers, vines, and jungle-grass.

But then what cared I, who was about to leave a spot which, in beauty, resembled a paradise, but was unendurable as a residence simply because I was alone.

CHAPTER LXXIII.

TRIAL BY WATER.

My breakfast consisted of a piece of dry meat, a hard biscuit of my own baking, and a drink of water, after which, anxious to reach the port whence I was to start on my perilous journey—most delightful to me—once more I sent the canoe gliding through the waters, the shores of which were no longer fiery furnaces, but banks of verdure, flowers, and creeping plants.

My spirit was buoyant. The dangers I had passed through gave a zest and charm to present safety, and the fine weather, the song of birds, the gambols of whole schools of monkeys, amused and even enlivened me.

My gun was close to my hand, but I shot nothing, though much came in my way. There were snipes in abundance in the marshes, and the pelican busy fishing, and once I fell over an old adjutant—the very king of fishing birds.

He stood about ten feet high, with a bill eighteen inches round and more, and about four feet long. He took no notice of me whatever, but strutting out into the water, stood like a statue, except that his head moved uneasily. Then down went his prodigious beak, and up came what looked like a moderate-sized conger eel. Then the bird lifted his beak, and went away rejoicing to his breakfast.

I could have laughed, except that just then I noted that my canoe was proceeding at an unusually rapid rate, with an inclination to turn round.

I leaped up, and saw at once that I was in a rapid, while at the same moment the din of falling waters came clear and distinct to my ear. A cold perspiration burst over my body. That I was approaching a cataract was undoubted, that my boat was doomed appeared certain, while I myself might not escape with life.

For an instant the thought flashed across my mind of swimming to shore, and abandoning my canoe to its fate. But my soul loathed the very thought.

And now it is too late

I am sucked into the vortex, and must nobly brave the danger, and succumb or escape as Providence and my own energy wills it.

It was not exactly a cataract that was before me, but one of those terrible rapids where the river descends a slope at a fearful rate, and where snags, rocks, and sunken reefs place the unfortunate traveller and his boat in such fearful peril.

I caught one last glance at the shore, I looked up at the richly variegated foliage that clothed the banks, and I dipped my hands, to quench their heat, in the rippling waters. The dark shadows then fell across, the sunbeam that chequered its surface, all seemed to catch the eye and vanish. I knew that the moment was come.

I knew my peril. That as fierce and boiling waters were safely shot by trappers, boatmen, and Indians, in the frailest of canoes, I was aware; but I also knew that there is no occasion in life when coolness and presence of mind is more required than when steering a frail bark through a current that runs with inconceivable velocity.

There is not the remotest chance of reaching the bank, the canoe can by no possibility be turned—all you can do is to go at it, keep a cool head, a steady eye, a strong arm, and put your trust in Him who holds the waters in the hollow of His hands.

I sat or rather knelt, in the middle of the boat—there should have been one in the bow, and another in the stern—with my pole balanced like a rope-walker.

On sped the little craft, away she rocked from this side to that, on dashed the white and curling waves, up went the bow and then the stern ; while I do believe that in this, my great hour of peril, the steadiness of my nerves, the firm position I sat in, and the delicate use of my pole, saved me from utter destruction.

It was the work of an instant, when suddenly, with a fearful jerk, my poor boat struck a rock, twirled, and began to fill with white boiling water.

With a beating heart I leaped out, and found myself up to my arm-pits in water, but protected from the fearful velocity of the stream by the very rock which had caused my shipwreck.

I looked around. I was at the bottom of the rapid, but not out of the tumultuous and turbid waters. With one hand I held my precious craft, with the other I sounded the river. I was on the rift, where, after a few yards, the depth was not over my knees.

Wading and guarding my precious craft with the care of a miser, it was soon safely housed in a calm receding channel, caused by the back water.

I have since then watched others heading the foaming torrent, making good their footing, and dashing headlong into the foaming breakers that boil and hiss, and I have seen them do it with ease; but I must confess that once was enough for me, and I did not repeat the dose.

My gratitude for my escape was indeed great. My poor canoe, which I had feared was ruined, was unhurt, so that it had escaped already the two most fearful of all ordeals —fire and water.

I crept on shore, made a fire on the grassy sward away from trees, and then taking off all my clothes, hung them to the blazing fire to dry.

A few forked boughs with transverse bits of wood, served the purpose admirably, and then seating myself, like any other Adam, in a perfect state of nature, I had while smoking my pipe, an opportunity of examining into the nature of the

---

* We have already noted the fact of the vulture coming hundreds of miles after a battle to feed on the carcases. The Rev. Mr. Cheever asserts, and so do other naturalists, that the albatross has been known to travel a thousand miles from its known haunts. "The capture of a whale, especially on the New Zealand whaling ground, and still further south, when eight hundred and a thousand miles from land, will bring them trooping from afar, as a carcase in Mexico or Lousiana will the turkey-buzzard."

feat which I had unwittingly and almost unknowingly performed.

The river for above a hundred yards was compressed by high rocks into a narrow channel, which descended by a rapid slope to the spot where I was seated.

Every now and then a huge globular swelling betokened a sunken rock, while those which could be seen were terrible enough, in all conscience, to make me wonder how myself and my canoe had escaped so many dangers. An old proverb crossed my mind. But I will not quote it.

Below, the danger was not quite over, for as is generally the case after rapids, there came shallows, which have to be steered through with extreme nicety.

The river here was very broad, and on examination proved in no place to be more than a foot and a half in depth.

When, therefore, my things were dry and I had dressed myself I was compelled for some time to wade through the water, and drag my canoe backwards, as the current swept it before me.

At length, however, I was again afloat, and towards dark reached my camp, after one of the most adventurous and perilous journeys in the whole record of my strange and eventful history.

My animals welcomed me with delight, and it was with no small satisfaction that I took a hot meal, and turned in under my tent or hut.

I had seldom been so utterly exhausted as on that memorable occasion.

CHAPTER LXXIV.

PREPARATIONS.

THE next day was well occupied. My canoe had to be packed with due regard to equilibrium as well as to space. I wanted to be able to move about freely.

For this purpose the mast was first set up firmly, but in such a way as to admit of being taken down without much difficulty.

The sail was to be hauled by a stout but not heavy yard, while it was held fore and aft to the larboard or starboard side, by sheets, that is, ropes fastened to the clew or corner.

That to my right or left was to be pulled aft, or taken forward, according to the tack I was upon; while when I went rap full before the wind, they were made sufficiently long to let the sail belly out in front.

Having stepped my mast and placed the sail in the right position to be drawn up at a moment's notice, my oars or sweeps were next laid ready for use. The short and wide paddle was fixed in its place astern, and then the craft was ready.

My provisions were placed in a great measure by weight, allowing for the additional weight of myself and the one dog which was to accompany me.

Fixing and unfixing, packing and unpacking, riding once to my cave in search of something forgotten, the day soon passed away; and evening, the last I was to spend on the island, at all events for some time, came.

It is not to be denied that there is something in that word—the last time—whether it be quitting a being we love, a home, or even this great earth itself.

It makes you sad, whether you will or no.

I could not help a certain amount of emotion from creeping over me, as I looked at my faithful dogs, at my cattle grazing near at hand; and I ate my supper and smoked my pipe

with a certain amount of melancholy which is not wholly unpleasant.

Then the thought of all that had happened to me passed close upon my notice. I looked back with a kind of awe to the various events which had taken place since first my barque was wrecked on that inhospitable shore, and I could not but be deeply grateful as I reviewed the past, for the mercies that had been vouchsafed to me.

But do what I would, try as I might, the one idea which filled heart, brain, and soul, was the Indian girl.

There were pleasant ideas associated with other things, but this was the acme of everything. Methought I saw her as she first presented herself to me in her virgin purity and beauty—and I could have wept with emotion.

But my thoughts necessarily reverted at times to more ordinary ideas.

A fancy came over me that my dogs had their suspicions of my intended exodus; for they cowered close to my feet and looked about uneasily.

Once now and then they ran about in a circle, nor did they return to me for some time.

The night was, on this occasion, close and sultry, without one breath of wind, which did not tend to promote sleep. A number of the most inveterate mosquitoes attacked me, too, a sure sign that the tendency of the wind was from the south.

All this while nature lay in a death-like sleep, which was imposing, though the never-ceasing hum of the smaller class of animals might ever be heard, while now and then the night-hawk and other nocturnal birds swept by, recognizable only by the sound of their sweeping wings.

To rid myself of the mosquitoes and sandflies, I made a fire and threw into it some cocoa-nut husks, which produced a smoke enough to have choked a dozen men, but it made no impression on the blood-suckers, until about an hour or so before daylight, a light wind from the north drove them away.

It was indeed a comfort, and now at least I could be still, and either try to sleep or think over the events of my coming adventure, which certainly seemed to swell in proportion as the hours passed.

When I slept, I was tossed upon the raging sea, now mountains high, now into the very depths of a deep and hollow gulph—but even in the distance I could see her holding out her arms to invite me.

CHAPTER LXXV.

I START.

MY heart was full to bursting, as cowering under my verdant roof, I gazed through the thick gloom at the spectral-like appearance of my little Stormy Petrel.

I had but one idea, and that was my journey. My mind was as full of it as a boy of his first visit to the theatre; but at last a doze relieved my weary brain from too much thought. It was not long I know, for when I awoke the day dawn had chased away the myriad stars from the blue and clear heaven overhead; the insect world, which had been so busy from set of sun on the previous day to the grey dawn, had ceased their shrill and twittering notes; the gloomy forest shook off its sombre and ghost-like hue, and dripping with the pearly drops of morn, glistened with light, while the smooth but rippling waters laughed a thousand smiles. All nature was awake and so was I.

Determined to allow no evil influences to weigh down my spirits, I bustled about, fed my animals, put on board the last of my cargo, made my own dog Tiger enter the stern sheets, and driving the others back, leaped in myself, and then suddenly pushed off.

But my faithful beasts were not to be deceived in this way. The she-wolf and her progeny came rushing into the water, while even my cattle looked at me with a wondering eye. But my heart was steeled against all these sentiments by one affection more powerful than any known in the world.

I struck back my followers with an oar, and saw them, in no pleasant mood, turn towards that shore where, doubtless, it seemed to them lonely to be without a master.

As for Tiger, there was a look half wise, half perplexed about him which was infinitely amusing.

My whole attention, however, was not given to my canoe. The wind was light and chopping, now blowing gently, then suddenly ceasing, which seemed to indicate an inclination to a change in the weather.

I was all the more anxious to reach the other island, over which hung a cloud of smoke, as there did, for that matter over mine.

The water in the river was perfectly smooth, and so it was out at sea, but on the shallow bar there was what is called a little bobble.

It behoved me, then, to be peculiarly cautious, as now my canoe had to be put on its metal.

There was some difference in descending rapids in a boat without any load and masts, and trusting to the same vessel rather deeply laden and with a mast and sail.

As the wind and current were now the same, I was half inclined to lower my sail, but on second thoughts resolved to try it.

The cargo was so well placed as to ballast the canoe perfectly, and next minute she was slipping through the waves with an ease and rapidity that was delightful.

Then the Stormy Petrel was on the waters of the sea, gliding with an easy motion off the land! The sensation was delightful.

But I did not venture just then to look back, being anxious to keep myself quite free from any latent regret or dangerous emotions.

Directly the influence of the stream vanished and I found myself in blue water, it became evident that there was a current to the eastward, which made me shift my sail somewhat and steer to the south of west.

I had naturally not omitted to take with me the compass, that greatest and most admirable discovery for the mariner on the seas.

This change of course brought my island in view to my right. But all I could distinguish was a mixture of rocky and woody shore.

I was at least three miles from it, and with that wind could not have returned to it if I would. To say that I was without dread of the consequences of my own action, is to say that which is untrue. The dangers and the perils were known to me.

I might land on an arid, sterile, and deserted island, without water or food; I might be detained there by contrary winds or storms, and in consequence might starve.

Many men before me had been punished for discontent; but then, there was the sweet hope that I might find myself among my fellow creatures, among those mild and benificent savages, to whose tribe Pablina belonged.

I did not insult her by calling her a savage. Heaven forbid! Indeed I often found myself wondering how she came into that part of the world, her skin, colour, and man-ners, being so totally different from anything I had ever heard of as native of that coast.

While giving way to delicious dreams, the wind was so slight I had but to steer and smoke; it became evident that I was making scarcely any progress.

The wind was fair, but very light, and at last ceased altogether. This was a very serious consideration, as calms are sometimes of very long duration. But it was useless making mountains out of mole-hills.

Having slept scarcely an hour the night before, I fell off presently into a heavy slumber, during which, however, horrid dreams of being for ever becalmed on a pathless ocean, of having only one tea-spoonful of water between myself and dog, of seeing that animal die, and then being driven to eat him, caused it to be rather painful than otherwise.

Then I awoke to find myself still becalmed under a calm and beautiful night, with the vast heavens overhead, re-splendent with stars, with the milky-way one mass of blue and white spots, the young moon sprinkling land and sea with a silvery light, and the calm, unruffled ocean gleaming here and there, as my boat turned round, with phosphor-escent light.

It was beautiful, but it was intensely wearisome, and I began to think of using my oars, when a low, rumbling sound was heard in the distance; a dark cloud, no bigger than a man's hand, overspread the horizon, rose to the vault of Heaven and made that cheerful, pleasant night hideous and black.

In a few minutes after there came overhead a dense black mass of clouds, charged with electricity, from which shortly there burst one of those thunderclaps and flashes of lightning which one ought to expect would herald the crack of doom. Down went my sail to the very gunwale, as a white streak of foam was seen in the distance.

Then all was still.

But on the edge of the horizon I saw a small, red and increasing light.

Then the squall burst.

It was lucky that my sail was down, for in one moment I was wildly tossing amid the spray, my boat whirled round, and myself rocked so violently that I could hardly keep my seat.

Then in five minutes it was over. It was a mere puff and it was gone.

But still on the edge of the horizon I saw a small, red and largely increased light.

CHAPTER LXXVI.

VOLCANOES AND WATER-SPOUTS.

Hope on, and murmur not,
In the palace and the cot;
Though the sunshine all be gone,
Let each human heart hope on,
In the dreamy hours of night
Hope can give thee visions bright;
When the heart feels all alone,
She can smile, and say, " Hope on!"
It is whispered by the breeze,
As it comes through waving trees;
In the song of every bird
Are the cheering accents heard.
Hark! the waters seem to say,
In their gentle murm'ring play,
With a soft and soothing tone,
Weary heart, hope ever on!

My sensations were those of great awe.

In a great sea, as it were, of black, at a considerable distance, appeared a small point of red, rather above the level of the horizon.

This point, however, grew rapidly, and then up rose to the wild weird heavens a column of fire, followed by an uproar, as if all creation were being enveloped in destruction. The noise was appalling—a mixture of artillery roars, with mutterings of agony and wrath, as of some immense power writhing under chains and darkness.

Then up went flames from a large cone, with red hot stones, cinders, and ashes, which were propelled to a great height with immense violence, and then the molten lava came boiling over in two beautiful curved streams, glittering with indescribable brilliancy.

Then again pale flames, ashes, stones, and lava, were propelled with great force and noise from the rugged and yawning mouth.

In the stillness of that night I fancied I could hear the hissing of steam, and the roaring as of a mighty fire.

The way in which my boat was shaken satisfied me that an earthquake had accompanied the eruption, while every now and then loud claps of thunder, with quick succeeding and vivid lightning, warned me to prepare for a storm.

My sail was closely furled, and then, for further safety, my mast taken down.

Then again my eye reverted to the burning mountain.

The action of the crater was intense.

One gory jet followed another in quick succession, its crimson hue darkening and deepening from its first issue, till it fell again into the hot pit whence it came.

It was as if nature were at play with the most fearful of its elements, that which prophets have said is at last to destroy the world.

This lasted about half an hour, when the centres of intensity seemed to abate their fury, the jets were less and less rapid, and soon a dusky light alone seemed to flicker on the top of the mountain.

A few minutes more and nothing was visible but a vast column of smoke, rising like some huge giant, black, frowning, and sombre, to the skies, where it hung—a dense, murky, and ugly cloud.

And still no wind.

All this time the dog, affected by the atmosphere and the scene in general, had cowered at my feet, but now, as the night became less infernal and hideous in its characteristics, he rose, and putting his cold nose against my hand, seemed to ask for my caress.

This he had freely, after which, by the light of the dim stars that peered out here and there, we took supper, which was very welcome, nor did any event of any consequence occur to disturb us until dawn.

It came heavy, dull, and menacing, the clouds did not clear away; the sun rose fiery red in a bank of vaporous fog. The sea looked a heavy blue, while the crater of the burning mountain vomited forth dense clouds of smoke.

It now became a question as to what was to be done.

The probabilities were very much against the volcanic island being inhabited; for if it had once been, might not that fearful eruption have destroyed the poor wretches who had made it their home? A fearful pang went to my heart as the thought flashed through my mind that I had been a witness of the destruction of the Indian girl and her friends.

But hesitation was not part of my character, and never did shipwrecked mariner long for a vessel to come and take him away from a desolate shore, more than I to feel a breath of wind.

It came sooner, and in a different way, from what I had expected.

It was about an hour after dawn, and I had been gazing at the distant island through my telescope for some time, without making out much about it, when, casting my eyes a little to the southward and eastward of the burning mountain, some showers of rain fell. The volcano,

Whose combustible and fuell'd entrails,
Sublimed with mineral fury, aid the winds,
And leave a sing'd bottom, all involved
With sulphurous stench and smoke—

is also the cause of rain.

It is from steam escaping from their yawning chasms, and immediately condensed by the cold mountain air, and falling in drops into hollows, that these regions are watered.

But this struck me afterwards, as the rain was moving swiftly, and I knew must be accompanied with wind that might prove fatal to my frail bark, now floating like a useless log on the waters.

I glanced uneasily at the coming squall, and prepared to steer my boat for the best.

I was half-way between the two islands, and could hope to reach neither.

Then my eyes were fixed with greedy curiosity on something out of the common.

I saw a dense cloud whirling round and forming its folds into a tube, trumpet shaped, but bent to an angle of sixty degrees or more with the sea.

Then I saw another, more fully formed, rise from the sea, in position and appearance like a cone.

Then the tube from the cloud, like a huge engine-hose, descended and joined the other.

In the centre the diameter of the column was about three feet, but seven or eight times as thick at the two extremities.

It was a water-spout, and moving in my direction.

I knew that, if it came anywhere near me, I should be sucked into its draught and lost.

I watched it then with an intense anxiety, which may be imagined but not described.

Having effected this junction, it became like a hollow cylinder of water and vapour, extended in a somewhat oblique direction from the sea to the cloud; thin, as I have remarked, in the middle, and broad at the two extremities.

I could distinctly make out, as the wondrous column approached, a whirling motion as of fluids being sucked up from below, clearly demonstrating the water-spout to be a cloud-feeder, like the suction-pipe of a fire-engine.

This I was well aware it was; but what the law in pneumatics was by which water was thus pumped up into the cloudy regions of the sky, I did not know, neither do I believe that it has ever been satisfactorily explained.

Then I saw the pillar become gradually small from below, and then vanish.

Soon it disappeared entirely, and the heavily-weighted clouds were rent by the weight of water, and a deluge of rain was seen falling immediately around the spot.

The origin of the water-spout seems to be a kind of whirlwind, whether they begin from above or below.

My delight may be conceived when the danger was over, and I at once removed my gaze from the one dark spot that had so much alarmed me; when, to my terror and astonishment, I found that I was surrounded by those remarkable phenomena, which, like the pillars of sand in the Great Desert, often submerge and kill dozens.

There were three, and in the gloom of that canopied heaven the sight was awful.

The one nearest to me was moving slowly, with a violent ebullition of water at its base.

It was about a quarter-of-a-mile off and coming exactly in my direction.

There was nothing to save me.

About half the distance, a rippling commotion in the water seemed to presage its power, when down it fell with a fearful flop, agitating the sea for miles around, and rocking my boat in a fearful manner.

It had providentially struck a reef, which I soon found to be only a foot out of water, and on which I found a number of dead fish, killed by the momentum with which the column of water fell.

It was a narrow escape, as I had heard of large ships being sent down by one of these columns, while they have been known, when breaking on land, to wash away houses and drown the inhabitants, while trees have been rent up by them, valleys flooded; eminences ploughed away, deep pits excavated, and habitations, harvests, and cattle, swept away with fearful force.*

CHAPTER LXXVII.

A STORM.

My mind soon recovered its tone; when, as a relief from the confinement of the boat, I began paddling on the reef, picking up fish, and amusing myself with the gambols of my dog.

But not for long, as a chill, which went to my bones, warned me of a change of wind, and a coming storm.

To set my sails was useless.

My poor canoe would have been submerged in a moment.

To attempt to land in the furious surf of a rocky island, while the wind was blowing a gale, would have been equally impolitic.

But here it came, and there was nothing to be done but face it.

The gloomy clouds above, the general darkness of the day, and the total blackness of the water, made the storm seem worse than it was; but as it was, it was bad enough.

First, from due north came a cavern-like break in the clouds, through which the wind, laden with the ices and storms of the far distant pole, might almost be seen pouring with stern and angry violence; then, underneath the sky, appeared what seemed a second horizon, so black, clear and defined was it.

This was a bank.

When the angry wind pours its fury on the placid waters, before it lashes itself up to a full conviction of its own power and vastness, and sends the waves towering and toppling mountains high, it raises as it goes a dark fore-running wave, that hisses and rolls like the surf on a sandy shore, changing the mirror-like surface of the water to bubbles and billows.

Seizing hold of the rudder, I turned the boat round, stern to the wind, as, had the storm taken her on her broadside she must have capsized.

The next minute I was riding on the boiling, seething, crackling, hissing and tearing waves, my whole energy being devoted to keeping the canoe straight before the wind.

It was no easy task, for as we flew—the billows from behind increasing in size and force every instant—it was with difficulty I prevented my canoe from being pooped, which was the danger which, in the first part of this strange and eventful history, was described as being incident to running before the wind.

It is this wise.

The waves came swelling up behind much faster than the boat could fly before the wind, and as a rule passed by, or rather under, after heaving the canoe right up on their summit; but now, instead of merely rising and falling, they were so elevated as to comb over, and had one of these fallen on to my stern sheets, all would have been over in a moment.

I did not dare look back, except with the most hurried glances, my whole attention being devoted to keeping the little craft dead before the wind, even a slight deviation from that course being likely to be fatal.

How long I flew before the blast, what hours came and faded away, what agonies I endured, how many times I appeared to die, and then to revive once more, I cannot say; but I imagine that the storm lasted at least forty-eight hours, during which time I did not sleep at all.

Exhausted nature could no farther sustain the struggle, when the huge black canopy of the heavens seemed rent in twain, the blue sky peered through clear and bright the sun danced merrily on the waters, and the wind gradually ceased.

But it was a long time before this was any advantage to me.

After a severe storm the sea is more dangerous than during its continuance, the waves bobbing and tossing you about in the most impolite and unmerciful manner.

My eyes were constantly on the rack, as I could scarcely keep them open—until at last the waves were beaten down by a heavy and refreshing shower.

Then, eating a mouthful or two, and drinking some water, I lay down and sought, beside my dog, that rest and slumber of which I was so painfully in need.

It was scarcely evening when I went to sleep.

It was long past sunrise when I awoke.

What a change! Not a speck of cloud, not a ripple on the wide ocean, that heaved lazily under the burning sun, as if wearied with the Titanic contest, in which wind and water are never victors one over the other.

The air was hot, fiery, scorching, so that my first impulse was to drink.

Not a drop of water was on board the boat.

During the furious tempest, I had emptied the keg, while the gourds and calabashes had cracked, and spilt every drop of liquid.

There remained nothing whatever to do but to subsist upon the contents of the cocoa-nuts, until I could make land.

But then the fearful conviction came, like a flash of lightning, to my mind, that not a speck of land was in sight, nothing but that fearful sky and water, and that awful sun peering down upon me like a huge eye of fire, and scorching me to the very bones.

My first task was to step my mast, and then hoist my sail in such a way as to give me some shelter.

This certainly was an improvement, but no one out of

* Some of our school-boy friends may recollect the lines of Lucretius, thus freely translated:—
Like a vast column, gradual from the skies,
Borne o'er the waves, descends it; the vex'd tide
Boiling amain beneath its mighty whirl,
And with destruction sure, the stoutest ship
Threatening that dares the boisterous seas approach.

the tropics can conceive the intensity of the heat which is experienced in those latitudes, with the sun above your head and not a breath of wind.

At twelve o'clock, the boat cast no shadow on the waters.

The sun was vertical above, plunging its torrid rays fiercely, awfully, below.

With nothing to quench my thirst but the contents of the cocoa-nuts, it became necessary to lean over in the boat and bathe my hands and face, than which no better way can be conceived of checking thirst in its earlier stages.

But, with my sailor boy education, imagine the shock which went to my heart when I saw, close to the canoe, a large bottle-nosed shark steadily swimming round the canoe, attended by one or two pilot fish.

Then I made up my mind that I was about to die, and that these awful scavengers of the deep knew it.

There is always a slight delirium attendant on thirst, so that the mind is unnaturally affected.

Be this as it may, I leaned back in my boat, and then caught the eye of my dog.

He was looking at me with a fixed and earnest glance. His paws were stretched out, his mouth open, his eyes red, fixed, and staring, while he panted horribly from the excessive heat, and from intensity of thirst.

My God!—there could be no doubt about it, the creature was going mad.

I felt sick unto death, but searching in my belt for a knife, determined to make some defence.

To be bit by the poor, wretched, canine friend that had stuck to me so long, was a horrible idea—and I knew not which to prefer, the alternative of being torn to pieces by sharks, or dying slowly of starvation, thirst, and rabies.

A whole cocoa-nut was close to me.

I contrived to open it without spilling a drop.

Precious as was the liquor to me, I held it out to Tiger, who lapped it up with singular pleasure and delight.

It was my last.

Awful, dreadful, and indescribable sensations now came over me.

I believe I laughed and cried alternately, then jumped up in the boat, glared over the side, struck at the shark, and did many other mad and foolish things, such as those who suffer from thirst will do.

Several times the frantic expedient of swimming was thought of, but, fortunately, I was too exhausted and weak to undress myself and try the experiment.

On sped the day, and still the incessant fever of that arid thirst tormented me.

I began to sing—a sure sign that my head was going— when, through my hot eyeballs, I saw the sun go down in such wild and gorgeous splendour as I never care to see again.

The last thing I recollect of that frenzied hour was tossing overboard a lot of my provisions, in the vain hope of propitiating the sharks.

Then I fell into a stupefied, heavy slumber, from which I did not wake till nightfall.

Then, over the still waters, came rushing the evening breeze, and I welcomed next

> "The cloud that burst
> Over my weary bones, and felt delight
> In the cold drenching of the stormy night."

A gentle breeze and one or two smart showers did indeed revive both myself and my dog; and then, by the light of a rude lantern I had manufactured on purpose, I examined my

compass, and steered in the direction which I thought right.

At daybreak the burning island was five miles to leeward, and the canoe hurrying along with a good spanking breeze.

———

CHAPTER LXXVIII.

A VOLCANIC ISLAND.

THE island, which I was now rapidly approaching, was arid in the extreme.

The shores seemed unapproachable, as the sea rolled in heavy, hoary breakers right up to a wall of lava.

Masses of wave-washed stones and masses of broken lava strewed the rude beach beneath.

The rocky wall for twenty feet and more above, was honeycombed from the action of the waves.

I sailed slowly on, watching for the first chance of landing, but all the coast was cavernous and precipitous, admitting in no way of being scaled ; while every now and then could be seen huge funnel-shaped blow-holes in the rocks along the shore, by which the spray of a great wave, and even stones, would sometimes be ejected with great force, and with a noise much louder, but not at all unlike, a spouting whale.

At length I came in sight of what appeared to be a little bay, or bight.

It was approached by a fissure between two huge rocks, and when I contrived, after letting down my sail, to pole the boat into the narrow channel, I found myself, in a few minutes, in a perfectly land-locked bay, the shores of which were entirely covered by stones and ashes, while no poet ever conceived anything more hideous, bleak, and desolate.

After eating a scanty meal—in my mad frenzy I had thrown away the greater part of my provisions—I took a gun, and, leaving my dog to guard the boat, started on my journey of observation.

No sooner did I set foot upon the shore, than I observed in front of me a large and deep subterranean gallery, which appeared to me to lead into the interior of the island.

It was evidently an old sluice-way to the sea for some pent-up stock of old lava.

It was about fifty feet high at the entrance, and soon became a cavern.

There could be seen the remains of shells and sea eggs, and many bones, as if it had been inhabited, but not lately, for the whole ground was strewed with rocks that had fallen from the roof in earthquakes, making the bottom of a most jagged and irregular description.

The cavern appeared to have no end, and how far it went inland, rock-ribbed and vast, I did not care to examine.

It was an awful place, something like the hall Eblis, described in Vathek.

There was nothing beautiful about it, but there was something Titanic and sublime in the silence, gloom, and vastness of a place seemingly in the bowels of the earth, where liquid fire had flowed ages ago, and where earthquakes had dislodged vast fragments of rocks from the jagged roof.

As there was no chance of this cavern leading anywhere, I turned back, and began to ascend the slope of the hills towards the hill whence the smoke still arose.

But it was a great deal farther off than I expected.

Never in my imagination had I conceived anything so dreary as this spot.

After climbing a small ascent, I came to an immense field of smooth, flat, unbroken lava.

It had evidently once been a huge upland lake of mineral fire, but had suddenly been congealed into a vitreous black rock.

The very billows, which had been raised on its surface by the wind were congealed in some places in large swells and hollows—in others, resembling the surface of the ocean when calm, or just as its surface is ruffled by a light breeze.

It was a dreary plain, "forlorn and wild, the seat of desolation."

I hurried on, unable to conceive how at any time this could have been the abode of any human creature.

Passing over this wretched place, where not a living thing bird, beast, or reptile was to be seen, I could note how the smoke and sulphurous stench from the crater was borne along by the south wind; and now as I advanced, the lava began to be more decomposed, and the ground was cracked and rent into fissures and chasms, from which ascended smoke and vapour, looking as if I had been in some old familiar region of smelting furnaces.

Then a little farther was a terrace, like a sunken plain, rent by earthquakes, and strewed with great boulders of lava.

Then at a distance I saw, not a truncated top of a mountain, with broad, bare, and furrowed sides, but the raised brim of a mighty cauldron—a hideous, gaping chasm or fire-pit, about fifteen hundred feet deep, and about ten miles round.

And this was raised about four thousand feet above the level of the sea.

I gazed for a moment with an idle, vacant ecstatic look, and then began to take in the whole scene.

About four million square yards of half-cooled scoria, hundreds of thousands of square yards of convulsed torrents of earth in fusion, of gaseous fluids, effervescing, boiling, spouting in all directions, like the disturbed waves of the ocean, while in the centre was the abyss of abysses, the cauldron of cauldrons, a frightful area of three hundred thousand square yards of bubbling red-hot lava, now rolling in long curling waves, now spouting up with terrific fury and a subterraneous and fearful noise.

It was an awful sight to gaze at the living fires and the boiling cauldron, at the blackened perpendicular sides of the vast abyss, steaming and smoking at a million pores, gleaming all over like a bed of live coals.

In order to look more about me, I ascended a mound or sulphurous bank, at no great distance, which could be climbed and travelled over in its entire length, but still was hot, emitted mineral vapours, and at times shook with the vibration of the crater.

At the extremity of this mound was a ravine, the bottom of which could not be seen, though its edges were overhung by trees and shrubs, completely whitened and crystallized over by sulphur.

As at any moment a fresh movement of the fierce volcano might be dangerous, I hastened to leave this spot, and by skirting the huge crater, reach the other side of the island.

But I was weary.

Fortunately, the steam furnished a copious supply of water, which I found in pools, and after travelling some time, near one of these I encamped.

A screen of canes and brakes hastily thrown up, served to protect me from the scud caused by the steam.

The sight, when night came on, was magnificent, and I never wearied from rising to admire the salient jets and coruscations and beautiful fireworks of the volcano.

In the morning I continued on my way, taking the east side of the crater, and coming on new scenes of wonder at every moment.

Soon I came to a wild region, broken by abrupt hills and deep glens, and thickly set with shrubs and wortleberries, while thousands of birds seemed to consider it a safe and warm retreat.

The crater kept in sight nearly all the time, presenting new objects of interest at every step—but not to me.

I was searching for that part of the island where Pablina and her friends had taken up their quarters, for sure I was that in that spot she had located herself—there being no other island within a reasonable distance.*

But desolate, arid, sulpurous, and wanting in rich vegetation as it was, it might not have been so previous to the eruption.

But what had they done when that terrific outburst of nature took place?

Had they retired to the farther extremity of the island and there crouched, trembling, during the earthquake, or had they launched their frail barks upon the waters, and sought safety in flight?

This was the more probable elucidation of the mystery.

As I advanced, the desolation seemed to me to be greater than ever; now and then there was a patch of coarse earth, where wortleberries grew, which were eagerly devoured; and here and there a spring of hot or lukewarm water, sometimes sulphurous, bubbled up, and trickled away towards the sea, but nowhere did I behold in this part the faintest trace of any living thing.

---

* The phenomena of volcanoes are still little understood. Humboldt, in his Cosmos, gives us an insight into the question. When the questions are asked, what is that burns in the volcanoes ? what excites the heat, fuses together earths and metals, and imparts to lava currents of thick layers a degree of heat that lasts for many years ? it is necessarily implied that volcanoes must be connected with the existence of substances capable of maintaining combustion, like the beds of coal in subterranean fires. According to the different phases of chemical science, bitumen pyrites, the moist admixture of finely pulverized sulphur and iron, hydrophoric substances, and the metals of the alkalies and earths, have in turn been designated as the cause of intensely active volcanic phenomena. The great chemist, Sir Humphrey Davy, to whom we are indebted for the knowledge of the most combustible metallic substances, has himself renounced his bold chemical hypothesis in his last work, "Consolations in Travel and Last Days of a Philosopher." So general, deep seated, and far propagated an activity as that of volcanoes, cannot assuredly have its source in chemical affinity, or in the mere contact of individual or merely locally distributed substances. Modern geognosy rather seeks the cause of this activity in the increased temperature with the increase of depth at all degrees of latitude, in that powerful internal heat which our planet owes to its first solidification, its formation in the regions of space, and to the spherical contraction of matter revolving elliptically in a gaseous condition. A philosophical study of nature strives ever to elevate itself above the narrow requirements of mere natural description, and does not consist, as we have already remarked, in the mere acumulation of isolated facts. The inquiring and active spirit of man must be suffered to pass from the present to the past, to conjecture all that cannot yet be known with certainty, and still to dwell with pleasure on the ancient myths of geognosy which are presented to us under so many various forms. If we consider volcanoes as irregular intermittent springs, emitting a fluid mixture of oxydized metals, alkalies, and earths, flowing gently and calmly wherever they find a passage, or being upheaved by the powerful expansive force of vapours, we are involuntarily led to remember the geognostic visions of Plato, according to which, hot springs, as well as all volcanic igneous streams, were eruptions that might be traced back to one generally distributed subterranean cause—Phrophlegethon. This Phrophlegethon of Plato plays much the same part in relation to the activity of volcanoes which we now ascribe to the augmentation of heat as we descend from the earth's surface, and to the fused condition of its internal strata. Volcanic scoria and lava streams are portions of Phrophlegethon itself, portions of the subterranean, molten, and ever-undulating mass.

ON THE VOLCANIC ISLAND.

No. 16.—Sailor Crusoe

And thus another weary day passed.

At evening, faint and weary, I lay me down behind a huge boulder, and having had nothing but a piece of cocoa nut, some wortleberries, and a little water, tried to sleep off my sufferings, sorrows, and regrets.

All night the heavy rumbling of the interior of the volcano could be heard, especially when I made the earth my pillow.

l rose on this day unrefreshed by sleep, and in no very pleasant mood.

My journey, commenced under such very pleasant auspices, was a failure.

I was as far off from the great object of my life as ever. All my dear and darling hopes were blasted, and I had exchanged a Paradise for a Pandemonium.

How that I had fallen on pleasant places was forcibly brought to my notice and recollection by the aspect of this place, accursed and deserted of man.

Up soon after daybreak and away, after breakfasting on berries and water.

CHAPTER LXXIX.

HIRUNDO ESCULENTA.

AFTER ascending a somewhat steep elevation, the character of the country began to change.

It was still vastly inferior to my own beautiful home, but it was a little more fertile.

There were patches of trees here and there, some blades of grass, and now and then some fragrant and pretty shrubs; but still no animal that I could shoot.

Soon my steps brought me towards the top of some lofty cliffs that looked down upon the sea, or rather, on a bay some miles across, along the shores of which vegetation appeared to have been luxuriant, though now trees were lifted up, their roots laid bare, and the whole economy of nature disturbed by the earthquake.

It must have been a pleasant spot, shielded entirely from the north, west, and easterly winds, and no doubt was rich as a fishery, and had its fair stock of birds and other small game.

But how to descend and explore the locality was a mystery and yet was I determined to do it.

Examining the whole of the bay, it was clear that the cliffs were everywhere solid.

My telescope was too accurate to allow of any deception on this point.

Still there was an instinct, a kind of loadstone attraction which told me that I must go down.

There is at times a magnetic influence in our souls which draws us on, whether we will or no—and I felt irresistibly determined to try the experiment of searching that bay.

It did not look inviting—it did not look promising—it held out no hope of any satisfaction—and yet I would go down.

The uprooted trees, whole acres covered with a thick crust of cinders, rocks up-heaved, and every sign of the power of earthquake and eruption, only determined me the more to be doing.

But how was the descent to be effected?

The cliff was of goodly height, but, peering over, it did not appear to be so very difficult of descent, if one could but get to a ledge about thirty feet below.

This did not appear difficult when I recollected that my lasso was wrapped round my waist.

To take it off was the work of a minute, and then I looked around.

Close above where the ledge was, stood a point of rock projecting out of the soil, which not a dozen men could have moved.

My lasso was, with a view to its being used for a variety of purposes, about fifty feet long.

This I knotted all the way along at intervals of about a foot, and then using some strong sinnet I had about me, I fastened it to the rock.

I proceeded to the edge of the cliff to make sure that the rope did not chafe, as a fall would have been fatal.

The cliff itself was about a hundred feet above the sea, with many deep fissures in its face, while around me was stubbly jungle, underwood, overgrowing rocks, fissures, and boulders in all directions.

As I prepared to descend, creeping over the cliff with my rope in my hand, and my feet feeling for the rope, I thought of the singular story of Don Quixote descending into a well, but recollect well that I had good reason to think more of it after.

Next to "Robinson Crusoe," "Don Quixote" was my pet reading as a lad.

Though on board ship I had never hesitated to climb everywhere, and could show great activity and courage, my present undertaking cost me many a tremor.

It was indeed quite a different undertaking; the cord not being fast below, and thus vibrating like a pendulum, made the task one of great difficulty; while the roar of the sea below, and the possible chafing of the rope above, made the position anything but pleasant.

It was swinging between heaven and earth with a vengeance.

But, thank Heaven! I was young, and bold, and active, and though "I was tossed in empty space like an idle and unsubstantial feather," I retained my alertness of exertion and presence of mind; though taking care to keep off the rock, I steadied myself as much as possible with my feet. I certainly, however, felt dizzy.

Still I persevered, when suddenly, being nearly at the end of my rope, I was startled to find myself at the mouth of a large and gloomy cave, from which there rushed, with a whirr and a wild twitter, some hundreds of small birds, which at a glance I recognised as the *Hirundo esculenta.*

I almost let go my hold, so much did this discovery move me.

I was hungry and athirst, and here was one of the greatest delicacies on earth within my immediate reach.

Novel and strange as the thing was, I knew that I had fallen on an article of commerce of extreme value, and which occupies a large amount of small shipping in all the islands adjacent to China, the more rocky and precipitous islands yielding the larger quantity.

The moment my eye fell upon these birds I knew them, and knew also that the cavern contained the better part of the treasure—the edible birds' nests.

I had often read of these little birds, and indeed often seen them, but had never before fallen over their quarters.

They might constantly be seen skimming about the surface of the sea near my home.

In form and feather they looked like a connecting link between the common swallow and the smallest of the petrel tribe—the Mother Carey's chicken, of which more anon—ever restless, ever in motion.

Sometimes you see them skim low to the edge of the water, as if they were taking up some substance with their bills from the surface of the waves; at other times they are beheld darting, turning, and twisting in the air, as if they were in earnest and serious chase of fleet-winged insects.

Yet it is asserted by all naturalists, and I can fully corroborate the statement, that the keenest can detect nothing upon which they really do feed.

The natives of the Archipelago, were they are chiefly found, assert that they feed upon insects and upon other minute creatures floating amid the scum of the surface of the sea; then, by some peculiar arrangement of the digestive organs, the bird, from its bill, produces the clear, glutinous, and strange stuff of which the nest they build is constructed —an opinion in some manner fully corroborated by the singular appearance of the nests, which, when examined resemble long filaments of very fine vermicelli, one part coiled over the other, without any regular system, and then glued together by transverse rows of the same material.

The shape of the rest is singular.

They resemble somewhat a bowl of a gravy-spoon split in half longitudinally, and in every way they are smaller than swallows' nests.

The little bird fixes the straight edge against the wall o rocks, in general selecting some dark and shady fissure in a cliff, or some cave high up in a cliff, or else where it is washed by the waves of the restless sea.

The only hypothesis which ever appeared satisfactory to me was, that the strange swallow that is the architect of these nests, is a night-bird, and that it never does really feed at all by day.

Indeed, it rarely happens that anyone has ever seen them except in the early morn or late at night, or perhaps now and then in the deep shadow of some tall and overhanging cliff.

They appear systematically to avoid the sunlight and the broad glare of day.

All this flashed across my mind as I hastily *ascended* my knotted rope, which I found safe above, but took care to make more secure against chafing by placing a lot of grass under the place where the pressure was most.

My reason for my hasty ascent was twofold.

I had seen near the top of the cliff the very thing I wanted.

Hastily peeling off the bark of a tree of a resinous character, I manufactured a torch or two—good large torches, that would give powerful and glaring light.

Then I cut a long pole, fastened a calabash to my side, and again descended, this time with less precaution then before.

I soon stood upon a narrow ledge of rock, which led into the cave, whence issued odours, not of myrrh and frank-incense, while a black, dreary, inky darkness pervaded the interior.

For this purpose I had made the torches, which were with great difficulty lit when beyond the reach of wind and daylight.

I thought I was in my serpent cave again, for no sooner did the torch blaze up, than it was the signal for the most infernal din human tympanum was ever attacked with; the tiny chirp of the strange little swallows was taken up and multiplied a thousand times by the beautiful echoes of the cavern, whilst huge bats, big enough to be vampires, flew at my torch, not only being near putting my flickering torch out, but threatening to shove me off the narrow ledge into the dark and gloomy depths below.

At length, however, the din decreased, and I was able to look about me.

It was a low cavern where I stood, but evidently rising to a great height at no great distance.

I could see the nests sticking to the roof, and soon, aided by my pole, got down as many as I could carry.

Then casting my lighted torch down the rocks, I hastened to descend, and though in places I had to creep down where only a gull could have obtained a footing, at last the beach was reached.

The torch, still alight, had fallen under a tree, where at once I made a fire, and as soon as there was nothing but live coals left, placed thereon two cocoa-nut shells full of the nests, with a little water, much of which was to be found about in pools.

While waiting for my cookery to be finished, I sat down and smoked a pipe, thinking the while what a fortune might have been made, could the contents of that cavern have been used to freight a schooner.

The trade is a most lucrative one, and employs a large amount of labour and capital.

But the loss of life from the trade is extraordinarily large —still the high prices obtained cause labour never to be slack.

It is said by old and experienced travellers, that on an average, two out of five men come to a violent death in the pursuit of this delicacy, which is sold at forty dollars a catty, or nine pounds sterling the one pound and a quarter weight.

The peculiar value and choiceness of the nests depends on their translucent whiteness and their utter freedom from feathers and dirt, the very best quality being of course those which have not been lined or used by the unfortunate swallow.

The fact is, these nests are nothing but a mass of pure gelatine.

They have no taste, but boiled in cocoa-nut milk are very nice.

On this occasion, about half an ounce of salt water had to be put into the soup to make it even palatable.

But why the Chinese should take such unheard of pains to procure them is a mystery, since they only use them with *beche de mer*, shark fins, and other gelatinous substances, to thicken their soups and rich ragouts.

However this may be, they brought me to considerably, and I rose like a giant refreshed.

Slinging my gun on my shoulder, I clutched the pole, and taking a hasty leave, by a glance, of my swinging lasso, plunged through the thicket which lined the shores of the bay, to explore its mysterious precincts.

No sooner did my feet touch the soft and silvery sand of the beach, than, with a wild exclamation, I fell upon my knees, beside a long, thin, and dark mass, jammed up between the rocks that had been heaved up by the upsurging earthquake.

It was—but my pen fails me, I must pause ere I record the awful discovery.

———

CHAPTER LXXX.

A TERRIBLE DISCOVERY.

I have seen one, whose eloquence commanding
  Roused the rich echoes of the human breast,
The blandishments of wealth and ease withstanding,
  That hope might reach the suffering and oppressed.
And by his side there moved a form of beauty,
  Strewing sweet flowers along his path of life,
And looking up with meek and love-lent duty;
  I called her angel, but he called her wife.—ANON.

IT was the broken, crushed, and mangled remains of Pablina's canoe.

Quickly my eyes were cast about, with a horrid sensation of fear.

If the canoe was thus ruthlessly destroyed, what had become of the girl?

I sat down, fainting and helpless, on the ground.

It was fortunate for me that the edible bird's-nest soup had invigorated my frame, or I verily believe I should have died.

My heart beat wildly and tumultuously, as if it would have broken, for never, in the whole course of my adventurous career, had such a dread come over my soul as this.

I had parted from her with bitter sorrow, but the hope remained that some day we might be re-united.

Now all hope appeared to have vanished into thin air, for there, where I sat on that sandy shore, I expected to find her mangled body, if indeed I did not soon fall over a pile of bones, at which jackall or hyena had been gnawing.

Raising myself on my feet, after some little time, I took the pole in my hand and began to beat the bushes, but with such a great horror and dread on my soul as made me shudder as I touched the yielding boughs.

One thing alone reassured me.

Not a sign was to be seen of the foul scavengers of the tropics, even in mid air, where, floating aloft, they look down in search of what next they may devour.

I had to scramble though briars, over rents in the earth, through chasms of uprooted trees, and over toppling and unsteady rocks; but I found nothing.

What did this portend, and how came that lorn and crushed canoe or dugout in that bay?

Where was its mistress, for that it was hers I could no more doubt than I could my own identity?

It was a riddle I could not solve in any way.

But I would not give up—I would search every inch of ground—I would walk over it in every direction, but I would unravel the mystery.

First, by way of an experiment, I shouted her name, and the huge rocks gave it back in rich melodious echoes that went to my very heart.

I had not heard my own voice for some time, and it sounded pleasant.

Hark! what is that distant cry?

I listen with all my ears.

It is the bark of a dog.

There can be no doubt of it—a long, prolonged bark and howl, which is to me incomprehensible.

It cannot be mine, for Tiger is miles away on the other side of the island.

I pressed my head in my hands, in order calmly to think, but it was vain.

Wild fancies would rush into my brain, and all but drive me mad.

Again I cried out, and this time, long ere the echo of the rocks had died away, the barking was renewed.

I sat down upon that sad and lonely beach, and thought. I was no time for hasty or premature decision.

There was some mystery, which was not to be fathomed in a hurry.

After awhile, calming my perturbed spirits, it became clear that night was coming on.

Nothing more could be done ere morning; and coming back, and for very shame alone, not stooping and kissing the bark that had borne her from my shores, I made my way again to where my camp had been fixed, and after another meal of soup, composed myself to sleep.

It came, but fitfully; not that long, heavy, and refreshing slumber which is more conductive to strength and health than even meat and drink, but little dozes, from which one is awakened with a start, just as you reach the still and silent land of dreams.

Some of the awakenings were cruel, for they tore her from my arms, and gave me again to despair and doubt.

There could be little doubt of one fact—unless she was with her friends, she must be somewhere on the island.

She could not swim such a distance as intervened between the volcano and my more fortunate retreat.

Such things have been recorded by travellers, especially of native women, but my Pablina was to delicate, too slight, too much wanting in physical power, do such a perilous deed.

And thus the night passed moodily and drearily until the dawn was welcomed with a delight such as I had rarely known.

My first impulse was, after hasty refreshment, to ascend to the summit of the cliffs, and by walking round on the top, find out some clue to the strange mystery that environed me.

With this view, using my pole with a dexterity that was the result of early habits, I clambered up to the cavern, at the mouth of which still hung my knotted lasso.

Just, however, as I was about to clamber up, happening to move a little on one side of the ledge, I saw a streak of light fall into a distant part of the cavern.

At once the idea flashed across my mind that this was the way by which the bay was reached, and that my best plan would be to pursue it.

The birds and bats were still flying about, but with less of a horrid din than heretofore; so passing my pole forward, in order to feel my way, I entered the dark and gloomy fissure.

The way was, however, smoother than I expected, so that I gradually neared the spot where the light began to prevail without let or hindrance.

I now became aware that this was the centre of the cavern.

It was lofty, and here and there fissures and holes let in a dubious and indistinct light.

I looked warily around, and saw that the cavern went on, and peering into the kind of passage which presented itself to me, again I perceived a glimmer of light in the distance.

This was then my road.

It had hitherto ascended towards the summit of the cliff, but now the path was slightly descendant, until at last it became level, when, gazing as through an open archway, a scene never to be forgotten came under my view.

CHAPTER LXXXI.

THE VILLAGE.

A SMALL lake starting from the immediate entrance of this strange tunnel, was dotted here and there with fairy-like islands, on which, through the trees, I could distinguish what were undoubtedly huts, and huts, too, erected with considerable care and pains.

Yes; it was a village, and undoubtedly the village of the gentle tribe of Indians to which my beloved Pablina belonged.

It was strange that no one should be stirring, that not a sign of any canoe or raft could be seen, or that no children should be fishing in the pellucid water, where a number of a species of trout were leaping in the tepid water after a kind of may-fly with gossamer wings, which hovered over the water and covered every rock near the lake in countless myriads.

Hastily wading through a shallow run, I made for a narrow ledge of land which skirted the water, and hurried with frantic speed to find some way of crossing to the island on which I could just make out the village through the trees.

In five minutes more I was startled by a fresh and hopeful discovery.

A bridge of rudely fashioned planks was laid from the shore to the first island, not more than six feet from the shore.

This proved to be the case with the channel between each island, until I was close to that on which the village was situated.

Moving with the caution of a man who knows not what may next occur to him, and clutching my gun with a determination to defend myself, if I were falling into a trap, I crossed the last bridge, and stood in the middle of a deserted village—deserted, too, in a hurry, for several articles of use lay scattered on the ground.

The great convulsion had evidently reached to this spot, as the huts were cracked and ready to fall.

I entered the first.

It was simply made of four upright sticks, from which withes had been passed endwise, with mud and grass to plaster it, while the roof was a kind of thatch admirably adapted to its purpose.

This was evidently only a sleeping place, and it appeared to my fancy the sleeping place of two young women, for on each side of the hut was a rude couch covered with hay and straw of a coarse kind, plucked from the neighbouring hills.

My heart beat with strange sensations as I examined this chaste retreat.

Is there some sympathy—such as people say we feel when walking over our grave—when we stand upon a spot hallowed by connection with something or somebody we have loved?

I know not, but true it was that then my sensations were of the strangest—what they became afterwards will be seen in its proper place.

Lingering longer in that room than was absolutely necessary, I, however, at last tore myself away to examine the rest of the island village.

Next to this little hut was a larger one, built very much after the fashion of the inhabitants of the prairies of North America, or of the copper-coloured, small-featured, long-haired Fellatahs of Africa.

It had a small door and two windows, this being a novelty; and a projecting roof, to cast off the wet during the rainy season.

It had a few rough stools; something in the shape of a table; while a truckle bed in a corner, made with coarse sticks and grass matting, proclaimed a certain degree of ingenuity.

Some fishing spears and rude landing nets, with certain half-finished hooks and points, were on the table, where also stood a pile of gourd plates, most certainly cut with a knife.

I sat down, overwhelmed with emotion.

There could be no doubt that the little tribe or family which inhabited this village, were of a civilized turn.

Not a sign of any warlike propensities could be seen, and doubtless with these did Pablina dwell, until the terrific eruption and earthquake of a few days back had driven them to seek some more hospitable shore.

Sorrowfully I came into the open air and gazed around.

The huts were seven in number.

In all were evidences of civilization of some kind.

There were in one a knife and axe of some rude iron, ozier baskets and grass mats, both ingenious and elegant; while there remained some scattered specimens of a red earthenware which is made by the women of certain African tribes, and burnt by stacking them with layers of wood between the rows, as bricks are baked.

There was abundance of the calabash pumpkin, both in its manufactured and raw state.

They had adopted the usual fashion of adapting this vegetable to their uses.

When the fruit had begun to ripen they had cut a hole in the small end to admit the air, which causes the pulp to decay without injuring the rind.

Some make the incision round the fruit, at about one-third from the smaller end, and thus a vessel with a neatly fitting lid is produced without further trouble.

The size of the calabash varies greatly.

Some are as small as a tea-cup, while others will hold three or four gallons.

In some of these vessels were the remains of a meal that had been in preparation when they were disturbed by the eruption, which had doubtless the more alarmed the inhabitants, that a cursory glance showed me a heavy fall of hot ashes had startled them.

It lay about in every direction, on the roofs of the houses and on the ground.

I gladly ate of one of the preparations, which I found to be Indian corn mixed with a strong sauce, made of beef and fish, and flavoured with salt and Cayenne pepper, which grew, I noticed, in abundance round the village.

It was very palatable and nutritious.

There were yams, too, piled up in a corner.

But it was in vain to stand by regretting the absence of the owners of this peaceful and calm retreat.

All I could do was to continue my search.

A pathway indicated that there was a second outlet to the village, which led in the opposite direction to that by which I had come.

It took me across one or two smaller islands, to the skirt of a wild and gloomy wood, over which the trees arched so densely as to exclude the light of day, but fortunately, the underwood was very slight, and did not in any way interfere with my progress.

What might have been the case had the eruption not have interfered, I know not, but the woods were utterly abandoned by every living thing, which added to their solemnity and grandeur.

About a mile from the village, *following a beaten path*, I saw before me an opening in the forest, where the trees were not quite so close together, and where a lovely little clearing exhibited its bright array of flowers and shrubs to the view.

But what startled me was a clear and pellucid pool, in the centre of which bubbled up a spring, and on the borders of which was a graceful bower all overgrown with creeping and flowering plants—a very faint imitation of my summerhouse on the island.

I hurriedly entered it and sat down upon a seat.

Then my eyes were cast down upon the ground, and I saw distinctly the impression of two pair of naked feet.

One mark I could have sworn was left there by Pablina, but the other—

It turned out the toes in a way decidedly European and civilized.

CHAPTER LXXXII.

TAILING A BULL.

THERE could be no mistake about this.

Nearly all savage or half-savage nations, when walking, turn the toes inwards.

This in part arises from their style of following and leaving a trail, always putting one foot right before the other, and leaving thus, as it were, the imprint only of a single foot. But whatever the reason, that they do do it is a well-known fact.

Now this little naked well-shaped foot was evidently that of one who had been taught to walk, and by a European teacher.

Who could it be, who, cast on that desolate shore, had taken up her abode with savages?

But why should I be certain it was a girl?

It might be the foot of a youth.

As this idea flashed across my mind, the sensation of anger, despair and jealousy, which flashed across my soul was something awful.

The very thought that the solitude inhabited by Pablina was shared by one of my own sex, was enough to drive me mad.

And yet, what right had I to be angry that she should prefer me to some one else?

It was the privilege of her sex, and why should she not exercise it?

But again my eyes fell upon the elegant footmark, and a careful examination convinced me that it was, after all, a girl, and undoubtedly one whose feet had been confined within the usual tight-fitting boots of civilized countries.

What could this mean?

A wild and almost insane idea had once or twice flashed across my imagination, but had been dismissed as soon as admitted.

It was impossible, it could not be true; and yet why had my misfortune, my unlucky fate, set me on my journey just at the moment when the mystery I would unravel was only deeper and more intricate?

My nature was hopeful, as a rule.

During my solitary sojourn on the dismal shores of an island which, however beautiful, was without my own kind, I had, except on rare occasions, never allowed myself to despond—never found fault with Providence for suffering me to be cast away, without hope of any further contact with my fellow-creatures.

But now, overcome with emotions of a mixed and strange kind, I sat moody and silent.

What my thoughts were, I would rather not reveal.

They were not exactly creditable to me.

The discovery of which I had a faint trace did not seem to please me as much as it ought.

My soul was turned towards Pablina, and anything which interfered with my hopes with regard to her did not please me.

I verily believe, as I sat in that bower, I thought myself the veriest deserted, abandoned, and lost wretch that ever lived, forgetting wholly all the mercies which had been vouchsafed unto me for three years.

I was awoke from my reverie by the song of a bird, and, looking up, I saw on a tree a bird the name of which I did not know, but which very much resembled a robin-redbreast.

A tear came to my eye as I gazed, and I recollected, with intense emotion, the words of a good and great traveller,* who, like myself, had suffered much, and who yet had never lost heart :—

"I saw myself in the midst of a vast wilderness, in the depth of the rainy season, naked and alone, surrounded by savage animals, and men still more savage.

"I was five hundred miles from any European settlement.

"My spirits began to fail me, and I thought I had no alternative but to lie down and perish.

"The influence of religion, however, supported me, for I was still under the protecting eye of God.

"At this moment, painful as my reflections were, the extraordinary beauty of a small moss in fructification caught my eye.

"The whole plant was not larger than the tip of one of my fingers, but I could not contemplate the delicate conformation of its roots, leaves, and capsule, without admiration.

"Can He, thought I, who planted, watered, nd brought to perfection in this obscure part of the world, a thing which appears of so small importance, look with unconcern on the situation and sufferings of creatures formed after his own image?

"Surely not.

"I could no longer despair. I started up, and disregarding both hunger and fatigue, travelled forwards, assured that relief was at hand; and I was not disappointed.

"In captivity, in solitude, in suffering, there is but one true consolation, and that is religion. He, who is armed with that has sword and buckler both.

"He can defy the worst of enemies, and bear the most fearful troubles."

But still my soul was not altogether restored to its proper tone.

Rising, then, with determination, I continued on my way, satisfied that having traced them thus far, I should again meet their trail.

The way through the forest was clear. These inhabitants of the volcanic island had adopted a plan similiar to that of the dwellers in the great backwoods.

They had barked a tree here and there on their way.

* The gallant, the chivalrous, the admirable Mungo Park.

This again convinced me that there was some member of a European race of the party.

But my reflections were suddenly brought to a standstill.

I had been so deeply absorbed in my reflections for some minutes, that I entered upon a clearing before I knew where I was; and, striking my foot against a fallen log, was tripped up.

As I fell headlong on the ground, still firmly grasping my double-barrelled gun, I heard a fearful roar, and rising, saw that I had fallen on a heard of buffalo cows and calves, which were quietly feeding on the short grass of a lovely prairie, guarded by a huge bull—one of those immense creatures that a lion will not attack alone, and which often comes off victorious in the conflict.

I levelled my gun, for I saw that he had discovered me, and was lashing himself with his tail into a state of fury; while, if he caught hold of me, my fate was certain.

My hand shook somewhat, and it was my after conviction that I leaned against a tree in my agitation.

This I do know—I fired.

Scarcely had I pulled the trigger, when my vision seemed obscured, except where I saw two red and bloodshot eyes fixed upon me, while the nose of the ferocious beast appeared to plough up the earth in a long furrow.

I fired my second barrel, but without effect, and the useless weapon fell at my feet.

At a glance—and the whole matter did not last two seconds—I grasped a branch of the tree, which was, as well as I could make out in my great fear and hurry, a young baobab. With a gymnastic bound I drew myself out of the animal's reach into the first branches of the tree, whence I hastily ascended into the topmost boughs, were, of course I was perfectly free from any immediate danger. Taking time to draw my breath, I gazed downwards.

The buffalo, larger and more powerful than that of America, had posted himself beneath the tree, and appeared about to mount guard over me.

For a short time the affair seemed rather amusing than otherwise.

I actually talked nonsense to the bull, and sneered at him for being taken in.

But, at the end of half-an-hour, the matter became serious; but still I felt no great alarm, until at last I began to be aware that the buffalo had made up his mind to try my patience, and to starve me out, if he could not slay me.

Every now and then he would lift his head, bellow furiously, and fixing his savage eyes upon my form, which he could plainly distinguish, allow me to see that he was in earnest.

Then he would move slowly round the tree grazing in the most quiet and calm manner, but with one eye still turned upwards every instant.

The cunning beast knew his power.

On the skirt of a fertile prairie he had food sufficient for him, while the copious morning dew would serve him for water.

I, on the other hand, must soon starve.

Thirst and hunger are assailants that we can only ward off in one way.

I must escape from the tree and the animal, if I would not be starved or gored to death.

But how it was to be done was a great mystery. My thoughts suggested no remedy, however, and soon a cold shivering fit proved the extent to which my danger had roused feelings of terror and alarm.

I gazed around; but no tree was near enough to admit of my leaping from one branch to the other. I had heard of these animals, when guarding their seraglio, watching an enemy for days, and this bull appeared to me one of this relentless class.

He never swerved from a certain circle, browsing coolly, however, all the time.

His persistence alarmed me.

Then, when he appeared to have satisfied his appetite, he lay down, with his head in my direction, snorted through his huge nostrils, and prepared for a regular siege.

The cows and calves went on browsing calmly.

Something must be done, that was clear, and a bright idea suddenly flashed across my mind, and I at once determined to carry it out.

I slid down the tree until I was not more than seven or eight feet from the ground.

Between my teeth was my long sharp knife. There was no time to lose—the buffalo was in the act of rising, when I leaped, cleared him by a couple of feet, and, as he got to his feet caught firmly hold of his tail.

I had heard of bull fighters doing this, and thus saving their lives.

Quick as lightning, and with furious bellowing, the bull turned round, but I was as quick as he was. Twisting, jumping, and grasping the place above the tuft with a resolute and firm hold, I grasped my knife in my right hand.

I was now a match for the huge and infuriated animal, which as long as I kept behind him, could not harm me.

His terrible horns were useless now.

His fury was something ludicrous.

Now he stood still and bellowed with vain and savage rage; then he would dart suddenly round to shake me off; then again he would kick up his heels; but whatever he did I was too much for him.

Still, this state of things could not be allowed to last, so raising my knife as high as possible, I drove at him with all my strength.

The knife went into his flanks to the very hilt, and then, bounding from the ground, he made a dash that nearly wrenched my wrist off.

But I held on, aware that if I let go he would certainly turn and gore me to death.

But to end the dreadful contest, I again repeatedly struck at him with my knife, now in one flank, now in another, according as I was tossed about.

It was a fearful race through shrubs, over a grassy plain, through a swamp, across a stream, until I came to a rugged plain.

The bull had gone at a fearful pace at first, but now could not move so quickly.

I looked about.

My hope was to let go suddenly and, falling behind some thicket, hide from his view. But what is this? We are dashing down a steep declivity.

The bull's head is down—his eyes are on the ground—he goes headlong!

Another minute we shall be dashed over a precipitous rock.

I had just time to let go and fall hastily back on the ground, when over rushed the maddened animal.

When I regained my breath, I crawled to the edge of the cliff and peered down.

The poor animal lay mangled and dead below. I was sorry for him, for he was a splendid creature; but amidst my regrets there was one satisfaction—I had done that of which I had often heard, but never thought to see—I had tailed a bull.

CHAPTER LXXXIII.

THE CHASE.

My mad race with the infuriated bull had brought me to a spot between the bay where lay the broken canoe of the Indian girl and another small harbour, for which I at once made.

As I already suspected, it was that where I had myself landed.

I had come back to the place whence I had started, after skirting a great portion of the island and crossing another. I was always, when on high land, within sight of the burning mountain.

My canoe lay perfectly safe about a quarter of a mile from where I stood, and my dog was close at hand, engaged in an occupation of a most singular kind, but which I could clearly make out by means of my telescope.

There was a very shallow part of the bay about twenty feet from my canoe, and when I first looked, Tiger was lying down as flat as he could make himself, watching. Suddenly he leaped up, dashed into the water, and seemed to be driving something before him towards the shore.

Tiger was fishing.

Then I saw him come out of the water with a good-sized salmon, or such like fish, in his mouth, which he there and then incontinently devoured.

My first act, on making this discovery, was to turn away once more.

My intention was to perform a journey round the island in my boat in the hope that I might find Pablina and her friends encamped on some pleasant spot on the coast, or somehow trace the mode of her departure.

But it was first necessary to fetch my gun and my lasso, which took so much time that I was again compelled to pass the night on shore.

At daybreak, however, I descended the rocks, and rejoined my faithful Tiger, who was delighted to get a drink of fresh water, that which he had discovered being so brackish as to be very unpalatable to any one not suffering from extreme thirst.

The canoe was then impelled out of the bay, the sail set, and with a wet sheet and a flowing sea, we started on our journey.

First, my attention was to visit the spot where the bull had fallen the day before, as some of his flesh would be found exceedingly welcome and useful.

As I expected, the place was easily found, a whole herd of vultures being collected round the spot.

These disgusting animals, before they go in for a gorge, sit awhile at some distance from the body to make sure that it is dead.

Aware of this peculiarity, I made for the shore with great rapidity and some dexterity, beached my canoe on the soft and pearly strand, and advanced towards the carcase just as the gory-beaked vultures, fresh from some carnage at no great distance, settled, one by one, round the bull.

My dog flew towards them, but dared not venture within reach of their talons or mouths.

I was compelled, therefore, to fire at them with my two barrels, which, killing one, sent the others lazily flying away to the neighbouring rocks and boulders.

My long sharp knife was now brought into requisition, and in a few minutes the skin was cut away so as to admit of the finest morsels being cut out, including the tongue. I was not so experienced a butcher but that it took me an hour to do the whole satisfactorily.

The choice bits were then strung together, and carried to the boat.

It was high and dry.

The tide had ebbed, and left her safe on the sands.

This was a very serious matter, but there was no help for it but to wait until the tide flowed again.

In the meantime, by way of occupying myself, I determined, if possible, to make a fire, which was not difficult, as a number of stunted palms and bushes grew behind a row of heavy boulders.

Dragging these up out of the arid soil, a huge blaze was soon made, and then, when the flame subsided, a goodly meal of buffalo-steaks, far more than was immediately required, was cooked, and partly eaten by my dog and myself.

The rest was placed on board the boat; it having been nearly high tide when we landed, we had to wait until it was nearly night before, by great exertions, I could get the boat afloat again. During the heat of day I had slept, so that I preferred starting, even though night was coming on.

The sea was tolerably smooth, and the wind steady, though with a tendency to head me in my course, which compelled me to run out a good distance from the shore, in order to get a good offing.

As I was close upon a wind, and not running before it, with a fair breeze, steering was comparatively easy, so that I jammed the tiller to starboard, and amused myself with smoking and gazing out at the wild and fantastic scene.

The moon shot like a glittering pathway across the waters that made its rays dance and tremble as the waves rippled and fell; while I could never lose sight of the dark column of smoke that rose everlastingly from the summit of the volcanic hill.

Suddenly I started.

Something, I knew not what, had shot across the silvery pathway beneath the moon.

Eagerly I clutched my telescope, and then saw at once that a canoe, manned by two natives, was paddling towards me with a caution and circumspection that seemed somewhat inimical.

But being well armed, I could not fear two naked savages, so immediately going about, steered direct for them.

With equal rapidity they turned and fled.

The swiftness with which they used their paddles was miraculous.

They were making for the shore at an angle which, steering as I now was on the contrary tack to what I had been, would bring us close together long before the line of white waves, marking a sunken rock or coral reef, were reached.

Still they plied their oars with intense earnestness, and though they lost ground, were not deterred from the most violent exertions.

Soon they were not fifty feet from me, and I was wondering what I should do with my capture, when, with a wave of their paddles, they appeared to strike.

But I was mistaken.

The perigua was twisted round, and ere I could make out their intention, they were paddling directly in the wind's eye, in which direction I, of course, could not follow them.

Still, it was not my intention to give up the chase; but going

TAILING A BULL.

No. 17.—Sailor Crusoe.

about once more, I trimmed my sail, and keeping close to the wind, followed relentlessly in their track.

As they must end by being fatigued, and as keeping in the wind's eye would drive them out to sea, my chase must surely end in being a successful one.

My motives for perseverance were of a mixed character. I had caught but a very faint glimpse of the two paddlers, but it appeared to me that the one in the bow of the boat was Pablina.

I had but seen the moon's rays fall once on her face, and yet I could not be mistaken; at least, so I thought, which made me strain every nerve in order to reach them.

For some time the canoe did not seem to gain on them at all, especially as, to keep any way on their track, I had to run up in the wind's eye every now and then, which naturally put me back in my course.

But just as we appeared to be getting quite out of sight of land, they altered their course, and made with increased rapidity for the island.

Round and after them with all speed, which, now being well-used to manage my canoe, was very great.

It was evident that the fugitives had been watching my movements with a keenness of observation quite wonderful, for they now took a course a little off the parallel, so that we should avoid meeting.

As they were to windward of me they could run down upon me when they liked, but I could not make one inch more to the eastward than I did, to save my life.

But what were these untutored children of nature about to do?

In front of them was a raging sea that threatened to submerge them.

Out half-a-mile into the sea were huge boulders, against which the waves dashed with incessant fury, while in the channels between, the waves ran twenty and thirty feet high, breaking in white foam and spray.

But sitting firmly in their tiny bark, the bold mariners made ready.

I, too, looked about me, and saw to the west an expanse of smooth water, by means of which I might turn the reef and catch the perigua ere they could reach the shore.

Up went my helm, and away almost square before the breeze I dashed, glided with magic speed through the smooth water; down with my helm again, and aft with the sheet, until I was round a corner and behind the boulders, and in still, smooth water.

But where is the canoe?

Gone.

No; yonder I can see something.

It is the canoe.

But they have been to quick for me.

They are within a very few yards of the beach—they run their boat aground, they lift it up, and disappear in the woods; at all events, so it appeared.

What was to be done?

To think of pursuing two natives, even with a dog and gun, at night was out of the question.

They would outstrip me without the slightest difficulty, while even they might lead me into some treacherous ambuscade.

For you must know, I was not sure of one of them being Pablina; only fancied so; and more than that, hoped so.

My best course, under the circumstances, was to anchor on that reef-protected shore, which I did in an original sort of way.

Seeking out the first rock above water, and selecting one that was honeycombed by the waves, I fastened my lasso thereto, and made all secure for the night.

Then, though anxious and nervous with thinking of her who was always uppermost in my mind, I lay me down, and went soon off into a sound slumber.

When I awoke, it was some time past sunrise.

I could make nothing of the shore, which was wrapped in one of the most singular mirages I ever saw.

Objects a hundred yards off were utterly without any definition.

A crow, a stone, or a bit of black wood, looked as lofty as the trunk of a tree; pelicans were exaggerated to the size of ships with all studding-sails set, and the whole ground was wavy and seething, as though seen through the draught of a furnace.

It was a most singular illusion, and did not last long.

When the strange mist rose, I pushed for the shore, which was very arid and covered by dried-up pools, near which grew bushes not unlike fennel, but not less than eight to twelve feet high.

There were also prickly gourds; the nara, with long runners, covered numerous sandhills; while high shifting sand dunes, or denes, as they call them at Yarmouth, completed the scene.

The sun was hot, and yet having secured my canoe as well as I could by means of my lasso, I hurried, with great anxiety and intense haste, to the spot where I had seen the perigua run ashore.

But the perigua was gone.

Could all the events of the previous night have been a dream?

No; I was wide awake enough, and the long chase of the tiny boat was no effect of the imagination.

Besides, here was the mark where the canoe had been dragged ashore, while the feet of natives, clothed in moccasins, were clearly visible.

I followed the track for some little distance, until on the other side of a large hillock I found a little fountain, in the shape of a hole seven inches across, of green stagnant water.

Hastily removing the surface, I drank some of the water, but it was so execrably bad, that, though thirsty and feverish, I had to desist.

But while stooping to see if a rill might not be found supplying this fountain with water, I saw a small print in the sand.

It was light, it was almost imperceptible; but I knew it was Pablina's foot.

Why did this girl thus persevere in fleeing from me—or was she forced to do so by her native companions?

What was to be done?

To leave my boat was dangerous, as they might come upon it and ransack its contents; but then, I could not bear the uncertainty under which I laboured.

My gun, my dog, and my lasso, was all I took, and with these I proposed to follow the trail.

Fortunately, the prickly gourd of which I have before spoken was here in abundance, growing in perfect hillocks. It was meat and drink both to me and my dog, who, like the hyænas, antelopes and birds, had taken a great fancy to it.

For some time the trail was not difficult to follow, and in a very few minutes I became aware, from the impressions on the sand and elsewhere, that the two fugitives were carrying a heavy weight—of course, their canoe.

This aroused me to active exertion, as it proved their settled determination to flee from me.

After a short period, they had entered a dense growth of underwood and bushes, through which I know not really how they made their way.

In this wood there appeared nothing alive but black-and-white crows, that disdained to move as we passed.

I pushed through, after fastening a piece of cord over the cock of my gun, for fear it might, in forcing my way through, be pushed up.

It was fearful work, and my hands and face were fearfully scratched, while every moment I heard the sound of snakes getting out of my way, which did not certainly add to my contentment.

After half-an-hour I came upon a wide and rapid stream, and here the trail ended.

CHAPTER LXXXIV.

THE CHASE CONTINUED.

MY chase after the infatuated Indian girl seemed to me to resemble that of some benighted toper making his weary way after an *ignis fatuus* or will o' the wisp, over bush, brier, and brake.

Though evidently attached to me, and feeling for me sentiments almost akin to my own, she fled from me like some forest Diana from the lover she feared and yet loved.

Woman is a riddle, and I at that time decided her to be the most extraordinary one.

But then, what right had I to judge this innocent child of nature, who, though to a certain extent a savage, had her feelings and her sense of right and wrong?

Young as she was, how knew I that she had not a husband? In tropical countries girls marry at eleven, and are antique grandmothers at twenty-five.

Why should Pablina not be married, and why should this not be the reason why she should have fled me.

The thought, I must say, went to my very heart, but still it was a suggestion not to be rudely dismissed, though that did not explain much that was essentially mysterious in her conduct.

Why, indeed, had she sought me out the second time?—why should she have stopped with me and nursed me, and then, after owning her tenderness for me, why had she fled in such a strange and mysterious way?

Why!—the answer that she could have given would have been sublime; but I could not even suspect it.

The river before me was swift in the extreme, swift enough to preclude all idea of my swimming it; so that my only plan was to go upwards in search of a ford or a rift, or a place where the channel was wider and less like a rapid.

Its banks were bordered by the ordinary trees, but scarcely any sign of animal life was visible, save where a few lizards basked in the sun, or little birds hopped about on the twigs.

The pathway along the river was not very easily travelled. I had to make long detours every now and then, but succeeded in keeping it in sight.

This was absolutely necessary for my purpose.

But as I advanced, the chances of success seemed to diminish rather than to increase, as the river grew rapider than ever, while the way was so difficult that I do not believe I made five miles in the whole day.

At eventide I halted, exhausted and worn out.

Where I selected my camp was under a steep over-hanging rock.

The space I occupied was not more than a dozen yards square, but it was sheltered, and did not necessitate a fire, which I wished to avoid, lest I might frighten away the fugitives, or bring more around me than I cared to meet.

The night was pitchy dark.

My dog lay at my feet, exceedingly wearied with his day's journey.

I was so myself, and yet it was a long time before I could go to sleep.

My rest was not for long.

I awoke with a severe headache, rubbed my eyes, and looked across the river.

As certain as I was alive, there was a fire on the opposite side—a fire, too, burning in a position which made it all but certain that I had fallen on my fugitives.

On the opposite side of the river, the banks were perpendicular, sheer down to the water.

The camp of the others was on the summit, and all I could make of it was the reddened under-branches of a tree that overhung the fire, and which branches were every now and then illumined by a red and flickering light.

I ascended to the summit of the cliff, and there, using my telescope, I saw all that was passing.

It was a camp-fire under an overspreading tree, and by it sat two figures.

There was no doubt about it, one was the Indian girl, the other a man of much darker hue—a negro, in fact, but with none of that air of ferocity, nor none of that revolting ugliness which had so disgusted me in the Fan negroes, whose cannibalism is to be read in their faces.

Now this man was strong and powerful, and had evidently compelled Pablina to fly from me, when our two canoes met upon the waters.

What was to be done?

I could have shot him easily as he sat up in earnest conversation with the Indian girl, but it was quite evident that though he exercised a very severe control over her, still they were not enemies.

They were conversing in an undertone, and they were serious, but still their actions, the expression of their countenances, was friendly.

Pablina was making an effort to persuade him of the truth of something he would not listen to.

He shook his head negatively, he pointed upwards, he made odd and unintelligible signs, but they were evidently of disbelief.

Then she laid her head upon his arm and looked up in his face with such a winning smile as I would have given worlds to have addressed to me.

And yet, somehow, just then I felt none of that bitter corroding jealousy which might have naturally assailed me.

That she was trying to persuade him he ought to have waited for the sail boat was to me quite self-evident, but he was hard of belief, and could not get over the fear my appearance had inspired him with.

To end the discussion, he cast himself down beside the fire, and was soon asleep, or feigning to be so.

We were fifty feet apart—a swift and rapid stream ran between us, a stream that no swimmer that ever lived could have ventured to affront, so powerful was the current.

There was no present chance of our being united, and yet I could not bear the thought of allowing the opportunity to pass.

She was seated by the fire in an attitude of deep thought, with the light playing on her speaking countenance, so that I could watch the emotions which preoccupied her mind.

Every now and then cast a glance at the sleeping or recumbent form of the man.

Presently she seemed to think him secure, for she rose and approached the edge of the cliff.

I could no longer restrain myself.

"Pablina—hist—Pablina !"

She started like some beautiful animal terrified by the first glimpse of the hunter.

Then she listened in an attitude of deep attention.

"Pablina !" I repeated.

She glanced across, and I knew that she saw me, for her hands were clasped together in an attitude of supplication.

But I was no more advanced than I was before.

No further conversation was possible.

She was evidently afraid to wake her companion ; I knew not what to say that she could understand.

It was most annoying and vexatious, as unless I could communicate with her at daybreak, her guardian would carry her off once more—never for us to meet again in this world.

It was a most painful position.

We were neither of us sufficiently advanced in each other's language to be able to have an explanation in a few short and pithy words.

And thus, with an occasional whisper across the gulf, as impassable as that of Tartarus, the night sped away, and then grey dawn arose.

I was on my feet with my arms outstretched towards her, while she, with downcast eyes, appeared anxious to avoid showing her own deep emotion.

My gun leaned on the hollow of my arm.

I glanced at the swift torrent below.

It was not to be crossed.

I pointed to it.

She shook her head gloomily and sadly, and then raising her finger, pointed upwards.

I understood her.

The stream was to be crossed at a point higher up the river.

I made signs that I would move on.

She nodded, and herself made similar signs.

At that instant, the man who held her in a kind of subjection rose to his feet, rushed at her angrily, caught her by the wrist, and dragged her out of sight ere I could speak or act.

My gun was at my shoulder in an instant, but it was too late, even if I could have made up my mind to have shot him, without having some better excuse than I had at present.

I was dumbfounded.

Which way this man would take her was a mystery too much for me to unravel.

However, irresolution would be of no avail, and my mind was instantly made up to return to my boat, to coast along until I passed the river, and then to land, and, aided by my dog, to hunt up the fugitives, and at any risk and peril to take Pablina from her guardian.

The journey back was performed with a rapidity and recklessness for which both my body and my clothes suffered for a long time afterwards, but I reached the boat in an incredibly short space of time, took a hasty meal, and seeing from the shore an opening in the breakers, started at once ; and, dashing through two combing waves, found myself in the open sea.

Away before a rattling breeze went the canoe—away, hope at the helm and impatience at the bow, until my vision was gladdened, in about half an hour, by the sight of an opening, which I saw and felt, from the excessive rapidity of its current, was the river I was in search of.

So quick did the water run, that it was impossible to enter the river ; but about a hundred yards beyond it was a convenient cove, into which I ran the canoe, and, fastening it carefully, took my gun and dog, and started in pursuit.

About a mile up the river, I came upon a solution of part of the mystery.

Across the river, where it was swiftest, perhaps, and where the water rushed so rapidly as to form almost a rapid and fall, was a rope of cocoa-nut fibre lashed each side to a stout tree.

By means of this it was that they had crossed the river.

Had I known it, what misery—what doubt—what suspense I might have been saved.

I did not stop, however, in my course, hurrying on along the banks of the river, until at length wearied, exhausted, and utterly out of breath, I cast myself down upon the spot where she had lain the night before.

This was some satisfaction ; but more remained to be done.

I had to find the trail, and to follow it up, until I was successful.

After a goodly rest, which was absolutely necessary, I rose, and commenced a survey of the camp.

There were the remains of the fire, and the marks where the bushes had been torn up, and small trees cut down, to make the fire which had guided me to their whereabouts.

But, as I required no one to inform me that they had been there, my whole energies were devoted to the discovery of where they had gone to.

As soon as my breath had returned, I scanned the whole scene with a cautious eye, and soon saw the path by which they had chosen to depart.

They had carried the bark canoe, as I had clear evidence of where it had lain upon the ground, and now it was not.

Laden even with a light bark canoe, their progress must be slow.

It was impossible to run, so that in this way it was likely I should overtake them.

Their trail was marked, the more that I saw Pablina had taken pains to indicate their progress, had plucked flowers, had broken twigs, had stepped in soft places, where feet could be clearly distinguished, and acted in other ways to facilitate my pursuit.

She knew, then, that I was after her, and was willing to afford me every assistance in her power.

This was a joyous fact, and one that gave me every hope for the future.

CHAPTER LXXXV.

A DISCOVERY.

THE country I was passing through was arid and rude.

Here and there were trees and bushes, and generally grass ; but the general features were bad.

Huge, jagged, rough stones—many as big as a small house —were piled up and thrown in all directions, with deep fissures between them—just the place for a man to fall through and break his legs.

But for the keen sagacity of my dog, such I believe would have been my fate.

I found several fountains, but scarcely one fit to drink from.

The stuff in them was horrible.

Probably, before the eruption and earthquake, they had been visited by doves of wild animals, such as zebras, which, after splashing and rolling themselves all night, had left the shallow pool, about twenty yards across and from six to twelve inches deep, in every respect like water pumped from a farmyard.

The hill sides were covered by thorned bushes, which were terrible to contend against.

Then it was very hot, and I had become very thirsty, as well as Tiger, who panted along with his tongue out of his mouth, until we came to a hill, perhaps the most rugged I ever climbed.

At length, however, the summit was reached, and just as my dog took to his heels, I made out with my telescope a kind of a standing pool, green as grass on the top.

Away I ran, but had just mounted up a kind of natural step, when, while I was balancing myself to keep my footing, I discovered, to my horror, that I had put my foot upon the tail of a great dark-green snake, who was up in an instant, and stood confronting me, his hideous head as high as my chest.

Fatigued and used up as I was with my run, I had just sense and quickness enough left to leap over the side of the rock, and roll myself amid the bushes.

The snake was after me, but I had gained upon it, and raising myself up, crushed its head with a great stone as it advanced.

For a moment or two, my sensations were such that I had to pause, having always an instinctive horror of the animal which is the native and natural enemy of man, since it was doomed to be bruised by his heel.

As soon as I recovered myself, I made for the pool, where I found my dog wallowing in the water with great delight.

By removing the green mantle off the stagnant pool, I was able to obtain myself a drink, which was exceedingly refreshing.

I had noticed, as I came down the hill, that some red and white geese had risen from this pond to take refuge on another small one of rain water, at no great distance, where I followed them, and shot two.

But when I had secured the game, it struck me that I had lost the trail of the fugitives, so I hurried away in the direction I believed them to have taken.

It was over a wide undulating plain, black with dense thorn bushes.

My progress was now extremely slow, as the way was so rude; but about evening, a last undulation having been surmounted, I saw before me the sea, and in the distance the coast of Africa.

But where were the fugitives?

I took my telescope, and swept the waters, already dark and gloomy under the influence of night.

There was the canoe—but what is this I see beyond?

A village, with numerous canoes hauled up on the beach.

My heart sank within me, for, in the company of a hostile tribe, would not Pablina be as much lost to me as if she were gone to the interior wilds of the vast continent?

But I was desperate, and would not be defeated, so determined to risk the visit, even if it resulted in my being taken a prisoner.

But to do this it would be necessary to return to my boat, and for this I was too utterly exhausted that night.

We had to camp once more in the open air, in sight of the distant hills and rugged shores of the continent.

I slept under a rock, without a fire, so fearful was I of putting the villagers on the other side on the alert.

CHAPTER LXXXVI.

A VILLAGE OF WHITE PEOPLE.

BEFORE the sun was in the skies, and while the chill that precedes dawn was on the earth, I took my way back; this time a different way along the coast.

It was an arduous task; but there was no danger of my being lost; and after a day spent in exertions which were almost herculean in character, I reached the spot where my boat lay rocked upon the slowly moving waves.

But great as was my impatience, I did not start until sundown, as I dreaded, above all, alarming the natives.

Once they took a start into the interior, all hope of rejoining them would be gone.

The night was cloudy and threatening; so that I had to be cautious in the extreme, especially as my boat was wanting in ballast.

The wind was light and puffy, which indicated a disposition to change.

From the moment I started, my eyes were directed towards the heavens; while my two hands were engaged, one holding the tiller, the other the mainsheet, to be ready to let go in case of any puff being unusually dangerous.

The sky was black in most parts, though here and there a break could be seen where the stars shone brightly, but the scud of the clouds seemed to indicate an excessively dirty night.

The act of a prudent man would have been to anchor for the night in some sheltered bay, where I could weather the storm.

But my brain was on fire—my spirits were roused to an unnatural pitch of excitement—and, in fact, I was in the mood in which men do desperate things.

My canoe, careering over to the larboard gunwale, rushed along before the breeze.

Soon after skirting the coast some time, the dim shadowy outline of the hilly coast of the mainland became visible, and I stood directly for it.

It soon, however, became evident that some other element than the wind was at work, for while I stood in direct for the land, I was being swept past it with a rapidity quite alarming.

Then I knew that there was a powerful current, which it would require all my ingenuity to stem.

Instead, therefore, of steering head on to the land, as I had been, I drew aft my sheet, and steered a little to the south of the course I intended to follow, in order, in some measure, to counteract the influence of the current, which swept me, almost hopelessly, to the northward,

In this way, I made but little leeway, though the puffs and light winds were very vexatious and annoying.

At length, however, I seemed likely to realize my expectations, for, by my observations, the land seemed only half a mile off, while, in the hazy light cast by the stars, I could see the village towards which I was heading fast.

But soon I found that, between myself and the shore, there ran a line of white water, which I knew to be a reef almost level with the sea, but over which the tide was running with intense rapidity.

That there must be some channel I was certain; but how in that dark gloomy night was I to discover it?

No time was to be lost.

The tide was sweeping me past, as if I had been carried down a mill-race; and, trusting to my Indian girl, to assist me in my trouble, I fired my two barrels as a signal.

In an instant the village was alive, I saw men and women, some undoubtedly in a kind of European costume, rushing about with torches, which were successively lighted at a fire that burned in the centre of the semicircle of huts.

They called loudly to me, they waved their torches, they ran right into the water; but the roar of the surf concealed every word they said from me.

Still the conviction flashed across my mind that these were English; and then my sight grew dizzy, just as, letting go the rudder handle, I took up my telescope.

Then, from a terrible revulsion of feeling, I became insensible.

When I recovered, I was gliding along the coast with great rapidity, wind and tide being both against me—the village was out of sight; the village which, I experienced a moral certainty, not only contained Pablina, but my father, my mother, my uncle, my sisters, and my cousin!

I do not say that I recognised them.

It was manifestly impossible at the great distance they were off; but it had long been my conviction that they were alive, and in companionship with Pablina.

It had often struck me that this girl was a kind of emissary from them to me.

She was better able to brave the perils of the deep than they were—more used to the management of a canoe; and thus to her, it was my belief, had been confided the important task of letting me know of their existence.

Then came the sudden discovery that I loved her, that I wished to make her remain with me and be my wife.

I was sure that there was a great struggle in her mind. That she returned my affection, I had not the slightest doubt; but she was too noble-minded, too good, to accept that which she thought to be the right of another.

Everything mysterious in her manner, in her actions, was now clearly explained, and my mind was in a frantic state of doubt and uncertainty.

But other things occupied my attention just then.

I was being swept past the spot where I had discovered the village with fearful rapidity, and by no ingenuity of mine could I control my fate.

Alas! how much depends in this life on trifles.

I had not left my anchor at home, as the Dutchman found he had done in the storm, but I had never thought of making myself one.

And still the gale rose, and I could not but look in some degree to my safety.

It is true that I almost felt that I had done with life, but yet instinct, in the case of our worst troubles, will prompt us to save that we affect to despise.

I looked to leeward.

The sky was hot and sultry looking.

It can be described in no other way.

I knew what that meant.

Unless I reached some shelter before the gale fell upon me with all its real might, it would be utterly hopeless to think of escaping with life.

But here it came, and I had just time to lower the sail of the canoe, when she heeled over, and away I flew before the still rising blast.

This lasted an hour, my only safety being that the sea had not yet been lashed to its utmost fury.

Then a dark mass loomed in the distance, and before I knew what was about to happen, the canoe struck, and I was cast upon a sandy beach, once more the shipwrecked Sailor Crusoe.

CHAPTER LXXXVII.

MY SECOND SHIPWRECK.

WHEN I came to myself—the night was passed under an overhanging cliff, where I lay half-stunned, half-sleepy—I found that I had been wrecked upon a naked and arid shore; my boat knocked to pieces, my powder all wetted, and everything else a ruin.

Nothing left me but an empty gun and my faithful dog.

This was a misfortune enough to have broken any man's heart.

All my labours were in vain, all that I had endured, suffered, and done, was undone.

The work of years had to be gone over.

I was as helpless as when cast upon my deserted island with nothing in the way of worldly wealth but a clasp-knife and a broken oyster-shell.

But despondency was of no avail, so picking up my now useless gun, to carry it as a club or defensive weapon, I determined to explore the interior of the island.

But one glance sufficed.

I knew were I was.

I was within half-a-mile of my cave.

Then I fell on my knees and thanked Heaven which had been so merciful to me as in this fearful strait to have brought me to the only haven of rest which existed on that part of the earth.

Even the regret I felt at other disappointments was palliated by this piece of excessive good fortune.

My dog itself appeared to be aware that he was at home, for he jumped about, gambolled, and then suddenly took to his heels in search of his mates.

That night I slept in my old cave, being too exhausted to look about me, however impatient I might be to examine into the state of my domesticated animals and plantation, all of which had been too long neglected.

In all cases of mental affliction, particularly when it affects the body, there is nothing like occupation; and I found myself cutting out for my future days an amount of work that was really almost impossible, but which it pleased me to think could be done.

If those who object to the Scripture instruction and order, that we shall earn our living by the sweat of our brow, would only think, they would know that it is the greatest of all dispensations.

If left idle, half of us would die of inanition.

CHAPTER LXXXVIII.

THE HUNT.

I WAS up early, as, despite the fatigue and exhaustion consequent on my shipwreck, my mind was in a perfect flutter of anxiety to know what had occurred in my absence.

My dog had not yet reappeared, but towards breakfast-time he came back followed by the whole tribe, looking rather shy and wild, it is true, but still evidently glad to see me.

I shouldered my gun and determined at once to let them feel the advantage of my presence, than which nothing more tames such animals; I took them towards the pig-pen, where I saw, by the wild way of the porkers, they had been before.

The moment they saw the dogs they came rushing to the rail, and put themselves on the defensive.

The array of tusks was rather formidable, and doubtless the dogs had found it so, for they held back yelping and shrieking.

I then shot two fat pigs, which terrifying the others, they retreated, so that I was able to provide myself and my beasts with a supply of fresh meat.

I took all that I required, and hanging it up, abandoned the rest to the dogs, who having waited patiently for some time while I did the butchering, then fell to and enjoyed themselves, evidently with singular delight.

I myself, however, proceeded on my way, being anxious to visit the beautiful valley of the gazelles, which now that there was some chance of my family being increased, did appear to me to be a most important feature in my domestic economy.

Yes, this was the notion that filled my mind.

If the inhabitants of the village on the coast were indeed my friends and relatives, they would certainly try to reach my island, which Pablina must have described in such a way as to make them fully aware it could bear us all.

Of course I could not be certain that they were the persons I had seen, but still my instinct seemed to tell me it was so.

After my own misfortunes and mishaps, it was scarcely to be expected that I should again take heart of grace and make me another canoe.

But they being many, would doubtless find it easy to do so, especially if they were the persons I fondly hoped they were.

I had seen many beautiful places on my island, but I thought nothing half so exquisite as my valley of the gazelles now appeared to my delighted eyes.

The whole was one mass of lovely vegetation.

The palm trees had sprung up, the grass was luxuriant, while the number of the gazelles had greatly increased, and I thought the little ones the sweetest and most beautifully formed creatures I had ever witnessed.

My ostriches stalked about with imposing gravity, evidently on the best of terms with the gazelles, though they generally kept themselves at the scrubby and arid end of the valley.

They had grown very much larger.

But what excited my attention most was the fact that all the does were amply supplied with milk, which made me drive two of them into the pen; that, having given them a goodly supply of food, I might on the next day myself enjoy the luxury of a bowl of milk, of which I was always wonderfully fond.

This done, my steps were retraced in another direction.

What had become of my zebras, or had my absence entirely deprived me of the possession of my steeds?

On this point I was peculiarly anxious, as, make up my mind to be calm as much as ever I would, my ideas would still run on that village on the vast African shore.

They were gazing happily and peacefully in the old place, but evidently very shy.

The sight of a gourd full of corn did not appear to incite them to any familiarity with their old master, who was, however, determined to recapture horse and zebra, even if the lasso had to be employed again.

But this proved not to be necessary, for after some delay the horse, with that instinctive fondness for man which so often characterizes him, walked up to me, and after rubbing his nose against me, proceeded to eat the corn.

The zebra was evidently watching him, so I too was quick and careful, and when the beautiful creature came up after his companion, I contrived to have a halter ready for him.

This done, I leaped on his bare back and rode him home, leading the horse, and followed by the young zebra.

My intention was to scour my island ere I settled down to work.

I was ill at ease, dissatisfied, discontented.

I did not know how to begin.

Sometimes the idea would creep over me, that at any sacrifice I would build myself another boat, and either search out the settlers on the shore, or sail down the coast of Africa, until I reached the straits, which, in fine weather, did not seem to be such a difficult adventure.

But first I would reconnoitre the coast, and find out if, indeed, it would be impossible to cross over to the mainland on a raft, and walk back to the settlement.

With this view, my preparations were made.

A supply of pork, some coarse cakes, a gourd of rum and water, powder and shot, were placed to my hand; while my very best guns were all examined, and one remarkable for its lightness, and yet the large ball it carried, selected.

At daybreak, the zebra was saddled, and myself upon him, and on my way, though at first I had quite enough to do to manage her, so wild and skittish had she grown.

As there was every sign of a change in the weather I took with me my lion's skin, for on rising during the night to listen to some strange noise outside, I had felt the night-air to be particularly chilly and damp.

The way selected was one almost new.

It lay between the lake of my summer-house and the sea-coast, towards some woods, which had excited my curiosity, from the peculiar appearance of the trees.

I did not hurry my steed this day, even dismounting several times and walking; so that, what with excursions to the right and left, very little, if any real, progress was made.

A fire was very welcome that night, the stars being clear, and the air very keen and bracing.

Near this it was pleasant to lie, while my zebra, duly hobbled, stuffed herself with reeds and green grass, which was all it had, except just one handful of corn.

Before me, in the morning, was a ridge, the ground of which was a kind of crisp gravel; while to my left lay broken, rocky ground; and to the right, a chaos of broken crags and rugged hills.

Then came in sight the woods I have already alluded to.

Suddenly I started.

What was this I saw in the soft earth?

I knew it at once to be what the Cape hunters call the spoor or mark of an animal, though of what nature I really could not tell.

Dismounting, however, a careful examination soon convinced me of its real character; and with a beating heart, I remounted, and forcing my steed to a trot, descended the slope towards the woods.

My hunting propensities were aroused, and in a very few moments my expectations were realized, for among a lot of bushes, and quietly browsing off a camel-thorn tree, was a splendid giraffe.

Away, like the wind, I darted, now urging my swift little zebra to her utmost speed, and succeeded in getting within fifty yards of the magnificent animal before she saw me.

Then, off she was at a great rate, crashing through bushes that were excessively annoying to my steed, which rather resented such rough treatment.

Not wishing to lose my first giraffe, and forgetting in my excitement how little use she would prove, I fired my gun, and, as luck would have it, hitting her on the quarter, she went at once at a much less rapid pace.

Still it was painful to follow, especially as I had to load as I galloped.

Hoping to take another mile or so out of the animal, I fired again, but without success; after which, having once more loaded, away my faithful zebra was started in pursuit.

Having become fat and bloated with too much rest and grass, she was soon blown, so that my only hope was to overtake and confront the animal.

I was riding parallel to my prey, which bled from its wound, but looking at the cameleopard, instead of before me, I was very nearly having a fall into a dried-up watercourse; but seeing it just in time, I managed to make the zebra carry me over, and, fully aware that everything now depended on the next few minutes, rode with all the skill I could, not sparing heel or thong.

My brave little zebra, now evidently excited by the chase, then beat her, and passed her.

But the great and somewhat unwieldy giraffe would not be checked.

Then she came headlong on; my steed stood firm, with her legs well out, very likely glad to be reined up and gain her breath.

My gun was lowered.

The giraffe came at me with a most vicious glance.

I fired just as her head was over me, and the huge beast tossed her head back; the blood spirted from her nostrils, she turned, staggered, and sought once more to fly.

But I was determined not to let the poor brute escape, simply from those hunting instincts which belong to all of my nation.

My gun was hastily loaded, my zebra urged slowly after her, and then once more a bullet, which penetrated the brain, settled the contest.

I had shot my first giraffe.

I verily believe it was chiefly to convince myself that I had not committed a wanton murder that I was soon engaged in the task of flaying the animal, and cutting off large steaks, as well as securing the marrowbones, which would, I knew, make a most delicious soup.

The meat required keeping, but to a hungry man everything is welcome, so I managed to make a meal.

My zebra was completely done up.

The chase had been a heavy one, and rest was absolutely necessary; as it was again necessary to prepare a camp, while doing which I fell upon some ostrich eggs, of which I ate one for a late supper.

I often used to think of the quaint old traveller who said, " I have read in some old-fashioned books of fiction, entitled 'Natural History,' that an ostrich egg will feed six men; but I know that I could finish one before supper. But then I enjoyed the blessing of a good appetite.''

Unless during illness, and under one or two circumstances which will be explained fully as I proceed, appetite was never that which was wanting; nor, through the blessing of Providence, the means of satisfying it.

There were all the animals, trees, plants, and streams of the island at my service, with none to interfere, or say me nay.

It was a sultry morning when I rose, and, as after breakfast, I made my way through the camel-thorn trees, thorn bushes, and stunty grass, I noticed a want of life in the landscape.

The grass was quite withered, and the bushes stunted and seared.

No birds could be seen or heard, and every feature looked quiet and dead under the most saddening of all lights, a blazing sun in an unclouded sky.

Then the scene changed like magic, and there were the distant hills of the coast of Africa, a sloping ground intersected with bushes and trees, and below, the shining gorgeous sea, as blue as the hot, unclouded sky above.

I had thus reached the temporary end of my journey, for it was with a view to examine into the capacities of this channel for being traversed that I had travelled so far from home.

I looked warily round, fearing every moment to find myself in the propinquity of a village of Fan Indians, whom I was quite sure were periodically in the habit of visiting its tempting shores.

This had not so forcibly impressed itself on my mind as it should have done; but now I was near the place where their tents and huts had formerly been, I began to be very wary and cautious, dismounting from my steed, walking it, and peering into every bush and thicket as I advanced.

In this way I reached the shore, and drew forth my most valuable of instruments—my telescope.

A large temporary town had been erected on the shores of the coast, huts had been placed in rather symmetric order, while a large spear, that I could distinctly make out, marked the tent of a chief.

Now, what could all this indicate?

Why had they come down to that desolate coast?

Was it to deal in gold dust, slaves, and ivory with the iniquitous traders? or were they about to make a raid upon my island?

In my nervous state of mind this latter idea prevailed, and, forgetting all else, I mounted and rode away towards the more deserted part of the island; nor did I stop until I had reached my cave, where I remained two whole days, collecting my thoughts, ere I ventured a hundreds yards from home.

Then, reflection coming to my assistance, I hit upon several plans to avoid meeting with the negroes.

In the first place, I determined to draw a line of demarcation between my own and that part of the island where elephants were found, as these were the prey they chiefly came in search of.

This line I would not pass.

I would trust to the lake keeping the secret of my bower; while my own part of the island having no game to speak of at all, would present so little attraction for them as to run little risk of being visited, unless my presence were suspected.

Now this was not likely; but still, as one cannot be too

No. 18.—SAILOR CRUSOE.

ALFRED FORTIFYING HIS HUT.

safe, it was my firm resolve to reserve my powder, and to depend on bows and arrows, traps, and even on the boomerang—such as I made in the early times—rather than use my powder.

This I now resolved to husband, for two reasons; first, because it was my only hope in a contest with savages; and next, because it might be the means of attracting their particular and curious attention.

I was not without hope of making gunpowder; but then I had many other things to do, such as extending my plantation, improving and extending my gazelle valley—this was a favourite idea—and completing my fortifications, which might, in the long run, be my last hope.

To this latter task I determined to devote my first energies; the preservation of our lives being the very first idea that presents itself to man.

CHAPTER LXXXIX.

MY FORTIFICATION.

HAD I consulted my own tastes, I should certainly have made myself a goodly rampart, have planted it with guns, and trusted to pure physical force for my defence.

But it would have taken one man seven years of hard and incessant work, to have achieved anything like the work I intended, so I had to be more moderate in my ideas.

My stakes and transplanted trees had progressed so much that it was a sight to behold.

They had shot upwards and sideways until they had become a tangled mass, and it was quite a task for me, every time I had been absent a little while, to cut myself a path by which to enter my retreat.

What more was there to be done I scarcely knew; but that something additional, in case of a furious onslaught, should be provided, seemed quite necessary—so having thought on the matter a long time, the following plan was adopted.

The great danger lay in the discovery of my pathway.

That once in the hands of an enemy, any number might force their way in.

As Pablina had done so once, it might be done again.

To obviate this a number of good stout, young trees were cut down, the branches roughly lopped off, and planted firmly with cross beams on each side of the entrance.

From one of these a heavy gate of bars was suspended and securely fastened, so as not to be opened from the outside.

This, at all events, guarded against surprise, which was one of those things chiefly to be feared.

This having been executed to my complete satisfaction, my guns were all taken down, and a stout frame having been made, they were laid at about three feet from the ground, in a way to point all at the gate.

But as in the rainy season they would be spoilt, I had to erect over them a stout and slanting roof, while their muzzles were corked and their pans covered by a piece of skin securely tied down.

Had this been omitted, they would soon have been utterly spoiled, for rain in these latitudes is a very different thing from rain in England.

First, you have a few passing showers, then these showers become more frequent and more copious until it pours torrents.

The fall of water on my island was wild, like everything else.

During six months in the year the north wind blows incessantly, driving over dense masses of clouds, which sweep heavily over the earth, darkening the sky, and preceded in their course by dreadful peals of thunder.

On reaching the higher lands a rapid condensation takes place, which destroys the equilibrium, and a veritable deluge ensues.

In a few moments, cataracts rush from the mountain heights, the smallest rivulets are turned into torrents, and the rivers, over-flowing their banks, cover the plains—this will last for a considerable time, during which, to go forth is impossible.

The natives of some parts of Africa abstain from lighting fires during this period, and even go without food, rather than come into the open air.

The more surely to guard my guns, I made the thatch and boughs very low and projecting, while a little rill leading to my pond carried off the water at once.

My next task was, for me, not an easy one.

I required a ladder, by which secretly to leave my retreat, and reconnoitre, in case of a siege.

This was very laborious, and when finished was not very handsome, but it served the purpose for which it was made.

Now I thought that I was a match for any amount of naked savages who might venture to attack me.

But there still remained the dangers of a long siege.

They might find traces of me, and unable to discover my actual abode, might wander about the island and render close concealment necessary.

It is true, I had ample store of water, I had my grain and dry vegetables, but I wanted animal food.

A spot under the cliff, in which my cave was hidden, raised an idea in my head.

On the other side of the pool from that which I occupied, was a space about seven or eight feet wide between the palm trees and the rock, where scarcely anything but grass grew.

It ran back seventy to eighty feet, while the lower part of the palm trees were so dense with shrubs, that with a very little addition it could be made impenetrable.

Here I proposed to place a gazelle or two, and as many fowls as I could, there being ample food for them by only scratching the ground, and by picking up seed and vermin, which abounded in this humid spot.

But though I had the gazelles, the other creatures had to be found.

I had seen nothing resembling the home hen, but it mattered little to me what they were so that they laid eggs.

As to ostriches, it was out of the question.

It became necessary, in order to obtain a supply, to go on a voyage of discovery, which I was very loth to do, being in constant fear of the savages, whom I imagined to be roaming, like fierce lions, about the place, in search of whom they might devour.

Cannibalism is a thing so horrid that it is not pleasant to talk about, but it is, nevertheless, one of those things which should be known, that we may be more fully aware of the blessings of civilization.

This horrible propensity, of which my first idea, when a boy, was conveyed to me by the story of the ghoul in the "Arabian Nights Entertainments" is common in many places, but generally among nations which have suffered intense privations. It then grows upon them, and the taste cannot be shaken off.

On this point my readers will pardon me, if I digress so far as to tell a story which lives in my memory, though I cannot recollect in what book of travels I read it, or to which exact tribe it refers.

CHAPTER XC.

THE STORY OF THE CANNIBAL CAVE.

THERE was, some years ago, say in the beginning of the century in which I write, a tribe of harmless and happy African savages, neither negroes nor Arabs, but probably a mixture of both.

They were very happy.

They had green pastures and steep hills, where the warriors and chiefs hunted the elk, the gnu, and the wild boar; they had pleasant streams, whence they drew an ample supply of fish.

They were not a warlike or a savage race, but quite contented with their lot; living to eat, drink, marry, and give in marriage, until death took them away to the happy land; like a great many other people would be if only let alone by those terrible butchers of men called conquerors.

But ambition, unfortunately, is not wholly confined to civilized lands, so that this quiet and peaceful community was not left long in the enjoyment of happy hours.

They were governed by a good king or chief who cultivated, as far as in him lay, the arts of peace, and who tried to make his people a settled, instead of a nomadic nation.

Then came news that a great chief, who lived beyond the mountains of the moon, was about to subdue all the nations of the earth; that is, all the tribes that came within his ken.

They would have defended themselves, but they could not learn to fight in a day; which is a warning to nations, and disposes at once of the doctrine of peaceful Quakerism.

They could not fly, for their enemies were on them.

Then this great chief, having conquered them almost without a struggle, did what other great chiefs in more civilized lands have done before—placed a lieutenant of his own over them, who also, like many other servants—overseers of slaves to wit—was more cruel than his master.

But he was very brave, which was something; but then he kept the people under a yoke of iron, so that they could scarcely call their souls their own.

But he was, I have said, cruel, and he subdued them and held them firmly in subjection, by putting to death, impaling, and poisoning without mercy, anyone who would not submit to his authority.

But even his own followers wearied of his tyranny, and many of them, leaguing themselves with the oppressed, secretly withdrew from his yoke, and fled to the hills.

But he, too, having escaped the yoke of a tyrant became a tyrant himself, and fought with the tribes which lived in his neighbourhood; being again a terror to his weaker and more peaceful neighbours.

From that moment the land became the scene of continual and unremitting slaughter; no one feeling the curse of war more than those very tribes who wished to live in peace.

This state of things lasted many years, the fields remained uncultivated, and the horrors of famine were added to the already fearful horrors of war.

Several tribes were utterly destroyed by this fearful and two-fold scourge.

The same has been nearly the case in more civilized communities.

The ties of friendship and consanguinity were soon wholly forgotten.

Every one lived for himself alone.

All gave themselves up to murder and pillage.

Then associations of cannibals were formed in the most inaccessible mountains—associations which knowing no longer any distinction of race, tribe, or party, went forth prowling everywhere in search of their wretched victims.

Years after travellers visited these caves in which the wretches lived.

The tradition, fortunately, only remained.

The ground was literally strewed with half-roasted skulls, shoulder-blades, and broken bones.

There were large red spots still perceptible in the most retired parts of these dens, where the flesh was deposited; the blood had penetrated so deep in the rock that the trace of it never can be effaced unto the end of time.

Nearly all the chief and influential men in the country were carried away by the terrible tide of war.

But one able and observant chief contrived to breast the stream.

He was a clever and a cunning man, endowed with remarkable strength of character, and knew effectually how to resist and to yield at the right moment.

He made himself allies even among his enemies; set other of his enemies by the ears; and showed himself generally a diplomatist as well as an able ruler.

So finding he had a following large enough, he retreated to the top of a mountain, where, in a huge cavity of the rocks, he was safe from surprise.

He had a tolerably good supply of flocks and herds, and laboured hard to procure more.

Soon many began to rally round him in the valley below.

His power grew great, and in order to ensure the gathering together of all his people, he restored tranquility as much as possible, and determined to suppress cannibalism.

He had to contend against the anti-cannibals, who wanted to slay them all without mercy, and against the cannibals, who were wedded to their habits.

He foresaw a civil war to which that of the Big-endians and the Little-endians was as nothing.

It would have depopulated a land which was already destitute of inhabitants.

He was also fully aware that cannibalism, being neither a tenet of religion, a national custom, nor a tradition, must be repugnant to most of those who indulged in it.

But just then there occurred an event which almost shook his faith.

The wife of a chief was carried away by the cannibals; but as there was a move in the right direction, the cannibals offered to take a ransom of six oxen.

The chief, who was very fond of his wife, at once acquiesced.

He, however, thought it wise not to venture in that direction himself, but deputed some young men to perform the task.

They started early in the morning and soon reached the spot they were in search of.

The cannibals had taken up their abode in a vast and immense cavern, which was protected from approach by thorny bushes and fallen pieces of rock.

The ambassador entered into conversation with some women, who were returning from the fields bearing baskets of roots upon their heads.

They told the envoy that the young woman they desired to restore to her family was still living, and added that the oxen would be willingly taken in exchange.

These words gave them some courage.

Their next step was to climb the steep ascent which led to the entrance of the cave inhabited by the Anthropophagi.

But no sooner did they reach the entrance of the cave than the envoy and his friends felt their legs begin to tremble beneath them, while a thrill of horror and disgust ran through their veins.

Nothing was to be seen but skulls and broken bones.

A woman was near the threshold cooking; she lifted a pot to stir the contents, and they saw a human hand.

They turned away after hearing that the men had gone out hunting.

They soon had good cause to know what this meant, as they soon came in—a horrid and hideous crew, armed with clubs and javelins, and driving a captive before them with loud shouts of " Wah ! wah !"

The prisoner was a tall, well-formed, and handsome young man, who entered before them with a firm and calm step, and most contemptuous expression of countenance.

No Red Indian at the stake could have shown more fortitude.

He sat down in the corner of the cave, and looked on with an air of the most perfect indifference, only listening with a satisfied air to the narrative of the envoy.

While this was being told one or two of the wretches approached and strangled the unfortunate youth, who made no struggle.

The envoy turned away with horror, and having, with much praying, obtained the exchange, went away, glad to leave the place, the cannibal remarking that he had done him a great favour, as one young woman was worth far more than six oxen.

But the upshot of the adventure shows the force of habit.

The chief was delighted to see his wife; but she soon escaped from him, and returned of her own accord to the den from which she had been rescued.

She had made friends there, and had acquired a taste for human flesh.

Now this exasperated the people so much that they could scarcely be restrained from rising up and annihilating the whole set.

But the wise king refused, and said that men-eaters were living sepulchres, and that no one could fight with sepulchres.

These words being repeated to the wretches, they saw a way to pardon, and gave up their evil practices.

The prevalence of the crime may be guessed when I add that some few years after there were thirty or forty villages peopled by ex-cannibals.

Still, strangely as this story ends, in Borneo, in Africa, and other places, cannibals still exist.

CHAPTER XCI.

A JOURNEY.

THIS is one of the many stories which my father had told me of a practice which I held in peculiar horror, and which, indeed, preyed upon my mind whenever I thought of savages.

I may as well add here, that ever since I had been on the island, I had contracted a very peculiar habit of spending my leisure hours.

When I was indisposed to work, and did not wish to smoke, I would fold my arms, and after thinking awhile, begin a story aloud.

Hundreds and hundreds of the hours which I spent on that island were beguiled by this practice.

I would get so interested in my narratives that I would gladly have preserved some of them, which, without flattery to myself, I decide to have been exceedingly engrossing and entrancing, at all events they were so to me.

But as yet I had not made me pens, ink, and paper, but how I remedied this in the end, and wrote this very manuscript, will be seen in its proper place.

Another very great amusement with me was to read out the adventures of the Skeleton, whose manuscript I had so miraculously found, and which, to me, was the most delightful book in the world.

But these digressions take me from my regular narrative, and prevent me from carrying on the story of my preparations in the eventuality of a siege.

This idea held such fast possession of my mind that it had scarcely room for any other, and I was eternally contriving and thinking how to evade being entrapped by them.

My deep desire to be again in company with my fellow-creatures was as great as ever ; but to be alone for ever was better than to fall into the hands of men who made a practice of devouring human flesh.

A few days after the completion of my fortress, which now assumed a most formidable aspect in my eyes, I again resolved on an excursion.

During the whole of this period, my horse and zebra, had remained hoppled, without having, however, a very good range ; but coming home at night to lie near my cave, to have some corn and salt from a bowl I placed within their reach.

I took the pains on this occasion to keep my dogs in a leash, so that they might not startle the birds which it was my firm belief I was about to catch, though how was not as yet exactly defined in my own mind.

I was determined, however, that I would do so, not only for use but for amusement.

It was my belief that it was in and on the skirts of the woods which were near my bower on the lake, that I should most easily discover that I was in search of, so in this direction I took my way early in the morning, mounted on my horse, and with Tiger—to his great disgust, kept within bounds by a rope—trotting by my side.

With a view to listen for the forest sounds, by which chiefly I could hope to track my hoped-for prey, I moved very slowly.

My accoutrements consisted of a gun, a net similar to that with which I had captured my gazelles, my sword-saw, knife, and a bundle of twine, a small supply of provisions, and a gourd for water.

Thus equipped, I advanced quietly and cautiously ; but for a long time nothing occurred to disturb my meditations.

when suddenly they were interrupted by an adventure of rather a startling character.

For some time no trace had been seen of any large wild beasts, which was the more surprising that my domestic animals appeared to promise them an easy prey.

One thing, however, struck me forcibly, and this was the fact of the abundance of all kind of game on my island, which, for a very long time, puzzled me inconceivably.

How natural and easy of explanation the circumstance was will be seen in a future part of my narrative.

It was towards evening; I was looking out for a fit station for my camp, when I noticed that my dog was uneasy, while my horse all but stood still.

Looking upwards, I saw several vultures in the air.

Curiosity in some sort over-coming prudence, I tied my horse and dog to a tree, and, clutching my rifle, crept on to where the scene of action seemed to be.

I advanced with all the due caution of an experienced hunter, and soon reached the summit of a small eminence along which ran a wall of thorny bushes.

Stooping to see if I could pass, the whole was explained at a single glance.

It was a huge lion enjoying his dinner.

The mighty master of the forest had killed a young zebra, which he was tearing to pieces in most unseemly manner.

He was stretched out at his ease, enjoying his prey, which seemed greatly to his taste, and also to the taste of a host of other animals, of a less lordly character.

Attracted by the scent, they had come rushing to the curée.

These were hyenas and jackals, which having stealthily approached, stood with fierce and envious eyes, watching the rapid motion of the jaws, which portended but a scanty remnant for themselves.

In addition to these already sufficiently repulsive animals, there were slate-coloured vultures, which had come whirling from the clouds, and which now, with folded wings, stretching out their bare necks and uttering the most piercing cries, jumped, in a most] ridiculous manner, towards the object of their greedy desire, something like some hungry men-servants watching the performance of their masters on a scanty allowance.

As long as the whole of this parasitical gang kept at a respectful distance, the master of the feast allowed them to growl, scream, whine, chatter, and make every angry mani-festation at their pleasure; but presently the ravenous circle drawing nearer, the front ranks being pushed forward by the weight of the rear ranks, the whole movement became at first annoying, and then alarming.

Of this the lion, hitherto so contemptuous in his manner seemed perfectly aware, for becoming strangely incensed, he cast a sidelong look at his parasites, and then, when least they expected it, leaped, with one bound and one terrible growl, into the midst, striking to the right and left with what might be called his mighty fist.

The scene was terrible, and ludicrous at the same time.

Away sped the jackals; the hyenas heavier and less agile, followed suit, while the hideous vultures made their retreat slowly.

Then the lion, as if satisfied with this moral chastisement of his uproarious court, returned leisurely to his feast.

Infinitely amused at what to me was as good as a play, I remained motionless.

Then reflecting on the danger of the vicinity of this beast,

I took a steady aim, and being now a first-rate marksman, hit the animal in the head, when he rolled over in con-vulsions, and soon after died.

For some time there was stillness; and then, slowly, cau-tiously, and with uncertain steps, the whole gang returned to the charge.

They evidently thought the lion asleep, for they halted now and then to watch him.

No motion.

Nearer and nearer, until, with a howl and a yell, they darted on their prey, when such a scene of confusion, fighting, and contention ensued, as never was surpassed.

I returned to my quarters, lit two fires to keep off the prowlers, and then lay me down to rest.

CHAPTER XCII.

THE LYRE BIRD AND LAUGHING JACKASS.

I WAS awakened in the morning by certain peculiar and singular sounds, which, while I was collecting my scattered senses, filled me with astonishment.

The sun had just risen, and all nature seemed suddenly to have awakened to life.

Close to me, I could hear the crowing of cocks, the screaming of cockatoos, the chattering of the common parrot, and the howling of the jackal, in delightful concert.

Unable to make out what it was, I crawled out, gun in hand, to elucidate the mystery.

Fortunately, my dog was tied up, so that he could not startle the game.

The noises appeared to proceed from a small, thickly-wooded ravine, or gully, which extended from my camp to the hillock whence I had watched the lion.

I crawled slowly along, and suddenly halted.

The sounds were close to me; in front, in fact, in a little open glade, covered with high grass.

All the sounds I have alluded to were again repeated, but one at a time.

Having a shrewd guess now what it all meant, I watched, and presently I saw a slight movement in the bushes, at no great distance from my hiding-place—say about twenty feet, followed by a scratching and picking noise in the high grass.

Then I saw, or thought I saw, some long feathers pro-trude now and then above it; and, carried away by an impetuosity which was certainly very foolish in my circumstances, fired in the direction of the moving object; when, to my annoyance and mortification, up rose a magnificent cock bird, his tail erect, and walked off into the bush.

A loud laugh startled me, and made me jump to my feet, when, on the bough of a tree, I saw a bird closely resembling what is commonly called the laughing-jackass, literally grin-ning at my misfortune.

I strode away, humiliated, annoyed, and angry with myself.

Though the eggs of this bird were of little use, yet I knew the young pullets to be very good eating.

After a little reflection, I determined to make an effort to capture this very audacious bird, with all his cunning, as well as the female, which was sure to be about.

After considerable reflection, I thought of a plan.

From its being damp, and knowing the habits of the bird,

it was pretty certain that the cock would return to his feeding-place.

Cutting two straight, long staves, I fastened them one on each side of my net, with another cross one, to keep them apart.

Then, carrying this machine to the little open glade, I fixed it in an upright position in the soil, having first fastened a cord to the upper part.

No sooner had I done this than I made a precipitate retreat, for I had discovered the reason why the cock selected that feeding-place.

It was a perfect nest of leeches, upon which this bird feeds habitually.

Not being sure as to the time at which he might return, I had brought with me food and drink, so as to be able to watch any amount of time, taking care to select such a spot of ground as was likely to be free from leeches.

This very peculiar bird, which is very plentiful in the islands lately discovered by Captain Cook, is called a pheasant, or lyre bird (*Menera superba*), but is, properly speaking, a thrush.

It is about the size of a small fowl, of a dirty-brown colour, approaching to black in some parts, while its beauty consists in the magnificent tail of the cock bird, which is in shape exactly like a lyre.

But what is this sound?

Again I hear its strange imitative voice.

It seldom cares about its own natural note, but rejoices in imitating all the sounds of the forest.

I gently raised my head, and there it was again, strutting round in a circle, scratching up the dead leaves and soft mould with its somewhat formidable claws, and then feeding on the leech, in which food it delights.

Quick as thought I pulled my string, and then darted into the open glade, to find, to my inexpressible delight, that both cock and hen were my prisoners.

This was no bad beginning, and now that my trap was provided, it was not many days ere I had a goodly supply of birds, with which I returned to my residence highly delighted.

Their wings were clipped, and this precaution taken, they were let loose in my fowl-yard, where, with some care, they throve and often supplied me with young birds, and eggs.

The nest of the lyre bird was about three feet in circumference and one foot deep, having an orifice on one side.

The female was a very unattractive bird, having a poor tail, nothing like the male.

It lays one egg, of a slate colour with black spots.

CHAPTER XCIII.

HOME AFFAIRS.

I HAD now done all that was in the power of one man to prepare myself against an emergency which might happily never arise, but which an imagination roused by my solitary life represented as very likely to occur.

It behoved me now to look to other things, and amongst these was the care of my plantation, which had been neglected and was running to waste.

I had fortunately housed all the seed, but not having replanted it, weeds, grasses, and such like, had invaded the space in such a way as to make it a very laborious task to renew my crop.

But there was no remedy for it.

Something had to be done.

After some little thought, a plan was hit upon, which promised to answer the purpose.

By great exertions, I tore up, destroyed, or cut down a strip on each side towards the woods I was anxious to preserve, quite wide enough to ward off the flames.

Then the rest was set on fire, to the great annoyance of snakes and other animals, especially rabbits, which had taken up their quarters there.

The task executed, another rude and very heavy plough was made, to which I harnessed my three beasts of burden, the young zebra being perfectly tame and very fond of me.

When I say plough, I should say something to represent a plough; for it was really a kind of rake, made of a strong trunk of a tree, with teeth of iron-wood set in holes close together.

These being very strong, and reduced to my size and use by means of fire, tore up the ground quite sufficiently for my purpose.

Such agricultural doings may make people smile at home, but in a country where the rain is so violent as to actually move and cake the soil, it is quite sufficient.

It has already been explained how sorely my cave was infested with rats, a set of animals which are, without exception, the greatest plague the husbandman can have.

Now my head had been at work for a long time how to remedy this evil.

I knew of several safe and patent remedies, but then they were very laborious.

One admirable plan of antiquity suggested itself to me, but it was beyond my power to undertake.

They would hollow out a kind of hole in the ground, of the shape of a stout-bottle with a very narrow neck.

This, covered over by a thick layer of clay, would preserve grain for many years.

I knew of the system, too, of many savage tribes, who make baskets almost in the shape of a globe with the two poles slightly flattened.

The texture of these contrivances was not firm, because it was intended to swell, stiffen, and become impervious to rain, by the very pressure of the grain, which was usually heaped into it by means of heavy levers.

They are not, however, of durable workmanship.

The way they are made is this; the workman places near him a few bundles of plaiting materials, and two or three sheaves of dry grass, very long and tough; in his hands he holds a large needle with two eyes, so that the material he interweaves should not get unthreaded.

He takes a handful of grass, and gives it the form of a small disc, which he interweaves in all directions, until it is firm and cannot become unrolled.

This done, nothing more remains but to go on sewing to the part already formed twists of grass of equal thickness, until the basket finishes in an orifice of six or eight inches in diameter.

I resolved to do something of the kind, and for this purpose made choice of a goodly selection of withes and of such grass and filamentous fibres as would twist well and serve my purpose.

My winter, or rainy season, proved on this occasion rather long, so that I had ample opportunity to carry out this part of my operations, which, after some trials, proved remarkably successful.

This success in the basket-maker's art led me to try my prentice hand at other things, and especially at a straw hat in which I was also tolerably successful, even to the making of a thick one, which would keep off both the rays of the sun and the severest showers of rain.

The substances used were straw and reeds, with inside, as lining, some gazelle skin, prepared only by lying long in water, and then being softened with grease.

My grain was all placed in these huge bottles, and the outside, at the proper time, coated with india-rubber, which proved an excellent preservation against rats, at all events, for some time to come.

Thinking always of the dangers of a siege, I looked much to the interior comforts of my hut—improved my bed-room and sitting-room.

My store-room was made as impervious to vermin as possible, while on all occasions two dogs were placed within it, day and night.

Here it may be explained that, although I had been compelled, for my own safety, slily and cautiously to make savage slaughter among my stock of dogs, yet had they multiplied in such a way as still to leave me eight.

It seemed very cruel to destroy whole litters of puppies, but it was absolutely necessary, or I should have been myself devoured, so great is the increase of these animals.

As, after the experiences of the bower—which I always regretted, but feared to dwell in, because of its exposed situation—it was impossible with any satisfaction to sleep in a standing bed place, so, as the rainy season waned, I contrived to make myself a hammock, which afterwards proved to be as pleasant as it was useful, being so much healthier than a close bunk.

It is scarcely necessary to say that on no occasion did I waste the produce of my hunting.

All skins were scrupulously saved, and prepared for use in the best way I could, which, after all, was rather crude but still answered all the purpose of coats, breeches, and shoes, or rather, those anomalous things, called moccassins.

A piece of skin of the proper size was cut, say a foot by a foot; then holes were bored all round, through which leather thongs were passed, drawn up round the ankle; and the shoe was complete.

In this, and some other employment, in reading, telling stories, and smoking my pipe, the winter season passed quickly away.

But still, one was glad to herald the joyous return of the warm sun, which once more gladdened and warmed all nature.

As usual, my first task was to visit my plantation, my piggery, and my gazelle valley.

The first was doing well, the second required considerable thinning, which was useful for my larder and for my ravenous dogs; while the last of all seemed to increase in beauty every year.

The trickling rill, the old rice swamp, the young palm trees, with the vivifying influence of so many animals, had made the place a perfect little paradise; while both gazelles and ostriches had vastly increased in numbers.

I could now allow myself an ample supply of butcher's meat and milk every day, while on many occasions an ostrich egg was added to my luxuries.

But it was quite clear that more space was required for them.

This idea had often entered my mind, but never so forcibly until it became evident how rapid was the increase.

The extreme end of the valley had been constantly examined by me, and the only outlet, a narrow gap in the rocks, so securely blocked up that they could not pass through.

Beyond this was another valley of even more curious formation than this one.

It seemed, for all the world, like the crater of an extinct volcano.

Towards the centre it gradually sloped to a lake, but the sides were precipitous.

From these depended the wild convolvulus, knotted shrubs and raspberry bushes, while below were rich green grass, aloes, and everlastings.

The depth of the vegetable earth was considerable, and nearly everywhere a foundation of clay was found, covered with a blackish soil of the richest nature, two or three feet in depth.

This may be seen where the little hill torrents had made themselves beds.

The grass was high and rank, but my herds, I knew, would soon reduce it, so that every day the whole party were driven in by my dogs, and the aperture closed, and in two months the whole valley was cropped as neatly as if had been artificially mowed.

It was a great source of amusement to my dogs to run down the young ostriches and capture them, which they did, after a little practice, without in any way hurting their prey.

The object of so doing was to clip their wings and otherwise disable them from escape to the extent of one half, the other half being let loose to shift for themselves, for fear that my flocks and herds should become far too numerous.

When first my singular lot cast me away on that deserted locality, it was little my expectation that I should complain of an abundance of riches, but so it was.

I was now so wealthy that it was absolutely necessary to thin them out, and had it not been for the ravenous appetite of my dogs, it would have been my duty to have allowed nearly all my pigs and some of my gazelles to abscond.

The pigs were of very little use, to me, further than for feeding my dogs.

I found, from observation, how right the Hebrews and the Mohammedans were to make eating pork contrary to the tenets of their religion. It is not at all wholesome in hot countries. My use of it was very sparing.

Since all my tea had been used up, a substitute for coffee had been made from certain berries, which, with the juice of the wild sugar-cane, served as a preferable beverage to water, at all events.

Then there were cakes, dried meat, fish, and cocoa-nuts, always pleasant; and in the proper season, ripe fruits, which experience, however, taught me to use sparingly.

During several days of the hot months, my cave not being agreeable from absence of air, I slept under an improvised hut in the valley of the gazelles.

I mention this because it caused me to be gratified by my first view of a delightful spectacle, that of the Southern Cross.

It was a beautiful spectacle.

It is to this glorious revolving cross, first seen by the traveller after passing the Cape de Verde Islands, that the southern hemisphere is indebted for its celestial beauty.

It is a perfect glory in the heavens, and by its means both the variation of the needle and the hour of the day can be told, though the latter was a complicated process which I could not carry out for want of instruments and the latest nautical books.

I knew that if one watched it from the summer solstice, which is on the 21st of June, to the northern autumnal equinox on the 21st of September, and noted the right ascension of the sun, with some small calculation the exact hour of the day might be told.

But I had little leisure for such speculations, and yet it set me thinking.

I knew that now I had been four years on the island, by the recurrence of the rainy seasons, but if I were to live there much longer even the years might be forgotten.

To remedy this I resolved to make myself a calendar, which was a thing which only the multitudinous duties which befall a man in my position could have made me forget.

For this purpose I set up one post in the valley of the gazelles for the years, upon which I made four notches; a second, much larger, was put up for the months; and a third for the days.

From that hour this duty was never neglected, and when I started on an expedition a tally was attached to my waist, on which I notched the days, and then transferred them, on my return, to my calendar, which, if it was of no use, was rather a pleasurable occupation than otherwise.

Thus passed the peaceful days on my return from my adventurous voyage to the volcanic island—peaceful days which were not to last long.

It seemed to be my lot that whenever there had been a season of quiet and peaceful labour it should be immediately succeeded by bustling and active hours.

And now to tell how, in a very curious and in fact extraordinary manner, I became at last possessed of that which I so much longed for—a servant to wait upon me and assist me in my labours.

It was so unexpected, and happened in such an extraordinary manner, that it must be reserved for a separate chapter.

CHAPTER XCIV.

A HOLIDAY.

> What security's too strong
> To guard that gentle heart from harm,
> That to its friend is glad to pass
> Itself away, and all it has.
> And, like an anchorite, gives over
> This world for the heav'n of a lover?—*Hudibras.*
>
> Shine but on age, you melt in snow,
> Again fires long extinguished glow,
> And charm'd by witchery of eyes,
> Blood, long concealed, liquefies!
> True miracle, and fairly done,
> By heads which are adored while on.
> *Green's Spleen.*

THERE is such a thing as feeling good.

Now, having provided against almost every possible contingency; having sown that I might reap; having fortified myself that I might be able to fight for my life; having seen to the interests of my flocks and herds, and done all that was in one man's power for my plantation; I had my time upon my hands; and, sooth to say felt very much like a wealthy English country gentleman, ready for amusement for amusement sake, without any reference to its utility or advantage.

I wanted to kill time. Many a man has done a worse thing. Every great statesman, ruler, and conqueror has been of the same opinion.

Some in their hours of recreation have taken to cards, some to tennis, some to jumping as high as possible, like a certain cardinal; some to fiddling, about the least sensible of ways; and some to wickedness to which I will not further allude.

Now it was always my opinion that that which you do purely from a sense of duty, of necessity, of utility, does not sufficiently recreate the mind.

All work is equally or more conductive to insanity than all play.

Let nobody persuade you, my dear boys, that incessant application is good.

On the contrary, it is a great evil.

The human mind is like a cart-wheel, and wants continual greasing, only that instead of grease it wants amusement.

The harder a man works, the more highly wrought are the faculties of his brain; and the more real and positive his labour, the greater should be the zeal with which he should enter upon any enjoyment that is not criminal.

Strain not the delicate fabric of the mind, which, like the panting horse dragging heavy weights up-hill, is all the better for those merciful halts which, in countries purely mountainous are always provided.

Not even the authority of a parent should condemn a child to grind ever at any work.

Perhaps all this may be only to palliate the fact, that it was with a sense of deep enjoyment I one day made up my mind I would have what was called at school, a "spree."

And what think you, boys, was the way in which I determined to enjoy the whole holiday which I had made up my mind to give myself?

I determined to have a day's fishing.

Now, it is of no use my concealing the matter; the preparations for the day did cost me many hours of preliminary labour.

But then—the truth be spoken—it was of an evening.

There was a rod to make, lines to twist, hooks to contrive and then bait, for had I not the audacity to intend flyfishing?

All this may appear very puerile; but let anybody reflect upon my forlorn and deserted condition, obliged to fall back upon myself wholly for support and amusement.

Still, open confession is good for the soul; and I must candidly say that my preparations for my day's angling gave me more delight than any great hunt of the *Grande Monarque* did him.

The rod was a masterpiece.

I selected with my eye a number of the very best bamboos of various sizes, which I cut down, removed to my hut, and seasoned.

Then they were cut in proper lengths, the points hollowed out, and so cut and shaved as admirably to fit.

It was wonderful to see the delight I felt in anything so simple, but I verily believe that I stood in actual awe of my own talents.

It may appear strange, but this day of boyhood, of real and intense happiness, had been hatching in my mind for many a day.

All the sly bits of gut which I put by, trying to persuade myself that they might turn up some day for some essentially useful purpose; and yet, sly old fox that I was, knowing all the time that it was to be one of the elements of my longmeditated day's pleasure.

The line or rather the lines —I had fished too often on the

A SUDDEN ATTACK.

No. 19.—Sailor Crusoe.

broads and rivers of Norfolk to trust to one, were made with the utmost ease of gut and cocoa-nut fibre, while the flies were artificially fashioned by means of feathers culled from my poultry yard.

But the hooks!

Here, I confess, I was at a *nonplus* for some time, until at length, I bethought me of cutting off, by means of a saw-knife heated, a piece from the top of one of my gun barrels.

This was a task which nearly overcame my courage and my resolution.

But at last I was successful, and by dint of mere hammering on a polished anvil of stone, succeeded in making some strong wire, which was then fashioned into hooks of various sizes.

This was a triumph.

Never, since the days when I had caught my first minnow with a crooked pin—and you know the excitement of that, boys—had I been so happy.

In my boyhood's joyous hours, when I knew no care or thought of sorrow, when trouble was a stranger to me, I had been passionately fond of this most entrancing of all amusements.

I knew every stream within twenty miles of home.

I could see them pass distinctly before my eyes as I was busy on my self-allotted task; there was one rapid, clear and sparkling, now gliding through some rocky gorge, where some separate fish moves in solitary majesty, and the current, angry at being confined, rushed with mad impetuosity on towards open meadows, fringed by alders and willows, through which, as the morning sun beamed on the broad and silvery stream, many a glorious trout and grayling might be observed glancing and leaping on its surface.

The other was quiet and sluggish, winding the slow and easy tenour of its way through green and grassy meadows and flat alluvial soil, its sedgy banks the hiding-place of many a colossal pike; while in the deep and quiet holes, were many a gigantic perch.

I thought of those other days when off the end of an old jetty in the queer old town of Yarmouth, I would, with a deep sea line, wait patiently for flat-fish and lobsters.

These were happy days—were they not, boys?

There was one great day in my young life, when, with the under-feathers of the partridge's tail for wings, a little red hackle for legs, hare's ear for a body, and a couple of rats' whiskers for a tail, I made a fly that caught no end of salmon.

But I am becoming garrulous, and in my thoughts of the halcyon hours of the past, forgetting the necessities of the present.

I started over night with my camp equipage fastened on my horse, for the spot which I had selected, and which was a river running to the northward; as I afterwards found, the termination of that which so unceremoniously left my bower lake by the great cavern cataract.

It meandered through the richest and most verdant meadows or prairies, with only a tree here and there. It had rapid falls, swift-running shallows, and every other sign of the favourite abode of fish. My dog Tiger accompanied me. He was still in his prime, and a powerful dog, upon whom too, I knew that I could depend.

The camp was reached about midnight, the fire lit, a hearty supper devoured, and then I lay me down to rest. I slept, but was up before the dawn, eager as a schoolboy for the fray.

It was a warm and sultry day, just as if I had selected it myself; while heavy clouds were scudding across the heavens.

I would not wait for breakfast, but hurried to the river side, put up my rod, which answered as well as one made by the most celebrated makers, and began.

I don't think I shall ever forget my first cast. I had fitted on three different kinds of bait on my line. It was in a pool beneath a fall. Down went my line, with a tug as though I had hooked a ten-pound salmon.

I ran along the banks, having never thought of a reel, for a little while, and then checked the progress of the fish. There was one on each hook.

They were two kind of graylings and a trout, or, at all events, a fish which answered very well for one.

I saw at once that the inhabitants of that river, probabl from never having been fished before, were disposed to be amiable, so I went at it with a will, and before sundown had killed some fifty or sixty pounds weight.

It was a happy day.

The feeling of perfect satisfaction—the scenery—the bracing air—the idea that it was a holiday, had in it something satisfactory of itself.

And then, the fish themselves were no mean addition to the pleasures of the occasion.

I know that many anglers affect to despise the produce of their labour, but that is unwise. I knew that I should have a splendid broil.

And so it proved, when my fire had become embers, and the coals were red-hot, I took four forked sticks and stuck them in the ground; laid others across, of hard wood, not two inches from the fire, and then broiled the fish, which, with salt and a rude kind of pepper—common all over the island—formed a delicious dish.

My dog and myself probably ate more than was good for us; but who thought of right or wrong that day?

Perhaps, when night came, and I sat smoking by my fire, I found out that never since my residence on the island had I been so fatigued, never had my joints felt so stiff, my limbs so full of aches and pains; but that was an additional pleasure, for it made me enjoy a sleep, which was delicious beyond measure.

It was many hours after sunrise when I awoke. I was fresh, invigorated, and full of life. Again, without any feeling of satiety, we enjoyed a broil, and then I sat some time ruminating on the past. I was sadder that morning than I had been, though still my memory of the day before was pleasant—so pleasant, that I would set apart one day each week for my pleasure.

One day each week for my pleasures!

How my heart smote me as the thought flashed through my mind, that I had never once, since I had been on that island, thought of giving one day in so very many weeks to my God.

I was ashamed, humiliated, vexed, and irritated at myself; so much so that I solemnly vowed never again would I omit this pre-eminent duty of a Christian. Not that I had ever omitted to thank the Giver of all good for all His mercies; but then, it was on occasions when I had escaped from some great peril.

I am no advocate for a gloomy Sabbath, which makes more irreligious people than anything else; but it is as well to have one special day on which more especially to fix the mind on religious thought, which in the bustle of active life we have no time for.

Besides, the Sabbath, as an institution, is one for health of body and mind. No civilized nation can do without it; and proportionately as a country keeps it as a day of rest, so is its greatness.

From that hour, unless under very peculiar circumstances, I always kept Sunday. I rose, breakfasted, let loose all my animals, and then read the Bible for about an hour; after which I would sit and ruminate on those early days, when my father would, in his own home, address the flock around him, and expound, with sincerity and energy, religious truths.

About twelve I dined, and after this, gave myself free liberty to visit my poultry yard, ride out to the gazelle valley examine the piggery, or do any little useful or ornamental work that came into my head.

I had no companion with whom to beguile the hours, and no books to while away the time, save those which I knew by heart.

CHAPTER XCV.

THE CHIMPANZEE.

IT was nearly twelve when I set out on my march; no home, but with a view to exploring the regions beyond the river, which I had never crossed. My horse was laden, so that I walked with my gun in the hollow of my arm, my eye always cast about in search of something that might be useful.

The country at once began to change. It was low and swampy, while on all hands I observed that wild rice grew in abundance. This was a discovery no less agreeable than important, as here was an article of food perfectly inexhaustible.

I had promised myself to spare my powder, but I could not resist the temptation of shooting some of the bird which rose. They were all varieties of snipes—common, painted snipes, of beautiful dark and variegated plumage, slow on the wing, and not very good eating; the large, or solitary snipe, as big as a woodcock; and the Jack snipe.

When I had crossed the rice fields I had six brace of snipes, which were plumed, and the fattest and best of them cooked.

The swamp ended, a slope of a kind of low jungle followed, with trees about fifty yards beyond. Having dined, and thrown the remains and bones to my dog, I now took my gun, and went forward to explore.

There is an ineffable pleasure in wandering where, probably no human foot ever trod, unless it were the naked foot of the savage. There is a pure and calm delight in sailing first up the river, the waters of which never before were cut by the prow of the silent canoe, which I always highly appreciated, and never more so than on the present occasion.

The forest was magnificent, and, I suppose from some peculiarity in the soil, devoid of creeping plants, though there were occasional bushes.

This was the more delightful because in all the years that I resided on that remarkable island the greatest drawback to my enjoyment was the constant fear of coming in contact with venomous snakes, of which I had an instinctive dread, though pretty well accustomed to their presence.

On all occasions when making my way through the dense undergrowth of the forest, this was my constant source of apprehension.

But what is this noise?

Some animals are in front of me. I can hear them plainly Clutching my double-barrelled gun, which was now loaded with ball, I peered through the bushes, and saw a sight I never shall forget.

It was a whole family of monkeys—and monkeys, too, of a race I had never seen.

It was the chimpanzee.

As it was always my desire in writing this narrative to give information, as well as to record my adventures, it will be as well for me to dot down a few facts relative to this animal—both from my studies and observations. The chimpanzee is a large black ape, almost confined to the western coast of Africa, and very common on the mouths of the Gaboon. It ranges, however, over a considerable space of country.

It is almost entirely black, with the exception of a few white hairs on the muzzle.

As it grows old it becomes greyer. The beard on the chin and face gives it a peculiar aspect. It, in common with other apes, can lay claim to a nose, though it is very flat; that feature, in its perfect shape, being the exclusive property of man.

The pig has a snout, but no nose.

In its native country the chimpanzee lives in a partly social state, and at night the united yells of the community fill the air with their reiterated yells. They are said to weave huts for themselves, and take up their residence therein. Now, it is a certain fact that the ourang-outang is able to make himself a shelter or platform of interwoven branches—and why not the chimpanzee?

But one is said to live on the structure he makes, the other under it. Travellers assert that the hut is for the females and young, while the male perches on the roof.

The ancients considered that they lived in caverns, and mistaking them for wild men who lived in rocky caves called them *troglodytes*. They live near the ground, and though splendid climbers, rarely avail themselves of the protection which could be afforded them by the higher branches.

Their strength, indeed, is such that they are comparatively unharmed by those members of the cat tribe which are usually so feared by the monkey race—such as lions and leopards. Not that any one would face a leopard, but they fight in schools.

It is solemnly asserted that these monkeys carry off negresses into the woods, and detain them there for years, sometimes even until death releases them from their miserable captivity.

A very extraordinary narrative is told in Borneo of a female ourang-outang who carried off a Dyak and kept him seven months; but we have no space for it here. The natives of Africa look upon the larger sort of monkey with a sort of superstitious dread, elevating them into a kind of semi-man, and telling the most wild and strange stories in regard to them.

They will not live in a climate like that of England. They are so susceptible of cold, especially where there are marine and saline exhalations, that they become afflicted by pulmonary diseases, and invariably die.

But where the climate agrees with them, they are gentle and docile, and, indeed, easily tamed. A most singular circumstance is their fondness for dress. A chimpanzee, who had a new coat and trousers given him of a bright hue, tore up the old ones, that there might be no chance of his wearing them again.

Now the group before me appeared to be composed of a grandfather, a husband and wife, and two large young monkeys, with one baby, which the mother was suckling. It was really a most amusing and not unpleasing sight to one who was such a lover of nature as I was.

The aged monkey, who appeared to have arrived at maturity (a very fine specimen of a chimpanzee, which was domesticated in its native country, lived to twenty-one years of age), sat with his back to a tree, looking on. He was evidently feeble and old, though what his age was nobody could have guessed.

The age to which it attains in its wild state is wholly unknown. But, at all events, this one was not young. The mother and father were full-grown monkeys; the young ones vigorous and supple.

They were rolling on the ground in play; they wrestled, hit out, bit; but did not hurt one another. It was all fun.

At this moment, with a roar almost terrible to myself, in flew Tiger, and I knew at once that a tragedy was to be enacted. The female, thinking more of the baby she had at her breast than anything else, flew to a tree, climbed it with one paw, and sat grinning on a branch.

The old chimpanzee showed his teeth, and snatched at a bough of a tree, but could not break it. The young and powerful monkey seemed prepared to defend himself solely with his powerful arms, and still more powerful hind legs. But the valiant dog, nothing daunted, rushed at him. In an instant the ape had him round the neck with such a powerful grasp as nearly to stifle him, while the young ones clutched him with their claws.

There was no time to lose, as even the aged ape was coming to the charge.

Firing one barrel directly in the breast of the younger monkey, I advanced to the charge. As far as he was concerned, it was unnecessary.

He threw up his arms, looked a look of deep and untold despair, fury, and impotent desire for revenge, *cast his eyes upwards* to where sat his faithful mate, and fell back, bleeding and insensible, on the ground.

The old monkey stood still, as if spell-bound, while the younger ones would have escaped to the trees. But one succeeded, the other being pinned by the arms by my fierce and powerful dog.

This made me think at once of a plan which had often entered my mind. I was well aware that ourang-outangs are taught to carry water and wood, and do many acts of domestic servitude—and why not a chimpanzee?

Throwing a noose round its arms, in such a way as to render it powerless, I made the dog let go; and then surveyed the field of battle.

The old monkey, who was really unable to join in the combat, stood on the defensive, leaning on a branch it had succeeded in breaking.

The male younger monkey lay weltering in its blood; the female sat, with a sad, frightened, and perplexed look, on a bough, while the twin of the prisoner had got about ten feet up a small tree, where it sat, jabbering and grinning at us in unalloyed terror. It was a complete victory, but one of which I was not proud.

But I knew that I had not brought it on myself, so had not much to regret; but it was many a long day ere I forgot the glance which the dying animal gave first to me and then to its once happy mate.

It lingered in my memory for years, and never, but from the most absolute necessity, did one of the tribe receive a shot from me from that memorable day until the present time.

But is was my firm resolve to capture and tame the two young ones, so fastening the one already taken to a large trunk, I pointed to the other, which was in a small tree away from any other, and bade my dog watch. Then I snatched my axe, and with one well-directed blow felled the tree in which the unfortunate animal had taken refuge. Away it ran, for dear life, but Tiger was too much for it. He pinned it to the ground, and there held it, until I came up and secured its arms.

Satisfied with these prizes, I turned backwards. In order to secure the captives from all chance of escape, I had tied the left wrist of one to the right wrist of the other, and then, with a stick to keep them in order, and my dog behind them, led them along. The dog, however, kept them more in awe than anything.

Having decided on a return march home, my horse was loaded with whatever camp equipage I had, including game and a quantity of rice, while I, leading my capture, walked beside the animal; Tiger also assuming a dignified and important air, as if he had been the main instrument in taking these prizes. They strode along with a mournful air, which was partly caused by their wounds, and partly from a sense of defeat. They refused all nourishment, and the idea began to cross my mind that I was taking a great deal of trouble for nothing.

Still it was of no use giving up so soon. At length we reached home, and here a new difficulty presented itself to me. Out came the whole tribe of dogs, and flew at the prisoners; I hastened to drive them off with a switch, but before I could interfere, they had placed themselves out of reach by leaping on the horse's back, and there grinning at the furious and barking troop.

Driving the dogs away, and casting to them a pig which I had killed by the way, the monkeys were led within the fortification, where they were fastened each to a separate tree by a very thick cocoa-nut fibre rope, which went both round their waists and necks. Then I dressed their wounds, which were very painful. This at once made a change, and I thought I could see each of the little brutes look up at me with a grateful and happy look, which was pleasing, indeed, to behold.

It gave me the key to the nature of these animals. They can be tamed only by kindness. Naturally enough, they are afraid of man at first, for in their native wilds he is even a greater enemy to them than the snake and the leopard, for the simple reason that monkey flesh, especially that of the small monkey, is popular.

It is said to be tolerably good eating, though extremely dry and sapless. The fault of this, however, lies in the inferior and primitive style of cooking, which is simply this—a sharp stake is run right through its body, and it is roasted whole thus. Though I believe it can be made palatable by proper culinary preparations, it was never my intention to try, as with me monkey eating seemed almost on a par with cannibalism, and was regarded so by many old travellers. No doubt much relative to the consumption of the human body for food may have arisen from mistakes of this nature.

Having secured the monkeys, I brought them some food, consisting of broken cocoa-nuts, vegetables, ground nuts, and other fruit, which, after some sulking, they ate, but only on this occasion, when I was at a distance. But on that, and many consecutive days, by giving them food at stated periods, by bringing them water myself, and by driving off the dogs with a whip, they began to look upon me as their natural protector.

From that moment they were mine, and I knew it. They allowed me to play with them; would never eat unless I gave them food with my own hand; and gradually began to obey me as strictly and immediately as any that ever were seen in the streets of a great city. By degrees, as they grew bigger, I used them to carry light burdens, until, as their strength increased, they willingly carried loads.

As they cannot stand quite erect, and require the constant use of their hands in walking, I devised a plan, which was plainly successful. I made for them a thing like that which the Welsh milkwomen put across their shoulders to carry milk with. These were made in such a way as not to hurt them, and in this manner they carried such considerable burdens as astonished me.

CHAPTER XCVI.

A HUNGRY THIEF.

MY attention to my monkeys, whom I called Castor and Pollux, did not prevent me from attending to my other duties. My plantations wanted continual watching, which I did with my whole kennel of dogs; who liked nothing better than to scamper after the birds, rabbits, and other animals which feloniously endeavoured to appropriate to themselves my goods and chattels.

Numerous crows and other birds were snared by my net, and duly hung in chains as an example to all and every evil-doer. This, carried out with spirit, was marvellously useful, and kept them away to a very large extent. Still, to my great chagrin, they devoured much more than would have lasted me for a considerable period. For this there was no help but resignation—and as there were at my disposal so many of the good things of this earth, it would have been ingratitude to have fretted.

Of course it will easily be imagined that all this time my thoughts were bent upon her who had vanished so strangely from my society, and on that village where I was sure were so mysteriously congregated all that I loved best in the world. But with all my courage, I had not the resolution to consume months in the construction of another canoe, when I recollected what had occurred on the last occasion.

Another idea, however, crossed my mind—that I would, if they should not be the first to visit my island, make a bold venture and build a raft, gain the mainland anywhere I could with my horse, and ride direct to the village. But there were very many reasons against the adoption of this plan. In the first place, it was a most fearfully laborious task to make a raft of sufficient size to bear myself, and my horse and baggage, across the bubbling sea channel six miles wide.

Then again, nothing could be more unlikely than that the dwellers in that village remained any length of time on that bleak and arid coast. If they were not able to gain my island, they would go into the interior and settle in some obscure and fertile valley, until such time as they could devise some means of escape from their horrid fate.

This time the risk appeared to me so great, that, though there was always a deep longing to be working, I had not made up my mind to begin. Even a considerable discovery which I made at this time, did not move me so much as it might have done at any other period.

This was my falling on that curious marvel of nature—which is after all marvels—the cork tree.

The cork tree is simply an oak (*Quercus suber*). In order to take off the bark, an incision is made from the top to the bottom of the tree, and, at each extremity, another round the tree, perpendicular to the first. When the tree is fifteen years old it may be barked for eight years successively; and the quality of the bark improves with the age of the tree. When stripped from the tree, which does not therefore die, the bark is piled up in a pond or ditch and loaded with heavy stones, to flatten it and reduce it into a tabular form. It is then removed to be dried, and, when sufficiently dry, put in bales for carriage. If care be not taken to strip the bark, it splits and peels off of itself, being pushed up by another bark formed underneath.

The cork tree, and the uses to which the bark may be applied, were known both to the Greeks and the Romans. Pliny informs us that the Romans employed it to stop all kinds of vessels; but the use of it for this purpose does not appear to have been common till the invention of glass bottles, of which there is no mention before the fifteenth century.*

Other vegetable productions have been sometimes employed instead of cork. The *Spondias lutea*—a tree which grows in South America, particularly in moist places, and which is there called *monbin* or *monbain*—was sometimes brought to England for the purpose of stopping vessels. The roots of liquorice are applied to the same use; and on this account the plant is much cultivated in Sclavonia, and exported to other countries.

A tree called *nyssa*, which grows in North America, has been found also to answer as a substitute for cork. The bark of cork is of some use in medicine as an astringent. It also makes Spanish black; and some people fancy cork cups. The Egyptians made coffins of cork, which, with a resinous composition preserved dead bodies uncorrupted. In Spain, they line stone walls with cork. Such are some of its uses.

But a truce to digression, of which, like most old men, I am perhaps too fond.

It was during one of those occasional days of rest, which were kept holy by me as the Sabbath-day, that, exploring my island as I now did in every direction, and always finding something new, either in the way of flowers or of plants, I gazed curiously at a grove of trees which were quite new to me, but which struck me at the same time as very curious. Approaching nearer, and being unable, from my previous knowledge, to make out what they were, I cut them with a knife, and the truth was at once apparent.

It often struck me what vast riches were concealed in that strange and outlandish district, and what mighty fortunes might have been made by many who were now poor simply from want of employment. There is very little doubt that the day will come when some will avail themselves of this mine of wealth, though it is difficult to make merchants go out of the beaten track.

While millions are starving, there are regions so fertile on the south coast of Africa as scarcely to want tilling. But the very poor can never hope to be delivered there, as one poor season carries off all their savings for any such purpose, and leaves them utterly destitute.

But these reflections, which often, with other such sage ideas, presented themselves to my mind, were merely amusing, and had no practical utility for me. The weight that was on my mind was, how could I communicate with the inhabitants of the white village? and then, why had

---

* This is a mistake of the ingenious narrator. Glass bottles were known to the Egyptians, to the natives of Pompeii, and to the Chinese.

Pablina not contrived once more, at all events, to visit me, and give me some faint idea of the real state of things?

Whenever these emotions of despondency came over me, there was no remedy but to lead an active life, or do something to pass away my time.

Though I refrained as much as possible from using my gun, living on fish, milk, vegetables, and an occasional gazelle, with ostrich and other eggs, I never went out without firearms, as my mind was never at rest as to the natives of the coast, who had already cost me so much care and trouble.

About three months or more after the enlargement of my fold, and when the gazelles had been driven back to their original valley, I went one morning, with my attendant monkeys, to milk my now numerous flock, as well as to take away a fat buck for the use of the family.

I always took care to slaughter those I was in want of at a great distance from their habitation, not wishing to alarm animals which I knew to be extremely sensitive.

Imagine my horror and disgust when I found the whole herd, less two, driven away to a corner of the pen, huddled up in a confused mass, from the effect of some recent terror; while on the ground in front of the enclosure were the mangled remains, and very little remains there were, of two unfortunate and very fine animals being pecked at by some vultures.

My indignation knew no bounds. I could almost have wreaked my vengeance on the vultures, but contented myself with driving them away with switches, and examining the state of things.

I examined the ground. I looked at the trail of the savage beasts which had done all this damage, and could not make them out. The vultures had torn up the ground around where the victims lay, and the rapidity with which the devastators had fled prevented their leaving sufficient marks to indicate their character.

But that which they had once done they would do again; of that there could not be the least doubt, so I revolved deeply in my own mind what was to be done. At length, after some reflection, I determined on a plan which should not only expose the true character of the robbers, but operate to their destruction and warning.

Milking my does, and, in disgust at what had occurred, neglecting to take a buck with me, I fastened Tiger and another dog in front of the pen, and went my way. The day passed wearily, so impatient was I for the night to come. Twice I visited the gazelle valley, once to see how matters were going, and once to remove the dogs, which would materially interfere with my arrangements.

At length sundown approached, and I made my preparations. Near the pen, into which all the hungry little animals were driven, was a grove of very fine trees, to one of which a choice gazelle of the brood was attached by a cord. Some grain and leaves were placed before it, and then, well provided with ammunition and my double barrel loaded, I climbed into the branches.

The night was dark and gloomy, but I could see round the valley for some little distance, especially as my eyes gradually get used to the gloom.

But for some time nothing came, not even any sound, save that of the soughing of the wind. Suddenly I heard the gazelle uttering little plaintive cries, intermingled with a sort of sneeze, which was, as it were, a kind of snarl of petulance intermingled with timidity.

Then came, in the distance, the sullen roar of a lion. My

horror may be conceived. I had not lost my respect for this mighty beast, and I do not believe, when in actual contact with him, you ever do.

With a wildly palpitating heart, I listened to the varied and lugubrious sounds of the ground below the valley. Then could be heard the heavy stamp of some animal, which I imagined was the buffalo, but which proved to be the gnu, and then the gallop of either quaggas or zebras bounding wildly on high, in order the better to snuff the air, and to make out from the scent which way the terrible enemy was coming, whose fearful voice they had heard.

Then came the screaming of the jackal, which rose shrill above the tumult, and seemed like a horrid laugh preluding the horrors of a general carnage.

Then there came a dead, almost a magical silence, and nothing could be heard but the plaintive cry of the gazelle at my feet, and the rustling of the tall grass and reeds on the plain. These moments of silence were not devoid of alarm, for the huge beast might be advancing upon us with stealthy steps, to attack when least expected.

I had just determined to ascend higher in the tree out of reach of any lion, when a longer pause than usual ensued, and I waited. Then I could hear, in the far off distance, the rush of many feet, as of gnus, gazelles, and zebras, and one majestic roar of the lion in pursuit.

My mind infinitely relieved, I was half inclined to descend from my elevation and return home; but reflecting that at all events in my tree I was safe, and might even on this occasion discover the real depredators, I resolved to wait. Firmly fixing myself between two large boughs, my gun was so placed that I could shoot when the thief, of whatever nature, came within a yard of the gazelle. In this position I lay peering out upon the plain.

Presently it seemed all alive; there were lions, and tigers, and zebras, and elephants, and hippopotami, and every known animal of the world, rushing about in a wild and furious stampede, which to my eyes was infinitely more ludicrous than horrible.

At length they all halted, and I saw myriads of eyes of every colour under the sun—green, grey, blue, black, bleared, and lurid, every tint between these that can be imagined—glaring at me.

I was as fast asleep as—to use the familiar expression—a church.

And in this uncomfortable position I, no doubt, slept for many hours, as I afterwards judged by the quick way in which the dawn appeared, after I awoke, on the horizon.

Suddenly a faint noise, I suppose, awoke me, and then I heard not only the gazelle whining and sneezing, but another sound coming across the plain.

It was a drove of hungry wolves.

My heart beat wildly. I knew well the extreme ferocity and tenacity of these fierce denizens of the forest, which, since my arrival on the island, I had never fallen on before. This mysterious appearance and reappearance of animals will be, however, strangely explained.

On came a drove of twenty, but in a scattered line, some twenty yards from the tree, some, fifty, the majority, a hundred. I hastily settled myself. The gazelle under the tree gave forth most heart-rending sounds, and then the wolf, with a hoarse roar, bounded to within three feet of its neck. I fired.

Back went the wolf tottering. One or two convulsive movements, and all was over. I loaded quickly the barrel I had fired, as I remarked that the nearest wolves had halted to reconnoitre. There they now were in a kind of circle, hideous in the breaking night, with their red tongues lolling out, and their eyes of fire gleaming in astonishment at the tree.

Then half-a-dozen made a plunge towards the gazelle. I fired both barrels, lamed one and quite killed another. Again they retreated; I reloaded, and again, after ten minutes, they charged the gazelle with, as it were, redoubled fury from being restrained so long.

Two this time bit the dust, and, as if satisfied with the fearful slaughter, the rest turned tail and fled, none the less quickly than I gave a hearty view hallo.

I prepared to descend the tree, when I felt a hand placed upon my shoulder.

CHAPTER XCVII.

ILLNESS.

Alp turn'd him from the sickening sight,
Never had shaken his nerves in fight;
But he better could brook to behold the dying,
Deep in the tide of their warm blood lying,
Scorch'd with the death-thirst and writhing in vain,
Than the perishing dead who are past all pain.
There is something of pride in the perilous hour,
Whate'er be the shape in which death may lower,
For Fame is there to say who bleeds,
And Honour's eye on daring deeds!
But when all is past, it is humbling to tread
O'er the weltering field of the tombless dead.
And see worms of the earth, and fowls of the air,
Beasts of the forest, all gathering there;
All regarding man as their prey,
All rejoicing in his decay.—*The Siege of Corinth.*

IT may readily be imagined that my very flesh crept, as dropping my gun, by a convulsive effort, I turned, and then immediately, and to my fancy, very fortunately, dropped myself to the ground.

It was a small, black, and rather savage African bear—a class of animal, the very existence of which was new to me I was not much hurt, as my fall was from no very great height; and then it was, moreover, broken by the body of the wolf, which lay stone dead at the foot of the tree. Hastily picking myself up, and looking into the tree, I perceived that the bear was rather irresolute, and having no doubt of his predatory habits, I determined on a grand execution all at once.

Having cut the string for the gazelle to escape, my gun was hastily loaded, each barrel with two bullets, so that even at the risk of bursting my gun, the chances might be in my favour.

The black bear is an animal not to be trifled with in his savage mood, but very gentle and playful when tamed.

He looked rather curiously down at me, and then at the dead wolves. It was quite apparent to me that, during the whole early part of the evening, this ugly customer, very likely after a hearty gorge, had concealed himself amid the leafy boughs of this or some other tree, where he lay heavily asleep, and had only, perhaps, come down in a friendly way to see what was the matter, when he heard the strange report of guns, to him something as novel and startling as his presence was to me.

After some delay, as if uncertain whether to affront this strange being, which stood calmly, as it appeared to him, surveying the scene, he began to descend, hind-quarters first, In a moment of haste, I levelled, and was about to fire, when it came to my recollection that a bear must be either shot in

the head or the heart. I waited, then, until he turned and made slowly towards me, with that shambling gait which is the peculiarity of all his tribe.

With as calm a nerve as I could collect, I took aim and fired. An awful growl; and the bear, wounded and savage, rose on his hind legs. His eyes were frightfully wild, and, fearful to lose the chance, I fired at his heart. The animal stood still, as if struck to stone, and then rolled over, a warm but lifeless mass of clay. I sank, myself, almost equally inert and helpless, at the foot of a palm-tree, to regain my lost breath.

After a few minutes, every drop of water being exhausted from my gourd, I crawled to the rill which supplied the gazelles, and along which my palms were rising beautifully—making a great increase in the volume of water*—and refreshed myself, both with a drink and a wash. This done, I returned to the scene of my terrible combat; and having, on the previous night, prepared myself for the emergency, hoisted by ropes the whole party of bandits, with their feet just away from the ground—a sight which I hoped would act as an example and a warning to other thieves.

This done, I returned to my cave, where my dependants were glad to see me, and here I remained all day, having been exceedingly fatigued with my night of combat and watching. Calculating back on that day, it came into my head to notice that I was about five years older than when I was cast away, which was a serious reflection, and drove me to think that in all probability I should end my days there. This was, when seriously thought of, a most melancholy and terrible reflection. Cut off for ever from all communion with my species, never to know the sweet companionship of a wife, never to call any warbling prattlers my children, were sad drawbacks, indeed, to the pleasures of this life, and enough, however much one might try to be grateful, to make one discontented with one's lot. It is not good for man to live alone, whatever hermits, generally worn-out men of the world, may say—and I felt that it was not, every day of my life.

This made me melancholy, so that I would gladly have risen and hunted or fished, but I was exhausted and feverish. I was, I foresaw it, going to be ill. Anxiety, the excitement of the contest, and the exposure to the night air, perhaps on this occasion more noxious than others, were about to prostrate me.

No wonder that I had instinctively hoped for companionship, for the gentle hand of a nurse. While, however, I had strength, I collected my gourds together, filled them with water, and placed them behind my bunk, which was safer than my hammock. Then every egg which could be found in my poultry-yard, with some light cakes, were put on a shelf. Then, cold shiverings coming over me, I lay down in a wild, feverish sort of ague, and in a few minutes either lost my senses or fell asleep.

When I first opened my eyes again, I thought I should have died, so weak, prostrated, and utterly without energy, I was. I with difficulty put out my hand—it was thin and white—to reach a drop of water. All the bowls were empty. Had I drank them, or had my animals helped themselves? This was scarcely likely, as they had plenty without. But water I must have.

But what is that shadow which darkens the entrance to

---

* This is a very curious and well-known fact; where forests are destroyed, rivers become rills. The ancients speak of large navigable streams in Greece, which are now mere rivulets. In former days the mountains were one mass of verdure, and attracted the water. The devastating and brutal Turks destroyed the trees, and left the country desolate and dry. Such is despotism.

my room, upon which a faint ray falls from the entrance of the cave?

I turned my eyes round. Heavens! what hideous monster is this? and I all unprotected and alone! It approached my bedside and peered at me with its fearful eyes. Then I knew it—it was Castor, and beside him was Pollux.

I held out my hand. The faithful creature, which was used to this familiarity on my part, took it, and uttered a grunt of satisfaction. Then catching up the empty bowl, and putting it to my mouth, I made signs to drink, and then turned the bowl up, and shook my head. As I fully expected, the intelligent animal understood me at once; the chimpanzee, and especially the ourang-outang, being very excellent servants in their way—fetching water and drawing loads.

Away he ran, followed by the other, which was so exactly a counterpart that I always shall believe they were twins; and soon returned with a bowl of fresh water; after draining which off, and eating an egg, I fell asleep once more. When I awoke all fever was gone, and I was able to crawl out of my bunk and search for some fresh eggs; those which I had by my bedside being quite stale and bad.

Several raw eggs, with a little dried fish, seemed to do me good, and I sat down under the shade of a palm tree, to revive myself by the action of the air, which is, after all, nature's best and sweetest restorer for the invalid.

All this time I had serious thoughts that something was missing, which I discovered in a few minutes to be my dogs, which, being tired and wanting quiet on my return from the gazelle valley, I had shut out.

Had they all left me, and gone away? Perhaps so. To all appearance, it was I who had deserted them. I could, however, not venture to see after them yet.

Towards evening I made an omelette with some salted gazelle dripping and a lot of eggs, which I ate with great pleasure.

Soon after this I went to bed, and woke in the morning quite well, only very weak.

But once the malady is over, a good dose of open air exercise is the best medicine, so I determined to have a ride. For this purpose, I opened my barred gate and went forth. The zebra and horse were nowhere to be seen. This was a disappointment, but it had to be borne philosophically, on the principle that what cannot be cured must be endured, so, leaning on a stick, I walked slowly about in shady places, until, quite suddenly, I came on my zebra and horse, grazing. They were close together in the most friendly way in the world.

I had a halter and a bowl of corn, but it seemed to me almost impossible for one so weak to capture anything so swift and skittish. Still, as nothing is to be done without trying, I advanced slowly towards them.

They did not move, but continued grazing without the slightest fear. They certainly walked away a little, but when they saw the well-known bowl of corn, they came slowly up to where I stood.

I gave them both some grains of their favourite food, after which I secured the horse and led it towards a stone, by means of which only could I mount.

The zebra followed quietly, though what had become of my favourite young one, was a puzzle, which in my own mind I wished particularly to unravel.

Having mounted the horse, I rode quietly towards my cave, where having arrived, I saddled the patient steed, and then once more rode forth in search of that which was now

so much needed—health and strength. That day I did not go far, but contented myself with a visit to my gazelle valley where, finding everything in order, I drove the gazelles into the inner valley.

I had not been long on my way towards the piggery, when there was a rush in the woods, and my dogs came bounding towards me with open mouths. Had I been on foot, in my weak state, they would very easily have overcome my strength, and as it was, I had playfully to drive them off.

On my return to the cave, where I was now accompanied by my live stock, I found that the open air and exercise had given me an appetite, which, however, I took care to satisfy only with eggs and light food generally, as the weakness of my stomach would have made me revolt against any more generous food.

By taking great care of myself, and being much in the open air, in one week I was quite well, and able, not only to enjoy my food, but to do anything that was necessary—and though a history of my daily experiences would be wearisome in the extreme, yet was there much to be done in the way of planting, reaping, snaring birds, fishing, and the like. Let no one fancy that my life was all play. It was as the life of any man who has to supply himself with food, clothing, and a habitation, full of labour and arduous occupation of every kind.

CHAPTER XCVIII.

I VISIT MY BOWER.

I WAS my own physician, it is true, but I was sufficiently reasonable to attend to my health, and to hold consultations with myself as to the wisest course of proceeding. Now that all traces of my disorder, whatever it was, was gone, there could be no doubt that there remained an uneasy feeling which could only be got rid of by time, and as it was all-important to me to have no relapse, I determined once more to take a holiday—this time for a fortnight, during which I would do nothing but fish, hunt, and stroll about.

Change of air, even from good to inferior air, is often conducive to health, so, despite my natural dread of cannibals, and, indeed, of any savages whatever, I determined to visit the bower in my lake home, which I had neglected so long. For this purpose, I loaded both horse and zebra with provisions, tools, and the materials for fishing and the chase.

What to do with the monkeys was a difficulty, but as, during my absence, they might grow somewhat wild, I thought it best to take them with me, particularly as on the little island of the lake they would prove companions. My dogs would not be left at home, so I had to let them follow me, which was somewhat annoying, as not to let them grow too wild, I had to kill game for them myself.

The journey to the lake took two days, as we advanced extremely slow. My cattle were much loaded. On reaching the shores of the lake, the stable of the zebras was found in excellent repair, only requiring the cutting down of exuberant shoots. This was pleasant, as to save myself trouble, I intended to stable them every night, letting them out again quite at early dawn of day. The first night I was glad to sleep in the enclosure myself, as I was very much fatigued, and not up to the mark enough to make a raft.

Whenever I thought of this, the idea would recur to my mind, that here had come the second heavenly vision of that girl, who, despite all my efforts, would not leave my mind.

CAPTURED BY CANNIBALS.

No. 20.—SAILOR CRUSOE.

When the illness, through which I was tended by her, was compared with that which had recently attacked me, and from which I had only escaped by a merciful interposition of Providence, the old saying, that it is not good for man to be alone, recurred to my mind with great force.

And surely it is not good. To think always, to brood, to have no one upon whom to lavish the rich stores of your affection, to know no companions save the beasts of the field, and the fowls of the air, is, beyond all power of description, wearisome and monotonous. What foolish men have done from choice is no mitigation of the evil.

As I awoke in the morning, the reflection crossed my mind, that as I was to be some time in my bower, and should be constantly crossing backwards and forwards, some means of conveyance more handy than a raft should be found; but, for the life of me, for some time I could not think of any remedy.

At last my eyes fell upon a tree; and the idea of a bark canoe suggested itself; not a canoe such as had cost me so much labour, and then been so disastrously destroyed in a moment, but a bark canoe, easily made and easily managed. I felt myself sometimes thinking of giving up my time and attention to another sea-going vessel; but always succeeded n withdrawing my mind from a subject full of so many deceptions.

I don't exactly know why, but, probably, because I always liked to be climbing and examining trees, I had brought my ladder, which was clumsy but not heavy, with me. This was fortunate, for it facilitated the process immensely.

Having placed it against the tree which I had chosen, I ascended and proceeded to cut a line half round the trunk, so as to lay bare the bark, which was solid and without a crack. Having loosened it all the way round, I proceeded to bore holes, in which I inserted several pieces of strong cord, to which I afterwards fastened my lasso, previously thrown across a bough and attached below.

My next plan was to cut the bark below; after which it was slowly loosened at the side, until, after much exhibition of ingenuity, it was loose everywhere, and, with much nicety, lowered to the ground. Then at each end the bark was slit for about eighteen inches, and the two pieces overlapped, and sowed with thongs, so as to form a pointed stem and stern. The whole was then gummed over, some sticks placed here and there across it, to keep it in shape; and my canoe was ready.

This, with the snaring of some birds, and other minor duties, took me two days. On the morning of the third, the canoe was launched; and, paddle in hand, I urged it swiftly to my bower, where once more, after so long an absence, I found myself. Everything was in order, save an exuberant growth of boughs and creepers, which were duly cut down and consigned to the flames inside my bower, in order that the heat and smoke might drive away all vermin of every kind.

Of course my birds—though unable to fly away, from want of the wing feathers I had pulled out—were pretty well as wild as when I caught them. But when once animals have become used to the society of men, they are easily tamed a second time, and the judicious distribution of some grain and other favourite edibles, soon brought them round.

It took me almost a day to put my cabin to rights, to clear the spring, and to make the approaches to the bower easy. But when the task was done, it proved very agreeable and pleasant. My holiday had as yet been rather fatiguing, but now, my duties over, I proceeded to lay out my plans.

One day should be spent exploring my island, wandering lazily about its pretty little woods and pleasant shores, and selecting a proper spot for a kitchen garden, such as I had long contemplated. The soil of the island was rich in the extreme, as I could see by the beautiful prairie, with its luxuriant growth of grass. The second day I would fish at the head of the lake, or up the stream which supplied my lake with water. The third, as then I should probably be still stronger, I would have a regular sportsman's day with my guns and my dogs.

This was a pleasant programme, and I at once proceeded to carry it into operation. Shouldering my gun, and taking with me Tiger, the only dog I had allowed to come over to the island, I began my tour of the island next morning. This was no easy matter, as the trees grew in some places quite into the water, and almost everywhere close down to the banks.

Still, by using my hatchet, the journey was feasible; and though many halts were rendered necessary, yet, at length, I found that in every place it was possible to get round. During this journey I found that my island was rich in fruits, for not only did I come across the guava, but also the pine-apple.

The guava is a kind of brushwood, which, however, where the soil is very fertile, is, as it were, a noxious wood, so rapidly does it grow. It is a very delicious fruit, and may be eaten freely.

The pine-apple, though not nearly so nice as the ones which we grow in our conservatories in England, were very pleasant. But perhaps the most striking sight was the bread-fruit, conspicuous from its large, glossy, and deeply digitated leaf. It is admirable to behold groves of a tree, sending forth its branches with the vigour of an English oak, loaded with large and most nutritious fruit. However seldom the usefulness of an object can account for the pleasure of beholding it, in the case of these beautiful woods, the knowledge of their high productiveness no doubt enters largely into the feeling of admiration.

These were pleasant discoveries—not so much from the mere fact of being able to enjoy the luxury of an agreeable dessert, but from the circumstance of my being exceedingly fond of the study of natural history in all its branches.

There was another feature about this, which was agreeable. When I chose to confine myself to my island, I could always be sure of some provisions. On the whole, my tour of the little island was satisfactory, and gave me a large insight into the wealth and luxuries of my singular residence. When I returned, and had supped copiously, I was glad to go to bed in my hammock, and slept the whole night.

CHAPTER XCIX.

A TRAGIC DISCOVERY.

NEXT morning saw me, at an early hour, launched upon the smooth waters of the lake. I had with me my gun, my rod, my rude landing-net, provisions, and some weak rum and water. In addition to this, I had fashioned an umbrella, which was, in such a climate, not a guard against the rain—which poured too heavily for any such weak protection to be available—but from the sun.

My canoe proved invaluable, as though at this end of the lake the current was not very strong, no raft would have been able to stand it. By judicious management, however, my canoe was taken right up into the mouth of the little stream, which at once manifested itself to be navigable for such a light craft. It was a deep and sluggish bayou* with sedgy banks, though I daresay, during the rainy season, it ran swiftly enough.

My line was very strong, and my rod a sturdy one, so that I was prepared for any strong fish likely to abound in that spot, which in England would certainly have been the resort of pike or jack. Still, with all the difference of climate, only a similar fish could be expected to be found.

My bait ready—I had caught some small fish in the lake with a hand-net—I was not long at work before my canoe was covered at the bottom with fish. Wearying of such easy sport, I went slowly up the stream, wafted upwards by a gentle breeze, which turned my umbrella into a sail.

Then my heart sank within me, my bosom beat with wild emotions, and my whole nervous system was upset by a most unearthly cry—a cry that seemed to curdle the blood in my veins and paralyze my every energy. It was a cry I knew not. What was to be done? It had arisen at no great distance in the direction of my stable.

My first idea was that a lion had attacked my cattle; but then, neither my horse nor zebra could have uttered such a long melancholy wail as that. Dreadfully and unnaturally uncomfortable, I pushed my canoe in shore, and landed, after fastening it to a tree. Then, clutching my gun, I crept under the trees, just as once more up rose the fearful and horrid wail—this time followed by a series of fearful shrieks in another voice, and that voice the voice of a woman.

What horrid thoughts filled my soul it would not be easy for me to say. I at once came to the conclusion that it was my Indian girl. Imagine my feelings, and at the same time, the feeling of intense wonder as to the nature of the danger in which she was placed. I rushed on almost heedless of the consequences, in such a frenzied state of mind was I.

Then all was still, not even the scream of a bird or the shrill cry of a monkey broke the dark solitude, and, indeed, anything, just then would have been welcome. I had nothing to guide me. Nothing could be heard but my own panting breath, when suddenly a whirr and a rush took place, and I saw my horse, zebra, and dog scamper past without taking any notice of me.

I halted. Just before me, sitting on a tree, were a pair of beautiful green pigeons, and in a few minutes nothing more could be heard saving the cooing of the birds, and then——

Heaven have mercy on my soul! for there is the fearful scream again, and close to me. I clenched my teeth, and stooping low, came upon the explanation of what I heard, which was even more fearful than I expected. At the foot of the very tree on which high up in the branches sat the pigeons, was a young girl, very good looking and gentle by nature. She was dead. She had been tied to the tree, and tortured to death. It is a hideous punishment performed by beings in the shape of man on females suspected of being witches, or of having caused the evil eye to fall upon any one.

They had fastened her to the trunk and lacerated her flesh all over the body, and in these cuts they rubbed red pepper in order to render the torture more horrible.

I knew, from books of travels, their common mode of tormenting their victims. The natives of Africa are nowhere behind the Red Indians of North America in their devilish ingenuity.

But who had done all this? and where were the fiendish monsters?

* In answer to inquiries, the Editor begs to state that a bayou is a small stream, generally without visible current. In Texas the Editor was often doubtful, upon cursory examination only, which way the waters ran; but this was in the wet season, and with very high tides.

I peered round, fearing every moment that they would attack me; and as I could do no good to the unfortunate and wretched girl, I resolved to escape as quickly as possible to my island, and there devise as to my future plans. To creep back to the river, to enter my boat, and to glide noiselessly down the river, was the work of a very few minutes.

Terror lent me wings, nor did I scarcely stop to think, until I was safely landed on the small island. That my home was invaded, that a large party of savage and ruthless natives had either made it a battle or a hunting ground, could not but be certain. The desolate thoughts which came over me scarcely find vent in words.

They would kill and slay all my domestic animals without a doubt; they would devastate my plantations, and throw me back into as wretched a position as I was in during the first fortnight of the shipwreck. But what chiefly occupied me, and indeed, made my heart beat with terrible violence, was the fear that they should discover my fort and cavern, in which case my ruin was consummated.

Still there was nothing for it but to lie close and watch—at all events, until night, when I might contrive to elude the vigilence of the wretches, and return with Tiger to my fort, where I determined to make one last stand for life and liberty. Indeed death was far preferable to falling into their hands.

The sight of the poor wretch of their own race, tortured and murdered for some supposed crime of witchcraft, was enough to fill my soul with such horror and dread as made any ordinary death quite a welcome thing in preference.

I ate whatever I could lay my hands on, muzzled my dog, loaded my double-barrel with ball, and watched. My island was only accessible from two quarters—one was the river which supplied the lake with water; the other, the landing-place whence I always started on my journeys.

This, as trodden upon, and leaving very clear marks of where I was myself in the habit of landing, was the most probable, and this I watched with intense interest. And then the hours slipped away; no sounds awakening the echo of the night, save when in the distance I seemed to hear the yelping and barking of my dogs, which, with my zebra and horse, had been terrified doubtless both by the presence of the savages and the fearful torture of the girl.

CHAPTER C.

A FIGHT.

THERE was a sudden hush of all nature as the sun went down, and was at once replaced by the silvery moon, which had long since risen. It fell on the slightly rippled waters, and then all the sounds which herald night in the tropics—the chattering of monkeys, the hum of insects, and the cries of different animals—might be distinguished.

Every now and then a dark cloud would speed over the moon and leave all nature in a deeper gloom. It was during one of these moments that I caught a sudden glimpse of a small fire under the leafy arches of the forest close to my stable. Then it blazed up on high, and I could see dusky figures piling on wood, and next minute, up went a clear blaze from the quantities of dead boughs which, lying about in all directions, are so easily collected.

Before five minutes had elapsed, I became aware that these reckless savages, with a spirit perfectly demoniacal were about to destroy my stable. It was pure, wicked, unadulterated mischief; and as I saw them—clear, distinct and naked—in the light of the fire, I could scarcely refrain from slaying two of them at once. But my powder was valuable, and besides, it would have been madness to have disclosed my retreat.

As soon as the fire was fairly made, and the green walls of my stable began to burn, the savages stepped back to view their handiwork. I have already described them. They were the same horrible Fan Indians who have been seen at work before in an early part of my narrative. They were huge and powerful men. There was one who struck me more than any, from the ferocity of his appearance and the "bravery" of his ornamentation.

His body was painted red, he had a very large shield of elephant's hide, and held in his hand a bundle of three or four spears, with a bag of what were probably poisoned arrows. He was giving orders. At last I saw him distinctly point to my little island. Half a dozen warriors immediately were detached from the group, who advanced to the landing. They had torches in their hands, and examined the ground carefully.

Then, with a great shout, they pointed to my footsteps, and to the mark left by the boat on the soft soil on the bank of the river.

They had found my trail.

Then I knew that their was little hope for me. I could fight as long as my powder lasted, but that would only be for a little time; while at every shot the fear of fire-arms would become less in the minds of these warriers, who were evidently used to fighting, and no doubt very brave and expert.

They now dispersed, and each man appeared to be making a raft for himself of the reeds; and in ten minutes more, six grim and terrible loooking fellows were embarked on the water, armed with javelin, cross-bow, and shield.

I had my double-barrelled gun, my flask of powder, twenty or thirty bullets, my pistols, a knife, and a heavy sharp axe. This I laid near to my hand, in order to be ready for that terrible emergency, a hand-to-hand conflict. Again all was still, and the whole appeared to me like a scene in a play or a panorama.

The fire made everything else dark, but wherever its radiance extended, one might have counted every leaf. It hissed and spurted, and crackled, and shot up on high with a force which sent the sparks and blaze thirty feet into the air; a lot of fresh fuel constantly piled on sending up a colume of black smoke to the very skies.

The warriors stood around in groups, and waited.

The rafts were altogether, and came on slowly, being paddled by small pieces of broken branches.

They were about two pistol shots off when I took aim.

They were in a crowd whispering. Evidently they were certain that I was on the island, and expected to catch me asleep. I took deliberate aim, my very heart in my mouth. I saw nothing but a dark and frightful mass, the furnace on the shore making the lake pitchy black.

I fired, and as the echoes of my gun woke up the forest, I gave them a second barrel. It was like magic. When the smoke passed from before my eyes, the rafts were empty, and floating slowly towards the current, where they would soon be sucked in by the waterfall. There were four heads in the water. The others had sunk.

The four who had escaped were swimming hard for the shore, though one I could see was lagging behind, being no doubt wounded.

But without troubling myself, I proceeded to load, putting two balls in this time without any extra load of powder.

Then I waited.

Three of the fugitives were soon upon the shore, where a great cry was heard, probably at the news that two had been killed. Then they ran to and fro, while one or two rushed into the water to assist the last man. But it was too late, his strength was gone; and in a few minutes more, three dark bodies, those of the killed, moved slowly past me, drawn on by the remorseless current.

For some time I was left in peace, the whole of the party retreating into the woods. I was at first inclined to think that they had had enough of the combat, but soon was undeceived. In about half-an-hour the whole gang reappeared, headed by their chief.

He alone did not carry a burthen, though all the others I soon perceived carried a number of trees and branches, with which to make a commodious raft. For so many, inflamed by the passions of hate and revenge, nothing was easier than to construct a machine that would float a dozen. In half an hour a large and secure, but unwieldly, construction was in the water.

Then at the end next to my island, they placed a rampart of bushes, grass, and turf, rudely torn from the ground. Then the warriors, some ten or a dozen in number, laid down on the raft, those who had the management of two huge oars kneeling.

Then I determined to shoot at them as soon as they were near enough to be aimed at, as, could the raft be moved out into the current, my task would be easier. To shoot through the rampart was wholly out of the question, it being thick and high. But I had more than one plan of escape.

And I determined to put one in practice, to escape from these cannibals.[*] It was the most feasible that occurred to me. My canoe lay at the landing. The paddle was in it and the water gourd. Now nothing could have been easier than for me to have fled, if the lake had ended in a river like that by which the water entered in. As it was, I had to slip round the northern extremity of my island, cross the current which sailed towards the cave cataract, and then glide away by the opposite shore.

Once or twice I thought of making for the cataract, standing up in my canoe and clutching at the overhanging bushes as the bark boat fell into the yawning abyss. But this was a great risk, which I was not at all anxious to incur. But all this time the savages were coming up, and, by some devilment which I did not understand, the raft came direct for the island.

Peering out into the darkness, I saw that there were four or five savages swimming in the water, and keeping the raft in the right directon.

Now my pistols were very good ones, and for mere practice I had taken a great deal of pains with them. I had shot birds on the wing, and so had great confidence in my

---

*Numerous correspondents wish to know if cannibalism still exists. Certainly; and is very common. This very day we receive the following:—" On the arrival of the Armenian mail steamer at Liverpool, we learn that when the vessel was in the Bonny River, on the 29th January, a report was circulated to the effect that a cannibal feast was about to be made in the town; but no one gave the rumour credence. However a party went on shore on the 1st February; and were horrified to see, when walking through the place no less than five human heads placed in a most systematic order on the grass, with a fire close by, and a large pot ready for cooking. At another spot, close by, lay arms, legs, &c., in the course of being prepared for the pot; while an old black woman was engaged in slicing a human liver for the ' stew.' It appears that previous to the return of King Pepple to Bonny, after his long residence in England, the population was divided into two powerful parties, one of which was opposed to the Kings return; but, latterly, both parties signed a treaty that no person's life should be sacrificed without his being brought before his majesty for trial.

ability to use them. I watched my opportunity keenly, saw a great black savage rise in the water, and fired.

With a cry, which was re-echoed by a dozen others, he let go his hold and sank. I had hit him in the head. Again I fired, and once more another fell. Then taking aim at one of the oarsmen, I fired, and, the oar falling out of his hand, the raft broached to, turned round, and the whole party of warriors came in view. With a fearful yell, they leaped into the water. Once again my gun sent forth its volley of flame, and then I fled.

Gliding along the shore, I soon came to where my canoe lay in the dark shadow of some cedars; I could see the savages making a rush, despite the mischief I had done. In a few minutes they would be on my trail. The boat was pushed out, and then, the overhanging boughs mainly assisting me, the bark canoe was pulled along without the use of oars. In this way I soon reached the end of the island, when, pushing my boat under some overhanging trees, I loaded my gun and listened.

The savages were on the land, searching for me everywhere. I could hear them tearing through the bushes, striking right and left with their clubs, in the hope of thus finding me.

Tiger, who stuck close to me, gave a savage growl, which warned me to be off; so, sitting firmly in my canoe, I struck out for the opposite shore, taking every precaution to avoid the influence of the current, which, now that I was round the point and on the opposite side of the island, was very strong.

Fear lends strength, I do believe; so that I did on this occasion prodigies, which at another time I might not have done. The canoe flew beneath the vigorous strokes of my paddles, and in a few minutes I was across, and under shelter of the trees which skirted the borders of the lake.

The bark canoe was fastened to the boughs which swept the water's edge, and then, creeping into the arches of the gloomy forest, I preferred trusting to all the chances of wild beasts, boa-constrictors, pythons, and all the other species of the family of snakes, to running the risk of falling into the hands of the cannibals.

For some time I continued on my way in impenetrable darkness, until at length a small clearing opened before me, and I saw at once that I had fallen on a village of monkeys. Every tree had a nest—that is, a rude platform, and a roof of slanting thatch. Tired, wearied, and scarcely knowing what to do, I climbed into the most handy of these, and curling myself round very much like the animal which erected it, fell asleep.

When I awoke, it was long past daylight, but nothing was in sight. Probably my large dog sleeping at the bottom of the tree had kept the monkey away. However this may be, I glided to the ground, and, without stopping even to pluck a berry, hurried on my way.

I soon reached the stream supplying the lake, and contrived to cross it by means of one of the many logs which lay upon its banks. I then struck out for the track which led to my cave. Once there, I considered myself a match for a hundred or two, even of such Indians as the Fans.

My dog, which I had again muzzled, suddenly stood still and whined.

I brought my gun to the charge, but at once saw that it was too late. Fifty warriors were upon me, and the death of one or two would only have exasperated the rest. I made a feint, however, of running, cast my gun into a thicket, and hen, facing about, met the howling, yelling, shrieking troop of savages with a firm and undaunted look.

It required all my nerve to do so; but though I had but little hope, yet, even at that painful crisis, it was, at all events, satisfactory to show them how a white man can die. They were lighter in shade, stronger, taller, and more active than any purely negro race; they were naked, except wearing a wild cat apron, while their teeth were filed, which gave their faces a ghastly and ferocious look, especially those who had their teeth blackened.

Their hair, or wool, was drawn out in long thin plaits, while on the end of each stiff plait were strung some white beads and copper or iron rings.

They clutched me with a yell of triumph, and at once tied me to a tree; after which they retired to a distance and sat down in a circle.

My feelings may be imagined. I knew my fate. There was the image of the poor Indian girl before me; but then she was one of their own tribe—I was not; they would certainly eat me.

Besides, had I not killed their warriors, laid desolate some of their homes, and, to their ideas, deserved death? I knew it was coming, for they began to sing a mournful heart-piercing chaunt, which seemed to say, "There is no hope!"—something which sounded like, *We che noli labellea pe na beshe!* Then up they leaped, brandishing their spears, hatchets, shields, and war-clubs.

Four rushed at me, and I knew that my hour was come. They halted facing me, their countenances exhibiting the utmost distortion which the human countenance can show; such countenances as one may imagine to belong to cannibals. But I knew I looked them full in the face with a most undaunted expression, which seemed to exasperate them awfully; for one raised his lance, one his club, another his poisoned arrow, just as I muttered a hasty prayer for mercy—not to them, but to Him who alone could save me in that strait.

Heavens! what is that cry? It must be madness even to think of it—and yet it seemed clear and distinct.

CHAPTER CI.

OVERWHELMING ADVENTURES.

My utter and overwhelming astonishment may be conceived, when on coming to myself I found hanging over me three Europeans, as I at once recognised them to be, despite their sunburnt looks and strange costume.

"It is—can it be?" said a voice which sounded like a dim echo of the past. "It is—my boy."

And I was clasped in the arms of my own dearly beloved father.

"This here is no time for speechifying," said a gruff voice. "I wants to know, master, if there is any place which we could hold against these rampagious savages. They're taken aback—but my name's not John Thomas if they'll not be on us again in a minute."

I rose to my feet, the circulation having by this time returned, and well aware of the exposed position in which we were, took upon myself to lead the way without any superfluous observations. I took care, however, to lead them in a direction which admitted of my recapturing my gun, which I took up without remark. Indeed I was too overwhelmed to speak. The miracle which had been performed in my favour was so astounding that I really could scarcely credit my senses.

One moment before, and the savages were about to immolate me without mercy, and now I was a free man, with my father, uncle James, and the skipper John Thomas. It seemed scarcely possible, and yet it was so. Yes. My hand was held in that of my beloved parent, as we hurried along without a word, the gallant captain bringing up the rear and keeping a good look-out.

He was right when he roused us to a sense of our situation, for we had not gone a quarter of a mile when we saw the savages hanging like a cloud on our rear, and preparing for an attack. With their spears, clubs, and almost impenetrable shields, our fire-arms, which they now began thoroughly to understand, were not so formidable as they had at first imagined.

We were, however, determined not to be circumvented, and retreated, therefore, in good order, keeping our guns ready. The savages do not all at once get over such a surprise as that we had given them, so that for a time the mere pointing of our guns sufficed to send them back in full and precipitous retreat. Then came a rushing sound through the wood, and both horse and zebra came galloping up, accompanied by all the dogs.

They had doubtless been attracted by the firing, and their curious instinct made them understand that with us they would be safe against the savages who had pursued them with such relentless zeal. I, however, took no note of this circumstance; but capturing them, we mounted, two on each, and though the burden was heavy, were soon out of sight of the furious and discomfited savages.

When we reached my cave, and they passed through my pathway into the fort, the delight and admiration of all knew no bounds. My artillery, my pond, my monkeys, my cave, my stockade, were all examined and applauded in turn, but I checked all this to talk of other things.

"My mother—my sister—my cousin?"

"All well," said my father, quickly, "but of that when we have leisure. Let us now think wholly of ourselves."

"Right you are!" cried old John Thomas, a grizzly seaman of three-score; "and first as to the larder."

All the dogs having followed us, two of the most yelping curs among the lot were tied at the end of the pathway, to give notice, while I led my delighted friends into my cave and gave them a hearty meal; of which, it appeared, they stood in ample need. My heart was very full all this time, and as I viewed them, I could not help taking their hands and pressing them to my heart, and by my looks manifesting my extreme delight at what had occured.

But our coming danger rendered it absolutely necessary that we should prepare for our defence. No sooner, therefore, had the meal been concluded, than we sallied forth and examined the state of our fortress. Everything was thought admirable, except that in case of a rush, it was thought advisable to leave the gate open, only fixing some bars across, that did not impede the devastating power of my infernal machine, which was fresh loaded and primed

This decided on, the dogs were called in, and with the monkeys fastened up within the cave, so as not to guide the savages to us by any imprudent noise.

Then, with a goodly supply of powder and ball, and with such arms as I could find them, such as axes and swords, my unexpected and beloved allies took up their posts. It was arranged that at the first rush of the savages, I should fire my infernal machine, and then one of the others would slam the gate and fasten the thick bar; when each would act according to circumstances.

Then climbing up by means of my ladder, at a spot well-known to me, I crept from bough to bough, until I came to a spot where I could overlook the plain; there was no hope whatever of our escaping their attack. The trail we had left was broad and obvious; all we could hope for would be fair warning.

It has been truly observed that the warriors of this part of Africa—not excepting the Fans—are not overstocked with courage. They invariably applaud tricks that are inhumanly cruel and cowardly, and never, in any instance, seek open hand-to-hand fight. To surprise man, woman, or child in their sleep, and then to kill them; to lie for hours in ambush for a solitary man, and to kill him by a single spear-thrust before he can defend himself; to waylay a poor woman going to the spring for water, and kill her; or for a large canoe to attack a small one on a river; these are the warlike and boasted feats of African savages.

Indeed, no rude or barbarous people appears to be really and truly brave. The head-hunters of Borneo trust almost wholly to night attacks, while even the North American Indians dealt in surprises, fought like the negroes, from behind trees, and were, with wonderful exceptions, rather cruel than brave.

In fact, all that we see of barbarous and civilized life is strongly in favour of the latter in every way. Savages may be picturesque enough, but that is all.

For a long time there was an awful stillness on the earth, which may have lasted an hour, when, as I had for some time expected, I saw the savages come out of the wood in small parties on the trail. As soon as they saw that the track led to a dense thicket they halted, while I eagerly returned to my position within the fort, making signs as I descended the ladder that the blacks were coming.

I received no reply, they having posted themselves in out-of-the-way places. From their after story, I always believe that, worn out with a fearful journey and much suffering, they had after their ample meal become fearfully sleepy, and were taking a doze. But this circumstance I kept to myself, as their waking was to be terrible.

I crouched down beneath the shed which covered my guns. They were all loaded, with the pans open, and a train of gunpowder communicating between all. As they were tried muskets, they had several balls. I myself was hidden behind some planks, which had, however, chinks in them, through which I could peer out and observe all that was passing. In my hand was a lighted piece of touchwood, in my belt two pistols, and by my side my double-barrelled gun.

But again all was still as death, and I should myself, exhausted and weary, have given way to sleep, had not I suddenly heard a suspicious cracking of dead and dry boughs in my pathway. In an instant, I saw a whole mob of curious faces peering one over the other through the open doorway of the fort.

Loud was the report, fearful the yells, and dire the destruction, as my train flashed on high, and the guns went off. In an instant, slam went the high gate—the bar was placed across, and my friends were ready. They said not a word, but each peered forth from his hiding-place.

I could see that the destruction caused by my artillery was great, while terrible groans of anguish made us aware that the pile I gazed at was composed of the dying as well as of the dead.

But our position was too perilous to take this consideration into account, so I contented myself with loading my infernal machine once more; after which I summoned the whole party to a conference, under the shelter of my palm-trees. This done, I expressed my opinion that there would be no attack for some time, so that it would be wise for all who could to take some rest.

"But we must have a sentry," said Captain Thomas.

"I will keep guard," was my reply, "while you sleep."

"No, my boy. I am an old sailor, and used to keeping my eyes open—snatch a little sleep. I will awake you all at the least noise."

Reluctantly, I yielded; but I was anxious not to prolong the discussion, as my father and uncle, despite the danger of our position, and despite the intense excitement they were labouring under, were dropping with fatigue and an irresistable desire for slumber. I led them at once inside my cave, gave them a cordial, and then, after one hearty embrace, they fell fast asleep.

CHAPTER CII.

THE NIGHT WATCH.

As for myself, I was glad to be alone with my own thoughts. The events of the last twenty-four hours had been so bewildering, that my mind was in a terrible whirl. I knew not what to think of. My capture by the savages, my narrow escape from death, my wondrous rescue by those whom I had little reason to think in the land of the living were scenes which surpassed all I had passed through during the whole five years that had elapsed since my wreck.

I could not sleep, except one calls those snatches or dozes which last only a few minutes—sleep; but woke every moment with a start, to fancy that all that had occurred was a dream. Then, at last, however, wearied nature overcame every other consideration; I became insensible to all around for hours.

When I awoke, it was black and dark without, and I crept into the open air, to find the grizzled old seaman at his watch. Nothing had occurred all night to startle him, while even the dying groans of the wounded were no longer heard. This stillness of the savages made me suspect some devilment, and I become uneasy.

"If attacked," I said, "you can rouse the others. This perfect calm alarms me. I will go on the scout."

"Not if I know it, boy."

"There is no danger," I replied; and explained to him the mechanism of my cave.

My project was to pass through, gain the heights, and, by following their edge, try and discover what the Fans were doing. Danger there could be none, as they would have miles to go round to reach the spot where the ravine could be crossed. With my telescope and gun, I should be far more useful than inside the cave or fortification.

"Why, my dear Alfred," said the grim, old sailor, "you beat Robinson Crusoe. This is indeed a most wonderful island!"

I could not help smiling, and then, after giving him certain directions, was about to depart, when we heard a strange noise outside the gate; and then the dogs flew with a yell, and began scratching underneath. As no attack was made, I would not fire, but climbing up my ladder with stealthy steps, peered down through the leaves.

It was a number of lads and women removing the dead bodies.

I had a great mind to fire, for I suspected the horrid purpose for which they were being taken. Then I recollected that no tribe eats its own dead. The Fans buy the dead of the Oshebas, who in turn buy theirs. They also buy the dead of other families in their own tribes, and besides this, get the bodies of a great many slaves from the Mbichos and Mbondemos, for which they readily give ivory at the rate of a small tusk for a body.

But another consideration also restrained me, which was, that the removal of bodies in that hot weather was strictly necessary from sanitary motives.

I descended from the ladder, and communicated my information to the skipper; after which I passed through my cave, drove back all my dogs but Tiger, and closing my door behind me, crept through the serpent cavern and soon again emerged into the open air. There was now a faint tint of dawn creeping slowly along the eastern horizon, of which I was extremely glad.

Taking my way along the summit of the rocks, a walk of a few hundred yards brought me to a spot which overlooked the plain, and there I saw the Fans had collected a perfect army in numbers, and one which it was almost impossible for us successfully to oppose. Stooping behind the arid bushes which grew on the crest of the ravine, I used my telescope, and saw that they had piled all the dead bodies, more than a dozen, in a heap, and were now about to go through some ceremony.

They were about to dance some dance to the music of a monotonous little drum, which is their favourite instrument. It was a wild scene, but did not last long, as they seemed in a hurry. But while it lasted, it was, indeed, a wild and horrible scene, to behold about ten hundred nearly naked savages whirling about with all sorts of frightful and hideous contortions of their limbs.

When this ceased, the women approached with food, which they ate eagerly, though—perhaps it was my heated imagination—they cast eager glances at the pile of human flesh.

No sooner was the morning meal consumed than they rose, clutched their cross-bows, lances, clubs, and spears, and advanced to the assault, this time with a fierce determination which boded us no good. They were soon about two hundred feet from me, and five from the gate of the fortress. With a desire to alarm the garrison, and without regard to consequences, I levelled, took careful aim at a tall chief, and fired. I saw that he bit the dust; and then expecting a grand onslaught, took to my heels.

When I gained the cavern I found all up and ready. Their sleep had refreshed them much, and when a hasty breakfast had been handed round, they all seemed to come forth with new vigour.

Still no attack from the savages.

I have already explained that when I planted the dense thicket, which was, as it were, the wall of my fortress, I left the trees which were there before, only cutting down for fuel any that came near the outer part of the wall. I now proposed that three of us should, by means of our ladder, climb into their branches and surprise the savages by a volley from the summit of the trees.

This was agreed to, Captain John Thomas remaining near his broadside, for which he had a considerable predilection. The others, guided by me, ascended the ladder, and then climbed from bough to bough until we were on the edge of the wall.

CHAPTER CIII.

A DAY FIGHT.

THE Fans were advancing gloomy and slowly in great force, though I remarked, with an inward shudder, that about a dozen of their slimmest warriors or runners had turned back and were evidently about to cross the ravine in search of an explanation of the shot from the rocks.

This was a terrible shock, as they were as likely as not to discover the shaft-like entrance to my cave; in which case we were lost.

Just as this idea crossed my imagination, another of such portentous character came to my brain, that I almost cried aloud for joy. But I restrained myself, and resolved to mature the plan in my own mind before I had recourse to so extreme a measure. The savages carried their huge elephant shields in such a way as to protect their bodies. But what puzzled me was this:—

The front of the column was composed of about a dozen men, who had fastened one great shield above the others in such a way as to descend to their very feet, while those behind appeared to be carrying bundles.

Bundles! Yes; they were about to attack my fortification by fire. This explained their long quiet. They had been collecting masses of reeds, bamboos, and dry wood, to burn us out. But this was not the only danger. These savages were extremely agile, and a cause of alarm of a very peculiar kind suggested itself.

As soon as the column was near enough, we held whispered counsel and took aim, each taking care to select a different man. We fired at their heads, and were so much in earnest that they dropped either dead or mortally wounded.

Then the whole body, without caring for their companions, made a desperate rush at the walls and cast down their bundles of faggots at the foot of the dense thicket. Again we fired with deadly effect, and then retreated to the inside of the fort, to wait the course of events.

I was fortunate, indeed, that I had during my stay on the island bethought me of saving up a goodly store of provisions, which, though salt, were welcome, as we had a goodly supply of water. Then there was my poultry yard, which on a pinch would serve us for fresh meat, should the siege be prolonged to any great extent. This, however, I doubted, as I was fully aware that it was the habit of savages if not successful when making a dash, to give up and retire in despair, before losing too many men.

As soon as we were all together in a sheltered corner of the hut, we began to devise as to the best plan of acting under the circumstances. That the savages would burn us out was a matter of great probability, as the amount of fuel they could bring to bear on the fort would be immense, and nothing would be easier than to make a clear open pathway to the inside.

My advice was, to take my infernal machine bodily on its frame into the very depths of my cave, which I thought we could defend against any amount of enemies. My friends had a tolerable supply of powder, while I had enough to last all our guns for a week. They readily acquiesced; but upon examination of the interior, the old sailor suggested that my battery should be fixed in the doorway of the upper cave, which would then be to all intents and purposes impregnable.

I thought this a very good suggestion, as it would sweep my cave and prevent an otherwise wanton amount of destruction on the part of the irritated and infuriated invaders upon my home.

Several cargoes of provisions were moved to my inner cave, with a thick deal box, the contents of which were now invaluable to me, though formerly I had scorned them as useless.

This done, the infernal machine was fixed on its frame in such a way as not to impede our exit or entrance; and then we again sallied forth to watch the progress of events, all being calm and collected, but at the same time prepared for the worst. It was a very sultry, hot day, and we could even hear in the distance the rolling of the thunder portending a storm.

Just as we heard this, in order to be screened from the scorching rays of the sun, we had crept under the shadow of a tree at some distance from the cave. Scarcely had we taken shelter when my dogs began to bark furiously, sticking up their noses in the air, and jumping in the wildest and strangest manner. As it behoved us to be very careful, and to omit no opportunity of watching the Indians, we broke off a low whispered conversation, and I peered up into the air.

My heart beat wildly as I remarked the infernal cunning and perseverance of these warriors. About half-a-dozen had crossed the rocks, followed the ridge until they had made out the region above my cave, and were now clambering into the tops of the palm trees. Only one of these, however, could be reached from the rocks, but that gained nothing would be easier than to cling to the next.

But the savages had no intention of adopting this means of attack. They were picked young men, who probably intended to show the great body of warriors what desperate deeds of valour they were capable of. The first warrior no sooner was on the tree, than, peering down, he began to descend. I whispered the state of things to my friends, and gave directions how to act.

We first cautiously moved the branches on one side and took aim, by previous agreement allowing four to get on to the tree first. With a whispered signal, we fired—all at once. A fearful fall, and the subsequent furious barking of our dogs, was all we could make out. Then the smoke cleared away, and on the ground we saw one warrior being torn to pieces by our dogs. But our eyes were then, by one accord, cast upwards, and we saw the three wounded, bleeding wretches using frantic efforts to re-ascend the tree.

At this moment a fearful crackling, and the rising of a dense column of smoke, informed us that the main body had succeeded in setting fire to their faggots. This decided our course of action, as the wood was all so dry in that hot season as to be very inflammable. Without waiting to see the result of the fearful struggle above, we entered the cave and esconced ourselves, after some few more preliminaries, inside the inner cave, where even in a hand-to-hand fight we should stand a very fair chance.

Now began one of those long and wearisome waitings, which make the heart sink. Of course, the action by fire we knew must be a slow proceeding, but, at the same time it was dreadful to be waiting all this time in the darkness unaware of their proceedings, while the labour and care of so many years was being destroyed.

We could hear, even over the noise of the fire, the cries and groans of those who had fallen from above, until at length our dogs came rushing in, as if unable any longer to endure the heat. We made them pass within the inner cave, where, as the reader is already aware, there was a magnificent spring of potable and excellent water.

AN UNEXPECTED CAPTURE.

No. 21.—SAILOR CRUSOE.

We conversed, and I learned many things which made my heart beat more wildly than it ever had done previously; but as I design, before continuing much farther my own extraordinary adventures, to briefly explain what had happened to them, I will not unnecessarily break my narrative. It was told to me by bits and scraps, so that it needed much explanation. And thus another day wore away and night came.

We sat round the entrance of my inner cave, with our weapons to our hands, occasionally taking some refreshment, while the skipper indulged in a smoke.

CHAPTER CIV.

A JOURNEY.

THEY all slept but myself. I could not feel that inclination to slumber which at other times I should have so freely indulged in. There were many reasons for this, the most important was in connection with certain revelations which had been made to me. All this time I kept my eyes fixed on the entrance to the cave, which, after having been some time lit up by the lurid flames, was gradually relapsing into darkness.

Suddenly I heard strange noises in my cave. Had I been dozing, and had the savages taken advantage of my brief slumber to creep in? It was a fearful doubt. But something must be done, so, without taking the trouble to wake my companions—indeed, I did not think of it—I fired.

The cavern was full of them. They were everywhere. They were groping about in the dark in my kitchen, bedroom, and store-room. When, however, my gun exploded with a terrible report, they made a furious rush towards me. But my companions were ready; they fired the battery and then single guns. Such shrieks and yells and groans, intermingled with the reports of the deadly weapons, surely were never heard out of Pandemonium.

"Keep them at bay a moment," I said, "and then do as I do."

I had lit a taper in a corner, and had opened the mysterious box to which I have already alluded. From this I took first a bundle of rockets, and when I and my friends had discharged one of these each, I followed up by such a shower of catherine-wheels, dragons, and such fireworks as fly about of themselves, as turned the cave into a very furnace.

Sparks, flames, with an awful odour of sulphur, added to the terrible nature of this cannonade, which being continued five minutes, we stopped and retreating into the inner cave some distance, lay down to allow the smoke to pass over our heads. This took some considerable time; after which, quite satisfied to trust to our dogs, we remained still, and slept until morning.

My cave, on examination as soon as we were all again up and ready, proved to be in a dreadful state. There were nine dead bodies, killed not all by our guns, but by heavy pieces of stone, which had fallen from the roof. The disorder was perfectly fearful, and then the very first consideration was to rid ourselves of what would soon prove a fearful nuisance.

But first we went out to peer into the country, to see if the savages were really gone. We used every precaution, being armed to the teeth, and taking with us all our dogs. We threw ourselves out in, as it were, skirmishing order, keeping, however, in sight of one another—creeping behind bushes, crawling at times—but not a trace of the savages was to be seen. My fortunate preservation of what seemed in my state so useless a thing as a box of fireworks had terrified them far more than the guns, which they had begun faintly to understand.

It was some time, however, before we became convinced that we were safe; and, indeed, we were not fully convinced of that until at length reaching the heights, we saw the savages in full retreat towards the continent. Their canoes were being urged through the water at a pace which plainly indicated the terror with which they had been smitten.

Still, the discovery by these warlike savages of my retreat was something to fill us with perpetual alarm, as once recovered from their present abject terror, they might take heart, and return in such overwhelming numbers as to utterly destroy us, and render any attempt at defence useless.

A council of war was then held. It had been already agreed that the whole colony which had been left on the mainland should be transported to my island, and well housed; while an effort was to be made to build such a ship as would enable us to reach a point on the African cost frequented by trading vessels, one of which would certainly give us a passage home.

The erection of such a fabric would, however, be a work of time, and it behoved us to be prepared to spend at least another year on the island. Such are human calculations!

The first thing was to be prepared to feed so largely increased a colony. But this, to me, offered no great difficulty; and to convince my companions of this, I proposed a survey of my island. This was readily agreed to, and my zebra and horse, both of which excited their unbounded admiration, being caught, were loaded with provisions and necessaries for our journey.

It was a change, indeed, from my solitary state, to find myself at the head of a cavalcade, composed of three men, two horses, and a drove of dogs. It was with a delight that may be imagined, but not described, that I pointed out all the different scenes of my mishaps and misfortunes, as well as of my many mercies and happinesses. Many things which had been forgotten now recurred to me, and I pointed them out with pride.

Nor did I forget to tell my father how much I had benefitted by the education he had given me, and how those early lessons of wisdom and courage had served me in my perilous straights, from the time when I was cast away on a bleak coast—my whole riches, a knife and an oyster shell—until now, when I had my herds and flocks, and all else that man could need here below.

My plantation first engaged their attention, which seemed to them wonderful, until they recollected the extraordinary fertility of the climate and soil, which only required to be turned up with a stick to produce anything that man could wish for. Still, with the prospect of so many mouths to feed, it would have to be increased. This was task number one.

My piggery both astonished, delighted, and amazed them, especially as the pigs were very lean and savage. Their rapid increase had begun to make food scarce, so we at once set to work to thin them, selecting the largest and fattest, which we concealed in a deep and secluded thicket, to be salted on our return, which would be the next day, if, indeed, the wild beasts and vultures did not in the meantime find them out.*

* We have already alluded to this subject; but it is so curious and interesting, that we make a quotation from Darwin's "Scientific Journey Round the World" on the subject. Speaking of Patagonia, he says :—"When any animal is killed in the country, it is well known that the condors, like other carrion vultures, soon gain intelligence of it, and congregate in an inexplicable manner. In

As soon as we left the piggery, I must confess that my heart beat with considerable emotion at the prospect of showing them the valley of the gazelles, and I determined that it should prove to them a perfect dramatic hit. These animals as well as the ostriches had been driven to Crater Valley before the eruption of the Fans, so that when they came to the end of the first valley, I cried a halt under a grove of palms, where I proposed that we should dine.

This settled, I left them, taking with me only my shepherd dogs and strolled up towards the partition which I had made in the feeding grounds of my animals. The intervening space was soon passed over, and in ten minutes more my extraordinary flock of gazelles and ostriches were bounding joyously into the fresh fields and pastures new, which they were evidently delighted to be allowed to revisit.

"My dear boy," cried my father, shaking me by the hand, "what perseverance, what courage, and what foresight you have displayed."

"I have been miserable and despondent enough, dear sir," I replied; "but heaven at last sent me resignation, and, believing that my fate was inseparably connected with this solitary island, I determined to submit, and to create for myself as many companions and as much occupation as lay in my power."

"Well thought of, my son; labour after all is the only cure for mental suffering. But tell us how it was you organized this beautiful valley."

We sat down to dinner, and while discussing that meal I recapitulated some of my more remarkable adventures, and described how, by means of the lasso, † I had procured myself my flock. I then added a description of my labours in preparing a pen for them, which narration agreeably occupied the time until dinner was over.

I now proposed that we should leave the animals and provisions here, where I proposed passing the night, and that we should spend the afternoon in exploring the neighbouring country in search of a spot where we might find both a dockyard and timber at hand to commence our vessel. This all agreed to, the horses were hoppled, the dogs, all but Tiger, were tied up, and away we started in a northerly direction.

My cave in the rock had given considerable satisfaction to my friends as a place of retreat in the hour of danger, but at the same time it was manifestly unsuited to the residence

of so many people; nor could it even hold them. One therefore of our objects was to select a place where a village could be erected on a spot both fertile and capable of defence.

For this purpose we kept our eyes sharply about us. My own opinion was in favour of a spot near the jungle of bamboos which had been of such great service to me, and in this direction I led my party. They were delighted at every step by some novelty that I pointed out. At length we reached the spot where I had first fallen upon bamboos, and here we halted.

The bamboos grew over a considerable space, perhaps a mile in length, and about two hundred yards wide. Behind this was a running stream, which, meeting with impediments of rocks, had spread over a very large space of ground. On the other side of this were some gigantic trees, which we only discovered by forcing our way through the bamboos.

These trees were the largest I had ever seen. Not a sign of brushwood was visible, but a green grassy turf rising in a gentle slope from the river.

"This is the spot," I cried, "here we may erect our village, and here shall we find both a place for launching our bark, with plenty of wood to build it."

"Yes," cried my father, "it is indeed a beautiful spot. I could willingly pass the rest of my days, Alfred, on your marvellous island."

At this instant, we were standing on the skirt of the jungle, a crush was heard in the bamboos behind us, and then something of enormous size came bounding in our direction. By a common instinct we ran up to our middles in water, and waited, our guns cocked and our hearts beating.

The very absence of all noise made us dread we knew not what.

CHAPTER CV.

THE LIONS.

DURING my residence on the island so many adventures of an extraordinary nature had befallen me that I was prepared to be surprised at nothing. Luckily, we were four together and well armed, so that the chances were whatever the nature of the interruption, we were fully capable of defending ourselves. But my alarm and astonishment may be conceived, when a whole troop of lions, as it appeared, stalked suddenly out of the bushes and confronted us. We exchanged rapid glances, and all but myself seemed disposed to fire.

"Hold!" I said, in a firm, low whisper, but such as could be heard at a considerable distance; "it is a male and female with her cubs. If we let them alone they may turn back, but if we attack them they will become furious."

The male, one of the most magnificent creatures I had ever seen, stood on the banks of the stream lashing his sides with his tail, while the lioness kept a little back, playing with her two cubs in a gentle and affectionate way that was very pleasant to contemplate.

The affection of this animal for its mate and its young is very great. Once the lion takes to himself a wife he will never, if possible, part with her, nor does he, like some animals are known to do, expel his young from his lair until they are quite able to take care of themselves.

These, however, were after reflections. The main object now was to get out of their reach, which, after some hesitation we decided on doing by retreating to the other side of the stream. This, the river being shallow and full of stones and boulders, we at length effected, and found ourselves

---

most cases it must not be overlooked that the birds have discovered their prey, and have picked the skeleton clean, before the flesh is in the least degree tainted. Remembering the experiments of M. Anderton on the little smelling powers of carrion hawks, I tried, in the above-mentioned garden, the following experiment. The condors were tied each by a rope in a long row at the bottom of a wall; and having folded up a piece of meat in white paper, I walked backwards and forwards, carrying it in my hand at the distance of about three yards from them; but no notice whatever was taken. I then threw it on the ground within one yard of an old male bird. He looked at it for a moment with attention, but then regarded it no more. With a stick I pushed it closer and closer, until at last he touched it with his beak. The paper was then instantly torn off with fury, and at the same moment every bird in the long row began struggling and flapping its wings. Under the same circumstances it would have been quite impossible to have deceived a dog."

† The lasso consists of a very strong, but thin, well-plaited rope, made of raw hide. One end is attached to the broad surcingle which fastens together the complicated gear of the recado or saddle used in the Pampas; the other is terminated by a small ring of iron or brass, by which a noose can be formed. The Gaucho, when he is going to use the lasso, keeps a small coil in his bridle hand; and the other holds the running noose, which is very large, generally having a diameter of about eight feet. This he whirls round his head, and by the dexterous movement of his wrist keeps the noose open; then throwing it, he causes it to fall on any particular spot he chooses. The lasso, when not used, is tied in a small coil to the after-part of the recado. The bolas or balls are of two kinds. The simplest, which is chiefly used for catching ostriches, consists of two round stones covered with leather, and united by a thin plaited thong about eight feet long. The other kind differs only in having three balls united by the thongs to a common centre.

on the other side, on the green sward under those enormous trees which had so much excited our admiration and curiosity.

Still, the lions did not move, and it now became a serious reflection with us as to what was to be done. Return in face of them we could not, while it was very dangerous to leave our hoppled animals undefended. We held counsel, however, and soon determined to return another way, not crossing the river until the jungle appeared to be open and clear.

That the park-like sward with those huge trees, would afford us a most delightful post for a village we were satisfied, while it was equally clear that the presence of man in any numbers would scare away the wildest of the animals of the forest.

The stream, a very little below the spot which was fordable, became deeper and evidently navigable, which, if it continued to be so towards the sea, would enable us to build a vessel here, by means of which we hoped to escape. There was another advantage too, that the jungle would not very much tempt natives to explore this part of the island, unless, indeed, they came upon our trail.

Examining the position we wished to occupy, we scarcely noticed our adversaries, until a roar drew our attention to them, when we found that they were quietly following the opposite bank of the river, watching our every movement.

This was very unpleasant, especially as the day was fast falling, and night would be upon us long before we could regain our camp. This caused serious reflections, and there was talk of forcing the passage of the river. But all knew the ferocity of this animal when in company with its young, so we resolved to try stratagem instead of force.

A pile of wood was soon collected at a point of the river where it was narrow, and as soon as it was dark this was set fire to. Round this we camped until it was black dark, cooking some of our provisions, and lastly, throwing a number of bones on the fire, which sent a pungent odour for a considerable distance. Then each man lay down out of the circle of light, and one by one we cautiously retreated without making the slightest sound, until we were congregated together about a couple of hundred yards below the spot.

Not a voice was raised, not a whisper uttered, as we sought a spot by which to cross the river, which was very deep. At length, however, we discovered a place which seemed suited to our purpose. The river here was about twenty feet wide, very deep, with steep banks, so that it could be only crossed by means of a bridge of some kind. Here we all stood in a group devising as to what was to be done.

The two banks were lined by trees resembling cedars, which leaned over and bent towards the other side, some of the branches even touching one another. I pointed up, showed my lasso, and intimated my intention of extemporizing a bridge of a suspension character, such as is used in the more southern parts of America.

As I was the youngest of the party, no great objection was made to my making the adventure, though all earnestly requested me to be careful. I promised, and at once selecting a tree which hung very much over the bank, so that to climb was easy, I crawled upwards, taking care to keep my eyes fixed upward, lest I should turn giddy. At length, however, I stopped and peered down, when to my astonishment, I found myself exactly above the edge of the opposite bank.

It now become easy to descend. My lasso was stout and

long, so that I could pass it over the bough of a tree, and then the two ends touched the ground. The knots, too, were a great assistance, and without communicating with my friends, I determined to make the first trial.

Clutching firmly hold of my double rope, I began to descend, and would in a very few minutes have reached the ground, when I was checked in my career by a terrible cry from my friends.

"Stop where you are, descend not an inch!" they shrieked, and at the same moment fired.

Then almost letting go my hold, so sudden was the start they gave me, I looked down, and saw sprawling on the ground the great male lion, which had, despite all our cunning, followed us steadily along the bank. At the same instant I felt that the cedar, the roots, as I have often before remarked, being fastened in a shallow soil, were giving way and that I was falling into the very jaws of the great beast.

I closed my eyes with a fearful cry, and next minute sank on the beast's side. But he was harmless, so that I was quit for my fright, which, naturally enough, was very great. As soon as I was able I rose to my feet.

"What cheer?" said the husky voice of Captain John Thomas.

"All well. The lion is dead. You can come over."

The cedar had fallen directly across the stream, and made a bridge; somewhat precarious, it is true, but still one which would serve at a pinch; for in a very few minutes they were again beside me, and viewing with wonder and delight the huge monster that but for their three bullets striking him would have made a meal and a sorry end of me.

It was now very late, and my exertion, combined with my very natural terror, having exhausted me, it was resolved to camp where we were for the night, though not without the necessary precaution of a fire. Besides, my friends were desirous of securing the skin of the animal, which only their excessively good aim could have destroyed thus quickly. We found afterwards that one ball had pierced his heart, when, of course, death was instantaneous.

As we were four in company, wood was soon collected in sufficient quantity to make two good blazing fires, between which we lay down; very glad at last to take rest, which, after our journey, we needed so much.

It was late when we rose next day, but still all went to work with a will to skin the lion; and while so doing, came to the decision that, as we had been so fortunate as to have one tree to aid us, we would here make a bridge, and call it "The Pass of the Lions." This was a very good idea, as the spot was one that could be easily defended, or the bridge even destroyed, upon the recurrence of any of those emergencies which in our position were so likely to befal us.

Our way was through a wood beneath which the grass grew in such a way as to make walking difficult; but we hoped soon to find some way of destroying this, and making ourselves a clear road to the bridge. When it is considered what wonders I performed alone, what had I not a right to expect now that we were so many?

CHAPTER CVI.

A NEW ESTABLISHMENT.

THE first important consideration, with a view to the transportation of many things needful to our new establishment, was the construction of some kind of vehicle that would take a good load, and which, drawn by our two steeds, aided by ourselves on perilous occasions, would assist so much in all that we wished to do.

For myself, I would gladly have crossed over to the mainland at once, and fetched my friends and relatives; but my father wished first to secure their comfort on their arrival. The season was passing, and it was desirable to have everything ready before the wet set in and interrupted our labours.

My heart was very much against this resolution; but it having been resolved on by older and wiser heads than mine it was useless to contend; so, instead, I determined so to advance our preparations as to hasten the time of meeting as soon as possible.

Our resolution was to have the cave set apart wholly as a retreat in case of accidents, as a last desperate redoubt when driven from our intrenchments by an overwhelming force of savages. The chief objections made to it as a residence, even in the winter or rainy season, were the confined space, the darkness, and other discomforts always attendant on a cavern dwelling.

For myself, it appeared like leaving home; but as I knew the others to be right I made no objection, especially as since the combat the place presented such a very different appearance as to have destroyed that early charm of association which hitherto I had felt to belong to it.

Besides, I knew that a small town such as that we were about to erect, would be more healthy, pleasant, and cheerful, than my old residence; while the cave could always remain as a shelter, and my habitation on the island of the lake be a pleasure bower to be visited on festive occasions, many of which, as soon as the deserted locality was more fully inhabited, would doubtless occur.

The plan we adopted for a sledge was to cut down two trees with trunks of a sufficient size to make the sides, with a curve in front to facilitate getting over grass, shrubs, and other obstructions. Then we laid across several lateral pieces of wood, and fastened them securely by means of fibre-cord and nails.

The harness was of the simplest character, but, at the same time, strong and able to bear all the weight which we could require. In the first place, there were tools to be removed to the new station, then such things as could be spared from the cave without exactly stripping it altogether and making it uninhabitable.

As soon as some other little matters had been attended to, such as preparing and salting some provisions which, during our laborious undertaking, might serve us, with fish and turtle, for our food, the whole colony started on their journey, armed to the teeth and accompanied by the dogs.

First marched myself and Tiger, as guides— knowing the country best, and being able to avoid a number of difficulties which, otherwise, might have impeded our advance. My father came behind me; ready at any moment to assist me did I stand in need of assistance—such as removing logs or stones from the path—and thus making the course of the sledge easy and smooth.

But though our vehicle was not excessively overloaded, and though we gave every needful assistance to the animals, yet did we not reach the bridge until night; so that we were once more compelled to camp on that spot, which, being so well provided with provisions and live cattle, we did with some little apprehension. But by means of a large blazing fire and one or two guns fired off at intervals, we escaped being attacked, and even enjoyed a tolerable night's rest.

Our first duty after breakfast the next day was to make the bridge, which would, indeed, have been an arduous task had we not have fortunately had the fallen cedar tree to assist us. By means of this the task become comparatively easy; for two of us were able to crawl over to the other side and guide the other trees, which had to be fitted in their fall.

About six trees, after a little chopping and cutting, made a firm and solid surface, over which we first placed a number of boughs and then covered the whole with a coating of grass and earth, mixed together, which made an excellent roadway, over which we passed in great triumph, the sledge and horses doing admirably.

The terrestrial paradise, which had so struck my father, was now before us; and, as I have already remarked, the turf being smooth and without undergrowth, our journey became both easy and pleasant, until we reached a spot which struck my father at once as that which would serve our purpose.

Several of the gigantic trees already alluded to grew at a considerable distance apart on the slope of a small plain, skirted by a deep but narrow stream that lazily meandered through this grove of trees, and which it was proposed should form one side of our stockade or wall. This once agreed to, a very peculiar style of house was, after some conversation, settled on.

The trees, I have said, were far apart, very lofty, and of considerable girth. My father smiled at my boyish desire to perch myself upon their lofty branches, but proposed a kind of tent house, which was not exceedingly difficult of erection, and, at the same time, was commodious and elegant.

By means of a ladder, some notches were cut in a circle round the tree, over twelve feet from the ground. Then a whole circle of stakes were planted round the tree, in distances of about a foot apart, strong powerful stakes, capable of supporting the weight of a man. Then, some stout poles, eight in number, were nailed by sharp wooden pegs into the tree, and then carried to eight stakes. Between each, there being four-and-twenty stakes, were placed two bamboos, and then laterally on these other bamboos were fastened.

Over this, by means of a couple of rude ladders, we carried a very strong roof, able to carry off the rain; but more by means of the slanting nature of the roof, than its own undivided strength. Some weights, such as stones and logs, were then added to keep the thatch down. For myself, I had misgivings, but my friends had not, as they proposed to improve, strengthen, and mend, even to giving a rude coat of india-rubber, of which I had told them such wonders.

The outside of the hut being thus finished, the building was divided into four distinct dwellings, with each a separate door, though with one inside, by which to communicate in bad weather. It is not to be supposed that the erection of such elaborate dwelling-places, well built, well fastened and plastered on the inside with a kind of mud, should have been concluded in a very short time; but, at the end of three weeks we had succeeded in erecting four of them, which it was calculated would suffice to lodge the whole party in comfort.

Then, a little way off, we built a log-hut for a common kitchen, as fire was a thing not often to be endured in these latitudes. Then there was a store-room, also built of logs, and very strongly and stoutly, so as to fly to it as a fort in case of an attack, and thus concentrate all our forces.

It was nearly six weeks ere we concluded these preparations; nor had we touched the stockade which was to surround the dwellings; that being a matter almost beyond our strength, and requiring the assistance of those dear ones for whom we were already labouring so hard, it was determined to adjourn that undertaking until we had fetched them to the island.

But rudely to furnish our huts and stock them with provisions, which were not perishable, was a task which was necessary, and which we performed with that resoluteness which all appeared to have acquired from the habit of shifting for ourselves which we had acquired since our shipwreck. Then another delay occurred. The season was unusually hot, and we had to take in all our corn and vegetables, and then turn up the ground for more. No sooner, however, had we sowed our seed, than we were surprised by a regular equinoctial gale, which threatened to shut us up in our huts for an early season.

This was very unpleasant, but there was no help for it; so we entered into possession of the largest and best of our huts, and there devoted our hours to the fabrication of tables, chairs, and such other articles of furniture as came within the reach of our mechanical genius. This kind of labour lightened our vexation and cheered our days; but in the evening, confined as we were, time would have been tedious indeed, if we had not found a delightful way of beguiling the hours.

My father, at my earnest request, began the story of his adventures and those of my family, since I had been separated from them, nearly six years before. My uncle and the skipper knew it all, of course; but my discovery of tobacco to them was delightful in the extreme, and enabled them not only to endure the narration, but to enjoy it.

For myself, these evenings were entrancing, more so than any of them could understand at the time.

CHAPTER CVII.

MY FAMILY.

When I made my mad and desperate leap from the wreck, it was the belief of all that I had sunk to rise no more; and though they made frantic and desperate efforts to reach the ship once again, the wind and waves were too much for them. At last, those who were in the boat resolved that to remain by the wreck was madness; and pulling the helm up, let her go before the wind.

The shore of the island upon which the vessel had struck was so bleak, and arid, to all appearance, on that misty day, that none cared even to attempt a landing, but flew right before the wind, in the direction of the continent, which the skipper firmly believed to be at no great distance. While endeavouring to take me off, they had lost sight of the yawl, and of it they never saw sight again.

The wind had much abated from the fearful gale which had been the destruction of the good barque Reformation, so that by baling and careful steering, they were able to keep themselves from sinking, until towards evening they espied a dark mass in the distance, which, on nearer approach, appeared to be a pile of rocks, against which the waves washed angrily.

The landing-place was difficult of access, but one of the negroes, who was a bit of a sailor, undertook to steer in the boat under the direction of the captain, who, moreover, directed everybody to look out, for there was little doubt everybody would be upset—a sorrowful look out for my mother and younger brothers and sisters. Every preparation was made to guard against this contingency, but the rollers were too much for them, and though the negroes leaped out to lighten the boat, it no sooner touched than over it went, without, however, any injury to anybody, thanks to the agility and energy of the blacks.

The boat, however, was so broken as to be a wreck, while very little was saved that was useful to the fugitives, whose desolation, dwelling as nearly all of them did on my loss, may be more easily conceived than faithfully described.

In deep darkness, on a bleak and arid shore, with a northerly wind blowing, they suffered all the same miseries which made my existence at first unendurable. They had some provisions, but no water, that having been lost in the staving in of the boat. In this condition, after some search, they found a rock of some dimensions, which sheltered them from the extreme severity of the blast. Thus huddled up together for warmth, the children pressed into their midst, they passed the weary night.

Nor did day bring them any sensible relief. They were in a land-locked bay, without any apparent means of ascending to the summit of the cliffs, while nothing could be seen save a thicket of very poor trees, and for eatables, a few mussels and cockles which clung to the rocks, and were eagerly taken off and devoured.

They, however, found water ere the young people began to know the horrors of extreme thirst, which was a great consolation to the elders.

This done, it was resolved that the strongest and most energetic of the sufferers should form a party to explore while the wounded captain and the women should stay with the children. There were two of my sisters nearly women, but the other two were much younger, while my brothers were mere children. All the rest of the party have been already mentioned.

My father, uncle, and the four blacks, with a youth who had been a midshipman on board, by name Andrew Gordon, the only one except the captain who did not join the crew in the yawl, for reasons best known to himself, composed the search party. They were wholly without weapons, none having been thought of in the hurry of escape.

They, however, cut long sharp-pointed sticks for their defence against wild beasts, and then began their peregrinations, which however, brought no other result for a long time but to show them the utter misery of their position. They were imprisoned in a space not a mile square, with no means of exit.

Suddenly, however, my father began to take notice of the birds which wheeled about at the mouth of the cavern—for he was in the very bay where I had been terrified by the discovery of the Indian girl's canoe—and knew them. This was a matter of considerable importance, as promising some food of a nutritious character. Some minutes after a negro, who had lagged behind, gave a shriek of delight; he had found a turtle benumbed by the northerly wind, and had turned it.

This was a great piece of good fortune, as not only would the flesh of the turtle be pleasant, but the shell would make a tolerable stewpan. On the strength of this a fire was made from great quantities of dry and drift wood on the beach—no negro being ever without his tinder-box—and a messenger despatched for the women and children, who, however, on first seeing the smoke had moved that way, leading the infirm captain.

Not a word was said of the adjunction of birds' nests to the turtle soup, which being salted from some natural salt-pans, proved most nutritious and agreeable to all. This unexpected cause of delay having been settled, it was resolved to explore the cave; and as it was at once found that it was a means of communication with the inner country, the whole party of men hurried through with great hope, delight, and satisfaction.

The aspect of the valley and lake with its many islands was grateful in the extreme, especially as the volcano being not burning, they were unaware of their fearful proximity to a volcanic mountain. Without a moment's delay, it was determined to let the women and young folk participate in the happiness which the discovery had generated in their minds.

While my father and uncle remained to explore the lake, and seek a place on its shores where something like an awning of leaves and boughs might be erected to protect them from the night air, the others hurried back to assist them through the cavern. Both my father and uncle were too sanguine as to the powers of so many to build something which would float them to a habitable part to feel any very great uneasiness.

This made them more sanguine and less uneasy at the idea of the fact of their having no firearms, which otherwise would have been a circumstance of serious moment. Besides, as they did not despair of repairing their boat, they purposed an early visit to the wreck, both to visit it and to search for me.

With knives, and by the exertion of main strength, they began to lay in the materials for two large huts—one for the men, one for the women—in which to pass this their first night in the interior of the island. And lucky it was that they had found it, for before midnight it blew such a gale from the northward again as would have frozen them to death in the bay below.

As it was, they passed but an indifferent night in such shelter, which all felt to be but poor protection against rain whenever it should come.

Next morning, therefore, it was resolved that they should erect huts on the islands, as they contained trees and bushes suited to such work, and being close to one another were easily reached by bridges. Before, however, proceeding to work, my father, uncle, and the captain had an earnest conversation; the result of which they communicated to my mother, who, though startled at first, soon agreed to the correctness of their notions.

They were outnumbered by the blacks, who, though hitherto good and faithful servants, had been in part doubtless restrained by the prestige of white power and dicipline. They were now their masters in every way, and should they become lustful of power would enact such scenes as had always disgraced slave insurrections.

But if they were conciliated the danger might be at an end. With this view they were all summoned to the presence of the whites, and thus addressed by my uncle:—

"You have all of you been in my family many years as faithful and attached servants. You were, in Virginia, my household property, as left to me by my forefathers; but misfortune levels all distinction. Here you are free, and free you will remain should fortune ever enable us to escape from this place; but should you desire to remain in my service, I promise, when we return, as I hope we shall, to Virginia, that you shall each have enough money and land to start in life with a fair prospect of success."

Loud cheers from the negroes followed this announcement.

"There is another point on which I desire to have satisfaction. You are young, and, I daresay, have all your affections, your dislikes, and likes. In a well ordered community, however small, the sooner matrimony is introduced the better. It is my wish that you one and all select your partners, and I as a magistrate, will at once marry you."

A Homeric shout of laughter from the men followed by conscious and downcast looks from the women, succeeded to this speech; and in another instant Peter stood hand-in-hand with Hagar, Jack with Bella, London with Sarah, while Crœsus took Venus, nothing loth, to the presence of their master; who with appropriate words and a repetition of proper forms, such as he had used a hundred times before in his own country, married them.

"That is a great load off my mind," said my uncle, as the loving couples moved away, no doubt scarcely knowing whether they were dreaming or awake. "A great source of dissension is removed."

And he was right. The negroes and their wives were from that hour the most faithful and obedient of servants. There was one whose eyes plainly bespoke a desire to follow their example, and that was the young midshipman; but a very timid hint was peremptorily stopped both by my father and uncle, and no more was said on the subject at the time.

The negroes were now set to work to prepare materials for permanent huts, while the three white men leaving Captain Thomas at home, determined to explore the island, in search of food of some kind, of which everybody stood pressingly in need. Now it was that they felt the want of firearms, as very many birds could be seen on all sides flying about, which would have been a very welcome addition to turtle and edible birds' nests, both very insipid eating unless properly cooked.

The negroes, however, soon found a remedy for this monotony of diet. The lake was full of fish of a goodly size, which they set to work to catch in a very original manner. They had neither hooks or nets, but in a very short space of time they divided off a shallow part of the lake with wattled stakes, leaving here and there narrow entrances. Here they fastened a number of supple boughs, in such a way as to form a kind of basket, wide at one end and narrow at the other.

This done, they stood watching, and when they saw a good shoal of fish, plunged into the water with long sticks in their hands, with which they drove the terrified fish forward until many of them were glad to escape into the enclosure through the long baskets, the narrow end of which closing as soon as they went through, there was no hope of return. The captured ones were of very many kinds, but one was new to all. It proved to be the armado, and was remarkable for the harsh, grating noise which it makes when caught by hook or line, and which can be distinctly heard.

This point settled, the three explorers, armed only with a stick and a knife, started on their exploring expedition, with the intimation that probably their absence might extend to the whole night.

CHAPTER CVIII.

A NEW ARRIVAL.

It was a remark made by all, that, considering the island was placed near the equator, it was very far from excessively hot. This appeared to be caused by the singularly low temperature of the surrounding water, brought there at certain times of the year by the great southern polar current. Of course, as upon my island, very little rain fell, except at stated seasons; but the clouds always hung low.

The consequence of this was that while the lower parts of the island were very sterile, the upper parts, at a height of some five or six hundred feet, possessed a damp climate and a tolerably luxuriant vegetation. This was, however, more perceptible on the windward side of the island, which is the first to receive and condense the moisture from the atmosphere.

But soon after they left the lake, nothing could be less inviting than the aspect of the island, which, it was at once apparent—to their great dismay—was volcanic. A broken field of black basaltic lava, thrown into the most rugged waves and crossed by great fissures, was everywhere covered by stunted, sun-burnt brushwood, which showed little sign of life. The dry and parched surface being also heated by the noon-day sun, gave to the air a close and sultry feeling, like that from a stove. Even the bushes smelt offensively, and the brushwood appeared at a distance as leafless as European trees in winter.

They had not advanced more than two miles, when they reached a sufficient height to become aware that they were upon a volcanic island, about a third of which was endowed with vegetation. Everywhere however, could be seen the signs of volcanic action especially in the form of small extinct craters, like circular pits, with steep sides.

The day was hot now, and scrambling over rough surfaces and intricate thickets, was very fatiguing. Suddenly, Andrew gave a cry. At last something in the shape of game had appeared. His companions turned, and saw two large tortoises, either of which could not have weighed less than two hundred pounds. One of them was devouring a piece of cactus; but no sooner did the youth approach, than he lifted his head, and stalked leisurely away; the second gave a shrill hiss, and drew in his head.

To allow them to escape was out of the question. They were too valuable as food, and as they afterwards found, abounded greatly on this island. They frequent, in preference, the high, damp parts, but live likewise, in low and arid districts. Some grow to prodigious size—the old males being the largest; the females rarely growing to a large size. Those tortoises which live where there is no water, and in the lower or more arid parts, feed chiefly on the succulent cactus. Those which frequent the higher or damp regions eat the leaves of various trees.

They are very fond of water, drinking large quantities and wallowing in the mud. The tortoises which frequent the lower districts travel long distances when thirsty; hence broad and well-beaten paths branch off in every direction from the sea coast. Many of the old *voyageurs* and buccaneers were thus able to find water when every other means had failed. When the tortoise reaches a spring, he buries his head in the water above his eyes, and greedily swallows great mouthfuls at the rate of about ten a minute.

When travelling, they go on day and night, never stopping until they reach their journey's end.

Knowing that to turn a tortoise is not, as in the case of the turtle, sufficient, a consultation was held, and a plan is she.

devised to secure the unexpected treasures. After some hesitation the midshipman cut his leather belt into two strips; and then, once on their backs, they were tied by the tail to a strong stake and left, while the explorers pursued their adventurous journey.

But I must return to the negroes and women, ere I give an account of my father's remarkable peregrinations and discoveries.

Each of the newly-married couples would necessarily require a cabin or hut; but with the fidelity of their race, when really attached to their masters, they set to work to build houses or wigwams for the whites, which they did in this way. Strong stakes were thrust into the ground at short intervals until a square was formed, when slighter boughs and withes were worked into them, in and out, until a pretty solid wall presented itself.

Between these were thrust grass, until the air was sufficiently excluded. They were roofed in the same primitive way, in order at all events to provide accommodation for the present against the weather and the heat, though, of course, they would be of no avail in the rainy season. The negro huts were to be on an island to themselves. This was their own wish.

They first made a hut for my father and mother and the two little boys. Next to this was one for my four sisters and my cousin, thus making one wall do for two huts. Then came a larger one, much wider than the others, to be used in the daytime; and after that, one for my uncle, the captain, and Andrew. They were not all completed in one day, but even the first night proved a welcome change from sleeping in the open air.

But when I visited the island another hut had been added, and as my very first question had been on this point, I will at once explain how it happened. The day had been sultry, and the little colony hard at work; when, towards evening, the women started, as they always did once or twice a week to bathe.

There had been a hurricane blowing for some days, but it was over now, and the weather had completely changed. Still, the wind was not down; and when the somewhat frolicsome party had descended to the beach, they found the surf running rather strongly on the shore. Still, by selecting a small, deeply-indented inlet, they thought they could enjoy an amusement, which in hot countries is, as it were, a necessity of life.

Polly had begun to cast off unnecessary clothing, when she gave a singular cry, and ran forward hastily in the water. She had caught sight on the coming roller, into which, as an experienced swimmer, she was about to plunge, of what at first sight might have been taken for a huge animal, but which, on a second examination, proved to be part of the mast or yard of a vessel.

But surely there was something living on it.

Polly saw it recede from her, but next minute it came up again with the roller, and my cousin, dashing forward, caught it in her hands. But it was too much for her strength, and had not the negresses rushed to her assistance she would have been carried out by the retreating waters. Their united strength, however, was enough to stay it; and the somewhat heavy log was dragged ashore, when the alarming discovery was made that to it was lashed the apparently lifeless body of a young girl.

All bent around her; and Polly, who seemed to look upon her as her legitimate prize, placed her hand upon her heart.

"It beats—she is warm—there is life in her yet," said she.

POLLY AND ANDREW.

No. 22.—Sailor Crusoe.

CHAPTER CIX.

WILD CATTLE.

To carry her to the huts, to wrap her in such things as they could spare, to rub her before a fire, was their first task; but only when some of the turtle soup had been poured down her throat did she seem to revive. As it afterwards proved, she was suffering from exhaustion and want of food, far more than from exposure to the merciless waves. When her eyes had opened once or twice and her heaving bosom began to inhale, with devouring eagerness, the air which apparently had left her for ever, she was placed in the girls' hut, and there nursed by Polly and Ellen.

Not a word was said to her. All she was allowed to do was to be still, and occasionally, when she awoke, sip the savoury and invigorating broth with which they continually supplied her.

Next day she was able to sit up; but when they began to question her, it was found that she could not understand one word that was said, while her language, though musical, was unintelligible. How this waif from the sea had been cast upon those shores, whence she came, and what she was, must then, for the present remain a mystery.

Polly looked upon her as her prize, and straightway got the negroes to build a special hut for the two, where she could, during every leisure moment she could bestow, devote herself to the education of the girl, whom my father and uncle declared to be no negress, but rather of some Arab race, though for want of a better name called her the Indian girl.

Gentle, docile, and at the same time ingenious, she was very useful. She could make snares for birds; while before she had been a month on the island, she had discovered a tree, which, by signs, she requested the negroes to cut down for her. They being now, in a way to be presently recorded, possessed of axes, did as she wished, and obeying her directions, cut it into a small canoe capable of holding, however, only one person.

No larger one appeared likely to made on that island, from a circumstance which is proper to nearly all volcanic islands—the smallness of the trees. This canoe was portable, and proved for fishing purposes on the lake exceedingly useful.

But let me turn to the regular order of my narrative, which I only interrupted in order to narrate an incident which I had so much at heart to explain,—how the Indian girl came among them.

My father, uncle, and Andrew, as soon as they had secured their valuable prey, continued their journey. It was satisfactory to know that the island abounded with animal food; but the elders did not feel satisfied until they discovered something which they could substitute for vegetables, without which it is well known that the human frame cannot exist. Exclusive fish and animal diet will not suffice to support life.

As they advanced they, however, did not seem to gain anything by the change. Having become entangled unwillingly in a narrow gorge, they turned away from the more fertile and happy part of the island, and came upon an undulating land, with a desolate and wretched aspect, which was everywhere covered by a peaty soil and wiry grass, of one monotonous brown colour. Here and there peaks and ridges of grey quartz rock broke through the smooth surface. In some of the valleys they saw small flocks f wild geese.

Finding that in this direction nothing was to be hoped for, they determined to turn to the right, cross the hills, and seek a more agreeable situation. The sides of the valley were very abrupt and steep; but after half an hour they were rewarded by reaching the summit, when they at once saw that they had reached a spot with scenery such as they might expect in that high latitude.

The slope of the hill was for some distance stony, and possessed of a very scanty soil; but as they neared the bottom, where flowed a small stream, they began to discover something like tropical vegetation; while on the opposite side of the water was an extensive wood. Forcing their way through the bushes, they were soon on the banks of the little river, when they made a discovery which was not without its pleasant side.

It was a small herd of wild cattle feeding on the edge of the stream. This was so far satisfactory that it appeared difficult to starve while so much meat was to be had; but the difficulty then occurred, how to take them; but as savages contrive to capture them with ease without firearms, it was a kind of reflection on their manhood, they thought, to have any doubt on the subject.

Now, however, the idea uppermost within their minds was, how to cross in face of the herd, which was guarded by one old bull and two young ones, which at sight of them had retreated with the cows, while the old bull stood still with outstretched legs, as if ready for the conflict. They had never seen such a magnificent beast. It equalled in the size of its huge head and neck a Grecian marble sculpture.

Their wish was to cross over, and the three shouted, in the hope of terrifying him; but, though he tossed his horns and bellowed at the unusual sound of the human voice, it did not make him stir from his ground. To cross in face of him was impossible, as he would gore them with his horns. After some consultation, it was agreed to retreat into the bushes and make a large circuit to avoid him, though all were eager to have a taste of buffalo for supper that very night.

This, however, was out of the question while in presence of the bull. So they retreated—the savage beast bellowing and roaring all the time—until they were masked from him by shrubs and cactuses of an extraordinary character. Some of a spherical character were six feet in circumference, while the common cylindrical or branching ones were from twelve to fifteen feet high.

In this way they were completely lost to his view; and at the expiration of a quarter of an hour were able again to turn to the river, which was in this place interrupted by a cataract formed by a rift of fallen timber, stones, and earth; which enabled them to wade over, knee deep, to the oppsite side. They were now in a wood with many bushes and creeping plants, that rendered their progress difficult.

It was proposed to halt here for the night if any kind of provision could be found, which, however, seemed difficult; so that they had to depend upon the pieces of roasted turtle which they had brought with them; and anything more nauseous to the taste after awhile can scarcely be conceived. The disgust with which a man even scents turtle after living upon it—as on one or two occasions they and I had to do—for days together, is something incredible. Turtle steaks for breakfast, turtle steaks for dinner, turtle steaks for supper, would sicken even an Esquimaux.

While devising in their own minds what was to be done, my father, to whose teachings I owed so much of my own happiness and comfort, was looking around him. He could not help admiring a huge thistle or cardoon, which grew on the banks of the river, in many places right up to the edge of the forest. Approaching nearer, he examined it carefully, and his companions saw him smile.

"What is it?" said my uncle.

"Well, it is only a thistle or cardoon," replied my father, who was still looking up at the gigantic plant, which towered a foot over his head; "but, with cultivation, we can make a fine vegetable of it. Botany teaches me that the cardoon and the artichoke are the same thing. Cultivated, the one becomes the other; while, if artichokes are left to grow wild, they degenerate rapidly into the common cardoon."

"But this is a matter for the future," observed my uncle.

"Not at all. All thistles are excellent vegetables, and until we can do better, these will keep off scurvy, which we have much to fear."

This discovery was, at all events, hopeful, but as not being of present use, was dismissed, while they looked around in search of a fit place for an encampment. With this view, they actually cut a way with their knives through the woods, until they reached a spot where the trees became loftier, being a kind of pine, under which no undergrowth is ever to be found.

It was something like the kauri pine of a large and celebrated island. How they could exist on this volcanic island was a mystery; but there they were, rearing their gigantic heads ninety and a hundred feet in the air, while many of them were thirty feet in circumference just about the roots. These trees are remarkable for their smooth cylindrical boles, which run up to a height of sixty and even ninety feet without a single branch. The crown of branches at the summit is out of all proportion small to the trunk, and the leaves themselves are small compared with the branches.

Here it was determined to camp, even if they were compelled to put up with turtle for their supper.

But such was not to be their fate.

CHAPTER CX.
ANDREW AND THE COW

ANDREW, whom I have so briefly introduced, was once a midshipman in the British navy; but being of a somewhat sullen and disagreeable temperament, had been compelled to leave from the simple fact of his officers making his ship too hot to hold him. He then, as was the case with many discontented spirits, determined on emigration to Virginia, a course pursued by very many gentlemen in those days, to the manifest and great advantage of his Majesty's colonies.

But his change of life not meeting with the approval of his friends, they had refused to assist him with money; so that he was compelled to take his passage on board the barque Reformation as second mate. Being, despite his defects, a gentleman of parts and education, he found some encouragement from the passengers in the cabin, which however, would not have long continued if the voyage had been prosperous, his attentions to my cousin being by far too marked to be pleasant.

Then came that fearful continuance of storms, such as surely no ship ever met with before, and which I have so fully described in the opening part of my narrative. Under these circumstances, all rivalries and differences were laid aside, in order that we might each and all look to our common safety; and the awful trials we met with, and the catastrophe that ensued, cast out all such thoughts from the minds of all.

But when the final event took place, Andrew, instead of going with the yawl, contrived to slip into the long-boat, so as to remain with a family in which he felt so deep an interest.

Thus much by way of explanation.

While my father and uncle were looking about with great anxiety, in the hope of finding even a ground nut to vary the monotony of their supper, Andrew had stepped on one side to pick up some wood with which to make a fire. He had scarcely gone twenty yards, when he came back on the points of his feet, his left-hand fingers on his lips, and his right raised in a warning way.

"Whist!" he said, as soon as he was near; "don't stir to help me, and you shall have a fine supper to-night."

They signified assent; and then, with the utmost caution, proceeded to follow Andrew, who was a Scotchman, and had had in his boyish days some experience of deer-stalking. In the present instance, however, the object upon which he was about to exercise his skill was a solitary cow, which, apparently attracted by the luxuriant grass of a small clearing, had strayed from the herd, and was enjoying a rich feed.

The cow, which was a very plump and handsome animal, was about a dozen yards from the edge of the pine grove, its back turned to those who were hopeful enough to look upon it as fitting prey. Both my uncle and my father, the moment they discovered the object of Andrew's solicitude, concealed themselves behind a tree, so as to leave him entire liberty of action.

The young man acted with a degree of calm deliberation which gave evident token both of courage and wit. The cow's head was so placed as to face the wind, which came directly from it to them; which was an element of success which all who have to deal with wild animals will appreciate. Both in the case of deer and swans, especially the latter, this is essential; as they will, when the hunter is to windward, smell him half a mile off, and never even allow of approach sufficiently near to give a chance of a long shot.

Andrew stretched himself at full length upon the ground, so as to be wholly concealed by the high grass, which, like all such rank vegetation, arose almost to the back of the cow. Then his sharp knife—his only weapon—clenched between his teeth, he crawled towards the animal by such slow degrees as scarcely to allow the grass to indicate his motions.

The lookers on were careful, by no act of theirs, to render his success uncertain. They did peer occasionally round the trunk of the huge tree, but with such extreme caution as to give no alarm. They, however, noticed with some anxiety that the cow was a little uneasy. Once or twice she flapped her tail, and even turned her head round, with a curious glance of her great eyes, but her intelligence failed seriously to alarm her.

Still she moved slowly onward, as cows will do when feeding, scarcely ever standing quite still for more than half a minute.

It was a time of great anxiety. In a situation like that in which my friends were placed, the bare question of existence was the first thing to be thought of, and all felt that to be driven to the nauseous food against which their stomachs rebelled, was not only unpleasant, but detrimental to their health.

At this instant the cow gave a great cry, as Andrew, rising

to his feet close at the animal's heels, and with a dexterity surprising in one who had long since deserted the sports of the field for the sea, gave the fatal touch with his knife to the main tendon of the hind leg.

The animal was powerless, and without almost any difficulty he drove his knife into the head of the spinal marrow, when the poor cow fell dead, as if struck by lightning.

Then his companions rushed forward and congratulated him warmly on his dexterity. Andrew replied with a mixture of pride and modesty becoming a successful hunter, and then bade them prepare a fire, while he got the elements of a supper, such as only a sailor having seen foreign parts could have dreamed of.

He cut good-sized pieces of the flesh with the skin to it, without the least intermixture of bone, and then proceeded to initiate his companions into the mysteries of an old buccaneer dish, known as *carne cum cuero*, or meat roasted with the skin on. The result proved to be as superior to ordinary roasting as venison is to ordinary mutton.

A large circular piece was taken out of the back, and this was placed upon the embers with the hide downwards and in the form of a saucer, so that not one single drop of the gravy was lost. As my father quaintly observed " if any worthy alderman had supped with them that evening, *carne cum cuero* would soon have been a celebrated dish in London."

Even allowing for the excellent appetite which exercise in the open air always gives, it is a fact patent to all hunters that the dishes made by experienced trappers and great Nimrods of the desert, are far superior to any which the utmost stretch of a professed cook's imagination could invent or carry out.

They supped with great glee, especially as, while waiting for his supper my father, with his keen eye made a remarkable discovery. He noticed while strolling about, a plant about four feet high, the leaves of which seemed familiar to him. He pulled them up, and, as he expected, found that to the root were attached some small tubers, the very largest of which were of an oval shape and two inches in diameter. *They were potatoes.* There was no occasion to be at all doubtful on that matter, as the very smell was enough. But on being roasted in the embers, they proved watery and insipid, but without bitterness. Still the discovery was important, as doubtless, with cultivation and manure, they would produce numerous potatoes and more leaves.*

CHAPTER CXI.

THE VILLAGE.

SATISFIED with these discoveries, the explorers determined next morning on taking the return road, as they would have something satisfactory to communicate to their friends. They were anxious, too, to see how the village had progressed. Determined, however, not to go back empty-handed, they loaded themselves with as much of the meat as they could well carry; indeed, even with more than was wise. But they halted in the middle of the day, and took such a meal as only hunters could put away.

Then, following the stream—not exactly coasting all its sinuosities, but keeping it in sight—they travelled as fast as possible in the direction of the lake, which was to the westward. In this, as in many other things, Andrew proved a good guide; but though they hurried as much as possible,

* This potatoe is found in the mountains of central Chili, and in numerous islands —See Humbolt and Sabine.

they still did not reach home that night; so encamped once more, and gladly enjoyed another meal of cow beef.

At early dawn—such was their impatience—they were again on their way; and, as they expected, before two hours were in sight of the village; where they were welcomed with all honours, and their news received with great delight. It must be frankly confessed, that to people who had been living on edible birds' nests, turtle, and fish, the meat was almost as welcome as the masters; but none ventured to make the remark.

The negroes, under the guidance of Andrew, started to the spot where the tortoises had been left; but, to their great disgust, they found that one—and that the bigger of the two—had succeeded in getting on his feet and escaping, after gnawing the leather away. But his brother in distress was secured and carried home in triumph.

For some days all hands were now engaged in completing the huts, in fishing, and in snaring birds; while the negresses, who were shrewd enough in these matters, scoured the woods for nuts, roots, and other substances which serve to vary the monotony of a diet solely composed of flesh—than which nothing is more insipid and wearisome.

The huts themselves wanted a great deal done to them, to answer English men and women's ideas of comfort. They had hitherto lain on the floor; but though this was perfectly satisfactory to negroes—who, as a rule, are quite satisfied with any place that will shelter them—my relatives had other ideas of comfort. At the same time, they only strove to raise their couches a few inches from the floor —the roof of the huts not being high, and it being well known that the nearer the sleeper is to the ground the less will the exhalations of the human body affect the human lungs.

All this, with hunting and fishing, took many days, but very pleasantly and agreeably spent, except for the constant regrets which were being experienced relative to my supposed unhapy fate. Then a grand hunt was decided on by all the men, which was the occasion on which the remarkable adventure took place which gave them another inmate to their village.

Now, my father was well aware that Pablina could neither have fallen from the clouds, nor have been floated from the opposite continent of America. He recognised her at once as belonging to one of those peaceable tribes, which being neither negroes or Arabs, travellers have given the name of Indian to, and he rightly judged that she must have been cast ashore from a wreck, though the whole terrible story of her misfortunes he could scarcely have imagined.

But a few days after the arrival of the girl, he took with him my uncle and the captain (now quite recovered) leaving Andrew to superintend the works, and walked to the very summit of the rocks, whence he had an excellent view of the whole sea, adjacent to the island. As his instinct had told him, Pablina had not come to the island by any magical means, but from a wreck which was floating at no great distance, at the mercy of the waves.

This was a source of such great hope and joy as they scarcely could realize to be true; and yet, she having been saved, what more natural? To those who read carefully the records of shipwrecks and losses at sea, it will be evident that one half the disasters which have occurred have been from the crews hastily deserting their vessels, which have been afterwards found and taken into harbour, to the great advantage of sailors.

Of course, as the wreck was afloat, there could be no doubt that on board were many treasures which, to the poor castaways, would prove invaluable. But how to reach it was a mystery which was not easily to be fathomed, until Captain John Thomas, whose voyages and perigrinations would have made a wonderful book, asserted that he could make a raft with which to reach the deck.

"All hands to the pumps," he cried, in his old-fashioned sailor way; "the weather holds good and will for some days, I'll warrant. Let's go to work at once, and we'll start at dawn."

The jolly sailor's enthusiasm was contagious, and away they went to the village to communicate the news. In ten minutes everybody was at work, tearing down trees, and collecting everything which could be useful to make a raft. This being done, they were dragged down to the sea shore, where the yard which had saved Pablina, and other driftwood, being put into requisition, a huge, heavy, and somewhat unwieldy fabric was manufactured.

Then great fires were made, and the whole party camped by the salt sea-shore, in order that the adventurers might start at break of day.

The dawn at length came. It was an extremely hot and sultry day, with very little wind, and that off shore, as otherwise the air would have been cool. Those who started on the journey were my father, my uncle, the captain, Andrew, and the negro boy Cudjie, which seemed as many as the raft would bear. But they had contrived a mast and a coarse sail of cowskin, which, with two large oars, enabled them to reach the vessel in an hour.

It was, as my father expected, a slaver and water-logged; so that all hope of reaching the hidden treasures out of its hold was out of the question. Still, their visit was not without its results. The captain's cabin was a perfect armoury, and the powder magazine being water-tight, they hoisted out every barrel, and found them undamaged. This was a delightful discovery, as it did away with all fear for the future as to a supply of game.

Guns, pistols, swords, and bayonets, were in abundance. These were placed upon the raft with the utmost care. Then a second raft was improvised from spars, tubs, barrels, and other pieces of wood—even the deck being broken up to make it solid. This was fastened together with some skill under the direction of the sea captain; who, moreover, though without any thought of immediate use, would set afloat, by the aid of empty air-tight barrels and cork floats, eight very handsome brass carronades, which he found on deck.

But the most treasured of their discoveries was the captain's chest.

The second raft was for the gunpowder, which it was determined to tow at a great distance. From among the spars still adherent to the masts of the slaver they rigged a mast, and also contrived a sail, so that they might go ashore easily in the dusk of the evening, when the cool sea breeze should set in upon the land. That there were other treasures in the vessel there could be no doubt, but the water had risen to a certain level, which rendered taking off the hatches dangerous, so they were obliged to be content with what they had, only plundering the steward's pantry besides of a few knives and forks, plates and cups.

Then, as the moon rose in all its beauty on the calm waters, and a still, soft breeze stole over the rippling waves, whispering, as it were, music to the miniature billows, they started, after noticing with satisfaction that wind, waves, and tide were carrying the heavy artillery towards the shore. The powder raft was towed a hundred feet behind; so that, despite every effort, it was many, many hours, ere they were in reach of the shore: so long, indeed, that they took watch and watch, and rested.

At length, however, just as the dying wind indicated a shift, Andrew leaped into the water and towed a line ashore to the head of a deep creek, where he made it fast. My father then followed, and as he did so a new discovery was made. The whole place abounded with seals. Every bit of flat rock and parts of the beach were covered with them. They appeared to be of a most loving disposition, and lay huddled together fast asleep, like so many pigs. Every herd was watched by the patient but inauspicious eyes of the turkey buzzard. This disgusting bird, with its bold scarlet head, abounded on the coast when the seals were in, which was only in those months when a regular northerly wind blew.

Andrew, and the rest of the party, now soon got the rafts into the deep creek and commenced unloading, being soon joined by the negroes, women, and children. The first task, before the heat of the day came on, was to carry the barrels of gunpowder into a safe place, which was found in the interior of the passage which led from the beach to the valley. About half-way, a moderate-sized cavern was found, into which, by great exertions, the barrels were carried and safely lodged for fear of accidents, the entrance being barricaded, and an arrangement made that Andrew should be the sole distributor of powder.

Never was there seen a youth so wild with delight as he was at having a gun and a brace of pistols. As to getting any reason out of him there was none. My father would have had him wait until the great heat of the day was past, but he was always wilful, and soon his companions could hear the sound of his rapid shots in the woods, and then all was still.

Until late at night no alarm was experienced, but then all began to have an instinctive dread of what might have happened. A party was at once organized to go in his search, all being well armed and provided with torches.

They had not far to go, for not a mile from the village they found what appeared to be his dead body, which they raised up. But life was not extinct. He breathed heavily, though in a high fever, and my father at once pronounced that what had befallen him was the result of a sunstroke, from which he might or might not recover.

He was carried home, treated as best they could, and did recover after some days' devoted nursing on the part of Polly, who, though she had no sympathy with his ardent affection at that time, was disposed to recognize his martial qualities and his many other virtues.

It was noted by all that when he began to get about there was a wildness in his eyes which boded no good, and it was resolved, under the plea that it would take a long time ere he could bear fatigue, to deprive him of the use of fire-arms. He accepted the prohibition sullenly, but seemed satisfied to make up for it by fabricating a rod, line, and hooks, with which he occupied himself half his time, doing thus great service to the colony.

CHAPTER CXII.

THE ABDUCTION.

DURING this time much had been done. With a view to the advent of the rainy season, the roofs of the huts had been strengthened with additional boughs and thatch. Then they were slanted over the eaves, and a ditch dug round to carry off the water. Care had been taken to have a due examination of the island, so as to find the line of high-water mark in the rainy season, and it was discovered that all the huts had been erected above it, which was a great consideration.

Then a field was planted with wild potatoes, and a large supply of salted fish and beef laid in, with every root and wild vegetable that might militate against the scurvy. One rather useful matter was found on some beech trees. It was a globular, bright yellow fungus, which grew in vast numbers. When young, it is elastic and tinged with a smooth surface; but when it comes to maturity, it shrinks, becomes tougher, and has its entire surface pitted or honeycombed. My father knew from travellers that it was eaten in Chili, Tasmania, and Terra del Fuego, where it is the standard article of food.

It is collected by women and children in large quantities; and eaten uncooked. It has a mucilaginous, slightly sweet taste, with a faint smell like that of a mushroom. With a people, who, with the exception of a few berries of the dwarf arbutus, make it their chief article of food, it must be wearisome enough, as fern was to the New Zealanders before the introduction of the potatoe; but, as an addition to animal food, it was well enough.

Such berries as proved on trial to be wholesome, were collected by Cudjie, the negresses, and sometimes by the children; and in this way a goodly store of provisions was prepared for the wet season.

Then a passage, with a roof, was made for each hut to the refectory, so as to render exposure to the weather unnecessary.

Meanwhile, another change was taking place. A friendship of the most close and earnest character had arisen between Polly and Pablina, even before they could utter one word that the other could understand. Now Polly set to work to teach the young girl, with a patience and energy which was delightful to behold. After they had completed the work of the day, which to them was light enough, they would retire to a little distance from the village; and then seated on a log, the schooling commenced.

As long as the lessons were confined to the names of things, it was easy enough; but when they began to attempt the interchange of ideas, it was another thing. The notions of the girl were very scanty indeed, but Polly was determined and firm in her resolve to teach; and ere two months they began to interchange sentences.

All this while they had a careful watcher in Andrew, who now openly, now stealthily, would walk around, as if desirous to join in their studies. But the severe coldness of Polly interdicted him. There was in her anxious desire to teach the poor Indian girl a partly selfish motive, which she treasured in her heart of hearts, and which, above all, she would not have him know.

Andrew grew more sullen every day, until one evening, with fire flashing in his eyes, he boldly addressed Polly, and asked her to be his wife. Hitherto, the colony, with one drawback, had been like a garden of Eden; but already had the serpent entered upon its precincts, as will ever be in this probationary world.

Polly firmly refused. She was engaged to another, and would never, no never, break her fealty. With a cry of rage and despair such as a demon might have uttered, he fled, nor was he more seen in the village of the lake. During my solitary residence on my island, at all events discord, and bad passions had been absent. But here, where a small nucleus of future races was collected the same could not be the case.

Let a hundred men and women land upon an island, divide it equally, parcel out every acre of ground; before twenty years one would be chief—either the ablest, the wisest, or the worst—some dozen would be a little aristocracy and court, and the rest would be, if not serfs, subordinates. In the record of the fortunes of the colony, both before and after finding me, it will be seen how, when some half dozen or more families come together, their interests must, in the end, clash.

When it was found that Andrew had absented himself every other man on the island, well armed, started in search of him. But not a trace could be found. He had vanished. As his sun-stroke had left decided results in the shape of weakness in the head almost approaching to lunacy, the general idea was, that he had committed suicide.

This was a terrible blow to so young and rising a colony, but worse was to come.

It was a whole fortnight before the excitement settled down, and the inhabitants of Volcanic Island came to believe in the death of Andrew. Then everything went on as usual, except that the elders spoke in whispers of the absent one. Polly and Pablina resumed their studies. The Indian girl began to understand English. Why had she feigned to know nothing when she first saw me? Ah, me!

Polly and Pablina, like all the young of their sex, began to be merry and mirthful. The Indian girl already understood little sentences. My cousin would still continue teaching her words; but, as a rule, contrived to initiate her in sentences.

"Now," said Polly, after a while taking up a new task, that of saying something the other did not understand, "I am thirsty—fetch me water."

Away sped Pablina, laughing heartily, for from some of the younger children she had heard this much. In about five minutes she returned with the cup brimming full. But Polly was nowhere to be seen.

"No hide—no fun," said Pablina; "water spill."

But no answer came. In a moment the mug of water was placed upon the ground, and Pablina was rushing into every corner. Still not a sign of the young girl. Wild with terror, Pablina rushed to the village and startled the peaceful colony from their quiet occupations.

Her signs, her broken English, were quite enough. They understood her but too well. In a moment armed and unarmed, with and without the resinous torches of the great pine trees, of which there was an ample supply, some went one way, some another; some crept silently about; while others shrieked and cried aloud.

Pablina was presently missed, which put the whole colony in an uproar. Traitors and serpents seemed to have entered Eden, at least so thought the dispirited and worn-out pursuers, when they returned after a fruitless search kept up in the darkness until midnight.

Then, and then only, utterly exhausted, they gave up the futile and hopeless search, and endeavoured to gain comfort and consolation from sleep.

It was grey dawn. All slept the slumber of the exhausted and the weary, when a loud cry, a cry that went to their very hearts, aroused them all.

It was Pablina, standing before the huts, worn, exhausted and footsore.

"Come," she cried, as soon as my father and uncle appeared before her.

They needed no explanation. They knew at once that the glorious and heroic girl had not startled them from their slumbers for nothing, and at once prepared to follow her.

Captain Thomas was left in command, with strict injunctions to keep good watch and ward.

The pursuers would have started without refreshments, but Pablina shook her head, and herself proceeded to take a hearty meal of prepared soup, which had only to be warmed. The others imitated her example, and in this way enabled her to obtain half-an-hour's rest.

No sooner, however, did she start than such was the pace at which she travelled, the men had to check her. Over hill, over dale, through valleys, through streams, she went, as the crow flies, without diverging to the right or to the left, and this for hours, carried on by that unerring instinct which seems to belong to savage races. At length she halted, and put her finger to her lips.

They were ascending a slope, which seemed to end in an abrupt and perpendicular rock, but in a few minutes the truth was revealed to them. They were on the edge of a deep but narrow gully, through which rushed a swift stream of water, while on the other side was a small platform; after which rose on high a very steep rock.

The sides of the gully were covered by bushes, and sloping upward from their side was a tree, which appeared to connect the two sides. Pablina signed to them to halt, pointing at the same time to a fissure in the opposite rock. Then, with a firm and courageous step, she placed her feet on the tree and began to cross.

"Back!" cried a horrid, wild voice, and a man clothed in the almost bleeding skin of a buffalo cow, with strange ornaments of boughs and tropical leaves, presented a pistol and fired, but without effect. When the smoke cleared away this was explained; Polly had rushed from the cavern, and, with the self possession of a heroine, struck up his arm.

This saved Pablina's life!

CHAPTER CXIII.

A SURPRISE.

THE young man turned round upon her with such a look that for a moment it was thought he was about to vent his rage upon her. During this interval Pablina was rapidly crossing the tree. Polly stood face to face with the maniac, looking him full in the eyes. Like many a man in his unhappy state, this cool and collected exterior was enough. Still, he was evidently not conquered, for, with a savage cry, he turned away, as if to rid himself of her influence.

As he did so, he found Pablina close to his shoulder.

The shock seemed too much for him, for, with a shriek of mingled despair and defiance, he turned and leaped wildly into the gulf below.

They rushed forward to see what had become of him, perchance to save him, but the waters had closed over him, and his body, in all probability, been carried away by the torrent.

This was, indeed, a sad tragedy for so young a colony, but there was comfort in the reflection that none of the survivors had anything to reproach themselves with. Indeed, there could bely but one opinion on the subject, and that was real no longer doubtful. His sun-stroke had weakened his intellect, and his naturally sullen nature acted on by fever, he had been wholly unanswerable for his actions.

Polly, whose energy and courage were all gone now, had to be assisted across the gully by the men, who then made a hand litter and bore her away. It was several days ere she could bring herself to speak of the events which had occurred during that eventful twelve hours, and when she did, it was with visible reluctance.

When Pablina ran away to fetch the glass of water, Polly burst out laughing at this practical proof of the progress the girl was making in English. This laugh was re-echoed close to her, and turning round, she saw Andrew in the act of putting out his hand to clasp her wrist.

His manner was sufficiently alarming, while his appearance was dreadful. He had been wandering through the woods, subsisting on roots and berries for days, until he had torn his clothes to ribbons. With the natural instinct of a man brought up in a state of civilization, and who, moreover, had his lucid moments, he had contrived to provide himself with a savage kind of dress.

Heaven only knows how it had come about; but there he was, with the skin of a fresh killed buffalo-cow clinging to his skin, while stuck in his belt were boughs of trees and tropical leaves fantastically arranged. His head-dress was of a similar character. In his hand was a huge club, a small tree torn bodily from its abiding place.

The precaution against allowing him to have fire-arms had been evaded. He had a pistol stuck in his belt.

Polly knew that the man was mad, and having, as she thought, least of all anything to fear from his violence, she rose firmly and faced him, looking him full in the eyes. Like all persons whose minds are affected, this was more than he could bear.

"So you have come back?" she said, gently but firmly.

"I have," he replied, in a hollow tone; "I have come to fetch my bride."

"Do I know her?" she said, gaily.

Andrew raised his eyes, gave utterance to a ferocious growl, and, before she was aware of it, snatched her up in his arms and ran away at the top of his speed, as if she had been a child, nor did he relax his rate of running until they were at such a distance from the settlement as to render pursuit almost vain. None of the pursuers thought of trying to track him by his foot marks but Pablina.

It must have been a picture, indeed, to have seen the Indian girl following the necessarily marked and easily found trail in the dark night by means of a torch. Probably but for this she would have come up with them, but the flickering of the resinous pine torch—this pine wood is full of resin—warned the cunning maniac, who made occasional detours to avoid being tracked.

It was in vain, however. Pablina, in the cause of friendship or of love, was a regular sleuth-hound, and though wearied from excitement and running, never once lost the trail. In this way she tracked them to the cave by the gully, and at once returned homeward.

Meanwhile, Andrew had been compelled to let Polly walk, to all her entreaties and prayers he replied only by silence and menacing gestures. Whenever she asked him to turn back and join the friends who would be glad to see him, he answered by pointing onward and flourishing his club. He was evidently in one of his dangerous moods, nearly all madmen of his calibre taking it by fits and starts.

Polly saw that the best way was to humour him, and, making no more resistance, walked onwards until she came to the cave. They crossed the bridge and entered the fissure in the rock. It was nothing more. A pile of grass in one corner, some dried meat and some bones, were all it contained.

Andrew, had, however, collected a good supply of dry wood, with which he made a fire at the entrance of the cavern, over which, when it had burned to embers, he cooked some buffalo beef and handed it to Polly. She with the greatest composure, accepted the offer, and ate. Indeed, she felt the necessity of keeping up her strength, as she knew not at what moment he might turn upon her.

But his manner soon became rather melancholy than ferocious. The fit was passing away, and presently all his savage tone subsided and he burst into tears.

"Polly," he said, sadly, "why is it I am driven out like a dog—why is it I have had to bring you here by force?"

"You left us, Andrew, of your own accord. For days you were looked for, until at length it was believed that you had perished. Then we all mourned for you."

"Mourned for me. Did you mourn, Polly?"

"Certainly—no one regretted your misfortune more than myself."

"I sometimes believe," he said, in slow, measured accents, while putting his hand to his forehead, "that I have been mad. But I am all right now, and shall remain so if you, Polly, will but love me and be my wife."

"You cannot," she replied, with great presence of mind, "you cannot expect me to give any answer to a man who confines me a prisoner. It is neither reasonable nor just. I will give no answer until I am free."

"You are very cunning," he said, with a strange light again in his eye; "but I will think of it. You may now rest in peace; I will watch."

And he went out upon the platform, nor did she see him any more until morning. How she passed the night she could scarcely describe, as though she fancied she slept she was not sure. But still, from the sense she felt of the shortness of time, she must have dozed.

Then he came in and gazed wildly at her, after which he again cooked some meat, and brought water in a broken horn, of which she made a breakfast. Suddenly he leaped to his feet, clutched his pistol, and rushed into the open air.

Polly followed him, and the rest has already been narrated.

CHAPTER CXIV.

AN IMPORTANT CAPTURE.

FROM this day, though all believed the wretched young man to have perished, strict injunctions were laid upon the girls to keep near the village and never to go about except in pairs. This injunction was scarcely necessary as far as Polly and Pablina were concerned, for they were more together than ever. A number of wicks had been prepared to serve them during the wet season from the pith of some bushes, and the two girls while doing such work as this would converse.

Then there were other sedentary occupations, such as mending and making. The clothes of European manufacture were put on one side by the men as soon as they had skins enough, which the negroes had a peculiar way of preparing so as to make them soft and lissome. They were then cut out by the experienced matron of the family and given out to the girls to sew, which they did with needles made of bone and coarse thread formed from sinews of animals.

Soon after the occurrence above related, the two young girls, while wandering together in the woods, discovered the spring which I afterwards found, and there erected a bower, where they and my sisters came to work in the great heat of the day. They did not, however, devote themselves solely to sedentary employments, often wandering in the woods in search of fruits and flowers.

Ada, my youngest sister, on one of these occasions made a discovery, which it is surprising had not been made before, as all these islands, and, indeed, the whole continent, abounds with them. She saw some curious things hanging from a tree, which on examination proved to be gourds. Now, as my sister and my cousin shared my knowledge of natural history, they proceeded to collect a number of the finest, with which they returned to the village.

Their return with their treasures was exceedingly welcome, as my father and uncle knew their numerous uses well. To the savages they are invaluable, as they use them to store their food and drink in, besides serving as cooking utensils. The great voyager, Captain Cook, it was, I believe, who explained how, when they wanted to dress food in one of these rinds, they would cut the fruit into two parts and scooping out the inside, would then put water into one of the halves with whatever article of food they desired to dress.

This done, a number of clean stones were made red hot in a contiguous fire, and thrown in one after another until the water was nearly boiling, when the meat was fit to eat.

This, however, was an experiment too tedious for so busy a colony, all preferring to be satisfied with broiled and roasted meat while there was so much to do on the island. They had no grain to sow as I had, but they had the potatoes to plant and even the cardoons to experiment upon, though not expecting much result at first.

My father, uncle, and two of the negroes, at the suggestion of my mother, started one day on an expedition, of which they said nothing to the young folks, for fear of failure, but which was of singular importance to their own welfare.

They started at early morning armed to the teeth, as if bent on a buffalo hunt, taking with them coarse baskets of withes, wove by the negroes, to carry the meat in. All visits to the territory owned by the buffaloes were made with great caution, as the bulls were very dangerous, and though in most cases fire-arms were effective in checking them, yet they had no desire to exercise any of that wanton destruction which is fast destroying the cattle of the Pampas and the buffaloes of the great American prairies.

Besides, the bulls were coarse eating, so that, except in the case of one or two savage old bulls, that were good for nothing, they were very cautious as to destroying the sources of their supply.

Crossing the river, they crept through the wood with extreme precaution. They were by this time pretty familiar with the haunts of the animals, and at length, after some search, found exactly what they wanted.

It was a bull, a cow, and a very young calf.

This discovery having been made, the three white men and the two negroes arranged their plans. It was in this instance absolutely necessary to sacrifice the bull; but as being very young, he would serve for meat, this would be the less objectionable. The bull was at some little distance from the cow and calf.

My uncle and the captain posted themselves in such a way as to be able each to aim at one shoulder of the bull, while, the negroes and my father stood behind some bushes with coiled ropes in their hands. Then when all was ready they fired. The bull roared and bit the dust, while the cow, to their great astonishment, came at his call, as if totally unconscious of the effect of the shot.

This placed the negroes behind her, while my father suddenly appeared in her front. The cow paused in her career and stood still. Before, however, she could recover herself

No. 23.—SAILOR CRUSOE.

FIRST MILKING.

and make any attempt at escape, a rope round her hind legs and one cast over each horn rendered it impossible.

While this was taking place the hunters had put the wounded bull out of his misery, so that they remained in full possession of the cow and calf. Still, the cow was very difficult to manage, kicking, struggling, and fighting in a desperate way. But the negroes soon remedied this, by fastening her fore legs together and bending down her head by means of a rope fastened to the horn.

Still the obstinate animal would not move, when one of the negroes, with a loud laugh, caught up the calf, which had stood still all this time, and carried it off in his powerful arms. The little animal set up at once a terrified bleating, and the cow, with a sympathetic low, made an effort to run after him. This, however, brought her to her knees. Having assisted her up, my father bade the negro go more slowly, and in this way the cow was able to follow.

About a mile off they halted at a stream, and allowed the cow to drink, and also gave liberty to the little calf, which was scarcely able to walk. It eagerly crept to its mother's side, and sucked. After this the cow appeared more resigned, and, after some considerable labour, they were successful enough to bring her to the village, where her advent was received with loud shouts of triumph and rejoicing, especially from my mother.

She had long dreaded sickness with her children; but what a precious resource had she not now in milk.

The cow was placed in a hastily-formed enclosure with the calf, and her head set free, though her fore legs were still kept together. Then an ample supply of grass and such herbs as she usually fed on was given to her, with a moderate supply of salt, and the care of her then delegated to the children.

This was the first white day in their calendar, and so important was the capture considered, that next day all hands set to work to build her a large and roomy stable for the wet season, as well as to cut grass for hay, that she might not want for food during a period when her milk would be of immense consequence to the younger members of the family in particular.

CHAPTER CXV.

BUILDING A STABLE.—FIRST MILKING.

THE few tools which had been found on board the slaver—such as axes, swords, and tomahawks—were divided between the whole party of men. It was the intention of my father to erect a log-hut for the cow, as now that proper tools were in their possession this would be comparatively easy.

Directions were given to all to select trees of moderate girth, and as much as possible of the same size. Two sets of these, as fast as they were brought in, were cut into lengths of twelve feet, and two sets into lengths of ten feet. Then, in the shorter lengths, a groove was cut, upon which the ends of the longer logs, their extremities slightly pared down, were laid and fastened by means of ironwood pegs.

By the joint hard work of all, even to the women and children, before night a very neat structure stood up; that is to say, the back wall and the two sides. The front had to be made in a different way. Two upright posts having been fixed to form a doorway, the next day's work would be cutting shorter logs, to make the two vacant spaces equal to the others.

At early dawn everybody was up and at work, this task being truly a labour of love. While one party were at work completing the front in a satisfactory manner, the other prepared the materials for the loft and roof, which it was essential should be water-tight, for the preservation of the hay.

As soon as the erection of the building was completed, the negroes, who are very ingenious and clever at this sort of thing, began to work at the roof. First, by means of wooden pins, they fastened a number of chips to some lateral thin poles. Then came a layer of huge leaves of certain tropical plants, placed as evenly as possible. Over this they plastered a mixture of sand, mud, and shells, which, thanks to the extreme heat of the sun, became so baked that it even resisted the tropical rains of that region.

People at home, who talk of a severe shower, have no conception of the character of a shower in the tropics. As the storm passes over the forests, the sound produced by the drops pattering on the countless multitude of leaves is very remarkable. It can be heard at a distance of a quarter of a mile, and is like the rushing of a great body of water.

My father said that nothing could equal the pride and delight of the children at seeing their cow-house completed, except that they all declared it was a much better house than any of them had. But my father indicated the immense importance to them of an animal which, during the rainy season, would provide both meat and drink.

My father would generally, while the evening meal was about, improve the opportunity to enlighten the minds of the young people; or, if they were at play, he would converse with my mother and his friends as to their future prospects. Besides, it was delightful and delicious in that hot climate to sit and watch the evening pass into night. The melody of home was, however, wanting, as nature in these climes chooses her vocalists from more humble performers than in Europe.

A diminutive frog of the genus, known as *hyla*, sits upon a blade of grass about an inch from the surface of the water, and sends forth a singularly pleasing chirrup, and when several are together they sing in harmony on different notes. Various *cicadæ* and crickets at the same time keep up a ceaseless shrill cry, which, when softened by the distance, is not unpleasant. Every evening after dark this great concert commenced, and often did I listen to it.

Then out would come the fire-flies, flitting from bush to bush. On a dark night I have seen their light quite two hundred yards distant. It is a curious and remarkable fact, that in all the different kinds of glow-worms, shining clusters, and various marine animals, the light is always of a well-marked green colour.

Soon after the erection of the cow-house, the children began to hold secret conferences. The cow and calf were their delight, and by degrees as they collected fresh grass and other vegetables for the ruminating animal, they began to offer her food from their hands. When she found that they did not attempt to hurt the calf she began to be very tame, and after a time it became a regular thing to feed them from their hands.

But the greater question which occupied the young people was as to the milking of the cow. Everybody wanted to be the first to attempt this rather serious operation, but after considerable discussion it turned out that no one knew anything practically on the subject except my sister Ellen, and so it was determined that she should be the milkmaid.

It was further determined by this little parliament that the whole affair should be juvenile, and that the parents and elders should not be admitted to the conference. They wanted to have the fun of a surprise, which would have been perhaps dangerous, except that the cow was so well fed as to have gradually come to be fond of its little providers.

One morning, accordingly, when my father and the elders rose, not a child was to be found. They had all vanished, even those who might rightly be called young women having accompanied them. At first my father and mother thought they had gone to bathe, but then certain mysterious preparations, which had been noticed, recurring to her mind, my mother had made a shrewd guess at the truth.

The children had sought out the very largest bottle gourd they could find, and having cut it in two, had made two pails, with withes for handles Then Ellen had manufactured herself a hat of palm leaves, and fancifully adorned the poor remains of the dress she had been wrecked in. Besides this, while the parents were out, the children had caught the calf and tied it away from the mother. Under these circumstances, my father and mother determined to hurry to the cowhouse.

This is, however, what had happened.

CHAPTER CXVI.

THE PYTHON.

THE children were anxious, above all things, to be able some morning to present their mother with a bowl of hot milk, and for this purpose it was that they entered into the conspiracy to which we have already alluded.

Ere day had broke they had sallied forth on what was indeed a most perilous adventure, for when they reached the enclosure, they found the cow in an almost frantic state. Not only was she bellowing for her calf, but the unwieldy state of her dugs showed how much she was in need of some removal of her milk.

They halted and looked at one another. My sister, who had a coarse three legged stool which the negroes had made for her, did not like the idea of giving up her venture, and at last, when the cow began to feed out of their hands through the bars of the gate, they boldly, or rather recklessly entered the enclosure. No sooner did they do so than Polly and Pablina caught hold of the cow by the horns and held it while the children stood back half amused and half terrified.

The cow was inclined to be restive, and would probably have disengaged itself from the hands of the two girls had it not been for the rapid action of Ellen. She popped down her three legged stool, placed the pails at her feet, and began to milk. The animal—which was evidently suffering great pain—stood still, as if instantaneously relieved, and allowed the necessary operation to be performed with a meekness truly wonderful.

At this moment it was that my father and mother came up, in some little alarm; they gently chided them all for attempting what might have been a most dangerous experiment; but the children replied by a shout—showing the huge gourds of foaming milk, which they proceeded to carry in procession to the village, where it was received with general applause.

The calf having at once taken to green meat, was allowed a small portion of milk and water, and then, after a time, allowed to return to its mother; which scarcely seemed to notice its arrival, but remained content to be milked twice a day by Ellen; and even quietly submitting to be let out to pasture by the children, with hoppled knees and a cord round one horn.

This was the last event of any consequence which took place ere the rainy season, which came on suddenly and drove them all to their tents. Lucky it was they had wicks and a supply of oil, which, though coarse and rancid, was still very useful. The only means they had of preserving it was in the bottle gourds, of which they had cut down and hastily dried a great many.

The wet season was a very dull one, except, perhaps to Polly and Pablina, who were never wearied of their conferances. They would, for lessons, retire to the small hut, and there pass whole hours in conversation. They began now to understand one another. The others employed their leisure in fabricating articles of furnature out of wood collected for the purpose.

There was another undertaking in which all felt a considerable interest. The negroes had found some fibres fitted to the fabrication of nets for fishing, and one of them being exceedingly skilful in such matters, had taught all the others; so that it appeared likely they would before the rainy season have a net capable of taking enough fish for the whole party.

Then there was the cow to be milked and fed, and now and then the fishery to be visited, as this was all in the way of fresh food which they had during the whole season. This enclosure had been much enlarged and improved previous to the rainy season. Its banks had been made higher; and numerous openings made by which every species of small fish could enter, without the large ones being able to depart.

In time—by extending it, pond after pond, and taking care to give them a constant supply of food—they became rich and valuable. Whenever a haul was made the large fish were thrown into the "parc," the middling ones kept for food, and the small ones returned to the water.

No sooner did the rain cease to pour down than forth ran the whole colony to gaze upon the sky so long concealed by clouds. The air was still delightfully cool and fragrant, and the drops of dew still glittered on the leaves of the large liliaceous plants which shaded the borders of the lake. Standing on its deep green shores, it was delightful to watch the various insects and birds that flew past. All were struck by the thin vapour, which, without changing the transparency of the air rendered its tints more harmonious and softened its effects. The atmosphere, seen through a short space of half or three quarters of a mile, was perfectly lucid; but at a greater distance all colours were blended in a most beautiful haze of a pale French grey mingled with a little blue.

But the horn of the hunter now sounded. Everybody was impatient to be stirring. The housekeeper clamoured for fresh meat, and so two expeditions were at once organized —one in search of buffalo, and the other of fresh vegetables. The former consisted of my father, uncle, and the captain, with one negro, Peter. The other negroes undertook to see to the cow and calf, now becoming strong and hearty; while the females devoted themselves to the plantations, where the potatoes and cardoons had been sown.

It was late in the day when the expedition started, as is was intended to camp on the edge of the buffalo grounds, so as to commence hunting at break of day. Towards evening the whole party were to join them, in order to carry home the expected produce of the chase in triumph. It was with no small difficulty that they succeeded in making a fire, and then only in a somewhat peculiar manner.

On the edge of the forest, and at no great distance from the river, was a solitary tree, that had somehow been left alone by the forest, and falling upon an arid soil, or rather, the fertile earth being swept away by the rains, had began to rot, and the inside was quite eaten away. The trunk was, however, only hollow to the height of about eight feet, so that the opening being to the leeward side, the inside was perfectly dry.

The hollow was, indeed, a kind of tinder-box, which they ignited with ease, and which soon was a cheerful fire. By degrees the trunk and bark began itself to ignite, and suddenly a flame catching the upper part of the tree, the pith became first red hot, then caught flame, and in an instant the whole trunk was a hollow tube, up which the fire rushed with a perfect roar.

This was rather serious, as did the somewhat tall tree fall in the direction of the forest it might set the whole in a blaze. To prevent this some stout stakes were cut, with which to guide it in its course, and as soon as the fire had sufficient hold on the bottom of the trunk they assisted the progress of the flames, and at length had the satisfaction of seeing the tree bend gently and fall towards the river.

They now had a glorious bonfire, behind which they gladly assembled themselves to pass the night, nor did any of the wearied travellers rise before the sun had risen an hour in the eastern sky.

My father shook himself and advanced towards the stream to sluice his face, when he saw, on a small black rock close at hand, a gaunt, nearly naked figure of a man, gazing thoughtfully, almost wistfully, at the camp.

"Massa Andrew!" cried Peter.

My father, startled in the extreme, waved to him to come into the camp, but he did not move, except to glance at the shelter likely to be afforded him by some very large trees with low branches, which were close behind him. A whispered conference now took place, and the whole party dispersed, determined to effect his capture, as in his present mood he was likely, while at liberty, to be very dangerous to the colony.

Though he saw them advancing towards him, he did not seem to intend moving, nor did he turn to go until they were within ten yards of him, when he leaped off the rock. All shouted frantically to him, for as he did so they saw the huge head of a python, which, uncoiling itself from a large branch, prepared to strike at him in the way usually employed by these hideous and frightful creatures.

The python is a native of Asia, and is commonly found in India. The dimensions of this reptile are often very great. Specimens have been seen measuring twenty-five and thirty feet in length.

But Andrew saw him not, and not until the huge beast had him in his folds did he become aware of his danger. The python now kept his tail only fastened round the roots of the tree, and commenced that kind of pressure which in five minutes would have utterly destroyed life. But axe, sword, and gun were brought to play upon him.

My father and uncle fired both at once, the muzzles touching his body, the captain and the negro chopped furiously with their sword and axe, until the frightful monster, cut in three pieces, was writhing on the ground. My father had drawn his pistol, and it required one more shot ere the vast monster lay in convulsive agonies on the earth.

Then they looked for Andrew, if Andrew it was, but he was nowhere to be seen.

CHAPTER CXVII.

THE BUFFALO CLEARING.

THIS incident, which did not take five minutes in all, caused great emotion in the whole party; and while they deeply regretted having allowed the maniac to escape, yet could they not but rejoice at the destruction of the snake, which would not have been so easily effected had it not attempted to destroy Andrew in the usual way adopted by this destructive and horrible race.

A silent horror brooded over the whole party as they moved away from the body of the huge python.

"Pretty island this," said Captain Thomas, with a hitch of his nether garment; "we shall be ate up one after another."

"I think not," replied my father; "such animals are very rare on islands. It is, probably, only a stray one from the continent, though how it came here is a mystery I cannot solve. My wish is, that we keep a good look-out when near trees, and never go out alone; but that neither the existence of Andrew nor the snake be mentioned to the women."

Every one having acquiesced in this, and it being now advancing day, all returned towards the spot where they were to penetrate the woods towards the clearings inhabited by the buffalo. But it was with evident reluctance that any entered the woods, and once they had done so, every eye was fixed upon the boughs of the trees, as if they were all nests or dens of serpents. The negro rolled his eyes, and twisted his body about in the most ludicrous manner possible; but being really a brave fellow, and still feeling within him the spirit of obedience to his masters, kept close to them.

The forest, however, was traversed without much difficulty, except what arose from the thick entangled bushes, but not a sight of anything larger than birds was observable. They were started at every step, and the sight of many of them suggested to my father another excellent source of occupation for the children—that of keeping fowls, which is always desirable, to say nothing of having eggs. But it was necessary for this purpose to select some appropriate birds, which had not yet been seen.

The clearing before them was that in which I myself met with my remarkable adventure with the buffalo, which had been so near costing me my life. It was not a circular clearing, but seemed to be carried through the forest a considerable distance, here half a mile wide, and then, perhaps, narrowing to a dozen yards.

On that part of the prairie which they had just reached not an animal was to be seen, so that they cautiously crept along the edge towards the passage leading into the next clearing, when their attention was suddenly arrested by a terrific uproar. They could not for awhile make out what it meant, until suddenly the whole scene became presented to their view.

Two huge buffalo bulls were facing one another with terrific roars, while a small herd of cows—the cause of contention—stood still at no great distance, evidently watching the affray with mingled anxiety and alarm. The bulls were pawing the ground, and tearing it up with great fury, all the time lashing their sides with their tails, and roaring in a frightful manner.

Then suddenly, with a furious bellow that made the echoes of the forest ring again, they rushed at one another heads downwards, and a battle began which seemed likely to prove fatal to one or the other, if not both. This result is very common in combats between deer with large horns, which, becoming inextricably entangled, both remain locked together until starvation ends their dreadful sufferings.

The rush of the buffaloes one against the other was so terrible, that they both fell to their knees as if struck by lightning, but getting up almost as quickly as they were down, there began a series of rushes, gallopings, feints, and attacks with horns, until both were running with blood. It was a very grand but, at the same time, terrible sight. One appeared more distressed than the other, and his opponent, apparently thinking he had had enough, was moving off in the direction of the herd, when the other, bending his head low for a last charge, caught him in the side, and inflicted so terrible a wound as to cast him to the ground, and almost immediately to cause death.

Then the victor stood still, gave another awful bellow, and walked slowly away towards his cows. But the hunters had by this time crept towards them, and selected two of the fattest, which they brought down by their guns. The bull for a moment turned round, as if inclined to make a rush, but influenced, perhaps, by his wounds, again turned, and fled with such incredible rapidity, followed by the cows, as to soon place them far out of their reach.

No sooner was the coast quite clear than they proceeded to secure their prey, which was very valuable both for present food and for curing for the future. This they had arranged to do on the spot; so leaving the negro to act the butcher, in which character he was very clever, the others proceeded to erect a kind of shed under which the whole party might pass the night. This was nothing more than a sloping roof of boughs and leaves of sufficient thickness to keep out the dew.

This took, however, some hours, and when they turned to examine the progress made by the negro, they found that he had already cut up the three animals into large joints, but had, by my father's instructions, selected a fine joint or two with the skin on to be cooked for supper, as none had forgotten the delicious roast which poor Andrew had formerly given them.

They were, however, excessively amused at the way in which Peter was about to make a fire. Let a negro be lost ever so far in the woods, without flint and steel, and let him have anything to cook, there is no fear but what he will make a fire. Peter was an example of this, for while the others had been at work, he had discovered a peculiarly white and light wood, well-known to him (the *Hibiscus titiaceus*), and which was the most common one used for the purpose.

He had then cut two pieces off, in one of which he had cut a groove, while the other he had sharpened. Then he began rubbing the blunt end into the groove as if to enlarge it until, by the rapid friction, the dust become ignited, when with moss and small sticks he soon made a flame. The fire was produced in a few seconds, but to anyone who had not understood the act it would have required great exertion. On or two occasions I myself, greatly to my own delight, succeeded in igniting the dust.

Necessity is the mother of invention, and this method is common; but each country has its own method. The Guachoes of the Pampas have a peculiar way of their own. They take an elastic stick about eighteen inches long, press one end on their breast, and the other pointed end into a hole in a piece of wood. Then they rapidly turn the curved part like a carpenter's centre-bit.

But Peter had, in addition to giving them this important lesson in woodcraft, made a great discovery. The whole circuit of the clearing, never before visited by them, was, as it were, one huge orchard. He called my father's attention to his discoveries, who was equally amazed and delighted. On every side were thickets of bananas, the fruit of which lay decaying in heaps on the ground. Then down towards the stream was an extensive brake of canes, which could not but be useful; while a rivulet that ran at one end of the clearing to join the larger stream, was shaded by the dark-green, knotted stem of the ava, so famous among travellers for its intoxicating qualities. It has an acrid and unpleasant taste, and would generally be pronounced poisonous.

"But, Massa, buckra, look at dat noo," said Peter, as he held up a root—that of the wild arum, which is good to eat when baked; while its leaves are as valuable as spinach.

"Upon my word, Peter," said my father, "you have made good use of your time."

"Yah! yah!" cried Peter, holding his left hand behind, "and what do yah tink o' dat?"

As he spoke, he produced an undeniable yam, one of the most excellent and valuable of fruits.

The yam is a large fleshy root, eatable when boiled o roasted, of which there are several edible kinds, all natives of tropical climates. They are very useful, as they will eat like potatoes, for which they are a good substitute. The negroes call them sweet potatoes. They keep a considerable time in the ground without spoiling; and are eaten instead of bread or potatoes, while the flour is made into bread or puddings. The people of Otaheite are said by the late Captain Cook to make a favourite dish from the root of the white yam, with the pulp of plantain fruit and grated cocoa nut.

There is nothing like the instinct of a negro to find out all that is worth eating. As, in general, his enjoyments are purely material, his whole mind is fixed on the best way of satisfying them. Had I been fortunate enough to have had one of the negroes with me, many of my severest trials would have been spared me.

All, however, now were hungry; and while waiting the arrival of the whole party, had decided on making a hearty lunch. My father would have hastily toasted some pieces of meat on the embers, but the negro checked him.

"Golly! massa," he said, with a sly look at his master, "him show you some nigger cookee. Dis child taste many in de woods round massa's plantation."

The negro had by this time made a good fire, placed a score of stones, of about the size of cricket balls, on the burning fire. In about a quarter of an hour, the fire was consumed to embers, and the stones hot. While this was being done the negro, with a skill and agility which surprised all wrapped up pieces of meat and yams and bananas in banana leaves. Then he placed these green parcels in a layer between two layers of hot stones, and covered the whole up with earth, so that no smoke or steam could escape.

In about a quarter of an hour their hungry appetites were rewarded by a most delicious meal, admirably cooked.

This over, further preparations were made for the night; and then, Peter being left as head cook to prepare a meal for the whole party, the others started to the place of rendezvous, which was on the edge of the stream.

CHAPTER CXVIII.

JERKING BUFFALO.

THE spot selected was where the stream, being extremely shallow, had spread out to a great width, which, it seemed, would not be easy to be crossed by the young people without wading, which would be injurious to their clothes, already not in a very good state of repair. But my father, uncle, and the captain, soon saw a way of remedying this, as the stream was full of large stones, which had only to be moved a short distance to make a line of stepping stones, just above the level of the water.

A bridge was even contemplated, as being both easy to be made, and comfortable; but, of course, that matter was reserved for future consideration.

According to a previous understanding which had been come to, three guns were fired towards evening, as a signal; and soon after, a shot being fired in reply close at hand, the cavalcade appeared, the negresses carrying my two little brothers, of whom more particularly at a future date.

They had all been at work all day, and were glad to be near the end of their journey, and equally glad to see the others all in safety. The river was crossed amid much merriment and laughter, and one or two mishaps, such as Hagar plunging into the water, with my youngest brother on her back, and thus exciting the jeers—good-humoured enough—of her companions.

Once on the other side, everybody was hurried forward as quickly as possible to the clearing of the two buffaloes, where a cheerful fire and a copious meal awaited all. The meat cooked in its skin excited universal admiration; but the bananas and yams brought down a torrent of questions and exclamations of delight, which were not easily repressed.

"You have to thank Peter for it," said my father; "and now, to satisfy these young people who desire to know what a banana is. The banana is of the order *musa*, and is one of the most important of those found in tropical countries, to which the species are confined in a wild state. It is, whether raw or cooked, rather a necessary article of food than a luxury. Three dozen fruits on an island where the mean heat is seventy-five degrees (Fahrenheit) will support a man instead of bread for a week, and is better suited to him than that kind of food."

This allocution being pronounced to hungry people, who were busily engaged in filling their mouths, was listened to without interruption; but no sooner was the meal over than the whole party scattered over the forest prairie, though with strict injunctions that none were to go out of sight of the fire. The elders, including my mother, occupied themselves in giving a finishing touch to the two sheds, which were to contain, one the men, and the other the women.

Soon that plain, once the abode only of the savage buffalo and other wild animals, resounded with the merry laughter of children and young girls engaged in games suited to their ages. My father and mother, however, observed with concern that Polly and Pablina were always accustomed to avoid all these boisterous demonstrations, and to walk arm-in-arm apart from the others, never by any chance joining the children in their healthful games and amusements.

They conversed in whispers, and they spoke of me.

Yes, this was the secret which had been so well kept, and which, now that Pablina began to talk with some little fluency, was the constant theme of their discourse. Polly had, during that awful moment which followed the leap for life, caught a faint glimpse of the island behind the rocks on which our good ship had been wrecked, and the faithful heart nurtured in her bosom a belief that I might still be alive.

Her sole thought, then, was that of coming, as soon as possible, to my relief.

This was the plan which for months had formed the staple topic of their discourse, and which was their thought both day and night. But hitherto they could not decide upon any course of action, though a boat was the only hope they could have of release. A boat they had, it is true, made for Pablina by the negroes; but it was small, and could scarcely hold two persons—certainly, not more than one, where any sea had to be contended with.

This was the difficulty which these two affectionate girls were ever trying to overcome, and which as yet they could not solve, especially as if they found me the canoe would become useless, and would necessitate a longer stay on my island than they would like without consulting their friends, whom they were afraid might be opposed to the trial altogether, as being very dangerous and of doubtful utility.

All the rest firmly believed me to be dead.

Night soon fell upon the busy scene, large fires were made to keep off wild beasts; while one grown person, with the whole armoury to his hand, watched in turns through the night, lest they might be attacked by some savage and dangerous animal. My father and the elders generally were in constant dread of the advent of another snake, which would be an event almost too terrible for reflection; when they thought of the terrible nature of an animal against which no amount of prudence can guard.

But the night passed away without any event of note, and again at early dawn the plain resounded with the sound of human voices, voices with which, could I have fancied them so near me, mine would soon have been mingled. Breakfast was made from water, fruit, and meat, all having good appetites; and then preparations were made to preserve the meat of the bull and cows, so as none of it would be wasted.

The day was very hot, which encouraged them to try a plan which Captain Thomas had seen practised in his travels, that of jerking or drying the meat in the sun. For this purpose stakes were cut, and large leaves of fibrous plants stretched from one to the other, over which the meat, being cut in long strips, was hung, to be dried by the mere heat of the sun.

My father, however, determined to add salt to it, for which purpose he despatched two of the negroes to the neighbourhood of the sea, where several spots were covered with a thick crust of common salt, which had been left there in past ages, when the land was upheaved by some internal convulsion. The salt was white, very hard, and compact, and was generally found in water-worn nodules projecting from the agglutinated sand.

In this way the buffalo proved, then and at many future periods, one of their most valuable resources, especially as they were now able to eat with it an ample supply of vegetables and fruits, thus keeping off scurvy, which is the terrible scourge usually following on a too great indulgence in salt meats, or on animal produce of any kind, without vegetables.

Here it may not be out of place to say a few words on the buffalo, which may more clearly define the animal to those who may peruse my narrative.

This animal, which proved so valuable to my friends, is a ruminating quadruped of the ox species, which it very much resembles it form and stature; the head is, however, larger, the snout longer, and its horns, which almost touch at the root, spread to a distance of five feet at their extremities; its ears are also larger and more pointed. The whole form of the buffalo, and no less its motions, announce amazing vigour and strength; but the enormous size of the head, the singular curvatures of its long horns, under which appears a large tuft of bristly hair, of a yellowish white colour, give a terrific ferocity and wildness to its physiognomy. The animal inhabits hot countries. It is, however, used in Italy as a domestic beast for tillage and drawing.

The method adopted for taming the buffalo is by fixing a ring in the nostril when about three years old. The operator contrives to entangle the leg with a string, and the animal falls to the ground; several men fall upon it, and confine the legs, while others make the wound and pass the ring; it is then left; it runs furiously from place to place and endeavours to get rid of the ring; in a short time it begins to be accustomed to its fate, and by degrees to learn obedience. A cord is fastened to the ring to lead the buffalo; if it resists it suffers pain; it therefore prefers to yield, and thus is brought to follow a conductor willingly. After a certain time the ring falls off, but the creature has, ere this, become attached, and will follow its master, and nothing is more common than to see a buffalo return from a distance of forty miles to seek him.

Their young keepers give them a name, which they never fail to answer to, and, on hearing it pronounced, they stop short in the midst of a company of their species. Troops of buffaloes are found together in the plains of America, Africa, and Asia, that are washed by rivers; they do not attack men unless provoked, but the report of a gun renders them furious and extremely dangerous; they run straight to the enemy, throw him down with their horns, and do not desist till he is crushed to death in the struggle. A red colour irritates them, and they are hunted with infinite care and precaution.

The negroes having been despatched for the salt, and the women and children instructed in the art of jerking buffalo meat—while my mother and the elder girls were strictly directed to keep up good fires, and to have several loaded guns by which to drive off wild beasts—my father, uncle, and the captain again determined on a voyage of discovery. The truth is, they were exceedingly anxious to discover even the faintest trace which might guide them in their belief as to the presence of any more such huge snakes on the island.

CHAPTER CXIX.

CROCODILE LAGOON.

On this voyage of discovery, they took a little more to the right of their former expedition, making their way as much as possible through the trees which had least undergrowth, and in this way, having travelled some hours, reached a stream about fifty yards wide, but with very low marshy borders and no wood on its banks. Immense fields of reeds and other water weeds covered the marshy soil, so that they were fain to cry a halt.

To walk along the banks, unless under the trees, was manifestly impossible; while, at the same time, they were very anxious to cross over and explore the country beyond. The stream had scarcely any current, the waters were turgid, and the smell of decaying vegetables very unpleasant; but beyond they could see some hills and higher plains. To wade, even if the water were not too deep, was out of the question, as such spots are always infested by crocodiles, a style of animal against which there is no possible protection in the water.

For a little while they followed the banks of the river, seeking a spot where there was a chance of their crossing, when suddenly they stood still in amazement. The river appeared just as wide as ever, and then abruptly stopped; though that it flowed in the direction was evident. What was to be done? The marshy reedy plain was still before them, and then a row of trees resembling poplars. Clutching their guns, and moving forward with extreme caution, they plunged into the reeds, and found, to their great delight that they did not grow in a swamp, but simply in a damp soil.

This enabled them to reach a small stream which poured, with a rapid current not more than six yards wide, out of what was now clearly a lagoon, a lagoon, too, which, if they could burn away the reeds, and thus render the soil more solid, would serve them for many purposes. They could see the fish leaping, and, to their delight, noticed that they were red mullet, while the presence of certain fish would alone have indicated the abundance of prey in the water.

The pelicans waded on the banks in prodigious swarms, gulping down all the luckless fish that come in their way. It was infinitely amusing to see them swimming about in grave silence, and every moment grabbing up a poor fish which if not hungry, they left in their huge bag, till sometimes there were three or four pounds of reserve food thus awaiting the coming of their appetite.

There were Egyptian ibis, too; but what struck the fancy of all was the abundance of ducks of various kinds, which built their nests in every little creek and bayou, and in every little inlet which appeared in the lagoon. This was a sight not to be resisted, and so my father fired, and was fortunate enough to bring down several, though, perhaps, the din which arose was such as had never before been heard in that place.

The cries of the pelicans and ducks was nothing to the hideous mewing and shrill screams of the sea gulls which had also come there to feed.

But there lay the ducks, dead or struggling in the water, at no great distance, floating very slowly in their direction. It was quite evident that once they were sucked into the rapid current of the stream they would be lost, so preparations were made to catch them by means of a hastily cut pole with a slip-knot at the end.

About five lay in a lump coming down close together, and there stood my father with his newly invented landing-net ready to capture what all had no doubt would add much to the enjoyment of their supper. The water where he was standing was shallow, so that, in his impatience, he at length waded in.

Then up rose a black slimy mass some twenty feet long, with wide mouth and hideous snaky eyes, which made at him with jaws that appeared capable of swallowing the whole party. But my uncle had his gun which was loaded with ball ready to his hand, and fired just as my father fell sprawling on his back.

The hideous beast tumbled back, struggled violently, and then sank into the mud.

My father rose to his feet, shook himself, and then taking my uncle's hand, pressed it warmly.

"That was a narrow escape," he said. "I had no idea that this lagoon was so infested."

My uncle pointed to a black mud island at some little distance, which was literally covered by crocodiles. Wherever the eye turned these disgusting beasts, with their dull leer and huge savage jaws, appeared in prodigious numbers. This was explained by the vast number of fish to be found in the lagoon, which enabled these animals to grow fat without much labour.

Meanwhile the captain, who had always an eye to the main chance, had caught up the pole and captured the ducks, which he proposed should be immediately cooked. But my father had no desire to remain on the spot. From that day he took a dislike to crocodiles, nor would he, I doubt have ever consented to have ate one, even at the very last pinch, though the negroes are so fond of it, and esteem it excellent food, and for this purpose hunt it with harpoons.

During the great heats of the day these animals will retire to the marshy reed banks, where they lie sheltered, but in the morning and afternoon they come forth in search of prey. They swim with great silence, make scarce even a ripple on the water, and yet make pretty good progress through their native element. The motion of the paws in swimming is like that of the dog—over and over. They can stand quite still on the top of the water, when they may be seen looking about them with their dull wicked eyes. They sleep in the reeds, but not for long in the same place. Their eggs they lay in the sand on islands in the lake, covering them over with layers of sand.

But how to get away from the spot became the difficulty. None were inclined to turn back, as the country beyond, though not extensive, was evidently pleasant-looking. But to cross over by wading was out of the question in the presence of so many of these hideous monsters. The stream seemed too wide for a bridge to be easily be made, while none of the trees were close enough together to admit of that method of getting over.

At this moment what appeared a log of wood come rolling over down the lake. It was crosswise, and, should it touch the two sides of the narrow stream might prove a ford. It was a huge black slimy mass so hidden by mud as to be scarcely distinguished. As it came near the mouth of the stream, my uncle pushed out his pole and proceeded to guide it, when it turned over, and they saw it was a dead crocodile.

They drew back with horror, but there it was stopping up the mouth of the stream, and in a few minutes with the water of the lake pouring over it in a kind of cataract.

My uncle laughed and said that my father had provided his own bridge.

"It is a hideous one," he replied, "but rather than stop here, I will try."

The crocodile was soon firmly imbedded, and by means of the pole already alluded to my father contrived to steady himself and to cross without peril to himself, in which example he was soon followed by his companions. They now found themselves in a very different character of country. They were soon on the side of a long hill, and close where a cool sparkling rivulet leaped from rock to rock down into the lagoon. Five huge ebony trees lifted their crowned heads together in a little knot just above them.

Here it was resolved to camp, as, after their journey, they were all tired and hungry. It was further resolved to pass the night in the place, though there was time, which they intended to avail themselves of, to explore the neighbourhood. A fire was hastily made, and the ducks prepared for broiling, which was done in a very summary way. As soon as the feathers were removed, they were split open, and in this way easily cooked. They pioved, with some yams that were roasted at the same time, to be excellent eating.

While having their supper none of them could help admiring the ebony tree, which is always met with along ridges or hills, and never on very low ground. It is one of the finest and most graceful trees of the African forest. Its leaves are long, sharp pointed, dark green, and hang in clusters, producing a most grateful shade. Its bark is smooth and of a dark green. The trunk rises straight and green to a considerable height, often fifty or sixty feet, when large, heavy branches are sent out.

Some of these trees have been seen with a diameter of five feet at the base. The mature ebony tree is always found hollow, and even its branches are hollow. Next to the bark is a white sap-wood, which is not valuable. This in an ordinary tree is three or four inches thick, and next to this lies the ebony of commerce. The young trees are white or sappy to the centre, and even when they attain a diameter of nearly two feet the black part is streaked with white. Trees less than three feet in diameter are not cut down. The ebony tree is always found intermixed with others in the forest. Generally three or four trees stand together, and no others are within a little distance, so that the cutters move through the forests constantly seeking trees.

When their meal was over, all rose in order to make a circuit of the neighbourhood. As they were about to camp there for the night, they thought it wise to be prepared for the worst, and to know exactly the character of the country they were now examining. From the complicated turnings and windings which they were compelled to make because of ponds, jungles, and undergrowth, they could form no opinion whatever as to the size of the island, if indeed it were one; while they could not form the least idea as to the ground they went over in the course of a day.

They were now ascending a slope, well wooded and yet green and grassy, towards a ridge from whence they fancied that they would be able to take a survey of their territory. For this purpose, when they reached the summit, which was one mass of intermingled vegetation, trees, and huge boulders, they sought out a tree, which they could readily climb and from its lofty branches peer out upon the plains below.

My father, as the most active of the whole party, selected a tree, not of very large dimensions; but which had its branches low to the ground and easily climbed. Having mounted into this as far as he could go, he made it a kind of step-ladder to reach a huge baobab tree, into which he ascended until he could ascend no farther.

But in vain. Nothing could be seen around him, but vegetation, in the shape of the waving green boughs, except that up in the sky, at an apparently marvellously short distance, up rose a dark column of smoke marking the spot where the women, children, and negroes were engaged in their domestic duties. This was certainly a source of some satisfaction; but, at the same time, it would have been extremely gratifying to have been able to make out the extent of the island on which they were located.

But this being impossible, my father began to descend the tree, and, the boughs being very close together and almost impassable in some places, at length espied one long bough, the extreme point of which appeared to almost touch a grey rock surrounded by creeping plants and bushes. Down this my father slid, using considerable caution, however, until he was near the extremity, when, with a fearful cry that woke the echoes of the forest, he strove to reascend.

My uncle and the captain ran to him.

"Keep back!" he cried; "be still—move not, if you would not affront certain destruction."

Then again he struggled, with convulsive shudders and trembling hands, to reascend the branch.

Just as he was about to leave go and leap to the ground, he had, by a very natural impulse, looked downward, and there, coiled up in a huge circle, he saw, not five feet below

BUFFALO HUNTING.

him, a frightful snake, which he at once recognised as the female of the python—the dreaded savage pythoness.

Sick, faint, and shivering with horror, he almost let go his hold from pure weakness.

The animal was in a kind of hollow, like a lime-kiln, surrounded by bare rocks, on the edge of which grew some plants and shrubs, while at one side of the hollow was an opening large enough for her to pass through. This was all my father could see, as, with a film spreading over his eyes, he made fearful efforts to reascend the branch.

For a time all his efforts were vain, but at last he succeeded in twisting his leg round the bough, and in this way gaining a position in which he could at all events take breath. Then with anxious, almost glazed eyes, he looked down at the hideous monster, which had never moved.

For a time the natural disgust and alarm which was natural to one in his position prevented him from making out why the pythoness made no effort at motion. For awhile he believed her to be in that state of torpidity which arises from what can only be called a gorge, when this animal will lie still and defenceless for weeks. Then however, other objects caught his eye, and he saw that the fearful beast was engaged in the maternal duty of hatching a large brood of eggs.

Taking care to select a spot where the turf was green, my father slid to the ground and rejoined his companions, to whom he gave an explanation of his sudden fright. They recoiled with horror, casting horrified glances at the nest selected by the mighty animal.

"We have no occasion to be alarmed," said my father; "the snake when breeding is almost as helpless as when it has swallowed a whole pig or deer. But it is the extension of the brood which I fear, and hence have resolved to destroy the whole."

"How?"

"I have my plans, but they must be carefully carried out—not one of the horrid lot must be left."

He then, after some consultation with his companions, began to collect dry wood, fallen branches, pine knots, and other combustible articles, which he piled up against the orifice which admitted to a view of the snake and her eggs.

She raised her head, hissed, strove to dart out her tongue, and then languidly laid it down again. She was evidently fearfully exhausted from want of that food which it totally abstains from during incubation. Once satisfied that she was harmless for the nonce, the work went bravely on, until a vast pile filled up the entrance, when a great quantity of bushes, light-wood, and leaves were rolled over into the hollow until the pythoness could no longer be seen.

Then, and then only, did they set fire to the whole, casting flaming pine-knots into the hollow.

Up rose a burning mass of flames and smoke, from which the three men retreated, having their guns ready in case the pythoness should be roused to any desperate exertion of her strength. But none came for some time, until the interior bushes were consumed, when an awful head peered over the hedge; and the snake, scarred, scorched, writhing in agony, slowly wound along the rock, and descended towards the green sward. The first impulse was flight; but then, all taking steady aim at the animal's head, fired.

The pythoness, which could scarcely crawl, lay insensible. Their victory was complete; nor did they ever, during their residence on the island, see any more of them. Their fortunate discovery of the nest before the eggs were hatched, probably prevented the island from being swarmed with them.

All wiped the cold perspiration from their brows, and moved away slowly, but not without warm congratulations at their timely and extraordinary discovery, which so easily enabled them to rid the island of a pest so horrible.

That night they slept in tolerable comfort under the ebony trees, having first made fires to keep off noxious animals; nor was one found, after the fatigues of the day, willing to act as sentinel. Luckily no interruption of their slumbers took place in the night, nor, indeed, until morning, when a sudden storm of wind and rain compelled them to keep beneath the shelter of the ebony trees, which, however, proved of little avail, as their fire was soon put out, and themselves soaked through.

The storm, however, was of brief duration, and soon as it ceased the sun burst out, the birds began to sing, and nothing remained of the storm but the dewdrops sparkling on every tree, bush, and blade of grass.

Resolved to explore somewhat further, the three travellers moved in the direction of the lagoon, the banks of which, on this side, were like a lawn, so close had the grass been cropped by some animal. It was a charming place, and would, but for its proximity to Crocodile Lake, have been a delightful place for a residence. As it was, a hunting and fishing box was proposed, and the idea pleasing all, was carried *nemine contradicente*.

About a mile and a half further down, the lagoon narrowed to a small stream, flowing over a bottom of pebbles. The water, too, was beautiful and clear, so that there was no difficulty in wading across. As they now found themselves on the trail of the day before, they determined to make the best of their way to the camp, which they did, arriving about evening, to find it in a fearful uproar, from a cause which seemed utterly inexplicable.

Polly and Pablina were missing, and had been since the morning. There had been no noise in the night. They had lain down close to my mother; but when she rose they were gone, leaving not a trace behind.

This was a catastrophe so sudden and so inexplicable as to admit of no explanation.

CHAPTER CXX.

A NIGHT ADVENTURE.

No sooner had the camp fallen into that deep slumber which so naturally succeeds the fatigues of the day, than Polly and Pablina glided from beside the other sleepers, and stood in the open air. It was a calm and beautiful night, and the moon's soft rays fell upon the clearing with a brightness which, for that pallid and cold luminary, was indeed surprising.

The girls spoke not a word, but acting, as it were, by some previous arrangement, took a supply of provisions, while Polly raised a gun from the ground, and then, with cautious steps, glided across the plain, regardless of the many dangers which lay in their path. Their route was directly towards the spot where they had crossed the river two days before, and they must have marked the trail well, for even when beneath the trees they did not, as my friends afterwards discovered, delay one moment.

Having passed through the woods, and forded the river, they found themselves on the return trail, making their way for the village on the lake which they reached about an hour before dawn. Still not a moment of rest did they seem inclined to take.

Drawing the canoe ashore, the two girls lifted it on their

shoulders, and made towards the mouth of the cavern which led to the sea, and through which they passed at a pace sufficiently rapid to warrant a belief that they were fearful of being pursued.

Their whole conduct had a guilty air, which would have been so judged at a casual glance; and yet never were young women actuated by better or more genially generous motives. They were devoting themselves to a task of difficulty and danger—the one from the pure generosity of the female heart; the other from deep and devoted affection to her adopted sister.

Softly the dark sea waves came rolling on the shore, brightly sparkled the little billows under the cold, chaste moon, warm blew a little breath of air from the land, and grandly still was all nature at that hour, when deep sleep was on the earth, and not even the marauding denizens of the woods were to be heard gambolling or crying to one another.

It was a night when anyone might have been freely forgiven for believing that nothing but peace reigned upon the earth. The sough of the tiny salt sea waves made music as they ebbed and flowed, now washing over the smaller rocks, now leaving them bare and shining under the moon.

Afar off the billows rose and fell with a gentle undulation which would scarcely more than have rocked a child to sleep.

The canoe was placed upon the ground, and then set afloat in a small cove, into which the waves came slowly and softly. Pablina entered, while Polly handed her some little parcels of food. Pablina's back was turned to Polly, when the latter moved a little back to fetch the gun. As she did so, the Indian girl gave a sweep with her paddle, which sent the little frail skiff dancing out upon the surface of the waves.

Polly shrieked, thinking at first that it was an accident.

But no sooner was the Indian girl at a small distance from the shore, than she steadied her little bark, and spoke.

"Pablina go alone—bring him safe or die!"

"Come back," cried Polly; "either we will go together, or neither shall go. I will not let you risk your life thus madly for me. I will share your danger, or you shall not go!"

"Pablina go—good-bye—back soon."

And away the devoted girl paddled, in spite of the frantic cries and supplications of Polly, which continued until the other was quite out of sight, when my cousin sank behind a boulder, insensible; nor did she—the faintness turning into sleep—recover until the storm broke, when she sheltered herself under a rock, watching the rising waves with a sullen and wild glance, which it would have been dreadful to gaze on.

She was speechless with horror. There could be no hope that such a cockle boat as that in which Pablina had departed could live in such a sea as was fast rising under the influence of the storm. Then not only was the hope of Alfred's escape and of his rejoining them gone, but she too would perish, a victim to her selfishness and the Indian girl's own devotion.

It was a fearful awakening of a long and fond dream, in which these two brave girls had long indulged, and the more terrible to Polly that, after always intending to share the dangers of her faithful companion, that dauntless girl had departed on her mission alone, and that, too, with a storm raging which might have engulfed a much larger vessel.

When the squall was over, and it did not last above half an hour, the sea was tossed in angry billows, which would have never allowed so small a canoe to have lived. Polly strained her eyes over the whole horizon, in the desperate hope of making some discovery, however, hopeless.

She would have been thankful even to have known that all was over.

There she was, a picture of remorse and of despair; her cheeks pale as death, her eyes streaming with tears, her hands clasped upon her knees, as, with the waves almost washing her feet, she sat, gazing silently, hopelessly out upon the vast wilderness of tossing waters.

And thus it was they found her, faint and weary from want of food, and utterly unable to give any explanation just then of her own conduct or that of Pablina. But when next day, after a night's rest, her head leaning on my mother's shoulder, she told her story, it was with difficulty that a dry eye was preserved in the whole assembly.

Polly had succeeded not only in imparting a knowledge of the English language to her friend, but had, during the necessary studies which had taken place between them, got to learn a very fair amount of the other's somewhat barbarous dialect. By this means it was that these two were able to understand one another completely, and in this way my cousin had come to know the other's history with something like correctness.

She now freely imparted it to her friends, as almost a necessary explanation of the perilous undertaking which they had so long been plotting.

CHAPTER CXXI.

THE HISTORY OF PABLINA.

SHE came from a land underneath the sun, but which no name by which she spoke of it represented any country known to modern geography. It was, she said, a fertile land, with many horses, cows, oxen, and even sheep, while the people dwelt in huts and tents, generally on the banks of rivers. They were a brave but not a warlike race, being rather fond of hunting, fishing, and snaring animals, than of contests with their fellow men.

They were utterly ignorant of the use of firearms. Their weapons were bows, arrows, and clubs, while much of their hunting was done by snaring. They did much in the way of elephant and hippopotamus trapping, saving up the ivory for an annual trip down a large river; where, at a town which she pronounced Ndina, they trafficked them for necessaries.

Their lot did not seem an unhappy one, as their softness of character kept them from all those disgraceful cruelties which appertain to the negro generally on the coast and in the interior of Africa, and shown in man hunting and eating, and in atrocious cruelties to their own people when accused of the monstrous crime of witchcraft.

One day—whether the pirates had had ill-luck elsewhere, or had travelled farther than usual—the village, of which Pablina's father was chief, was surprised by an inroad of the Fan Indians, who, after killing some of the warriors and all the old people, carried off the rest into captivity. The marauders were in vast numbers and had collected an immense booty, which they drove before them as they would have driven cattle.

Many perished by the way from want of water and food, as well as from fatigue; but at length they came to a river, where a large number of canoes awaited them, and where food was in abundance. The able bodied had still to walk, but the women and children were placed in the boats and rowed forward amid beautiful scenery, which, if it did not cheer them, reminded the poor prisoners of home.

Palms lined the river banks and the numerous tiny islands which studded its smooth and glass like-bosom, whilst the occasional deer, which started away from the river side as the fleet of canoes swept past, the shrill cries of whole schools of monkeys little and big, who gazed at them with mingled astonishment and fear, the clear blue sky, and the magnificent solitude of those mighty forests, which swept back miles upon miles, and now and then a distant smoke curling through the trees, marking the site of a village, so reminded the captives of home that they wept bitterly.

Their brutal captors only laughed and sang songs in a strange dialect, as if ridiculing their weakness.

Then came, after many days, their arrival on the sea-shore and their sale to the white man, more cruel, more brutal, more debased even than the negro captors, who themselves do not treat their slaves very affectionately or tenderly, except when they actually fatten them for the purpose of immediate consumption.

Having sold their slaves, the Fans retired into the interior, when the transfer to the ship commenced. It took place from the old barracoon to which I have already referred, and whence it was that Pablina was able to see the island on which I was wrecked, as well as that with the ever smoking burning mountain, which she at once recognised on her landing.

It would be painful to record here the terrible story of the sufferings these wretched slaves endured during their short journey, sufferings not one-tenth part of what they might have suffered had they had to endure the horrors of the middle passage. But a fearful tempest arose, which drove them towards the land, and lasted several days; at the end of which the seamen took to their boats and left the ship, imagining it was sinking.

Then a large party of the negroes, aided by some black sailors belonging to the crew, who had been left behind, made a raft, which took nearly all the slaves upon it, being very large. It was made of ship spars and masts, with empty water casks, of which there was an abundance on all sides.

Those who were unable to leave the ship were left to their fate, which, as the ship was unmanageable from the breaking of its rudder, was a cruel one. The last remnant were chiefly women, and being attached to one another, did their best to save one another's lives. Seeing, from the burning mountain, that land was not far off, they lashed one another to spars and committed themselves to the waves.

In this way was Pablina washed ashore. The others met with a very different fate.

As soon as Pablina and Polly could understand one another thoroughly, it came out, in the course of conversation, that there was a fertile wooded island to the northward, which at once roused hopes in the young girl's bosom which had never been quenched. She had seen, as they were swept away in the gust of mist and rain, that there was an island at no great distance from the ship.

Then Polly was well aware how many a man had lived for years upon a deserted island, by dint of courage and perseverance; such as Selkirk and others—to say nothing of Robinson Crusoe, who was nearly forty years alive on an island. My cousin had sufficient faith in me to believe that with a wreck under my hand, I might, despite every difficulty have survived all this time.

Then it was that Polly confided her hopes and fears to Pablina. She was sadly afraid that any attempt to enlist other sympathy, in what might appear so utterly hopeless a cause, might cause the total defeat of her purpose. Besides, there was a kind of grandeur in doing it all herself, or else a canoe or raft might have been constructed to transport others to the island.

But Pablina had great faith in her own powers. On the lakes and rivers of her native country—which she said had big seas, but not salt—she had crossed more than twenty miles, in even rough weather, and she was quite sure she could cross over, search the island, and return. But no sooner did she understand the fixed determination of Polly to accompany her, than she kept to herself the fact that the periagua would not contain more than one.

Her stratagem, it will be seen, was successful, and away she sped on her mission of gentleness and love.

For some hours her task was easy, and she succeeded by keeping well out to sea, and thus avoiding currents; in this way she reached the northern end of the volcanic island, after which she paddled in an oblique direction to that which appeared a dark cloud in the distance. But she was fully aware that this was her destined gaol.

But presently the lowering sky, the distant thunder, and the flashing lightning, warned her of her great danger. But she faltered not. She was determined to succeed, or to perish in the attempt.

Then down came the storm, not at first very violently, but still enough to raise mighty waves in comparison with the size of the tiny craft, which was all that intervened between her and death. Still she urged her little craft forward, until the waves began to swell visibly, and she could now fancy herself down in the deep depths of the ocean, or then up on the very summit of the waves.

But her bold and gallant heart knew no fear. On! on! she sped, as the rain fell, and the thunder roared, and the lightning flashed, and the wind blew, until everything seemed to prognosticate a fearful gale. At this moment, as if by magic, though the darkness was still over the face of the deep, and the elements were still in mortal strife, the water became stiller, and the wind was unfelt. She had been swept by a current under the lee of my island, into smooth water.

Then away she paddled with might and main towards the shore, which she at length reached by means of a river, and utterly exhausted and fatigued after her perilous and adventurous journey, lay down to rest, after carefully concealing her canoe under some bushes.

CHAPTER CXXII.

ON THE ISLAND.

SHE slept many hours, even unto dawn, and when she awoke the sky was so blue, the sea so smooth, the wind so light, that she determined to attempt a tour of the island, in the hope of finding some trace, either a hut or smoke, or some other sign of my existence.

Unfortunately she took the wrong way, and paddled along the shore in the direction where, afterwards, the Fan village was temporarily erected. On this occasion, her eyes being intently fixed on the shore, she moved along with extreme slowness; so that by evening she had only reached the mouth of another small stream, on the banks of which she at once noticed several of her friends and late companions on board the slaver, bathing.

Next minute almost, she was alternately clasped in the arms of her father and mother.

Before, however, she could enter into any explanation as to her presence on that island, and in possession of a canoe, a number of Fan Indians came rushing down, with loud shouts and laughter; for these were the very men who had sold her and her friends into slavery, and who now were once more in possession of the whole drove, for which they had been already so handsomely paid.

The arrival of Pablina was a great triumph, as it was so utterly and totally unexpected.

One of the young chiefs, who came down to welcome her in the ironical way which such brutal savages were likely to adopt, seemed, however, struck by her appearance. The life she had led with my friends had elevated her intellect. The mere study of a language will react upon the brain. Pablina looked glorious.

It has often been the fashion of writers to decry civilization, and praise up the virtues of a state of nature. Such persons know little of savages, who are in general cruel, brutal to women, tyrannical to children, and utterly selfish, indulging in every form of vice and debauchery which is known to man.

The one who looked so keenly at Pablina was a chief. The poor girl at first, knowing the awful habits of these atrocious negroes, fancied that her plump form, so different from the gaunt shape of her friends and relatives, had attracted his notice, and that she was to be immediately sacrificed and eaten. She was right in one way; her graceful appearance had taken his fancy, but he did not want to eat her. He wished to make her one of his wives; polygamy, of course, being common with savages so demoralized.

When Pablina understood the object with which the chief was gazing at her so earnestly, she was no less alarmed than if he had intimated his intention of eating her for supper. She had an intuitive horror of these fearful cannibals, and her intercourse with my cousin had not tended to increase her desire to mate with a Fan negro.

But she dissembled, and when the hunter-brave paid her compliments, feigned to receive them with modest diffidence, and thus gained time.

The hunters had been on the island several days, and had had considerable luck, but they next day moved more towards the interior of the island, when an idea struck the poor captive, of which she at once determined to avail herself.

She kept her eyes ever about, and during the course of the day observed that there was continually to be seen, in certain places, the mark of footsteps, which, like those of her friends on the volcanic island, were covered by something in the shape of a shoe, such as she wore herself, the gift of my cousin, who had saved several small articles in a bundle when the boat was loaded.

Once the discovery made, she knew that her journey had not been undertaken for nothing. The youth about whom Polly was so anxious was there.

The prisoners were not very securely guarded. The only canoes on the island were in the hands of the Fans, and under the charge of diligent sentinels, so that an escape into the woods would be, indeed, of little avail. But Pablina had another belief. She had, not unnaturally, a somewhat exaggerated idea of the whites. If she could but communicate with me, her father, mother, and other friends might be saved.

This thought it was that made her resolve on an escape.

Pablina was indeed fleet of foot, or she would not have gone a hundred yards. As she started sauntering on her way, the eye of a savage Fan sentry was on her, but he suspected nothing until the girl, having discovered the general direction of my trail, took to her heels. It must have been a sight to see her bounding over the plain with a dozen or more yelping savages in her train, foremost of whom was the youth whose eyes had been captivated by her bright and pleasing countenance.

These cries it was that alarmed me, and enabled me to give the savages such a welcome as taught them to respect the power of fire-arms for some time to come. My feelings have been already fully explained, but those of Pablina were difficult to define. How difficult it was to analyze her sensations may be judged from the fact that she did not reveal her knowledge of a smattering of my language.

I believe that my successful repulse of the Fans, my wholesale massacre of their warriors, had imbued her with an amount of respect for me amounting to idolatry, while still her mind was full of the pitiful state in which her parents and relatives were placed. What made her abstain from communicating her intentions to me, can scarcely be explained, except that she feared I would not allow her to attempt the rash task of rescuing her friends from such a horde of fearful savages.

Be this as it may, her escape is still in the memory of my readers, as well as the events which immediately followed her flight from the shelter of my cave. But what followed is yet not known.

CHAPTER CXXIII.

ANDREW.

WHEN Pablina and her friends were hurried into the canoes, the terrified Fans, who had been carefully kept from the knowledge of fire-arms by the traders, moved as rapidly in the direction of the mainland as they could, but so carelessly as to take little heed of the currents which always ran between that island and the continent.

Not so Pablina.

In the great hurry of their departure it was not noticed that she was in her own canoe. Terror had deprived these terrible savages of sense, and it seemed to be a race who should get quickest away from my murderous and destructive weapons. Pablina, who had none of this wild dread of what she was used to, gradually edged her periagua to the right of the little fleet.

The savages had at length discovered that the current was taking them out to the northward and for this reason urged their canoes as much to the south as possible to reach the shore. Now Pablina knew very well that nearer to my island was a back-water, and could even, with her quick eye, see the ripple where it was separated from the current running in a northerly direction.

By keeping some distance to the right of the canoes, and still apparently making for the continent, she was able at last to make a dash into the back-water, which turned her periagua suddenly round, and when she headed for my shore it was too late for the savages to capture her, while her determined efforts to reach my island might place them under the guns they so much feared.

They, therefore, continued on their way, content to lose only one captive. She was sad enough, but she felt that what she had done was only her duty to Polly, to whom she had devoted herself, in order to succeed in rescuing me from solitude.

But the tide which swept past this part of my island was too strong for her, and she soon found herself sweeping along the coast helpless, indeed glad that she was not carried out to sea.

The trade winds, too, had set in, so that it was only by great good fortune that she reached the volcanic island without accident. The place where she landed was a splendid specimen of tropical vegetation and scenery of a somewhat unpleasant character. A small river flowed into a bay, into which the tide swept with the flood, so that Pablina was, for a time, almost stationary. The shore, the mud island, the trees, which came nearly down to the water, were crowded with birds.

There were pelicans, there were strings of flamingos, there were herons, cranes, and gulls, and then one vast mangrove swamp, such as one might have expected only to have found on a great continent. There was a fearful smell of decaying matter, which with the hot sun, made Pablina feel quite ill. But she determined to push onwards, so anxious was she to rejoin my friends with her great and important news. A short way up, however, the tide ceased to affect the river, and the swamps disappeared.

The mangroves themselves soon disappeared, and the banks of the river becoming higher, the stream rolled along with a life-like current between well-defined banks. There were palms and the usual vegetation of Africa, while here and there large trees projected over into the middle, and formed a fine arbour, beneath which she paddled, relieved of the burning rays of the sun.

But the current became strong, and Pablina felt that she must go on shore and make the rest of her journey on foot, leaving her canoe to be fetched at a future period.

Then fastening her boat, the brave girl cast one upward glance at the heavens, and, totally unarmed, entered the woods, which were not very dense, making for what appeared to be a clearing of some extent. Scarcely had she come upon its borders than she heard a noise behind her; she turned round and saw what appeared to her a huge gorilla of the largest species in chase. Now Pablina was firmly convinced, as are all the people of the interior of Africa, that the gorilla is in the habit of carrying off girls and women; so, with a fearful cry, she rushed away at the top of her speed.

She need not have done so, even had it been a gorilla, as that beast, which lives on vegetables, seldom if ever lurks behind trees by the roadside, nor does it drag unsuspicious travellers in its claws and choke them to death in its vice-like paws, nor does it attack the elephant and beat him to death with sticks, while it rarely, if ever, carries off native women.

Still Pablina ran, her pursuer coming close up behind her, until she found herself on the ground, entangled in a huge net, with Andrew, the midshipman, standing over her. He was still more ragged, still more gaunt, still more wild looking than ever, while hair was growing all over his body, as it did with that ancient castaway who might truly be called the First of the Castaways.

Deprived of arms, and from his half wild, half mad, and savage nature, determined not to yield to those who had, as he believed, ill-used him, Andrew all this time had been wholly dependent upon himself. Not deficient in ingenuity, and having more practical experience than myself, he had adopted a plan of hunting common among the Mbicho negroes.

They make nets of the fibre of the pine-apple plant, and also with the fibres of another kind of tree, which are twisted into stout threads. The savages make them about sixty or eighty feet long and four or five feet high, and every village owns several. But as no individual village has sufficient to make a great spread, like the *battue* of more civilized regions, several unite in one grand hunt and divide the proceeds, the game caught in any one net being the property of the owner.

Then the animals of the forest are driven in this direction by means of dogs, loud shouting of men, and firing of guns.

Andrew—who was very clever at all such mechanical contrivances, and who, before he was sailor, was an adept in the mysteries of net-making—when he found himself cast upon his own resources in the wild and gloomy forest, with no weapon but a club torn from the earth in shape of a small tree, had set his half cracked wits to work to manufacture the only kind of trap by which he could hope to keep himself supplied with food.

When Pablina rose to her feet, her heart beating wildly, she found herself not alone entangled in the net. A gazelle of a very minute size—a beautiful little animal, worthy of being a pet, and not so large as a pointer—and some partridges had been captured. These were the *Norhuta major*. They do not go in coveys like the English bird, nor do they conceal themselves. They are very silly birds. A man on horseback, by riding round and round in a circle, or rather in a spire, so as to approach closer each time, may knock on the head as many as he pleases. The more common method is to catch them with a running noose or little lasso, made of the stem of an ostrich's feather fastened to the end of a long stick. A boy on a quiet old horse has been known frequently to catch thirty or forty in a day.

Andrew quietly wrung the necks of the partridges and strangled the gazelle, without apparently taking any notice of the young girl, who, having extricated herself from the fibrous net, was endeavouring to make off, when a savage roar and menacing gesture restrained her. Then Andrew motioned her to take up the gazelle, while he tied the partridges together, and then follow him. All the while he spoke not a word.

Some who have been alone, as the ancient Crusoe, have in course of time lost all power of speech, and have had, when found, to be taught their native tongue again like children, but this could not be the case with the midshipman. The time that had elapsed since his escape from the colony was too short. It appeared rather that the semi-maniac was possessed of that control over his actions which is the property of many of his unfortunate companions—that of effectually concealing for a time his own weakness.

Andrew probably felt that had he spoke, he should not have spoken coherently. Besides, there was a sullen ferocity in his manner which was sufficiently alarming. Pablina, however, showed no fear. She was already too much of a woman not to believe in her own power of conquering the obstinacy of one of the other sex.

Andrew's habitation was simply a small, clear space burnt away by fire under a tree, with a confused mass of skins coarsely dried in the sun for a bed, while all about were spread bones and feathers, indicating the numerous captures he must have made. His mode of lightning a fire was one not uncommon in country places all over Europe, and universal in agricultural districts in France, where the wood fire at night is allowed to burn down to red hot embers, which are covered over by ashes, that preserve the same until morning, when, by the addition of a few small sticks, a fire is easily relighted.

Andrew had done the same. How he had first procured fire was a mystery, but since he had done so he had taken care not to let it go out. It was made near the trunk of a large tree, the branches of which kept off both wet and dew. Stooping down and removing the ashes, the embers were then blown upon by the young mate, dry chips, decayed wood and leaves placed thereon, which being fanned, first by the breath and then by a branch of palm leaves, soon burst into a flame.

Good stout wood was then added until a goodly fire was made. Then Andrew pulled from his breast a pipe, made from a small cocoa-nut and a reed, which he proceeded to load with some substance, in appearance resembling tobacco, which he proceeded to smoke with much seriousness and evident enjoyment.

Pablina quietly sat down, and began to prepare a couple of partridges for his meal. She did not cast her eyes towards him, and yet saw all that he was doing. Women have a marvellous power of eye-sight, when we think them totally inattentive. She knew that Andrew was watching her keenly, so she went to work with a will, and as soon as the fire gave forth no smoke, cast some coarse salt on it from a bag hanging from a bough, and proceeded to cook the partridges.

As soon as they were ready, the young man pointed to a receptacle in the trunk of the tree, where were concealed some fruits, and allowing himself to be waited on by this graceful Hebe, ate his meal with a wild and savage relish, that showed he had degenerated much from his original manhood. Still there was a remnant left, shown by his forcing Pablina to take one of the partridges herself, though, as it was afterwards proved, he could eat three.

Having despatched this rather copious meal, he washed it down with water from a spring close at hand, and again proceeded to smoke, eyeing Pablina all the time with a strange expression. She, however, apparently took no notice of him, but proceeded to put to rights his disordered and uncomfortable couch; after which, with a firm step, she proceeded to the skirt of a small thicket, and began there to erect herself a hut.

Andrew looked at her with a stern, ironical expression, but made no remark whatever.

Pablina all the time was as joyous as a bird, thinking in her own mind how she should escape, for escape she would, ere night lent new horrors to the scene. Still, no idea suggested itself. She was fleet of foot, it is true, and not much encumbered with dress, but Andrew, during his terrible and solitary career, had become remarkable for his running powers; so that this was not to be thought of.

Still, the other smoked, watching her movements all the while with evident pleasure, as what man in his senses would not have done? Every now and then Pablina, plucking a branch here and a branch there, glanced over her shoulder at him, and noticed that whenever she went beyond a certain distance, he raised himself from his recumbent position, as if prepared for a start.

But Pablina always returned to the spot where she had selected a resting-place, so that at last, he seemed less watchful.

Now Pablina had remarked that through the thicket was a wood, the trees of which, though not lofty, were thick in girth; and on this fact she rested her hopes of escape. Suddenly his eyes were closed, as if in excessive enjoyment of the nicotine weed. This was an opportunity not to be lost. Under the bushes, first to the right and then straight forward, until she was in the wood, and safely ensconced behind a tree

Then with a yell scarcely human, with a wild and savage cry which resouded through the forest, startling the small green parrots of that locality from their nest of sticks, away the young man came, plunging through the woods, his club waved above his head, and his whole mien denoting the utmost fury and rage.

How her heart beat as she passed from behind the tree and saw him running here, there, and everywhere like a dog who has lost his scent, moaning, cursing, swearing, and uttering such unearthly cries as were horrible to listen to. Then he stood still, and, in a calm and natural way, implored Pablina not to desert him. He was a lone and solitary man; he would be her slave; he would not harm her.

Then he gnashed his teeth, tore his hair, and renewed all his furious expressions, while Pablina, at every opportunity, glided from tree to tree. Then she saw that Andrew had taken up a position where, by standing still and keeping his eyes about him, he could discern almost every movement in every avenue of the forest. At once, with the instinct of her race, she cowered down and thought.

At the edge of the forest was an open glade, terminating in a small stream.

How was she to reach this, and not be overtaken by the wild and ferocious maniac? A wondrous idea entered her head. From a point where Andrew stood to where the open glade was seen, ran a regular avenue of trees almost as straight as if they had been planted by art instead of nature.

This Pablina determined to use as the means of saving herself. Looking about her, she selected from among a mass of similar plants a long thin fibrous vine of the india-rubber species. Then crawling on the sward, and taking advantage of the inequalities of the ground, she passed the fibrous vine round the trunk of a tree about two feet from the ground, and then lying perfectly flat, crossed the avenue and did the same on the other side.

Then she rose, and walked deliberately in a straight line towards Andrew. She affected not to see him, but when at last she could feign no longer, she gave a shrill cry, turned, and fled, using as she did so, those leaps and bounds which are common to savage races. In this way her flying leap over the cord was not noticed, and ere Andrew could check himself, he was pitched headlong forward sprawling on the ground.

For a moment he was stunned, but rising and rubbing his forehead, with terrible menaces he rushed down the bank again, and searched every possible and impossible place for the fugitives.

But he found nothing, not even a footstep marked the way she had taken.

Water leaves no trail.

CHAPTER CXXIV.

HOME AGAIN.

WHEN Pablina escaped from the clutches of the maniac, and fled, with the lightness of foot belonging to her age, sex, and country, by a rapid exercise of that instinct which was native to her, she plunged into the stream; nor ceased running until she had placed two miles between herself and her pursuer. Then finding that she heard nothing of him, she slackened her pace and began to reconnoitre.

One glance was enough. She was at no great distance from the lake village, the stream she had been following being one of those which supplied it with water. With a beating heart, that throbbed with varied emotions, Pablina followed the banks of the stream, until at length the village was in view, and she could make out its inhabitants engaged in their usual avocations. It was nearly evening, and all had come in. Some were cooking, some were searching the fish preserves, others were disposing of the captures of the day.

Seated by a fire, with a sad and melancholy aspect, was Polly. For some days she had not been well. She bitterly reproached herself with having been the cause of the death of the Indian girl; and, from sheer fretting, was wasting away to the condition of a skeleton. Still, she would rouse herself to do something; and, as superintending the cooking, with the assistance of the children, was the easiest work to be found, she was allowed to have her own way.

Suddenly there arose a loud cry of triumph from the two boys, who then, without a word of explanation, bounded in the direction where they saw Pablina standing.

The camp was immediately in an uproar—a confusion like that of Babel ensued—and then the welcome fugitive was surrounded, feted, and made a perfect goddess of. But Polly soon induced them all to moderate their transports. Rising from her seat, she took Pablina's two hands in hers and looked in her face.

"Well?" she said.

"Alfred lives," replied the Indian girl.

Polly turned to the astonished and almost incredulous group, with a look of heavenly triumph which none of them very easily forgot. Now was the time for Pablina to be overwhelmed with questions; but as Polly was the only one who could thoroughly comprehend her, it was arranged that she should hear the story first, and then relate it to the others.

And this was done; and when, after supper, the happy dwellers in that secluded and unknown village heard all the wonders which had befallen me—how, taking example of my great predecessor, Robinson Crusoe, I had striven to do all that one man can do, imitating him in some things, as every cast-away, who has had the fortune to read his book, must always do, improving on him in others, where my opportunities were better—the delight, gratitude, and joy of the whole party may be better conceived than described.

There was but one opinion. They were not any of them prepared to undergo the delay of building a canoe, but all agreed that for such a journey as that contemplated a raft would be sufficient; and to the construction of this they all agreed to give their minds.

In the first place, it was decided to build it at the mouth of the river where Pablina had fortunately found a port. This necessitated a great supply of provisions; and a migration of the whole party to the sea-shore, as neither women or children would hear of being left behind. During the absence of Pablina great advances had been made in domestic economy.

An exploration taken on a day of holy rest had revealed to them the fact that the southern end of the island was one great nest of birds. As in the case in all countries where man first makes his appearance, they were found very tame. Mocking thrushes, finches, wrens, tyrant fly-catchers, the dove, and carrion buzzard, have been commonly killed by the switch, cap, or handkerchief of a sailor. One old traveller found a gun quite useless, as a hawk allowed himself to be pushed off a bough with the muzzle.

On my own island, until I began to use my gun rather freely, I recollect once, when lying down, noticing a mocking thrush alight on the edge of a large gourd which I held in my hand, and begin sipping the water; and it even did not fly away when I moved the vessel. But all old voyagers and discoverers record the same experiences. In the reign of his late Majesty Charles the Second, one says:—"The turtledoves were so tame, as that they would often alight on our hats and arms, so as that we could take them alive, they not fearing man, until such time as some of our companions did fire at them, whereby they were rendered more shy."

My friends did not find them quite so tame as this, but by a little exertion of patience and ingenuity very large captures were made, and many proved to be exceedingly good eating. The most important take, however, was that of some doves, which were alive, and were placed in a kind of rustic aviary, where, being well fed and tamed, they readily took up their residence; at last even being allowed to fly out and in.

All these were very important considerations, for although the stock of powder on board the slaver was exceedingly great, yet still, with such a community, the day would come when it must be exhausted. They would then become wholly dependent on domestic animals, pitfalls, and such contrivances as that which they heard with so much surprise had been adopted by Andrew.

The adventure of the Indian girl with the semi-maniac was heard on all sides with great distress, though the news of my safety invested it at first with secondary importance. On reflection, my parents, whose elation at the news of my escape from death is almost too sacred a subject to be touched on, saw the danger of allowing this man to be at large; but what was to be done?

The negroes, it is true, undertook his easy capture, but my father was fearful lest they should, in their anxiety for the general welfare of the colony, do him a mischief, which, as he was clearly not responsible for his actions, would have been great cruelty. All that could be done, then, was to keep a good look out.

Pablina had some difficulty in explaining to Polly how it was she had not explained everything fully to me; but the Indian girl declared, with touching simplicity, that she had been so terrified at all that happened, and so bewildered between the desire to save me and to save her parents also, that she knew not exactly what she was about. She added that she firmly believed terror had tied her tongue.

Polly was at last satisfied with this explanation, and then showered upon Pablina such a multitude of questions relative to my appearance, my state of health, my comforts and hopes, and my dress, that the other had enough to do to answer them. However, she did her best, and Polly came to have a very fair idea of the domestic economy of my island home and empire; for truly, indeed, was I monarch of all I surveyed.

All hands were set to work to prepare for the expedition to the coast, which was by no means a trifle, as they had to make such vast circuits to avoid hills and dense thickets. Both food and water were needed in abundance; and after some time, it was decided that one essential was, that the cow should go with them, and the calf as well, which was not quite independent of its mother. This was done for many reasons. In the first place, they did not find anybody willing to stop at the village to tend the cow; while, in the second place, it was determined to make it carry the water skins.

These had been made from some skins of cows, well cleaned first, and were very essential, as there were many places on

No. 25.—Sailor Crusoe.

the island quite destitute of water, but where circumstances might induce them to camp at times.

Clothes of European make were now rare, but as all clung to them with that fondness which is engendered by civilization, they were put on one side for high days and holidays; while the best substitute that could be found was made from skins and grass, in the weaving of which into mats and such-like things, Pablina was very clever and ingenious.

My mother and the negresses had enough to do to make all these clothes, and would, indeed, have found it an almost hopeless task, had not Pablina have shown them how to make thread both of fibres and sinews, as well as needles from fish-bones. In this way their labour was much lightened; but, despite all their ingenuity, their clothes were but coarse, yet satisfied all the requisites of decency and comfort.

CHAPTER CXXV.

THE JOURNEY.

JERKED meat, salt-fish, dried birds, having been provided in abundance, the whole colony prepared for their march to the opposite coast, where they hoped to be able to open up a communication with my island. My father, uncle, and Captain Thomas, the elders and leaders of the party, marched first, armed both with gun, axe, and pistol. Close behind them were the negroes, also armed, and carrying heavy axes and other loads without any apparent effort.

Then came the cow, with her load of water-skins, which she did not at all seem to appreciate, but which were kept on by dint of management. Polly marched on one side, with a cord round one horn, while Pablina did the same with the other. My mother, the anxious queen of all this flock, came last; the negresses, Cudjie, and the children, forming the main body.

Their advance was necessarily slow, as the weather was very hot and sultry; while the cow would not be urged beyond a certain pace. About noon they halted, under the grateful shade of a clump of palm-trees, for members of their family very ugly ones. Their stems were very large, and were thicker in the middle than at the base or top. But they excited no more notice than that their shade was very grateful, until my father noticed that Pablina was examining them with considerable attention.

"What is it?" said my father.

"Cut one down—see!" replied Pablina.

As the Indian girl generally had a very good and efficient reason for all she did, there was not much hesitation in obeying her directions. The axes were heavy, and amid a shout of delight from the children, who always, I fear, delight in destruction, the tree fell. Then Pablina caught up a small axe, and chopped off the crown of leaves from the top.

The result was almost foreseen by my father, who, while the negroes were so busily engaged, had been endeavouring to make out the girl's object. These palm-trees are so common in some parts of the world, that people have attempted to count them on one plantation; and having come to a hundred thousand, the task was given up as hopeless. They are cut down at certain periods, and as soon as the crown of leaves is cut off the sap begins to flow from the upper end, and continues to flow for some months. It is, however, necessary that a thin slice should be shaved off from that end every morning, so as to expose a fresh surface.

A good tree has been known to give ninety gallons, and all this must have been contained in the vessels of the apparently dry trunk. It is asserted that the sap flows much more quickly on those days when the sun is powerful, and likewise, that it is absolutely necessary to take care in cutting down the tree that it should fall with its head upward on the side of the hole, which had been done by Pablina's direction. They found her to be quite right, although one would have thought that the action would have been aided instead of checked by the force of gravity.

The juice is chiefly used after boiling, when it becomes a kind of treacle, but it was very pleasant when fresh, and was indeed one of the very many useful discoveries which they owed to the young girl who had been cast like a waif upon their shores.

After dinner, which—what with milk, meal, and palm-sap, and cocoa-nuts—was both plentiful and refreshing, they again started upon their journey, the children making parasols or sun-shades with the leaves of the palm tree. They also made fans with different bushy boughs to keep off the flies, which mercilessly assailed the cow.

The country they travelled through was rather barren than otherwise, though now and then a wood, thicket, or collection of bush, would intervene, where always a slight halt was declared previous to crossing through any arid plains. In this way they did not make more than twelve miles the whole day. But, at all events, no one was fatigued beyond measure.

The halting-place was near a spring. The setting of the sun was a glorious sight, the valley in front of them being black, while the peaks of the volcanic mountains still retained a ruby tint. They made a fire—wood being very scarce, except green wood—of bamboos and the bones of a small cow which had been shot on the route. The evening was quite cool enough to be agreeable, and when a hasty harbour of bamboos, with green boughs for a roof, had been made, everybody was very comfortable.

All felt the mysterious and inexpressible charm of thus living in the open air, such a life adding a buoyancy to the spirits and a cheerfulness to our nature which nothing else can. The evening, too, was calm and still, with nothing to be heard but the occasional cry of the goatsucker or the hum of insects.

At an early hour, a march being decided on at daybreak, the whole party retired to rest. It had been resolved, for the children's sake, not to travel during the great heat of the day, but to take advantage of the cool mornings and evenings.

Fatigue and health gave sleep to all save Polly and Pablina, who conversed together for some hours in whispers as to their hopes in connection with my island. At last, even they were exhausted, and fell into a deep slumber.

Before daybreak some of the negroes were on foot, with the intention of preparing breakfast, but they found the two elder girls before them. Despite the late hour at which they had fallen to sleep, they were up while all the rest slept.

They were stooping over the fire attending to some domestic duties, when they were startled by an exclamation from the negroes, which made them look sharply round. At a little distance, in the direction of the rocky and volcanic part of the island, was what old travellers call a bluff, about twenty feet in height, and on this stood a figure which, in the grey morning light and shrouded by a mist that rose from the valley below, looked gigantic.

It wielded a large stick, and appeared about to descend in the direction of the camp, when suddenly the negroes made a dash in his direction. They were armed with muskets and ship cutlasses, but the young heart of Polly was too tender to allow them to do the poor man hurt. It was only Andrew, and it was no crime that heat and a fanciful passion for herself should have turned his brain.

"Don't hurt him," she cried.

"No hurt him," replied one of the negroes, "but em catchee!"

And with rapid steps they pursued the half naked and unhappy maniac.

In vain. He had, since he had been without arms, acquired such habits of speed as to be not easily run down. It was afterwards found that there was scarcely any animal which a man could venture to attack, that he would not beat in a race, to such perfection will practice in any art bring the patient man.

No trace of the unfortunate youth being found, the discomfited negroes returned to the camp, where their absence caused some anxiety. The morning meal being hurried over it was determined to start while the day was yet young, when suddenly there spread a darkness over the face of the sky, and almost ere they could cower under their extempore huts, which the negroes hastily strengthened with new boughs, a storm of thunder, lightning, and rain overtook them, which gave them a foretaste of what was to happen in later days.

But it was of short duration, and when the sky again became blue, and they started on their way, the air was balmy in the extreme, and a delightful coolness pervaded the atmosphere, which made the journey extremely pleasant. In this way, journeying slowly, examining every object of interest, and noting down places which were worthy of future examination, they at last reached the sea, and halted on the banks of the river where Pablina had arrived on her escape from my own island.

Hasty huts were at once erected, while my father and uncle searched the woods for such trees as might be suitable to the formation of a raft.

CHAPTER CXXVI.
AN ADVENTURE.

EVERYBODY worked with a will. They were all desirous to reach the island upon which my fortunes had fallen. The description which Pablina had given them was such as to make them feel a wish to join me, not only from natural affection but because they saw it in a better realization of their idea of a residence.

None felt safe on a volcanic island, where, at any moment, an eruption might take place, and lay waste and desolate even that portion which had already been spared during the ages since the fires below had upheaved that small space of earth.

This idea it was which made all the family come down to the shore to be in readiness to move across the channel, should the attempt by the elders prove successful. It must be recollected that the space between the two islands was as great as that between England and France, or nearly so, so that the construction of a raft was of itself of great importance.

The mouth of the river, as has been already said, was very wide, while the current was rapid. Still, a spot was readily found, a kind of cove in the river's bank, where the frame of the raft could be built. It was made of four of the longest and straightest pines they could find, dovetailed together in something of the same way that was adopted in making a block-house.

This took them the whole of the first day, as to cut down four suitable trees was no easy matter. Then the boughs had to be removed and the logs drawn down to the water's edge. The women, meantime, employed themselves in fishing and snaring birds, which were plentiful and easily captured, especially the small, fat kind of rice bird, which is common to all this class of islands.

As the raft was not the work of a day, and as few of the men had any leisure to devote to any task save the one great object, the children and girls devoted themselves to collecting fruits and other provisions, while the negresses, who were very ingenious, were engaged in fabricating from bamboo, fibre and creeping plants a huge lateen sail, that the travellers might be spared the labour of rowing.

Pablina and Polly, naturally enough, were all but inseparable. They had a common subject to speak of. They were, as I afterwards found, never tired of talking of me. The Indian girl had taught her friend the use of the bow and arrow, both for the purpose of killing game and fish, which latter proceeding was singularly ingenious and clever.

About a mile up the river, was a small cascade, which came down from earthy hills, carrying with it, probably, worms and other food which suited the palate of the larger fish, for they crowded round it in droves. Pablina, and afterwards Polly, would walk up to this spot and proceed in this way. A good bow and half-a-dozen arrows, the heads made from bone well barbed. When a shoal of fish came up she would take careful aim, the arrow having a thin coil of gut fastened to it. In no instance did she fail to strike a fish, which she nearly always landed with perfect success. This mode of fishing was very profitable and agreeable.

One day, after sending down an ample supply for dinner, by the boy Cudjie, the adventurous girls determined to explore a little farther, and going up the river, were soon stopped by a creek, very narrow, winding and deep, with on each side a wall thirty or forty feet high, formed by trees intwined with creepers, which gave it a singularly gloomy appearance.

As by leaping from root to root, and holding on now and then by boughs, there was a possibility of following its windings, the girls turned up towards the interior of a dense forest, such as they had not yet seen, being composed, in a great measure, of evergreens, which gave it a peculiarly sombre and dull character.

Presently the bayou or creek began to narrow very much, when it suddenly opened into a small, swampy, half-drained lake. The banks were low and yet dry, but Polly would soon have turned from it, had it not have been for her attention being attracted by a singular bird. It had short legs, web feet, extremely long pointed wings, and was about the size of a tarn.

The beak of this extraordinary bird was flattened laterally —that is, in a plane at right angles to that of a spoonbill or duck. It was as flat and elastic as an ivory paper cutter, and the lower mandible, different from every other bird, was an inch and a half longer than the upper. The half-drained lake swarmed with small fry, and there were these birds in small flocks, flying rapidly backwards and forwards close to the surface of the lake. They kept their bills wide open, and the lower mandible half buried in the water.

Then away they skimmed over the surface, ploughing it in their course. The water was quite smooth, and it was a most curious spectacle to behold a flock, each bird leaving its narrow wake on the mirror-like surface. In their flight they twist about with extreme quickness, and dexterously manage with their projecting lower mandible to plough up small fish, which are secured by the upper and shorter half of their scissor-like bills.

This was frequently repeated, as, like swallows, they continued to fly backwards and forwards close around the two admiring girls. Occasionally, when leaving the surface of the water, their flight was wild, irregular, and rapid; they then uttered loud harsh cries. When these birds are fishing, the advantage of the long primary feathers of their wings in keeping them dry is very evident. When thus employed, their forms resemble the symbol by which many artists represent marine birds. Their tails are much used in steering their irregular course.

Watching these interesting birds, they wandered round the lake in search of a place to rest, as they were both fatigued, and presently found themselves under some trees that made Polly start. They were apple trees growing in a dense thicket. All the lower part of almost every branch, small conical brown wrinkled points projected, always ready to change into root.

Polly sat down, after plucking some of the crude fruit, which Pablina assured her was very poor eating, but which the other would eat from old association. She explained this to the dusky skinned girl, who laughed heartily at the sentimentality of her white sister.

Suddenly Pablina started up and listened, with gleaming eyes and a face expressive of both anxiety and alarm. Polly asked her, in a low tone, what was the matter. The other pointed to two trees where were the marks of the claws of some powerful and ferocious animal. Polly gave a frightened glance at the forest, expecting to see the gleam of a pair of ferocious eyes, but Pablina stayed her, motioning with her lips to be silent.

She cast up her eyes at the heavens. Beneath the shadow of the trees they had omitted to notice the time. It was nearly sunset. Pablina did not hesitate a moment, but having always the materials with her, at once made a fire on the borders of the lake, which she fed until the blaze reached to a tremendous height, and the smoke sent birds, monkeys, and owls, crying, squalling, and hooting in all directions.

Pablina then explained that it was quite common to find such trees on the banks of rivers, to which the puma or jaguar regularly repair to sharpen their claws. In front the bark would be worn smooth, as if by the breast of the animal, and on each side there would be deep scratches extending in an oblique line nearly a yard in length. The scars would be of different ages. The natives would adopt this plan of finding out whether there were jaguars in the neighbourhood.

To a certain extent there is truth in this idea, but, in all probability, the habit of the jaguar is similar to that which may be seen in the common cat, as with outstretched legs and exserted claws, it scrapes the leg of a chair, or even the trunks of young fruit trees in an orchard. But in the jaguar the object is, probably, to tear off the ragged points of their claws.

Now, the girls were brave enough for their age and sex, but they knew enough of these animals to be aware how little chance they stood with a beast that will carry off a strong man. They therefore cowered on the ground behind the fire, which they kept continually supplied with fuel, composed of bamboos, small bushes, and dry reeds from the borders of the lake, which made a crackling noise sufficient to have startled and alarmed a whole forest of animals.

And thus the early hours of the night passed away without any further interruption than a number of false alarms which, naturally enough, were raised by the natural sounds of the forest.

Presently the girls, after making up their fire afresh, stooping low to listen for any noise, dozed off. It was but a fitful kind of slumber, but still they did sleep. Suddenly Pablina laid her hand on the arm of Polly.

"What is it?"

"Listen!"

Polly bent her head, and distinctly heard the footsteps of some heavy animal advancing leisurely towards them.

CHAPTER CXXVII.

THE JOURNEY.

THE two girls, whose courage was undoubted, but who necessarily knew their own inability to cope with the ferocious denizens of the forest, held their breath, and stooping low, pierced with eager eyes into the gloom, which because of their own circle of light, was so dense. Then they saw two huge and blazing eyes fixed ferociously in the direction in which they lay. The animal, whatever it was, appeared to hesitate. All wild beasts recognise the power of man and of his subtle agent, fire.

But the girls gazed with awe at the creature. It was a kind of panther, but of a large and curious variety.

At last it seemed to make up its mind. It drew back for its spring, a shrill shriek was torn from them both in their last mortal agony, and then a gladsome shout from half-a-dozen throats proclaimed that assistance was at hand. The animal turned to face the new enemy, when two heavy axes descended with terrific force, wielded as they were by the arms of powerful negroes, and the savage animal lay still upon the ground.

The fire had guided their anxious friends to the place where the girls were camped. It proved to be a very small distance from where they had started, fortunately for them, as in any other case the search must have been deferred until the morning.

After the hearty congratulations of all, they started on their return, my father however taking on himself to insist on no such explorations for the future, unless attended by some of the armed men.

No further adventures of any consequence happened until the raft was completed, when my father, uncle, the captain and one negro, started early on a splendid morning to commence their adventurous journey. They were amply supplied with provisions, they had a small mast, and rude mainsail, a couple of heavy oars, a rudder and other necessaries. The raft had sides to keep such things as were absolutely necessary, in place.

By sundry experiments made at different times, the strange currents of that coast had been carefully examined. When the tide was at the ebb they seemed to flow in the direction of my island, so that the ebb was selected for a start. All the family stood on the shore, some with eyes streaming with tears, at the prospect of the perils the brave voyagers would have to undergo, while every heart beat high with hope that I might be found safe and sound upon my deserted shores.

The morning was warm, the sky was blue, the heavens without a cloud, while a soft and balmy breeze came from seaward. It was, however, very hot; this should with more experience have made them hesitate to start, as in those seas, the extreme sultry days are often squally. But the bold mariners, nothing daunted, sped on their way, and were soon lost to view as they turned the point of a promontory.

Working steadily at their oars, and assisted partly by the sail which counteracted the current, they headed directly for my island. Of course with such an unwieldly machine, their progress was slow, not more than a mile and a half an hour. A raft is always difficult to manage, and in this instance, being unusually strongly built, was all the more awkward. Luckily the skipper of our old bark was a first-class seaman, and as all obeyed orders and tried to emulate his ability, everything was done that could be to advance the progress of the craft.

The wind, which had never been much lowered, until at length it ceased altogether, the raft advancing solely by the use of the oars.

"Humph!" said the skipper, "I don't like this. If any it's a shift of wind. That sail must come down, and we must work with a will before a squall catches us."

They were now about three miles from their own island; while mine was but like a cloud in the distance. The old skipper shook his head.

"If there were time, I should say," he began, "let us go back; but there isn't time. We must make the best of it. I see a cloud rising on yonder hills"—pointing to the main land—"which is uglier than I could wish. If the raft can live, we shall not be long before we find young Sailor Crusoe."

His experience was right. A squall was evidently coming down upon them, and they could see the surf beginning to break at the bottom of the cliffs of their own island. In half an hour more the wind was upon them, the raft was nearly submerged; while everybody was wet to the skin. All lay down to meet the first force of the blast, and when the raft, righting itself, they could look around, their horizon was limited by the sheets of spray borne by the wind. The sea looked fearfully ominous—like a dreary plain with patches of drifted snow.

None spoke. The skipper kneeled at the rudder, keeping her head to wind; and thus they went on for several hours, scarcely exchanging a word, until the squall subsided, and they found themselves tossed wildly about at the mercy of the waves. Still darkness brooded over the face of the deep, and night fell before they could discover where they were.

They now took some refreshment, and the sea gradually going down, were able to seek some repose. Presently they were rocked upon the wild sea waves as gently as in a cradle, and all slept, until awoke by a kind of shock. All leaped up and gazed anxiously around. They had been floated by the current or wind to what appeared to be a kind of shoal.

Nowhere else could any land be seen. This was, indeed, a trying event; but my father and his friends had gone through too much to be terrified and cast down by any trial, however sore or terrible.

They accordingly waited until morning, when, gazing eagerly about, they saw my island, as it were, hull down; while of their own, they could distinguish nothing but the conical mountain.

As for themselves, they had drifted to an atoll or lagoon island, the work of that wondrous thing the coral insect. These islands are mere circular reefs, surmounted here and there with islets, on which grow some cocoa-nuts, that serve to nourish a kind of huge land crab. They were near a narrow opening in the reef, through which they impelled themselves into the land locked lagoon, when the scene was very curious and pretty. The shallow, clear, and still water of the lagoon, resting in its greater part on white sand, was,

as the sun now fell upon it, of a vivid green. Finding their way by means of their oars to one islet, a strip of dry land, about a few hundred yards in width, they gladly dried themselves and eat a few cocoa-nuts, the trees of which, without destroying each other's symmetry, were mingled in one wood.

There were a few birds, and a kind of rat; but what delighted and surprised them most was the discovery of a well, from which they procured a supply of fresh water. These wells ebb and flow regularly with the tides, and it has been imagined that some had the power of filtering the salt from the sea water. These ebbing wells are common in some of the low islands in the West Indies. The compressed sand or porous coral rock is permeated like sponge with salt water, but the rain which falls on the surface must sink to the level of the surrounding sea, and must accumulate there displacing an equal bulk of the salt water.

As the water in the lower part of the great sponge-like coral mass rises and falls with the tides, so with the water near the surface; and this will keep fresh, if the mass be sufficiently compact to prevent much mechanical admixture; but where the land consists of great loose blocks of coral, with open interstices, if a well be dug the water will be brackish.

There were plenty of turtle in the lagoon which might have afforded good sport, but they were too anxious to indulge in any such amusement. Their whole minds were given to one thought, that of returning, or rather of gaining my island. They, however, crossed the little islet, and gazed out upon the vast ocean. It has been well said that there is grandeur in the outer shores of these lagoon islands. There is a simplicity in the barrier-like beach, the margin of green bushes and tall cocoa-nuts, the solid flat of dead coral rock, strewed here and there with great loose fragments, and the line of furious breakers, all rounding away towards either hand.

There is the ocean throwing its waters over the broad reef, and appearing to be an invincible and all powerful enemy. Yet is it resisted by means which seem to be weak and inefficient. Let the hurricane bear up its hundred huge fragments—yet what will that tell against the accumulated labour of myriads of architects at work night and day, month after month.

I have already alluded to the crab which lives upon the cocoa-nut. It is very common, and grows to a huge size. The front pair of legs terminate in very strong and heavy pinchers, and the last pair are fitted with others weaker and much narrower. Most persons would think it impossible for a crab to open a strong cocoa-nut covered with the husk. But my father saw it done. The crab began by tearing the husk, fibre by fibre, and always from that end under which the three eye-holes are situated—when this was completed, the crab commenced hammering with its heavy claws on one of the eye-holes till an opening was made. Then turning round its body by the aid of its posterior and narrow pair of pinchers, it extracted the white albuminous substance. This appears as curious a piece of instinct as any that ever occurred to me, being the adaptation in structure between two objects apparently so remote from each other in the scheme of nature, as a crab and a cocoa-nut.

This crab is diurnal in its habits, for every night it pays a visit to the sea, no doubt for the purpose of moistening its branchiæ. The young are likewise hatched, and live for some time on the coast. These crabs inhabit deep burrows, which they hollow out beneath the roots of trees, and where they accumulate surprising quantities of the picked fibres of the cocoa-nut husk, on which they rest as on a bed. Certain natives and fishermen take advantage of this, and collect the fibrous mass as junk. They are very good to eat, having no animal matter to feed on.

The wind was very slight but fair, as with their sail, they once more pushed forward in a direction with my island. They were much struck at the constant column of smoke which rose from their own residence, which made it all the more desirable they should change their quarters, as volcanoes portended both eruptions and earthquakes.

The sea was now as beautiful and calm as the day before it was turbulent, but they soon discovered that, despite their oars, despite all the steering abilities of the captain, the raft would make towards the volcanic mountains. My father often said it put him in mind of the story in the "Arabian Nights Entertainments," when the ship is drawn by magnetic force towards the great mountains of adamant.

In these seas there are mysterious currents governed by causes which are not easily explained. They are influenced by the winds and tides, also no doubt by the subterranean fires, which end in those violent eruptions, one of which so terrified me, and so nearly cost me my life.

At length they saw that any attempt under present circumstances to reach my island was totally out of the question. The current was steady, and any effort they made to get out of it only resulted in their being, when just on the edge, whirled round and sent quite backwards. At length with a deep sigh, and much regret, as I afterwards learned, they once more made for their volcanic island and at once found that all difficulty as to their progress ceased.

They landed in a kind of cove, which went in some distance between two rows of high rocks, and abandoning the raft to its fate began their journey through the woods in the direction of the river, which would guide them to that camp where all they held dear, save myself, were congregated. They were exceedingly down-hearted and low spirited, almost afraid to face the light hearted girls, who no doubt were by this time expecting them, with good news of me, perhaps with me in their company.

They marched along in silence, their guns upon their shoulders, the negro, who was least affected, leading the way and showing something of that marvellous power of instinct, which is generally believed to be characteristic only of the North American Indians. He seemed from the way he strode along, to smell the trail, and at length with unerring eye brought them out upon the borders of the river, on the opposite bank to that on which the colony was collected.

CHAPTER CXXVIII.

HOME.

MEANWHILE the colony has been in a state of the most terrible alarm. They had seen the raft depart with such bright prospects, and then a very short time after they had heard the dull moaning of the trees, they had distinguished the dark clouds which were overshadowing the waters and the clouds. They were all too well experienced in the changes of the weather in tropical climes not to dread the consequences.

Then came the pattering of the rain drops on the tree tops; then down came the sweep of the tempest, laying many a forest tree low, and telling them of the awful dangers which others had to endure who had not their shelter, and not dry land to trust to. They were little aware that the land they trusted to was far more treacherous than the most tempest-tost sea.

They retired to their huts, the white women to pray for those at sea, the negroes to talk of the dangers which menaced their friends, and the whisper of dark warnings and signs which always occur to credulous and half cultivated minds, in days of danger and difficulty. And so the hours of the storm passed, when all went forth to the shore to gaze with longing eyes for any indication of the return of their friends.

But nothing was seen.

At early morn all, unwilling to own their fears even unto one another, set about their ordinary occupations, milking the cow, preparing breakfast, searching for nuts and fruits, as if nothing had happened. No conversation was interchanged, as all were too full to speak. It is said, out of the heart's fulness does the mouth speak, but there are occasions when the heart is too much moved for utterance, and so it was now.

Breakfast over, the negroes went fishing, or attended to a pond they had made, or cut down trees to improve the huts of a village which was to be their occasional residence during their stay upon the island. My mother and my younger brothers devoted themselves to a garden, which they had made in a nice shady place and which was both useful and ornamental. They had made it in this way. A small patch of ground had been when they arrived covered with reeds, which in a watery soil rose to a great height. A number of these had been cut down all round by the negroes, and the rest burnt. The soil below was good, and exposed to the air soon dried up sufficiently. A very large quantity of sea weed was then procured, which was also burnt, and cast over the ground for manure.

But the negroes, while my mother and brothers were searching for seeds and flowers to transplant, made a notable discovery, which was a kind of tradition in their country, and by means of which they asserted certain parts of Africa were in former days fertilised. In the mouth of the river, and about a hundred yards out at sea, was what appeared to be an island of white stone, much frequented, indeed, wholly covered, by birds. It rose in chalk looking cliffs from the water, and here the negroes went, by means of a large but rudely constructed raft, in search of eggs.

In this search they were much aided and assisted by the boys, who, like all boys are extremely fond of this amusement, even when not accompanied by the excitement of climbing trees. Now, when the garden had been laid out with its walks and beds, the boys started one day with the negroes in search of eggs, of which they procured a goodly quantity. To their surprise the negroes did not join them, but devoted their whole time to putting on a special raft a quantity of dirty white stuff, composed of nests, feathers, and birds' dung, which they seemed to think particularly valuable.

The boys laughed heartily, but the negroes only smiled, and were right. In the days of my wonderful colony, the history of which is a kind of second part of this narrative, it will be found that this material was excessively valuable, and produced most marvellous results. But of this, more at a future day.

My cousin, eldest sister, and Polly, were, strange to say, charged with the defence of the colony, and, at the same time, with hunting after game. It was my father's wish, that under the circumstances in which they were placed, they should learn the use of fire-arms; and as powder was tolerably plentiful, they were allowed a certain amount of practice every day. With quick eyes and fearless hearts, they soon became excellent shots, as on many future occasions will be seen.

These three together were so little apprehensive of the consequences, now that they were armed, as not even to fear a panther, though the animal killed had been a male of considerable size. Still, they were not fool-hardy; and Polly, who was the best shot, and also the eldest of the lot, carried her gun loaded with ball.

For some hours, however, they did not meet with anything worth wasting a shot on, as they could now, by nets and bird-lime, snare as many birds as ever they liked. It was determined to shoot nothing less than dangerous beasts, a deer, a gazelle, or a pig, of which they had found many signs, though they had as yet seen nothing of the species.

At length, still keeping the banks of the river in sight, though at a distance, they came to a spot where some monstrous trees rose into the air, almost without a bough, until they had reached a height greater than that of any columns in any portico in the world. They gazed at them with perfect awe, sitting down even to enjoy a full sight of them.

Pablina, who was more practical than any of them, began searching in the long grass until she found that which she had suspected would be there. Without ceremony, she began eating a delicious fig, and handed many to her friends, who, following her example, enjoyed the delicious fruit.

"There would be a bower of bliss," said Polly, pointing thoughtfully to the wide spreading branches.

"Rather difficult to climb," replied my sister, "but poor Alfred used to tell me of persons who had made their homes in such places."

Polly rose and turned away towards the river, her eyes at once suffused with tears. She was a little in advance of the others, with her gun in the hollow of her arm. Suddenly a strange noise startled her. It was a sound of something human, and yet not human.

She started, and there on her pathway, kneeling, nearly naked, though tanned and hairy, was Andrew, his hands clasped together in an attitude of supplication, the tears streaming from his eyes, his whole aspect forlorn, miserable and broken-hearted.

CHAPTER CXXIX.

ANDREW.

HE was quite calm now. Fever and illness had done their work. For some time he had been unable even to walk, crawling about the forest in search of berries, which, with water from the pools which were left by occasional rains, formed his whole sustenance. With this prostration of his physical powers, the madness which had affected him had passed away. He was, at the same time, perfectly conscious of the past, and felt deep regret for all that had occurred.

"I am ill—very ill," he said humbly.

"Heavens!" cried Polly. "Can this be Andrew? Do get up and come with us."

He rose assisted by Polly, and seated himself under a tree. They had with them a flask containing some brandy and water, which my mother always insisted on their taking with them on excursions in that hot climate. They handed it to him. He took it greedily, and then with no less relish ate some dried meat which Pablina took from her pack.

His story was a terrible one, and but that I am anxious to come to what I believe to be the most interesting part of my narrative, I would find space for it here. Suffice that the story of his sufferings brought tears into their eyes. When he was a little restored by means of both food and drink, he rose and offered to accompany them home.

At this moment the sounds of many footsteps were heard in the forest, and before the courageous girls could put themselves in an attitude of defence they were surrounded by the return party—without me, as Polly saw at a glance and fainted.

She thought they had visited my island with a fatal result and it was with great difficulty they could make her understand that their return without me was due to their failure to reach my island, and not to any accident which had befallen myself. This was a consolation in its way, but still not satisfactory, as the hope of being reunited to me seemed more and more distant every day.

However, there was nothing for it but to return home, and adjourn any present attempt to reach my island, as the rainy season was coming on, and it was necessary to regain the village which had been erected on the islands of the lake, with a view to such a contingency. The whole of the colonists were delighted to see Andrew so rational; while after a day or two of quiet living and careful diet, he was in as good health as ever, and endeavoured in every way to make up for the past by labouring industriously in the cause of the colony.

It must not be thought that they had any intention of abandoning me to my fate; on the contrary, they were more determined than ever, but they had lost all faith in a raft, and determined to build a boat, a small ship capable of bearing the whole party. This was the only way in which Polly could be at all reconciled. Being a good and reasonable girl she could expect no more than this—and so full of hope and trust in the future they went into winter quarters.

Their occupation during a season which was unusually wet were exceedingly monotonous, but they were not, like myself, exposed to the dull weight of solitude. At all events they had the most satisfactory and pleasant part of human intercourse, that of communication with fellow-creatures, while I was in a situation only second to solitary confinement in prisoner's a cell.

Despite the severe nature of the weather during this rainy season, there were moments when they contrived to come forth and take exercise. They were, however, few, and were looked forward to with intense longing and anxiety, as nothing was more disagreeable than to be cooped up in huts, barely large enough for their dwelling place when they were only required at night.

This made them resolve on a change of residence, and the selection of a spot where they could erect a number of superior houses, with a common hall where they could take recreation and exercise.

At present, when not inclined to be wholly cooped up, they were driven to the cavern passage, where my father, uncle, and the skipper generally smoked their pipes of an afternoon, their tobacco supply, thanks to Captain John Thomas, being tolerably good. Andrew generally remained with the girls to whom, however, he was simply attentive without pressing upon them his affections in any way to raise their terror again. Indeed, he had plainly told my mother that he should not obtrude himself on Polly any more—indeed, that her conduct had quite alienated him, so that he even hoped in time to persuade my sister Ellen to share his lot.

My mother gave him little encouragement, but told him if he proved himself to be thoroughly rational, the subject might be renewed at a future period.

Andrew acquiesced without a mumur. The intensity of

his sufferings, had, at all events for the present so tamed his character as to reduce him to a state of humility very foreign it might have been thought to his character.

The rain began to fall less continuously, and now and then, as my friends sat in the mouth of the bird's-nest cave, they saw strange glimpses of light in the heavens. They were fond of occupying this look-out, while they worked at such sedentary occupations as making plates, dishes, and other articles of domestic use. One afternoon, the rain came pouring down in fearful torrents, the wind howled above their heads, with an energy and roar that seemed to betoken a fearful tempest, when suddenly all was still as at the Creation; the rain ceased, the wind died away, and all was peace.

Then all started to their feet, as about three miles out to sea they saw a great wave come pouring in as if about to overwhelm and destroy the whole island. On it came with a smooth outline until it broke with a fearful line of white breakers, and next minute it was whirling rocks, boulders, and large trees about as if they had been straw and feathers. Then came another and another, and at the same time, the earth rocked, and my friends were cast to the ground, while huge rocks thundered from above, and they were nearly choaked with rubbish and dust.

There were several shocks of earthquake before twelve at night, but none so bad as the first, and towards morning the younger people even ventured to sleep, cradled in the arms of their elders. But these latter shocks were accompanied by rain, which soaked them to the skin. The misery they suffered that night, both mental and physical, was appaling. There is nothing which so utterly prostrates the human mind as a sense of weakness—and what else can it feel in the presence of such a calamity as that which they had to contend with?

Just before dawn there was a very severe shock; they were all lying down to rest themselves, though few slept. It lasted about two minutes, came on very suddenly, and ceased the same. The rocking of the ground was clearly discernible, while the undulations appeared to come from due east.

But when day came, and they glanced around once more, they saw, indeed, how terrible had been the shock. Looking down towards the sea they perceived huge and numerous masses of rock, which from the massive productions adhering to them, must have been before lying in deep waters, now cast high up on the beach.

The ground was fissured in many places. Some were about a yard wide and of unknown depth. The superficial part of some ridges were as completely shivered as if they had been blasted by gunpowder.

CHAPTER CXXX.

HOME.

A CONSULTATION was held by the male whites of the party, during which they retired to a spot where they had even a better view of the burning mountain, which smoked and sent up huge masses of rocks, that rose and fell like the balls in the hands of a conjuror. They could see, too, that a steady stream of lava was pouring over, and the nature both of the eruption and the earthquake was such, that they could not tell any minute but they might themselves be submerged and destroyed. The consultation was very brief. They would, at any peril, leave the island and reach the main shore, whence they hoped to able to communicate with myself.

No sooner was the resolution come to than preparations were made to carry it out. All the arms and ammunition were collected, the latter being strapped on the cow; every scrap of food which could be carried was collected together, and such other things as in the emergency were most necessary; and then hastily the whole party made for the sea shore on the opposite side of the island.

The channel was six miles wide, and evidently the current was swift. But there was no help for it. A very loose, clumsy, but substantial raft was made after a whole day's work, a raft not only capable of bearing them all but of supporting the cow. It was concluded about nightfall, when after a hearty meal, the night being clear with a bright moon, they determined to start. Long poles had been cut for oars, but, to their great delight, they found that they were able to pole the raft. Whether they had accidentally hit upon a ford, or whether the earthquakes had raised the bed of the sea, they could not say, but they touched the bottom the whole way across.

Everything had now to be done over again. The shore where they had leaped was desolate near the water, but soon grew fertile inland. Indeed, they discovered close behind them a very charming valley, full of trees and fruits. But they adhered to their original plan of building their huts on the shore under some palm trees, as more likely to attract my attention and from an anxious desire to be within reach of that sea by which alone they could hope to escape.

They were the more gratified to have gained the mainland that all the rest of the night and the next day the volcano continued in action, now pausing a moment and then beginning again, in this wise: the top of the cone, a minute before black and dark, would look like a large star gradually increasing in size until it really presented a magnificent spectacle. Then, amidst a huge glare of red light, dark objects were seen to be thrown up, and then to fall down.

When morning broke, all set heartily to work to establish themselves in this village. It was disheartening to have to begin life again, when, to all appearance, they had been so comfortably settled, but there was no help for it. After a brief exhortation from my father they set cheerfully to work, and within a week their huts presented a cheerful and pleasant aspect. They were so built as to afford shelter even in case of attack from savages, which, along that shore, was not at all unlikely.

There was abundance of game in the valleys and forests behind the hills, while the sea afforded fish in great quantities. Much time was spent in hunting, in order to leave the colony well supplied with food during the period of the excursion which had been decided on in search of my humble self. Then occurred my visit to the volcanic island, the discovery of my friends on the shores of the mainland; after which the impatience of the whole party could not be much further restrained.

The four started, as has already been explained, leaving Andrew in command of the colony.

When my friends reached that part of the coast which was nearest to my island, they at once made a discovery which explained the character and size of the animals which frequented my territory. It was low water and the tide being unusually so, there was a ford all the way across. This is the way in which elephants and such-like animals reach Ceylon from the continent, the space to be crossed being very many miles.

The delight experienced by my friends at finding me I need not further dwell on.

THE END OF THE SAILOR CRUSOE.